WYLDINGWODE

- BOOK FIVE OF THE WODE -

Being a tale of Robin Hood (a.k.a. Robyn Hode)

⊕

J TULLOS HENNIG

Forest Path Books

WYLDINGWODE

Published by

FOREST PATH BOOKS

Forest Path Books publications may be purchased for educational, business, or sales/promotional use.
For information please email the publishers at:
info@forestpathbooks.com | https://forestpathbooks.com
or address:
Forest Path Books, LLC
P. O. Box 847, Stanwood, WA 98292 USA

Stay informed on our releases and news!
Join the reading group/newsletter at:
*https://forestpathbooks.com/into-the-forest/*This is a work of fiction.

Cover design © 2022 Mahli (https://bookdesignbymahli.com)
Cover content is for illustrative purposes only, and any person depicted on the cover is a model.
Pi Rho Runestones font © Peter Rempel (licensed for use)

Library of Congress Cataloguing: 2020912735
ISBN:s

978-1-951293-38-3 (hardcover)
978-1-951293-66-6 (trade paper)
978-1-951293-10-9 (e-book)

This is for all those
who question 'authority'
who resist, even in the smallest-seeming ways
for
We will always need Robin Hood
We will always pursue legend
We will always create stories that question
and
Challenge
and
make Dreams in the shadows
We will sing back the light
We will hold hands in the darkness
and Dance
when they would have us on our knees

We are *werran*
We understand
and accept:
There are indeed things worth dying—and living—for.

WYLDINGWODE

- Prelude -

Mam Tor, the Peak,
Derbyshire/Hallamshire
Fête of Beltane (May Eve), 1201 CE

A tug at his sleeve—*come away, it's done.*

Only for now—he'll see to that, he will—but aye, for now it is done. Over. He should retreat, 'twere merely sensible. Of course, his best friend—only friend left, truly—often made sense.

But 'tis as impossible to leave as to, in the end, stay away. He'd held out, he had, for a brace of years. Loath to return. Unwilling to believe.

Drowned in the black of Barrow Mere, it was said . . . or, more likely, *poisoned by the Templars . . .* or *ta'en awa',* as Arthur would say, *to the Fae and the otherworlds . . .* Aye, the rumours were rife the farther south they'd returned, telltales to one ill wind: the Hooded Green Man was lost to the Shire Wode.

Why, Rob? I told you. Told you the treacherous sod would be t' death of you. O, Rob. . .

He'd burned his own nest to give those warnings, was reduced to crouching a stone's throw away from the Maiden stones, nursing bruised ribs and a bitter heart.

"He'll come." Firm, the Maiden's words; her eyes gleaming gold against the flames, her chin held high despite a troubled swallow.

"But if—"

Those gleaming eyes slid sideways, quelling. Beside her, the younger lass bit her lip and lowered her head. To the Maid's other side, an elder woman muttered a sigh. Silence lingered, and crept across the stones where they sat: an honoured—if troubled—triumvirate.

And that was why he'd challenged, truth be told. Because sommat needed to be upheld. Especially since one who should protest just stood there, supposedly Guardian to the women with hand to sword hilt but not acting . . . noble's lackey! Whilst one who'd have stood up to any noble who thought to take their forest—save the one, damn him to his Hell . . .

Robyn was gone. It was over.

Drowned in the black of Barrow Mere. . . poisoned by the Templars. . . taken away to the otherworlds by the Fae. . .

Yet May Day still blazed with light—somehow, and the Horned Lord's power all about them—somehow, pricking even the most dulled and unused senses. The flames licked high into the starless night with that power, reflecting against heavy clouds to shimmer the sand and scrub about them, flinging dancing shadows across the hilltop. The gatherers, nearly fifty strong, circled, capering, singing . . . and if 'twere more shouting, really, it held its own merriment and music, and wasn't that the proper way of things during the feast of Beltane?

That, and the challenge to the god.

None had shown any signs of knowing him as he'd challenged the cocksure noble bastard. And thank t' Mother none had recognised who'd slunk away in defeat . . .

"Will." Once more, Arthur tugged at his sleeve. "Come away."

Instead Will glared through his greasy forelock at the victor, who stalked the hilltop like he owned it. A lord, right enough. Not the man Will had expected to find—hoped to find, take down, defeat, *humiliate*—but this one just as foul, a newcomer wearing a greenman's face that sprouted tiny goat's horns. Stripped down for the wrestling, hair skimmed crimson in the firelight, anointed as challenger for the god's right—the cheeky bastard had neither height nor heft on his side, but he was deceptively strong, and more treacherous-quick with the staff than Will'd believed any of his like could boast.

Noble-bred bastard.

He wouldn't've taken Will, if—

"I know. He'd not've taken you if you weren't drunk." Arthur's hand landed firm on Will's shoulder, proof he'd spoken the last aloud. "Faith, lad, you've *been* drunk one way or another since . . . since . . . Well, it's done. No use staying. I've no stomach for rites like t' these. Letting such folk in . . . the lass has turned away from our Lady's true face—"

"Marion did nowt!" Angry, clipped harsh. "I wain't believe that from her or any our folk! 'Twere that ginger bastard, letting his kind run over our places like vermin! Taking, allus taking, just as he took *Rob!*"

"*Bendith*, friends."

Drunk and slow Will might be, and Arthur soft from keeping a tavern by day and a wife by night, nevertheless both of them whipped around, hands to weapons, as quick as it took the speaker to finish the blessing.

A cool customer, he was. A blink of pale eyes beneath a grey cowl, and a slight tilt back of head, but his gloved hands stayed steady where they were, resting at his belt.

"It is blessing time, friend," the stranger repeated, stressing the last with a smile curving his lip. An old Saxon tilt coloured his speech—it even coaxed a fond smile from Arthur as he fingered his granda's axe hanging burnished at his belt. Yet Will could dredge up no like affection even for an elder tongue; the stranger's clothes, though of plain woollen, lay with a fine sheen no peasant hereabouts could afford.

And of course, he'd an opinion. "Tha fought well. But sadly, tha also fought as one with too high a stake—and too much drink in the belly."

"What's it to you?" Will snarled.

"I'm . . . drawn to lost souls." A shrug of the grey-cloaked shoulders. "One might say it's my profession."

"Your *what?*"

"He's a bloody priest!" Arthur spat. "It en't enough that nobles can take up the god's horns, now Herself's letting *their* like in here?"

"The Church can lay no claim to me or mine." Saxon warmth went flat and cold. "Why else would I be here, but to witness the elder powers? Refute the Great Lie?"

The man was raving. Great Lie? Will started to speak, scoff.

Instead a bellow from the fire reclaimed everyone's attention. "Come now! Are there *none* who dare challenge?" 'Twere the Motherless nobleman in his bold greenman's mask, crowing like a bloody cockerel and brandishing his staff.

The silence hanging from the trio seated in state upon the Maiden's stone trickled outward, damping the gathering's songs to whispers, shouts to murmurs. Bare and booted feet scraped and shifted. The fire became the only sound, still crackling high but hissing as, from the heavy clouds, droplets began to fall.

The nobleman smiled, broad and entitled. Cruel.

Will wanted to wipe it from his face and break the mask over his head.

O, Rob, better you be dead than see this.

"You're Scathelock, aren't you?"

This time they did draw daggers, whipping about towards the stranger. Who merely cocked his head and continued, still a murmur, "And this fellow must be Arthur, the famed one-armed axeman." A *tsk* as the daggers inched closer. "The time of a Great Rite, and you would profane it with unconsecrated blood? My, but you have wandered far from the Hood's people."

"How do you know who—?" A sharp jab from Arthur stiffened Will's drink-supple tongue, twisted it in another direction. "What gives you t' rights, judgin' us?"

"I make no judgements, I merely observe. And you seem overly edgy for one no longer wolfshead. Or are you so again?"

"I'm freeman, so is he," Arthur growled. "We're respectable folk, makin' our way."

"And here to defend something dear to you. So, good fellow, am I." A bow, graceful. "It so happens I represent a cohort of, ah, *respectable* men, both common and otherwise."

Will rolled his eyes.

"It is our desire to return to . . . older ways. To re-open paths many would prefer eradicated."

"Rad-ih . . . " Will shook his head, growled, "Twere better when you were speaking the old Saxon."

"Well enough," the stranger answered, in that tongue. "Dost tha miss wild Robyn? There are rumours of his return."

"Robyn's dead!" Arthur hissed. "Else he'd be here, protectin' what's his!"

Will couldn't speak; the words had lodged, quivering, like an arrow to the gut.

Beyond them, Marion rose, graceful and self-possessed as any queen, to face the challenger. Behind her, Much the bloody noble's lackey remained, useless hand to useless sword.

Not that Will's hands had proven any more capable . . .

"Harrogate is a peaceful vill, and the Preening Peacock at the foot of Bland Hill well known for an excellent brew. But pray think on what I've said." With another bow, the stranger turned away.

"Wait!" Arthur hissed. "You know our names; we know nowt of yours."

The man hesitated, cowled head betraying a flash of teeth in the dim. "I am *Chevalier Déguisée.*"

"That en't Saxon," Arthur challenged.

"We often must use enemy devices to achieve good aims," the man rejoined. "Enjoy the festivities, good freeman. *Bendith.*"

As he disappeared into the murk, Will found himself staring after and wondering: how had the man known of Arthur's tavern?

"He'll come." Firm.

"But if—"

A look quelled Aelwyn's protest. Doubt, however, remained, an insidious weave around the great, sandy rock upon which Marion, Aelwyn, and Gunnora sat.

One could only be grateful that past the stones, in stark counterpane to any doubt, raucous merriment echoed across Mam Tor and into the night. Indeed, as the last beaten opponent slunk away, bruised and limping, the newcomer brandished his staff and gave a roar. The crowd roared back, smitten. Wagers flew, sure and swift as the man's staff.

"Never thought he'd make it so far," Aelwyn muttered, and her hand crept into Marion's. "Why is he even here?"

But Marion knew. All of those tightest-bound to the Shire Wode covenant knew, from the small and waiting semicircle keeping watch just past the fire's bounds, to their Maiden sitting with her women upon the altar stone.

The price of sufferance, this particular aspirant to Kingship, whilst the Wode's true Kings bided absent.

Marion hadn't agreed, at first. But her Summerlord had been persuasive—and surprisingly, old Gunnora too, harkening back to tradition older than any of them. Finally, Marion demurred. Surely any nobleman would prove inept to the challenge, complete the farce she suspected him of playing out.

A Fool deserves honour, Gunnora had said.

Yet this particular nobleman Fool had foxed them all, beating four challengers already, and stalking the wrestling grounds looking for more.

"He *has* to come." It escaped Marion's tight throat, desperate and fraught with shameful things.

"But if he don't?" Gunnora's filmed eyes turned towards the fires. "I nivver thought . . . but if he *can't. . .*"

"Then," Much growled from his place amongst the tight-knit group guarding the altar stone, "'twill be mine to—"

"—Challenge?" The Fool bellowed, his voice a little too shrill, patrolling the firelit clearing as if 'twere his. He rolled his shoulders, staying limber—narrow and stooped, they were, but nonetheless overlain with a soldier's muscle. Barrel-chested, bandy-legged . . . and that last betraying a horseman from the cradle. Marion wondered how many had caught the hints, scattered like coins from a royal tour.

"Who will challenge, I say?" The gaze behind the greenman mask slid, mocking and arrogant, towards the Maiden.

Aye, and his like saw nought in their Lady but a stepping stone to what power could be taken from Her. *I can unman you with a word,* Maiden's eyes answered, her back straight and proud as Mother and Crone gathered closer. As Guardian put a hand to his sword hilt.

Fool's gaze flickered behind the mask, at first unsure, then thwarted-furious. Lifting the staff, he whirled and shrieked, "Are there none who dare challenge?"

Silence began a slow trickle, from the Lady's stones and over the gathering. It damped song to hum, shouts to murmurs. Bare and booted feet scraped and shifted. Soon the huge centre bonfire was the only sound, crackling high but hissing as, from the overhanging clouds, droplets began to fall.

The Fool smiled, broad and entitled. Cruel.

The Guardian started to unbuckle his sword belt.

Instead the ring of shod hoofbeats upon shale and sand resounded—*ke-tump, ke-tump ke-tump*—across the heights.

Everyone turned as moonlight crested a bank of clouds, revealing a rider and horse ambling the ridge of Mam Tor. Closer they came, hoofs striking rock all the faster. Threat or boon? Cause to flee? To fight?

The people looked to their Maiden, saw she merely waited, unafraid. 'Twas then the murmurs started; first on the far edge of the gathering, forward and rippling back. Awe replaced any wish to panic as the rider crested the last rise and passed the peripheral bonfires.

He wore a hood, and upon his courser's saddle hung a tangle of bone, black, and silver.

It drew more whispers, rising into the night as he loomed closer, as the moon drew a veil of cloud across her face and sent Him into shadow.

Lord. Horned One, some acknowledged, whilst others entreated *Hooded One!*

And many others *Robyn. . . Robyn!*

This last plainly angered the Fool. It stabbed Marion like a dirk to the belly, but not from anger, nay. 'Twere wild and forlorn, her reaction: an unending ache, a scab nearly healed only to be torn to bleed. Even as thisnow changed about her; as her brother's memory shifted, inexorable, into something other. Something legendary.

Horned Lord. . . Hooded One. . . Master. . .

Robyn Hode.

I can't be dead or gone, aye? Robyn's voice tickled her ear, borne upon a shadowed moon and specked with rain. *Not as long as memory lasts and stories are told.*

All of it, part of their purpose.

The rider stopped upon the edge of the shadows. As the clouds chased past, he held aloft in one fist what had been hanging at his saddle. The skull was painted with woad and weld; a horse's bony carapace made into a mask, its long mane a fall of ebon and silver.

The *Mari lwyd.*

Astonished whispers rose, became hoarse cries of approval. Another string to the bow. Another legend to hallow the past:

And Robyn Hode defeated Guy of Gisbourne, took from him both head and name. . .

Aided by another gust of shadows, the rider replaced hood with mask, nudged his horse forward. The revellers parted before him like rainwater upon rock.

"My Champion," Marion greeted, stern. "You're late."

"My Lady, I must apologise. I encountered . . . difficulties. But I've ridden, the Hunt on my heels, to do you all honour." A soft voice, resonating outward from mask and hunch of cloak, incongruous with the broad-shouldered warrior. Boyish-fair. Beloved.

Her heart swelled within her breast, and from behind her, Much breathed "Milord" as if in benediction.

The eyes behind the mask regarded them both for a long breath, then he put two fingers towards his concealed lips and shared a kiss. A scathing, sideways glance towards the bonfire followed as he threw the reins. The stallion stretched his neck and shook, a shuddering jingle-flap of hide and kit. The hunch of cloak proved itself another rider, slight and a-pillion, sliding from his perch and down the grey's haunches. Their little John, gliding forward to take the rein, stroking the grey's steaming neck.

John shared with Marion a quick, cheeky smile as their champion swung down. Much was already there, helping shed the garb. Aelwyn too, waiting with filled ewer and bowl.

Beside the fire, a Fool stood waiting.

"You," he said.

The *mari lwyd* mask dipped, acknowledgement. Or perhaps to

merely allow Aelwyn to lift away the long front carapace, leaving a smaller one beneath. "Aye, my lord. I've come to defend my crown."

"*Your* crown?" Raked with disbelief and—threaded undeniable—trepidation.

'Twere one thing to defeat young men who thought to grasp the horns from a noble-bred newcomer who claimed rights to their Rite. But now a Fool who would be King faced the Lady's own Champion, a sorcerer's powerful gilt behind the mask's hollow gaze, and a shimmering cord girdled at his bare hipbones, knots and tassels brushing his left thigh.

Silence held, broken only by soft whispers and the shifting of bodies, as Aelwyn placed the carapace beneath the horn crown at Marion's feet. Gunnora took her time braiding the ebon-and-silver mane, and John with the oiling. Finally the Lady's Champion rose, his eyes beyond the mask flattened dark as a seasoned cookpot. One hand gestured towards the largest of the bonfires.

It roared upward. As one the crowd gasped, tottered back.

"Japes and sleight-of-hand?" Fool mocked. It yipped upward, self-betrayal, as Champion flung his hand outward again. This time, however, Much simply tossed him a staff. Caught one-handed, it was spun midair.

As the Champion sprang forward, another roar lifted over Mam Tor and into the cloudy night.

Wagers were lost in the first few paces, and more frantic on the sidelines as, in a breathless-quick, furious grace, Champion sent Fool sprawling and flew after. Another few breaths, another flurry of hammer-blows and dodges, and Fool tumbled on his arse with a shout. He didn't stay there, rolled just in time; the Champion's staff stabbed the ground a mere half-breath after.

Champion pursued, cool and predatory. Fool dodged sideways—clumsy with fear, it seemed, for he stumbled and scrabbled in the dust. The decisive blows were dealt—all too quick, from the audience's groans—one to the leg, then the shoulder, then the small of the back. Fool spun, staggered backward, tripped to land flat on his back.

And Champion ensured it with one bare foot to Fool's breastbone, with which he shove-stomped. His staff lowered, grazing the pale throat.

Fingers clawed at the rocks. "I am your sovere—!" It cut off, from shriek to choke, as the staff pressed closer. As the Champion leaned closer, the mask of the *mari lwyd* stark white, and the Horned One's voice breathing heated menace.

"Not tonight."

A quirk playing at her lip, Maiden took the cup from Crone, rose and strolled forward. Her smirk must have been contagious; her Champion caught and answered it. Beaten and cornered, the Fool's mouth quivered in a mix of fear and outrage.

"Mind your place"—a savour lay beneath Marion's words, sweet as the honey mead cupped in her hands— "or lose it forever."

The eyes behind the greenman mask narrowed. Doing battle with awareness: who—*what*—she'd been versus what she now represented. Furious at the necessity of it. The staff nudged even closer, hovering above the windpipe, threatening the pulse hammering just beyond. The Fool's throat spasmed in a swallow, and finally a nod: grudging but there.

Removing his foot, the Lady's Champion trailed the staff up to tap at the mask. The Fool snatched at it, holding it close.

Again, the tap, and again, the deceptively-mild voice. "Those horns, however small, are not yours to keep."

A stiffening of spine, a snarl of lip. But as if realising he'd chosen this moment, this possibility—even whilst never believing it would come—the Fool slid it upward and flung it into the fire.

He expected to be recognised, it was plain. He wanted the reactions, the awe. Unfortunately, many of the gatherers had never seen him, save, mayhap, as some remote figure riding their country, a well-dressed untouchable staying with their lords.

"You may possess one crown." It was a purr, so soft that only Marion heard. "But this one is lost to you. Be grateful, my lord, that for now someone else takes your place in the dance . . . and pays the teind."

King John met Gamelyn's eyes, his own narrowing at the underlying threat. Then, a strange little smile twitching his lip, he inclined his head.

"Indeed," he answered, wry-sharp. "My liege."

"You had me worried."

"I had me worried." Gamelyn's teeth flashed, more snarl than smile, against the ebbing firelight. "The ambush took some time to sort."

"Ambush?" Marion nearly sat up; Gamelyn tightened his arms, rolled onto his back, pulling her against his chest.

"Shh. It's done. I think our guest wanted to stack the odds in his favour."

"He would've won. I . . . well, I wasn't looking forward to the prospect."

Gamelyn knew the sudden rise of fury in his chest was improper, considering. Still . . .

Marion leaned forward and kissed his cheek, chide and consideration both. "Thankfully the blessing cup can turn sweet many a sour partner. Or so me mam said. I think she'd only a few aside from me da by which to judge. So far, I've had her luck." Another kiss, this time to his chin.

Fairer emotion filled his chest: fondness, inexplicable joy . . .

comfort. The mead that was his Maiden sipped more potent than any blessing cup. Gamelyn closed his eyes and held her close.

"I've missed you," she said against his chest. "Much misses you."

"I've missed . . . " Joy hiccupped, letting in the ache. Subjugated but never gone, the latter, and too potent here, in their place. "Everyone."

"I know, love." She traced a slow circle upon his breastbone, stirring gilt fur, fine-damp. Then, nigh silent, "He'd never consent to any of this."

"Robyn isn't" —and damn, but his throat kept closing all thick-tight— "isn't here. And when he is—"

"He will be. So must it be."

"So must it be." Another ache, this against the necessities of time, and practice, and skill.

"Even though *that one*"—scorn laced Marion's words, and well he knew who she meant—"would no doubt hold you back."

"Master Wymarec can't hold me forever. He's beginning to realise what he's loosed."

From the gleam in her eyes, Marion knew as well. "We go to the Mere upon dark moon. We'll take Robyn back from Them. From *Her.*" Again, bitterness in that last.

Gamelyn kissed the top of her head, breathed the scent of Marriage boughs crushed by their bodies, the fresh-tilled loam, the waft of wild roses. "We'll take him back however we must. And . . . well. He'll come to understand. What price, survival."

She chuckled, rue and sweet. "You do know my brother, aye?"

And it was either join in or concede the sudden burn behind his eyes. "I survived before I knew him. I survived when I thought I'd killed him, and you. And I will survive long enough to see this done." He took in a deep breath, let it out and watched it quiver the ringlets flung across his ribs. He reached to let them curl about his fingers, cinnabar snagging at his calluses like raw silk. Didn't—quite—wish them black as the night sky. "It seems to be what I do."

She kissed his neck, kept tracing her fingers in a sunwise circle on his pectoral.

A rustle sounded, beyond the fire and creeping closer. Gamelyn tensed and reached for a knife only to realise he had none. Straightaway he was glad he hadn't. The needfire's ebbing embers limned two slight figures, one topped dark and another, the smallest, with a telltale carrot-hued thatch.

"You knew it was them," he whispered.

Marion smiled as the children pounced and burrowed in.

Words akin to *Missed you so much* and *Wanted to coom but Aderyn wouldn't,* and *You bedded Mam 'stead of coomin' to see us!* babbled indignation in little Rob's reedy voice, while Aderyn's excited gestures flew too quick to take in, her smile rivalling any Bel-fire. Long in the caverns below Temple Hirst, learning other equally arcane languages and bereft of even John's company, Gamelyn realised he was rusty as an ill-kempt blade with the signing talk.

Marion, laughing, held up her own palms, a clear *slow down, pet!* Aderyn grinned, sat halfway up, and treated Gamelyn to a darkling glance and twist of eyebrow so akin to her uncle Robyn's, it stuttered his heart in his breast. Swift and fierce, he snugged both children close, and this time let the tears come.

"Aye," Marion's voice was soft. Satisfied. "We've more than the one reason to pay *any* price."

- II -

"**Y**ou should have given your liege the win."

"Yet he is not my liege within the Rite unless he *does* win. He must earn it. He mightn't like it, but he understands the . . . necessity." Gamelyn bent closer, speech tilting even softer. "As above, so below, my Master."

And England's Master Preceptor couldn't argue with that, though he wanted to. With a disapproving sniff and glance about the barn—complete with stern regard for the five Templars waiting just out of earshot, Wymarec de Birkin continued on to the next subject. "Then we return to our preceptory. We will wait a short while, allow you time to prepare."

"I beg your forgiveness, Master Preceptor, but I must tarry at Tickhill a while longer. I've several important matters to attend."

"And those would be?"

"Matters of political necessity—"

"Political necessity! More like an indulgent feast at an over-filled board, complete with a show akin to pissing on each other's boots!"

"Mayhap, but I cannot abstain from this. My presence has been specifically requested, Master Preceptor. By the King." He let Wymarec chew on that for a beat, then added, "And there are other matters of management, ones I need to see to."

"Management!" Another huff. "Hardly. Whilst the witch woman regards herself too equal in many things, she at least possesses a man's mind when it comes to practical matters. Surely she needs you not."

Marion would have something to say about that, though indeed it were praise, in Wymarec's view.

It also meant that Gamelyn was winning, this time. "There are things Tickhill's lord must personally attend. From our first infiltration of the woodland cult, it was agreed by all—including you, my master—that my role would by necessity be that of walking two worlds."

Walking a tightrope, more like. So far—thank the Lady!—his balance had stayed sound.

Wymarec seethed—not obvious to any but the most observant and familiar of acolytes—but, still. Finally he stepped closer, his toes nigh treading upon Guy's soft indoor boots, his voice a hiss. "If you are at last to be initiated into the innermost circle, you will be within Temple walls before the sun sets on the se'nnight of St John. There is one world that will not wait for you!"

Aye, Gamelyn thought, as he bowed the Templars to the stable entry, and watched them depart through Tickhill's massive carved gates. *There is, indeed.*

To hold a King's banquet was, supposedly, a sign of the highest approval. And it was the first held at Tickhill—one of King John's favourite castles—since he'd come to the throne not even a year previous, with a guest-list long as a clothyard.

Such favour Marion could have well done without. It meant no little organisation of resources, including the depletion of carefully-filled storerooms and a glut of wood-cutting, hunting, and fishing—with the latter in particular organised on a scale destined to interrupt the salmon's breeding cycle for this year and mayhap the next.

If that wasn't enough, it all had to be organised in between preparations for more important rites. Beltane's blessings had by necessity been submerged beneath the tide of a King's residence. The Great Hall had been laid with fresh rushes and sprinkled with sweet herbs. Fresh paint gleamed beneath the best tapestries Tickhill possessed—or could borrow—and torches blazed in tens of sconces, expunging the shadows of cloud-heavy afternoon. Every table had been dusted and dragged from storage, with extra props between the normal clothyard's span—and a good thing, that latter, since the boards had been crammed with a meal made from every sort of fish, fowl, beast and grain England could grow. Some England couldn't, come to that. And the foolery that went into 'presenting' said meal?—well, Marion had never gotten used to that. If 'tweren't peacocks stuffed with game hens, 'twere pork rolled up and stuffed into pike, and the pike placed as if escaping downstream from a great granddad of a sturgeon. And that stuffed with rabbit.

All in all, a finer example of conspicuous and pretentious consumption Marion had rarely seen.

Not enough t' just honour the animal in its own way, aye, pet? some internal chide bade Marion, in a voice so like to Robyn's it made her eyes sting. *Nay, everything has t' be all scrambled t' sixes and sevens. And our folk making do with one snared coney and roots shared amongst six. . .*

The leftovers go straight away to those as need 'em, she told her brother. *Your sister sits at the same board with a King, wived to a lord. . . and in result, our people are fed. Safe.*

As if kenning her discomfort, Gamelyn's hand snuck into her lap, found her fingers, and squeezed. Above the board, his face scarcely changed; his green eyes made a constant roam of the Great Hall beyond them. Still, that gaze returned to hers and held for a breath, complete with a tiny, well-satisfied smile that made its own promise.

A successful Rite held upon the Tor, a show of solidarity and strength in their home, and when the last of the noble intruders had departed Tickhill's gates, that Rite would fulfil another . . .

"As I was saying to your lord husband, your table is beyond splendid, my lady." King John leaned on one elbow, jaw against his fist. A smirk suggested he'd noticed her woolgathering. "Your wine, superb. However, I must say, the company is somewhat less so."

Gamelyn's hand gave a tiny twitch within hers; Marion addressed the King with some real dismay. "My liege, how have we offended you?"

But the King waved that away. "Nay, you are both excellent hosts. I merely mean, that whilst my late and lamented brother would no doubt be well satisfied," King John eyed the several male servants standing and waiting his pleasure with a wry twist of brow, "I find that I might become easily bored in the next several days. Your home, my lady, has less . . . feminine company than I would have imagined."

Gamelyn's hand twitched again. Marion slid a glance his way, saw him looking up and into the Hall rafters. He seemed to be fighting a smirk. No doubt remembering how she'd sent to the outlying crofts any women unwilling to fence King John's attentions.

Aelwyn had stayed, of course, but in garb purposefully drab. Acquiring the throne had but encouraged their liege's legendary appetites. All of them. Being lady of Tickhill—well, it *might* discourage even a king's lechery, but Marion's power as the covenant's Maiden protected her all the more.

For now, anyroad. And whilst Marion thrived in the management of a busy estate, the games required in noble halls strained even the quickest pupil. Endurance only lasted so far.

"My lord King, a lone woman charged with her castle's security needs plenty of male protection. I do apologise for the—"

"Milord Gerard de Furnival and milady Maud de Lovetot, of Sheffield and Hallamshire! Milord Otho and milady Alais, with sons Ian and Nicholas and daughter Edyth, of Stainton Grange!" David enjoyed his role as seneschal all the more when calling out visitors in his broad, Scots-laced tenor. Yet he seemed to pause before announcing the next visitors. "Prior Willem of Kirklees! Milord Brian de Lisle, castellan of Knaresborough!"

And if the last name stumbled—nay, curdled—upon David's tongue, the sound of it iced Marion's blood. She slid a quick gaze down the main board. King John seemed unsurprised; indeed, he watched his hosts keen as any hawk. Gamelyn's expression clearly disappointed the King, nigh malleable as stone. Yet, beneath the board, fingers clenched at Marion's. Her own shoulders had rippled tight. Aware of the King's notice, she forced her countenance to sport a mildness of which her da would have approved.

Behind them, Much and Aelwyn barely twitched, but their stance suggested they were nothing less than an honour guard looming behind their Maiden and Lord.

"They're late." King John gave a dissatisfied smile and a lift of his empty goblet to the servant who hovered, attentive. "How predictable. How boring."

Otho was fifteen years Gamelyn's elder, and had always equally surpassed him in physical might, solid as the motte supporting their father's keep. Unfortunately, birth-rank and muscle had both waxed soft in the fallout of a five-year gaol sentence ordered by King Richard. Otho had made the mistake of holding Tickhill against said king's return.

So Gamelyn, unable—or, admit it, also unwilling—to challenge Richard's edict, instead gave Otho's wife a fee worth ten of her husband. Alais had made a spectacular go of it. And when Richard had died at Chalus and John had ascended the throne, Alais had kept on managing it, even after Otho received his freedom for much the same reasons: holding Tickhill against Richard. John made fierce policy of rewarding loyalty.

Still, Otho walked Tickhill's paving stones as if the castle were his . . . unsurprising, mayhap, since it once had been. *Not any more,* Gamelyn growled into his wine, albeit soft and silent.

Marion would chide him for being arsy, stiff-necked. Unforgiving. Well, then, mayhap she was right. What lands Otho did hold were in fealty to Tickhill. And since Tickhill and its surrounding honour was held by consent of the King, it naturally followed Otho and Alais, Lord and Lady of Stainton, would attend that King, showing kin-homage and affinity to their designated overlord.

However.

Entering in de Furnival's wake could be construed to mean

somewhat less than that. And as to who had entered in *their* wake . . .

"My liege." De Furnival bowed low, his Lady following suit. Maud clung to her husband's arm like a jessed falcon, or a decorative bracelet—this despite the lands he held by the grace of her inheritance. She'd influence, yet she conceded it, claimed no affinity for it.

Thinking like a Heathen, Gamelyn chided himself. He tried to imagine milady of Hallamshire holding off a troupe of attackers with carnyx and longbow, and failed. Miserably. A smile creeping across his mouth, he drew Marion's hand upward and brought it to his lips then rested it, interlaced with his own, upon the table.

Both smile and affectionate demonstration seemed to unease de Furnival. He tipped his head in the barest of courtesies. "My lord and lady of Tickhill."

Maud, smiling prettily but eyes flat, did likewise.

Alais made an honest show of homage, smiling at both Marion and Gamelyn. But Otho seemed more truculent than sincere, following Hallamshire's absent iteration with a muttered "My lord and lady" as if beneath the glory of the Royal Presence he'd disremembered himself.

Dismembered would be better, the Horned Lord steamed, silent, from the corners.

Again, Gamelyn smiled.

All the while, their King kept watch as first Prior William, then Brian de Lisle, started their own tribute, King John interrupted the former's apologetic claims of difficult roads and lame horses.

"You're late." Brusque. "All of you, a day late, so perhaps it shall take Us a day or so to make time to speak with you. Be seated."

The small group hesitated then, beneath the glare of their sovereign, bowed and turned away. Not much could subdue Gerard de Furnival's sense of self-worth, true; still, he seemed the most chastened.

Gamelyn started to press Marion's hand the tighter, only to find her, for a wonder, staying put. She always considered it her sacred duty to personally attend her guests' comfort, and that despite his persistent reminders: Heathen hearth-right, firmly sustained in the crofts, for the castle held a different meaning altogether. Such tasks were to be delegated, unless one intended open tribute to a guest's greater rank. With Marion's usual answer being, of course but guests ranked higher than a host!

Yet now? She nodded to Aelwyn and returned her attention to the guest at her left hand.

Aelwyn's smile mirrored Gamelyn's as she descended to settle the arrivals, and a slight flame licked at de Furnival's cheeks. Message received, no question.

De Lisle alone showed no reaction to any slight, subtle or otherwise. Instead his eyes strayed to Marion and held, seething with something Gamelyn well recognised.

"Be careful around him," he murmured, beneath the pretence of pouring more wine into Marion's goblet.

"I aim to." Cool, the response, but warmer than the indifferent stare with which she acknowledged de Lisle's regard.

"An insult," the King muttered. "And surely their company is not accidental."

Gamelyn turned, conceded, "Coincidence is rarely that, my liege."

"And your brother. Once he held this very castle as Our staunchest of allies. Yet now he arrives in company of those lazy and late to Our court." The King accepted a serving lad's offer of more pork, but kept peering after Otho's retreat in particular. "Is the man becoming troublesome?"

"Nothing I cannot handle, my liege."

"Well, and I've little doubts of that. More I should resent it, yes?" A bark of laughter, to which Gamelyn forced a chuckle. "Well. We must love our brothers, even as we detest them. Even after they're gone. Particularly after they're gone." King John's dunk of fingers into the washing bowl was of biblical proportion. "But trust them? Never."

Guy of Gisbourne would have thoroughly approved. But that skin had long been shed. "Trust must start somewhere, my liege."

"Particularly when there's something to hold it hostage." King John gave Otho another hooded glance, and Alais. "The eldest, mayhap."

Gamelyn frowned, uncertain. "My liege?"

"Mayhap We shall request their eldest son be fostered here at Tickhill. See that your brother's loyalty remains . . . unfaltering."

Ah. This was something Gamelyn could nip before it budded. "My lord, fosterage has already been arranged. My brother's lady requested it."

"Excellent!" King John smacked a hand on the table and sat back, nodding. "Mayhap de Furnival's, as well. He's sired one already—and with a girl like that, why wouldn't he?" He tracked Lady Hallamshire's richly-gowned form, and the light of it kindled memory behind Gamelyn's eyes.

Another king, with the charming, darkling gaze of a predator: Richard, watching Robyn.

"A fighting cock, that one, who needs his spurs trimmed, eh?" King John shrugged away Hallamshire, turning to Gamelyn. "My lord. Pray share with me your thoughts."

When I finally stand in hell, mayhap . . . Gamelyn tilted his head, let a pleasant quirk tilt his lip. "If they are of interest, my liege."

"How stand you upon the rise of the one who was once Nottingham's Sheriff?"

Marion's hand twitched beneath Gamelyn's, despite her earnest and homely conversation with the lady past. She got along well with Pontefract's second wife, who possessed both a tender heart and a forthright will.

"We know your, ah" —the King's mouth quirked, excising and replacing even while ensuring Gamelyn knew exactly what he'd meant to say— "your . . . wife's late brother had a few issues with the man. We indeed trail in the wake of many stories, yes? *Robyn Hode and the Sheriff of Nottingham*—of such things my brother Richard's catamite trouvère made many a tale! But." The hazel eyes narrowed. "The past is past, yes? Some things are best left there."

Gamelyn's memory prompted again: a would-be king's boot staving already-broken ribs, and the furied satisfaction of wrapping his fingers about that same man's throat, albeit brief. Of the man slapping Robyn down like a dog, or contemplating Marion's death by burning, and for nothing more than an evening's entertainment.

"Some things, my liege." Gamelyn met that man's eyes, demeanour coolly respectful.

"Indeed. So We thought it best to see to de Lisle's return from Normandy. He has served Us well there, risen from cast-off disgrace to a valued tool of warcraft. More, your own Master Preceptor recommended him to Us." The King still watched like a fox at a mouse's burrow, seemed put out that his words had no greater effect. "My lord de Lisle has been gone some time, my lord; surely you yourself have . . . thoughts."

"Thoughts?" Gamelyn reached for his wine. "Forgive me, my liege, but you assume I bother to think of him."

The Royal Gaze blinked, startled, and the tight mouth twitched. Thankfully it broadened into a smile, gave way to another bark of laughter, this one sharp.

As always, with any king, there was no telling.

"My lord King?" Marion's query held a soft and faultless courtesy. "I beg your pardon, but my lady of Pontefract desires music, and I confess it would be a delight to me as well. May I indulge a whim, and suggest some dancing?"

King John's brows furrowed. Always, it seemed, he was trying to parse whatever riddle the scions of Tickhill provided.

Mayhap, Gamelyn considered, it meant they weren't 'boring'.

"Of course!" The King sat back. "I, too, would welcome some music and movement."

"Then pardon me, my liege. My lord," Marion added, quieter, with a squeeze to Gamelyn's hand as she rose and made a graceful way down the dais.

℞

With more refreshments sweetening even the most peevish of temperaments, Tickhill's guests took some ease. The children, both guest and resident, were being shepherded at one end of the Hall by Aelwyn and several others. The King's musicians encouraged dancing with a few lively tunes; indeed, their liege himself led the first several dances before retiring to watch.

It fell to Gamelyn, as host, to lead the following carol, hand-in-hand with Marion.

"'Tis my understanding," she murmured, "that Himself intends to leave day after the morrow."

"He wishes to hold council first thing," Gamelyn confirmed. "Then open court."

"Wain't be soon enough for me. We've work to do, but if the King's hearing court here, we'll have supplicants coming for days. Even after he's on to the next shire."

"We can leave those to our people." Gamelyn stepped out, then inward, placed his hand palm-to-palm with hers. "You're right, we've work to do."

"In our own place."

"Ah," Gamelyn answered, purposefully light, "but it isn't 'our place' at present, is it? We're surrounded by those who'd alight upon any chance, hawks upon the hares of weakness."

"You're out of sorts."

"Hopefully it isn't so plain?"

"Only to those as know you. You allus spout wry poetry when you're fractious."

He couldn't help the chuckle that burst forth, hugged her close and swung her about, careless of the couples close. "Ah, fair Maid, I do love you."

"I know. I love you, too. But set me down and fetch me shoe before those hawks of yours start pouncing on *it*."

He obeyed, with a shrugged apology to their dancing partners. Most were lubricated by good spirits of several sorts. Alais, who had barely dodged Marion's slipper, had a smile tucked sideways. Otho seemed torn between resentment and mirth, while lord and lady Hallamshire were Not Amused. Their liege lord gave a lazy toast from the dais.

Marion rejoined the dance, reshod and with a whirl of skirts just as the music changed. The dance followed suit; participants shifting sunwise in a change of partners. Gamelyn held out his hand, found Alais placing hers there, light as catkins blown from a willow branch.

"My lord."

"My lady Alais. How does your household? You've brought the children, of course?"

"Ian would have mutinied otherwise. He's quite taken with your horsemistress, you know."

"I do." He grinned. Alais echoed it as they glided forward: toe-heel, toe-heel, and a rise upon tiptoe with a graceful arc of arm between.

"We've a few rounds of this dance, 'twould seem." Her voice lowered. "I'm glad to be able to speak with you without subterfuge."

"About your . . . companions?" Gamelyn knew, with the

certainty of a hungry predator, where the other dancers were. In particular de Furnival and his wife, who had bowed out from the dance for now, and Otho, who partnered Pontefract's lady.

"I'm sure you know they've been our guests this past se'nnight. I've no qualms informing you of Gerald's overtures towards Otho. They've spent many an afternoon hunting, and most evenings drinking. Commiserating, as if they don't have enough to occupy them without coveting others' allotments fair and foul."

"And Otho is . . . influenced." It wasn't really a question.

Alais dipped her head, seeming lost to the dance. "You know your brother, my lord."

Aye, he did. Well-intentioned, tenacious . . . and until of late, quite satisfied with what his wife's management and his brother's largesse had regained him.

"Gamelyn. You should cultivate him more. He is willing to give you respect instead of resentment, follow your lead."

He always has been. Any voice stronger than his own, no matter the consequences. Strange, how amongst uneasy choices made and sordid paths taken, this should be the one at which he baulked.

Alais glanced at his face and sighed. "I'll talk more with Marion later. Since we're speaking of . . . ah, family things?" She hesitated as the music began to quicken; a warning of the coming change in partners. "Excuse my frankness, but I'm relieved that you've . . . well, that you've kept to your wife in the wake of . . ." Flustered, no question. "Despite the . . . loss of . . . the rumours of . . ."

His body longed to betray his affront. Gamelyn forced it pliable, steady into the music's rhythm. Replied light, though his molars ground with the effort, "He was my wife's brother, the most beloved of my family and friends. More brother to me than—and you must pardon *my* frankness—my own ever were."

"Of course. I understand." Alais' voice remained circumspect, quickening as the music gained like pace. "Please appreciate that I speak from respect and concern, for you as well as the place we've both fought so hard to repair. You've made excellent maintenance of the King's regard—and for some time, considering." She gave a light shrug to the vagaries of monarchs. "But there are many who are—shall we say—dissatisfied? with that regard. Many do not fare half as well as we and eye Tickhill's abundance, not only of fruit, but royal favour. Trust to this, my lord, there are those who'd leap at any hint of degradation or deviance, simply for the chance to discredit or unseat you."

Degradation. Deviance. Thankfully the music demanded a release of hands, a small turn. His molars didn't likewise unclench, though he managed a light half quote, "'When I became a man, I put away childish things'."

Again, of all the lies he'd spun and lived, this one tasted of burnt ash and despair. Alais accepted it whole-cloth, with a smile and curtsey to his bow, moving away as the music changed once again.

Roger de Lacy's wife held out a small, plump hand. She proved an agile—and thankfully silent—partner.

ᛦ

"There must be something you can do," Alais protested. "Gamelyn simply refuses to listen to *me* about this."

"I'm not sure I've the rights to make him listen." Marion frowned as her companion started to mouth another protest. "Alais, you know the past better than I. You witnessed it first-hand."

Marion herself had guessed most, seen the results of some, and with slow patience unearthed the remainder of Gamelyn's youth. What had started as a lark, visiting forbidden peasant friends at the forester's cottage near Loxley, had become an earnest escape from a situation grown untenable. A father's illness and loss of authority had empowered an elder brother's jealousy against the beloved youngest, releasing an all-too-willing tendency to spend it against Gamelyn's hide. As to the middle brother, watching . . . well. Otho might have occasionally deflected Johan's ire, but never had he drawn it. More often than not, he'd been complicit.

All this, whilst *her* younger brother had borne—*nay, bore, he isn't dead only gone!*—scars both visible and otherwise. And those garnered in deflecting ire from those less able to take it; all as effortless and artless as he breathed.

Otho had been a coward, pure and simple. And didn't look as if he were stepping up to anything less the now, save for the love of a woman worth ten of him.

"The past cannot be helped!" Alais bit her lip as her voice began to rise, slanted a wary gaze towards several other women chatting nearby, and leaned closer to Marion. "It led their family to ruin. Otho understands that. He'd listen, if he'd only the opportunity."

"Would he? Or would he rather follow a bitter trail laid by others?" As Alais' mouth tightened, Marion quickly furthered, "Gamelyn's given more than he should, considering—"

"And he'd lose further opportunity because of pride?"

"Mayhap," Marion said, gently, "he recognises pride all too well, and knows not to trust it."

"Trust?"

Alais had started another protest, instead turning away, mouth tightening, as Maud de Lovetot came closer, repeated:

"Trust what?"

Marion had been aware of her as she'd crept closer; no doubt she'd been brought by her husband for this very reason. Not that she was any use for nowt *but* prying and listening. Did the woman ever think for herself, or just echo whatever she was told? Maud wasn't stupid—at least Marion didn't think so—but nevertheless she clung to shallow devices like a drowning person.

"Pride," Alais retorted, severe. "Something your lord husband should hearken to, and beware."

Well, Maud might be younger than either of them, but treating her like a child wasn't the answer, either. Even if she reacted to a reprimand like one, looking down and hunching her shoulders beneath a costly, embroidered gown trimmed with even-more-expensive silk. Alais had no doubt suffered exasperation up to the eyeballs and beyond, staying at Sheffield and enduring such company for over a se'nnight.

"Excuse me, please, my ladies," Alais continued. "I see my son is instigating."

Marion hid a smile behind her hand as Alais set off. Ian was a good lad, though he'd a nose for more trouble than his mother cared to see. A noblewoman's upbringing seemed inadequate to the task of wayward children, male *or* female.

Oddly enough, it seemed to spark Maud's dull expression. "He seems a handful, does young Ian."

"All children are, in their own time," Marion answered. "How does yours?"

"I wanted to bring him, but Gerard said . . . nay." The last word faded as, no doubt, Maud realised the implied insult. One did not bring one's son and heir into an untrustworthy house.

It fetched sharp as a slap in the face. Marion retorted, composed but no less sharp, "I don't ken how your lord runs his holding, but here we don't offer hearth-right to betray it. And only cowards would take anything out on a wean!"

"There aren't many who'd agree with you. Babes grow into men. As the sapling is bent, so grows the tree." Maud's gold-brown eyes fastened upon the dais where King John, mellowed by good wine, had finally consented to her husband's approach. A wealth of expressions crossed her face, from curious, then dread, and finally settling upon anxious. She gave a self-conscious brush at her crème-coloured veil, and the movement pulled at one snug sleeve, betraying telltale splotches of green and yellow along that wrist.

It bade Marion speak with a solicitous honesty she'd never thought to give a de Furnival. "You and your husband have plenty. Why do you want *our* home?"

Maud blinked, slid her eyes sideways. The frown didn't lessen. "You seem to forget it was once mine."

"How so? You never lived here. Never ran in these halls as my children have."

"And as lord Otho's children have done?"

Marks to Hallamshire on that one. Marion flicked a glance upward at the rafters, counted the everpresent gwyllion perched there before she replied. "As they still do." A gesture over to where Ian posed and laughed amidst the younger ones, his brother beside him and hanging on every word. "Ian is to be fostered here."

"Convenient."

It was Marion's turn to blink.

"Oh, come now, lady Marion. You might have been raised late to your station"—and my, *that* scathed—"but you can't be that ignorant. Ian is security, nothing more, against Otho's intent."

"How interesting," Marion countered, tart, "that you know so much about Otho's intent, yet persist in believing I know so little."

Maud let her gaze retreat to the dais once again. De Furnival still lurked there, hopeful.

"I also know that your lord husband has overmuch to do with Otho's seeming discontent with his situation."

"Seeming? Forgive me, but you don't know much about men, do you?"

Mayhap being a snotty cow made for a proper weapon, but it also showed weakness. A smirk played at Marion's lip. "I'll wager I know a bit more than you, lass."

Maud peered at her. "I meant high-born men."

Another slight, that; Marion chose to ignore it. She'd been called names by the best. "I know enough to realise when a man's trying to prove sommat. Having a piss on another's leg might be in his nature; what I can't abide is why anyone would bother going from that to ploughing ower others. It proves nowt. Senseless twaddle neither low nor high, and all of it weakness. Sommun who's secure in his own situation has no need to step on weaker toes."

Maud's nostrils tightened.

Marion didn't give her the chance to protest. "Who's the more daft, then? The one acting it, or the ones who'd follow him, blind-like?" She leaned slightly closer, well aware of being a full head higher and a good ten years older than her companion. "I recognise your man's like, believe me. I've seen too many like him, fearing sommun might whip out a knob bigger than his, all eager to nick another's share to pump up his own lot. What I truly want to understand is you, milady Maud. You en't stupid, though you like to pretend you are. Why stand for it?"

Again, Maud had gathered herself up to reply; instead she deflated with the words like wind pricked from a bladder. "Who's the fool, now? You speak like we've choices."

Only noblemen speak as if they've choices in life. Robyn had said it many a time, and Marion had just as often appended: *The key word bein' noble* men.

She reached out and touched Maud's sleeve. "What choices we do have, we need to make count."

Maud looked ready to twitch away, but Marion's tone seemed to gentle her, like a skittish horse.

"Milady Maud, I think you're forgetting who brought the power to your marriage."

A short laugh, far too bitter for such a young woman. "Do you think he lets me?"

"I think I understand that you've enough enemies in your own home, milady. You've no need to see one in me and mine."

The everpresent frown had lessened, albeit slight.

"I en't against you, milady. I never have been. All I want is what most women do: a place to call her own, where she can do good work and raise her family, with enough food, shelter, and spirit to stand firm when times come harsh." Marion patted Maud's arm. "What I'm saying is you needn't covet Tickhill. Because you've a place here already. Understand? Should you need it."

Turning away, Marion walked over to the dais, aware of how Maud's gaze—confused, fascinated, conflicted—followed her the entire way.

The pool is wide and black, a shimmer of half-light stretching out, lapping gently against his bare toes. The other side beckons, thick with undergrowth, heavy with trees in first leaf. A wet fog meanders, hanging upon this limb, that bush, plastering his hair to his skull and leaving a velvety scrim upon bare limbs. Fireflies illuminate the moon-spackled mists in fits and starts, skimming reflections upon the opaque mirror of Barrow Mere.

Yet something else lurks as well. A passage in the underbrush, a promise of adversity trails ghosts against the water, gleaming. Eyes regard him, winking-wet, reflecting the fireflies dancing in the murk.

Watching.

Gamelyn, too, is watching. Waiting for it.

And, in a whirl and *whuff* of breath, sharp tines rise from the mists of the opposite bank. The god-man abandons His cloak of shadows, eyes glowing like a beast faced by torches. The fireflies cut swathes of gilt against ivory skull and horns.

Games, a Voice croons, *are not enough.*

And the eyes, one by one, wink out. The Horned figure's immense rack dips, green withering, skull-face stark from beneath. His cloak falls, turns to ash, sprinkles in a gust of chill wind to scatter the Mere's surface . . . yet the skull remains, stark and cold. Colour leaches from the grass, grey and black, and the skull seems akin to that of the *mari lwyd* . . .

Yet beneath white bone spreads a carpet of green. As if flame has been set to dry grass and instead of incineration, there is blossom and leaf, unfurling. The skull shivers, then rises, with a cowled figure beneath its bare, antlered crown, and fire leaps upward behind Him, blown upon the wind and spreading. Still, the woodland does not burn. It illuminates, gilt and green, the Wheel's turning.

Rebirth, the Hooded god-man whispers. *The reason. . . the truth. . . of Sacrifice.*

He lurched upright, fingers tangled in a horse's mane of grass and fire and . . .

"Gamelyn?" Soft and slow, the query against his neck, with familiar hands tangled firm in his hair and a lean-muscled leg thrown across his hips, for good measure.

Tie a knot and hang on, Much had once said.

Plainly, their little John had been listening. "Coom by," he said, this with a sharp tug to Gamelyn's hair.

Not horsehair, grass or fire clenched in Gamelyn's hands, but soft, linen sheets. Not a chill wind whistling through the Wode, but his gasps echoing against stones and draperies. Not the company of fireflies and a full moon against the Mere, but the whipcord of a lover cozening him back from a ride on the night mare, and gluey eyes opening to see, past John's worried expression, the lord's solar at Tickhill, dimly lit by a pair of squat candles spiked upon a wall sconce, against the faint light of another dawn.

Gamelyn sighed into John's hair. "I've not had that dream in . . ."

Years, it had been.

John merely laid a line of kisses down Gamelyn's breastbone, slid a hand down his belly. A flash of teeth in the dim, and with his free hand John signed, *Some benefits to dreaming of the Horned One, at least.*

Stretching to meet that clever, nimble hand, Gamelyn started his own reciprocation. He kept to his wife, yes. And to his lover, both of them finding immeasurable comfort in the taste, touch and smell of what an absent beloved had once held close.

And after, John sat up, peering at Gamelyn with eyes that gleamed all uncanny.

Mayhap, he signed against the growing light, *it's finally time.*

Marion rose before dawn, seeing to her demesne and the day's events. Council first, then Court, then the King's exit.

First thing, though, she had a meeting to attend.

Hugh de Neville, veteran of the siege of Jaffa, heir to several southern counties, chief forester to not only King John, but King Richard, was not a big man, though his power implied otherwise. Middling height, truly, with the shoulders and thighs of a lifetime horseman and a mane of thick, gilt hair suggesting more than a few Gaulish forebears. Of an age with Marion, de Neville nevertheless seemed older, canny as any Celt trader—and as vicious, when it suited him.

He'd come with the King and asked, most courteously, for a room central and large enough in which he could do business. Marion had given him this room—off the Great Hall and central, to be sure. More important, one which assured he could be watched.

Her superior he might be, but she trusted the man about as far as she could pitch him. Even with an archer's arm.

He'd approached her at last night's banquet and asked for "my lady Keeper's presence upon the morn". So she'd sent David on first, as Tickhill's seneschal delivering a statement: Tickhill's lady would not be snapped to heel like a mere lackey. Garbed neat and elegant, keys heavy at her belt, Marion made her arrival as the bells rang in St. Nicholas' chapel.

David gave her a dip of head—nothing untoward, it seemed—and retreated to stand just inside the door. Marion inquired as to de Neville's situation and comfort, all the while making it plain: he stood as guest to not only her place, but her husband's successful fiefdom.

"My lady, your hospitality is as legendary as your household." First volley, giving due notice of the notorious background surrounding Tickhill's lady.

David shifted by the door, hands upon his belt, expression thunderous.

A cool one, de Neville; he didn't so much as glance that way. "Your man's diligence does you credit, milady Keeper, and I ask that both of you kindly receive my regards, and give them to your foresters in turn. Sherwood and the Peak remain well stocked, and as peaceable as we could hope for in such times." He bent over the table set up beneath twin tapestries—one of St George, the other the Dragon—and stubbed a beringed finger at a parchment over which his clerk hunched with quill and inkpot. "*Et dominus,* you fool." It scorched, yet de Neville didn't raise his voice—or change his expression, which rarely amended itself from a bland, fixed courtesy.

Had Crusade schooled such control? De Neville and Gamelyn had been amongst those rare few who'd fought and survived both Acre and Jaffa; despite such, they remained the most distant of acquaintances, would share an occasional drink yet no reminiscence.

Of course, Gamelyn had once said the ones who'd actually seen battle rarely wished to reconjure it. Only the aged soldiers gave open memorial to past manifestations, the reality softened, mayhap.

Or mayhap the sharpness sought, to reconnect with a life passing all too quickly.

"Although," de Neville turned his attention back to her, "there is a matter which concerns me, regarding Sherwood in particular."

Marion clasped her hands over the peacock fan hanging at her belt—the same one, albeit with some replaced feathers, that Queen Eleanor had gifted her—and tilted her head. Said, smooth as cream, "Sherwood?"

"There are rumours that poachers have been encroaching into the King's park at Clipstone." De Neville's eyebrows arced, ever so slight. "Your jurisdiction, Lady Marion."

"Rumours are not fact, my lord." It had taken time, and effort, but Marion could tilt her voice posh as any noble's, did she have the need.

"In my experience, there is seldom smoke without fire, preceding or in the afters. And other rumours go even farther afield."

Marion heard David shift against the door, slight.

This time, de Neville deigned to notice, a tiny flicker of gaze to the door then back to Marion. "The people seem unrestful. There are tales of another hooded man roaming the forest."

"Tales, milord, are just that."

"But these rumours are tied to the poaching incidents. Several villagers have confessed how others in their midst have received gifts."

Confessed. Some, then, had broken faith. Unease tickled the back of Marion's throat. "Gifts?"

"Of poached game."

"My lord, surely you can't blame people for taking in food that appears on their stoop!"

"I could, but there'd be no point, would there? At any rate, cattle are witless; 'tis the one responsible as matters. It frets me, my lady. So I appeal to you for understanding. After all, considering your previous existence—"

This jab travelled a path altogether well worn. *Outlaw drab. The Hood's sister.* And, *Cattle are witless.*

"—I would hope you'd have some feelings about this character."

She met de Neville's gaze. His brown eyes flickered, but did not drop. She had to be satisfied with that. "My lord, I feel for anyone who has to watch their children go hungry. I'm sure you have reports of the various—and lawful—ways I go about easing my tenants' plight in times of need."

"It speaks to your management, truly, that you keep your people so well fed. Of course, when one has lived certain realities" —a shrug— "it is difficult to stay detached."

Crofter's daughter. Peasant. Again and aye, but he was well prepared to put her in her place, wasn't he?

It spoke to his discomfort with her other, former place. And beneath that lay other assumptions.

"My lord de Neville. When you have proof of any rumours, kindly send such on to me. Rest assured I shall deal with it." Marion's smile merely edged the words tight. "You have no reason to suspect otherwise, or that I shall do any less than I have done regarding any offences in the forests over which I am Keeper. And better, I might remind, than my lord's foresters, as my brother, rest him, outwitted those for *years.*"

De Neville's nostrils flared.

"Not to mention *our* father, who were forester to the North when you were a wean toddling across a polished castle floor."

"My grandfather," de Neville answered, just as edged, "was head forester when your ancestors were squatting in a hovel scraped together from mud and shit, squabbling over mouldy roots."

Right, then. "Take care, *my lord*, with your scorn. Lest I slip one of those . . . *mouldy roots* into your drink some evening."

He paled—slight but there. Unlike most of the few lords allowed to playact with the old ways, finding excuse in them for debauchery and excess . . .

This one had been at Nottingham, when the Wild Hunt rode. Had heard it howling in his nightmares.

Hugh de Neville believed.

"I will do my best," Marion assured him, "to curtail lawlessness in my forest. One thing I can assure you: this man, whoever he is, is not Robyn Hood."

- Entr'acte -

Bright, it was being, a twinned presence brilliant-hot as the shining memories of a sun long dulled. Heat and rage and fury, repeating the geas of the Iron. Faltering not, in pronunciation or intent . . . even when elder words were making but ripples. Even as the possibility of failure began sinking doubt into souls hot and heavy-sharp as the Iron with which they sought to claw the borders asunder.

The acolyte moved forward, drawn to the flame despite herself, then shuddered and retreated a step.

So. These were being the invisible ones, those who would . . .

She wanted to see Them, mark Them. Perhaps she could be twisting Sight from the magics seeking to penetrate the Veil; some danced familiar, softling elder breaths curling about her senses, as if to sooth the foreign gasps that wielded the glittering edge of steel.

"Care." Softer, this voice, and softer still the presence, her Priestess gliding into the vast cavern quiet and tense as a hunting fox. "The magics be stronger, thisnow. Even the Ancient One stirs."

Indeed, the great wyrm couched within the Deeps had roused, albeit slight. Black hide shivering, eyes lidded but twitching, the iron shackles upon his neck vibrated, and the silt upon which he lay drifted upward, casting thick clouds about his slumber.

Only a handful of times could the acolyte remember such a thing happening.

A graceful hand rose, and square, indigo-marked fingers sketched against the damp air. In response the Veil rippled, blurred. Instead of an unseen presence heating one's face, or lost spell-speech tickling one's ears, a vision wafted into muzzy focus.

Conjured of outworld fire against the misty fabric of the Veil, it brought tears to the acolyte's eyes—so bright, so painful!

A woman, standing upon Mere's-edge. Bare arms raised, a sword glinting in her hands, her hair blowing like flame. Mother, Sister, whistling up the wind with Iron Speech growling: an angry, cornered wildcat with kits in her den and one in the belly.

"She be strayed. Once a danger to our purpose, now being lost. But that one . . . " Another breath and gesture; Priestess conjured sharper focus. "Threat, *he* be."

And aye, the man-Magician shimmered more gilt than crimson, alien despite the Horned shadow upon his pale shoulders, dressed in a white sparking too many colours. Too pale, he was being; white-hot like . . . like . . .

It came into her heart, memory from her mentor: like a forge of the conqueror-folk. "But . . . She. She be of Mother-blood, speaks our tongue, bears in thatworld the blessings of vine and fruit."

"Thatworld." Flat. "Not ours. As I am saying, her heart be turned. To the iron and bells, and away from our Mother. Be looking to these usurpers, dearest mine. Be wary. They will not be resting. They be thieves."

"And if they succeed?"

A smile. "They can be trying."

And the hand closed, swept the vision into blackness.

- III -

The eastmost door lay open, welcome to the dawn and any early comers, yet the chapel at All Hallows seemed to hunch, dark and solitary, upon its hill a few miles south of Tickhill's keep. Battened down, in preparation for the coming storm.

Grey Hilal danced between his knees as Gamelyn drew rein at the chapel door, twisting in his saddle to ponder the horizon. Sparks and shards of light chased across a mass of indigo and green-black, forerunning the low, billowing front, stalled south. The dawn, still clear, fingered its way from the east.

The past fortnight had been thus, a disparate competition of opposites: chill and wet slashing across the shire every other day, with in-between bursts of sun glinting across the sodden land, a promise of jewels in a dank pouch.

Promise, aye. He'd come home with such promise, with the spells and the methods for delivering them . . .

Only to the same, sad ends. Again.

"This storm en't natural, milord." Much cued his bay close, off knee nudging against Gamelyn's. From the other side John also drew near, one hand making a curt gesture—a sign against evil. Horse as well as man stared into the gathering distance, fascinated and a little fearsome.

"All-Father en't happy you're leaving." The harsh bursts of light lit Much's profile white-pale. "Mayhap we should just go return home. The storm's stalled for t' while, but once that wind turns?"

Return home. Put off leaving for another day, another several. Return to Marion, travel to the Mere's edge again . . . for what? More failure? Better to keep going, face the admission of that failure, slink with tail between legs to his waiting master and the fortress of Temple Hirst. Find more answers.

Wasn't the very definition of idiocy demarcated when one kept on, unchanging, in the face of mistaken actuality?

A hand alighted on Gamelyn's knee and squeezed, hard. Gamelyn turned, almost unwilling to John's gaze. Yet no blame there, either. Instead the peat-dark eyes lit slow fire in Gamelyn's belly, reminding him of the previous night. As much struggle as satisfaction, that last coupling, and John's fierce attentions both chide and reminder: while he didn't approve of his lover immuring himself in a monk's white habit and disappearing into some preceptory for months upon end, he knew why. Had even more reasons to see this through.

Aye, it was past time to return. Not home, but on north, to Temple Hirst, to the initiation he'd strived for. Gamelyn had tugged the leash overmuch of late. Hubert's patience would be tested. And Wymarec's.

The latter ticced a tiny, insolent smile to Gamelyn's lip.

But there was no denying he'd tarried overlong as it was. The solstice was fast approaching, and he'd been warned. He couldn't afford to wait another day, storm or no. More fool him, for insisting upon this small side journey.

What would All Hallows give him that he couldn't find anywhere else, at that? What was he seeking here? Comfort? Affirmation? Of what? He'd thought he had the answers: the Saxon rune-poems, the spirit names, the iron spells, cold and clever.

Gamelyn turned to Much. "Mayhap 'twould be best if you return to Tickhill. John is with me. And I know she never says it, but Marion expects you back in timely—"

"Marion 'spects both me and John to see you safe to Temple Hirst" was Much's laconic counter, as he returned a wary gaze to the lingering storm.

As if in reply, lightning traced a jagged arc against the clouds. Gamelyn counted five breaths before thunder rumbled, accompanied by the sharp scent of fractious light hanging midair. Hilal tossed his head, and Gamelyn laced fingers into his mane, tugging to quiet him. His own neck hairs stood on end. John dismounted, with a pat to the neck of his black gelding, who stood steady as he took Hilal's rein, humming beneath his breath. The grey quieted, and Gamelyn swung down with a jingle of mail and kit.

"I shan't be long," he promised, and melted into the chapel's gloom.

It took his eyes some time to adjust, but Gamelyn's ears caught the whisper of draperies against stone, following him up the aisle. She who roamed All Hallows no longer bided, chained, within one chapel, though Her relic—the dark Madonna—presided over the altar, dark eyes measuring his progress.

Yes, you have set me free. But My other face turns aside, heeds Me not save within the Rites.

He halted before the altar but did not kneel—not yet, not just yet—his eyes drinking in the relic. Her hands, graceful and strong, held Her son at suck. Her face and form sculpted of burnished, rarest mahogany, She remained like, yet so unalike his flesh-and-blood Lady. Her 'other face', cinnabar-pale and defiant.

Marion.

The children.

He clenched his fists, resisted the urge to bury his face in his hands.

God, but it was *so hard* to leave.

"My lord!" The voice boomed, filling the church and making Gamelyn start. "I surely wasn't expecting you!"

"Surely," Gamelyn replied, turning to see the priest, "we're long past 'my lord', Father."

A wide, wolfish grin, and Dolfin's startlingly blue eyes met his with the same empathy of always . . . and, as always, feet unshod and sandals tucked beside the brown tail of his robe and into his belt. Gamelyn's smile turned fond; it had been David who'd first dubbed him *Brother Tucked-Up-Robe*. The remaining ex-outlaws still called him Brother—well, Father Tuck, now—which Dolfin endured with waggish grace.

"You are my lord of Tickhill, and well deserved after so long a fight. But," Dolfin acknowledged, "as you wish. I did not mean to disturb you, Gamelyn, but what with the weather turning, I thought you'd already be up the North Road."

"Until the wind changes, I have time." Flinging his cloak back from plain woollen travelling clothes, Gamelyn strode forward to the priest, bent his head and knelt. "*Ignosce mihi, Pater, quia peccavi.*" Looked up. "Please."

One eyebrow crept upward, puzzled, but Dolfin merely nodded. "Give me a few moments to prepare."

"*Accedia.* You speak of despair, when to truly despair is to turn one's back upon God."

"A fair quandary, aye?" Gamelyn retorted, wry. "To turn upon oneself."

Dolfin sighed, taking this with the same aplomb as he'd taken other avowals, however edged with blasphemy. Wood creaked as he shifted where they had settled upon the bench nigh to the Lady's chapel. "A familiar one with you, my son, without drawing down either god or goddess. Nigh so as *superbia* . . . pride oozes through the cracks of any mask. Indeed, many are built upon it, while the scars of self-rending lie mostly invisible."

"To my relief. Yet . . . " Gamelyn's folded hands pressed firm against his chin, ready to smother injudicious speech. Thankfully the language of confessional made some candour simple—and tolerable. "I fear this as I've feared little else. To leave here, the home and sanctuary we've made . . . it grows past cruel, hardens into a despair past any rending. I fear I'll endure the pain too long, and in the enduring—"

"Give up?"

Gamelyn hadn't yet dared to speak that aloud, or bring it to being: of all the conjured spirits, this refused to be claimed, or tamed. To cede their years of battle as unwinnable. Allow content to hold him, and bide comfortable in their hard-won place . . . only it wasn't *their place*, not truly. Not since a vital third had been taken from Tickhill's Lord and Lady, leaving only a black-haired ghost to lie beside Gamelyn at night and vanish come dawn, a memory to creep up in random hallways as only the Thief of Sherwood could, and slay him in his tracks.

He had to guard against many enemies, and this the greatest of all. Acceptance. *Capitulation.*

"Gamelyn," Dolfin countered, soft, "would it be so terrible?"

"To give up? Give *in*?"

"Nay, to face the truth."

"And what is truth?" Gamelyn murmured against his hands.

"Mayhap one you yourself tendered your Masters, my son: that six years ago, Robyn Hode drowned in Barrow Mere."

Gamelyn clenched his teeth, eyes sliding upward. "The Fae exist, Dolfin; not as mere apparitions, but a reality trapped in an otherworld. I have seen them, surely as you have seen Our Lady walking this chapel."

Dolfin's gaze fled to the dark Madonna, discomfited.

"Answer me this, O Father Confessor. How is it those of the Church would beg for visions, yet when they actually have them, they doubt and turn away?"

"Gamelyn, it's not so—"

"Simple? Nay, this much is: the Fae took from me what is mine, and I will have him back. Robyn is *not dead.*"

"Would you know even if he were?" Dolfin didn't quail, though Gamelyn could see, reflected in the too-blue eyes, the fiery backlight of the Horned Lord's ire within his own.

The words were startingly gentle. Dolfin had long ago accepted what he'd once termed *my lord's ill-starred predisposition*, and—mostly—abjured the adjective, with the same deference he tendered that same lord's role in a cult of magicians, and the power of a faith more ancient than his own. He even consented to the familiarity of hearing Gamelyn's confession; though it had, over the years, become less absolution for sins unimagined than the honest counsel of a respected advisor.

But never before had Dolfin questioned this.

"I would know!"

"But now, unlike any other time you have come and tended confession to me, doubt lingers, and heeds the prickings of despair."

To that Gamelyn had no reply.

"Small wonder and smaller blame, to contemplate turning away from another soul-crushing crusade and seek comfort in what you do—"

"I will not turn away! I've endured all this for . . . for *him*."

"Not for yourself?"

"Aye, of course, for myself as well! I want him back, at my side, in my life, *in my bed*!" Gamelyn flung it at Dolfin as if throwing it in the teeth of the Church. Not the pure faith of its messiah, but rather the men who'd used His words to build a citadel unto ambition; who would call him unclean, unnatural; who turned their faces from any regard or oath they couldn't tax, beget, or control. "His sister longs to hold him close. The children deserve to know him."

"There are many who deserve to know those who have come before. Alas, such things are often impossible."

"The *Ceugant* cannot thrive without its Archer. The wild magic is his, embodied within him more than either myself or Marion. We need Robyn. His people need Robyn."

"Do they not have him, after all?"

"Do they?" Gamelyn murmured.

"You forget I was there, at the rites, when they called you Robyn Hode."

"Marion said it; it's a legend beginning to take hold."

"And beneath that, perhaps sacrifice was the more pressing need."

"I don't believe that!"

"Yet the land thrives."

"After he was taken, there was the hardest winter in memory. Famine ravaged the North; we're only now recovering."

"But we are recovering. Have been since your return to the rites and your goddess' call. The land, and Her people, have *you*."

"I," Gamelyn said through his teeth, "am not enough."

"Perhaps, in this time, you are." Dolfin spread his hands. "King John took his brother's throne with some controversy, and made promises, many as yet unkept, to a nation bled white by foreign wars. The remembrance of famine lingers. Another war looms likely with France. The land shows her bounty, and her present champion is no pagan peasant, but one who can walk both ley lines and court halls."

"Yet the land remains unsettled."

"Aye. The land is the King, and the King is the land." This time it wasn't King John that Dolfin meant. "You said it yourself: weakness and despair, those are the enemy. You've lost so much, my son, but in the losing you have gained. You have wealth, and holdings kept despite the fragility of royal promises. A position amidst the Templars' highest circles despite—or because of, perhaps—your transgressions."

Gamelyn met the gleam of curiosity within Dolfin's eyes, and answered it not. There were indeed transgressions the Templars would not permit.

Dolfin didn't let it go, a mastiff growling over a meaty bone. "Moreover, you've a household truly loyal to your family—and that family includes a wife and children to continue the respected place you have made amongst your people, both rich and poor."

"Respected? Or feared?"

"In our world, they go together."

"In *our* world," Gamelyn repeated, wooden. "Alas, what of the others?"

"Those aren't within my powers of advice."

"Bollocks! You're a priest!"

"As are you, my lord," Dolfin chided, and returned the slight, caustic smile that crept across Gamelyn's face. "Unlike you, however, I'm quite content with mundane paths. In my time I've carried sword, shield, and cross; been a warrior, then a humble monk, and now?" He leaned forward, smile broadening, "Now, my lord of Tickhill asked specifically for me, to take charge of a chapel that many consider haunted by ancient demons."

Gamelyn snorted. Just beyond the Madonna's ebony visage, he glimpsed stars and indigo. Smelt desert roses, and felt a ripple of humour.

"But neither have I have I carried a mitre and walked the path of prophets, nor" —Dolfin met and matched Gamelyn's gaze— "worn the horns and hood of the old gods and lain with a goddess."

"Lord?" Quiet, insistent . . . and accompanied by a ripple of distant thunder. Not Much, who wouldn't interrupt save for a cadre of bandits galloping over the nearest hillock. Gamelyn turned to the slight figure pacing up the aisle. John gave respect to this church because of those ancient 'demons', humility affording a perceptive and brilliant inner star: he knew when to act, and how, and didn't go on about it.

The wind has turned, John signed, undaunted by Dolfin's heavy sigh—the latter did not lightly tolerate being interrupted in confessional. *If you mean to travel north today, we must go.*

Dolfin gave John a grimace—which he ignored, being John— then rose and said, quiet, "*Bendith,* friends. Go with God."

Near Barrow Mere & the ruin of Loxley village
Hallamshire/Yorkshire
Waning of Winter Solstice, 1194 CE
Or, mayhap, none of the above.

He smelt smoke, at the first; the dull, dry tang of wood long seasoned. Then acrid musk—both beast and human—and smouldering herbs, and smoking meat, and . . .

Something else as well: unfamiliar, sweet, vague.

Echoes quivered within hearing: the drip of water, thick with silt-milk into cavern pools, the muted rumble of some activity vibrating through stone, the pop and hiss of fire speaking against chill and darkness.

The utter pleasure of that last, warming one bearded cheek, tracing his left arm to ribs and hip. He was naked beneath soft plush: rabbit fur? Aye, a stitched-together coverlet of skins warming him where fire didn't. His hair fell in ringlets across his eyes, still damp.

And he *remembered.*

Taking in a guarded-silent breath, Robyn let his eyes slide open, slow. Firelight threw coppery spears past twinned shields of dark lashes and darker forelock; it glanced against pale, scarred skin of one pectoral, scattered sideways against the pit of dark fur joining an upflung arm. He willed his exhale slow, unremarkable, the even pace of sleep. Something flickered against pale stone walls. From the fire? From something else? Instincts quivered, pervasive upon the latter.

He was not alone.

Robyn coiled, akin to one of those desert serpents Gamelyn had once recounted, and struck. His hands seized hide, fur, and hair; in the next breath he slammed the shadow figure against the cavern wall. A small cry; Robyn choked it silent with one hard hand, the other groping for his knife to find only the tail edge of the fur coverlet, slithering down his body to crumple at his feet. He kicked it aside.

The 'shadow' had thick, fair hair, with grey eyes white-wide through a smudge of chalk and kohl. The hands gripped tight-corded to his wrists were painted, too, as if for the spellmaking, and woad swathed broad cheekbones, blue snaking across taupe. Bits of tooled copper gleamed against flared nostrils and along one ear.

Frightened. Young. Female.

The last two made Robyn hesitate. The lass took the opportunity, and with an oath shoved him backwards. Another set of hands reached from the shadows and twisted his arms behind him—or tried to. Others rushed in, and the fight was on.

All several hands smaller than he, but no matter there; they were stouter, painted and oiled as if going into a wrestling ring, and moreover, fought like battle-hardened warriors. Robyn twisted, kicked, punched; in short used every trick in an ill-gained lexicon of dirty fighting. They merely piled on like wolves attacking a wounded bear. Hard, woad-vined hands immobilized him and, with a twist as nigh wrenched his teeth from his head, had him facing an elder. The elder spat something unintelligible, and gestured with one lean, pale arm traced with woad—snakes. Grey twist-locks bounced about his waist with the movement.

Another male sauntered forward. Built like a bull with pate half shaved, half braided locks, tied back from a face painted to resemble an indigo skull.

The skull grinned, and dove head-first into Robyn's midsection. The breath drove from him in a painful *"Chuuh!"* of spit and air.

Those tens of hands kept him upright . . . barely. He sagged, hoping they'd drop him, loose him, something. Instead Skull Face went for him again. Another blow, another in-close tussle Robyn couldn't hope to fight. Amidst a twist sideways, his desperate eye fastened upon a coppery glint: a broad knife stuck in Skull Face's belt, athwart his right buttock. Robyn ducked again and managed to wrench one hand free. Snatching the knife and heaving upward beneath all the prisoning hands, employing the muscles used to pull a longbow's might, Robyn slashed outward.

The knife made contact: thrice, if the sudden shouts and loosening of his left leg were anything to go on. Sucking desperately at the air still refusing his aching lungs, Robyn writhed again, whipping his new weapon through the air. Another cry from behind, and in front a bare miss of the elder, who leapt back and hissed a command. Robyn flung himself forward again. His antagonists parted in a small wave before the knife edge; Robyn ran up against the painted cavern wall, using it to ricochet back into the fray.

He merely dove through another wave of avoidance. Then another.

So Robyn halted, crouching, the fire at his back and knife at ready. The painted warriors ringed him, a silent and gravid semicircle of predators.

The elder issued another quiet command. The clot of warriors backed off, albeit slight. Robyn frowned, peering at the elder. A half-smile twitched the elder's lip; he nodded and extended one lined hand, plainly asking for the knife.

"Nay," Robyn said, returning the tiny smile. "I don't think so."

The old man tsked, shrugged, then gestured.

"Aw, bloody damn . . ."

For sure enough—and Robyn had to admire the discipline—the warriors whirled and leapt for him.

No time to kick his own arse; it was plain they were going to do it for him. An elbow aimed for Robyn's nose and he ducked, slashed with the knife. A fist cracked into his ribs before he could dodge. He staggered sideways into a waiting trio. They seized Robyn's knife hand; hard, thick fingers dug into his wrist tendons, forcing his fingers open, nerveless. The knife clattered against the stone floor in shrill, brassy plaint as a thick, tattooed arm snugged around his throat.

At least by the time they forced him to his knees, he'd taken five more out of the running. But they kept coming. And coming.

Robyn took some comfort in how it took seven of them to spread-eagle him on the floor, writhing and bucking. The stone abraded his naked back and buttocks, but he refused to stop fighting. Skull Face—unfortunately not amongst those Robyn had taken out—growled out what surely had to be a curse. He straddled Robyn and sat down hard.

"I'd rather be knowin' you a bit better before we have a quick tup, thanks aw . . . fly!" It trailed into a hiccup as Skull Face whipped out a copper dagger and held it beneath Robyn's chin. No question, but the fellow's next spat-out comment bided less than complimentary.

Their speech sounded familiar, somehow.

And bloody damn, but Skull Face was *heavy* for all he was shorter than little John . . .

John. Where was John? They'd been heading northeast from Mam Tor and the caverns, stopping at the Mere before they returned home. And odd, so odd that Robyn should ever think of a nobleman's castle as home of any sort, but Gamelyn was there, and Marion, and the rest of their people, all comfortable and tucked up, badgers in an odd burrow.

He'd left John on the edge of Barrow Mere, intent upon seeing to a sacred place. Instead . . .

How fitting, that the Mere had taken him at the last. Had he drowned, then, with this some sort of dream-drunk afterlife? Because these people didn't look anything like the aloof Fae of tales told to a wandering child who refused to stay in bed. They looked more akin to his mother's people: dark and small and solid as the stones. Particularly the elder who strode forward, shoving up the bone-bead armlets on his thin, powerful arms. He spoke, seeming all the while too reasonable.

Skull Face grinned a reply, this time with his own small, white teeth, and leaned closer.

Robyn grinned right back. And head-butted Skull Face with all his might.

Skull Face collapsed backward with a harsh grunt. Robyn saw stars himself. Bloody *hard*, the man's head, and the proof of that as Skull Face recovered. With a furious howl, he lunged back atop Robyn, slashing the copper dagger across his chest.

The elder's stoic calm finally showed damage: he lurched

forwards, his snarled shout echoing into the cavern. A collective gasp sucked back and forth amongst the other warriors. Robyn blinked, surprised more by that than any strike.

And then the pain hit, a deep sear of acid in the knife's wake.

It felled him flat, the burning . . . nay, the agony, twitching his limbs and heaving sickness up into his throat. 'Twas all Robyn could do, for long moments, to not puke like a bairn too long at the mead.

Another voice, a whip-crack from the darkness to make the elder's fury seem tame. Robyn blinked, shook his head. Watched as Skull Face flung the knife away and scuttered sideways like a kicked cur, fear scrawled thicker across his face than any paint.

The knife clattered against rock and into silence. Robyn's head grew heavy, heavier; the next thing he knew he was flat out, limbs twitching, gut heaving, *helpless* . . . all from a nonsensical, shallow slice that shouldn't cause such pain, that must be a gaping wound from which his heart sought to burst through exposed ribs.

Poison. It must be.

Myriad shadows drifted into one. Looming large and well defined against the far wall, it ran the curve of cavern roof to dance closer. Gritting his teeth, Robyn again tried to raise his head. Hard, callused fingers tangled in his forelock, preventing it, forcing the back of his skull against the cavern's floor.

And he couldn't do a bloody thing to stop it, staring up and gasping into the thick silence like a landed fish.

The interior hum gave way to an exterior rattle-ring; something glinted and swayed just above his forehead, blurred then coalesced into a clutch of tiny copper bells, tangling with beads of stone and bone and wood. The sharp-sweet waft of some herb filled his nostrils, edged with smoke. Another command rang deep against his ears, this holding a power that set a distant dance behind Robyn's eyes.

Darkness parted then drew closer, flitted and played with his vision, dove a hum deep within his skull. No poison, no blood on his tongue, no nausea; this held an inky, familiar taste of earth and rain, of rot and fecund green: the magic, old and deep. Numerous skeins of possibility twining, twisting . . . *there*. Tynged's familiar loom plaiting and unravelling futures into the black.

Robyn snatched at the strands, gained hold, *hung on*.

The hand upon his forehead loosened. His hearing, abruptly, worked, letting in a small whispered chant echoing against the rocks. The breath of bodies swaying. Skull Face's whimpers against the wall. Sensations crowding, suddenly—too much, *too much*— and Robyn nearly heaved again. Instead he gritted his teeth, sucked in more air, and levelled his gaze upon his would-be benefactor.

Amber eyes met his, pale amidst hair and skin, the effect heightened by the careful brush strokes of char and woad. The antlers of a brocket seemed to grow from thick, chalk-streaked black hair, the latter braided into innumerable plaits, hung with dried mistletoe berries and oak galls, gilded with hammered copper discs and bird skulls. From neck to nipples, swirls of crimson, indigo, and chalk adorned her, with more permanent sigils spiralling along ribs and belly, trailing down beneath the fur knotted at one hipbone.

She was—and was not—familiar. She was—was not—the Wode-wose Girl he'd Seen within the chapel of All Hallows. This bore no resemblance to his sister. This was no girl.

The paint about those pale eyes creased, here and there, in tiny, telltale lines. Her hands hadn't the plump sleekness of youth, instead flexed sinewy, capable. Old-white scars traced one muscled bicep, and her breasts and belly confirmed a woman's honours: softened and scarified from bearing and nursing children.

Robyn had known he wasn't a man for women from the time his body had started quickening to its own hungers. But he knew beauty when he saw it, could respond to the ache of what this woman represented. No impossibly-unbroached Virgin Mother, this, or even a Spring Maiden flush with new green, seed, and blossom—*Marion,* the thought flickered, forlorn, *where are you?*—this power was practiced, primal; as natural and unpredictable as a sow with young. As close to a mother-goddess walking as Robyn had ever seen . . . and even his sister hadn't carried this. Marion's light had only begun spilling through mortared cracks, stunted and enslaved within Church walls for too long. Not even, mayhap, his mother . . . though Robyn abruptly remembered a long-ago May Eve, Eluned holding the Rite in her small, capable hands, sending his father to the Hunt. Robyn still remembered the tremor it had instilled within him: as much fear as love.

There was no love here, in this foreign, oddly familiar place. There was only fear. And, in its wake, anger.

You took me away! From my sister and her bairn-to-be, from my little John, from my family, from Gamelyn. . . Why?

As if in answer, the priestess smiled, and held out her hand for Skull Face's knife.

-IV-

Never was he denied this vigil, even if swept in the bow wave of some demanding rite. This always remained, as the first thing he did upon returning to preceptory walls.

Well, first thing after seeing to his horse.

Still dusty from the road, blunt-cropped, russet hair tangled with sweat and wind, Gamelyn left his garb and weapons—save one—piled at the door to the chapel of the Magdalene. He approached barefoot, clad only in braies. Normally he would place the quillion dagger before Her altar and kneel; after a silent communion would he sing, low, the Song of Songs as offering. This time, he prefaced obeisance with a kiss, then a length of cord, unbound from his hipbones beneath Her dark eyes. He laid both at the carven, ebony feet of his Lady.

Pristine and newly-plaited when he'd left for the Feast of Beltane, the cord—new-stained with earth, and sweat, and seed— had ripened into a true measure. Drawn to the sacred geometry of each individual, girdled in service of the magicks of a new existence—and in clandestine honour of another lying deep in the caverns of Mam Tor. His first measure lay twined with Robyn's and Marion's, cushioned amidst those bound to the Shire Wode covenant. Hidden—and protected.

A slight breeze lifted Gamelyn's hair as he finished his devotions; it wafted sandalwood, desert roses, and Her voice. *Aye, My love, your oaths bide safe and your people prosper. You have made the* heiros gamos *with your Maiden, and defended your crown.*

Summer returns, to enrich the land. A tiny echo of Marion crept in, lax with mead and sex. *You have done well by Me.*

Gamelyn raised his eyes. No longer trapped in ancient wood but breathing, *real:* Her skin gleaming like old honey, Her black hair tumbling, burnished with a trace of coppery light, Her body draped in stars and indigo. The rigid-cool feet he had but a breath before kissed still shone akin to burnished mahogany, but they were warm, hennaed like a new bride, and jingled softly with hammered rings of gold and silver as She stepped down from the pedestal. Tucking the alabaster urn snug in one bare arm, she knelt, indigo pooling upon the altar as she riffled breath and fingers through his hair.

He shivered and held Her gaze, pulse pounding with thick heat behind his ears. Whispered, "Why, then?"

Black eyes gleamed, lined with more henna, kohl, and dots of chalk. They seemed . . . curious? Chiding?

"It should have worked. The Rite should have given our workings strength. I prepared so carefully: timing, formulae—"

The Rite is for the Land. When you think to winnow power from what gives you life, you must choose altogether carefully.

"Lady, I took the greatest of care."

All of you within My Temple are so careful. So shrewd. Yet you would tether a wild horse, only to be astonished when either rope or neck breaks.

Gamelyn rocked back onto his heels, peering at her. "I don't—"

Understand. How can you, here, so far from the source of all you would try to shepherd? Gaze sweeping towards the entry, she shrugged and turned, mounted the step. *Alas, it seems we have little time. They come for you.*

He heard footsteps—a slow and hesitant approach—but didn't move. The acolytes would not come past the door until he was finished, for some of them saw Her. More, saw to whom She gave such attention.

Your 'Master' has given the orders, as usual. Fool of a man, to think he can scrub My touch from you.

Aye, particularly upon this return would the bath be waiting, scalding and poured over his head like baptism. And the stinging scrub of salt, ablution and—blatant—absolution. A recurring prescription of purification, intended to counter what the Master Preceptor considered an 'overindulgence' of pagan ways.

It matters not, for they cannot, he answered Her, silent. In truth, discomfort held its own solace. Habit—preference, really—to compartmentalise intent into such neat and isolated parcels. Focus. Endure. Survive.

As he'd told Marion, he was very, very good at it.

Aye. So who is truly master? She countered. *One who deems the magic a puppet to dance upon strings, or one who draws down the moon and stars upon his brothers' places? You hold the reins and fondle the keys to eternities, even as the Winterlord wakes to rattle his chains.*

The Lady rarely made reference to Robyn, and it set every nerve tingling, desperate. Gamelyn started upward, a hundred questions on his lips; at the last moment remembered the ones waiting. Instead, he clenched his teeth and hunched down, silent.

Even the blind magus will soon heed Us.

And what was 'soon' to a divinity, anyway? How much more would he have to endure?

Initiation is endurance, She chided, *and failure but one teacher amidst the many. Aye, it is indeed past time you should met* My brother-King.

The words ran another frisson down his spine—this chill, uncertain.

Have no fear. You will know Him, love Him as you have Me. Her smile, albeit small, was contagious. *It is your nature, your. . . predisposition.*

Gamelyn ducked his head. Smelt desert blooms, and spikenard.

Then kissed the indigo hem and arose, to meet the white-clad elders waiting at the entry to the Magdalene's chapel.

◁

"Milady Marion?"

At first, the voice would seem only one more person in need; one more amidst the cacophony, both human and animal, filling the great castle bailey. Vendors shouted directives and promises, hobbled geese tootled, cows lowed at their ties. Hens complained and roosters challenged, punctuating the blat and mewl of goats and sheep penned in withy paddocks. Any passage rose a haze of dust from the green sward that even the previous rains couldn't deny; in fact, damp made it worse: clinging in one's nostrils, leaving a skim upon skin and a dull drag-line upon even the best-brushed hem.

It smelled lovely. Damp earth and stone and, just about the edges, the hint of summer leaves upon a nimble wind taking any storms far into the North . . .

"Marion!"

Recognition set in, and Marion turned to see her lover striding across the grass. Much dodged a clutch of marketgoers, several children playing tag, and an unfortunate loose cockerel who squawked and barely avoided the hoofs of the horse trotting beside on a loose rein. Much had straw in his beard, muddy boots and leggings, and a damp-mottled cloak, but also a smile on his face. He was *home*.

In several long strides he'd caught Marion up into his arms, swinging her around 'til she was dizzy.

His palfrey snatched the opportunity to graze, whilst several bystanders greeted the display with enthusiastic claps and more than a few whistles. Marion noted a few, however, who peered askance at a common soldier, however well dressed, being so free with the Lady of Tickhill.

'Tweren't sommat she could afford to forget: market day brought in judgemental outsiders, who'd weigh a woman harsher than any man and find her wanting. Particularly if she held any authority to threaten their own mean existence.

So while a kiss was what she wanted, one hard enough to weaken her knees, she settled for Much bowing over her hand. At that, his smile promised the weak knees and more—later, in the privacy of her chambers.

"He's back safe, then." More statement than question; she knew Much wouldn't have returned so soon otherwise.

"Aye." Much fell in behind her as she ventured on. "Where are t' little ones?"

"Likely in the stables goggling over a new litter of kittens. Even market couldn't compare with that!"

He laughed, blue eyes calm and missing nothing. Scanning the walls and defences—noting how many and where, ticking off the nobility, freemen, and peasantry with much the same mien—Much focused on a corner vendor stall that had taken up a little more than his fair space. "Shall I talk to that 'un? His neighbour en't too happy, and the bypath's squeezed tight."

"That's where we're going now." She gave him a sideways smile.

"Makes me twitchy, like, t' see the front gates wide open."

"Me, too. But we can't exactly up the bridge and heat the pitch on market day!"

His eyes lit, teasing. "Might be a lark at that."

"A lark, aye, but we don't want to scare off good custom. 'Tis only our first market since regaining the license. Though" — Marion gave his arm a light squeeze— "your second commander thought it mightn't be bad, to prepare for the worst. So he did. Minus pitch, I must say. Too bloody expensive, that."

A chuckle. "En't it just. But Tom's a good Heathen, and he remembers t' past several years. Before Himself decided to nose in."

It had been a blessing amidst the undeniable curse to have a royal entourage in residence, complete with Templars and the King flying the golden lions. But Marion was glad 'Himself rarely stayed in residence more than a day or so.

"A foolish proposition to take this castle, even without a lot of royal soldiers." Much's blue eyes caught hers, teasing. "Milord might be away, but milady has her own ways of dealin' wit' thieves."

"Having known my share, you mean?" Marion smirked back, then shrugged. "I'm just glad the majority of the horde's well away." She'd watched her plenteous stores dwindle beneath the weight of the King's retinue with something akin to panic.

Five years ago, the blight and resultant famine had descended, as if in the wake of Robyn's disappearance. Its effects still lingered, here and there. The crofts hadn't forgotten, and neither had a crofter's daughter turned nobleman's wife.

The market stall proved easily settled. The offending vendor, true enough, bided a good Heathen and complied with his Maiden's decision. Marion smiled behind one hand, sure that Much's presence—all dark and handsome brawn, girt with mail and sword—hadn't damaged her cause, either.

"I'd hoped John would return with you, at least for these few special days, and . . ." Trailing off, Marion returned the bow of Pontefract's lord as he passed. Called, "D'you and your lady still plan t' sup with us tonight, my lord Baron?"

Roger de Lacy smiled, boomed, "It would be our honour, my lady."

"Better the devil y' know," Much muttered as de Lacy and his small cohort passed.

"We each keep one eye hard upon the other, I'm sure," Marion agreed.

"Huh. As long as y' wain't trust his like further than y' can throw 'im. That one and his brother both."

"The Baron has two brothers."

"You know which one I mean, and it en't the Prior."

"You yourself ensured de Lisle's journey back to Knaresborough."

"Aye, and I've a man detailed to make sure he stays there." Much gave a quick nod. "But lass, I fear our Johnny's away, back to the Hermit's caverns."

She'd feared as much, but, "I so wish he would have come back here."

"I wish he would, too. But t' holy places need him."

Aye, well, no question but someone had to guard that gateway. "I worry after . . ." She lowered her voice, looked around to make sure none was within earshot. "I'm feared They might take him, too."

"If They"—Much forked an evil eye somewhat southeast —"mean t' take our Johnny, They'd have done t' first time."

John had gone into the Mere after Robyn, but the Barrow folk had tossed him back into thisworld like a too-small fish. Marion was merely thankful John held enough of Their blood to not have drowned in the attempt.

"Fewer and fewer reg'lar folk go nigh t' Barrow Mere. None with sense, leastways."

And how sensible had their latest attempt been? Gamelyn had been so sure they could take Robyn back. Marion herself, still fair humming from the Beltane Rites, had thought nothing could stand against them.

Back to back, nothing can stand against you. . .

Yet there had been no answer from the otherworlds. As if Robyn was not even there.

It should have been the answer! The Rite and its triumphant aftermath had pointed the way. The otherworld beckoning, ripe for its barriers to be broken and all the while seeping a slow bleed into this one: from the Mere casting an eerie spell, to as far away as Nottingham, still teeming with the effects of the Wild Hunt.

Although—Marion grimaced—the newest Sheriff bided too heart-blind to notice anything but hard tender and hardy villeins working his fields.

Tickhill itself housed its own contingent of little Fae spirits, all following their Maiden and courting her attentions. Even now one of the gwyllion perched on her shoulder, making contented burblings and nuzzling at her ear.

All the signs had been clear. In good faith they'd prepared, worked an alchemy of ancient magic set upon those barriers by a Heathen Mother-Maid and a Templar Magician who wore the Horns by right and Rite . . .

Merely to fall. To fail.

Gamelyn's despair had been raw as a new-skinned carcass. Her own despair had long ago leached itself into cold, righteous anger. If Gamelyn had work? Well. So had she.

"*Bendith y mamau*, milady." A young lass, passing by with a gaggle of shod geese obedient to her crook, acknowledged those powers with a quick curtsey and a subtle, reverent sign.

Those were fine and healthy birds. Marion marked where the lass headed . . . ah, with the three sisters who farmed nigh Maltby.

Work. Aye. Whilst otherworldly influences continued to spread, settling into places long left fallow or made over to newer gods, whilst the gwyllion on her shoulder might be invisible to most— with those who did fancy seeing sommat averting their eyes— Marion set to heeding, and channelling, the old powers. More and more drew nigh to Tickhill: displaced villeins seeking refuge; outlaws escaping the same royal forest within which they'd broken or breached the law; cunning folk turned from their village beneath Church persecution; free Heathens paying homage to the lord and lady who'd made the land bear fruit again. Often her covenant found them, through Gilbert's forestry duties, or David's travels to procure necessities for the castle, or Gunnora, who held the ancient lines running deep along the ridge of the Peak and down through the village of Hathersage.

And all the while the network grew, a spider's web spun one strand at a time, woven witness to the rising of the Shire Wode. No longer bound to obscurity, the forest spirits blinked lamp eyes open against the harsher aspects of thisworld and progressed outward. Evolving.

They all were. Even Robyn, surely . . . though he lingered astray with the passage sealed behind him. Her fists clenched. "I hope—"

"Milady Marion?"

The call came from the stall they'd just passed; a wizened pig farmer, hat yanked from his pate, gesticulated for attention. His stock snuffled about his feet like friendly puppies, scrubbed pink and bedded fresh. "Milady, beggin' your pardon, but I've the pork y' ast for. I've sent boy wit', up t' kitchens."

"Thank you, George." Marion returned to the stall, digging in her purse; when he thought to protest, she put the coins in his cap. "For your wife and the wee one, then. You've tithed your share and more this season. Anne's fettling, I hope?"

"Your tonic did t' trick, thank you, milady. Me good wife's up already and on the mend. Plenty of milk, so our babe's fat and strong as a fine piglet!"

"Good. I'll bring my kit, come see her and t' bairn once all this" —Marion gestured to the market— "has come and been."

They continued on, hadn't gone far before Much, voice bespeaking what tenderness he couldn't openly impart, prompted, "What d'you hope, pet?"

"I hope . . . " She trailed away to smile and bow thanks as a merchant came forward to hand over a basket of dried apples. Finished, tight and low, "I hope Robyn's well. Wherever he is."

◈

Caverns were never truly silent. Always they echoed, always betrayed the *drip-drip-drip* of silt and water, or the tumble of calving rocks both small and large, or the passage of air: earth-breath, wafting comfort or prickling one's nape.

Yet even the cavern held its breath as the Priestess rose and held out both hands, palms-up, for the knife. Skull-face's hands trembled as he relinquished the weapon, and he didn't meet the Priestess's eyes.

Robyn took the opportunity, however small, and tried to rise.

The Priestess didn't even turn, but spoke a soft word. Tens of hands took hold of him again, yanked his limbs to all points. Robyn couldn't help the yip that escaped: surprise, fury, and aye, pain.

Still the Priestess refused to turn, but her next words snapped like a quirt. The hands shifted, no reduction of tensile strength but less pain, more accommodation. Robyn belatedly realised the several warriors holding him were female. The males formed a loose semicircle beyond, breaking ranks then reforming as the Priestess came forward—and aye, but she deserved those bloody royal capitals Prince John had so annoyingly craved.

The dagger flat upon her palms, deliberate, she put one foot against his right hip and one against his left. Then she knelt, straddling him not unlike Skull Face had done.

A smile—rather unpleasant to be sure—quirked Robyn's lip as

the Priestess leaned in, nose almost touching his. Plainly responding to his challenge, she leaned in, thighs tightening against his ribs and bare toes curving beneath his buttocks. Balancing the dagger upon one hand, she used the other to push the curls back from his forehead and trail her fingers along the left side of his face, riffling the beard curling along his jaw and neck, the fur tracing his collarbones and breastbone.

He let her. Not that he'd much choice, those hands holding him had turned to stone in a protection Robyn well recognised and respected. But it wasn't in him to remain sullen—that was Gamelyn's fancy—and a quiver of worry and longing flickered at the name, tailed by a hope, fleeting, after the safety of his own.

Not that he could do anything about it if he didn't make it past this . . . well, whatever it was. Robyn tilted his chin up, let his grin slide broad and purred, "Happens I've been tried by some proper fancy whores. You'd have to sprout some tackle to hope at takin' me on."

A tilt of head, a return growth in her smile; she tightened her knees and slid to lie upon him, belly to belly. Yet no disappointment flickered her expression as he remained flaccid without even a promising quiver. The Priestess merely sucked in a deep breath and let it whistle out between her teeth. The breath, at first warm, went to frost, trailing across his ribs and down. Robyn's smile faltered as she carefully laid the dagger below the wound it had tendered. Warm, the blade, as if it had been laid in the fire— which no longer bided a pile of ember and ash, but a blaze flickering gold.

She pushed back, spat just above the dagger slice on his chest. Robyn leapt like a hare as she traced her three middle fingers in a sigil cold and plain upon his breast:

The horns of the moon-crown, within the full moon spiral. The latter—slow, precise—throbbed with a magic that only Marion should possess in thisnow.

Where in bloody buggering hell was he?

The Priestess pinned him with a flat gaze. Robyn refused to drop his own. He'd often claimed the Lady didn't much like him, and it was as if in that moment both of them—Horned Priest and Mother Priestess—acknowledged it.

Holding to the stare-down, she rocked upright and extended one hand, palm up. The hands upon him obeyed with a rough manoeuvre that lurched Robyn halfway upright. The young grey-eyed lass he'd first encountered glided into view. She'd a tiny hank of dark wool teased across her fingertips, which she untangled, altogether serious and reverential, into her Priestess's outstretched palm. The Priestess nodded, smiled at her acolyte—the girl was that and more, Robyn could see the *tynged* tying them—and brought the wool to her lips, whispering. She used it to clean the seep of blood beginning to clot along the shallow knife-slice.

The wake of woollen passage against his ribs left no pain, eased the sting, and drew from him an inexplicable, deep shudder.

The Priestess smiled, and held the blood-streaked wool to Robyn's lips.

Robyn answered the smile, tight, with a tiny shake of his head. She already had his blood through accident or design; unlikely she'd tap his seed no matter how much she ground down on him, so neither would he willingly give over anything else.

Other than the sweat he'd rise in getting the hell out of here. Wherever here was.

The Priestess raised her white-dotted eyebrows, tilted her head and smiled.

Bent over and fastened her mouth to his.

Flabbergasted for a mind-emptied brace of heartbeats, Robyn let her. Outrage finally set in; he lurched sideways, clenched his jaw, even tried to bite down. As if he were a disobedient horse refusing to take the bit, the Priestess merely poked her knuckles into his jaw and held his mouth open against hers, twined her tongue with his and finished the job.

And bloody *damn* but she was good at it.

Then his knob, never adverse to a bit of rough rut in the teeth of danger, actually started a feeble and humiliating protest: no doubt that mouth had other useful skills, and an arse was an arse, after all; mayhap if he'd a go from the back . . .

Down, lad, he growled. *Bloody traitor.*

With a wet *smack* that echoed into the caverns, the Priestess loosed Robyn. Putting the small hank of wool in her mouth, she swabbed her tongue with it, pulled it free, and held it between them.

Teased a full, hissing breath upon it.

A skein of ice shivered its wake, belly to nose. Robyn juddered and fell back. His captors released him, and as his head hit unforgiving stone his eyes went black, a rainbow clutch of skeins and threads flying past him, curling about him, wrapping about him, *strangling.*

Again, Robyn was deathly afraid.

Then he was livid.

He sank within, captured the tynged dancing wild behind his eyes, and swirled it into a thick, multi-hued swath. Plaited it, unthinking, into puzzle pieces of sound and Sight, flung it around him like a flail, spun it into arrow and string and took aim.

In a blur of motion, Robyn lurched up and flipped his captor onto her back, fingers streaking her throat pale, other hand prisoning hers with the blood-soaked wool.

Belatedly the snick and slide of armaments registered, the startled animosity of her people reflected in the glint of not only bronze and copper, but bared teeth.

They didn't attack.

Neither did Robyn release the Priestess. She didn't so much as struggle, peering up at him with a considerable, shrewd waiting. Comprehension niggled deep, more puzzle pieces fitting and resolving themselves with tiny, nigh-audible clicks.

"Aye, then." His tongue slipped and slid into the Barrow-speech—another knowing, deep within, that he refused to question. "If my blood has this sort of power, I'm thinking none of you've the rights to spill it. En't my time, woman. More, you know it."

She smiled. *And what is being Time but meaningless, here? You be misconstruing. All of it.*

Her lips hadn't moved, her throat hadn't so much as vibrated beneath his fingers. Nonetheless, Robyn heard the words. Like the god and goddess speaking silent behind his eyes . . . the tiny, unformed thought-flickers from his sister or his lover . . . the not-speech of the otherworlds formed into the Barrow-tongue of his mother's people. Yet this was far, far older. He had, until now, only heard it with his mind and heart.

Aye, until thisnow. Thisnow, you be listening. Knowing. Be releasing me, boy, I must be completing amends.

Robyn wasn't sure he liked being called 'boy', and neither was he sure he should release that blood-and-sputum streaked wool. He did, however, release his grip on her throat.

"Easy be, my own." The Priestess met his eyes as she spoke to her people—slowly, allowing Robyn to untangle the odd tilt of Barrow-like speech. "He will not be hurting me."

"Great Mother!" Skull Face, a growl of protest.

"Easy be!" The decree rang soft, but final. Her people lowered their weaponry, stepped back.

The Priestess sat up beneath Robyn, propping on one arm. She raised her hand, still caged with his, the wool flattened in their palms. "I must be amending my own's mistake. Blood-price paid, final, in fire."

It was an old, old rite, twitching nigh-forgotten in Robyn's memory. His old mentor Cernun had once spoken of it, how blood drawn heedless in a place of power must be neutralised. Doubly so, if it was the blood of the god's chosen.

The Priestess reached up, tangled hard fingers at Robyn's nape and drew him down close. "Be of trust in this much," she whispered against his cheek. "I be knowing you, Hooded Lord."

He stood, pulling her with him. "Burn it, then."

For several breaths she considered him. Then, lips a-quirk, she strode over and gave the crimson-streaked woollen to the fire.

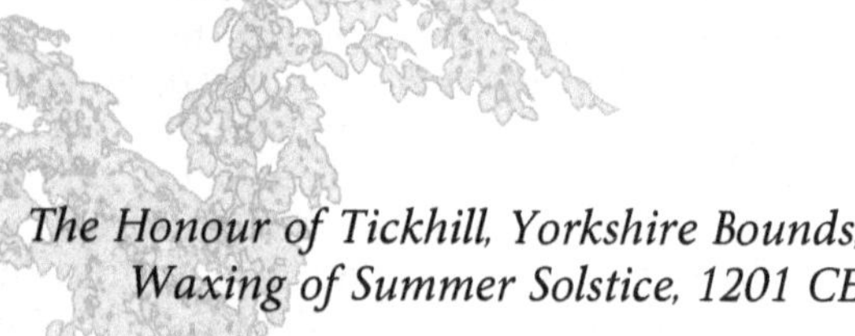

-V-

The Honour of Tickhill, Yorkshire Bounds,
Waxing of Summer Solstice, 1201 CE

*M*arion's Book of Hours:

6 years, 6 months, two weeks and 8 days –
<u>*Our Lord Shall Return*</u>

My lord husband is back to his preceptory, the land bides quiet, and none knows if our new liege will rise—or fall, more like—to the level of his crown. May Eve gave some answers, but only the Templars know how they'll play him in this strange game. All I know is I'd rather not play.

There's precious little liking in me for this path we so carefully tread, but we've been left with little enough choice. Things have to change, else we'll be ground down to dust and drift away, nowt but folk tales to hint where and how our people walked this land. Something has to survive—even if only in these words I pen and hide away. Even the Templars understand that much, revering such secrets. Even if held by a green Wode-gotten Maiden.

Some of them, anyway.

Mam always said it: often the goddess asks a price, so that we might better understand what gifts we're given, but...

She's played us all, hasn't She? From Robyn's disappearance to the failure after May Eve. She's lied to us, stolen my brother and bidden him walk the Barrow Lines for some hidden purpose... and aye, John would fork an evil eye at me for saying such things and tempting fate's hand. Sod that! I'll not only say it, but write it down like the conquerors would; give it that power as well, see it's never, ever forgotten.

And our new forms of cunning work. The land prospers, and this year's harvest comes a definite promise: fields heavy with grain, apple trees and brambles a'bud, and...

And I feel certain I am with child.

May our ways endure, and the land accept our oath, blood and heart, to remain fruitful.

Tickhill's secretive corridors—the same that had meant ruin and betrayal to Gamelyn as a boy—now gave immense benefit to Marion. In particular a narrow stair, leading from a forgotten exit in the undercroft and to a half-door beneath the bed in the castle's main solar, had become a repository, to conceal her most precious things. Like her Book of Hours: outwardly a religious salter, but with inward sentiments altogether treasonous—blasphemous—to Church and Crown.

Come the winter, though, likely t'would be difficult to shimmy on her belly beneath the bed. Sliding the door open, she wriggled closer and slid the parchment roll into a leathern bag next to another. Giving her cache a fond pat, she scooted back, slid the small door shut—

"Marion?"

—and jerked, bumping her head on the bed slats.

"Marion, are you here?"

A small mutter of relief escaped her chest as she recognised the voice. Gilbert knew of the tunnels, even used some of them, if to different purpose. She rolled from beneath the bed and stood up, shaking out her skirts.

"Gilly, I didn't expect you so soon. You look well!"

And he did; beard trimmed to a point in the newest style, overtunic and breeks brushed to a sheen, and not merely a pheasant's feather in his cap but a peacock's as well, with arrows fletched as gaily in a quiver 'crost his back. Many called Sherwood's Head Forester a dandy, more set upon impressing his lady Keeper than anything. Gilbert frankly encouraged it, too, a flirting sendup meant to fool those who'd scoff at said dandy's history. Despite being a noble's brat, Gilbert's archery had well earned his place with Robyn Hode's outlaws.

"You look positively radiant." Gilbert turned from the writing table with a bow, flashing the smile that stopped many a lass's heart. "There remains none so fair as our Maiden, Marion."

"Pull the other one, aye?" Marion snorted, once again brushing at her kirtles. "More like I need to have a go under my bed with a good besom."

He laughed, turning back to the table and dusting his fingers over the remaining parchments. "You really ought to give these figures over to David's remarkable clerk. You've enough on your platter already."

"But 'tis lovely, to ink all those positive figures into neat rows!" Even moreso, to tally the end results and see, laid out before her, the increase of the past few years. Almost akin to writing the spells of a Templar magus—Gamelyn, wresting *tynged's* wild doings into some control . . .

Even if she knew in her heart it scraped close to the unnatural and the impossible. Life remained uncontrollable: from famine to feast, from two living and loving bairns to the one as had bled from her the same ill autumn that famine swept the North.

Nay, she had to keep believing; in her Summerlord's ability to sway the magics if nowt else.

"I know, I know," Gilbert was laughing. "Mayhap at least let him tally the accounts and check them every fortnight?"

He'd a point there. Better to see it done soon; if indeed another bairn had kindled from Beltane, she'd need to delegate more than this. She'd never been bilious early on, but forgetful?

Oh, aye.

Gilbert lingered at the table, his attention no longer held by the accounts, but another smaller spread of parchments. "You're trying them, then?" The size of one's hand, these wee parchments, and covered with strange illustrations, they'd been made more substantial by gluing several layers of thick-scraped skins together.

It was soft, with a wary glance over one shoulder and towards the open door. Gilbert had been out from under the castle's protection and wandering their Wode these past years; he'd caution slung across his shoulders like the forester's cowl he'd flung from his wavy, umber hair.

"They're starting to work for me. Not better than runes, but I wain't use the runes, not now." To his puzzled frown she paced over, voice lowering. "Saxon ways and All-Father magic, the runes. What we're wantin' is older still."

"But this . . . this is newer, aye?" His fingers hovered over the parchments, his brow still furrowed. "Aren't these the ones Gamelyn's Commander gave you?"

"Hubert, aye. These are all but unknown, and new enough, but the signs upon 'em are elder ones, eastern ways. They're a mix of proper strangeness." She touched one, felt it waft against her Sight all full of odd omens and unfamiliar symbols. In the rafters, never far away, several of the gwyllion crooned—not unease, not quite. Almost accepting, which flew just past understanding. "These broke the Saxon magic even as the Saxons broke the Barrows. Another possible key." With a quick gesture, she blurred the spread and gathered the small parchments. "'Tis a love-hate relationship we have, me and these tools, to be sure. Did Aelwyn or David see you arrive?"

Gilbert blinked at the change of subject, but perked up as Marion strode over to the sideboard, where a clay-fired pitcher and several cups waited. "Aye to both. Aelwyn told me to come up and find you."

"Then food's coming. If you're hungry?"

"I could eat half your stable!" he avowed, coming over and rubbing his hands together. "And is that . . . faith, but it *is* mead! Mayhap you'd best hear my news before you serve me from the finest labour of your bees."

"Now, then, I've never been one to punish t' messenger," Marion chided. "Set up the board and drag a bench ower; we'll have ourselves a tipple whilst awaitin' sup."

"Brian de Lisle. Again." It was musing.

Gilbert peered at Marion over the rim of his goblet. "Aye. Slithering his way back into favour, and finding allies right and left."

"Sheffield, for one." Sheffield, and de Furnival. That one meant worry enough on his own and coveting Tickhill, doing his best to suborn Otho. "I knew fifty miles north wasn't enough distance from us by half." Not while Nottingham's ex-Sheriff persisted on her heels like a deranged hound. "This fair smells of trouble."

Gilbert nodded, all the while making further inroads into his repast. He gave a wave of knife, his sigh heartfelt. "Faith, but this pigeon pie is worthy of kings!"

"Aelwyn's taken over the kitchens with a vengeance," Marion agreed. But having brought the feast, Aelwyn had declined an invitation to sup with them. The miller had arrived and needed oversight. He'd already been caught selling the scrapings once.

Marion resisted the urge to go down and assist. She didn't need to; Aelwyn enjoyed her role of 'Bad Sheriff'. "Keep an eye sharp, Gilly."

"I'll do better than that, fair Maid." Another wave of knife, Gilbert's grey eyes tilted all merry. "I went to Sheffield, as you know, and received the tallies from the Park. Milady and milord were riding there, and spent some time speaking to me—very kind, they were. In fact, I think milady Maud fancies me."

Marion blinked. "I'd certainly think Maud's like t' be above eyeing up an ex-outlaw Head Forester."

"She has excellent taste!" Gilbert pretended outrage. "I'm handsome! Moreover . . . blast, what was it milord de Furnival said to her, when I wasn't supposed to hear? Ah, yes. 'Outlaw scum', he called me, and told milady Maud how 'Such a man is beyond loyalty. He might prove a valuable spy amidst Tickhill's odd assemblage of peasants, misfits, and undesirables'." Gilbert's clipped mockery of de Furnival's way of speaking wavered, seemingly forgotten as he peered into his cup with a hangdog expression. With a heavy sigh, he turned that same look upon Marion.

She poured more mead, grinning.

"If only milady Maud had the least instincts for the chase. 'Tis like wooing a stone." He shrugged. "The things I do for our Wode."

"I can't imagine that child's willing to any chase." Marion knew she should stamp de Furnival's wife as a threat. But the memory of old bruises upon the girl's skin kept trying to convince her otherwise.

Even if a beaten hound could be the most dangerous when someone attacked its master.

"Gilbert, you take care with that girl. Hear me? Sounds like her husband's doing nowt but whoring her to suit himself!"

Mirth fading, Gilbert nodded. "Well, milady of Hallamshire has other concerns at present. She is rumoured to be carrying her lord's second child." A shrug as Marion's gaze met his. "They hope for another son. Of course."

"Of course." It was dry.

"It could well work to our advantage. Keep the husband focused upon hearth and home instead of listening to de Lisle or inciting Otho. One of milady's maidservants is a bit more willing to my, ah, ingress. Though *she's* less charming than she'd like to believe. A tool of her lord, always telling tales about her lady even when she's on her back."

"Just don't 'ingress' y'rself into a case of the pox. And de Lisle can spit venom all he likes, but his fangs are pulled."

"For now. The King did, after all, give him Knaresborough."

"The King believes in the ancient powers more than de Lisle's sanity."

It was Gilbert's turn to snort. "For now."

"Aye, well, now's all we have. I only bring it up to reassure. You needn't endanger yourself overmuch."

"Life is danger!" Lifting his goblet in a toast, he gave a wild-quick smirk—one so akin to Robyn her heart ached. "I enjoy *all* my duties, fair Maiden, and trust to the magic of your spells, and salves. Should I need them, of course."

She kept peering at him. He finally demurred, with a nod and a kiss brushed to her knuckles.

"I also stopped at Stainton. Just checking, mind. My lord Otho begs your indulgence with this season's tithe; his lady Alais is unwell."

"Unwell?"

"She, too, is with child, it seems."

"Again." Marion sighed. "I'd wondered, when the King held court here. She'd a look to her."

Alais was well over forty, and though she keenly desired her husband's attentions, the results were chancy. Too, Alais remained under the sway of that wretched Father Matthew over to Rotherham, and dared not contemplate even the most commonplace of a wortwife's solutions.

Only a celibate crow of a man would dare think he could tell a woman such things!

"I fear looks weren't deceiving you, O wortwife." Gilbert seemed pensive. "Milord Otho swears the tithe'll come before the Feast of St Margaret."

Over a fortnight, that. "But you doubt it." So did Marion, come to it. Particularly if Alais remained abed.

"I'm the suspicious type. So I nosed around a bit, spoke to the people of his manor—"

"Alais' manor," Marion said, firm. "Well, Gamelyn's. But she's made a proper go of her grant with little enough help from Otho. Even since he was released from gaol."

"The people of Stainton would agree with you. Quietly, of course. They thrive under their lady's management. But" —Gilbert laid one finger along his nose— "many disapprove of their lord's manner."

"Do they, then?" Marion broke off more bread and offered it to Gilbert.

He accepted, but his brows were still drawn, pensive. "Most think him ungrateful. That he's more after 'drinkin' and gamblin' away milady's hard work'." His accent broadened, uncanny imitation of Alais's cotholders. "Others shrug and say 'Nae wonder, as marster's wearin' skirts t' now'."

Marion rolled her eyes.

"I'm only the messenger, fair Maid."

"Aye, and I should have paid more attention. Alais has become not only a loyal vassal but a kind friend. Otho, on the other hand . . . " She shrugged. "Likely that one's chewing over a bait of unpleasant truths, and the largest of those being his wife and children rendered subservient to a younger brother—"

"By his own actions, making it all the worse, I'm sure."

"Neither has it escaped Otho that his brother's wife is of proper peasant stock, once an outlaw—and from the same lot of outlaws he believes ruined his family's fortunes."

"Any of it, enough cause. Even an under-ambitious man might find incentive from a distant fire—especially if sparks are fanned his direction."

"You're turning into a proper poet, Gilly." Marion tilted a grin at him, though her stomach lay fair knotted. They'd enough vipers lying in wait from out country—now this, close to home. All of it brewing, but unlike the drink gracing her table, turning proper sour. She poured more good mead to smooth Gilbert's frown.

It helped, a little. "Well, the man's a malleable fool."

"Aye, that, and more stubborn than Father Tuck's old riding mule once he does arse himself to hearken sommat."

"Well!" Gilly smacked his goblet on the table. "Enough of that. I've the summer tallies for you, as well as the rolls from most of the agisters and woodwards. I traversed our Shire Wode from Nottinghamshire's southwest hundred to Barnsley and the Peak."

"And the Mere?" She said it soft, though the burning of her gut yearned the query to twist all angry.

"Ah. Barrow Mere." A frown quirked his brow and settled in. "It still seems . . . untimely. This year all has been late in coming, the holly unberried, the apple and hawthorn still unblossomed. As odd as the last two autumns, with snow icing the Mere and falling nowhere else. You remember."

Aye, and she did. Had travelled to see it, scooped the cold stuff into her palm whilst winter's spirits had flitted across the icy pool. Tasted it, and thought: *Robyn.*

After a brief, shared silence, Gilbert continued. "Our demesne burgeons with frond and leaf. The streams are filled with fish, the deer are fat and the fawns growing. So much, in fact, we need culling rights of the latter."

"The King tendered those this past spring, at the same time we petitioned for the market and reopening the tournament field." She smirked. "I thought it prudent to ask *before* Beltane."

"Well played, m'lady!" Gilbert dipped his head and grinned. "No sense gaming at his loss!"

Her grin widening to match Gilbert's own, she rose, dipped a curtsey and, moving to peruse the parchments upon her desk, snatched up a smaller one and extended it between them. It hung bottom-heavy with a flattened—and inscribed—wax disc. "The numbers we must exceed before culling are detailed in the second paragraph. Those who are to receive the benefits are in the third."

Gilbert took and scanned it, nodding. "Aye, and we're well past that. Best to see it done before rut. We'll have enough to placate the aforementioned nobles *and* skim a bit on the side. Feed our own," his eyes met hers, grin sobering, "with suitable cunning and care."

She read his intent, moved closer and resumed her seat, offering more mead. Prompted, barely a murmur, "Another successful journey, then?"

"More than the last one, thankfully. I never should have trusted that new man." The grin returned, this time wolfish. "Careless sod, to not heed his footing on a cliff's edge. But despite the detour, Auckley received their tithe." Gilbert peered up at her. "And what of Auckley mill's youngest son?"

"If Much knows, he en't saying. Which is proper. The Head Forester's notice was a warning, we'll take it as such. None's to speak of this; none's to *know* of this 'cepting us, Gilly. See it stays that way."

He nodded acceptance of the subterfuge. Fewer knowing, fewer risks. Hard times had sparked the forays, quick as a lightning strike in dry woodlands; now, 'twere as chancy to control—or stop. "I'll be off on the morrow. Shall we fetch David's lad to record the tallies?"

She stood, nodding. As he started for the chamber door, she meandered over to the window. Sunlight filtered down through the clouds, promising a warm—if rain-chanced—afternoon. Pork for supper, thanks to the hunt's return yester's even. Much and his team were providers any castle would be proud to claim.

She turned to find Gilbert still in the doorway, watching her. "Gilly?"

He met her eyes, gave a tip of his head. "Robyn Hode's justice thrives. We'll see to it, you and I."

The Preceptory Church of St John the Baptist,
Halifax, Yorkshire
Summer Solstice (The Festival of St John), 1201 CE

The crescent moon filters through the overhead vaults, spilling graceful—swanlike—upon the Relic. As if to deny the world will change this night, with winter-dark's returning.

Winter *should* have returned. Instead, Gamelyn has learnt—again—the price of failure.

"*Ad me ablutio.*"

I am divided, estranged. I have sinned, been unrepentant. Have walked the Shadow and the Nigredo, watched a world die and begin to fade into the dark.

"Nigredo," It is a paean into the darkness, against the sandstone floor. "*Fac de me absolvium.*"

I have been the raven, the chaos, the massa confusa.

"*Ad me ablutio, fac de me absolvium.*"

Bring to me the absolution. Make of me forgiven. Let me be worthy of this honour.

Honour indeed. For he has always known of the Relic's existence; has long suspected it lay within Templar control, Temple realm. But never here, so far away from its own place . . .

Secrets: the necessary means by which power-filled objects keep that power.

His voice, hoarse, chants the incantations while his mind, untethered and riotous, wanders. Wonders. Did the relic travel westward on the very ship that carried him and his master, Commander Hubert, back to England?

Had it in truth been merely seven years ago?

Merely a lifetime since his master had spoken, upon the westward decks of the Templar Galley: *"We will go home to Temple Hirst together, then. There is much our Grand Master has bidden me to, and therefore much reliance I shall place upon you."*

The seventh year. Apropos.

Ominous.

But no moreso than spending a night vigil at the dark, rouged heels of the Magdalene, to then be brought cross-country to do homage before the most revered Secret of the Templars.

That Secret watches Gamelyn. Has watched since he was brought here for the vigil. He knows this, despite not seeing it uncovered, and also knows he mustn't look, not yet. He is not ready, not prepared. Not when he lies upon the stone before a hallowed altar, lips moving but mind unquiet, brimming with undisciplined thoughts and raw emotions.

My soul repents. My heart is divided.

"I have been the raven, the chaos, the *massa confusa*. The Nigredo and the dark night of death. *Ad me ablutio, fac de me absolvium.*"

Mayhap he will never leave this place, will grow old here, never fulfil his purpose. Linger in this other time . . . well enough for that, perhaps he'll wander across from ghostly chapel underkeep to Fae darkling forest; it's sure he's lost track of any time so more the better for the wandering. Untold hours on his belly, or on hands and knees as the white-robed Masters bound and scourged him, smeared his face with char, mixed the salt, sulphur and mercury and poured it to bead-blacken upon the altar. They had retired, to chant and throw resin into the fires guarding the sacred entry, to draw protections against the smears of golden light and watch, as he himself had traced the sigils in cassia, myrrh, and frankincense before prostrating himself upon the warm stones.

Aye, warm, for the massive, underground chamber remains heated through by another sort of miracle: that of geometry, and ancient engineering.

Hubert had anointed him, and the Masters had uncovered the Relic, and Gamelyn had been left alone beneath its gaze, clad only in oil, char, and sweat, his measure, and a ring of onyx and silver.

This latter, a new weight spiralling the third finger of his left hand, tingles like breath, throbs like a beating heart.

How apropos that it is his left hand, and him naked in the wilderness, with memory more shroud than any cloak.

My soul repents. My heart is divided.

"I have been the raven, the chaos, the *massa confusa*. The Nigredo and the dark night of death. *Ad me ablutio, fac de me absolvium.*"

Hours, it seems, with time spiralling out from obeisance. Sometimes a call and sometimes a hoarse whisper, Gamelyn makes the spells that will open the doors to the underworlds. Hours, lengthening into days . . . mayhap less, mayhap more, he cannot be sure . . . then finally—*finally!*—air lifts within the still chamber, stirring the braziers' sullen coals into open flame.

Yet no spectral doors open for him, beneath or beyond. The stones seem to rise up beneath him like a lover, and he realises, again, his mind must be wandering.

He cannot fail! *Will not.* He must open the door, claim this Secret as well. Mayhap it is the key She taunts him with, the answer to a thorny, desperate problem.

"*Fac de me* Albedo. *Ad me ablutio, fac de me absolvium.* My heart is divided, my soul repents, separate."

But none answers.

What was he expecting? He will fail, will fail, will . . .

Cannot. Fail.

Please! Arms tremble towards the Relic, lips quiver with the spells, fingertips sting raw from tracing sigils upon stone. *Do not leave me, alone in this wilderness!*

And just as Gamelyn is about to scream, a breeze lifts and spills his hair forward to tease at his ears.

Surely he imagines it. Any wind in this sealed chamber is impossible!

Half a thought later, he growls scepticism to its belly. Nothing is impossible where the stones whisper his name and, beneath his splayed fingers, leach cool despite their heat.

Where another voice echoes within the chamber: *Bring me home.*

The soft baritone ripples across his hearing and softly echoes across the chamber; warms the backs of his eyes and tickles his throat, slides down to lodge in his belly, burning. Recognisable, the voice. So soft and homely-familiar that he wants to weep.

But nay, it is a dream, a cruel phantasm to move him from his purpose. It cannot be what—*who*—he hears. For Robyn has never, even in the depths of wild and sweat-soaked dreamings, spoken ancient Aramaic.

Gamelyn blinks away the burning in his eyes, presses palms and forehead harder into the chapel's stone floor as, inexorably, the voice sounds again:

Bring me home, o favoured of the fire djinn. Call not upon the waters, but upon fire and sand.

But it is Robyn's voice, he would swear; surely he hasn't forgotten.

Raving. He must be, light-headed from his vigil, no food or drink passing his lips from the time his toes had touched the inner sanctum. Madness is insistent, though:

If you love me, my heart, bring me home.

God! Gamelyn refuses to look up at the altar, grits out, "It is because I love you that I'm here, to bring you home!"

Then we have an accord. Laughter ripples through the chamber. Suddenly—thankfully—it is not so like to Robyn's. *Ah, Gamelyn, why must you constantly insist upon doing things in the most difficult fashion possible?*

Gamelyn remains silent. What to say . . . what to *do*? If it isn't Robyn, what . . . who . . . ?

Shall I tell you a story?

He nods—who is he to refuse?—yet keeps his eyes screwed shut. For if he does look, what will he see?

There was once a boy. A strange and gentle boy, one whose will nevertheless lay like cold iron behind soft eyes and softer voice. None suspected at the forge that burnt, sullen, within his heart; none so much as imagined he might have an ear for enchantment and wonder, that he peeked through his hands at Mass to see the Host. None would have guessed him for a Fool—a Sacred Fool who would dupe even his own heart. . . until an expert trickster teased it from him and caused his fall.

But it had not been, altogether, falling. There had also been flight.

And what is a fall but the attempts at flight? Finally, Gamelyn, you have come before me to be fully fledged. You would seek the al kimia, *the Secret of Secrets. Would you truly know me?*

Know me can mean so many things, and those setting his nerves afire, longing and dread and a hundred other possibilities. Fire and ice writhing under stone and, further inward, an *al kimia*—alchemy— of molten rock running like a fiery river, seeking to shiver upward and converge with a power that would rightfully call upon earth and stone. *His* power.

So, strange and powerful boy, would you bring down the stones about us just because you refuse to look into my eyes?

Gamelyn falls silent. The last syllables float into the arches and pillars of the chamber, wisp quiet. His breath echoes sudden-hoarse against the flooring, seeping into the earth's risen power thick as spilt blood.

It eases, goes to ground.

Slow—very slow—he opens his eyes and peers upward.

Beholds a lithe, dark figure with curly hair tumbling black against the impossible breeze, ebony eyes searching his . . . all familiar as the voice. Gamelyn's limbs go weak.

Nay, my own, I am no dream become flesh. Though you would clothe me, somewhat, in the flesh you love and desire. Quite the compliment.

Again, the voice is not quite Robyn's. And neither is the man . . . only just. Sitting almost casual upon the altar, one leg curls graceful beneath him, one hand resting upon the Relic. Well, and surely, he's the right, as a longer glance proves him of desert, not forest: his hips wrapped with a gazelle's skin, long limbs bronze from a harsher sun and fingers tapping the Relic, umber against ivory.

We are not that unalike, I and your absent lover. I, too, am called the wild man, the ascetic virgin of the wilderness; the one to hold—but not practise—the crown of opposites, and wield it to anoint Kings.

"Will I see him again?" The words escape, faltering, and not only from a language learnt but seldom used.

We will all see each another again in Paradise. Anything else is left to the gods.

"Even if we, too, can be gods?" Gamelyn rises from hands to knees, holding the black gaze. Deep within, that 'strange boy' feels somewhat faint at the very thought of sassing the Baptist.

But the Baptist smiles, a wry-wide, boyish tease so akin to Robyn that Gamelyn's heart shivers and cracks. *Just so.*

Silence, again, as the Baptist strokes his Skull, tender and contemplative. Then, *You have called me, Brother, and promised yourself to my truths. We have one accord: what others would you make with me? What would you give?*

"What I must, I will give, in exchange for your wisdom. For your spirit, guidance, and blessing."

All of those? A good bargain, indeed!

Gamelyn's cheeks heat, but he does not lower his gaze.

A soft laugh. *Even whilst you make things hard for yourself, you ken how bargains cleave true only when each side gives value. Mind this: the Great Work would have us all venture the wild alone and unshriven, unwashed and uncozened. Power has value when given freely, but such generosity can blur intent and sap vitality. The power you would challenge is far older than my own, and even more reclusive. Your heart is broken separate; it must transcend to dwell in one place, one pledge, do you wish to triumph.* A smile. *One is All.*

Slowly—his body stiff and his limbs uncooperative—Gamelyn rises to hands and knees. "I don't—"

Understand. But you will. The Baptist leans forward, black eyes intent. *Give me a year and seven days, as eremite to the desert.*

The desert? Gamelyn stiffens. "Already the forest is without—"

The forest has her Lady, a Horned Goddess, and she remains as apt a protector as any landed queen mother guarding her children's rights—

How odd, that the Baptist would know of thisworld's politics.

—and a wide retinue of guardians, thanks to the Wild God. And

little godlings, one yet to come. A smile, teeth flashing pale, and so Gamelyn is told of another child coming from May Eve.

It makes the prospect of heading to Outremer all the more unpalatable.

Ah, but my world has secrets you have only begun to uncover. The fires of Summer touch desert as well as forest, stone as well as tree. You are what you are, but that can be a coat of many hues, yes?

Gamelyn crouches low beneath the weight of the Voice.

Silence. Then: *How badly do you want this, my own?*

Flame stutters in his belly, flares and steadies hot. Gamelyn lifts his head to peer into the dark-dark eyes.

Again, the Baptist smiles. One hand lifts, a graceful gesture into the air. A wooden bowl appears in one hand, brimming crystalline with fresh water.

Shall I, then, anoint you, Brother?

- Entr'acte -

"I think we were unwise, Hubert."

Rolling his staff back and forth against his propped-up leg, Hubert pulled his gaze from the rafters of Hirst's main hall and slid a gaze past the hearthstones to the one who'd spoken.

England's Master Preceptor also partook of well-deserved leisure, seated across from him with a tot of wine, the fire flickering across his face. Yet for much of the evening, Wymarec had been perched on the edge of his chair—contrasting Hubert's relaxed sprawl—with ivory robes spilling over the flagstones, and the goblet balanced in one thinly-gloved hand. He'd drunk but a few sips; Hubert could see the stain of it, still two-thirds up the translucent surface.

"Unwise? How?" Even has he spoke, Hubert knew. The past few years had merely underscored the cause of Wymarec's subterranean, unremitting disquiet.

But its direction, this time? There were so many winds to lift this banner, after all.

"Unwise to allow it. Gamelyn is not ready for the Inner Temple."

Ah. "Overly ready, I should think."

"You are always quick to shield him."

"Even as you are ever ready to take him down."

A sideways swipe of glare, which Hubert received with equanimity. He offered another pour of the wine, as Wymarec refused, Hubert topped off his own then leaned back, grateful for the small comforts allowed those of rank. Like French wines, cushions and chair backs. The crossbow bolt injury from the Nottingham siege six years ago had healed well, but it—and a few other old injuries—had begun plaguing him, particularly when it rained. He rolled his staff up and down his aching thigh. Thank God he could still sit a horse even on his worst days. Riding made him feel a proper man again. Gimpy, mayhap, but not ready for pasture quite yet. Hubert smiled and drank his wine.

"Nevertheless, Hubert. Something is false."

Hubert loosed a small sigh into his cup. Wymarec listened to his demons too often when it came to Gamelyn—and vice versa, did it come to it. "Wymarec. No lie can withstand the Initiation of the Cauldron."

"That is what I mean. The Cauldron reveals all, bringing darkness into brilliance, yet . . . still. There remains something of deception."

"Surely you don't suggest he lies about the Relic?" This indeed travelled beyond any Pale.

"Indeed not. That bleeds over into everything he does, haunts his days and plagues his nights. He cannot lie about the Relic. This . . . other thing? It is different. Hanging over him, a stillness, a . . . cloak, dark and secretive. I'm surprised you've not perceived it. Or" —a darkling glance sideways— "mayhap you have."

"We all have our secrets, Wymarec."

"But this one keeps him circling just outside control! Not a cloak, more a barrier, made of iron and stone . . . a cloak, I could rip from him." Wymarec tossed down another gulp of wine. "He thinks to elude us. He could escape us. He has before."

"And returned. If we do indeed lose Gamelyn, mayhap we have never truly held him."

"Don't spout such infantile rubbish, Hubert! It isn't good enough, to deal in mere possibilities. His talent is too . . . prodigious."

And it galled, no question. Both Master and Acolyte held enough pride for a preceptory's worth, but the Master in particular had a twist of bitterness amidst: envy.

Mayhap the fire that had nearly been Wymarec's death—and granted no enlightenment, only emptiness—had indeed twisted his heart as irrevocably as the flesh upon his torso and arms.

Mayhap it was too simple an explanation, and angels could indeed dance upon pinheads. Hubert contemplated the stain of wine left in his cup, said, light, "Is this not a marvelous thing? A large nut hard as the wood from the tree it was taken, sanded and thinned to make such a beautiful vessel. I hear the things even give milk to their harvesters!"

Wymarec's gaze slid sideways, disdainful, eyebrows raised. Tenacious as any terrier at a burrow, he kept it up. "The boy has access to more power than any of us have dreamed of in our lifetimes, yet—"

"Come, old friend. Even what we have now is sufficient to any ends. He is no longer a boy, but a man. Our man."

"Is he?"

"He has done everything you asked. Even brought us the forest cult."

"Traded pieces of it, more like, for his own purposes."

Hubert chuckled, lifted the goblet. "A true Templar, our Brother."

Wymarec turned with eyes gleaming, and Hubert held up a hand in apology.

"I do not make a jest, Master Preceptor; and truly, what else do you expect? Gamelyn has well learned beneath your tutelage, has he not? And embraced what is left to him."

"Left to him. He's everything at his fingertips, and still that damned forest holds him!" Another sip of wine, another grumbling mutter. "The druid's death changed him."

"Of course. Did you expect it would not?"

"I expected it to change him for the better." Wymarec shook his head. "A waste. Not only of our Brother, but the druid. Talk about power! Robyn Hood! He had the secrets; he'd faced and found his death, accessed the ultimate—and the fool gets himself drowned! Drowned, and with him all that raw, unsounded power, lost to us for good! And the unholy bastard's leavings are a . . . a man but half ours, who takes a witch wife and revels in drunken pagan orgies."

"That, too, is well within our needs. Mayhap it is the primitive beliefs that enable our Brother to heed the Baptist's plea, eh? He, too, preferred the wilds to any civilisation." Hubert waved a hand towards the chapel and the underground chambers—the latter known to none, of course, save the Orders who'd dug them. "The waking of our most holy of Relics is a blessing upon us, Wymarec. And listening to its Voice by the grace of one of the Inner Temple's most powerful? That will bless us both here and into the eternities beyond."

Wymarec's frown had begun to subside; he took a drink.

"We grow old, you and I. Our time in this world is fading into twilight. Is it not a comfort to know that the Order continues, in whatever form it must? Brother Gamelyn will find what he needs . . . and that, my friend, is what *we* need."

Again, those pale eyes slid towards Hubert, demanding. "What have you Seen?"

Hubert shook his head; for some things, words remained inadequate. And in this much, Wymarec knew better than to press.

"Gamelyn is upon the Path. He will find his own end—and beginning—in the desert. What is baptism but transmogrification, eh? The Great Work!" Hubert tapped his staff on the ground; it rang into the hall. "I tell you, old friend, his time with the Heathen folk is well given. It has taught him to speak with hallowed spirits as unthinking as he breathes. In consequence, he converses with the most holy Relic of our Order!"

A pause. Then, careful, "Do you believe him, Hubert?"

"Do you not?"

Silence. Disquiet flitted behind the cool expression. Wymarec turned, focused upon the fire.

Said, "Would that I did not."

- VI -

"You tendered unto us this obligation, and now you'd have us abandon it?"

"Impossible, I tell you. Impossible!"

Denials rang into the still air of the torchlit crypt—the same, secret chamber where Gamelyn himself had fasted and prayed and, finally, understood. It had split the gathering in two: the gathered Hospitallers protested, lining alongside their leader. He stood unspeaking, solemn with hands in sleeves, eyeing the Templars who stood in loose semi-circle behind Wymarec.

A gathering indeed, and one called to the hidden, torchlit vaults of St John's of Halifax, their number thirteen including Gamelyn. A proper coven, this, made up of and parsed between the inner circles of two orders, adepts both shadowed and illuminated by flames and pale sandstone. The Templars had made their decision several nights previous; the Hospitallers, complicit with the hiding of the Relic, remained undeniably—perhaps understandably—apprehensive.

Obligations. Always, always *determined to see such things as scripted in stone.* Cocooned in silks, cradled within a gilt and glass reliquary upon a simple altar of stone, the object of their disagreement filled the underkeep with a soft baritone. It altered, ever so slight, and faded, as if with some remembrance. *Nay, even better to weigh, to learn then turn aside from what wicked trails our ancestors walked. To. . . make amends, and ken what came before, but allus, choose love ower hate.*

Robyn's voice, trickling though or from the otherworlds? The Baptist, wearing Robyn's guise to cozen Gamelyn's own accord?

"Not impossible unless," Gamelyn kept his voice soft, controlled, "we choose to deem it so. And ignore the rightness of—"

"Of your delusions?" the youngest of the Hospitallers snapped. "Why would the Baptist choose *you?*"

Gamelyn wasn't foolish enough to answer in the affirmative, though some wilful portion of him yearned to.

After all, it was preposterous, wasn't it? The Baptist had chosen *him* to perform this task? The Lady spoke to *him?*

I do, She purred from the alcoves, *and He has.*

And what are chosen ones anyway, but poor deluded souls desiring attention? Gamelyn riposted.

Only when they think themselves the only ones who have ever been. . . 'chosen'.

"You come here,"—the young acolyte had obviously also heard nothing—"make claims we cannot substantiate, and demand we merely hand over the most precious of our Relics?"

"It is not," Wymarec's voice rang against the stones of the underkeep, "*yours* to 'merely hand over'."

"Is it merely yours to take?"

"It is certainly not *yours* to substantiate any claims." Hubert's deep voice sent the acolyte into flushing silence. "Nor, indeed, do you have the right to trivialise a vision given to one of our most powerful adepts."

"Brother Remegius speaks with honesty, however ill-chosen his words." The eldest of the Hospitallers, head shaved to a bare frosting of white, stepped forward. His florid face tried to deny composure, but couldn't; the man was cool as the caverns about them. "Your Order found the Relic across the Sea and elected to bring it here for protection—no false decision, considering. You shared this bequest with our Order, knowing as you are soldiers, we are healers, two sides of a coin that would honour the Baptist and His mission. With the Relic's power, our two Orders together lifted this simple church into a worthy house for one of our greatest treasures."

"Things cannot be cut and parcelled so easily, Fra' Dominicus," Hubert replied, smooth and respectful. "Both our orders hold warriors, sages, and physicians."

Dominicus looked as if he would argue; instead he sighed.

Between them, the Relic kept up its lament. *Bring me home.*

Gamelyn closed his eyes, gritted his teeth.

"The competition that keeps our warrior Brothers at their prime has no place here," another of the Hospitallers allowed. "Yet to ignore the world is not for any of us, either. Fra' Dominicus mentioned the matter of Outremer. How can we willingly consign the Relic to such chaos? Even now the torch of another crusade is being carried; its fires fan outward and we will, no doubt, be asked to serve the Cross."

No matter, no loss. The measures swing, from darkness to light, ignorance to enlightenment, but this much can be remedied: bring me home and I will give you what you desire.

Could they not hear it? Gamelyn gave the small gathering grave consideration and considered further: perhaps they heard nothing because he'd finally and fatally skidded over sanity's edge. No longer holding on by faltering, bloody fingertips, but in free-fall.

The world is mad, aye. What can come of such but *madness?* The Voice—whoever it mimicked, whatever guise—had over the past fortnight grown from soft susurrus to the pound and crash of surf upon a sandy, arid shore. *You know me and my home better than any who would keep me here. You have sworn yourself to me, to my lone wilderness, for a year and a day. Fulfil your oath and bring me home!*

"The Relic could well be lost, did we release it. The desert is peopled with ignorance. It could be seized, destroyed by the blindness of zealots." Dominicus was nodding his agreement. "Surely, your Brother Templar who Sees the Baptist—and I cannot deny he Sees truly—has also Seen to what His Relic shall be returning."

"Do you mean to perpetuate the Great Lie?" Gamelyn shot back, and before any of them could voice the shocked protest upon their expressions, continued. "For make no mistake, that's what this is. The deserts of Outremer are peopled by *people,* no more and no less than any of us! To claim their ignorance is to merely prove your own . . . forgive me Fra' Dominicus"—this as the elder frowned—"but I have been there, lived with them. And to blithely sweep in and to . . . to appropriate such magics, as if they're mere things we've the rights to claim?" Gamelyn's gaze slid to Wymarec, who stared coolly back, not so much as bending to the admittance that such words applied to him. "More, to keep their spirit . . . mortified? Closeted away? To hold them apart from *their* source, *their* home? That is the Lie we face here!"

The gathering bore varied expressions, from his own Grand Master's unconcern to the blatantly-unnerved youngest— Remegius?—whose cheek had flushed even darker, and who kept up a considerable glare in Gamelyn's direction. Dominicus folded his hands into his white sleeves and tucked his chin against the ebon cross emblazoned on his habit. Murmurs echoed softly in the undercroft, more discomfiture than any acceptance. Even Gamelyn's own Brethren seemed taken aback by his outburst; accustomed, mayhap, to the *tabula rasa* of a god-struck oracle, but not a firebrand.

More Robyn's specialty, that.

And yours, the Relic insisted. *You are born from Anglic farms and forests, yet the djinn of fire also acknowledges you.*

Wymarec in particular watched him from the other end of the Templar's impromptu line, the light in his eyes beginning to flicker more in caveat than gratification. As if, Gamelyn pondered with no little satisfaction, he wasn't sure how to advance an uncanny circumstance he himself had nurtured.

Hubert, on the other hand, showed an intrinsic, implacable serenity that even outpaced the eldest Hospitaller, Dominicus. Never one to betray surprise or resentment when student outpaced teacher; instead, Hubert expected it. Demanded, even.

That demand did as ever it had done; encouraged Gamelyn upon another step, and the next. And then, Robyn's most precious gift: that of sidestepping expectation, surrendering his being to a godling Voice, and letting its spirit speak through his own. "Does not the Great Lie merely encourage us in more lies? Supposed rights and dominion, of invasion, theft . . . all things leading to power, but also to madness."

"We all well know these things," Dominicus agreed, solemn.

"Then we can never forget our susceptibility to them!" Gamelyn couldn't stop a narrow glance at Wymarec as he spoke; thankfully his Master watched the Hospitallers.

Dominicus, however, saw the glance; his eyes twinkled. "And so?"

"So, in our power, we take an artefact from its proper place, tell ourselves we're protecting it. We sift through the gifts of ancestors who are not our own, twist truths to our own purposes. And all to take over, aye?"

"Nay! To preserve what is falling away!" another Hospitaller retorted.

"Yes!" Gamelyn agreed. "But only *if* we turn aside from the Lie that says there is one faith only, one way only, one purpose only. Why are we here, Brothers? To do the Great Work, to hold the balance of all faiths, all powers! To find transcendence! Otherwise the chancre fills our bodies with rot and plague, from England to Damascus!"

"The balance has been disturbed by bringing the Relic here." Wymarec spoke up, soft but stern. "Our Brother hears its cry waking and sleeping; if you will not believe him, believe me, Master to the English Temple. I have heard it, through him."

"As have I." Hubert rubbed his thumb along the eye of the peacock carved upon his staff, a tiny back-and-forth motion. "We made a mistake that must be owned and rectified. The Relic must be returned to the Holy City and Solomon's throne."

"If it can be."

"Brother Gamelyn served with the Assassins." The Templar who spoke from beside Hubert tipped his head with grave courtesy. "He is best prepared."

"And if he fails?" the acolyte Remegius persisted.

"I have sworn the Relic will be returned." Gamelyn returned the acolyte's frown.

"But if you fail?"

"I will not fail."

Another quiet sifted through and took the small group. Then: "Mayhap, since Brother Remegius is so concerned, he should accompany you," Dominicus suggested, eyes still twinkling. "At any rate, it wouldn't be proper for either of our Orders to send a lone Brother into the desert wilderness, be it forty days and nights, or a mere fortnight."

The Honour of Tickhill, Yorkshire
Waning of Lammas, 1201 CE

Marion's Book of Hours:
6 years, 8 months and 14 days —
<u>Our Lord Shall Return</u>

The Tower beneath: upheaval, disaster

The Heirophant reversed behind: rebellion, new ways

The Fool ahead: new beginnings, innocence

The Priestess over, reversed: inner voice and centre, lost… Of course we've lost our way, lost our voices! I need no nobleman's divination to tell me any of this!

Hubert came yesterday, bringing a message from Gamelyn. Who has left for Acre and some damned desert pilgrimage. Away from here, his land, his place! A fool indeed; more blind irresponsible action than any 'recapture' of lost innocence!

"The answers are nigh, Marion. Our Lord shall return, and I come closer to finding the way, with this. Only a year and a day, I swear this to you. Only a year and a day. I shall come back to all of you — and this time for good."

By the Horns, I've heard it all before! This could be the answer. I'll find it, soon. I'll return for good. We'll get Robyn back, and then…

But all of it teeters on other ifs:

If the ship survives the voyage. If the Saracens don't slay Gamelyn just for daring to wear the blood cross in their homeland. If he finds any answer! He should know by now that he cannot find that outside himself, only inside! Won't he see?

We'll never find the answers, never... we've lost... we're lost...

We should be watching the Mere, dredging it, draining it! The Mere has to be the answer, more than any handful of 'keys' dangled by a deceitful master who wants nowt more than to hold our Summerlord away from us. Yet where he beckons, Gamelyn follows, like a moth for a candle and heedless of the damage it will cause!

He doesn't even know...

"Mam?" Little Rob's voice, and the quick thump of little boy feet—surely shod horses would step lighter upon the floor. "Mam, what's wrong, why're you crying?"

Marion barely had time to set her pen down and turn. Not only Rob, but Aderyn coming into her bedchamber and running across the smooth wooden floor. Marion only then realised she'd indeed tears down her face, her throat all thick-tight—and would have a lap piled with worried bairns if her lap wasn't already so full . . .

"Come back here, lad, you—Robbie! Aderyn!" The maidservant burst in after, in no less a flurry than her charges, with one woollen hose clutched in one hand and a comb in the other. "Wicked children, don't be barging in on your lady mother in such a flurry, can't you see she's at her desk and workin'?"

And aye, Aderyn's dark mop of curls stuck out at all angles, whilst Rob had only one leg clad, the other bare and plump and freckled. Marion laughed through tears and opened her arms, gathering her son and daughter close.

Mayhap they were all she'd have of their father and uncle.

No laugh, this time; the sob escaped before she could stifle it and the children clung tighter.

"Mam? Mam, what's—?"

"Faith and fortune, milady, is it the babe? Shall I call for—?"

Marion stoppered the unreasonable gout of self-pity with a sniff. "Surely not! 'Tis 'nowt more'n your mam being a silly mope of a breeding dame." With this reassurance, she gave the children a fierce hug and pushed them back, eyeing them. "Mayhap the bairn's havin' a visit from the night mare, makin' me take on so. Everything's fine, see?"

While the littlest allowed himself to be swayed, the eldest stayed chary, eying her mam. Marion stroked down Aderyn's hair and chucked Rob's chin. "Half-dressed and wild as any forest sprite, the pair of you! Don't you be giving Berta trouble, now . . . here." She gestured for the hose and comb. "Mam will see you right, and there's to be no more rumpus, aye?"

"Milady's surely too busy, and I'll have 'em out of her way in a heartbeat."

"They en't in my way, Berta."

"Lass, you'd have 'em sleepin' wit' you iffen you had your druthers—"

And she had her druthers, exchanging a secretive smile with her offspring, because how often had they crept in and piled in atop her and Much?

"—but you're Tickhill's lady, aye? You've your status to think on, and Berta's here to help."

Funny, how Marion's own mam had managed to run a small holding and a thriving wortwife's trade with nowt but her man and, early on, *her* mam's help . . . old Grandad, too, before he'd died and Gramma had followed after. 'Tweren't natural, to have little ones bide so separate from their parents; how were they to learn proper respect of others' space if they weren't in it, and being taught?

But she knew better than to say such things to the maidservant. Berta might be proper Heathen—otherwise Marion wouldn't have agreed to give her stewardship over Tickhill's children—but the elder woman had been brought up nigh to the castle, with rigid ideas of what was proper for peasant folk and for nobles, never the two meeting.

So Marion settled for "This lady says her bairns can stay as they like" and, true to form, Berta pursed her lips.

"You're tired, milady, and not finished with your papers; anyone can see that."

"And none of it more important than my children," Marion replied, dry, and extended a hand. "Thank you, Berta."

She'd learnt at her mam's knee how to be the Lady's vessel; being *a* lady wasn't that unalike—on the surface, 'tennyrate. While Marion's heart would never be any other than the peasant lass from Loxley, Berta's sort never would ken such things.

The maidservant tilted an eyebrow and a curtsey, handed over comb and hose, and heaved herself into both a gusty sigh and a departure. No doubt she'd be telling her cronies how Herself made an odd bundle of contradictions to be sure, but a pregnant Herself bided even more, so they'd best indulge her, for the while.

Not that Marion cared, already bent to her little Rob who, graceful as a fire-topped crane, balanced on one leg and consented that the other be clothed. His chatter, however, resembled more a magpie; just as musical and nonsensical. She let him natter on as she gathered up one hose and started to skin it over his leg.

Hesitated, smirking. "You've the one ochre and one blue, you know."

"Berta weren't findin' a match and me neither."

Liar! Aderyn signed. *You hid them. You* like *not matching.*

Rob blinked wide blue eyes at her, then his mother, all transparent innocence.

"Well?" Marion peered right back.

"We-eelll. Mayhap."

"Then *mayhap*" —Marion pulled the hose up and secured it— "you'll be starting a new fashion. But I'd rather you not display it at Hallmote. Understand?"

Rob nodded, took in a huge breath and started off again; at first nigh unintelligible, it rambled into something about the bailey, then swerved to the barn and horses and cousin Ian, and how he was going to ride Ian's horse, just wait and see . . .

"I'd rather you wait," Marion put in as he took a breath. This new mount, a gift from Hirst and Ian's Uncle Gamelyn, had proved overmuch for Ian's present skills. Otho's disappointment, hanging like a cloud upon his eldest son, had prompted Alais to send the lad here—not only fosterage, but so Tickhill's talented horsemistress could work them both in.

Gamelyn'd had trouble with his first warhorse, too. And been proper miffed how Robyn could handle the stallion with such ease.

Don't look there, Marion told herself, and gave her brother's namesake a fond smack on his recently clad haunch. "There you are."

Babbling more about the stables, Rob kissed her cheek and was away.

"Shoes!" Marion called after, and turned to Aderyn.

Saw her scanning the new-penned lines, dark brows furrowing more with each word.

Marion reached out and flipped the leathern cover onto the parchment. Aderyn blinked and peered at her mother, eyes large and culpable; she knew she'd no business looking at her mother's desk and papers. The frown remained, though. She'd read enough.

Da's not ever coming home? Those eyes glimmered.

Marion sighed again and curled an arm about her, pulled her close. Signed back *This is why you shouldn't read things not meant for you.*

You weren't going to tell us?

That en't true, pet. Marion cuddled her daughter closer with a slight sway, chin against black curls. *I was to tell you today. See, sometimes I need to say things in my Hours; work them out, like. They aren't always things I mean, exactly. More like my own worries and fancies, nowt more.*

More than nowt, else you'd not write them! Is Da coming back?

Marion pushed her daughter back. "I wain't lie to you, love, any trip east is dangerous. But aye, I think he'll come back. Your da's a fierce knight, aye? Not many get in his way."

And those who do, regret it. Pacified by the reassurance, Aderyn nevertheless seemed more thoughtful than Marion found comfort with.

"I'm worried after your da, aye, but I think I'm the more angry he didn't come to us, tell us himself."

Mayhap he couldn't, Mam. The Templars give him all sorts of hard rules, don't they? I wish he'd leave them.

Marion did, too. It didn't help that, knowing Gamelyn, he'd had the choice and made this one, thinking it easier on all concerned. Damn his eyes. *He'd* not had to see Much's face as she'd handed the letter over. Hadn't witnessed the conflict there that made Marion tell him: *Go. Take care of him.*

And Much's glum answer: *I'd chase him and never catch him, more like. And betray you in the doing.*

Marion bit her lip, fighting the sting of tears behind her eyes. It was easy to mask the cause as the bairn rolled beneath her ribs and kicked, hard.

Aderyn, diverted, smiled as another ripple passed across Marion's gravid belly. She trailed fingers in the ripple's wake and hissed a soft breath between teeth and tongue—singing, in her own way.

"Well?" Marion asked. "What do you think, my little midwife? Boy or girl?"

And thank the Horns that proved more diversion. Marion breathed her own music of appreciation; though Beltane-gotten with a raw talent surpassing many twice her age, Aderyn was still a child.

I think it's a girl. I hope it's a girl. We've enough boys here! You?

Marion smiled it away, shrugging. For the first time, with this one she bided unsure. Gunnora said she'd been straying too far from the Lady's voice, bearing the Horns and shutting Her away save for the Rites.

But what choice did she have now, other than take up the Horned Lord's place? With her consorts left and lost—one by the Lady's own hand? It was betrayal, nowt more; a sore, oozing and burning.

The only balm? Guard what was hers. Gunnora spoke from custom, but some things needed changing. If Robyn could convince their god to yield choice to the Lady and challenge His rival with a very different sort of struggle, then why shouldn't this Lady take full advantage of that choice? If Gamelyn could belong to both Lady and Lord, why couldn't Marion do likewise: take up the Horns, display them as hers to control, and in the doing protect her own?

She snugged Aderyn close. "All right, then?"

I'm all right, her daughter said, with another darkling glance towards her mother's book. It was too adult—too knowing—for a lass of barely six winters. *I'd best go after Robbie, aye? He'll talk Sarah into letting him on that horse, you know he will.*

Well, and Sarah possessed a few robust opinions regarding little boys on half-broke horses. Marion had no worries on that score. She relented, however, never of a mind to gainsay an older sister's protectiveness.

She well understood it, after all.

"Why am I here?"

A pause, hanging heavy as the stone above their heads, broken only by the fire, crackling as the Priestess tended it with wood and sweet-smelling resin. "You be knowing."

Nay, he really didn't. Robyn crossed his arms and propped one leg, hipshot. "And where is here, then?"

"You be knowing that, as well."

Aye, mayhap. Though he didn't quite believe it.

"Belief, belief! As if that being all that matters. Hob-Robyn, for you outworlds have been as poison." A sigh, and a shake of head.

Robyn wasn't too sanguine about how easily she read him. Not for the first time, his gaze flitted about the cavern, taking in who, and where, and what might be a decent weapon in a pinch.

Tens of eyes glimmered in return from the darkest corners. Not human eyes, though people still bided about the edges, wary and well-armed. Nay, these glittered like lamps, or mayhap the pale glow of lichen in the Hermit's Caverns. Only lichens didn't blink, or scry a man like a hungry wolf.

"You be home. That be all that matters, Hob-Robyn." Echoing on and on within the cavern, the name in particular scraped against Robyn's senses like a blade flensing skin from meat.

"Don't—"

"—Call you that? Why not be calling you by your Spirit, giving life in naming? Spirits be dying if forgotten, so They be going into outerworlds when they begin the fading. Your dam be naming you aptly . . . *Hob-Robyn.* See, even caverns be knowing it." A gesture of graceful fingers, and aye, it still echoed—*Hob-Robyn, Hob-Robyn*—past where human faces glared at a newcomer's cheek, and filled shadows where inhuman visages blinked and rustled.

A smile tucked itself into one corner of the Priestess's indigo-traced cheek. Robyn didn't fancy it; more, he grudged the way it made him feel, like a lad caught skiving when he should be mending hedgerows.

He tried again. "Begging your pardon, Lady, but Shire Wode's me home. Home and family, and as to that, me own'll be worrying. I'd best return to them."

She kept fussing with the fire, paying him about as much mind as she would that skiving lad. A shudder claimed Robyn as something flared within its depths; he recognised the last of the blooded wool.

The Priestess rose, regarding him. "What be your thoughts upon this?"

Robyn started to answer, realised she wasn't speaking to him. The old man came from the shadows with a grumbling sigh, his voice rising soft and too quick for Robyn to follow. His expression, on the other hand, told plenty. He eyed Robyn as one might a horse at market—and offered, mayhap, by a crooked dealer.

Meanwhile, the trio of remaining warriors glared, altogether unconvinced. Only the Priestess's young acolyte remained serene.

The elder strode over to Robyn, peered up at him, and snorted. "Be climbing a pasty mountain, with this."

Pasty? It was winter—what did the old one expect? Not that even a desert sun would tint him dark as they were. Though mountain, mayhap, were a fair cop, considering. All of them, shorter than John.

At least they'd started talking slowly enough he could follow.

"He be having the blood," the Priestess said.

"Precious little!" the elder snorted again. Small, aye, but the shoulders with which he shrugged away his twist-locks were all sinew and yew. "Sire be of enemy."

"Matters naught, when dam be thoroughly ours," the acolyte said, soft. "Counting sire right and blood tally ye be, Uncle. Like conqueror-people."

If the old man had horses' ears, he'd pin them. His nostrils curled, though, making up for the lack.

"He be of Spirit," the Priestess added, as if this were even more important.

"Hob!" Yet another snort, and the elder shook his head. "Of course. Who else be playing so with us?"

Robyn hadn't been talked over like this in years. "You still en't told me why I'm here. Or even where *here* is."

"And I be telling you, you be knowing both."

"*Hob* be having the knowing," the elder put in, sly. "This . . . mountain, he still be boy, nose to knees. All he'll get on be oversized and scrawny bairns!"

Bairns? Now hold on . . . "You've kidnaped me just so's I can sire *bairns?*"

The Priestess and her watching retinue chuckled—except the acolyte, who watched Robyn with great, grey eyes.

Those eyes reminded him of Marion. Which just proper brassed Robyn off. "Well, then, you've fetched y'rself the wrong man, O Priestess. I don't fancy women. You should've taken Summer, not Winter. He's more susceptible to a lass's charms."

Not that he'd wish any of this upon Gamelyn . . . unless they were here together. Gamelyn'd fancy that, he would: a timeless Eden, with gods and spirits walking the evening shadows.

"Huh!" the Priestess snorted. "So both of us be preferring a man for Rites, so may it be disappointment due both of us."

As insults went, it was fair enough, but the surge of anger that filled Robyn's belly wasn't just for that. "You . . . you took me from my place, from my people! From my *time!*" The words exploded from him, the old dialect filling his head and out into the caverns, power ringing the stones and wiping the smile from every surrounding face.

"Time." The Priestess's mirth, in particular, had sobered. "Which you gave us, Horned One, in your oath. I be holding it still."

"My—?"

She put two fingers to her lips, bidding silence even as she extended her other hand. The young acolyte lurched into action, scarpering down a torchlit tunnel. The slap of her bare feet retreated, silent as the ones waiting, then sounded again, returning.

In her arms she cradled a carefully wrapped bundle of fabric.

Robyn knew it even before the girl passed it—reverently—to her lady. Before the Priestess unwrapped it, held it up to the firelight.

A weapon, fashioned to fit a tall longbowman's reach, from a bough of willow rubbed dark with ash and blood. Runes curled stark-white about the shaft, to the sharp flint tip and back downward, where peacock tufts and split goose vanes fletched it for unerring flight. If it had writhed with power before, now, in this hallowed otherwhen, the Arrow spoke to Robyn in a multitude of tongues, and recognised him with a fervour that sprang heat behind his eyes.

The others gave way, murmuring. Several darted looks at him that suggested wary surprise—how he'd made such a thing, or that he could?

And no question he'd given it to them; loosed it into Barrow Mere with both invocation and promise:

My magic is yours, as much as me own. I have called you to ask this much: keep it safe until I return for 't.

As memory came into the caverns, Robyn once again heard the sough of breath that had wafted across the Mere, both longing and assent.

"You swore it to our keeping," the Priestess told him, and began wrapping the Arrow back into its coverings, reducing its Voice to a soft, warbled hum. "We are keeping it safe, until ye returning be, at proper time and proper place, the oath being fulfilled."

"The time *en't* proper!" Robyn retorted. "I en't finished with tasks in *my* wor—"

"Tasks left undone be falling to others." Implacable, the interruption, as the Priestess handed the Arrow back over to her grey-eyed acolyte, who took it, scurrying away. Robyn nearly followed, but a multiple of stern gazes halted any such impulse.

As if he could trip the lass and take it back, here and now, with Herself knowing just what he was thinking, Robyn was sure of it.

A wry smile twitched at the Priestess's lip. "Your task is in otherworlds, thisnow, to be loosing iron shackle-charms and ill-tuned bells. Hob-Spirit be knowing this. He returns to this-world—not merely for sire's place, but rightful home. You have slept long enough."

What did she mean by that? His time, their time, what time? Robyn blurted the question, unthinking, "How long?"

The elder looked to the Priestess, who shrugged assent. "Here," he said, "we be measuring by Goddess Moon, and no faint red Sun Father. You be sleeping for three nights of frosting moon. But be easy. There, your Maiden bides Mother, and the god's children be growing hale and well, brimming with first-magic."

"*Children?*" It forced outward past a sudden, great knot in Robyn's chest. And then, regret: he'd promised to be there for the birth, at Marion's side . . . well, mayhap not exactly, no midwife with sense'd let him nigh, but he'd promised to *be there.*

"O and aye." The milk-and-sienna gaze held an abrupt compassion. "Things be different here, Hob-Robyn. You be remembering this, too, anon."

The Priestess spoke, too swift for Robyn to follow, and the elder man shrugged, answered in kind. They fell silent, even as the rest of their people stood quiet. As if waiting . . . for what?

"I'll honour the Arrow's oath," Robyn gritted into the silence. "But I mean to go back to *my* people and my forest. I canna stay. *Wain't*, not after I've finally found—" He broke off, unwilling to mark that trail; not yet, not yet. "I'll leave here, one way or another."

"Foolish, foolish boy." The elder turned away, delivering the remainder over one shoulder as he left the cavern. "None of us be leaving here. Ever."

- VII -

Acre, in the Kingdom of Jerusalem, in the land Outremer
Waxing of Hallows, 1201 CE
First se'nnight of Muharram, 597 AH

If you love me, take me home. . .
Even through wrappings and leather, the precious cargo vibrated athwart Gamelyn's back. In waves, like the lift of the boat beneath his bare feet, or the sun battling the wind against his nose and cheeks with welcome heat then salt-wet spray, misting as he drew it, deep, into his lungs.

It would be the last moist air he would taste for a while.

His eyes ached from squinting against countless miles of reflections; a relief every evening to have the sun sinking into its fierce mirror. Cheerful voices echoed off the water and against the sails of the Templar galley, and lads scattered amongst the rigging, angling or shortening sails to their master's orders—all of the crew expressed unguarded relief at another successful portage. Even the sea's mood had changed, her swells welcoming as they drew towards a pale shore.

The city rose as if in challenge to the wide bay reflecting endless sky. With curtain walls and buttresses jutting proudly, the port of Acre seemed all white and gilt and crimson, licked into sacred flame by the setting sun.

In its way, Acre was home to the man he'd been, even as the Wode was home to the man he'd become.

"Look after them, Hubert," Gamelyn whispered into the hot wind. Heard, as if his mentor were there, his oath:

I will see the fêtes secured, whilst you wander. The King has Normandy and Aquitaine much upon his mind, and little time at present to give to the land he does, indeed love. If an Angevin loves anything other than his own power. More, he will have just as little time to attend the Rites that truly made him this land's sworn King. You have my promise, Gamelyn: your Brethren shall protect the Maiden, though she likely needs it not, being well secured by her own folk, non?

Indeed. Gamelyn had no need to whisper a plea towards Tick-hill and the Wode; Much, as always, stayed fast there, and the others of the covenant gathered round . . .

Nay, he couldn't think long upon Marion and the children, else turn about and be foresworn.

"How many years have you been away, Brother?"

The question, both courteous and curious, came from beside him. Gamelyn turned, also courteous, to the ship's captain.

With wiry dark hair confined against sea winds by oil, braids, and an intricately knotted scarf, the captain's gold-brown eyes squinted against the water's glare, acknowledging Gamelyn whilst minding his crew. At his direction, the first mate barked a relay of orders; the galley gave a pretty dip and scut sideways, sails furling.

"Too many," Gamelyn replied. "Not enough."

"Aye." The captain nodded, leaning one hard-callused hand upon a rig. "Unlike your comrade, I should think." A sideways glance aft, and a tiny smile. "Spanish, is he? They usually have better sea legs. Your Brother Remegius has spent much of our journey contemplating the railing."

Gamelyn shrugged. "We've all been there at some time."

"Never I, friend!" The captain flashed a wide grin. "I left Mombasa on one of the trading ships as a lad and never looked back! But my Lady Sea is a fickle mistress, aye?" He scanned the bay, sobering. "One never would guess what these waters have witnessed."

One never would guess, indeed, how this wide, beautiful bay had once transformed from crystalline to pitch, fouled with the gore of three thousand corpses. Gamelyn slid a glance to the captain's profile, watching his nostrils flare wider as if catching a scent of copper-salt.

King Richard's vengeance upon Acre still had the power to engender nightmares.

"Violence lurks beneath the fine skim of tranquillity," Gamelyn murmured. "Unrelenting hostility vibrates this city to its bones. It keeps watch: stalking stone walls, skulking the perimeters into the land beyond, and squabbling with its rivals over insufficient prey."

"Commander Hubert did warn me you'd some poetry to you. But I'd say you've it just about right." Another grin, swift and approving. "We'll take you with the second lot, Brother. Better to fetch a few supplies ashore. See the lay of things before you venture inward, aye?"

Gamelyn nodded.

"Fair skies to you, Brother Gamelyn, and return safely home." A nod as the captain turned away, calling directives.

Gamelyn shifted the pack upon his back. It hadn't left his side the entire trip. Its inaudible descant had changed, from plea to hope to fierce satisfaction. And now, giving voice.

Rivals over insufficient prey?

Not the Horned Lord; He had, over miles and furlongs of watery separation, fallen silent. Still, this Voice sidled against Gamelyn's heart and lay there, so akin to Robyn's it caught heat behind Gamelyn's eyes as he answered *What would you call it, then?*

Silence for long moments. The boat dragged, wallowed, and lurched as the anchor caught bottom and dug in. Then:

A shame, that all has come to this.

"Yes," Gamelyn murmured. Invasion, possession, blind dogma . . . it didn't have to come to this! He himself was testimony of it. His Order—those sworn to the innermost Temple, at any rate—had spent years of searching both inner and outer planes to achieve it. Innumerable prophets from this land had died for it.

Nevertheless, the followers of those prophets all insisted upon seething in the same, damned, and narrow pot: a handful of faiths that would rather kill each other than admit even the slightest understanding over their shared origins.

Fear is a powerful thing. Fear of losing boundaries thought safe and inviolate, fear of a world in chaos. Fear of being wrong. If the head had shoulders, it would have shrugged. *What do you fear, Gamelyn?*

That was easy. *That I'll never see him again.*

He'd been left in the small grotto with a goodly fire, a large meal on a wide board, and dry, warm clothes as companions.

Not so much as a guard. Robyn considered this, contemplating the other peculiarity: a sturdy flint-and-bone knife. Short, merely for eating, but it could do some damage did he try. It gave the elder's pronouncement all the more impact.

Foolish boy, none of us be leaving here. Ever.

Hunger gnawed at Robyn's belly, but when he thought to tuck in, his mam's voice whispered in his ear: *never be partaking of Fae offerings.* With a grimace, he turned away from the board.

No sense, though, in refusing the tunic of soft woven fabric, even if it barely reached his hipbones. Sleeveless, at least, and it wrapped his ribcage well enough. The leather leggings, on the other hand, were a proper length, wrapping snug from ankle to thigh as he laced them. Stolen? Made? Who could tell? Provided also was a length of cloth that might suit as a belt . . . nay, a belt had been provided. Mayhap a clout? Whats'mever, 'twere one now; he didn't fancy wandering a strange place with his knob dangling to the wind beneath a skimpy tunic.

If they'd wind, here.

He also tucked the knife in his belt. Wished he'd the Arrow, to braid into a lock of hair.

Not that the latter would of any help; he'd no bow. But it was his magic. It wanted to be nigh. Or mayhap, merely he to it.

How difficult would it be to find, at that?

Robyn saw no one as he padded outward, but encountered torchlit tunnels complete with commonplace signs of habitation: a hide drapery thrown back from a sleeping area; a fire banked about a covered stew pot; clothing hanging from hooks. Odd. Like they'd all to once headed somewhere.

Odder still: no signs of children. Not so much as a flung-aside toy.

Doubt crept in, rippling sudden chill between his shoulders and down: was he the only one left in the entirety of this place?

And if so, could he find the Arrow?

He cast his senses outward, searching. Felt nowt. Closed his eyes and let out a small breath to echo in the caverns, followed as it misted outward, seeking—

Voices yanked him back into his own skin, echoing from down one of the more well-lit areas.

Robyn veered away and into a darkened corridor, melting into the shadows as they passed. Three women carrying baskets, one white-haired. The younger two matched, considerate, their elder's pace.

Robyn realised he was sweating, wiped his upper lip and rested one hand against chill stone. He still hadn't felt the Arrow. It must be warded, or taken away. His fingers tapped the cavern wall, mirroring his frustration, and he started to step from the passage.

Instead frowned, sliding his fingertips over the stone. Incised in some places and—he looked closer—painted as well. The light being so faint, his fingers could easily trace them. Some sort of runes, albeit unfamiliar.

Still frowning, Robyn paced out into the corridor, eyeing the walls carefully. He was rewarded. More of the runes appeared, here and there, and soon enough their use became plain.

Robyn found a likely shard, and used it to mark his own path.

He well knew caverns. Disrespect them and they'd spin you round, tumble you arse over tit and never let you find your way into the light again.

The farther out he went, the fewer torches he found, and those few blue-white with the magic; it danced strong and brilliant here, the smell and feel of it lingering after he'd passed. Tunnels led, here and there, many of them dark and utterly forbidding. Robyn wasn't foolish enough to try them, not until he knew the place better.

Not that he intended to be here long enough to do so. At that, should he lose himself, the Fae would, no doubt, find him.

If They hadn't been following him all along. Because sommat tailed him.

After the third time of whirling on one heel and seeing only the torches wavering in the aftermath of escape, Robyn sighed, and crossed his arms. "Coom by, then, pet. I know you're there."

Nothing, at first. Then rustles, and hisses, and a scuffle or two. A few high-pitched growls. Finally, one by one they came out of hiding, either hovering a-wing or creeping upon the stones.

Gwyllion, Marion had called them, while *little beasties* had been Gamelyn's description . . . and memory speaking in the past tense sent a mournful chill down Robyn's spine.

As if in response, one of the little spirits hovered closer and gave a soft chirrup, then landed upon his shoulder, nestling into his hair. Robyn blinked; no bare feather's weight, this. More the heft of David's ferret, Tess. Warmer, too.

He reached up, half-expecting it to be as insubstantial as the ones that followed Marion about Tickhill—and juddered as the gwyllion nosed his fingertips not unlike a curious pony. Its nose was warm, and its pale skin radiated heat as it rubbed into his palm.

"Well," he murmured. "Is it you're the more real here? Or I'm the less?"

The gwyllion chirruped again, and snuggled down in Robyn's hair, tail curling, light and warm, about his throat. Its companions weren't quite so bold, flitting about his head and shoulders. Every movement raised tiny glints and ripples, as if rainbows were caught and captured, muted-deep in sleek-soft hide.

Longing dipped and hollowed his chest: for the rainbow after a storm, with trees all wet with rain and the sunlight shining after.

"Mayhap," he murmured, slow, "you can show me the way out, then?"

The one upon his shoulder gave a strange trill that ended in a tiny yip. Some kind of directive, it seemed, for the others loosely gathered, chattering. Finally, with a scamper and a leap, they were airborne, soaring past Robyn to disappear into the last of a narrow trio of tunnels.

When he merely watched them go, the gwyllion upon his shoulder nudged his cheek.

"Are you telling me you really do know how to fetch me from this place?"

The gwyllion purled deep in its throat and nudged again, launching from his shoulder to soar ahead. It paused and peered his way, hovering, eyes gleaming.

"Well, then, whats'mever. I've nowt to lose."

They went a fair way, all the while the torches thinning, Robyn following and making sure to mark his way. The shard broke against the cavern walls, dusting his hands pale. He stowed the pieces, rattling, in one palm; just in case none would be had further in.

His tiny guide gave an abrupt swerve, darting down a side corridor. A bunch of trills echoed from the distant black. Plainly the gwyllion had found his friends.

Nevertheless, Robyn lurched to a halt.

This threshold had its own torch, but seemed narrower than many of the others, shadows pulling outward from a darkness to rival the deepest oubliette. Faded, fine sigils marked it. He didn't have to read them to ken their consequence, further proved as he reached out to lightly trace them. The marks flaked, left an oil-and-powder residue to stain his fingers scarlet.

His breath escaped in a teeth-clenched hiss. Blood-runes. Akin to those with which he'd marked the Arrow, but even older. Mayhap more ancient than the original ones for which old Wotan had paid teind upon the World-Tree.

A small form came fluttering from the darkness, cheeping at Robyn. When he didn't respond, rubbing his fingers together and frowning, the gwyllion darted about his head, chittering at him all the while. When that didn't move him, it darted down and nipped at his right ear.

"Ow!" he yipped and, as the gwyllion kept scolding. "Aye, *mam*, all right then!"

Nevertheless—his guide telling him off the entire while—Robyn snatched the torch from its holder before advancing into the dark.

ⓝ

The tunnel ran long and narrow, beneath . . . something. Robyn could feel the weight of it above, more than earth but also less, somehow. He held the torch aloft, breathed his own fire spells as the extant ones tried to gutter. The gwyllion crooned on his shoulder. Mayhap song was its way to ward off the impenetrable gloom that sought to crowd their tiny, torchlit circle, lending darkling lustre against devastating, empty blackness.

Nay, not empty.

At the first he merely felt it: presences, creeping the edges of perception. The air turned chill, wafting against his face with a heavy, dank-silt smell. As they passed farther in, more of his senses cognised. Hearing, first: a stamp of hoof; a whine of an unlucky wolf pup; a starveling cry of a bairn long unfed and, chasing those, a slow gathering of faint, lost whispers. Sight played tricks, what with the torch glittering against close walls that would, just as unexpectedly, widen into chambers of pitch . . .

There, a glitter-gleam of eyes. Robyn nearly ducked into a nearby hiding-hole to avoid them, then realised these felt wholly unlike what spirits bided native to this place. Nor was it some Wilding Hunt whistled by elder gods, or strays of Fae ghosts.

Yet ghosts all the same, confined to the shadows. He remembered seeing their like before, drifting. He'd roamed the otherworlds with them, trailing the shades of his mam and da when Loxley had burned and a crossbow bolt had nigh ended him, too. Robyn kneaded at the latter's remnant, a numb-slick hollow of scar tissue, and eyed the revenants evading the light of his torch—they were backing off, slow, milling aimless as cattle droved and awaiting market.

The comparison disturbed him. Even amidst the dead, he'd never felt penned. Never felt as if there weren't some path to follow, or a destination.

These weren't waiting. They were trapped.

The gwyllion nosed the scar along Robyn's shoulder, curling its warm tail along his nape. Robyn whispered to it, soft, and kept following the other little beastie guides by sounds and the occasional movement past his torch.

Realisation came, gradual: he could see past the small confines of his torch, and more than shadows. The darkness made its retreat unwilling, but a faint grey began filtering through. First as a hint of gloom in pitch, it began filling itself into milky swathes that drifted like fog on a cold, clear morn.

Robyn hesitated, head cocked sideways as the gwyllion one by one disappeared around a narrow bend in the cavern, some winging, some crawling. A huge pile of stones blocked the way. The gwyllion on his shoulder gave a short chirrup, and he frowned. "I'm a lath of a fellow, no question, but that passage looks too tight even for me little John."

His passenger didn't agree, nipping a curl from his beard and tugging. When that didn't work, it swiped his cheek with a pinion and pecked his ear again.

"Hoy, you!" Robyn muttered, rubbing at his beleaguered ear and sliding a glare the beastie's way. It stared him down with eyes awhirl, clearly peeved by the delay.

"Whats'mever, then." With a shrug, Robyn propped his torch into a gap in the wall and ambled towards the passage. It took some careful doing, many of the boulders too heavy to so much as tilt, but there were plenty smaller ones that rolled beneath hands and feet. A rockfall, mayhap, and an old one.

Bit by bit he cleared it, and upon the wriggle and heave of a large stone gained the reward of seeing it totter and roll aside. In its wake brightness flared, darting tears to his eyes. Hazarding he'd moved enough rock, Robyn began wriggling his way through the opening. He endured several scrapes to his chest, bruised knuckles, and a barked shin—that one he swore at—all the while

blinking and squinting. His eyes finished adjusting soon enough—
this wasn't sunlight, not even close, but still, he needed no torch
to take in his surroundings. On the far side he staggered to a halt,
heart hammering with sudden and conflicting impulses:

Bewilderment.

Retreat, and one fast as possible.

But mind-bending, genuine wonderment stayed him, left him
standing open-mouthed.

It opened before him, surrounded him; all filled with half-
lights, damp, huge. A grotto from some ancient tale, a magical
cavern echoing every breath and humming with the magic. For
magic it had to be, to hold what lay at the far end.

The cavern walls . . . weren't, exactly. They halted midway up
and out . . . or more, submerged themselves in something akin
to watered-down milk or whey. If whey or indeed any liquid
could hang midair without so much as a quiver, to form half the
ceiling and the far wall.

Light filtered down, green shot with clouds of silver-grey. The
floor beneath his feet seemed solid enough, though it didn't look
it, flickering in waves and surges. He had to look up—and quick,
before his head disagreed with his gorge.

The gwyllion weren't so inclined; they darted and called and
danced. A bolder pair soared into the . . . the whatever-it-was,
performed slow aerials in its depths, then exploded back the way
they'd come with a small *pop!* As they shook midair, a fine spray
moistened Robyn's upturned face.

Robyn licked his lips, tasted . . . Water? It couldn't be.

But he were in the otherworlds, weren't he? Where *couldn't*
meant *mayhap after all.*

Deliberate, slow with head cocked sideways—no doubt he looked
a horse ready to spook—Robyn padded over to the . . . aye, and
calling it a wall didn't seem fitting, though it might be one by any
description he could come up with. Or mayhap a curtain, even if it
wasn't, not really.

The gwyllion settled down on his shoulder and began to preen
itself with little scratches and burbles.

"Glad to see you en't worried," he told it, perversely comforted
as it merely flipped its tail from his nape and began to groom that,
too.

And all the while the watery-curtain-thing rose above and
beyond, alive and quivering and for all the world looking as if it
might come crashing down at any moment. Mayhap fill the caverns
and drown him. It had to be water, though it surely couldn't be.
But what else could it be? Creeping forward, one tiny step then
another, and another, as curiosity began to creep just as steadily
along his nerves, smoothing panic.

Extending cautious fingers, Robyn touched the thing. Drew
back as it quivered.

The gwyllion kept up their aerial display. The one on his shoulder kept up its grooming, unconcerned.

"Wellaway," he muttered, and reached again. Slick and soft—congealed, almost—as he touched it and pushed in, submerging to his knuckles before meeting resistance. Try as he might, he couldn't go any farther. The . . . water? . . . aye, it slicked cool, but not cold. A fascinated smile playing at his lip, Robyn wriggled his fingers. The movement detached tiny air bubbles from his skin, made the watery thing shudder. Startled, he drew his hand back with a small and pressured *pop* of exit. Wet. He rubbed his fingertips together, sniffed, tasted. Fresh, to be sure, albeit weighted with silt.

Several more of the gwyllion went for a swim beyond the "curtain", shearing off a wake of bubbles. Robyn trod the periphery, peering in. Light filtered down, describing shafts of gold to grey over rocks to touch, here and there, a bottom of pebbles and sediment. In the depths, strange shapes flickered and flared; gliding from darkness to light and back again . . . nay, not so strange, after all. Merely moss and weeds wafting upon a slow current. They danced shadows upon a great grandfather of a sturgeon as it drifted closer, big as Robyn's torso and idly eyeing a silvery flash: a group of smaller fish lingering in a thick weave of weeds. Something darted downward like an arrow's flight made visible: a frog, diving in a wake of bubbles that proved it had come from air, and some sort of surface.

Deeper still, beneath a cavernous overhang of moss and water bracken, a huge shadow stirred.

Robyn's eyes widened. Indeed the stuff of dreamings—or nightmares. Yet as recognisable, if not as commonplace, as the other watery denizens. Lying black and sinuous, hide shimmering as the light flickered and wafted across its bed, breathing water as surely as Robyn did air, the creature betrayed what the waters were.

Barrow Mere. Where drowned ghosts lingered beyond its depths. Where a spirit old as the land itself slumbered, its truest form evoked—and prisoned—by an iron weight of forgotten spells. Where ancient magic conjured against the hope of waking, and drowned winged freedom just beyond the surface.

Where he'd come from.

Where, surely, he'd find his way back.

Robyn reached out both hands this time, and splayed them against the barrier. Reaching aggressive, this time, but unfortunately with the same effect: to his knuckles and no farther. And the harder he pushed, the harder, it seemed, the Mere pushed back.

So he sucked in a breath, let the words curl upon his tongue and outward. *Release me*, he told it, silent, and whispered aloud the Barrow tongue, "*Rhyddhau mi.*"

The strange, luminescent barrier misted from his breath, but otherwise made no response. Beyond, the water lay placid, streaked with murky light.

The wyvern lay serene, its only movements those of deep-set slumber.

"*Rhyddhau!*" Fiercer, but it lay quivering against the barrier. Seeking, asking . . . *penetrating*, absorbed in tiny, blue-struck bubbles, merely to skate sideways, as if skimming the strange curtain that contained the Mere.

The wyvern quivered in its sleep, as if a gentle hand had stroked its wing, or whispered at its ear.

What is your name? Robyn thought. *What do I call you?* 'Tweren't a he, exactly, or a she, more like both and neither, rather like the tiny gwyllion, only calling an Old One "it" seemed somehow less than respectful. Robyn suddenly mourned his lack of book learning. Mayhap there was a word, and he just didn't know it. Mayhap "tha" would be enough, for now.

And those gwyllion kept sliding through the thing as if greased, innocently taunting him from the other side.

"How does your like fetch through, then?" he asked the one still riding his shoulder. It blinked at him, gave the beastie equivalent of a shrug, and kept cleaning the end of its tail.

"Would you be forswearing your oath so quickly, Hob-Robyn?"

And bloody *damn*, but his heart nigh leapt from his chest. He did fall against the barrier, which—of course—only gave him enough admittance to reap a wet face.

The beastie shrieked and launched upward, leaving two sets of claw marks seeping behind. Growling, wiping at the scratches upon his wet cheeks, Robyn turned to face the Priestess.

Crouched on the rock slide with arms laced about her knees, she sat resting her chin upon them, studying him.

Tempting, to ask how long she'd been skulking there.

As if she heard the thought, her lip quirked. Leaping down graceful as a hind, she paced from the slide to him.

"Passage being easy for the little spirits, aye. The magic thisnow be letting their kind through what doors you and yours opened Hob-Robyn. But for our kind, 'tis not being so easy. The iron and the bells drive us, farther down and further in."

"But you . . . how did you bring me here?"

"Only just, and spirits be aiding. Through your spells you opened the way, through your blood the Veil let you pass."

"Aye, then, and if that's all it takes—" He drew the knife and whipped it towards his arm.

Just as swift the Priestess grabbed his wrist, strong fingers pinching his tendons, and the knife clattered to the ground. It narrowly missed their toes.

"Foolish boy!" she hissed up at him, shoving his arm aside. "Would you be ruining us all?"

"I am no boy," Robyn growled, "but the Lord of the Hunt. Ruin happens to be my other name."

She slapped him, open-handed and stinging, spat, "Boys be thinking of nothing but themselves!"

His fists clenched. "And what were you thinking, when you gave orders to take me from my place and my people?"

"Of my place! My people! A future!"

"With me as buck to your doe?"

She itched to slap him again, he could tell. Robyn glowered beneath his damp forelock, a dare. *Do it.*

Instead she clenched her fists, glowered right back. "Things are not being so simple! And now, you be entrusting your magic to us whilst in the next breath be searching for ways about it. Typical! Father's blood be running deep."

"Me da were a kind and just man!—for all the good it did him."

"And his son? Or his fathers? Magus be naming you aptly. Tall as any mountain—and thick as one, head filled with stone! Even mountain kings must be giving way when time be nigh."

"Yet mine en't nigh! Else all that show wit' your skull-faced lad cutting me, the 'amends' . . . that were nowt but some act, then?"

Amber eyes shifted dark, yet just as quickly anger wicked away, leaving a steady, resigned calm. "There be no 'act' with the magic. Insulting us both, you be, with such foolishness. Pardon I'll be giving, for our fate be biding cruel and hard to bear, at the first."

"'Tisn't our fate. Yours, mayhap, whilst my fate—my tynged—en't here, or . . ." Robyn trailed away, puzzled, as he sought the skeins—fates pulsating with colour, futures tangling or smoothing—merely to find them muted, quivering. Like strands of hair floating in water, sleepy as the Mere beside them, stretching into unending grey, shadows cast from a faraway, brilliant bend long since passed.

"Now," the Priestess said, gentle almost, "you begin to be seeing what your sire's people gave us. Took our future, the conqueror people did, all the while ensuring we be having neither it nor our past."

Robyn stared at the Mere, silent. The gwyllion came drifting back to land upon his shoulder, eyes whirling at the Priestess, who returned the scrutiny as if puzzled. "Is that why, then?" Robyn finally said. "Why you've done it to me? Taking some sort of revenge?"

She drew in a huge breath and let it trickle slowly outward. Calling upon patience? Or persuasion? "Revenge be in the hearts of those who've the means for 't—"

"Well, you've time enough for any means here, en't you?"

"—in foolish man-games of blood for blood, as if blood be not sacred to our Mother, nor spirit-shades returning with its price upon their souls!"

Robyn looked away, cheeks stinging as if she'd slapped him again.

"From your birth, Hob-Robyn, you be calling us. Your voice sings strong and uncommon, enough to be defying Horned Spirit in a great game He could not be resisting. As you lay in the ending, we are hearing, gathering to listen where we cannot be touching, and your voice be changing again. From random dart to an arrow's deadly point." She ambled over to the water wall, reached up to stroke it like she might a favourite hound. Turned to peer at him. "We knew when you found the powers called shaman, magus, druid, witch—the ways of the otherworlds and the endings. We heeded, for with such things are you making your magics. Even as the other spirits of your triune be answering. You be holding them, Spring and Summer, even when they be stumbling, failing."

"Then you understand why I must go back to them!"

"They not be needing you anymore, Hob-Robyn."

"You don't know that."

"Legacy and legend always more important be, than any who would be making and waking them." She paced back over, eyes holding steady to his.

Robyn refused to drop his gaze, made it a challenge.

"Your voice, Hob-Robyn, be teaching your consorts the song to be waking the eldest ones, to be opening passages long abandoned and shut. Aye, you even be snatching from slumber the ancient wyrm who is being the deepest heart of thisworld—our earth—freeing him from places he is being long forgotten. Calling upon the Barrow magics. Why?"

"They wanted us dead!" His answer came instinctive, though its sharp edge blunted against the water wall. "Nay, not just dead, but obliterated! We had to survive!"

"Yet survival not being enough!" she snapped back. "We who once were being dryw and magi to the Atecotti have . . . survived."

Atecotti. Robyn knew the name from his mam's first lessonings—the most ancient ones, it meant; given to a vanished Barrow tribe supposed more legend than reality.

They had vanished, all right. Not only into another world, but into gaol.

"In surviving we be . . . undying, thisnow stretching inward, not out. Our children long be grown, with no more being born unless outworld seed be planted here, or outland bairns taken from their cots or from where they be exposed on the hills. Survival never be all that matters. Even you and those once yours would be making places, conjuring the magics not just for surviving, but thriving. For fighting back. Aye?"

As if her words conjured their own magics, a memory floated in the Mere's depths—a copper-haired man driven desperate and loose-tongued:

"A place to call our own, a. . . a sanctuary where we can all be safe! Where your people can live free. Where you won't be hunted like

an animal, or Marion, and you can be that forester, she can have a wisewoman's prestige and hearth! Where you and I. . . where we can be together, with no fear of gods or judgment or. . . or a fate that would see us set against each other again, betrayer and betrayed. . .!"

A whimper escaped, hoarse. "Gamelyn."

"Even that one"—the Priestess forked a sign, and of its intent there was no doubt— "fated Enemy, *your* Enemy, his heart corrupted by iron and bells! Even *he* kens what he would be conjuring."

"Enemy he might be named, and more than the once," Robyn countered. "All the while everyone demanding we were that and nowt else. Didn't stop me from wanting to singe me fingers in the light of him, 'cause part of me knew what he could be. Didn't stop me from loving him, any more than what me da's people did kept me mam from loving *him*. 'Tis the obligation of those who come during and after bad times, to honour the challenge of fair paths . . . nay. Even better to weigh, to learn then turn aside from what wicked trails our ancestors walked. To . . . make amends, aye?—and ken what came before. But allus, choose love ower hate."

"And so, Hob-Robyn, you also be choosing to replait tynged into new patterns, new thoughts. Dangerous, those are being." Her head tilted; she crossed her arms. "And you be wondering why thisworld's Spirits called you home?"

The gwyllion chirped, faint and seemingly curious. A soft smile touched the Priestess's face, and she reached out to stroke the little beastie's neck. It purred, for all the world like the cat Robyn's mam had kept.

"See. Even now They be heeding you, Lord of beasts and Wode. As Their shades in otherworld heed your sister and her consort—and her firstborn. See?"

The Mere's reflections began to coalesce into more—no memory bittersweet, but possibles, never yet seen, perhaps not even yet done . . . his sister: proud sentinel upon the gates of Tickhill dead-dropping a horsed cadre; dancing with Gamelyn at the Bel-fires; seated with John in the Hermit's caverns scrying the stones; walking the stone halls dressed warm against the winter chill with a carrot-topped bairn on one hip and a black-haired little lass at her skirts. Robyn reached out, as if he could touch her. Instead it drifted away to revealed several more: a cloaked, solitary figure walking an expanse of sand broader than Robyn's imagination could ever conjure; a slight figure crouched at a fire within the Hunter's caverns; a hooded ghost wandering the green Wode armed with a longbow, leaving parcels at village gates . . .

Sorrow twisted his gut, wrung him dry and shuddering.

"It was you, or the little wren."

"The little . . . wren?" Somehow, this chilled him even more, despite wondering exactly what she meant.

"And Hob was being so weary of the otherworlds, spirit weighed beneath a war none of us be winning."

Not when you took me, he thought. *We had won.*

The battle, the Horned Lord suddenly whispered, faint and flickering downward in reflections of sunlight. *Never the war.* Then He sucked away into the thick, wet air, leaving Robyn to fully process—nay, realise—the silence.

It was the only time he'd heard his god since coming here. The only time, and he'd not . . . felt him, not even in those sparse, faint words. Not been filled/emptied with Him since he'd woken here, in these caverns, into silence.

Like when the crossbow bolt had nigh ended him in his fifteenth year, with his sixteenth one spent battling death in the Hunter's caverns. But that had been John's doing, to save him the weight of godling possession when he could barely hold his own thoughts . . . and even there had been openings to the sky, roots of trees in the upper lofts. Whilst here, nothing but rock and stillness. Was there indeed no green Wode here, teeming with life and death? No balance upon which the sky-wheel spun?

The gwyllion stopped its preening with a satisfied chirrup, extended its wings and dropped from Robyn's shoulder, soaring up just before it would have hit the floor to dive into the waves with its companions.

Robyn watched the little creatures sport amongst the fish and weeds of Barrow Mere. "I don't even know your name."

"Thisnow, I am being Priestess." It was sharp, inviting a quick, sideways glance. "But once . . . " It softened as she studied the Mere, a slight frown twitching at her brow. As if memory were difficult, or uninvited. It came sudden, from the way her eyes blinked. "Once, I was being Arianrhod."

Of course. The silvery moon . . . and the ravening sow.

- VIII -

M arion's Book of Hours:
Waning of Oimelc, 1202
7 years, 2 months and 25 days –
Our Lord Shall Return

I have debated how best to write to you, husband, and have finally decided upon this most private of my writings, with earlier, smaller parchments settled snug within. For I fear letters can neither reach you nor arrive complete and unread. Even through the auspices of your Commander, who graced Tickhill with his presence a se'nnight ago.

Hubert is dear to me as he is to you, but neither can he lie to me. Nor does he try. He worries after you, follows your progress as he can, and tells me what is tellable—not much. Only that you have spent the past months scouring what libraries the Templars still hold within Outremer, and that the holy object you are trying to return cannot be placed where most think it belongs. He admits the Relic speaks to you and, since it is as amoral as most spirits, worries where it will lead you.

I don't trust it, either. I wish you had returned here, to tell me in person. Though I might have smacked your silly head from your shoulders, but I'd hang your skull where it belongs, trust me. On the sacred Oak, not buried in some faraway desert.

Well. This lack of communication means I also cannot tell you of our daughter, nor describe how beautiful she is, nor how late she came—other than when she did decide to make her appearance, it was all too quick. I have named her after your mother, and I can only hope that you will see this Marjory as you never did your own mam.

We will all see you again, and I shall give these letters to you myself.

We have wintered well, and spring has come as early as Marjory did late, warmish with fair skies and enough rain to set, not soak, the land. We've put ploughs in the ground fair early, all the while hoping it won't decide to nip back cold and delay the planting. Though, 'tis true, we won't be oversowing; it's early days yet.

All the children are happy and healthy, though we had a scare with Aelwyn's Tom over the winter. He's never been the strongest of our lot, and the ague nigh took him from us. Aderyn spent as much time nursing the boy as his mam and David did; there was no need for me, with such capable wortwives in our midst. Tom is well now, thankfully, and none of the others caught the sickness. Aderyn's been unsettled with night frights of late, sleeping with me (to the consternation of Berta, who says cozening her won't solve anything. I don't agree, and neither does Robbie—sweet lad, he insists on sleeping beside her so she doesn't wake alone. Either that, or he just likes my bed, little scamp.) And our newest addition to the Tickhill brood, Ian, is settling in well. Away from *your brother's stern regard, his eldest has begun to spread his wings. I sometimes forget the lad's of the Christ, though Father Tuck, as always, reminds me they all aren't the butchers who killed my parents. He gives a fine example in tolerance and true Christian behaviour. Ian's parents visit him with some regularity— save for this past autumn, when Alais lost the bairn she'd hoped for. I tended her after, and she recovered well, though slowly. I was frank with Otho, told him if he'd needs, he should find himself a likely lass to tend them. A mistake, that; he acted as if I'd given dire insult. As defensive as a bairn caught chipping a sliver off the sugar. But Alais understood.*

I prefer homely matters, but the world closes in on us more and more. I wish you were here and safe, with what's going on. War with Louis of France seems likely, and it's taking all the diplomacy of the Marshal, Archbishop Walter, and the Templars to quell it. "No more'n dogs pissing their claim" Robyn would say, and this time he'd be no more'n right. Neither looks to back down, and I do fear war shall come.

The king loves England, has sworn blood oath to it. Of course, he seemed just as smitten with the young lass who was to be Lusignan's bride... only that one he married and made his Queen. Which, of course, helped make the situation we're in. Our liege is as spoilt and 'mine-mine', as any of his like, doesn't think 'consequence' belongs in his lexicon, aye? And while he follows the Templars' advice when it comes to that magic, and that with nigh-fearful fervour, I suspect he believes more in his right to the ancient Kingship than he has any will to wield the powers themselves. Thinks he's but to reach out a hand and they'll come by, obedient as a hound.

We have indeed made bargains with devils, my beloved friend, and it's a proper jongleur's rope you've left me to tiptoe. You seem to have more faith in my balance upon it than I...

South of Tyre, in the Kingdom of Jerusalem
In the land Outremer
Waning of Ostara (spring equinox), 1202 CE
Month of Jumadal Akhirah, 598 AH

A great-grandmother of a storm blew in, turning sun-drenched blue skies into dark and ill-tempered gauze.

"Surely we can make it!" Remegius protested, pointing to a smudge due north. "I can see Tyre now!"

Gamelyn didn't answer. He dismounted, his eyes upon the dark clouds approaching across the sea. Cloak whipping in the wind, he led his skittish mount over to a tall cluster of rocks.

Remegius followed. "There's a storm coming!" His shout measured itself, not only against the fierce wind, but in a plain attempt at reason. "We have to get to the city!"

Still, Gamelyn didn't answer. Instead he handed his bay's rein over to Remegius, tied his cloak ends together, and began unlacing a hide bundle from his saddle. Controlling two wind-spooked horses stoppered the young Hospitaller's protests, at any rate, whilst Gamelyn, in the lee of the rocks, unrolled his bundle into a tarpaulin complete with ties and pegs. It would make adequate shelter behind the rocks.

Well, as long as the wind didn't shift and shred the thing, or lift it like some great Eastern kite and sail away.

Remegius watched with no little dismay. "But the *town*—"

"Is at least another half-hour's ride away." Gamelyn's words came terse. All his attention lay fastened upon prohibiting the tarpaulin from billowing into the wind and panicking their horses past any hope of Remegius holding them. "The storm will catch us much sooner."

Once the wind eased and rain started to fall—well, sheet down, more like—the horses put their broad rumps against it and, heads down, half-dozed.

Gamelyn was in no mood for dozing, though he should. His spirits had plummeted, as inexplicable, as dark and evil-intentioned, as set against them as the storm seemed.

Here he sat, off on some doomed and ridiculous quest, stuck in a tiny half tent with a damp-eared squire of a Hospitaller. Whose opinion of him, over the past months, had gone from 'vexingly dotty' to 'brain-boiling mad'.

"Why are we heading north, at any rate? Everything we've researched so far—"

And had they researched. Every dusty, dry and dim cache in every Templar castle up and down the coast of Outremer.

"—shows Damascus to be the place. Shouldn't we head south, take the valley there? Not this way where we'll have to cross the mountains?"

A damp-eared squire of a Hospitaller who kept asking *questions*.

Mayhap, the skull in the bag against his ribs prompted, *if you'd arse y'rself to give some answers. . .*

Stop talking in his *voice!* he snapped back.

"—cause, don't you see, Brother Gamelyn?" If nothing else, Remegius had learned prudence during his time with the Hospitallers. "We should—"

"We aren't going to the Umayyad, or Damascus."

That shut the lad's mouth with a sharp pop. Remegius considered the damp tether in his hands, coiled it for the tenth time, seemed to count likewise. "But it's where the Relic was found, after all. If we're to return it—"

I do not belong in the Umayyad, penned and displayed like—

Like a Relic? Gamelyn sniped.

A brief silence, informing Gamelyn that the Baptist was Not Amused. Then, *I do not belong in a cage. Not in Halifax, nor Nablus, nor Damascus. I belong to the sand and the wind.*

So you keep saying. Unfortunately, that describes a lot of places hereabouts.

You will find the way. You must.

It wasn't the first time he'd received that answer. Gamelyn just wished the Baptist had figured that out before they'd crisscrossed half the Kingdom of Jerusalem. Covertly. Salah al-Din's untimely death might have spawned half a dozen scuffles for control; his shrewd brother Sayf ad-Din had crushed most of them and was, according to rumour, amidst immobilising another. Gamelyn had no wish to fetch either of them into the midst of that.

"Brother Templar?" Insistent. O, and aye, but Remegius was insistent. Earnest, plucky, grudgingly patient . . . and definitely without a sense of humour.

"We must be sure." Curt, though Gamelyn tried to tilt it otherwise. "The Relic . . . it does not desire Damascus."

Thankfully Remegius—not without a grim look out into the rain—let it go.

At the end of the tether, Gamelyn's bay shifted. His sorrel companion snorted a steam of resignation. The downpour drummed harder against the makeshift roof, and Gamelyn cocked it a wary eye. Reaching upward, he poked several fingers at where the middle was beginning to sag. A small torrent poured over the edges.

Remegius' gaze, as resigned as their mounts, followed the water's course off their shelter and traced the runnels of wet at their feet. He sat upon a rock just out of reach of Gamelyn. So perched, they'd kept reasonably dry—and their boots were well oiled. "I never knew it could rain like this in the desert."

"Outremer is a place of extremes."

Again, quiet, with only the rain—and that was enough, to be sure, to fill the tent with sound.

"Where are we going?" Remegius finally asked.

How interesting, that in coming here Gamelyn should be the elder, with his own captious lad in tow. *How did you manage, Hubert? To not kill me, that is?*

You were much, *much quieter,* he imagined his mentor answering, with that sly grin.

True enough. He'd been unwilling to open his mouth in case all the past should come blithering out.

Think of your son, Gamelyn rebuked himself. *Your bold wee Robbie, with all his questions.*

It didn't help. It only cracked open the ache, and fouled his mood further.

At this rate, he'd not return for Beltane.

A year and a day, the skull reminded, and Gamelyn shivered.

For the first in a brace of years, he'd not be there. Not feel the primal, purest of magics wash over him, not do his part to keep the old ways and the dream—*Robyn's dream*—alive. He was a wandering monk, indeed, celibate and abandoned. Not his, this time, to dance and drink and slough off any shell. To lie with his Lady in a Marriage more sacrosanct than any he'd be blessed to openly know . . .

Take care of her, Much. Even when she doesn't want or need it.

"Brother?" Remegius prompted. "Where are we going?"

Gamelyn tilted the tent roof once more, watched the water flood over its edge, splashing at his toes. "We're going to what, in Syria, stands in for the Nest of Eagles."

Remegius' dark eyes limned white. "You mean—"

"Aye. The Old Man, his Mountain, his 'assassins', the lot. We're for Masyaf."

◌

"You're to follow me, to the Painted Grotto."

Skull Face's entry seemed totally out of character in that 'twere proper meek and almost respectful. More of the latter, in truth, as he noticed Robyn's bedmates.

Particularly when the one who'd appropriated Robyn's shoulder raised its head and hissed at the intrusion.

They'd not left his side, these five gwyllion, since leading Robyn to the Mere's cavern two nights . . . three . . . how many, at that?

Mayhap not so long. He'd not eaten since . . . when? Surely he'd be hungry by now, had it been so long.

Trying to process it, Robyn agreed to Skull Face's demand more easily than he might have otherwise—for 'twere one, no matter the man's put-on humility. Robyn had always dreaded the possibility of imprisonment, though it surely came with the territory of outlaw life, and this place more a dreary gaol than any refuge. He knew they watched him, so after seeing the Mere, he'd stayed in his little cavern just to bore them, put them off guard. Leave himself some breathing room. Plan.

Gamelyn would snort indulgence. *Plan, Hob-Robyn? You?*

I do plan, y' arsy ginger sod. When I have to.

And now, he had to. Not done, not by a long shot; there'd be a way to fulfil his oath *and* fetch himself from here. He'd find it, conjure it . . . cobble it together from whatever bits he could find, did he have to.

Not to mention, Painted Grotto? That tickled a curiosity despite his slight arsy bent of *Who are you to summon me, any road?*

His gaoler, that was who.

If Robyn had any doubts as to who'd likely decorated the Horse Caves nigh to Whitwell? Well, the walls of this 'Painted Grotto' settled them.

It also begged more questions, and the largest of those: how long *had* the Fae been here, trapped?

The Grotto presented those questions and gave few answers. It spanned out beyond its entrance, large as an oxgang of clearance ready for the plough. Indeed, it demanded attention, and far more than those who peopled it—small groups, here and there. Where torches and fires lit, Robyn could see colours—markings simple to wildly complex—adorning the vast walls. A wide, indigo sky had been painted overhead, its stars glittering and glowing against the flickering light.

All of it seemed muddied . . . nay, muddled, and by what had to be centuries of silt and drip water. The signs of that, of course, lay everywhere—'twere the manner of caverns to form their own decoration—rising from the floor, grown down from the ceiling, dripped and joined to form pillars.

But this cavern's artistry had been enhanced. Carven and shaped by hand, an array of creatures rose beneath that imitation sky, many depicting animals long gone from Robyn's own world.

Did they still exist here? Was there a place where they ran and rutted, ate and drank?

There had to be. Otherwise, how did these people live?

A bird in flight here, a rearing stag there, a huge pillar towards the back seeming a jumble of intricate shapes piled atop each other. Beside the entry and so close Robyn could touch it, an upward growth had been shaped into a horned dancer—long ago, at that, for the wet had eroded his horns into lacework, and melted his shoulders and outstretched arms into eerie, wavering stems.

Once Robyn started looking, he found others like to it, works fading/building into another form—and some still being formed. One small group lounged about, watching an elder woman do her work with copper tools. Against the far wall another man sketched something; again, people watched. In one alcove a pillar stood, remarkable not only for the odd sigils upon it, but the wide berth everyone gave it. Robyn didn't blame them; even across the wide span, the pillar—reminiscent of a chapel font, at that—made gooseflesh rise up his spine. He twitched his shoulders, shuddering it away. The gwyllion perched there burbled a protest, then took wing and disappeared into the ceiling shadows.

But the murmurs echoing throughout the cavern seemed contented enough. About thirty of them all told?—in their finery and painted up for something, to be sure.

Well, what else did they have to do?

"You be seeing the talents of our people here." The grey-eyed acolyte materialised from behind the melted dancer and came to stand beside Robyn. "Such beauty, aye?"

"I'd find it hard, trying to create sommat so tricky with a whole roomful of people eyeing me up."

Grey Eyes smiled up at him. Her fair hair fell down the back of her long, yellow tunic, and the woad stains upon her skin had been highlighted in like hues of yellow and white. She looked a burst of sunshine; 'all her spots on', his mam would have said, just like the rest of the gathering. Robyn was beginning to feel rather dowdy, as if he'd arrived for a fête barely dressed and combed.

'Twere plain Skull Face felt the same. He returned the girl's smile then resumed his glower at Robyn. Grey Eyes flitted a hand at Skull Face, plainly saying *Shoo!* Skull Face's frown deepened; just as plainly he wasn't about to shoo. He muttered something to the effect that he didn't trust the tall one to behave with any decency. Grey Eyes raised his frown with a scowl and a swift comment that brought a flame to Skull Face's cheeks.

With a grumbling sort of growl, the man slunk away. Not without, however, a sneer up at Robyn that said *Behave yourself, you Motherless git, or I'll do you proper.*

Robyn believed him.

"Do you be having such skills?" Grey Eyes asked.

"Skills?"

"Are you being a maker?"

Robyn snorted. "Not the likes of this, lass. Me little John, though . . . " It clogged in his throat, his fingers rising to stroke the delicate wooden charm that hung from his left nipple. A maker, aye, and John had more power in his nimble carver/ conjurer fingers than, mayhap, even Barrow folk could summon.

Grey Eyes followed the gesture, curious. She cocked her head sideways, as if kenning the whys and wheretofores, then nodded. "Aye, I be remembering that one. Herself be sending him back when he was being taken."

Sending him back? Robyn turned on the lass and started to question her.

Instead she grabbed his arm and pulled him in her wake. "Herself be looking. Come!"

As they progressed into the caverns, the gathering abruptly shifted. Some ambled forward whilst others remained in their places, wary and watching. Even the artists left off their work, staring. The warriors—plain by their spears and demeanour and including, emphatically, Skull Face—edged close, their attention in a different bent: waiting for the inevitable.

Robyn wasn't about to give it to them. Not now, anyroad, though mayhap later.

Murmurs sank into bare whispers as the folk shifted, making a path for Robyn and his companion. In the doing they revealed their crimson-clad Priestess, rising from a well-lit mound of furs in the cavern's centre. She was flanked by a smallish, informal court. The elder—Magus, she'd called him—eyed Robyn and raked his hip-length twist locks to spill over one fur-caped shoulder. He was seated, sinewy legs folded, to his Priestess's left. A duo of ancient grandmothers had settled in just behind her, one with spindle in hand and dressed in a white that echoed her snowy braids, the other garbed in an indigo that nigh matched the painted ceiling. Robyn kenned the hallowed threefold arrangement, though their particular tree seemed to be missing a younger branch. A brace of warriors made a standing semicircle behind them, each holding either torch or copper-tipped spear. A small fur at the Priestess's feet moved, betraying eyes that glowed like coals in the dim. Baring sharp, gleaming teeth in a yawn, what looked like a diminutive northern wildcat gave fair dismissal to their guest.

"Being well come to the Horned Lord's vessel." Dubious, whether the Priestess shared her feline companion's opinion as her gaze lit upon Robyn. Her movement, however, shared that companion's grace as she rose to kneel, heels beneath hips, folding her hands and tilting her chin down with no little respect. "My people, he is of us. He brings to this hall what has long been absent. Be giving Him due before the feast is being brought."

Robyn stood fast as they came to him—both sides wary but accepting—to murmur his name, touch his hands and feet, finger his sleeves. Some even reached up to lay a hand just over his heart.

There were no children. Even the youngest of them looked to be his elder—except, mayhap, Grey Eyes.

"Come, be seated with me." Less a request than an order.

Robyn eyed the Priestess, considering it. With a tilt of head he gave way, padding over to sit between her and the elder man. Not for him, to have the brass to sit amongst that duet of grandmams to her other side, and they exchanged pleased smiles at daunting him, however slight.

Grey Eyes took up an earthen jug, lifted it to first the grandmothers and her mistress, then Magus, then the gathered people. She acknowledged the cavern ceiling last of all; Robyn heard the gwyllion rustle, saw eyes glowing. Only then did Grey Eyes pour off the liquid into a copper goblet, touching it briefly to her forehead before holding it out to Robyn.

The mead teased his nostrils, sharp-sweet. Heathen hearth manners demanded a host's offering be accepted, and those so inbred he nearly took it. Nearly. Robyn closed his extended fingers, rattled by not only his mam's stories, but every warning told by firelight, every fork of evil eye, every *instinct*.

"Lies, told to frighten," the Priestess said, soft, meeting his gaze. "We be having no need to trap you into accord with a sip of drink or bite of food."

"Since I'm already trapped?" Robyn countered.

Grey Eyes frowned, and a murmured growl rippled through the watchers. A hint of scorn lit the Priestess's eyes, still locked with his.

"If we be having ways to conjure our own to stay with drink?" the indigo-clad grandmother spat out. "Surely we'd be conjuring our own escape."

"Is the Hob fearful?" The Priestess spoke it sweetly, with venom beneath.

"When I've sommat to fear, aye," Robyn's answer came just as amiable, just as acerbic.

"It was being hard, at the first." With one sinewy forefinger, Magus began tracing a cross-nap spiral against the fur where he sat. "Nights were being longest, and days flowing endless, raindrops upon a swollen spate of river."

"Hob is being insolent!" the indigo grandmother retorted.

"What is being Hob *but* insolence?" Magus shrugged, his eyes upon fur and fingers.

The Priestess raised an eyebrow, and the white-braided grandmother twitched at her spindle with a smirk, eyeing Robyn. It bided a mite too akin to lusty appraisal for any comfort.

Magus swept his gaze across the gathered remainder. "I repeat, when first we came, it was being hard. We mourned. We were being angry. I be remembering this. My task since the Parting, to be memory's keeper."

Small sighs and murmurs of assent echoed softly through the Grotto.

"But I am not forgetting the lies." The Priestess settled back onto her heels, peering at Robyn. "Little, they are being at first, or little half-truths, told to make us be seeming as less. The conquerors be saying we are ignorant savages dwelling in darkness. They even be taking our own names and twisting them cruel. Heathen? It be meaning people of the heath, naught more, but they be giving it other meanings."

Her words fell into a heavy silence.

Magus, finally, was the one to break it. "Those of us who were being Britons were called *wealas*—their word for slave, and outsider. Lower. Barbarian. So said people who be moving into *our* territory, taking away what be given us by our Great Mother! *Þa wealas flugon Þa Anglan swa fyr.*"

The last words echoed, turned so shrill that many hunched their shoulders, covered their ears.

The Priestess spat, "Magus, be not speaking that tongue here!"

"Nay," Magus countered, eyeing Robyn. "He be knowing it."

"'The Welsh ran from the Anglic like fire,'" Robyn whispered. "Aye, I do."

"No doubt this boy who refuses our mead also be knowing how his father's people took ours as slaves, sired their get upon our women." This from the indigo grandmother, glowering at Robyn. "They be still. As *your sire* did."

"Me mam loved my da—she weren't his slave!" *Weren't anyone's slave,* he started to say, but the words died on his tongue. Freewoman, aye, but keeping her head down all the while: wisewoman, witch, Heathen. And murdered for it during their most holy Rite.

"After," the indigo grandmother countered, "her people—our people!—be banished. What choices be women having in such a world?"

"He is of the Hob's spirit," Grey Eyes countered, her eyes upon her Priestess.

"Aye," the Priestess answered, not only the acolyte but the entire gathering. "There is no doubt in me; Hob-Robyn is being clever enough to recognise such ways."

"To be *remembering*," Magus inserted, quiet, "such ways."

Robyn did. Aye, even in his own lifetime the memories piled up like rotting corpses. And beyond?

"To be scorning them," the white-braided grandmother added, soft, "while knowing their secrets."

This seemed to penetrate the gathering's collective ire. Robyn frowned.

"So the lies repeat, being memorised like to truth." Magus leaned forward, the torchlight burnishing his face into deep bronze, his grey twist locks into gilt. "Soon, we are not even being people. We are being Other. Called *Fae, Pagani,* unbelievers, barbarians, thieves. Savages. All to excuse our destruction as something righteous. And those lies become"—he smiled, and it was not pleasant—"legends."

The Priestess stood, walked forward and took the goblet from Grey Eyes. She took a sip from it and held it out to Robyn, her gaze still measuring. Challenging.

Robyn's own slid away, unable to answer—or to move, towards or away.

"We merely be winning the god back," she continued. "Requiring Him to be holding to *His* promise, given to us through His manifestation. Be Himself remembering it?"

"That we should be holding His magic safe, from those who be wishing it destroyed or spoilt," Magus answered, the words echoing with their own magic against the stones, fading beneath the drip-drip of water against stone and into silence.

It cradled the soft breaths of her gathered people, spun them out.

"Be drinking with us," Grey Eyes pleaded from beside him. "You *be* of us."

Robyn reached out, took the cup, and held it aloft. "*Bendith,*" he said, hoarse, and downed it all.

- IX -

The rain had long gone, sliding into the gullies and ravines to vanish as if it had never been.

But it had been. Beneath it the landscape transformed, quick as flint to tinder and just as afire with colour. First had come tens of shades of green, spiking upward from ever-present fawn and ochre, and through which their mounts picked their way daintily, as if mindful not to trample the rich shrubs. Then had come the blooms: whites and yellows, purples and reds, leaving powdery swathes across hoofs and worn boots. The horses also took every given chance to browse, sometimes spitting out what was too bitter, sometimes curling back their lips to snip tender leaves from thorny bush.

Gamelyn drank it in like well-aged wine, and found indulgent satisfaction in the unguarded awe of his Hospitaller companion.

They were climbing, had been for the past two days, the air of the Lebanon's hills redolent with the fragrance of cedar and cypress even as it grew thin against their lungs. Gamelyn had explained the normality of that to Remegius, who confessed with some chagrin that he'd never been as much as forty miles from Halifax. The horses stayed mostly unaffected; Gamelyn had ensured their mounts were hill-bred.

On the third morning of tree copses and rocky promontories, switchbacks and seldom-used trails, they began a slight descent, Gamelyn on point and afoot, his horse following on a slack rein, whilst Remegius trailed, still astride. The ridge kept on, farther north, into more hills, fawn and green nearer, then fading: a dusk of distance. Before them, the trail disappeared into a copse of cedar, reaching upwards into an escarpment of rock that nature had built into its own fortress. To their right yawned a deep, craggy ravine, promising a long fall and a quick death should one step unwisely. Beyond that lay the plain, a stark shock of pale fuzzed with faint slats of aubergine, and those disappearing into a sunrise that blinded the horizon.

"It's the edge of the world." Remegius had a hand to his brow, squinting against the sudden brilliance. His horse slipped on some loose shale; letting out a gasp, he grabbed leather. Several flat stones ricocheted against the cliff edge and into freefall, and he muttered a brief prayer.

Memory trickled in, once more. A sixteen-year-old's wonder, with Hubert's patient explanations of how foliage became desert, how mountains could make their own weather, or even hold it close when ocean moisture ran up against the elevations and held, with some making their occasional way over to settle in sparse mists across a welcoming, parched expanse. Nearly a decade since, Gamelyn's first journey to this land . . . yet so little had changed, enduring and scoffing at the trials of men.

Gamelyn put his toes on the ravine's edge and his face into the sun.

Thought of Robyn, defying the edge of Mam Tor, aiming arrows against the sky . . .

"Look!" Remegius pointed out over the plain. "That must be it."

With a start and shake of head, Gamelyn let gaze follow gesture. A wide upthrust of rock had appeared, as if rising from the vast plain beneath the sun's conjuring fingers. In the space of several breaths, condensing shadows revealed more: a citadel, atop the stony plateau, heeled faraway by hills. It seemed more mirage than reality, spreading broad and rising tall against the sky, its walls shimmering white and gold and crimson.

"Aye," Gamelyn confirmed. "Masyaf."

"Where the Old Man of Alamut's Syrian court lingers, a main position from which to send his assassins to his bidding. Where the Templars took you during the last Crusade, bound for Alamut along with several other lads. Trade, it was said, in knowledge." Remegius pinned his gaze to the amulet Gamelyn had pulled from beneath his tunic to display openly upon his breast. Clearly he sought affirmation despite knowing the story.

Well, part of the story, at least. Gamelyn nodded. "Asāsīyūn," he reminded softly, in that language. "Or of the Nizārī Ismaili."

Remegius nodded. He'd proven a quick and able linguist; his grasp of Arabic had grown from faltering curiosity to reasonable proficiency. "How do we . . . " He seemed to reconsider, tried again. "Wouldn't it be prudent to let them know we're coming? Somehow?"

"Oh, believe me." Gamelyn began picking a careful path down the narrow trail. "They already know."

A given, that they'd not see anyone coming.

Some assistance, mayhap? A query of the Relic, without much hope of answer. The Baptist had been more silent than not, of late.

But of course, He foiled expectation. *I don't think you truly need my help, O wanderer.*

Well, fine. Gamelyn rolled his eyes and led on. Instinctive, by now, to press into service every bit of tracking lore learned from both desert and forest, from beloved ones and foes alike. Add to that the abstruse learning gained from a variance of spirits and temples, natural and otherwise. Travel until sun became punishment instead of discomfort. Take rest, food, and water beneath some sort of shelter, then continue once the worst abated. Advise one's companion to follow his lead, and make no sudden moves. Pay closer than normal attention to his horse's reactions, and equally scrutinise the terrain. Keep weapons—all of them—concealed and ready. Contemplate every quiet step.

Wait for the inevitable.

In consequence, Gamelyn knew they were being followed long before his ears registered anything. Not brigands—none of those would dare chance the wrath of Alamut. And these presences—five, maybe, or six?—lingered weightless as smoke, flowing just as hushed across the countryside. He kept on, kept waiting—albeit with a smile of appreciation for the craft that not only gave them such silence, but had trained him to realise it.

This was the chancy bit. It had once been the policy of the Nizārī Ismaili to not murder out of hand any small band of wanderers. Gamelyn could only pray to whatever god would listen that all such indulgences still lay in strict reserve for the 'Old Man' himself. But no question that the ambush would happen before they reached the wide expanse of plain, the centre from which Masyaf rose, impressive and formidable.

Whereas here, in the foothills . . .

Terebinth and broom threw sharp, fragrant shadows upon the winding path. Rocks sprouted from the hillocks, some wide enough to hide a quartet of mounted Templars plus their kit and squires. And every hillock possessed some sort of ledge, fitting a swift strike from above.

The mare tensed, ears pricked and one nostril curling. *They come,* said the Relic. But Gamelyn already knew.

Three dun-draped figures materialised from behind a cypress clinging to a carmine-streaked rock. Remegius' sharp intake of breath proved the presence of the other . . . four, it was. Damascene steel glittered in the waning sunlight, and hanging from at least one abaya glinted the same sort of amulet Gamelyn wore at his own throat.

Gamelyn halted. A slight turn—palms upward, open—so they

could see the amulet, and so he could see them. The visible ones, at any rate—that others lay in hiding he didn't doubt. Pitching his voice low, but carrying, he uttered the catch-and-pass phrase of the Nizārī Ismaili. Well, that of a decade ago, anyway.

Two of the forward assassins slid wary glances to each other, puzzlement obvious despite that only their eyes were visible beneath the tuck-and-wrap of scarf. The third one gestured with knife and fingers, too swift for Gamelyn's memory to supply any translation. Not that it was for him, anyway. One of the rear guard answered it just as quick, then directed a swift query— Arabic, of course—in Gamelyn's direction.

"Who are you, cunning stranger, who approaches our fortress and speaks of brotherhood with an outlander's tongue? Leading"— a gesture to the wide-eyed figure of Remegius—"a noisy boy, like a lamb to slaughter."

No open laughter, but the ones nearest to Gamelyn had crinkly eyes and a stretch to their face scarves suggested smiles. Remegius' kaffiyeh had slipped, exposing not only the wide eyes but the sparse beard he'd tried to grow upon his youthful face. And a sulky expression. He'd understood.

"I seek the wisdom of the Elder, may he be exalted," Gamelyn answered, "for I was once a Brother."

"Were you?" The speaker kept advancing, slow. He seemed older than the others. Likely leader of the troupe, supporting younger ones as they gained experience on patrols such as these. The giveaway lay in how he held himself, confident as a lion. He'd no sword, merely two beautifully-lethal daggers—one at his belt and the other in hand—and it merely amplified his poise. "Interesting. For one is either a Brother, or one is not."

"Your point is well taken. But as it has been nigh two handspans of years since I walked the ramparts of Masraf, and even more since I was fledged in the Nest of Eagles, I feel I must choose my words with reverence and restraint."

A small mutter was exchanged between the members of the troupe. The leader hesitated midstep, head cocking to one side, gaze keen upon Gamelyn. Light brown, his eyes were, and one splashed with a shard of gilt. It rang alarm bells in Gamelyn's skull—but not fearful. Memorable.

He knew this man.

"And when," the leader returned, "were you at Alamut, O green-eyed one?"

"Not just green," another suddenly dismissed. "My sister has such a colour, and her skin ivory as any Persian eunuch, but this one's eyes are different. Pink around the edges, pale-lashed, like a hare. Like Ifranji."

The last word growled out. One could sense the troupe's hackles rising. Save for the leader, who kept peering at Gamelyn as if puzzlement were trying to pick memory's lock.

Gamelyn rather felt the same way. He returned the steady gaze—all the while aware of the troupe circling closer. Remegius hunched upon his mount, loath to do anything foolish. Thank god for that. "Ten winters have passed," Gamelyn ventured, "since I came with four others. All of us, tribute to the knowledge of mighty Sinan, Elder of Alamut, may his deeds be extoled and recounted into Paradise."

The leader's breath hissed out from beneath his teeth, giving a tiny puff to the dun-coloured keffiyeh. He came closer, pulling the cloth from his lean, sun-bronzed and bearded face.

"Masud." It tried to burst from Gamelyn's chest; he bade it quiet, reasonable. "Masud Abbas ibn Malik al Abd-El-Kader."

The gilt-edged brown eyes sparkled; the mouth fringed by the well-trimmed and -oiled beard tilted. "Gui," the leader acknowledged, just as quiet. "Gui abd'Hariq aljinni alshier al-ghaba."

The troupe had either heard tale of him, or else recognised the subtleties of reunion, albeit wary. They drew closer, curious. Remegius started to do likewise, but several turned and made it plain: such a liberty wasn't allowed.

Remegius turned pleading eyes towards Gamelyn.

"Yes, and what of the boy?" Masud jerked his chin at Remegius.

"He is not of this land; nevertheless my companion is oath-bound to the Hospitallers and our journey. Brother Remegius has watched my back since my return to the land of the Prophets."

The brown-gold eyes narrowed upon Remegius, thinking, and crinkled in a smile. "Then we shall welcome him, this one who has watched the back of my Brother." A few quick hand signals, and the remainder of the troupe backed down.

Masud, still smiling, gave an abrupt buffet to Gamelyn's arm. "Ah, but only those marked by the fire spirits would dare travel before the sun sets behind the mountains!"

Western legend had it that the word *assassin* had come from *hashishin*, with that, in its turn, generated from reliance upon the hashish. Yet personal experience had taught Gamelyn how *Āsāsīyūn* actually meant *people of the foundation, of the faithful*—and how, when Alamut's legions did imbibe the hashish, it was for relaxation and leisure, to calm the senses after a hunt. Never whilst *on* the hunt, for it did just that: slowed the reflexes, dulled nerve, relaxed and spun time from a relentless hurl forward, sinking it into thisnow.

Also, occasionally, it smoothed over threat beneath the offer of comradery.

That last made Gamelyn hesitate as Masud held out a small piece of honeyed cake towards him. If there was a time one needed one's wits gathered close, this was it. Yet to refuse could be construed as insult. More, it would suggest betrayal, since his companions had extended their own trust.

Masud met Gamelyn's eyes, kenning the bent of his thoughts. His smile twitched broader as Gamelyn accepted the offering.

They'd travelled the foothills in companionable silence. Once dusk had begun spraying the skies, Masud had begun to speak of personal things: his joy at seeing Gamelyn—Guy—again, his own successes in rank; his love for his faith and his master. And Masud listened, openly attentive and compassionate, as Gamelyn shared his own.

The rest of the troupe, as if given permission by their leader's conversation, had begun a back-and-forth try at befuddling Remegius with a quick-paced, if quiet, banter in Arabic. Remegius seemed to be adequately holding his own, at that. One of the lads even led his horse and walked beside him, smitten as a hound with a new toy. They had continued on as the moon had risen, a lovely sharp waning crescent throwing shadows upon the rocks. It was only when stars had begun to peek through that Masud had ordered a halt and his troupe had made camp with spare efficiency. No fire—nor was it needed, the mountain path nigh bright as day, leading down to the crag of Masyaf which, despite its proximity, lay a morning's travel through the remainder of the foothills; the plain made deception of distance.

Gamelyn peered up at the stars—even more distant, more deceptive. Behind him, his horse snorted on its tether, munching, content. Watered and fed from the Asāsīyūn's own stores, and several of the youths had drawn lots to see who would be allowed to take the mares to a level spot for a good roll. Taking a small bit of the cake, he tasted honey and dates, emmer and nuts, all cooked together and shaped, with the hashish laying a subtle, savoury buzz upon his tongue.

Remegius, however, was frowning, eyeing his own bit. He took a sniff, shot Gamelyn a questioning look.

Gamelyn shrugged, leaned back upon his saddle, and took another bite.

"All the Ifranji cling tight as fleas to what they believe is their virtue!" One of the lads, still hot upon the mischief trail, pointed at Remegius and nudged his neighbour. "Yet they are sinners and infidels, all."

"We are, *all* of us, sinners," Remegius retorted.

"That much is true," another commiserated. "God is merciful, for which we are thankful."

Remegius slid Gamelyn another questioning look, then followed his lead, taking a tentative bite of the cake. The lads cheered him on—albeit hushed.

Masud chuckled, his eyes scanning the impromptu hearth and the small ledge where they'd laid camp, then over his troupe and upward, outward. Making sure, no doubt, that the several lookouts he'd placed were still observant. Again, not for brigands. Four-legged predators gave no notice of the Assassins' lair; they'd their own, equally powerful territory here.

Leaning forward, Masud broke another piece from the hashish cake nestled in its cloth packet, then halved it to share with Gamelyn. "You may or may not have heard," he ventured, only for Gamelyn's ears, "that our honoured mentor, the da'i Sinan, may his name forever be exalted, has left us for paradise. As God wills."

"As God wills," Gamelyn repeated, one hand to his breast. "I'd heard many rumours. He lived a long and fruitful life. May his name be sung and his memory lift those he has left behind."

Masud's smile had grown sombre. "He is greatly missed, my brother."

A grave quiet fell between them, broken only by the sound of the night, and the few scattered whispers and japes from the younger men.

"I had hoped against hope to find the rumours untrue," Gamelyn ventured, soft. "I need the boon of his wisdom in an important matter. There is a relic to return."

"Returning? Here?" The gold flecked gaze flickered sideways; he'd already taken notice of the bulky pouch Gamelyn kept by his side. "Usually Templars covet such things for their own uses."

"And thusly have appropriated many of them from their true places. This one has mourned overlong for home; I have sworn I will return Him there."

"Him."

Gamelyn realised the slip of tongue even as he made it. Not that it mattered, here and now, other than Masud might think him less than rational.

Mayhap that shouldn't matter. But it did.

"You always were," Masud ventured, "one whose heart called to the otherworldly Ones." A grin flashed in the firelight. "At least you are not compelled, heart or head, to carry some maiden's captured spirit. I have heard some Templars have such ill luck."

Have they, then? Not from the Relic, this; decidedly wry and feminine, wafting spikenard and attar.

And where have you been, Lady?

Waiting for you to become. . . susceptible. More of fire, less of ice.

Well, the drug was giving him a warm tolerance amidships, no question. *Sometimes men are stupid.*

Really? You astonish me. As full of mischief as the lads with Remegius, Her fingers ruffled through his hair just before She faded.

Masud remained oblivious. He'd always been more stoic than fanciful. "You would ask our master for wisdom about this relic, then?"

Foolish, mayhap, for Gamelyn to be straightforward instead of shrewd. Had it been any but this man, he wouldn't have even considered it. But Masud . . . they had trained together, feared then loved each other, had survived both the harsh realities and sybaritic luxuries of Alamut's training ground.

Gamelyn had once prevented three *fida'iyn* from rushing into a foolhardy death. He'd been whipped for the presumption, then for his loyalty sent to recover in a hamman that was straight from some romantic tale.

One of those *fida'iyn* had been Masud.

So he told Masud, in quiet murmurs, of the Relic: who and why and how. And Masud listened, his eyes growing wider with every word, finally narrowing as Gamelyn finished, "I would ask the da'i for his wisdom. It is important to both our peoples, that the Relic be returned to His proper place. Mayhap that is not some grand mosque, after all. I have spent months looking for written evidence, to no avail. Mayhap the Relic belongs to some place known only to the verbal lore of the Nizārī philosophers."

Masud, mouth pursed sideways, thought it through.

Gamelyn waited. A whine rose that could only be a pack of jackals, but no one moved. Again, 'twas farther than it sounded, echoing across the plain and against the hills.

"Guy, my brother. Many things have changed in your absence." A warning lurked beneath Masud's words—oblique, but there. "Our place is no longer so . . . independent. Many of Alamut have not . . . comprehended the righteousness of da'i Sinān's exalted example. Alamut has since determined to regain a . . . a constancy of influence."

"Yet is it not true, my brother, that the only constancy *is* change?"

A chuckle and a shrug. "My masters are no longer so well disposed to outer influences. I do not judge them, nor do I criticise ways that keep us strong and unassailable. But mayhap it is wise to judge the manner of such changes, and determine whether it is wise to place oneself in their path."

"If we have the choice, yes. Often we do not." Gamelyn finished the cake, licking his fingers and savouring the feelings: calm, before a storm. "I'm running out of options. My task is a sacred one."

"I understand." Masud sighed, and it seemed that there was an echo of that sigh; either the Lady or the Baptist, Gamelyn couldn't be certain. Mayhap even the jackals, their voices snatched upon the breeze. Or the younger lads, with Remegius now joining in their soft laughter, overschooled reserve bent by comradeship and a tiny portion of hashish.

Gamelyn's own share had been more substantial. He leaned back and contemplated the stars, whilst again, Masud thought it through.

"Guy, my brother. It is my duty to take you before the da'i, even as it is my *personal responsibility* to remind you that we trained together. Therefore anything is entirely possible, should you wish." A cheeky grin accompanied this, clearly substituting *anything* for *escape*. Gamelyn acknowledged it with his own even as Masud sighed. "However. Clearly, you do not wish such a thing. So we go. With care."

"With care," Gamelyn repeated. "The blessings of the Prophets upon you, brother."

"And upon you, my brother." Masud extended another hashish cake towards him. "You're going to need them."

Rashīd al-dīn Sinān, the Old Man of the Mountain who'd sent assassins after both Conrad and Saladin, had little use for the spectacle of display—or any need of it. There were the stories, to be sure, of zealots leaping off parapets at Da'i Sinān's slightest whim; of hidden rooms mimicking Paradise to where he'd send drugged-up recruits, presumably to let them know what they were in for when they died in his service; of his hypnotic power and influence over the assassins of Syria, giving them more-than-human abilities; of the massive court where outsiders paid tribute.

In truth, the Elder had walked amongst his people like an equal, all the while knowing, as they did, that he wasn't. And while he might have had a bit of the magic, the true power of his reputation had been gleaned from an intelligence bent upon efficiency and order, leavened in personal charisma and cunning.

As Gamelyn was ushered into the Presence of this newest of the Elder's successors, the 'why' of Masud's cautions gained stark emphasis. Sitting upon a dais in a thick-cushioned divan, garbed with costly fabrics and accepting supplicants like the great lord he was, with a bevy of attendants surrounding, waiting upon the slightest order, Da'i Nasr al-'Ajami was no charismatic holy man, but a religious bureaucrat down to his silk-shod toes.

Gamelyn had met his share, and knew them to be bloody dangerous.

So he genuflected as was proper—Remegius had been instructed to cool his heels in the outer chambers with several of his newfound acquaintances—and waited, haunches nestled upon heels, as Masud made introductions. These, of course, came with such elaborate descriptions as 'the best of a successful exchange that broadened the knowledge of both', 'survivor of many assignments', until coming to the last—and most important—'our brother in all but blood'.

The attendants remained respectfully silent throughout, which made a refreshing change from many a Royal Audience across the sea. As did the da'i, whose attention upon a valued commander seemed absolute.

More silence after, then a short command to Gamelyn—Persian, instead of Arabic. "You may rise."

There was the slightest hint of surprise as Gamelyn did so.

Mayhap the da'i had hoped to prove the infidel brother ignorant in some fashion. Aye, a bureaucrat, one playing a game his predecessor would have scorned.

"You honour me with this audience, O Da'i." Gamelyn continued on, polite, in the language his host had spoken. "My brother has told you, somewhat, of why I have come. If I might be permitted to elaborate, and in doing so, hopefully partake of your wisdom?"

Al-'Ajami nodded, folding his hands across his stomach. "Please elaborate. We will speak Arabic, so all present might understand."

Gamelyn took his time, spinning it out not unlike a tale, and making it plain that his mission was holy, necessary. He was interrupted, several times, with detailed questions. Marking testimony with keen insight, weighing the answers like any magistrate, with the last one in particular its own judgment.

"The pride of the Templars is legendary," the da'i said, severe. "Is that what made you, an Ifranji of the cross, believe yourself worthy to this mission? Were there none of the Prophet's own within your orbit, to whom you could rightfully pass such an obligation?"

"The Nabi Yahyā, may his name be blessed, is a prophet to many peoples, O Da'i, not just a few. He was kept in a very secretive place, hallowed, where only the elect might go."

"And you are one of these . . . elect."

"I am." Pride, mayhap, but truth as well, and Gamelyn could afford no less now. "Mayhap I was merely convenient. I'm not sure why he chose me."

Are you not, my own?

A jerk and blink from al-'Ajami, then a frown and a minute shake of head. As if he'd heard, then dismissed it. He settled in his chair, eyeing Gamelyn. The light behind his eyes turned, from incisiveness to . . .

Surely it wasn't fear. Yet the impression lingered, nonetheless. It didn't ease Gamelyn one whit. The beginnings of apprehension could turn even a sage to unreason. Sliding a quick glance to Masud, Gamelyn found reflected in his expression even more unease.

"So you have returned here, a Templar accompanied by a Hospitaller, your name spoken with fondness by one of my righteous Own. Not to seek welcome in a former home, but to seek privileged information."

"I had hoped for both, O Da'i. But none that would endanger Masyaf, may it rise."

"That is not your place, O Templar, to judge what endangers our holy citadel. We are no longer in the time of da'i Sinān, may he rest in paradise, where we can afford the luxury of welcoming outsiders to our gate. Too many of my Nizārī Ismaili have been slaughtered at the whim of those who would see our most holy beliefs obliterated."

Then we all have common cause, the Relic chided.

Again, al-'Ajami twitched. One of his attendants started to speak, concerned, but al-'Ajami shook his head, continued. "These days, the mere presence of an Ifranji is dangerous."

"I understand. None of this is usual. It is why I made such a journey—"

Alone in the wilderness, the Baptist prompted, in Robyn's voice.

"—Alone in the wilderness," Gamelyn repeated, denying the impulse to grit his teeth and tell a saint to shut it, "with none but a trusted companion. Why I approached the citadel that was once home to me with such care and caution. All I desire, O da'i, is that the great philosophers who once shared their wisdom with a young Ifranji would aid a task that, in truth, touches us all."

"Alone," al-'Ajami murmured, his fingers running an arpeggio along the belled sleeve of his robe, "in the wilderness."

"Aye, for God is everywhere, God is nowhere. We know everything, we know nothing. I have not forgotten, O Da'i, and I honour the Way."

The recitation, one encouraged in Sinān's time, was a grave mistake. His successor angled abruptly forwards in his seat, eyes narrowed. "Do not think to instruct *me*, Ifranji, upon the true faith!"

Gamelyn shot a look towards Masud, who was looking down, away. "I did not mean to . . . Holy Da'i, I beg forgiveness."

Silence hung after. Continued as, slowly, al-'Ajami leaned back against the well-padded divan. Contemplated his court for moments that seemed hours.

Said, "Bring in the Hospitaller, to witness."

Gamelyn didn't dare look Masud's way, nevertheless saw him tuck his head in acknowledgement, turn and obey.

Witness suggested that Remegius, at least, wouldn't pay for a fool's mistake.

Tailed by his faithful new comrades, Remegius entered. His gaze darted to every corner of the room, taking it all in, but his expression betrayed little until he turned it upon Gamelyn, then opened into uncertainty and questions. Gamelyn gave a brief nod, and Remegius let out the breath he'd been holding, composed himself once again and bowed, very low, to the dais. Aye, the lad had learned fortitude upon this road.

"Alone in the wilderness," al-'Ajami said, quiet. "It buzzes just past hearing; akin to a voice but not. It is a sign to me, as to what I must do to test the heart of this man, once brother to our fida'iyn.

"He says the Nabi Yahyā ibn Zakarīyā has made His wishes known to him. So the Nabi Yahyā will prove the veracity of his claims. The Ifranji will be cast, alone, into the wilderness of the Badiyat ash-Sham. There he shall stay, as the Nabi Yahyā himself did: truly alone in the wilderness, neither horse nor companion to aid him, until the moon fades dark. If he does not make his way back here after that time, we will come looking for him."

He eyed Gamelyn. Gamelyn didn't speak, didn't drop his gaze.

Remegius, unfortunately, had no such qualms. "We are your guests! This man was once your brother—or do you treat your own so—?"

"Silence!" the da'i snapped, and one of the heretofore unmoving guards stepped forward, hand upon sword hilt. "You are spared any ordeal, young Ifranji, as you were never of this place. You have no opinion here, in our halls. Mind that you are allowed in here merely to witness and, if necessary, to carry word back to your own people that your companion, at the last, proved unworthy."

Remegius had sucked in a breath, at this last let it whistle impotently between his teeth.

Gamelyn still didn't drop his gaze, remembering last night's crescent moon throwing shadows upon the plain. Even with travel time, it meant he was looking forward to over a full se'nnight alone in the middle of the Syrian desert.

He and the da'i stared each other down, like . . .

Like two wolves facing down over a carcass. And all Gamelyn heard was Robyn's voice.

Fear does y' no good. You show throat, they'll only sense it, and then you're nowt to 'em.

Am I not worth this? the Relic asked in Robyn's voice. *Am I not worth any sacrifice?*

Gamelyn didn't have to answer.

"You have been long away, and must prove yourself as one of us again. That is all I ask." Al-'Ajami's voice rippled light, as if he asked some mere and effortless feat. "If the Prophet is truly with you, Gui alshier nar al-ghaba, then I myself shall offer you water in the hamman of the Faithful. If the Prophet is not with you"—a shrug—"then you are truly an infidel and will not walk our holy stones again."

Masud, who had remained strangely silent during all of it, stepped forward. "O Protector and da'i of my house, I would claim the right and honour of taking my brother to the place."

Nasr al-'Ajami peered at him, gauging, then nodded. "It shall be so." He broke eye contact, started to rise.

"You cannot do this, my lord! You will regret—ah!"

Gamelyn's hand shot out, grabbing Remegius' arm and halting him midsentence. The grip tightened as Remegius turned on him, starting another protest.

"You do not help either of us this way," Gamelyn interrupted, low. "Obedience, Hospitaller."

"Obedience," Remegius repeated, slow. "I'll wait for your return. Here, as he said, as his . . . guest." The last word slurred, cold, towards the da'i's retreat.

Gamelyn smiled.

Ⓜ

Two days' ride to the oasis at Palmyra, then another day and a half riding farther south into the desert, with Remegius as witness, and three fida'iyn besides Masud.

Or at least Gamelyn thought it was south. To ensure that he didn't merely home in on some wadi they'd passed, the da'i had insisted he be blindfolded.

Though Masud had ensured it was loose, and thin about the eyes. Gamelyn could see, somewhat, how they travelled.

"He fears . . . something," Masud had whispered as they lay companionably beside each other on the second day, sheltered from the growing heat upon the outskirts of Palmyra. "Something he sees in you, mayhap. Or what you represent."

Or Me, the skull whispered.

Are you happy now? Gamelyn sniped back.

Ecstatic. I'm returning home.

Home. Gamelyn rolled his eyes.

That evening, Masud tied his blindfold even looser than normal, allowing him to see the moon lighting their backs and their way. They were heading south.

When the first grey light began to streak the east, they stopped.

Remegius was allowed to come near, and to untie Gamelyn's blindfold. He flung it on the ground, hissed, "What can I do? What should I do?"

The fida'iyn began offloading the meagre bundles the da'i had allowed.

"Survive," Gamelyn told him, holding his gaze. "I will do the same."

Remegius peered back, lugubrious, for long moments. "Well," he finally murmured. "If anyone could survive this, it'd be you."

Mayhap. "If there is need," Gamelyn said suddenly, "see that Hubert is gently told. That my family is told, and taken care of. To tell my wife . . . " It wanted to break; he refused it the privilege. "Tell Marion I'm sorry. I never meant to fail her. To fail *him.*"

Remegius tried to speak, couldn't. Instead he sucked in a deep breath and lowered his head. Croaked, "God be with you, Brother," and fled back to where the fida'iyn were starting to once again mount their horses.

"To show fear is to show weakness." Masud approached, voice soft. "So the holy da'i means you to be lost, and keep his hands clean in the doing. You must defy him, my brother, for I cannot."

"I understand, my brother." Gamelyn leaned forward and kissed his cheek, was surprised as Masud hugged him close, held him tight for long moments.

Until he felt the skin, cool and damp, being slipped into his robes.

"Water means life, my brother," Masud pulled back, held his shoulders. "Go with God. May Nabi Yahyā protect his servant."

- X -

Drunk, he's drunk as a monk—and he laughs to himself at the silly rhyme but it doesn't matter, nowt matters but purging the memory from behind his eyes: of what his people lost, of what they still were losing.

The fire burns, hot and high, and music fills the halls. It's so beautiful but also in some way bloodless; there's no sap in it, no true rhythm to make a dance. And only a few small drums that think to reckon a heart's beat, yet somehow fail.

Robyn tries one, nevertheless, threading steps about the bonfire. Only Grey Eyes joins him—she at least seems to understand the attempt—whilst the drums falter, uncertain, leaving only the bone pipes in a strange, unearthly melody that lingers unending, without cadence, blank as the eyes of the statues not-watching.

What sort of people can forget dancing? It might be all his own people have left—the dance and the singing—and even though the conquerors would try to forbid it, they can't halt what rhythm rises from the earth, filling hearts and tickling bare feet.

Mayhap the Fae have become deaf to the breath and beat, nowt more than statues frozen in thisnow, never stepping forward or back. Only the fire's leap and the resultant wink of golden eyes, watching from the shadows, seem truly alive: the gwyllion and their like, side by side with two-legged kin, as it had once been. As it is still, here and in small, vanishing pockets of an existence he can no longer touch.

He must have been mad to think he could change any of it! Mayhap there isn't any place for his kind anymore, only thisnow, this . . . Other, Outside. But if that's so, then why do the shadows keep watching him, with golden eyes that seem to be trying, desperately, to tell him sommat?

What do you want? he asks, and they answer:

You will know, soon enough.

Night is never-ending, lit by fire beneath a painted, starry sky. The grandmothers come to him, take his arms and draw him closer to the fire. Magus paints him fit for their company, stripping him down as if for the Beltane wrestling, girding him with a copper belt and heavy golden torc that matches the eyes glimmering in the shadows. The Priestess hums a wordless lullaby and combs his hair with oiled fingers, braids disks of wood and bone into ebon curls. The grandmothers keep plying him with mead, while he wonders where they fetched such a thing. It's good mead. Powerful, giving a pleasant twist to his sensibilities, floating them slightly sideways of normal.

Grey Eyes kneels down before him, traces with her thumb a slick of oil across each instep. As he frowns, she says, "Let us be honouring you, Horned One. You have come to us; it is fitting."

"It is being fitting" echoes throughout the caverns, agreement. The hands upon his hair soothe. Grey Eyes watches him, her mien soft, respectful. Even the watching eyes seem softened, somehow, and the weight of torc and belt negligible. Any frowns melt into languid, unhurried ease.

Grey Eyes bends over him, makes the sacrament. Scented oil upon his belly, his palms and breast, his lower lip and forehead.

There's all the time in the world, here, after all.

Grey Eyes takes his hands and kisses him, draws him back into the not-dance.

And it is more floating than any dance, wafting upon the uncanny sprawl of the beautiful music. The shadows still watch, but this time, amidst the golden-eyes, other presences start to appear. *Familiar*, these, their approach spiralling closer and closer.

Ghosts, hovering just out of reach. Past shadows conjured into present tense.

His mam follows, staying to the shadows but spiralling with him in the dance, a gwyllion perched upon her forearm like some noble's hawk. Then his grandsire forms beside a pillar of a half-melted wyvern, no longer stooped from years behind a plough but hale, and strong. He holds out a bow rarely seen east of the Barrow-lines: Welsh, she is—*Briton*—and Robyn couldn't so much as pull her until his voice had broken and, by then, his grandsire was long gone . . .

"Gone," he murmurs, and it seems a scrim of fog scuts across his eyes, to linger at the word.

As long as memory lasts, naught is gone, his mam answers. *You can be conjuring it before you always, Hob Robyn. It's always yours to hold, and reverence.*

Reverence. This from Magus . . . nay, no Fae wizard here, but the old hermit who'd moulded Robyn into *dryw,* into the Horned Lord's avatar? *You must reverence from whence you come, and what you will be.*

"Cernun," Robyn says, kneeling as mists gather upon the Mere.

You are the Great Stag, Hooded and Horned. You are the last and best of us, Hob Robyn!

A strange, unmusical laugh overrides the old man. It sounds like to Scathelock, but that's impossible . . . yet the voice gives it away, plain. And the form striding to shadows' edge, firelight glinting upon fair hair. *The best of us. . . yet still, you turned against us. Let their like roam our Wode. Let* him *put his grasping fingers to what no nobleman should ever touch—*

"He'd the right, as much as you!"

The rights to make a dog of you? Leash you, claim you, kennel you!— like all of his bloody murd'ring kind?

Robyn starts to rise. "You never understood. Never. The others, they did their best, let me be, but not you. I wain't let anyone set us against each other, never again! I love him, wain't you see?"

Do you? And this voice drops him back to his knees. *Do you love me, still?*

Robyn's protest castrates itself to a whisper. "Gamelyn?"

And a copper-gilt vision comes stealing from the shadows, a silent, dangerous gait as familiar as Robyn's own breath crowding in his chest. And that breath seizes even tighter as his lover comes into the light, swift and close, to kneel before Robyn and close his eyes with kisses.

Fogs his mind further with a soft, hoarse query: *Will you love me, now and after?*

A gormless question. But about this one thing, the clever Templar has always been less than brilliant.

Robyn doesn't answer, instead lurches against Gamelyn, kissing him with small, animal noises in his throat, pushes him down into the furs upon the dais. Pale skin soft against his callused finger-tips . . . and when at first he wonders where the freckles are, suddenly he sees them, blinking against the mist hanging about . . . or is it smoke, smoke from the Bel-fires?

And if they're Bel-fires, then shouldn't Gamelyn be lying with Marion, willing gift to the goddess?

Not thisnow. Thisnow is ours. Our place. A breath against Robyn's temple. *Walking together with our gods, in the cool of evening.*

Robyn starts to push him down into the furs upon the dais, but Gamelyn twists in his arms and rises up, knees aligning with Robyn's own. Back arching, Gamelyn hoves back against him; there's no question what he wants. Languor shreds and is cast aside. Robyn is so hard he thinks he might explode then and there. If it is Beltane, he's dreaming, he must be. But if he is, he isn't sure he cares.

Aye. Dreaming. This voice jars, as another shadow draws close.

Robyn hesitates as his fingers find curves instead of hard angles, muscles, aye, but somehow . . . different.

And squinches his eyes against the scut of mist.

For the mist lies *everywhere*, within and without, scented heavy as any drug. It films his senses and nigh obscures the shadow—the one that spoke to him. Then the shadow *touches* him, small lights illuminating brown curls, reflecting deep in peat brown eyes, and says, "Coom by, you've allus known the difference between dreams and waking, love."

Dreaming. Waking. Surely this is a dream, for never does this presence speak so clear. Nay, if he speaks aloud, 'tis with words bitten carefully, lest they stutter into the same gibberish that gave his da cause to send him east. Better to sell the service of a bewitched lad who spoke to animals easier than humans; he'd been born with the caul over his face, after all . . .

"John," Robyn breathed, and breathed again as the skim slid back from his eyes and heart. He let that breath hiss out between his teeth, grabbed a shoulder and a handful of coppery hair, and forced Gamelyn to face him.

Only it wasn't Gamelyn. The illusion runnelled away—not unlike the lacework and meltwater slowly destroying the statuary within the Grotto—to leave a grey-eyed girl who clung to him, growled soft, "Nay! Not yet, not—unh!"

The last burst from her as Robyn shoved her away; she hit the ground with another grunt, hair in her face. It still glinted copper—but more a trick of light, now, than any remaining illusion. Robyn shivered, chilled to bone. Not with fear, but fury.

"And you call me trickster," he growled. "How dare you, girl?"

"How dare you?" The Priestess hissed, rising from her couch, face pale and limbs quivering with the magic. She'd been waiting. All of them waiting, spinning and holding the magic made, conjuring their own Beltane Marriage with a drunken Fool who, aye, was King.

But not like this.

Grey Eyes, still sprawled naked on the floor, threw the fair hair from her face. Her expression, as she peered up at him, was just as naked, pleading.

And why should that look hurt him so, make him feel as if *he'd* wronged *her*? "This is sommat you can't tease or trick or fake." More to the Priestess and her lot, and less to Grey Eyes, for those eyes were beading up with tears. "Else it makes you no better than the ones as bound you here."

The white grandmother bared her teeth at him.

He wasn't moved. "But then, *you* put *me* here, aye? So mayhap you en't!"

The indigo grandmother spat, "You be giving oath to us, O man!"

"Not that one!"

"You be swearing your magic here, thisnow, to us." The Priestess's gesture encompassed not only the Grotto, but the entirety of her realm. "What do you think your magic is being, *Horned One?*"

Silence. From behind him, Grey Eyes made little whimpered sounds, scraping culpability against Robyn's nerves. He hardened his heart to it and stalked over to the Priestess. Easier to ignore the palpable menace that rose from every one of her subjects—that, he was accustomed to.

Yet she stood them down with a gesture, eyeing him coolly, as if she didn't even contemplate the possibility that he could pick her up with one hand and throttle her.

It might be worth it, at that. "*You* set her up to this."

Silence.

The slap set his ears ringing and staggered him back, stunned and furious and wondering how she'd done it *again*, even as instincts rocked him forward on his toes, fists clenched and ready for a scrap.

"So you be making further insult, denying her rights to choose?" Fury curled the Priestess's nostrils with white, bared her teeth and made her next words into a curse. "Making sounds of Motherless North-man despots, and your dam's shade sorrowing be! *She. Chose.* In thisworld, women be given choice as right!"

Soft murmurs began rising in the corners, agreement and protest. Yet as Robyn glanced about, not many dared to meet his gaze.

Save Herself, of course.

And Grey Eyes, who rose to stand beside him. "It is being my fault. You should have been the one, Mother. You warned me, but I was being wanting of the honour. Overconfident of my prerogative, I was, but you were being right. His magic is biding too wild and strong for my abilities."

"Nay, Maiden," the Priestess said, expression and voice gone soft. "It is being the Hob who be choosing to reject you."

And how was this *his* fault? "Fancy *you* speakin' of choices! After giving me none at the first and now, again. Like y' think it's some heedless choice to be as I *am?*"

"You are the Horned Lord's power!" The white grandmother had risen, fists clenched.

"And you'd mock Him, make the Marriage no more'n a lie?"

"How *dare* you?" The Priestess rounded on him, her expression hardening into a chill stone even Gamelyn would be hard put to equal. Behind her, Skull Face and his cohort crept forward, plainly itching to mop the cavern floor with Robyn's face.

Bring it, he thought. "How d' you dare t' think of having me shrug off what oaths I've sworn?"

"Your oaths are to the Horned Lord!" one of the elders snarled. "Is He here?"

Robyn felt it like another slap, snarled right back, "He *canna* live here, more like!"

"Then *be bringing Him!*" Magus slid between them, facing Robyn with a staff wielded in both hands. Both expression or the staff seemed an equal weapon, and his words wielded a blunt, broad shield. "We welcome him with open arms! Bring Him here, *to* us! *Be* Him here, with us!"

"They tried to take Her from us, but that they hadn't the power to do." The white grandmother reached out, laid a hand to her Priestess's shoulder. "They didn't believe enough in Her. So instead, they took Him from us. From their ravages were you bred, and born. The Hob has returned to us, and if his face has changed, it is what He does. It is what you were bred to do, is let in the green Wode and protect the wild places!"

"Aye, but that has nowt to do with what I've sworn to you! I never gave oath that I'd bed any Fae Quean. In fact, I gave oath I wouldn't."

This took them all by surprise. The Priestess frowned, and her companions muttered to each other, while Magus merely looked solemn.

"The Lady's face is my sister, not my lover," Robyn told them. "I hold the magic in my heart, my rival as my lover—and hers— and uphold Her honour upon the string of my bow and the flight of my arrows. So I swore the Great Hunter. I'm his Winter avatar, clad in holly and Lord of the Wylding Hunt: death-rider, not life-bringer. I've my own people; I've my own world!"

"What you be having," Magus growled, "is death."

A hiss as the last word echoed into the caverns; warding, warning.

"If that's what you're wanting, I'll bloody well—!"

Magus snatched upward, fingers snarling in Robyn's hair before Robyn could so much as duck. And held him, too; parting his companions, Magus answered Robyn's yip and twist with a growl-ing brandish of his staff, tightened a grip that surely belonged to a man twice his size and wielding a longbow, and proceeded to drag Robyn like an errant child across the Grotto. The gathering, once again with that uncanny silence, parted before them like so much grass in the wind, and just as Robyn contemplated ignoring any sense of respectful good manners, mayhap pick the elder man up, or sommat . . .

They lurched to a halt against the same waist-high and care-fully evaded upthrust of rock upon which Robyn had earlier bestowed a wary eye.

"What you be *having*, O North-sired Barrow child," the Magus growled, shoving his head down into the depression, "is *death.*"

The word echoed into the hollow bowl, as Robyn nearly snorted up a nose-full of milky water. He squirmed, tried to shove upwards, almost succeeded. The pillar foiled him, slick as sheep dung on sodden grass. He scrabbled sideways, would have fallen but for the fingers in his hair: the old man's grip, stout as a tree.

More hands laid upon him, and a second set of fingers tangled tighter at Robyn's nape. Together they hoisted him back over the bowl, to peer at his reflection.

Aye, for he abruptly had one. The silt had gone uncanny clear, revealing a dark gaze gone white-wide, a winter-pale, woad-marked face with bone-braided hair spilled and snarled 'crost it darker than spilled ink, tip of nose dripping . . .

Yet no ripples spread as it dripped, slow. Behind him hovered the white-clad Grandmother—she seemed the Crone indeed, in this moment, all merciless expression and her grip moreso, one snarled at his nape with the other combing his hair like a loom. Beside her crouched not only Magus, but two of the warrior lads; they held him spatchcock against the chill stone, and Herself the Priestess nowhere in sight.

Several elbows to his back shoved Robyn hard against the stone, barking the low edge of his breastbone against the well. An unwilling breath stuttered out past his tongue and teeth. It bounced within the bowl. And tore the still-quiet image into ebon shreds.

Ceiling silt dripped onto Robyn's temple, traced an icy, thick tear down his cheek.

"Making your peace you must be, ever-waning King," the Crone hissed. "You say you know who you are? I say you know *nothing!*"

He sucked in a half breath, trying to wind a charm that would release him; instead an icy *drip-drip* of ceiling melt splashed his nape, sucked the gasp back inward, turned it into a bare, hoarse whisper. "I know what I am."

"The Hob of tripled spirits, brined point and wintering Son, Horned Lord's creature, He Who Rides the Hunt to ruin and release, your crown twined with holly and mistletoe, your rack tangled in ivy and oak." A singsong, mocking almost, softening as the Crone continued, "Guise, those be. Robes to be donned and shrugged away even as Horned One be possessing you then letting you be. Already, you were forgetting your true guise and purpose. Aye, 'tis being the way of overworlds, the forgetting—but do you think thisworld be forgetting *you*? That we have not been watching you? That there is being any amongst us who would let this be forgotten, or be letting clouds take the reasons why you went back there?"

"Tell him, Magus." The Priestess's voice—somewhere behind Robyn, he thought—echoed back and forth across the stones.

"Spin the magic," agreed the Crone, and her grip, tangled so fierce in Robyn's curls, softened into a caress. "Read the past. *Tell him.*"

Magus began a soft, discordant hum.

It vibrated just nigh to unpleasant behind Robyn's ears, whispering more akin to threat than any sweet promise. Beneath him, the bowl quivered—the stone, not the water, and that staying flat-calm.

"Be looking into the Bowl, Hob. Be Seeing. Be *Making*."

"I'm no—"

The Crone's hand went hard, nigh shoving Robyn down face-first into the milky wet; he stiffened, managed to deny her, but it forced the breath from him . . .

And the breath turned chill. It curled, puffing and coalescing like mist from a sun-touched pool as the Magus' hum began to travel outward, the gathered folk taking it up one by one. The mist—the breath—began to move. Kissing chill across Robyn's cheeks, his own magic spiralling in the bowl.

"It be making its beginning with a goddess," whispered the Crone, rubbing the salt-chill from his nape even as the magic kissed warmth across Robyn's cheeks. "Always."

Time sinks. His breath stuttered. His heart slowed and filled his vision: *one-and two-and three-and—*

And . . .

And . . .

Ceases.

Maiden be first drawing her lot—

magus says

—and spirit be making the Walk to Otherworlds. She be the one choosing; She be the one to lead the way and hold fast. Only. . .

only water ripples beneath-around-behind, making imageries: milk and mist shimmers to a sky so brilliant blue, a sun so golden-bright . . . a mother sits by a mere, hat thrown upon the grass and black hair braided-wound in a kerchief, singing nonsense rhymes to a babe upon a blanket, laughing as wee hands reach for hers . . .

mam—

hob-robyn whispers, his breath rippling away the image, and a whimper rising to choke his throat silent

Mother being of us, but lets earthly sire claim Her daughter, made of Maying and born midwinter beside her people's mossy mere—

magus says

—so instead of godling child, Mother be raising child of two peoples, two worlds, and goddess-babe be torn, betwixt and between. . . even captured be!—ripe spring made mute by iron and bells and heavy, barren robes!

But what is creiddylad-spirit but of two worlds, two purposes, two choices. . . two hearts?—

crone says, old and wise as the time that cannot bide here, thin fingers plaiting his hair

—the magic is coming to her easy-bright, and she is being strong, beloved, born of water and wave; He cannot be hampering her. . . yet

Maiden be lonely and alone, and raises Her voice to be calling forth the Summering. . .

Summer!—

magus drops it into the water like a stone; it boils, hisses, changes

—so Adversary is called forth; winged Guardian be opening his eyes, allowing another spirit to Walk. . . but upperworld be changed, cursed cold, spinning newborn spirit lost. . . with two hearts, Adversary is formed—one resenting, one longing—will he be saving, or will he be destroying? be following new ways, take woman-right for his?. . . or cleave to old, heed Her voice and his Dance within Spiralling, be making battle with respect and love?

pool reveals all: white, cold-fire keep, mother-spirit labouring unto death, her birthing-blood sinking into stones to buy a summering babe time . . . needed time, for bound fast into brother-anger and sire-guilt he is . . .

but strong!—

hob-robyn protests

—strong enough to shrug away chains of bells and iron, strong enough to learn their secrets!. . . strong enough to love me, to love marion, to turn towards the sun!

crone accedes—

mayhap

and lets hob-robyn take in another desperate breath as magus agrees

—Spring and Summer together be calling, needing a lodestone in their breaking land—

another shove sends hob-robyn's taken breath into the bowl, quivers and quakes water-magic whirling from white-hot light to cool dark, green and auburn and grey, snow falling from grey and blue, forest and earth carpeted with a different white . . . surely a sight to wrench a heart with *home. . .*

and so hob be answering—

magus continues

—donning his darkling hood to brave the overworlds. . . and brave he is being, for he knows he will die twice and mayhap thrice. . . tricking Guardian to open his eyes, mould a singular purpose from a trebled spirit, so that they be making their Walk as one—

magus pauses, breathes in to let it swirl further within the scrying bowl

—for he means to throw the bones and send Spiral widdershins. . . he means to be returning choice and voice to Maiden-sister. . . he means to be teaching Adversary love instead of fear. . . he means to be rising Ceugant, be singing a song to be colliding Allworlds, to spill ancient magic out around the Veil where Guardian sleeps

but he cannot—

crone whispers

—for the golden shaft and fletchings of hob's Arrow be darkened with iron curse. . . so spun in their plight, hob begins to forget why he

is being. . . sacrifice and trickster, who behind eyes black as a flight of ravens, be holding a secret, cursed and bound to otherworlds!
    secret?—
hob-robyn growls, thin
    —no secret that we rise the old ways, the old stories, the old gods, ways and leys. . . with me as gywn and gamelyn as gwythyr, with marion as his bride and my sister. . . but instead we'll tear away the soiled cloth of rape and abduction where our goddess is nowt but mere prize in a game of toss-stones?. . . no secret i'll burn that and use the ash to make my bread!
    crone kisses his temple, strokes his hair, murmurs
    —he's right, he's right
yet priestess says, unwavering
    —show him
and crone, sorrowful, braids *tynged* from his hair, whispers against his ear
    —see it, hob. . . be knowing what you spend blood and oath upon
    as milky ripples shatter even that, ebon scattering into strands while the bowl fills itself with darkness . . .

Sound, first: the familiar, dull crack-and-thud of iron axes, and the buzz and bite, back and forth, of frame saws. The crackle of fire and scrape of rake. Sight, at the last—though he does not care to See this: landscape stripped away like beard-growth beneath a well-honed knife, for fuel, for housing, for arable land, for so many needed things and after all, the trees are plentiful, are they not?
    Until they are not.
Though some ancient-deep Wode lingers, also are there hillocks where only memories remain, roots dwindled to humus or stone long before Robyn uttered his first cry.

    i know what my father's people did, what many still would do! the taking without return, no respect nor honour nor obligation and i've sworn to my last breath to not just. . . let them. . . keep. . . taking!
    waiting be—
crone whispers, obdurate
    —for more be waiting

The Wode returns—it always does—in brambles and broom, then rootlings, then saplings reaching for the sky. *The Wheel comes and goes around. Comes and goes around,* a mother's voice reminds from a childhood past—and aye, the Wode is the Returning, the Circle/Spiral of darkling, uncanny beauty and danger both: predators, ha'nts, copses to lose one's way. But in lingerings of fear lies an ultimate protection: respect, tendered in tithes and blessings, in whispered prayers to gods undying, in wine given to the hearth and bowls of fresh milk set out for the Fae.

    less and less, the now—
magus reminds

Fires in the night, tens gathering then tens of tens, then more. Shelters, homes, crofts. Villages, towns. Lives worth living, making, *thriving.*

Until they are not.

Scorched earth and burning villages: the remains of plague and famine. It remains Her most effective practise against over-infestation. Sometimes the strong survive.

More often, merely the most rapacious.

hob-robyn tries to turn away . . . cannot, as ribbons of *tynged* snug him close, spiralling out into futures

See what comes—

the murmur against his ear, relentless

—face what you would be foolishly giving yourself for. . . be remembering what you are and why. . . for old ways and not for ones who have been taking, will be ripping outerworlds into fragments. . . and you want to be returning when there will be nothing left when they are done and those who are being lucky will die and deny rebirth even as cursed outlanders think to be controlling our sacred Wheel!

Horned Lord banished, twisted into a parody of guilt and shame. Huntress made barren, separate from the balance of life, shamed from sex and blood and making-magic. All Their children: all the needs, all the longings, all the spirits and colours of flesh and form, separated further from their Mother; stripped from her power.

Even plague and famine are not enough to quell this infestation.

propping against his palms . . . gasps echoing in the bowl . . . hob-robyn tries to turn away, close his eyes, deny it—

and can't as it follows and lingers behind his eyes, slithers into his soul and in its wake leaves putrid trails . . .

Great, shining trebuchets with jaws of iron roar like thunder across the waste. Forests levelled, wood and green burning . . . *his* Wode diminished until it is no more than a fairing roamed by curious crowds, surrounded by metal and stone, its eldest tree not even a sapling in thisnow. More machines belching smoke, creeping along hundreds of measured oxgangs ploughed and planted O-so-alike, exhausting fecund soil into parch and ash. Tall, mirror-flash of dolmans upon plains of stone, no green save what can squeeze itself between the cracks of the smoothed-off stone pathways. Deer blinded by the piercing, uncanny lights of small siege engines, running headlong into a grinning mask that growls like a cornered wolf.

Nay, no wolves. Only dogs, starved and skulking beneath bright night torches on tall metallic posts. No birds save stunted pigeons and sparrows . . . and crows, feeding on refuse instead of carrion. People, no better fed than the stray curs, wander and sleep bare upon the stones, becoming prey to the same sort of outlaws Robyn has always sent to the otherworlds: rape and plunder hold *their* thoughts, whilst they prey on the weak with no honour other than what they can steal.

This future holds nothing but theft: of resources, of souls, of bodies, of unbending minds stolen and shrunk to meanness, of a world once beautiful. Symbols gone or twisted, made into mockeries and sparks for hatred; a spectrum of spirits held sacred no longer. Love twisted into hate, freedom twisted into oppression, hell shaped by warped visions of heaven beneath dogmas that twist nature into the ultimate corruption: no more than a thing to be conquered, parcelled, marketed.

A vessel to be used, and cast aside . . .

"Make it . . . *stop* . . . " Robyn whimpers, for he cannot stop it, cannot so much as will a retreat; he is trapped into the dreaming, struggling like a moth braving the silken strands of a spider's web, all the while aware but heedless until its powdery wings foul, then bruise, then *break*.

"What you be having," the Magus hisses for the third time, "is *Death!*

And he is released, to stagger and slip against the pillar, while silence falls, waiting, watching.

With a strangled howl Robyn tears away. Flees, with the stumble-slip of his feet echoing against the watching, the waiting, and the silence.

Into darkness.

- ENTR'ACTE -

Temple Hirst, Yorkshire
Day after Feast of the Ascension, May 1202 CE

"Where do you think you're going?" Wymarec demanded.

A half se'nnight since Remegius had arrived, thinner, browner, and hard, with harder news. A half se'nnight since Hubert had excused himself from Hirst's main hall, closeted himself into his own chamber, and refused to see anyone, not even venturing forth for prayer or meals.

Or so Wymarec had been informed when he'd ridden in from London yester's even. Remegius had, of course, left for his own place, but the Commander left in charge had given Wymarec the Hospitaller's message, word for word:

"We returned to the place where Brother Gamelyn had been left. His assassin brother—Masud was his name—refused to believe it and ordered a search, he and his assassins and myself. We searched. I've never seen the like of them, tracking where there was no trail left. But Masud had to believe when we found Brother Gamelyn's cloak, nigh buried in a drift, all ripped and filthy and crusted with blood.

"Aye, my lord Captain, I fear the Relic was lost with him. . . But from what he said, that was what it must have wanted. Just like he. . . Gamelyn. . . told me to survive. To tell his Master. To send word to his wife, and tell her he was sorry he failed her."

That last still galled. That the man's last thoughts should be on a witch woman instead of . . .

No matter. What mattered now was that on this, the seventh morn, Hubert had finally emerged. He'd attended communal prayer, broken his fast, and headed straight to the stables.

Wymarec strode closer, yet Hubert didn't so much as turn in any greeting, merely kept tending his horse as if he were all alone in the world.

Wymarec made as if to speak again.

Hubert beat him to it. "I'm going to Tickhill. She must be told."

And damnation, but Hubert's fascination with pagan doxies would be the death of him, too. "If she's so bloody prescient," Wymarec drawled, "surely she already knows."

"Wymarec."

Hubert chiding him. Hubert. Chiding the Master of England.

When Wymarec thought to return the favour, Hubert turned to face him. The set to his expression bit off any words before they so much as passed Wymarec's tongue.

A se'nnight's worth of solitary prayer and fasting surely couldn't age a man like this. Hubert seemed . . . ancient. Lost.

Do you think I loved him any the less than you? Wymarec wanted to fling at him.

Hubert's expression arrested that, too. *Aye. I think you did.*

Words of reprove twisted into a comfort that came, surprising and unbidden. "It mightn't have ended there."

"Remegius saw the cloak left behind. The assassins kenned signs of a struggle . . . a lion, mayhap."

"We don't know *anything* for certain, Hubert. Gamelyn knows the desert nigh well as any Saracen assassin; he lived with them, according to you was all but one of them. He could still be alive. God knows, he's been lucky before."

"There comes a time," Hubert said, slow, staring at the girths and billets as if he'd forgotten how to work them, "when luck runs out." He leaned suddenly against his mount, who, being a well-trained warhorse, shifted sideways at the pressure. Hubert tottered then went along, murmured, "Whoa, *petit.*" The stallion nudged at him, obedient but sensitive to his master's mood. Hubert ran one hand along his neck, the other lingering at the girths. "Surely I'd know. If he were dead. If he were still alive. Surely I'd know. But there's . . . nothing."

Wymarec moved closer, gently shoved Hubert's hands aside and snugged the girths. "I think," he said slowly, "that it is cause for hope. That we don't know. Cannot See his fate."

"Have we ever, truly?" Hubert slid a wry, glimmering gaze Wymarec's way. Just a breath, then with a nod, Hubert bridled the stallion. The horse took the bit like a fish after a fly. Chewing his contentment, he nosed Hubert, who tucked the thick black forelock into the browband and went on to fasten the throatlatch. "I shan't be long, Wymarec. But she is the Lady of the Beasts and Woodland. She is his wife in the Great Marriage, and the mother of his children." When Wymarec started a reply, Hubert shook his head, said, firmly, "She deserves to know. Mayhap she already does know, has scryed what we're unable to. Mayhap she has . . . hope for us."

Wymarec wasn't too sure of that. But he remained silent on the subject. "You will take an escort." And when Hubert started to protest, said further, "It is the Rule, Commander. You will take at least one man with you. Preferably two." Wymarec allowed concern to colour his voice. "You cannot go alone, Hubert. Not like this."

So Hubert waited, whilst Wymarec himself rousted not only a trusted squire, but a full-fledged Knight. But he didn't wait long—Wymarec also saw to that.

The sun had barely risen another half hand before Wymarec was bidding Hubert and his companions Godspeed upon their journey, watching them trot outward and through the gate of Temple Hirst. Kept watching, as they picked up a gallop across the fallow fields.

And, all the while, his thoughts whirled.

Deserve to know or not, when the Maid found out—and God's beard, but if Lady of the Beasts wasn't an apt description, what was the girl but some broodmare to a pagan god, anyway? Mayhap she'd earned the right to know, at least, of her lord's disposition. But when she found out, mightn't she decide to sever ties with the Temple? She'd thought herself a cut above her betters for far too long, and she'd a knack for finding powerful allies. On her back there too, like as not, just as the harlot she had, no doubt, been named for.

His children, Hubert had said. Well, no doubt the boy was Gamelyn's. Overindulged, but a likely sort—and as like to his sire as shoot from root. No doubt who'd sired the first child, either. And supposedly there was a third—the timing of that suspicious in itself—and their latest unholy, if powerful, Great Rite had been held despite the absence of either the King or Gamelyn, that much Wymarec knew as fact.

His lip curled. As he watched his Templars dwindle to black specks against the southmost trees, his jaw latched tighter and tighter.

He didn't like it, not at all, but with the druid dead, and Gamelyn . . . gone, 'twas now the witch woman who remained their only tie to the pagan demesne. The reawakening of those powers had been funnelled into the Temple's own, a potent asset they couldn't afford to lose. The Great Work might have turned into a longer game than Wymarec had bargained for—mostly due to the idiocy of the druid—but the lot had been cast. Wymarec wasn't about to let years of work slip away, particularly on the whim of some peasant-bred *whore*.

Hubert disappeared, as if into the earth, and Wymarec turned back to his Temple. Business to deal with, after all.

And past time, mayhap, to set a few ancillary plans in motion.

- XI -

Marion's Book of Hours:
Waxing of Beltane, 1202
7 years, 5 months and 20 days —
<u>Our Lord Shall Return</u>

To my lord husband, greetings:
The Rites shall be held and hallowed, though Summer and Winter both are absent. Perhaps that explains the arrival of summer weather, as early and mild as Spring's coming. The fields are already green, and deer have waxed in such fat numbers that we've had to order culls within the Shire Wode. Gilbert and his foresters have hunted 'crost Sherwood and the Peak—with a share 'taken' by Robyn Hode, of course. And in consequence, those villages in need have extra meat for their larders.

Thankfully, the King's absence shall lay well timed with yours, dearest friend. Well occupied with France, he is satisfied to wage his battles there, leaving England's field ploughed by sacrifices and substitutes. A more pleasant and fortunate outcome for your Lady, to be *sure. I've no doubts Much would easily win against the King, does it come to that. As always, after, we shall look to any quickening within fields and fruit, not my belly. Both Much and I know we cannot kindle a child, and while he accepts it as he always accepts the will of the Lady, I do not. I am resigned, aye, but I do not accept, not quietly nor easily. She has taken enough from me.*

What matters is the Rites being proper held, our own oaths loving and solid, our folk well satisfied.

Their lords, however, are not. Unease lingers over whom the King has chosen to hold several of the royal fortifications. We all know the King rewards well those who serve him—including outlaws and peasants, to our gain—but mercenaries? I confess to sharing the views of the northern barons over this, though no doubt mercenaries and Heathen Cunning folk bide one and the same as any outlaw to any nobleman. And our people are much more secretive. Not that we have any choice.

Marion travelled the road from Conisbrough as bold as only the Lady of Tickhill might. The somewhat-dubious reputation of being the Hood's sister preceded her, for one thing—as did six of Much's most capable guardsmen, wearing her colours of green and silver. She'd a dirk at her belt, a sword hanging at her left leg—skirts hiked over to the right, so as not to tangle—and a short, Turkish-made bow athwart her back with arrows ready.

Aye, those who'd tried her in early days hadn't carried on the tale.

Much and Gilbert themselves had ridden with her to Conisbrough, and headed up north. The fierce repute—and loyalty—of Tickhill's captains had also travelled wide, so the Earl of Conisbrough had asked their Lady if he might borrow such capable men, to investigate a skirmish towards Doncaster.

Nowt better to sort mercenaries than a couple of ex-outlaws.

Marion's own business had been to present the forest tallies to the gathered lords of Skellow, Thorne, Sheffield, and Langthwaite—plus her own castellans of Laughton, Stainton, and Kimberworth—and discuss the round numbers amidst several days of good food and drink. A subdued meeting, to be sure, in the wake of Hamelin de Warenne's demise. He'd surely been a good man who'd lived a useful life. Marion sincerely mourned him. His son, William— another decent sort, for a lord—had postponed the gathering for several fortnights, but ended up carrying on with host duties in his father's memory. Marion was glad of that. The alternative would have been Sheffield. Keenly aware of Gilbert's warnings on that score, she didn't fancy trusting de Furnival in his own place.

"Lady! O, Lady, kindly wait for me!"

Marion jerked back from tumbling into her own thoughts, focused upon the peasant woman trotting along the verge, and halted. Her guardsmen, knowing well the difference between foe and folk, halted. Several eyed the hill beyond and another the woodland surround, whilst three flanked Marion, curious and watchful. The peasant woman trotted boldly over and grasped Marion's off stirrup, tugging at her kirtles.

"Have a care, dame!" The youngest of Marion's companions mightn't be amongst Much's "best", but he'd taken to riding out with her—and Much, whom he adored—with some regularity. Beginning to master the stallion his uncle Gamelyn had given him, Ian considered it his duty to accompany his fosterer when she rode out to hers.

"It's all right, lad." Marion bent down. Not uncommon, that they should have several stops along the way. The Wode's petitioners knew their lord and lady would heed them.

This girl, however, she didn't recognise.

"Give us your blessin', milady, for there's fever in our village!"

"Where's home for you, lass?" Marion quickly ran down the nearby vills. Mexborough, mayhap?

"There's fever!" the girl insisted. "We're in your hands—"

"Ware the woods!" the farthest of the guardsmen yipped, spinning his horse to face the western copse.

A group of rough-clad men slid from the tree. One took the lead, called out, "Off your horses. We'll take what you have, and you can go on alive."

Nigh in unison, her guardsmen lifted their own weapons. "I think not," the lead guard drawled. "I'd be the one turning back, were I you."

Mayhap he'd reason to be blasé. They'd quite a range of successes to their credit. But Marion's senses ramped upward, sudden and buzzing-mad as a captured wasp. Details started to add and subtract themselves—and nowt adding up.

This wasn't mere robbery. Their attackers were rough-clad, but their kit wasn't. Their knives were too fine, for instance, and while one had a rough crossbow, several others carried swords. Fine ones.

Ian drew his sword and started forward. Marion growled out a stern "Nay, wait" and started to raise a hand to her own bow.

And the lass—the same peasant clinging to Marion's off stirrup, nigh forgotten—tangled strong hands in Marion's kirtles, hauling her sharp and sideways.

Marion would have come off, if she'd been riding one of those new aside saddles. The lass was that strong. Instead Marion grabbed mane, thighs and calves gripping her horse's barrel, and hung on.

As if on signal, the attackers gave a yell and lunged forward. The guards leapt to meet them. Crossbows engaged, metal and wood click-humming. Steel clashed. Ian kicked his horse forward, no doubt intending to run the treacherous lass down; unfortunately, the nappy stallion decided he was having none of it. Whirling, he bumped against Marion's mount. The mare staggered sideways with an offended grunt. Thankfully it was the opposite of how Marion already tottered. The lass lurched backwards into the bracken, assisted by not only Marion's horse, but a boot in the ribs.

Just as quickly, it was over. Horses dancing, bodies fallen, survivors fleeing—or dragging themselves—into the woodland. The lass found herself hauled up and strong-armed against a tree by the second-in-command—still fighting, she was, and swearing a blue streak. Everyone accounted for, save . . .

Ian's riderless stallion danced with two of her guards, evading capture.

Marion's heart gave a lurch up and into her throat. Swinging off her mare, she ran forward—and just as quickly halted. Ian leaned against one of the guards, holding one arm. His tunic sleeve had been gashed open, and blood seeped from between his fingers.

"I got him," Ian insisted as she strode over. He looked a bit green.

"Let's make sure he didn't get you," Marion said, relief tilting her voice into exasperation, and started to peel his fingers away from his arm.

Nothing spurted, thank the Lady, but it streamed down his arm. Ian blinked at it, frowned. Then his eyes rolled back in his head, his knees folding.

"Whoops, lad!" the head guard said, holding him up. As Ian kept sliding down, the guard followed, settling him down and saying, wry, "I think he's gone menseless, milady."

"I think you're right." Marion tilted her head, a grin trying for her lip. "Let's get that arm wrapped *while* he's all menseless, aye?"

"Wellaway," another said, gruff, "apples don't fall too far, do they."

"'Tis his first time in a real bout," the head guard chastened. "He did take down t' bastid, at that."

A sudden squeal and *thump!* made them all whirl.

No new combatants. Instead Ian's stallion had trotted over to Marion's horse. The mare still possessed pinned ears and a wrinkled nose, and had obviously just served notice that if the stallion ran over her again, she'd do him but good. Whatever swagger her erstwhile paramour might have possessed had fled; with tucked tail and lowered head, he meekly allowed himself to be caught.

Marion chuckled, and the second captain joined in with a big guffaw. It faded as one of the men came up, a sword and several daggers in hand.

"Good steel, milord," the man said. "En't proper outlaws, for all of 'em to be kitted out so. They en't Robyn Hode, now, are they . . . ? Um, beggin' yer pardon, milady!"

"Nay, you're right. They en't Robyn Hode." She held out one hand and took one of the daggers, inspected it.

"Sheffield steel, milady," the head guard put in, warning.

"Aye, but many a man who can afford it, carries it," Marion cautioned. "'Tis that fine."

And, her eyes reminded, silent, *the girl's still listening, aye?*

The head guard wasn't her Much, but he was good; his eyes slid over to where the lass had been wrestled to her knees. He nodded.

As one, they turned and paced over.

"Who sent you?" Marion knelt down, eyeing her.

The girl merely returned Marion's flat stare. No wonder she'd nearly pulled Marion off her horse; she'd shoulders and forearms akin to a blacksmith—and blackened calluses upon horn-hard palms to further the comparison.

Mayhap she'd made those blades her comrades carried. But in that case, surely a lass with such a valuable trade didn't have to skive about with thieves.

"Moreover," Marion continued, reasonable, "who thought to use you like you were nowt but a tool, lass? You, who has such a valuable livin' to be made? You're a smith, en't you?"

A toss of her kerchiefed head, with the fair tips of her short braids bouncing. Six of 'em, plaited tight against her scalp, and another clue to her trade. You weren't likely to leave a headful of very flammable hair loose when you were bent over a forge.

"Give her to Ralph," one of the men offered. "He'll sort her proper, have her talkin' soon enou—"

Marion whirled on him. "I will *never*," she gritted, "give any woman over for abuse. Nor will I permit any to remain in my household who do. Do I make myself clear?"

The second lieutenant and several others nodded approval. The one who'd spoken looked abashed. "I just thought—"

"Nay, man, you weren't thinking. And aren't," the lead guard growled. "Shut your sodding face."

The blacksmith's eyes had widened; now they narrowed, peering at Marion. Puzzled, to be sure.

"You were after me, aye?" Marion persisted. "Why? What did I ever do to you?"

The girl spat on the ground near Marion's toes, said, "Witch." Let out a grunt as the guard twisted her arm with a growl.

"Show respect, girl!"

Marion held up a hand. "Only words. En't the first time I've heard 'em, and I'm sure it wain't be the last. Only," she bent closer, peering at the lass, "mostly I hear 'em from people who don't know their head from their arse. You might've done sommat foolish, girl, but I'll warrant you en't stupid."

The lass remained silent.

"Long ago, 'twere thought smiths were witches, too," Marion said, very soft.

"I'm no witch!"

"And honoured, then, you were. Just as wortwives, before the men decided they wanted our crafts and trades as theirs. A blacksmith was proper magic, using the forge fires to turn plain rock into beautiful things. Deadly things, too.

"What's your name, girl?"

The smith almost said it; her lips began forming it, with the breath filling her chest. At the last moment, she clamped her lips tight shut.

"Well, Mistress Smith who lets men use you to take down another woman, you're coming with us." Marion rose, dusting her hands on her kirtles.

"I've work to do!" the smith blurted, lurching to her feet despite the guard's hold.

"It can't be so important, if you can leave it to be a man's plaything."

"I en't his plaything!"

"So he loves you, then?" All mocking, and fluted soft.

"He does!"

"Does he? Not just for those strong hands and thighs to please him? Mayhap he loves you, aye? Or so he says."

Angry, now, the lass was, and not thinking. "He does say! More than any other!"

O, child, Marion thought, and folded her arms. Aye, she knew where this was going—and likely, from whence it had come. If the blades were Sheffield made, the girl wasn't; her talk curled more akin to Dales folk.

Knaresborough was on the edge of the Dales. Knaresborough Keep, and Brian de Lisle.

"So. This . . . paragon of manhood, he loves you so much that he asks you to do his dirty work?"

"He wanted to! He'd like nowt better than seein' you hung as the witch you are! But his lord said 'tweren't fittin', that he should capture a woman. Better such as I do it—an' I almost did, aye?"

"You did indeed, lass. But I en't without my own resources."

"So let me go. I've him waitin' for me, and m' work unfinished—"

"Fancy that. So do I." Marion turned away. "Tie her on my mare. I'll ride with Ian once he wakes."

Ⓗ

Visitors, Marion was informed at Tickhill's gates as she rode in. Much and Gilbert had only that morning returned, accompanied by my lord the Master Templar of Hirst.

Mayhap Hubert had news of Gamelyn. Mayhap he'd already boarded a craft, was sailing homeward!

A bit breathless, Marion nevertheless bade herself calm. She gave orders for the smith lass and the other prisoners to be confined in the underkeep, and ensured herself that Ian had conquered the wobbles—and enough that he insisted on tending to her mount as well as his own. She let him, heading out the bailey stables and towards the keep.

But the grain allotment had come, and the man wanting her approval as she passed the granary—"since you're here, milady"—so she didn't head up as quickly as she'd planned. Neither did Much come to greet her, and that was odd. Though there'd been one time he waited in her solar, with good French wine and a musician playing for their supper's entertainment. Aye, Much was as much a soppy romantic under that chain mail as his master, and not half as embarrassed about it.

The sun peeked out from behind the clouds as Marion mounted the inner keep bridge. She began to hum, taking the stair two at a time and through the main door, which had been flung open, no doubt with the mild weather.

The main hall was filmed and filled with light, she remembered later, and the gwyllion greeting her nigh frantic, as if sommat were wrong. Food and drink fit for guests had been laid upon the massive side table, with Much standing and Gilbert sitting—both oddly still—next to the hearth where Hubert sat. Both rose as she came in: Gilbert pale, somehow, and Hubert leaning heavily upon his staff, looking . . . ancient, all to the sudden.

But Much's face sank her. He turned and met her gaze with red-swollen eyes and nose. Tears began to run, unashamed, down his sunbrowned cheeks.

Marion spoke the only word that came to her, tilted all high and dry, like a small child denied food and drink.

"Gamelyn?"

"I don't know how long any of this'll keep." Much led the horses beside her, shadow long and strangely lean against Tickhill's gatehouse, sketched by the rising dawn. It was the first he'd spoken since last night.

"It has to." Marion halted at the bridge just beyond earshot of the attentive guards, and spared a glance backward, gathering up her rein.

She couldn't believe it. Didn't want to believe it. Had spent the night second-guessing herself until she was proper dizzy, and that had frightened her the most.

Gamelyn couldn't be dead. Surely she would *know*. It was her purpose, her right, to know such a thing . . .

Wasn't it?

She looked back towards the keep, saw a lone, white-clad figure standing upon the curtain wall. Seeing her off. Hubert had accepted her invitation for himself and his three companions to stay a se'nnight at Tickhill. He'd seemed encouraged when Marion had told him she had to make this trip, his assumptions filling any gaps. Obviously, she meant to travel to a sacred place, in order to receive the Lady's advice.

She hadn't the heart to correct him. She hadn't spoken to the Lady in several years. And Hubert looked awful.

Marion had left David and Aelwyn with strict instructions towards their guest: plenty of well-doctored wine, good company, a soft bed with plenty of furs. There were only so many fissures and cracks even the most solid of foundations could manage before breaking.

"All hell'll break loose. There's been rumours already, and now?" Much moved over to the off stirrup, holding it whilst she mounted, and lowered his voice all the more. "Put the proper finish to it, this. There's enough'll take advantage, even with a king's grant and an heir in residen . . . " His voice slipped on that last, and wobbled silent.

And it hit Marion sharp as a blow from a whip handle. *Robbie. My five-year-old son. Heir to Tickhill.*

Her hands trembled upon the rein and the mare danced. It wasn't easy, but Marion bade both horse and her fingers still.

"I'll see to the ones in the underkeep. We'll have the truth from 'em." Hard, Much's voice, and distant.

"Take care with the lass."

"She weren't so cautious about takin' care with you."

"She doesn't know any better. She's young."

"Old enough to run a trade and hike her skirts, love. Don't you recollect what you were about at that age?"

Aye, well.

"What if . . . " Much turned away, took a deep breath and continued, "If the Horned One wain't show Himself to you? Beltane's coming, after all, and Gamelyn en't here."

"We have His blessing. You know that, love."

"Aye, well." A tilt of head, and Much's cheek went dark.

"Aye, well," Marion repeated, and with her eyes sent the kiss she wasn't allowed to tender in public. "He's always easier for me to approach before the Rite. But even if He's . . . difficult—"

"There's Johnny."

"Aye." Marion snugged her reins and cued the mare on. "Either way, I en't telling my children their da's never coming home. Not until I know it for certain."

Ⓗ

If Much seemed surprised that their first stop was All Hallows Church, he didn't comment. Instead he took the horses to graze nigh to the ancient yew at the side entry as song rose upon the air.

The monks, coming from mass and ready to tend the day's chores.

There had been some discussion over finding the monks another place. Gamelyn knew the church belonged to older powers—and Marion had agreed. She'd no pleasant memories of abbeys, or their residents.

Robyn, oddly enough, had made an argument as to why the monks should stay. *They tend their bees, their gardens, and their fields. They took in the Dark Lady*—this with a gesture towards the ebony relic removed from Worksop's possession—*and see Her in all they do, callin' themselves the Mother's children. 'Twould be ill done to turf 'em out, considering.*

So Gamelyn had called in several favours. One had entailed procuring a promotion for a certain Brother Dolfin. As a Christian who truly heeded the altruistic teachings of his Christ—and in Marion's experience there were few enough of those, to be sure—Father Dolfin made a perfect go-between for monks and parishioners. As a result, the monastery of All Hallows transformed further under his management. Not only as a well-managed concern, but as one more precious and liminal space, where could roam spirits both ancient and new.

The chapel lay deserted at present, lit only by a few candles remaining from dawn prayers. Well accustomed to the social obligation of attending chapel since childhood, Marion nevertheless had her own prayers.

Especially now. Though they weren't exactly prayers.

"And so." Marion halted before the altar, standing before the ebony Madonna. "It was not enough to take my brother from us. Now you would take the father of my children?"

Silence. Small and dark, She seemed in this moment even more akin to Marion's own dam-line. Certainly more than any tall, pale invaders who'd first conscripted, then set awry, Her aspect.

"Mayhap that's it, in the end. Robyn was right: 'tis us and them, and they've won. More, you're one of 'em, now, en't you? Letting 'em destroy what they don't understand, and all the while you stay here, content to be contained. Kept in your place. Controlled. *Owned.*"

And you are not?

The Voice filled and knocked within Marion's chest. Nigh forgotten; certainly foreign . . . how long had it been?

Not 'one of them'? Not a woman kept in your own place, wielding and walking the stones and called 'milady', giving hearth-right and room to kings, lords, and bishops.

"I have to protect what's mine. I have to survive—"

Do you, then?

It fair took the wind from her. Still, she gritted her teeth and continued "—since you've taken everything that matters from me!"

Not yet, my dear.

A sudden fear parched Marion's mouth as dry as sucking wool. She'd no answer for this; only the impulse to chuck it all in, and ride like hell back to Tickhill. Up the drawbridge and fire the pitch . . .

Protect Our own, aye. But the day comes when you cannot. Sacrifice is inevitable. Our children are not ours. They come through us, but We have no claim upon their destinies, be We the poorest and hungriest, or a goddess draped in velvet, pinned upon a pedestal.

It tried to rise sympathy in Marion. Failed. "If Gamelyn's . . . gone, then we'll mourn him until we join him. But at least we'll be with him again, at the end. Likely play the whole wretched thing over again—"

And over and over. The Wheel comes 'round, and 'round again. Sacrifice is inevitable. It is your tynged, is it not?

"Not if Robyn is trapped away from us! You canna mean to—"

Ah, but if you think I steer the steps of the pwca, *you are sore mistaken, sweet. I have only ever grasped at the wind of that one's passage. And while I can breathe that wind into Our Summerlord's sails, often pain and deprivation are the only methods he chooses to heed.* Laughter filled the chapel, soft and rueful. *How did We end up with such consorts? Agitator and Apostate, both walking the fine line that draws itself between thisworld and the others.*

"Then they're both alive." Again, dread nigh glued Marion's tongue to the roof of her mouth. But this time she feared the asking—and the response.

Silence. Then, as if considering, the Lady ventured, *They are both. . . lost.*

Which was no answer.

In the lengthy, resultant silence, footsteps scuffed their way into the chapel.

It had been a bad se'nnight. Marion whirled, ready, hand to knife.

Dolfin lurched to a halt at the chapel's back, lamp-bowl in hand. "My apologies, my lady. I heard voices. I didn't mean to disturb you. I'll leave you to your meditations."

Always more comfortable with Gamelyn than the woman Gamelyn had taken to wife, Dolfin had long ago determined an overabundance of odd baggage came with the latter. As Marion also possessed her own parcel of mixed feelings concerning the head of any Church outpost, however tolerant . . .

Well, she and Dolfin found each other pleasant company, and that was about it.

So it made no sense that she should stumble forward as he turned away, and utter a half-strangled "Wait!"

Dolfin turned, frowning. When she didn't say anything more, or come any closer, he frowned all the more. They stood for some time, peering at each other. Then, with a grumbling sort of sigh, the priest padded up the aisle, silent on bare feet. Stopping an arm's reach away, he held up his lamp, seemed to further contemplate her expression.

"My dear," he said, quiet, "whatever is the matter?"

She told him. It spilled out, unlike the tears she still found herself unable to shed, words fearful and unwilling to belief even as she spoke them.

Dolfin sat on the altar step, with a small *whump!* that suggested his legs had given way. With a careful, shaking hand, he set aside the lamp, and looked down at the step, as if wondering how he'd gotten there. "Dead. He can't be dead."

Dead. Even Hubert hadn't dared to voice it. Indeed, it seemed an unhallowed word to be coming from a priest. Of course, while claiming they venerated death and rebirth, not many of the White Christ's followers seemed to truly believe in the latter.

Hubert's anguish she could understand, and his words: *I shouldn't have outlived him. He is the son I never had. I haven't the. . . the* right *to outlive him.*

If Gamelyn had indeed walked on . . . aye, and she'd mourn it the rest of her own life, hollow and uncertain. Yet the stark truth? She'd grieved, over and over, every time he left her behind. Did death finally catch him, they'd meet again, upon another rung of the Wheel. Had done so, over and over. Another sacrifice. Another strand of *tynged.*

But if her brother remained . . . *outside* their time?

She would never see him again. Gamelyn would never see him again. They'd be condemned to spin upon the Wheel, 'round and 'round, without a vital third of their existence.

How many times had they passed through? How many times together? How many times separate, lost?

They are both. . . lost, the Lady had said.

And Marion left helpless, with no concept of how to find them.

She hated it, worse than the Church that had killed her parents. Hated the helplessness, the uselessness.

Dolfin rose, took Marion's hands. "You have come to Her, haven't you? For guidance. Thank you for interrupting your own prayers to tell me."

She'd nigh forgotten his presence. Her mind flailed, blank, devoid of anything save the most banal of pleasantries. Marion took grateful refuge in them, squeezing his hands.

Said, with the soft, compliant graciousness every woman born had to acquire—either from childhood, or through harder means, "You needed to know. But you must keep silence, aye? Until we know for certain."

He peered at her, turning from confessed to confessor. "It's hard, to believe the worst."

"I don't believe it, Father Tuck." She said it as purposeful as the use of his old nickname—and aye, a quirk played at his lip. "I'd know, wouldn't I?"

Wouldn't. I.

"Gamelyn said that," Dolfin countered. "About your brother. But I wonder . . . " He paused, then continued, delicately, "Marion, I know you have the elder powers behind you—"

Do I? She eyed the ebon visage past Dolfin's hunched shoulders, and received no answer.

"—but there are some things that are past even the understanding of old gods. And goddesses."

"Survival," she whispered before she thought, and thought she saw a reflection—a hint of moonbow despite a sunny dawn— sparking the flat-black eyes.

"Aye. Souls live on, and so must we." Dolfin misunderstood, which was just as well. "You've your children and people to protect. We'll mourn our beloved lord as is proper, and meet him again in paradise. But I'll stay my grief, remain silent until you give me leave. That I swear to you." He laid a reverent hand upon the altar. "I understand the . . . precariousness of your situation, my lady."

My situation.

Beyond that altar—beautiful, enigmatic—She spoke no more. Merely stared through and past Marion as if she no longer existed.

Sod that.

"I would not say my situation is precarious, Brother. Dangerous, mayhap. But there is no doubt over Tickhill as to who controls Tickhill. And as long as I still have my children, I pity those who'd come against me." She eyed Dolfin. "En't a cornered wolf-bitch with pups the most dangerous, after all?"

His eyebrows rose—agreement or dissent, at first she wasn't sure—but then a smile lit his face. "I am pleased to hear it is so, my lady."

Marion smiled back, and told the ebon image, silent: *And my pups'll grow up knowing what you were, not what you're becoming. It wain't be forgotten. I won't let it be.*

Marion.
  John.
  Gamelyn.
  Gilbert. . . David. . . Aelwyn. . . Mam. . . Da. . .
  Waking, not dreaming, Robyn saw them.

Because when he thought to sleep—nay, more acquiescence to exhaustion than any inclination—'twere then the nightmares came, raking iron-forged claws against darkness, crushing the sweet evergreen of memory into solitary wasteland.

Robyn muttered their names into the dark, and the caverns whispered back:

Marion. John. Gamelyn. Gilbert. . . David. . . Aelwyn. . . Mam. . . Da. . .

And kept whispering, a litany of souls—all his people, none left out—until they all came to walk alongside him, silent as ghosts.

Mayhap they *were* ghosts. Already walked on, gone ahead, long rotted into his forest. Or what was left of his forest, where forged machines like twisted predators despoiled their graves, ripping earth and trees, belching smoke against a yellowed sky.

Robyn couldn't rip it from behind his eyes, though small crescents scarred his eyelids from several desperate tries. The sting of that, and the cold leeching into his bones, reminded him he was alive, and wandering aimless, unable to escape either the waking or the visions that lay in wait should he even think to sleep. Nowt to mark the passage of any sort of time, save a heart as beat no proper rhythm. Spastic, too slow or too fast. No rhythm, no pattern . . .

No *wheel.*

Just a lost and staggered progress through an endless wind of tunnels, where nightmares bared sharp teeth and memories whispered. Where despair lingered, dark-hot and waiting in the corners.

It had always been his fiercest enemy. The one he never failed to stare down, or when necessary wrestle down and throttle. The one he never let win.

There was no winning this.

Robyn bowed before it, showed throat, let it throttle him. For he truly was alone. He'd never return, never dance another Bel-fire, never again wend the Spiral. Instead he'd wander through a never-ending fog without his beloved ones, without his god, stumbling a tightrope of bleak-black threads, his *tynged* spilling endless into an empty dark.

- XII -

John was waiting, seated cross-legged upon the large rock that guarded the entrance to the Hunter's Cavern as casual as if enjoying the sunny day, his face raised to the massive rise of Mam Tor. Only when they picked their way into the valley and halted before the cavern mouth did he slide from his perch and welcome them with a hard hug apiece.

Much prolonged the embrace with a shudder and sigh, and John's eyes met Marion's, concerned, as they parted.

Come in, he signed. *See to the horses and come in, warm yourself. Eat.*

"Johnny," Much started, "We en't here just for—"

I know why you're here. John ended with a tiny flick of fingers. Marion would have called it negligent if she hadn't seen the shadows, around and within, those peat-brown eyes.

It was the perfect rejoinder. Much uttered the same mix of sigh and mumble-grumble he always did when surrounded with *too clever cunning folk.* Taking Marion's horse, he shot her an aggrieved look as she began to unsaddle the mare. When she didn't take the hint, he kissed her hair and gave her a firm push towards where John already had disappeared into the cavern's mouth.

Aye, well, and her man would be all the better for the soothing work of tending the horses, giving them each a good groom and hobbling them to graze. No doubt he'd also make a quick recce uphill and shoot a wary, jaundiced eye towards Peveril. De Lisle was no longer castellan, but neither was William de Ferrers. The

King had assigned some Brabançon hire soldier to hold the castle for him, despite de Ferrers holding much of the Peak. The latter would have made a less antagonistic neighbour, no question, as he and Gamelyn had gotten on well.

Had. The past tense of it shook her. If she didn't believe it, why . . . ?

She stumbled, bade herself to pay attention. The cavern entry-way could be daunting, even to one who knew it well. It zigged this way and zagged that, stone jutting outward with no warning, at times seeming no more than a dead end or a turn into pitch darkness. Without a torch, no chance. Thankfully, John had rushlights tucked here and there, their telltale lingering in the nostrils once passed, hanging thick upon approach.

He'd known they were coming. She hoped he knew more. Enough to wholly banish that past tense from sneaking in and gutting her thoughts.

One last, glittering overhang to duck beneath, and the cavern opened out before Marion, lit with torches, protected by depth and warm with the hearth, which crackled and echoed faint against the caverns. She smiled at the furs laid, thick and thought-ful. The rich aroma of cooking pottage overtook the necessities of smoke and reeds dipped in pongy fat.

John also knew that she didn't care for the deeper places. Her memories of Nottingham's oubliette lay buried with time, but never deep enough.

He saw her comfortable with a full bowl warming her hands, then squatted, staring into the fire. *You'll want to know what I've Seen.*

"Hubert came, and I don't know what to think."

Thinking's nowt to do with this.

"It's all I have left, John. Thinking, and staying one step ahead."

Yet you chose the path where the predators lurk, and the crows spiral, waiting.

That stung, though they'd had this discussion before, every bit as circular as the crows. "Seems to me either hand holds its choice of predators! To make a safe haven within what place we've made, or stay outcast and outlaw, with every hand against us? Or mayhap immure oneself in a cave, hermit to a god's memory?"

John shot her a dark look.

"What have you Seen, John? Tell me."

What have you Seen?

"I'm asking you! You know why I'm here, yet you're refusing to—"

Slower this time—but vocal. "What . . . have you . . . Seen?"

Gritting her teeth, Marion fumbled at the purse hanging from her belt, drew out the silk shrouded bundle and began to unwrap it.

John's hand darted out, a snake's strike that fanged her wrist and held. The cards spilled across her lap in a riot of muted, hand-crafted colours, and a few slid altogether close to the fire. When Marion went for them, John's hand tightened, stayed her.

"Nay," he voiced again, tried to speak further, gave it up with a growl. *Nay. Not what a magician's tools tell you! What. Do. You.* See, *Mother to the Shire Wode?*

"I *don't.*" She wrenched her arm away. "Don't you understand, I can't See *either* of them! Not clear, not enough! Sometimes those 'magician's tools'"—it was sharp with sarcasm, pointed to the scattered cards—"aid me, but even then it's as if sommat hinders me. A curtain. A veil, drawn thick across . . . " Cheeks heating, she looked away, angry, but also mortified. She'd held it too close far too long, with darkness lingering in the wait.

A cavern with the lights guttering. A gaol.

Her hands shook. Clasping them tight, she raised her gaze, slow, to take in John.

He stared into the fire, tears glittering in his eyes, and didn't notice she was peering at him for a few breaths. Signed, when he realised, *How can I trust what I See when the Lady's so hindered?*

"Because you *do* live here, in our sacred places, holding close beside the Horned One."

Holding close to *Him. Yet, sometimes, He fades. More, now that Summer has left as well.* John shook his head. *But I fear that if He goes, then mayhap the last of Robyn's spirit goes with Him.* The brown eyes flickered with gilt: mayhap the hearth, mayhap something more intimate. But definitely cross. *I won't let Him. The Lady can draw into Hallows and away from the Mere, but I won't let Him go until we make Them give Robyn back.*

The casual power to what he suggested took her breath away, and what prompted it filled her throat. Of course, but their Little John would hold fast, refuse to let the Horned One diminish. He remained the only one besides her brother who'd stood firm beneath the Horned Lord's fierce possession. Even Gamelyn, taking Him within for the Rite, found Him a heavy, oddling weight.

Marion reached out, brushed fingers through brown curls. "Oh, my dearest . . . I don't know how we can. Without Gamelyn—" *All is lost,* she thought but didn't say. Wouldn't.

We didn't have Gamelyn's power before. Aye, definitely cross. *Not enough of it to matter, leastways.*

"Come back with us," she blurted out. "For a while, anyways. You spend too much time here, alone."

I need to be here. And if I spend too much time alone, you don't spend enough. You don't believe Gamelyn has walked on. You know you don't. But you're doing like him, thinking too much about things as wain't bear thinking. John cupped his hand against hers, kissed her palm. As he did so his gaze dropped, dark lashes smudging gilt. *He'll come back, and we have to be ready when he does.*

"I wish I'd your faith." Marion began to gather up the cards.

John didn't move to help, even when she reached across and took up one beside his ankle. He'd refused to touch them from the moment he'd first seen them in her possession. *Woman-magic,* he'd said, *more ancient than the trees as had made them, and not mine to wield,* complete with a roll of eyes that said *Arrogant twats!* plain as plain when she'd told him the Templars had given them to her.

But in a world where Maids wore horns, and Summer and Winter rutted instead of rivalled each other, what belonged to whom?

Nothing is ours, she thought, shrouding the cards in their silk. *Not even a love to hold a spirit hostage. But it means we're supple, when thisworld shifts about us.*

"You have faith." Again vocal, to catch her attention. "You don't have a choice."

"Aye, and I've precious little of either, anymore."

That isn't what I mean. Summer has retreated, and Winter has been taken from us. If you have no faith, Maiden, then what does it mean for the rest of us? For our people? You haven't the luxury of losing faith. Any more than I've the luxury of loosing the Horned Lord's spirit.

Marion sucked in a harsh breath and stared at him.

With a shrug, John took her bowl, scooped up more pottage and handed it to her. As she took it, he cocked his head, frowned, and started scooping up more into a third bowl.

Sure enough, the air shifted around them, with boots scuffing against the stones. Faint at the first, then closer, and Much rounded the last bend.

"Some of those rushlights are burnt nigh to nowt, Johnny. Aye, thanks, that smells proper good." With the meal John handed him, Much settled across the fire and pointed to Marion's full bowl. "I hope that's your second. You en't had enough today t' satisfy a bird."

John gave her a smile, rose and filled the cups all around.

"My second, aye," Marion managed to say as Much started to wolf down the pottage.

"Aye, well, then. I took a pass at Peveril. 'Tis nigh deserted, just a few left to run t' place."

"Is it dark already?" Marion asked, sudden and soft.

"Nay, there's a while yet." Chewing, Much peered around the caverns. "But you're right, 'tis easy to lose track of time down here."

Marion put her bowl down and stood. "I'm going up Tor."

"Now, love?"

"Aye," she answered, firm. A glance towards John showed the tiny smile still quivering at his lip. "Now."

Marion took the southmost path, alone.

Clouds were gathering to the east—they'd likely have a wet ride home come the morn. But for now, those clouds were spattered with copper heat and cool ash, the sun angling fire as it settled lower in the sky.

A gradual ascent, but considerable, emerging from a copse of trees clinging to the hiked-up hem of Mam Tor's skirts, climbing up onto the moorland that truly made up most of the Peak. Stones marked the way. Each one held a memory, some harsh to fill her throat, others gentle-soft; she touched each, blessing and petition. Received the answer: *You are welcome here, Lady Huntress.*

Became aware, with senses that might sleep but never fade, of a silent Presence tailing some paces behind.

Marion kept walking, her breath catching not only from the climb.

Do you remember, Maiden-Mother, when you first beheld Me?

She did. Her brother had just endured initiation into the Wode covenant, at the hands of the old hermit Cernun. The crème-coloured stag of Gamelyn's dreams and her father Adam's reality had transformed into a darker, more predatory shade as Rob of Loxley became the weapon known as Robyn Hode; both of them an eldritch mirror of the betrayal, anger, and longing through which they had been winnowed.

He brought Me into thisworld. I remain.

Reaching the small circuit of stones—some left overturned, a grace to memory—Marion paused and brought her hands to her face. Breathed across her palms, honouring those memories.

Just as She remains, a ghost behind your grief.

"She remains?" Marion turned to face Him. "She's abandoned us!"

Has She? Antlers arched sharp-broad against the fire-filled sky, full twenty points all tangled with ivy and dried-out mistletoe, velvet shredding dark against pale tines. He stood upright, with—perhaps—a man's torso and arms, but in truth He remained a buck in his prime, rank with heat and haze, prepared for the yearly battle.

However . . .

Her breath tremored within her throat. Despite any promise/threat, the Horned Lord seemed but a shade of His true self. Unlike the vital presence conjured by the Beltane fires and hundreds of hearts, in thisnow, dappled by sunlight, He, too, faded. In and out. Sunlight to shadow.

You are, in truth, become my Shadow in thisworld. You, and the Maker-Seer, who holds the hem of my spirit robe. I but seldom feel My avatar's presence in that barren otherworld and as to Summer? A growl that oozed into a sneer. *He prefers a barren desert, does he not?*

Marion wanted to make a defence. Couldn't.

He will wander and call his death, become something. . . Other, and mayhap in doing so end all hope that we could ever win this war.

"And what if we cannot?" Marion retorted. "*I* cannot, not alone!"

Mayhap. Mayhap not. What, Maiden, is loneliness? Crouching in a cavern, wandering the otherworlds, trudging desert sands, walking the parapets of a castle? What if we should not? Will you flee the shrieking stones, abandon yourself to Sight, join what remains of your brother's heart within the only stone haven our folk trust?

"I am not ready to retire to any caverns. I have a home, and children—*our* children, O Great Stag. What becomes of them?"

The Horned Lord turned towards the setting sun. *You must watch over them. Danger lurks, always, for the god's children. They attract adversities like flies to a blown carcass.*

Marion clenched her fists.

Yet, I cannot See so well, thisnow. He paused, turned from the sun to mark the gathering clouds. *Shelter them as you must within the nobleman's stones; it remains that My forest shall protect them all the more. You—*He fastened gleaming eyes upon Marion—*must remember what you are. Come to Our places with an open heart.*

"My heart is open."

Your heart is angry. Oft your Wintering brother finds his power in heat, be it anger or passion. But you? You are not he.

Marion set her teeth. "So even here are women scorned for emotions unseemly?"

This is not about Woman. The Horned Lord's voice rumbled ire across the Tor. *This is about you. Resentment is not an emotion the Maiden Marion bears with ease. It does not drive you to action and pass through you, as with your brother. You do not use it as fuel for inner fires, as does the Summerlord. Instead your ire simmers, a pot left to boil which dries and cracks. It is choking you.*

"How can I not resent what She has done? She took Robyn from us! She took him, and could yet take Gamelyn, and not even You know why!"

The Horned Lord peered at her, silent.

"You know as well as I that it weren't Robyn's time! That were *Yours* to plait and unravel!" Tears too long unshed threatened; instead words spilled forth. "And Gamelyn—how can it be his time? Is he dead? *Is he?*"

What if he is?

"Stop it!" A scream, barely smothered. "Bugger your riddles! If he's gone, then Robyn's lost, and if Robyn's lost, neither of us will ever see him again!"

You speak as if the wastrel Summerlord is our final prospect. As if you truly believe he has entered the otherworlds. Do you think, O Mother-Maid, that we would not know if that were so? That there is hope in not knowing?

Marion's knees tried to give way; she wilted against the altar stone, let it support her as the tears, finally, came. "It's been so long . . . so much to do . . . so many . . . failures! One after another, we've done nowt but fail, every try we made! How can we win, with Her against us?"

A pause, then warm breath upon her crown, riffling back the

wrap over her curls. It lingered, sweet and warm as summer, to kiss her salt-damp cheeks.

You have not failed in all things. But heed this, My own: it is yours to parse the ways and means of Her. You must find your own peace, within and with Her, so when We see Summer returned. . . A long, heated sigh gusted across her nape. *We will have My avatar back, at the least—We* must *have him back. His task in thisworld is not yet finished. What She requires, we will give to set him free.*

Marion's gaze, smeary and salt-clotted—*wary*—slid upward to meet His. "And what does She 'require' that She has not already taken?"

Her people asked of Her that the Green Man's oath be honoured. Your dam's people required that what was stolen from them long ago be returned. They did not understand the pwca's *own oath in thisnow, made to Us, that he and his leman would send a thousand little deaths into the darkness, to make the world whole. Yet once the* pwca *sent his magic into their keeping. . .* The great head shook, velvet tatters dangling and twisting. *Foolish, mayhap, for while the Fae keep it indeed safe, they no longer have the means to wield such a power. They are. . . imbalanced. Or. . .* A heavy intake of breath. *Mayhap very wise, if untimely. He alone could call that magic into being, there. He knows what he is and must be.*

It was no answer, really. More like she'd stepped into some mummer's play and, given tambour and gown, shoved onstage with no idea of her lines.

The wren has supplanted the robin; inevitable, but untimely. We are all but in thisworld short and sweet, returning even as the sky spins above us and earth below. There is no denying the Sacrifice.

More riddles; she met them with her own. "Have we not sacrificed enough?"

Canines bared, more wolf than stag. *Have you, then? And what of all those failures?*

She couldn't hold his gaze, instead pondered the hills turning purple about them. "I can't change what has passed. I have to look to the future. *Our* people's future."

Aye, and what is that?

Marion fell silent, uncertain.

Robyn is the last of druid-kind, in truth, and the Summerlord Our future, but what is that? What lies ahead for 'Our people', when you yourself have abandoned the goddess for the keeps of the conquerors? When you scorn Her, and in your fury settle for the negligible power of being wived to a lord?

"I've settled for nowt! If I've turned from Her, it's because She's turned from us! But not from our forest, not from You! I give You Your due! I keep the Rites! My children are conceived in the Sacred Marriage, sired by the god, consecrated to the Old ways. Because of what Gamelyn and I have built, they are safe in the New, also!"

What is safe, Maiden? Now you are alone in a stone keep, a target of men. Your. . . 'lord husband' will be believed yet another casualty, and that of a foolish war those same men would claim their New Religion demands. In the crofts, at least, you had freedom.

"Aye, the freedom to have me home burnt, and me family slaughtered like pigs!" She stood, gesturing to the stone. "Even here, in our holy places!"

Danger lurks for the god's children, always. You were free to roam the Wode. Free to lie with whom you chose, without some cult conjuring threat from it. Free to practice Our ways, with the Hooded One's authority keeping Our places sacrosanct!

"It still remains so."

For how long?

"Help me get them back, and we'll make it so!"

It will take more than My power to do that. More than yours. Yet, still, together. . . The Horned Lord turned, looked out across the rolling, copper-and-aubergine landscape. His eyes glowed, gold against endless ebon.

As if in answer, fog began to roll in, creeping upward from the bottomlands. Lights flickered amidst the shadows, drifting across the moors.

Fireflies, where there should be none. Soul-lights, searching, and whispers echoing in the Sacred Wode.

Marion took in a long breath, held it. Waited.

The door will be opened. Dreamers roused from torpid blood and forced flight. Yet to hold it open needs the grace of Allworlds, the consent of She who conjures the Hob's spirit-bonds, and bids the Knight wander in sand and heat.

Marion's teeth clenched, a grit and scrape against the heavy, approaching mist. The Horned Lord glided towards it, raised his arms.

Accept Her. Consent to Her. You will need the Ceugant's power in fullness, when the Veil 'twixt the worlds lies thin. You will need the Blooded Dart to fly, the consecrated blade to break the iron, the wren to open the door and walk the crossroads when the Rade draws nigh, when the World-Tree's leaves draw into slumber. With blood, and fire, and wild, wild magic.

His voice boomed against the hills, as if conjuring the mists—and those kept ascending, reaching damp fingers for Marion's skirts. The fireflies, tiny groups of illumination, danced a wreath upon the great antlers, winking into darkness as He spoke again.

Hold fast, to keep your consorts bound to thisworld. 'Ware the prodigal, weaving traps to damn a soul. Guard the heartlines spun deep within the caverns. Heed the child, walking the path between, to speak with spirits of fire and water.

And in the time it took Marion to blink, He had vanished.

Badiyat ash-Sham (Syrian desert)
Waning of Ostara, 1202 CE
Month of Jumadal Akhirah, 598 AH

The extra water was what saved him.

At first, anyway.

Gamelyn's knife and sword had come in handy, as well, when the solitary lion attacked.

The brief and brutal battle had cost him his outer cloak. And after, precious water used, with more of that ruined outer cloak, to clean and bandage his thigh where the beast had clawed him. Gamelyn had scrubbed his bloodied blades in a drift of sand, and forced himself to walk—not limp—away.

The carcass would buy him time against the jackals he'd heard yammering in the night. The limp could cost him more, did they so much as sense it.

Three days and four nights. Sweltering days spent cowering in the shade of his abaya and what rock or cliff shelters he made it his business to find during the frigid nights. Sparing tiny sips of water, shifting with the moving shadows as a white-hot ball of fire slid, O-so-slowly, from horizon to horizon. Eyelids nigh glued to his eyeballs, the sun tracing a red-gold ghost against them as he closed them against the worst of the glare.

And the bag, hanging strangely light at his hip. The Relic lay silent, as if realising he'd no strength to make small talk.

Still sweating, thank God, though it dried too quick to give him the scarcest cooling. Still pissing, though scant and foul, his body telling him it needed more of what he did not have to give it.

Water was, indeed, life. He dreamed of it at night: a wide, impossible, moon-grey and milky wall of it hovering over him, quivering, waiting to submerge and drown him . . . aye, impossible. Instead, water splashed, too light, in the last skin. He had to eke it out as best he could. With what Masud had given him he just might have enough.

Gamelyn stumbled across the cave on the fifth sunrise, and collapsed into exhausted, twitchy sleep. When he woke, it was late in the day. His stomach grumbled—feebly, as if it knew complaining was hopeless. His skin tingled with every movement and his mouth cracked and bled as he chewed on the dried dates. Only a handful left, and four strips of the dried meat. Two insufficient swallows from the waterskin.

He had to find water. There was a wadi north of where they'd come; he'd smelled it as they'd passed.

The cavern was cool, but its rocks remained dusty as desiccated bone. What it did hold were markings—not that Gamelyn could see them, but his hands sensed the rise and dip of them as he felt along the cavern walls, searching—hoping—for the least bit of damp.

The markings buzzed against his fingers. Even in his weakened state—mayhap because of it—they seemed to react to his touch, recognising . . . something within him, promising secrets to be traded. Runes, of a kind . . . only not, for runes were of the Northmen, they'd no place here, in the Syrian desert.

Coptic, some of it, and some of it even older. One said *wind* and another *wave*, and yet another *serpent . . .*

My people were here, the Relic spoke, soft. *I have been here, in this Cavern of Spirits.*

Spirits. Mayhap they could aid him. Trying to decipher the markings by feel occupied his mind and, for too short a time, aided forgetfulness of his body's demands. But nothing rose to his whispered questions; if there were spirits, they had long slept. Gamelyn closed his eyes and leaned against the wall, fingers scraping.

Again the image, burning behind his bleary eyes: a wall of water, quivering, waiting. But in the end, nothing fell but darkness, and he had to leave the cavern.

He had to find water. He had to get to the *waha*, and onward, return to Masyaf.

The claw marks started burning. Gamelyn knew the worst was yet to come.

- XIII -

The gwyllion found him. He wasn't sure when, or how, but there were at least seven of them this time, their hot-sleek little bodies curled and piled over him with insistent . . . companionship? Guardianship?

It didn't matter. What mattered, finally, was that Robyn slept without dreams.

After, the gwyllion led him upward, in an unhurried pace from the bowels of the dark places, into another world.

There were, after all, places past the caverns.

The woodland was unlike any he'd ever seen: massive, black-green conifers rising into a bleak sky, their trunks as big around as twenty of him, roots sprawled like gnarled fingers digging into fresh tilth. This earth had never seen a plough—or if She had, 'twere so long ago She'd forgotten any tillage save the scattering of seeds and the burrowings of small creatures.

The sky, scratched by those reaching evergreen fingers, squatted bleak and heavy over its land, lit fitfully by a sullen, crimson sun. It threw bent and twisted shadows; even the gwyllion cast misshapen images as they darted here and there. His own shade—aye, 'twere more that than any living, natural shadow—seemed to react just that much too slow, biding along in some listless rhythm nigh its own. The air lay damp, but . . . smoky, almost. It hung stolid as if some village lay nigh, with a clutch of smoking hearths to desperately fend off a damp and wind-stalled winter night.

What moisture clung to his uptilted face tasted faintly of salt.

Something forced him to keep moving. Mayhap the gwyllion followed/led him. Mayhap the forest, which welcomed and took him in. Recognised within him some traces of an absent Lord, even one whose horns and hot blood and sap had been winnowed from mad gallop to this lost amble beneath a hoary sky.

Small wonder that the Barrow folk could grow nowt here—had they ever, in that faraway time? Well, no matter, 'twere a life familiar to him. Subsistence akin to outlaw life, this; the gathering and the hunting, the raiding and the thieving as necessary . . .

And it would be necessary, in some uncertain future, with this woodland lying so silent about him. Only the flit-flight and calls of the gwyllion and, rarely, some occasional scratch or rustle of something out of sight. Game scarce as hen's teeth, no doubt, though it did seem stomachs and appetites had also been . . . diminished. Including his own. He couldn't remember when last he'd eaten.

Had what few beasts as roamed here sprung from what had been trapped when the iron spells had descended? Did they wander in, somehow? Push up from the earth itself?—like blades of grass between the cracks of unnatural and slick ribbons of stone?

When he fell beneath the nightmares, the gwyllion made him rise. Small, they were, but fierce. He'd bruises from falling, but also scratches and teeth-marks from the little beasties forcing him upright.

Eventually, amidst the tumbles and the droving, he began to realise what he searched for. Recognised the faint, feral quiver that began to simmer all slow in his chest.

It resembled, sommat, hope.

Yet it, too, quivered and sank as he found no bounds, no telltale rent in the fabric of this place, not so much as another impassable wall akin to the Mere's barrier. The ravening sow and her litter had told him true: only the gwyllion and like spirits could find the way outward. *Protection*, she said, yet 'twere no more than a gaol of rusted spells, and while the Fae might've once ridden out in Rides and Rades, empowered to do so through the spells of his own kind, going back through the generations . . .

Now, they couldn't.

now? when is now. . . is it now? is it then?. . . and a hand rises to the thick vein on his neck to make sure it still throbs. . . how easy to open it, ensure the sacrifice, save his Wode. . . only this weren't his place, no true woodland—no reality bides here, aye?—so surely 'twould be merely another sad and useless gesture. . .

Those ancient spells whispering within the grey moss and the dying trees lay too long unspoken—even old Cernun had forgotten so many of them. Winnowed from existence by easier promises and uncomplicated salvations, all girded round with iron charms and cold bells. Only his own kind—few, so few—remained to so much as give breath to the powers set a-slumber. He was the Fool, thisnow, the Hob acting upon a whim—*making a last and dying gasp, nowt more*—from a feral triune of magics who'd failed. Nay, no Fool, merely a poor, deluded simpleton, to think to rise the *Ceugant* into thisworld! How could a mere small battle triumph over an unwinnable war? It had merely allowed a huddle of trapped spirits to coax their way through the Veil and snatch up offerings, with himself the latest, falling inward whilst his world turned to the soporific, despoiling incantations of the newest clutch of gods.

Like being outlaw. The Lady said—had said? once . . . sometime . . . mayhap thisnow, mayhap another—with Her voice growling like distant thunder from the ancient, ghostly trees. She, at least, remained in this oddling wood.

I am everywhere. Everywhen.

Aye, and he'd warrant She liked him even less, here.

Wherever *here* was. *When*ever here . . .

Time is/was/could be. . .

"Is this . . . this . . . not-Wode," he ventured, voice creaky with disuse, "the only thing to be left, in the end?"

Silence.

The gwyllion riding his left shoulder smoothed its muzzle against his cheek, making soft burbles. A second, winging just ahead, cheeped what might have been an answer. They kept him in his body, kept his senses from flying away. Particularly the leader, who rode Robyn's nape with forewings tangled in his curls and tail wrapped about his throat, all the while humming some descant to itself.

The woodland, also, tried to hum. It longed to speak to him. It wanted to be alive.

It wanted *him*, somehow. But he'd nowt to offer but lies he couldn't conjure, and forgotten . . .

What?

Is this punishment, then? he asked, and in the next breath nigh choked on his own laughter, because damned if he didn't sound like Gamelyn and *his* like, with their penances and demands for attention disguised as prayer. Surely a bairn of two summers wasn't as needy-jealous or as like to throw tantrums as Gamelyn's god; no wonder Gamelyn lived and breathed spectacle, worse than Robyn himself, and . . .

You wanted me out t' way, he accused Her. *You've decided to go the way of Gamelyn's god, and like him, you en't up to any contenders. You want to pluck hearts, count 'em and cage 'em, call 'em yours alone!*

Only a man would think so. One adequately caged and already despairing, like a prey animal ready to gnaw off its own foot to escape a trap. But you, my Hob-Robyn, are also too much the predator; willing to the wait and the possibility of chance.

"Are you saying there's a chance?" It cracked upward and thinned, there and not-there.

You will not return without some price, Hob-Robyn. So you have promised. So you will deliver.
But I will return to them.
No answer.
Was it Gamelyn who'd once told him how one of the peoples from the lands far past the sea believed resentment and gratitude all bound together, like? He fancied himself in agreement, because while he recognised the weight of the oath as had brought and bound him here, it didn't mean he'd to like it.

all will know us, and none find us. We'll walk together with our gods, in the cool of evening—
gamelyn says, soft and fervent
—if only you stay here with me.

If this is the Lady's game, it's a cruel one, and no surprise there . . .

you en't here—
hob-robyn insists, and
are you sure?—
is gamelyn's reply
—for is it not the duty of a dryw *to wander the otherworlds? to bide and return with some illumination, like the sun and stars and our land's promise?*
well, and en't you learnt sommat, milord—
hob-robyn snipes
—took you long enough, at that!

and his heart answers, maddeningly slow: *one-and two-and three-and. . .*
ad me ablutio, fac de me absolvium—
the song comes, soft . . .

or is it a song? Robyn didn't understand the words, but he recognised the voice, and the russet-haired figure that stepped out from behind a withered evergreen. Knew the slight roll of hips, the panther-like gait. Knew the damned colours the figure wore, white with a splash of scarlet against a broad chest . . .

none shall find me, all shall know me—
gamelyn walks in light, as grey and oblique as the promise of its presence lies transparent, fading in and out amidst the desiccated trees—
—i am divided, estranged. . .

"Fancy that," Robyn snarled into the stillness, more a wolf's growl than any human utterance. "Like you en't allus choosing that ower anything else you could've had."
The lead gwyllion, draped about his throat like a protective torque, gave a soft, worried trill. Robyn realised he hadn't spoken since . . .

Since . . .

since monsters crushed and gnashed the forest, fire devouring a yellow sky, and ebon dust sending the very air into choke and stench and burning. . .

More stings and nips, and Robyn lurched back into thisnow, found himself curled motionless in the withered bracken with the gwyllion diving at him, shrieking, and him thinking *Nay, you'll let them find me, give me away!* as if he were a fawn awaiting its dam's return.

He dragged himself to his feet. Kept on.

wait for me!—
he urges the white-clad figure that ghosted the tree ahead of him—
we'll find it together. . . allus better together, best with marion. . .
why?—
gamelyn taunts, and—
are you sure?

And the figure stopped, allowed Robyn to catch up, grab hold of the white cloak. Hand shaking—weakness . . . fatigue . . . fear?—Robyn grabbed harder, pulled.

The cloak tore in bloody rents, came away. And the figure turned.

No face, beneath the sweep of russet-gilt hair . . . or a face of a sort. A skull, still rotting, sat upon a neck of sinew and bone, with a mailed cowl sitting askew. The scarlet upon the limp, white surcoat formed no cross, but splashed a pattern of old, dried blood, the Templar's habit fouled with gore, torn and dragged open as if carrion eaters had already been at it.

mayhap we are all long dead, all of us—
it says with grinning, hollow mouth—
walked on, gone where you can never follow or find us. . .
And it all collapsed within itself, tumbling to the sere earth in a mouldering pile of bones and ash and meat, as dead as a forest long abandoned by gods and men.

Robyn fell to his knees, unable to so much as cry out. Only his heart, filling the silence. Beating too slow behind his eyes. Counting moments that . . . *weren't.*

what are moments?—
marion whispers and the goddess echoes, a breeze that lifts and ripples faded fabric, dingy white and old-old blood—
what is time, after all?
all we have—
hob-robyn answers, and touches the bony, broken skull—
is thisworld, thisnow.
Yet all worlds are Mine—

goddess-voice ripples like wind in faded trees—
all are one, and their realities a mirror, and. . .
and mayhap, you will finally come to understand

Before Robyn's empty gaze, the bones cracked and mouldered further, fading, changing, *dissolving* into the faded earth.
Mayhap you will come to understand.
So, too, the Fae had said, whilst beholding the wreckage of a world.

O

Fire.
Across pale-freckled skin, rashing blisters. Upon his tongue, thick-dry and coated with sand. Behind his eyes, slitted against wind and glare. Against the wide pan, heating rocks and sand and shrub like a cob oven. Surrounding his leg, throbbing and sweltering. In his heart, melting any remaining ice into a simmer, boiling it dry.
Fire . . .
Gamelyn longs for it in the night, shivering, with only gestured incantations and the gleam of steel to deny the jackals. He hides from it in the day, unravelling his head-wrap as makeshift tent or scrabbling from rock to rock, taking what shelter he can.
And you were allus on about the bloody wet!
The bag sears his shoulder, tugging down all hot and heavy—but it is not as weighted as the voice accompanying it.
Stop it! he would say, and *you're cruel,* but his voice is dried to a husk. He saves what croaks and whispers he has for the night, and the conjuring.
Instead he answers in rote silence, cold as the nights, as the never-ending diamond swath of fire above.
Ad me ablutio, fac de me absolvium. I am divided, estranged. I have sinned, been unrepentant. I have walked the Shadows of Nigredo. I have clothed myself in the Albedo, and watched a world die.
Clothed? Nay, you've cowled yourself in both darkness and light, Robyn's not-voice is mocking-soft, *and understood neither. Like a corpse in their winding sheet, waiting for the time of awakening.*
You aren't here. It's a trick, a cruel trick to weaken me.
Only a cruel god would claim love a weakness. No wonder you're so betwixt and between. Head and heart, allus separate. Neither of the Christ, nor of the Heath, nor—
And your god is so known for his benevolence!
Nature en't cruel, or kind. It just is, Gamelyn.
So reasonable. As if the mocking voice means what it says. As if a hand will take his arm, or steal about his ribs, caress and support. As if Robyn walks beside him . . . nay, not Robyn, for this apparition is clad in lionskins, limbs dark as good earth, not

pale as any forest dweller.

There is wind where there is no wind. There are waves where that are no waves.

Not waves of water—

Water is the life. . . you must find life, therefore water.

—but waves of heat, and the voice dances upon them, drawing runes that are not runes, like in the cavern long left behind.

It is Iao who unbinds you, Yahyā whispers as Gamelyn stumbles, and helps him to heave himself upward. Again. *It is Adonai who sets you free.*

It makes no sense. He is hallucinating. It's all nonsense.

Not nonsense. I led you to the cavern, Gamelyn. The most ancient of spells lies there. I would lie there.

"And have me lie there, too? Forever, no doubt?" Gamelyn tries to say. Instead he tumbles again.

Hands steady him, let him rock from hands to knees and back again. Gamelyn he watches his own filthy, blistered hands clench, dig into the sand for the coolness beneath the sear.

Knows he's finally—fatally, perhaps—gone mad.

And what is madness but the way within? What is madness but the inner spirit desiring flight?

But of course, this was inevitable. Not Robyn, nor Yahyā the godling Baptist, who dons the mask of an English archer with surprising ease. Nay, this was the divine Feminine; come, no doubt, to get her own licks in.

Gamelyn looks up, squinting. The Magdalene is clad in filmy gauzes . . . and nay, not merely her but Marion. Limned golden, body shadowed dark against the setting sun, she extends one arm towards him; the other holds a nursing babe.

And his own thirst is that fierce, surely, to contemplate shoving aside a god-gotten babe to quench the fire upon his swollen, cracking tongue.

Or mayhap not, because he still can reason with unreason.

I think you are not there yet, nay. Not hungry enough, not dry enough, not weak enough to give in.

He tried to speak. Again, a bare croak emerges. Instead he resorts to the sign language he shares with his lover—both of them—and his daughter. *You would have me give in, give up?*

What is the purpose of a journey, sweet, other than to strip you of all you have and know, and force you to face yourself? You will hold fast to pride and waste yet another opportunity?

Another?

Ah, but you have had several already, have you not?

Her words are . . . sorrowful? Why should She feel sorrow? She has what she wants, surely: his heart still beating behind his ears and against the hot sand beneath him, tight-taut and dry as any *darbuk.*

Do you always see the face of god in your mates? Yahyā kneels beside him, voice as soft-musing as night's slow approach. *How terrible. How lovely.*

All of us can be gods, Gamelyn argues, just as reasonable. *All of us, with all the requisite honour and malice.*

Just so. And incredibly, Yahyā kisses his temple.

The sun wanes in the distance. Night approaches, darkness licking at Gamelyn's bare, raw heels. Fire retreats, slow, from his Maiden's hair, shadows her face, lights her eyes and turns her robes to midnight. From Marion . . . to Mari . . . and to the Magdalene . . .

His eyes want to close. Need to close. His body shivers, racked with chill. His breath echoes into the stillness, hoarse. The prey, run to exhaustion.

Yet all he feels is the fire, burning.

You've won. You've killed me. You brought me here to die.

To my place, at the last, I have indeed. Mayhap you must die to live, She rebukes. *Mayhap the rule of your jealous god has been twisted far from true love or justice, but trust Me, My own, the time soon comes when an even harsher ignorance shall prevail, and cruelty reign the stronger. Mayhap, after all, the truest refuge for you and your wild-god lover is death.*

And isn't that the ultimate betrayal fit for any god or goddess? No place for us but hell, no compassion, only curses for our love, so just die? He flung back his head, glared at Her. *Only I won't be with him, will I? You've seen to that. Because he isn't dead, is he? I have to live, to find him. I have to live, return to my family. My children shan't grow up without a father.*

Mayhap your children are what will be left of you, and you have fulfilled your task in thislife. Mayhap you will see them again in paradise.

Mayhap I'll see you in hell!

An arpeggio of sound across the pan; a laugh, and there is danger in it—even Yahyā recognises it, stiffening, his hands upon Gamelyn strangely protective.

Hell? the Magdalene asks, soft and mocking. *Nay, My own, you have already once cast yourself there, remember? Offered the ultimate initiation, the final turn, the winnowing of leaden stone into gold. . . yet you could not recognise it. Instead you chose Hell. And it took every bit of will and witchery of your Ceugant to bring darkness and light together, to walk the way between and bring you back, did it not?*

It wasn't—

O, sweet, but it was. Like your sad and thwarted mirror of a master, casting the blame upon everyone but where it belonged, you turned from enlightenment and cast yourself into your own egocentric, self-imposed torment. You chose ash instead of fire, refused rebirth. You chose the mirror, Gamelyn. Will you choose it again—unthinking, unbending, unbelieving? Will you continue to believe in nothing but the necessity of the gaol?

His hands, deep-dug to the cooler sand, are shaking so fierce they cause the sand to vibrate, cascade inward. Arms weak, face drawn towards the tiny quakes and shivers. His head falls, one cheek into the sand. He jerks up.

It is well. Yahyā's voice seems faint, as if the nearer the Relic has come to its own place, the less real it is. *There is wind where there is no wind. There are waves where that are no waves. It is Iao who unbinds you; it is Adonai who sets you free.*

Hands make signs upon the sand—not his own, these are a sienna shadow where his clench freckled-auburn-pale. They burn against his eyes, back into his brain.

We wander the wilderness, you and I. No great halls shall honour me, I will be left to the mercies of our desert. Where none shall find me and all shall know me. . . and that is your doing, O son of many gods. You have brought me back to the wilderness; therefore, it is in my power to give you what you seek. So I ask: What do you seek? Will it be the ash, or the fire?

There is no "either". There is no "or". It fills his heart and brain, even as long, agile fingers trace another sigil in the sand. *There is only the alchemy of possibilities. Fire formulates ash from destruction. Amidst the ashes, the winnowed charcoal is the rebirth of flames. The raven of chaos becomes the swan of purification becomes the. . . the phoenix of. . .*

Death, and rebirth.

Even delirious, your mind keeps working, the Baptist chides, and sketches another sign. *Release it. Cease thinking, measuring, arguing. Life is not a debate, sweet Gamelyn, nor is it some mere lot cast, win or lose. You aren't here to make a 'better' world. The world is not ours, neither sway nor say. It does not need us; it merely wants us. We exist, swaying upon strands of hope and fate, to make the choices. To decide what matters, even when it seems we have no choice.*

Gamelyn looks up, meets those dark-dark eyes.

What do you choose, Gamelyn? What would you believe? What do you believe?

The answer comes without thought. *I believe in her. I believe in him. I believe. . . in what we* are.

Blood oaths, the purification of fire, and the wilding magic of the wilderness, where Earthly loves promise Earthly delights, and also Earthly sorrows. Not cruel, nay, the Baptist smiles when Gamelyn would protest, a flash against the coming darkness. *It merely is.*

Something cool touches Gamelyn's crown, and trickles down to his cracked, parched lips. He tastes water, for a brief, impossible breath.

I bless you, son of the gods, and thank you, and commend you to your fathers.

Then He is gone, into the darkness.

Fire, and ash. Blood, and wild, wild magic. A love not merely from thisnow, or this earth. Bare, hennaed feet pad over, bangles softly tinkling, and She, too, kneels next to him. Scoops sand into Her palms, and lets it spill into the wind, dust his cheeks. *Will you choose this life and fate, Gamelyn, and honour the others? Or turn aside, flee like a tortured animal and leave it, spin into another existence and forsake this fate as yet another one, unmarked and forgotten?*

She holds out a hand. He reaches for it. Falters. Grits his teeth and reaches again. This time he finds Her, and finds himself gathered up, a mother's tenderness enfolding him. He finds himself responding to it, clinging to Her.

Embraces fire, and lets it burn him down to ashes.

For there is only thisnow. Thisnow, and Her . . .

And, finally, the darkness.

O

Wandering the wilderness, She had said, and *you, too,* as if 'twere sommat familiar.

It weren't familiar. Not that Robyn cared. But he did wander. Sometimes stumbling, sometimes running, sometimes retracing his steps, spirals and circles within a hazy dream of trees and earth. Sometimes he remembered, clapped fingers to his throat just to see if he still lived, still breathed, still had the rhythm— *one-and two-and three-and—*

Anything to suggest time marked him, albeit sluggish-faint.

When he finally did leave the forest, it was from necessity: his stomach finally making a twist from forlorn complaint to empty ache, and no game in sight. Save, of course, for that hare which, behaving like no true hare, bloody followed him and his gwyllion companions. And as Robyn stopped, it humped over to him, stood on its huge hind feet and peered up at him.

Mayhap it were sick. Mayhap he were sick, and dreaming.

Either way, he weren't about to consider it as a meal. He'd not even a knife upon him, though he could have knapped a makeshift one, or even fashioned a bow . . .

Or mayhap not, considering the twisted, sickened trees.

The Barrow folk had food. So he stole back into the caverns, avoided any hint of company, raided a few baskets, and found himself going on. Further in, farther down, with the gwyllion making excited shapes as they realised his destination: the Veil's chamber.

Beneath the quivering stasis of the Mere, Robyn slept through another night and into the morning . . . there *was* morning, here, unlike a forest holding its breath with a sun barely stirring. This sun filtered down through the Mere's unreachable surface, another world moving . . . *changing.*

Doomed.

Robyn woke, sweated-warm as if he'd been tangled with

Gamelyn—but 'twere more of the gwyllion curled and piled atop him, and the weight of the wyvern's gaze.

Not that he were altogether sure of that last. More a tiny glimmer through clouded, half-lidded eyes, the promise of it slippery as fresh-caught eels.

There were eels in the surrounding caverns, leeched white and blind in the deep pools; he knew because the gwyllion caught them, brought them to him, seemed put out when he cooked them with a conjured fire.

Magic enough to burn, in thisworld. Neither did his benefactors refuse their share, though they pretended to fuss that it wasn't raw.

How was it no magic in thisworld seemed enough to make a rent in the Veil?

The gwyllion had the way of that, to be sure; once they brought him a fresh round of bread. Though soggy from its dunk in the Mere, its interior bided dry and light as he'd broken it open, its smell so filled with a world of warmth and sun that he'd eaten it all and greedily licked the damp crumbs.

Morning dawned here, though he couldn't tell if 'twere too slow or too fast.

Four days and five nights.

On the sixth, he heard what might have been footsteps and he stole away, uncaring if they saw he'd been here but knowing, with the whispered echoes, they sought him.

Good luck with that.

The need for counting slipped away, blurred from numbers into runes, and from that into pictures that burnt like fire behind his eyes. All that quenched it was waking, and the water reflections hanging about him, sometimes heavy as mist.

His thoughts simmered in turns: empty to full; futile to begrudging. Resentment turned, slow as the wyvern in its endless dreamings, to a strange, lethargic comprehension: the Wheel did not turn for thisworld's Wode. Or if it did, it turned too slow. Or mayhap too quick, he wasn't all that sure. Nor did it matter, not any more.

And, upon one of the endless, wet-grey mornings, the wyvern opened its great, glittering eyes.

- Entr'acte -

Barrow Mere, Hallamshire
Waning of Beltane, 1202 CE

She couldn't hate this place, though she'd been ready to, the first time.

Her mam had birthed her here, after all. Her mam, and hers before her, and hers before her all the way back to the people who'd first lived here . . . or so everyone said, anyway. *Their* people, who'd been banished from thisworld by the iron and bells . . .

Yet her mam refused to come here—*a sad place for us all, you understand?*—and wanted to *dredge it, drain it!* No one would tell her why, until Uncle John had come for a visit. After Beltane, that had been, and all of them together for a short, sweet time . . .

Save her da, still away over the Sea. Some said he was dead, but Aderyn knew they were wrong.

It had been Uncle John who'd told her about Barrow Mere, and even taken her pillion to show her the place—from a distance, mind, and Aderyn was sure her mam wouldn't have liked even that, had she known they would stop there on the way southeast. John had taken her on to Hathersage, and then on to Mam Tor. She'd been to the latter before, of course, during the Rites, but never had she seen the Hermit's caverns below the Tor. She'd held her uncle's hand in a darkness almost breathable, followed him by torchlight through vast, underground halls glittering like dew on dawning heather, and slept at his side, surrounded by magics that thrummed against her skin like a thousand heartbeats.

Aderyn still didn't understand, not really. There were too many contradictions. How Uncle John's ready smile would go . . . grey, really, as they'd passed here. How mention of it hung a cloak heavy enough to weight her mam's shoulders with some silent lament. Or how iron and bells could be a curse even when her da wielded iron so capable-fierce, and had grown up 'neath the bells—*more's pity for him*, Auntie Aelwyn would murmur with a sidelong glance and gesture, and *that* like-yet-different from the sign she always directed at the chapel of St Nicholas as they passed. Contrariwise, Auntie Aelwyn'd no such way t'wards All Hallows up on the Hill, and never failed to breathe a blessing upon the quillion dagger hung over the mantel when Da were away. Clearly the dagger spelled protection for Tickhill, same as the sound of All Hallows' bells, drifting soft-sweet across the fens . . . but t'were confusing all the same.

Though, to be fair, Aderyn didn't herself care for St. Nicholas' chapel. Its bell rang flat and anxious, and when Da were home and spent time there, he always emerged smelling of a bitter-old grief that even Mam or Uncle John couldn't cozen away.

But here, the contradictions began to unsnarl. Here, with her Mirror.

Of course, it were called M-e-r-e, Barrow *Mere*, though Aderyn had first kenned it otherwise. Even after she'd realised her mistake, she decided Mirror suited it better.

A long trip, there and back, but she could do it in an afternoon if she rode. She'd started her wanderings as the cold began breaking into spring. Warmer weather meant that the goatherds took their charges browsing out farther into the fens and growing brambles, and also that her friend the stable lad often took a string of horses out to pasture. A curious sort, and friendly, he'd learnt enough of her talk early on to have some understanding when she'd convinced him she'd every right to take Rutterkin for a ride—some advantages to being the lord's daughter, after all. No need for either of them to breathe a word to anyone, aye? Short trips, at first, to reassure both the lad and herself. And as the days grew long with the summering, and Aderyn always returned by the time he'd to take the horses in . . .

She'd set her pony's nose westward and made the try.

Thankfully, memory had persevered of that first, brief trip with Uncle John; only a few wrong turns the first time, with Rutterkin snatching grass as Aderyn pondered, yet somehow it seemed the closer she'd come, the more she'd . . . *known*. In her bones, like; even as she'd known Mam's newest bairn would be a girl. Over the next several visits, finding it had been easier, quicker there and back. And now . . .

The smooth, peaty-dark surface of her Mirror glinted. The

Wode here lay thick and tangled and ancient, allowing only a glimpse of sun, and then mostly midday. Especial friends defended the Mirror's edge, their reflections drifting in the shallows. The guardian Trees leaned in as she wandered them, as if trying to hear her voice—not that she had one, but the wind rustled the leaves in summer and creaked the branches in winter, so no need. The Trees understood; they too had no need of spoken words.

Auntie Aelwyn'd once said a darkling Fae had visited Aderyn when she were a wee bairn sleeping, and would have taken her but instead took her voice to keep them company. Mam's rebuke had been uncommon sharp, and Auntie Aelwyn had never said it again, but Aderyn knew it for truth.

Because she *remembered.*

So many things she remembered, even if Da once muttered how he wished memory'd leave him be and let him get on with it, whatever *it* were. She wasn't able to see him often enough to so much as ask, and even less this past turning of the Wheel.

Like knowing, just *knowing,* how to breathe a blessing into the surrounding thicket, and how to acknowledge the guardian Trees, which shivered like puppies as she petted each of them. Like how she knew their names: Rowan scouting the perimeters fierce-loving as Uncle Much; Yew reaching up all tall and thick, promising a bow when she grew strong enough to push it; Elm squatting broad-girdled as old Grandmam Gunnora, willing tether for a fat grey pony; Alder swaying slim as Auntie Aelwyn dancing the fires with Mam. All the Thirteen, really, were old friends within her memory. Oak, who both awed and comforted her, broad and golden and hung about with honour skulls. Even Holly, whose branches seemed more and more to reach outward, as if seeking. Aderyn always gave him special attention; he rose a slight distance from the other trees. Mayhap he were lonely, bereft even of the crimson fruit other hollies often bore. But ivy clung to his trunk, at least, and a swath of mistletoe seemed a soft tether between him and Oak's topmost branches.

But 'twere Willow as made green fingerling ripples in the Mirror, branches teasing at Aderyn's black hair as she knelt to trail her fingers in the cool, copper water.

She'd catch it, did anyone know she came here. Not even Robbie knew, though it grew more and more difficult to outwit him.

Something buzzed past her nose; she jerked back, wet-fingered and startled. Nowt more than a bee, mayhap?—but it returned to hover a good arrow-length from her, its wings brushing the Mere's surface with nary a ripple.

Aderyn frowned. This were no bee.

But what were it doing here? The gwyllion never went outside the castle's bounds, though they trailed her and Mam and, sometimes, Da. It drove Robbie distracted, because he couldn't see them most times . . .

Wait.

This weren't anything like the ones she knew from home. *They* glimmered as rainbowy as the inside of the shell Da'd brought from a far-off land: many colours and none, all at once. Whilst this one bided dull as unscrubbed pewter, its eyes like saucers and its feet webbed for swimming.

Sure enough, as she watched, it turned on its long tail and dove into the Mere. More a *pop* than any splash, and Aderyn leaned forward on hands and knees, trying to see into the murky water. Still more Mirror than Mere, she saw only her own reflection, and one to make Auntie Aelwyn press her lips and shake her smooth-plaited head. Tousled, sticky-outy hair escaping a slept-in braid, tunic and belt hitched sideways, knife shoved only partway into its hilt. Aderyn hadn't overlong to contemplate those transgressions as her reflection shattered every which way. The pewter-faded gwyllion returned with an even bigger *pop!*—and this time with a companion that could've been its twin.

They soared upward, sped through the trees and skimmed the breeze, tangled midair like mating hawks, spun and twirled and danced in the slats of sunlight. A breath escaped Aderyn's throat in what would have been a squeal had she voice; instead emerging as a round *Ohhr* of delight.

They must have heard, for they checked and rolled, came to a halt and hovered just above her head. Those great eyes whirled then fixed upon her, considered her for long moments.

Slowly, carefully, Aderyn extended one hand. A mistake, for the movement sent the pair wheeling once 'round the Trees before, one then the other, they dove and disappeared into the water.

Aderyn waited. Surely they'd be back? But several moments passed with no result. Even the breezes hesitated. Willow's water-logged leaves hung lank in the water, while the soft creaks and rustles of the other guardians stilled, fell silent. No bird calls, no squirrels chittering . . . nowt. Aderyn frowned, sitting back on her heels, disappointment congealing into apprehension.

Too quiet, it were.

And then, between her knees and palms, her Mirror . . .

Weren't.

- XIV -

The great ebon beast's gaze opened wider still, spanning wide as a longbow's reach. A mirror, aye, but one all of brass and darkness, lensing images into the water.

Indeed, it seemed Robyn's own reflection peered back at him as he drew closer. Distorted against the draw and spill of undertow, pale face nigh obscured by unkempt black hair, dark eyes glinting through, white-wide with curiosity. Only . . .

Only the image moved. Rocked back, though he himself stayed still, to disappear behind the tall withies.

Withies?

Robyn lurched forward and splayed himself against the Veil, fingertips wet as they dug in—only so far, so far. "Don't go!" It rasped from his throat almost unwilling. And foolish. As if it were anything but a reflection, or a dream conjured from his own delirium.

No response. Only the translucent inner eyelid of the wyvern, first sliding forward and then retreating, whilst the mocking dream reflection of the bank above vanished, then reappeared, floating in the deeps. Only the swallowed-silent murmur of his words against the Veil, and the sound of his own heart thudding behind his eyes and into the caverns, to dull upon the current: *one-and two-and three-and. . .*

Yet, mayhap no dream.

First two hands—small and plump, clutching at the grass. A dark mop of hair, a pale face with those large black eyes, all made slow appearance: a curious and wary child peeking over a withy hedge, unsure of what they might see.

It *was* a child. One that seemed to be watching him as intently as he watched in return.

Impossible, Gamelyn would say.

But what was impossible, where god-touched lads could die twice and still be walking, or worlds could bide shoulder to shoulder and never touch?

Save this . . . surely this were touching, mayhap more akin to what Alundel had once said: the eyes-meeting-eyes, the connection across a room—or across, mayhap, a Veil between worlds and all of it, mirrored by a water-drake's enchanted gaze.

Something caught and held the child's attention. Again, with a glance back towards Robyn, the child seemed about to retreat.

Again, his voice tried to hold them. "Can you hear me?" It barely moved the Veil's surface, hoarse from disuse.

No way he could be heard; mayhap the child saw his lips move. A frown and lean forward with head cocked, glints of copper and green fetching from the dark curls. Sun, brilliant and warm, lay overhead; it picked out more details: dark loam upon podgy fingers, the green fingerlings of a willow tree brushing a narrow shoulder clad in light, chaff-coloured stuff and, just beyond, a rowan protective, an ash trembling tall, an oak hung in mistletoe vine and ivy.

The child knelt upon the banks of Barrow Mere.

The wyvern's eye membrane slid across, its translucent curtain flickering and shading the child as ghostly as Robyn's own surroundings. He feared the tenuous contact would break, cover access with more slumber. Yet the eyelid quivered and slicked back, fully revealing Mere, sunlight, and a child still watching.

Something familiar teased at him. Surely the child looked like to his mam's people, but he'd never seen this one before. Never noticed much about any bairn, truth be told, though he liked them well enough. Particularly if they didn't get too close.

Likely no danger of that, here. Why was he persisting with this, anyroad? The child could see him, somehow. Likely had the magic, or the sort of artlessness wee ones possessed, to see spirits and such in spades . . . at least until they had it burned from them in chapel walls. What good was it, after all, other than some rich tale to be told and disbelieved?

The child rocked back. Robyn lurched forward, hands splayed and chest straining against semisolid damp. Said "Don't go!" all foolish and quick.

The words proved unnecessary; the child wasn't retreating, but plunking down on the grass beside the Mere. A lass?—a lad?—he wasn't sure. The child's left hand waved in the air in a gesture, albeit small and unsure. As Robyn stared at it, thinking it familiar but just as uncertain, the child did it again, and—

And the wyvern's eye sealed itself shut, as a hesitant voice filled the cavern.

"Hob-Robyn, we have been worrying after you."

Even coming on t'wards the longest of days, even though wee Marjory had outgrown a pre-dawn feeding, Tickhill's management this time of year made extra light into necessity. The valley would be marked with bonfires dotting the valleys this night, and Tickhill's tithes would be made over the next days with especial prayers. The season waning uncomfortably hot, their lord still missing past the horizon . . .

All the heathen folk mourned Summer's passage and offered gifts to ensure His return.

The day's heat lay well upon the pastures and fens by the time Marion returned to her solar, intending not only a small nap for the bairn upon her hip, but mayhap herself as well.

Her eldest waited there—likely waiting for the youngest. Aderyn, unlike Robbie, hadn't tired of her newest sister's company.

Aderyn also looked as if she'd been on one of her early morning wanders—like Robyn, Marion thought, the ache always there. But then, what with the glorious weather, 'twere hard to keep anyone indoors, especially Aderyn. She must have snuck away after breakfast and then back in, else Berta'd be here, fussing over the grubby toes and hair sticking every which way. Berta's latest crusade entailed trying to make A Proper Lady out of Aderyn. It was as doomed to failure as the last one, where Berta had tried to convince her mistress to hold to some propriety and bring in a wet nurse for Marjory.

"Milady, you need t' stop carrying a newborn about whilst at your duties. 'Tis too like some peasant drab workin' the tofts with a bairn latched to each teat!"

"I worked tofts in my time," Marion had reminded. "As have you."

The woman had spluttered to that like a kicked hen despite that Berta's people had farmed several hides' worth nigh to Maltby since Saxon times.

Marion nestled the baby into her basket. She'd nursed recently, which meant another bout of hard sleep, with Berta carping all the more about how babes who slept too much were likely Fae changelings. She would have included a slide of eye towards Aderyn, too, if the lass had been around.

Bloody damn, but if the woman wasn't so skilled at her work within the living quarters—and a trustworthy Heathen—Marion'd assist her back to her family's farm! With a boot chasing her backside!

Marjory, as if in comment, started to snore.

Aderyn shot a glance towards the basket and smiled. Returning the smile, Marion put Berta's stubborn—and revisionist—rectitude from her thoughts, ambling over to where Aderyn had settled herself, cross-legged in the mattress's middle. Marion's peacock fan lay spread out before her—a favourite trinket since Aderyn had grown old enough to not destroy it—with the child's fingers tracing it as if scrying a cerulean-framed rainbow. Aderyn's focus lay not only upon the fan, but the polished bronze mirror that usually lay upon Marion's dressing table.

Marion's own focus set itself upon the grubby bare feet that belied the clean linen shift. No doubt a set of muddy shoes and overkirtles had been shed in the stables. With a small sigh, she hitched a hip onto the bed, fished the comb that had permanent residence in her pocket—a necessity, with a keep's worth of hey-go-mad children—and began the familiar process of untangling her daughter's hair.

Aderyn gave her own equivalent of a sigh, complete with an eyeroll in nigh-perfect mimicry of her sire, but submitted with shoulders still hunched; this time in grim anticipation.

"If you'd let sommun braid it—"

—*Before you go haring off,* the girl finished with a wince as Marion found and tackled a knot.

Well, she'd hair so thick the knots would hide for days if Marion let them. But since Marion didn't, her daughter's mop soon enough separated into some semblance of order, and Marion began plaiting.

Aderyn bore it with uncommon grace. She seemed more taken with tracing her fingers upon shiny metal. A small frown reflected back. Unexpected, that, since a good wander always made for good spirits.

"You broke your fast early, I take it."

A nod.

"But back in time for supper, aye? Where to, then? To see the new foal?" Marion often employed her daughter's signed language, but just as often her hands were busy, so she resorted to vocal speech.

I went out with the stabled horses, rode Rutterkin up and down whilst they grazed. Aderyn turned, so quick that Marion lost hold. *Mam, is it true?*

Retrieving the braid and tying it off with a bit of cord, she let it fall between Aderyn's narrow shoulder blades. "Is what true, pet?"

Is it true that I look like your brother?

"It is indeed." Marion leaned forward and kissed her temple.

Aderyn eyed the fan. *Mam? Did a queen really give you this?*

"Aye, indeed. Queen Eleanor, King John's mother, gave it to me. Do you want to hear the story again?"

Shouldn't we wait for when Marjory's awake to hear it?

"Well, that's thoughtful, pet, but you know your baby sister. You could be waiting the while. And she's really too little to proper heed."

A satisfied smirk, and Aderyn gathered the fan up, ready to listen.

So Marion told, this time with plenty of her own embellishments to make it fresh, the winter's tale of which the trouvère Alundel had written: *Robyn Hode and Queen Eleanor, or: The Rescue in the Fog.*

Aderyn listened, rapt, and once her mother had finished, added, "She gave you the fan later, though."

"Aye, she did, and never did I expect it."

A pause, Aderyn fanning the feathers out and stroking them. "Who's Arthur? And Will? I don't remember them before."

And of course, sometimes embellishments could make trouble. But surely, they deserved their place in the story, even if they'd refused to take part in later chapters.

They were part of Robyn's band of outlaws, too? Why have I never heard of them?

Marion stroked the fan, considered and lamented one too many complex things, and settled for the simplest. "Sometimes people quarrel. Will and Arthur, they didn't agree with some things we had to do. So they both left. It was before you were born, even."

Aderyn frowned, then peered at the fan again. *Why would the Lady put sacred eyes upon the cocks instead of the hens?*

Well, and that had been easier than she'd thought. Marion grinned. "Hens have too much work to do, aye? Feathering nests and watching young'uns. Whilst the cocks are all ower strutting about and preening, keeping watch for rivals and danger with all those eyes fanned and ready."

Like Uncle Much, all fierce in his sword and mail.

"Aye, pet. Like our lovely Much."

I'd rather go with him to ride the bounds after supper. Better than making cheese.

"Ah, but he's more than enough soldiers to accompany him, whilst Auntie Aelwyn has only you, me and Edwina to help. The others are all out in the fields today, aye?"

A shrug. *I could help in the fields.*

"I'm sure you could. But cheese is important, too. We've a sight more cows and goats fresh this year than last, and milk's too precious to waste. Moreower"—Marion gave a tug to the neat braid—" you never mind getting a sample here and there, aye?"

Another shrug. *I s'pose. Mam, did Uncle Much find out why that blacksmith was after you?*

"She was in sway of a wicked man. Another reason you can't go with Much. He's taking her back home." With plenty of guardsmen and a return threat for the castellan of Knaresborough Castle. They'd found out from the girl she was smith there, but little else. Tough and tight-lipped. Marion couldn't help but admire her. It had been one of the captured men who'd called her de Lisle's whore, and let on further how de Lisle had been the one to hire them, though the money had come from elsewhere, as he was a skinflint well known to make tuppence shit a shilling.

De Furnival? Would he stoop to hiring men to attack a fellow lord's castle just because he coveted said castle? Or someone else?

Much would find out what he could, but Marion had some questions for Gilbert, next time he came this way.

Mam? Did Uncle Robyn have the magic?

While Marion thought herself well used to the rapid twists and bends of children's thoughts, this one poked her in all her tender places. She put her attention to Aderyn's braid, as if she'd not properly tied it.

Mam?

"Aye," Marion answered, soft. "Robyn had the magic. So strong and fine and all hues . . . like a rainbow breaking between storms. Or a deep, velvet-black night."

And mourned just a little more, how they had all started speaking of him as something belonging to the past.

Aderyn tugged at Marion's gown, her manner suggesting she'd signed several times to no avail, fingers flying as her mother turned to her. *Is that why the Fae took him?*

This fetched more a slap than any twinge. "How did you know that?"

The black eyes were wide. *Mam, everyone who knows, knows that. Even the crofters know Robyn Hood en't dead. They say he's still around, that they see him, sometimes. But if he's so close, can show himself to his people, why doesn't he come back?*

Marion sidestepped the latter for the former. "You en't been asking these sorts of things away from our family, now?"

Nay, of course not. I promise! the child furthered as Marion peered closer, eyes narrowed. *People allus talk around me, Mam. They think 'cause I en't talking like them, I en't hearing them.*

Marion abandoned her stern mien, pulling Aderyn close. "Well, people can be proper daft, aye? Think of all the things you'll overhear, and them never the wiser!"

A smile tipped Aderyn's lip; clever lass, she'd clearly already recognised that much. Still . . .

"If you hear owt that you don't understand, ask me, aye? What's prompted all this about Robyn, anyroad?"

Well. People tell stories, and I was just. . . well. Wondering.

Clever, aye, yet Aderyn was hiding sommat. No great shakes at prevaricating, and thank the Lady she took less after Gamelyn there.

Mayhap sommun in the villages had flapped their tongues. Again. Marion would find out who, how, and what . . .

A tug to her sleeve, and she turned to see Aderyn's face all set. *Is Da coming home?*

This hit her in the gut, and hard enough to nigh make her gasp. Unfortunately, her clever daughter read that as well, clear as ink on parchment. The dark eyes filled, spilled.

Marion reached out, started to gather her close. "Coom by, pet. It'll be all right."

It can't be! Aderyn pulled away, gestures suddenly wild. *Not if he's never coming home! That's what they say, when they think I en't listening. That he's lost over there, and never coming home. But I don't believe it! I* don't!

She burst into tears and flung herself against Marion's breast.

Marion hugged her tight, swaying, swallowing hard against the lump seeking her own throat. The tears she couldn't stop. Worse—oh, *so* much worse!—to face her bairn's sorrow. And the way Aderyn sobbed—so dreadfully soundless and hoarse, red-faced with great gasps for air and rattles of mucus instead of the cries that stoppered themselves silent. Her hands clenched and shook and beat within Marion's kirtles, but Marion could make out the words, stuttered tight and angry:

That's why. . . Uncle Hubert came! To tell us! And you didn't tell us!

Marion kept rocking her, murmured, "I didn't say anything to you because I don't believe it." Another tiny shake as the words didn't seem to penetrate. "I don't believe it, do you hear me, pet? I don't."

Only you do some days, don't you? a snide voice taunted. No gods or goddesses or spirits, this, but her own.

"I don't believe he's dead. We'd know, wouldn't we?"

And when doubt would slither through certainty, Marion envisioned Mam Tor. More, the caverns beneath, and the harsh truth of John's words:

You haven't the luxury of losing faith.

She didn't, particularly when her daughter depended on it.

Slow, almost unwilling, Aderyn's sobs were lessening. She nestled tighter, turning her face up to her mother, eyes wide. Wanting to believe, too.

Marion kissed her forehead, took a kerchief and wiped her face, held it to her nose. Obediently, Aderyn blew, then reached up and touched the tracks upon Marion's cheeks.

"Aye, pet. I hate it, too. I worry after him. I wonder if I'm imagining things when I believe your da's alive and coming home. But I do believe he'll come home to us. Home to stay. No matter what anyone else says."

Aderyn peered at the moisture on her fingers, frowning.

A flutter of nigh-silent wings, and one of the gwyllion arced down from its perch in the rafters to land on Aderyn's extended arm. She jerked, surprised. It merely eyed her, then bent to lick the tears from first her fingers, then her face. Aderyn's smile came small, but clearly delighted. It broadened as, once the gwyllion finished its ablutions, it gave a nuzzle to her cheek before it crept to the bed edge, dropped and soared back to its place.

They've never done that before. Aderyn watched the gwyllion. *Mayhap they know something we don't.*

"We have been searching, but you have been disappearing, always, as we think we might be seeing you."

Did Grey Eyes not realise that he'd wanted to disappear? Not see her, not see any of them— particularly now, with the wyvern's strange waking and the child upon the bank reaching out instead of running away.

But nay, she kept peering at Robyn with cow-moony grey eyes.

His gaze fled, seeking the wyvern, which seemed barely to breathe. Nowt more than a huge, submerged stone. Had that, too, been a dream? It seemed dreams were more real than any waking, of late.

And as if conjured, they rose from dream to waking, pounding behind his ears in a mad race:

—ravaged, raped, sown with salt and barrened by monsters, flesh-eating soul-destroying mind-searing
fire-burning—ash—and—flame. . .

Nay. Let be.

With a tearing gasp, Robyn came back to himself, found he'd fallen to hands and knees beside the Veil. The gwyllion had fled its normal perch. Instead soft, nigh insubstantial fingers caressed his nape—and gave rout to nightmares.

"Sha-sha," Grey Eyes said. "Let be, Hob. Let be."

The warm milk of her hands echoed the soft exhale of breath and intent. Beneath their weave and wax, the too-taut rhythm of his heart also began to slow, subside beyond notice.

"Come back to us, Hob-Robyn. We need you back with us. You be needing your people, too."

"I can't . . . they aren't . . ." And plague take him, but he couldn't even mutter fit speech! What was happening to him?

"I know it was being unpleasant, what our Magus gave you. I know you are being hurt, even if I am not understanding why. It is having nothing to do with us. There is being no need to hold this in your heart or—"

"No . . . *need?*" He lurched up, jerked out from under—not without a stagger as his heart gave its own lurch, no longer cozened by Fae magicks and anxious after . . . fight? or flight? Or mayhap curl up, a hedgehog in a meadow being pawed and rolled by a highlands wildcat?

And bugger him sideways if the lass didn't stare after him, her expression so blank he had to clench his fists to keep from smacking the bafflement from it.

"It has"—grating, through clenched teeth and an ever-tighter throat—"*everything* to do with me. And with you and all who bide here. How long d'you really think this pale shadow of a world can exist without the one past the Veil?"

"Underworlds—*our* worlds—have always been. Even though we have not been always bound here, still they are existing, on and on. Thisnow." Grey Eyes peered at him, hands folded together, brows furrowed. As if she were giving it a proper go at understanding, even did she think him mad as any hare in spring.

Mayhap he were. But . . .

"Underworlds? This is some otherworldly lair, I'll give you that, but it en't any underworlds."

No more of bemusement; this elicited a frown.

"Look, I don't know what that lot has told you—bloody damn, they might even believe it themselves by now. But I've walked Annwyn's halls, lass. Whatever this place is, it en't akin t' that."

The frown pinched harder. "Where else could we be? In the shadowed lands, where spirits come and roam, waiting for their time."

"Those unfortunate sods'll wait forever!" Robyn motioned outward. "Their time never comes, does it? They don't move on, do they? Spirits move on, return; they follow the Wheel. When it en't stopped, that is. Tell me, lass, have you ever seen a one of 'em leave here?"

A shot in the dark, aye, but he'd always been the sort of archer who felt more than saw his target. And this hit square with the same shudder and jerk. She slumped but didn't fall, her gaze faltering away from him to linger towards that dead-end cavern filled with ghosts.

He ran her down, knowing he had to stay it despite a ripple of uncertainty as to why. "They en't changed. Their numbers might grow, but they don't lessen. No more'n any of you—of us—bound t' shadow worlds. They're trapped, don't y' see? Trapped as sure as me and you and t' Fae folk, in some dismal mirror as does nowt but reflect what it came from, back and forth and ever inward, never a flicker and allus t' same."

"Of course we're trapped! It's why you've been brought here, to be returning life to—"

"You canna breathe life into sommat dead!"

"Says the Hob," she insisted, sudden and tenacious as her mentor. "Says the winter-white Brother-consort, who dies and returns again each Wheel's turning. Says the Horned Lord, who has been missing from our halls far too long. Only you would be cheating us of that, too! Cheat *me*—"

"The only cheating 'twere what *you*—"

"I gave you your oath, in flesh and form!"

"You gave me a lie."

"Not if you be holding the belief."

"But it weren't real!"

"And what is being real, in any worlds we walk?" she snapped. "Belief is being all we have, to be making the ground beneath our feet not go spinning wildly into the sky!"

He wanted to protest further; found, beneath that last, the words clogging his throat.

"I was making the decision, Hob-Robyn. My belief, how I would be giving you what you wanted, and making the Rite as needs be happening, and you were believing it. You loved, wanted . . . but I—" Tears sprang, sudden, in those great, grey eyes. "I was being weak, unable to hold to't. I should have been listening to my Priestess; she told me your powers were too turbulent to be capturing. I should have left it to her. To her, and all would not have been ruined!"

As sudden as she had come upon him, she turned and fled, her feet slapping bare against the stones until they, too, faded into the darkness.

He'd no wish to follow, though contrition niggled at him; he'd hurt her, unwilling.

Mayhap, though, in prodding her, you have planted a different sort of seed.

The whisper came undreamt of. Robyn jerked and stiffened as it floated in, nigh-forgotten, but familiar. *Real.*

He whirled, beheld sunlight wafting down through the black waters, to dance upon the even-blacker form supine there. The gwyllion began to trill and flit about the cavern.

A gleam caught, betrayed the wyvern's half-open eye.

And a deep, faint and faraway Voice. *Not only one Child, to be woken by Chaos. It is what you do best, My Own.*

The words tried to fill his chest but quickly faded, even as sunlight shifted into shadows, and the wyvern's gaze shuttered.

With a hoarse cry, Robyn flung himself against the Veil, not just once but again and again, until he staggered back, spent and panting, sobbing and drenched. Only then did he notice the panic of the gwyllion, darting at his head with shrill, maddened cries.

He fell to his knees, arms over his head, curling up against his thighs, and tasted salt, hot-wet, upon his cheeks. "Coom by," he whispered, rocking back and forth. "Coom by."

Only silence answered. The gwyllion, as if they too had sated their passion, gathered about him with tiny, curious cheeps. He rose, stiff and slow, with them nestled in his hair and clinging to his tunic and leggings, their warmth rising steam from the sopping fabric. The one that seemed more his familiar than any of its own kind circled his neck once, then twice, not unlike a dog by the fireside, and settled down in its regular place around his neck.

"Woken two children," he muttered to them, building a fire more from habit than any desire. "Woken *two*, He said."

Grey Eyes, who seemed little more than a child. Had probably, he realised, been stolen as a child. He passed a hand over the carefully-stacked peat, began to speak the words to bring fire to them—

Halted. Another faint memory visited, flickering and fetching like dawn in deep forest, or a tale told half asleep. A child, kneeling at the Mere. The child, from the outer worlds.

And how could he have forgotten *this*? Hadn't it just happened?

Hadn't it? He teased at the memory, like yarn from his mam's spindle, and twisted it.

The child had gestured to him. Been speaking to him. With gestures, like John. So akin to John, in fact, that Robyn could belatedly parse them.

Who are you? the child had said, with the sun gleaming crimson in black hair.

Before the eye had closed. Before Grey Eyes had found him.

He glared after her departure, fists clenching. But they relaxed, slow, and even slower he turned back to the slumbering wyvern.

What would it take to wake you, *then*? he wondered.

- XV -

Fire.

Pain.

All of it, lighting his days and nights, filling his heart as he wakes . . .

For Gamelyn is waking. Somehow.

He basks in the heat, feverish and racked with odd pain—not, yet altogether his—curled like a babe in Mother's womb, a tiny chick in its egg, with feathers of fire, formed in heated ash.

Fire. Pain. The taste of blood at the back of his throat. Voices echoing, sigils floating, drifting upon waves of . . .

Life.

Nay, not just life, a soft baritone informs him. *Rebirth. Your last chance, this, in thislife. You have tasks still undone. Wake!*

He's trying. It's hard, harder, mayhap, than it should be. But he can hear life beckoning to him: heat radiating beneath his body, wind upon his cheeks, the throbbing of his leg, four scores that seem to cut to bone. Can smell the rot of infection, and the fear-sweat upon his body.

But.

He hears the soft, tinkling sounds of a brook over rocks. Can also smell the moisture lifting and filling parched, dust-caked nostrils. Can *taste* it.

Not fire, this. Water.

Life, in a land of parched rock and grit.

And an unfamiliar voice accompanies life. Tenor instead of baritone, and sounding upon his ears, not his mind or heart. The words twist, oddling and familiar, unlike to any flat Anglic. Instead they spill, a lovely liquid of words; he hears sounds like *djinn* and *Yahyā* and that last brings him into awareness with a shock of light and heat and . . .

"*Alma'hu ya alhaya'tu*," it says, and again, as senses finally—finally!—translate: "Water is our life. Guests are revered above all others, so you must accept this gift from these my people, even in our time of holy fasting. Drink."

For the first time in Gamelyn's life, his primary adult instinct abandons him. He does not defend, reach for a weapon, or think to strike. Instead, he acquiesces. Lets his jaw drop in a soft sigh, feels tepid liquid sting cracked lips and lave his tongue.

Hears more encouragement in a familiar/strange tongue. "That's it, just a bit more."

Swallows.

Falls back into the darkness.

ᛗ

The wyvern might have been a rock upon the bottoms, save for those sporadic breaths—one for every twenty of his own—and the twitches of slumber: a tip of tail, a minute unfurl of wing, a dull glint from the corroded iron about its neck.

Its eyes remained shut, as if they'd never opened, never reflected a child framed by sun and sky. As if it had never transpired that worlds should meet . . .

Nay. Robyn had to believe what he'd seen. To remember how it happened, that it *had* happened. Otherwise he'd truly go mad. He leaned over the fire, traced a cupped hand over the new flames, and pulled the smoke close. It wafted over him, rich, and stalled in his hair. He drew a long breath, tasting the peat deep in his throat, holding it there as he rose, slow as a stalking wolf.

His gwyllion familiar purred, for all the world like a cat content at a hearth. The others hung close by, fascinated, as Robyn padded over to the Veil and laid both hands flat against it. For a long moment he tilted his forehead against the slick-wet, then he lifted his chin, breathed the peat smoke against the Veil, lips shaping a whisper:

"*Enynasai.*"

The hex-breath hung against the Veil for long moments, then sank within merely to dissipate, fire smothered by rain.

The wyvern didn't so much as twitch an ear.

Too easy, of course, just to speak the awakening and imagine 'twould work. Nevertheless, Robyn said it again, pulling it sharp as flint across steel.

The wings quivered, drawing tiny fluxes of silt and stream. It could be nothing—another dreaming twitch—yet hundreds of tiny bubbles, more foam than anything, sprang upward, as if seeking light and air.

Heart hammering up into his throat, Robyn leaned harder into the Veil, whispered the awakening one more time. This hissed sparks across oiled chaff: a call upon the belly-fires, the thoughts to kindle, the heart to beat stronger heat.

Tarnished metal rippled, and a gleam of bronze pierced the murky bottom as the wyvern's great eye skimmed slowly open.

"*Pwylloch, Ysgawen,*" Robyn urged, as the dark slit of pupil expanded then narrowed.

Focusing. On him.

"Be calm, Old One. See me. We have spoken before. Dost tha' remember?"

The wyvern regarded him for a long moment, then moved, rolling its black head upon the bottom silt, clouds of the stuff rising to nigh obscure it, the visible eye closing halfway.

"Nay," Robyn pleaded, leaning so close damp misted his cheeks. He denied it with another fire-called curl of breath, tracing misted-mystic signatures. "Stay, *Ysgawen.* Remember me. Remember otherworlds. Blue skies, green trees. Flying through sodden mists, and diving beneath a fierce sun, warming your wings?"

The gwyllion reposing across Robyn's shoulders raised its head, gave a soft, purry growl that sounded almost . . . curious?

"See me, Old One. See *for me.*"

Another blink, and another, almost as if it were considering Robyn's words, then . . .

If Robyn thought those eyes had gleamed before, now they illuminated the murk, the blaze growing—*kindling*—as if some forge bellows stoked a forgotten ember to light the Mere as a mirror wide and black and trimmed with bronze.

Nay. No mirror, this. A window, more like, and a child looking in.

The day had changed. The light was different—less overhead brilliance and more angled, with the grass gone from soft green shoots to tall sere, and the trees from full leaf and flower to the fade and crackle of autumn.

Yet it was the same child, sloe-haired and nigh bursting with the magic. Silent and watching. Waiting, it seemed.

Well, then, but hadn't his whole life had been equally comprised of *Sod you* and *Bring it?* So he dove into this gamble as well, raised his hands and signed: *Who are you?*

And the child answered back: *Who are you?*

ⓜ

Badiyat ash-Sham (the Syrian desert)
Waning of Summer Solstice, 1202 CE
Last days of Ramadan, 598 AH

Surely he is dead; he has lost all that matters, has failed, and so this must be . . .

Hell? Nothingness?

Not again. Nay, never! Let him wander aimless a thousand wastelands, but never again will he willingly turn to hell and think it justice!

I . . . am . . .

" . . . safe. You are safe, O guest, O wanderer who speaks to spirits, who guards our beloved prophet and has brought him home."

Gamelyn opens gritty, gluey eyes and tries to focus . . .

And focus came, slow but determined.

The last rays of sunlight reflected behind his shadowy companion in wide, rose-copper rectangles seated here and there, deflected by the shade that arched overhead. Gamelyn had seen the like of the tent before; sprung wide and round, large enough to offer protection for not only humans, but their most valued horses. Indeed, against the far curved wall several of the latter stood hipshot, one a mare with a foal lying beside, flat out. Several children were lying there as well, heads pillowed against the foal's furry sides. The mare, only half-dozing, guarded them all.

Slowly, Gamelyn became aware that he, too, lay nearly supine, albeit supported by cushions, not a suckling foal. His feet were bare and washed-cool, his robes loosened lax, his head and shoulders propped. A young man who sat cross-legged beside him, wiping the cloth over Gamelyn's face when it was nearly squeezed out, then dunking it, wringing it carefully into his open mouth. Gamelyn swallowed, found himself staring. Aye, the lad had a beauty the poets would sing to, but more unsettling, he looked altogether akin to the Baptist: angular cheekbones and chin; full, sensual lips shaping the Arabic and framed by a scruff of beard; the large dark eyes occasionally hidden by an ebon forelock.

And therefore, of course, he also resembled Robyn.

The Relic! It flooded through him, jerked his hand to grope at his side.

"It is here. You have spoken much of it." The lad reached out and took his wrist, guided his fingers to the familiar sackcloth over its precious box.

Gamelyn let out a relieved sigh, then frowned, wondering. He had spoken of it? What had he spoken?

A sweet, gamin smile—reassuring, and thoroughly unlike Robyn's, thank any god or goddess listening—suggested the lad could be thirteen or thirty. This black-haired lad also expressed no anxiety at a surrounding gaggle of children, all peering at the prone stranger from over the lad's shoulder. A few leaned on said shoulder to do so. This lot seemed older than the ones napping with the foal, but only just. Their eyes sprung wide, watchful—but also curious and unafraid.

One shot the lad a question, too quick for Gamelyn's muzzy head to follow. Again offering the gamin smile, the lad shrugged, saying—not Arabic, but the Badawī tongue, "I think he'll live."

Gamelyn's eyes must have echoed uncertainty, for the lad furthered, soothing, "God is merciful, fire-hair. You have been long ill, and nigh lost your leg, but we have—"

His leg. Memory flooded over Gamelyn, a great wave. Lost in the desert, killing the lion. Food, then water running out. The caverns full of mystery—had they been real? He wasn't sure, but one thing did remain: infection had broken him, let the spirits fill him . . .

His leg. He couldn't feel it, couldn't move it.

"All is well." Again, the firm hand grasped his, guided it down to brush against loose, cotton fabric and—thank all the gods that were and are!—a length of too-thin, bandaged thigh. "You have your leg, see? It was a long fight, but we saved it, and you. You are whole. You are our guest, and safe."

Gamelyn sucked in a halting breath and let it out, slow. Took another drink as it was offered, gulping noisily. His vocal cords finally loosened enough to let him speak, politely, in Badawī. "I thank you, beautiful friend."

The young man nearly dropped the rag. Blurted, "He speaks our tongue, Grandmother!"

"Of course he does!" snapped a voice from behind Gamelyn's head. "He is favoured of Nabi Yah'yā. Nabi Yah'yā favours our people, the people of the wilderness. How would it be otherwise?"

Again, Gamelyn's muscles tensed and tried to pull him upward before his mind registered the wisdom of such.

"Note you, third of my son's sons, the way of him? It is in truth a sublime warrior who possesses the hawk's instincts; he never lies easy. I know warriors. And such a rare one he must be! His adversaries did not leave him naked to the kites, no. They respected him. Respected him, I tell you, for they left him with his weapons to hand, so he should not die like a dog. They let him keep the amulet of the Ismaili about his throat, the cord of the infidel magicians at his waist, and a bag carrying the most holy and blessed of burdens."

A presence followed the words, swathed just as soft, brown and black gliding from the darkness and into Gamelyn's line of sight. One of the youngsters moved towards the woman and reached for her arm; she shrugged away the touch and turned her head in Gamelyn's direction, as if to measure the sight of him.

Yet it was unlikely she saw much of anything. Her eyes held a

thick, milky scrim within the leathery folds of her eyelids, stark-
pale against her face. The latter, framed by black woollen, had
been sculpted and pitted, burnished deep bronze from a lifetime
of desert heat, sun, and winds. Yet she crossed the tent with ease,
all the while keeping her head tilted Gamelyn's way—courtesy, or
listening for him, or both? But not towards him. Slowing as she
reached the horses, she'd a pat and soft murmur for each of them,
until at last she came to the mare and foal. The foal had risen on
spidery legs to nurse, and the children scattered in the elder
woman's wake as, with a tiny bow, she spoke to the mare.
Black-tipped ears twitched, and black nostrils fluted in the tiniest
of welcoming nickers as the grandmother patted the mare's neck,
fingers stroking a small, doeskin bag braided secure into the ivory
mane. Tens of bangles, silver and copper, glinted upon the woman's
bony wrists; indeed, hands—and, of course, that remarkable face—
were all Gamelyn could see within the black and brown robes.

"We did not disturb your blessed burden, fire-haired one, but
we did divest you of your weapons. For your safety, as well as ours,
in our place."

Again, the tension drained from Gamelyn. It was odd, the lack—
usually ever-present, *warrior's instincts*, no doubt the old woman
would say. A ... submission, and one he'd become wholly
unconversant with, even in the presence of his masters. In its wake
came relief, and gratitude—and certainty. Gamelyn well knew
what he must say and do. "I accept the necessity, respected host,
and the gift bestowed. You do me great honour."

Her chin tilted upward and she turned to him, faultlessly
formal. "The sun sets, and fasting ends. Wilt thou, then, stranger
from the plains of Yah'yā, sit to my son's hearth and eat with
thine hosts?"

"I am here to guard my family!" boasted the boy Ahmad—or,
Ahmad ibn Malik ibn Karim al-Banu Sulaym, as he'd introduced
himself. In the next moment he slid a glance to his elder brother,
adding, "Myself along with Tariq, of course."

Tariq, eldest of the old woman's grandsons sitting to the meal,
once again gave that gamin smile. The lovely young man just
starting to grow his beard, who'd woken Gamelyn with water.

How wholly apropos that his given name should mean *Star of
the Morning*.

And how strange, that loneliness should bubble up like this,
so sudden and strong. Gamelyn had lain alone for much longer
of a time, though even then he'd claimed the fraternal comfort of
a beloved companion.

He was glad Much had stayed behind. He could have been in
Remegius' place—and Gamelyn could only hope that Remegius

was, indeed, already back in England. What whim might have taken the Elder of Masyaf once he'd disposed of the brother Ifranji in the desert—and, thusly, cleared his conscience?

What must Marion think, and Hubert, and John, and . . . ?

"I and my two younger brothers were given this honour whilst the men are away," Tariq was explaining, with another of his ingenuous smiles as one of the younger women brought—with a graceful sideways avoidance of Gamelyn's bandaged, propped-up leg—and presented a well-filled fired-clay platter, lowering it with some gravitas to the rug. Suckling kid, spiced hot-sweet with plenty of spongy flatbread, and so tender it nigh melted in the mouth.

The girl's dark eyes, resolutely polite and downcast, nevertheless kept flickering to their guest. Gamelyn didn't miss the elbow nudge and disapproving hiss another woman gave her—nor the soft reply the girl gave as excuse: she was curious, nothing more.

This, of course, incurred a rash of droll chuckles from the women seated in the corner. Gamelyn did the polite thing: he ignored them. And was grateful how the remnants of sunburn hid the worst curse of a fair complexion. He was too old to flush like a wet-eared squire!

"They're raiding!" Ahmad put in.

"We're too young to raid," another of the boy-children admitted, wry.

"But soon!" yet another supplied around a mouthful.

"All of you chatter and chortle like jackals!" The grandmother, like the small group of women, would eat later at their own hearth. Unlike them, she had fully introduced herself—Adila, daughter of Rahman, son of Mahmoud, of the Banu Seleym tribe of nomads—and sat at the foot of the wide rug that served as board, riding herd on the lads. "Heed the wisdom of your elder brother, and of your mothers and sisters. Be respectful. Let our honoured guest eat in some peace."

Quiet settled for a while. Gamelyn ate slow, careful. No hardship, there; his appetite wanted to be ravenous, but didn't quite remember how. It was the first real meal he'd had in . . . how long?

"How did you find me?" he asked.

"We were hunting," young Ahmad supplied, whilst snatching up another piece of flatbread. "We saw the kites."

Pointedly, Tariq offered Gamelyn the basket of flatbread. Ahmad muttered soft apology at his inconsideration.

Tariq slid him an eye any younger brother could well recognise, and Gamelyn hid a smile as Tariq continued, "It is well we did find you. You might have taken the lion, but he nearly took you, as well. My sister's medicines are the best in Syria." His gaze slid over to where a veiled woman stood at a table in the back, her back straight, her strong, veined hands busy with a wide-mouthed mortar and pestle. She nodded, but didn't look their way.

"You were very sick for a long while." Tariq refilled Gamelyn's cup with fresh, tepid water. "We took you, hid you in one of our most secure places; 'twas too dangerous to move you very far, at the first. My sister said you would lose the leg, did we do so. So," a shrug, "I sat with you, kept watch."

"All of us sat guard upon you!" Ahmad pointed out with a wrinkle of his nose at Tariq.

"All of us, indeed," Tariq consented, with a fond fluff at Ahmad's sun-streaked mop. "It has only been the past few days that we could bring you here." He seemed pensive.

"We had to wait until his father was gone," one of the boys said, and was hissed silent.

"It was not disobedience," Adila remarked into the quiet. "You obeyed my instructions, and I could do no less once Tariq told me of our guest's holy burden. It is *my* responsibility as to what might follow, should my son come to know we harboured one of the Ifranji. And I say again, it is the way of my father's fathers, to do no less than honour and acknowledge the blessing in the wilderness, the Nabi Yahyā, may his name be revered. It is moot that exceptions be given in His name. It is well."

It is well. An echo, very soft, the Relic stirring at his side. *I am in the wilderness, in my place. We have found my home. You will take me there. They will build no great halls to honour me, but leave me to the mercies of my desert, where none shall find me and all shall know me.*

"How did an Ifranji come to be here?" Ahmad's query wavered as the grandmother hissed at him.

"Kindly forgive him," Tariq told Gamelyn, with a smack to the back of Ahmad's head. "He is of that age, where the mouth overruns manners."

"It's a reasonable answer for a guest to give their honoured hosts," Gamelyn replied. "But it's a long story."

This, of course, had everyone angling forward. A good story wasn't to be denied, be it told within temporary havens of hide crouched upon arid plains, or mortared stone castles limned with moss and wet.

"We would be honoured"–this from Tariq, after a silent and subtle query towards his grandmother—"if you would tell how such an ordeal, and such a marvellous chance, came to pass."

Thoughts. And too many of 'em, whirling through Robyn's head. Waking. Sleeping.

Time was. Time is. Time could be . . .

Could be. Was. Speaking through a Veil of thisnow into . . . what?

But *speaking,* with John's way of talking. The girl knew the same signs as only John and Robyn and their closest compatriots used. Which meant that John still bided there, still alive. And Marion, too.

For the child was Marion's daughter.

And aye, the girl had the magic in spades, not only from her dam, but her sire. It might be unmannerly to claim a god's child had any earthly father, but things had changed since the old days. And no doubt, 'tennyrate, who'd fetched her that peculiar wilfulness, one to bid a child ride her pony nigh twenty miles to the Barrow Mere.

Oh, all right then, Marion'd no doubt claim that sort of wilfulness as his own. But he'd kept all his, surely, not given it to his sister's bairn like a whispered secret.

And this was a secret, even more. He'd not give so much as a hint of a girl-child peering through a drake's eye and a mirrored Mere. Not to the Barrow folk. Not a breath of her existence lest he endanger it or they decide she was some abandoned chit as needed a home in purgatory—weren't that what Gamelyn's people called a place where no one changed and no one died? He'd made the secret proper unmistakeable, with a growled threat to the gwyllion as had made them hide in the grotto, silent and still, for . . .

Hours? Days?

He wasn't sure.

Despite that when he'd first come here, he'd known time's passage by the sun slanting through the waters. Of late it seemed to move . . . parlous, like; at times treacherously fast, and others slow. And whilst he seemed to sleep seldom, 'twere deep, and who knew what had passed whilst he slumbered? Like the wyvern, waking only when he and the girl-child were both present, and looking.

The child had changed, too. From the first time through this latest—only three days, surely?—but again, the difference there, even if chancy, and Robyn trying to grasp it only to have it go *pfft!* through his fingers like smoke.

Mayhap that was why the Fae didn't come looking for him all that often—and what meant *often* here, anyroad? Did they only remember him as a faint dream that hadn't turned out well? Mayhap they too didn't know arse from tit when it came to marking the days, let alone years . . .

Years. How many here? How many . . . *there?*

He'd never thought to mark them, before. Never needed to. Thisnow had been enough and plenty, with stories and memories to mark before and runnel through after, all of it coming back around.

Nay, he had to think more like Gamelyn. More like Gamelyn's people, who had the brass to try tallying the spokes of a Wheel that would shrug off any count like the contrivance it were.

So. How long? The girl child—Aderyn, she'd told him—looked to be . . . bloody damn! As if he'd any proper idea on how to judge a bairn's age by looking at 'em!

More the question: would she return? When? And if she did, could he find some way, somehow . . . mayhap give her a message to take . . .

To Marion.

He hardly dared think it. Didn't know how 'twere possible, and did he get some kind of message to Marion, would it do any good? Change owt, or shift the bounds about this place? Or more, line it up with that one?

Yet sommat had given way—why or how, he didn't understand—but did the understanding matter? The wyvern had woken, kept waking, albeit brief but long enough to give this strange, mute connection, and . . .

Not only one Child, to be woken by Chaos. It is what you do best, My Own.

So surely it followed, there must be more to wake. Somehow.

Badiyat ash-Sham (the Syrian desert)
Waxing of Lammas, 1202 CE
Month of Shawwal, 598 AH

In the woodland, in the desert, it didn't matter. The *scrape-ting-scrape* of steel being sharpened remained a sound no child could resist. Shy at first, these young Badawī, albeit quite curious and friendly, which certainly suggested their clan was a loving one.

As Gamelyn took no notice, and kept to his work, the children kept inching closer, all agog. Soon the rock upon which he sat was ringed like a trouvère at court by at least twelve of them, standing and kneeling and sitting. One bold lad about eight years of age leaned against his knee.

Not the injured one, of course, cocked sideways. The infection had passed, the deep scores and lacerated muscles mending, albeit slow. It seemed, sometimes, that tiny, invisible imps lurked in wait, their daggers sharp and taking him unaware. Sleeping, waking, and particularly walking. Well, limping.

None of the children had offered to so much as touch the dagger.

Nephew Ian had not been so restrained—or respectful, come to it. He still bore a faint hairline scar from cutting a podgy wee palm upon Gamelyn's sword. Tom and Tibba—less entitled or self-indulgent through literal generations of peasant stock—had taken longer to openly display their fascination, more comfortable with the blacksmith's presence than any lord, even if that lord bore the Horns upon the Rites. And their little bird, Aderyn, had at first been shy towards the tall, white-clad stranger everyone said was her da, while Robbie had never been shy a day in his life . . .

God, but he missed his family. Mayhap, with the grace and goodwill of this clan of nomads, he would return to them.

One more duty. Gamelyn whispered it, silent, along the blade with every scrape, every swipe. *One more promise.*

Remembered how Much had been so insistent that he should perform this task as well, only giving way when he realised Gamelyn wanted—nay, needed—to do this. The motions soothed, the act of tending his steel its own kind of prayer and charm.

Remembered Marion taking to the blade unlike any woman he'd known. But then she'd arms hardened from a childhood of hard work and pulling a longbow . . .

"Sayyid alshier nar?" The reedy voice broke into his thoughts; for a moment he had to consciously translate it, and couldn't help smiling as he did.

Sir Fire-hair. . .

"Sir, why are you crying?" one of the girl-children asked, not for the first time. She traced fingers down her own cheeks as if to demonstrate.

And only then did Gamelyn taste the salt trickling down his cheeks. He smiled at the girl, said, very soft, "It's only that I miss my own children."

This caused quite a sensation. The boy-child leaning upon his knee shot upright. *"You?"*

"Aye." Gamelyn punctuated it with a scrape at his sword. "Me."

"But . . . but . . . !" The leaner had no words; another of the boys supplied them:

"But you cannot have children of your own!"

"I've heard the Warrior Magicians of the Ifranji aren't allowed to have any earthly desires!" another cut in.

A quick back-and-forth babble, both agreement and not. One of Gamelyn's eyebrows rose into his forelock. The tiny smile still quirking his lip, he waited it out.

"That cannot be so!"

"It is! It is!"

"I've heard the Warrior Monks geld themselves like eunuchs, so they cannot sire children!"

"Ai, such things are against the laws!"

"Unnatural!"

"The Prophet forbids such things even to beasts! The Ifranji ways are wicked!"

"This Ifranji is our guest." The patient rebuke came from the open tent flap, Tariq emerging into the light of the setting sun. "And blessed of Yah'yā."

The children fell silent. But their wide gazes spoke volumes, warily fastened upon the fire-haired, pale-eyed, possible eunuch.

"Nay," Gamelyn said, voice and whetstone both a soft scrape into quiet. "I'm no eunuch. I promise. And I do have children of my own. Three. One's still a babe in arms—"

Is she? Still in her mother's arms, still alive? One lost to us, after all. Do our children still thrive?

"—and the other two are about your age"—he pointed to the bold one, then another girl—"and yours."

"Have they hair like yours, sir?" One of the girls again. "And such skin, pale and spotted, like a good chestnut horse turned grey?"

Well, he had to admit that was a polite—and accurate—description of his colouring. "My son does. My daughter is black-haired, and the babe . . . I'm not sure. She was born after I . . . left."

Speaking it aloud just intensified the ache.

The children were making suitable sounds of pity and sorrow even as Tariq began shooing them away. "Let our guest have some peace, wretched ones!" He sounded ferocious, but the affection beneath his voice was plain.

The ache settled deeper.

As the children scattered to their own doings, Tariq ambled over and hunkered down next to Gamelyn. They sat in companionable quiet for some time, only an occasional call from the children and the *snick* and rasp of the whetstone against steel breaking it.

"It is of the Nizārī Ismaili, this blade, is it not? Like the amulet at your throat." Tariq shook his head. "You are a spirit indeed, to survive the judgment of the Silent Ones."

"I'm no more spirit than eunuch, Tariq."

The dark eyes met Gamelyn's, considering. "When we took you to the Cave of Spirits, you were nearly that yourself. And when you spoke . . . it was not to us, but . . . others."

The whetstone gave a slip and skitter. "The . . . Cave of Spirits?"

It floated stray memory behind Gamelyn's vision. Cavern walls covered in runes . . . runes, nay, ancient script, more like: burning cold against sand and rock. An impossible, glimmering wall of water held midair.

"It is . . . an unsettling place." Tariq peered at him, a tiny frown upon his brow. "You are distressed. We had little choice, I promise you. It was closest to where you had fallen, and my sister said you should not be moved any more than necessary. My family uses it as a hiding place but seldom, so we knew you would be safe there, for a time."

"Nay, that isn't it," Gamelyn assured. "It's just . . . you called it by name, and I . . . I knew the name."

Tariq merely nodded. "Such things happen in that place. Many of my people avoid it, but I found long ago that if it is given due honour, and I take care when there, for it . . . " He trailed off, frowning again.

"It is lonely," Gamelyn said, soft.

The frown vanished, replaced by a slight smile. As if Gamelyn had confirmed something Tariq dare not say aloud. The lad leaned forward, seemed about to say something.

Instead he glanced aside, gained his feet, and loped over to the tent as his grandmother emerged.

A quirk replaced the frown that had started to twitch at Gamelyn's brow. Tariq took Adila's arm—gingerly, as if sure she would shrug him away with a growl. But she leaned in, speaking to him. Tariq nodded, leading her over to where Gamelyn sat.

Sheathing the knife at his hip—a fine belt had been gifted him along with loose shalwar, keffiyeh, and robes—Gamelyn came to his feet with a bow as the old woman approached.

"We have been honoured by your stay, Gam'alīn alshier al-Nar," she told him. "You have survived your own *bisha'a*, and have proven through it, virtuous and strong."

Mayhap he had done. *Bisha'a* meant judgment by fire—nay, an ordeal, if Gamelyn remembered it correctly.

"You have not faltered in your holy purpose. The prophet, may his name and remains be blessed, is home—and this after he was taken away by infidels. But you cannot stay any longer, O honoured guest, even though your heart finds itself at home in our land."

"Grandmother, you—" Tariq protested.

Adila put a bony finger to her lips, then gestured to Gamelyn. "Come, my guest. See what awaits you."

Gamelyn followed to the far side of the main tent. Beneath a hide lean-to, three of the youngsters were putting the finishing touches to saddling a fine-limbed beauty of a chestnut mare.

"Grandmother?" Tariq was surprised, this time—and again she gently shushed him, spoke to Gamelyn.

"This is Lioness, whose dam escaped and bore her in the teeth of a storm. Ah, but her dam, Jewel—*she* was a mare! Blessed is her memory, for she'd the heart of thrice her kind—and in our horses, that is much, eh? She escaped our watchful eyes to foal on the plain, and a lion found her in her straits, even as one did you, eh, my guest? So the blessed dam of Lioness fought and vanquished her enemy even as her life's blood drained from her. We found the foal with a full belly—and defending her dam's body from jackals."

"I myself shot the jackals," Tariq supplied as Adila nodded. "I wrapped the foal in the lion's skin, and brought her home."

Indeed, the saddle was blanketed with a fawn-coloured skin. Gamelyn moved closer and patted the chestnut neck, fingers sliding down, curious, to the mottled white splotch upon the mare's shoulder.

"She has had it since birth. It is favoured," Tariq explained. "My father thought otherwise and would have left the foal for the jackals. I pleaded with him to bring her home, as gift to his honoured mother. The foal's dam had been Grandmother's favourite, you see. The mare was blessed amongst the Prophets; she had the bloody shoulder. It seemed to me a sign, the foal's marking, that her brave spirit lived on."

"It would have been treachery to condemn one her dam died

to bear." This from the grandmother, tracing the roan shoulder hairs as if she could see them. "My son is a righteous man, but often only sees what is before him. Eh, he can afford to, as he is a man, with two good eyes. But this ghost-wind mark is a blessed reminder: we are no more, and no less, than what we leave behind.

"Tariq goes with you." Her change of subject came abrupt. "And will forget where the Nabi Yahyā goes, as He wishes. As far as the mountains and the sea, should my grandson choose to guide your return to the west. But you must go soon."

"I, Grandmother?" Tariq queried, softly.

"We have an obligation to our guest. He cannot yet walk, but surely he will manage riding. You, son of my son, can see him safe where he must go, ride hard, and return to us. Your father and the first of my sons has no reason to love an Ifranji—nay, not even one who has as companions the Nizārī Ismaili. Saddle your horse."

"Forgive me, mother of my father, but the first of your sons left the seventh of *his* sons to guard our family. Surely he will heed your wisdom about our guest, even as he did with Lioness."

"But Lioness is a mare, and thus of much more account to a Bedawī chieftain. Forgive my words, O guest, but that is how my son will see it."

Gamelyn nodded. Tariq started another protest.

"Ah, but hear me, grandson." Adila snugged closer to the young man, shaking his arm just a little. "Our men thought to return upon the last sliver of the waning moon. It could be longer, or it could be tonight. Knowing that, it is in my power to release you from your oath, give you leave to go. Our guest does not know our territory as we must, and his errand is most holy; I see it even if others would see only with their eyes. I say it is best if both of you depart before the sun sets. You, Tariq ibn Malik ibn Karim al-Banu Sulaym, and I, Adila bint Rahman ibn Mahmoud al-Banu Seleym, elder of this clan and dam of our respected chieftain, shall make this decision. Your father shall be angry at what he sees as an old woman's meddling, but he shall also uphold the wake of it when he understands. Even if he would contradict the decision itself, were it left to his making."

Gamelyn stayed silent, scratching the mare's withers. She, in turn, had stretched her neck to nibble and groom at his near hip.

"As you wish, Grandmother." Tariq tilted his head, gathered his young brothers by eye, and went to do as bidden.

The old woman took something from the voluminous folds of her robes, began braiding it into the roany hairs atop the mare's tail. "You lay as if dead for some time, fire-haired stranger. Your holy errand gave you leave to tread the streets of Paradise, where there is no Law. I shall remind my firstborn of this.

"And remember, Gam'alīn Alshier al-Nar, should we meet again in another time and place: you were a guest of the Hamid clan of the Banu Suleym."

"May my heart be cut from my body do I forget the tent of Adila bint Rahman ibn Mahmoud al-Banu Seleym," Gamelyn told her, quiet. "I shall tell stories and blessings about our fires at night, and my children's children shall know your names. I am in your debt. You have made a return to my loved ones possible."

"Then any debt is repaid." Adila turned away, voice wafting behind her. "All we have is family and God. His grace be upon you."

Gamelyn watched her vanish into the tent shadows. Another memory stole in, honey and rue: *It's time to come home, Gamelyn.*

Aye, mayhap. Again, a whisper that had been the Baptist's voice. He was gone, with only His skull weighting the bag, yet something of His presence lingered. *You have succeeded where your Masters have failed, found answers.*

Save within the one, remaining riddle.

The most beloved one, whose face you see in all things.

"I will find you," Gamelyn whispered, peering at the ghostly shoulder of the chestnut mare, but seeing another spectre, just out of reach. "And this will be my last journey across the Sea, ever."

- XVI -

Marion's Book of Hours
Waxing of Lammas, 1202
7 years, 7 months, 9 days
11 months, 9 days
<u>Our Lords Shall Return</u>

I've had no heart to so much as open my Hours for some months.

The weather has been mild and pleasant, and the harvest continues early, plentiful... spectacular, in fact, and that still has the power to seize my breath upon the word: Sacrifice. Perhaps it was made upon your bones and blood, my husband, and mayhap even now you and Robyn are somehow together in the otherworlds...

Nay. I cannot believe it. I won't. I have to believe you are alive, beloved friend, as our Robyn is alive. As John said, I have no choice. The Sacrifice is made in our separation and pain of longing, and the riving of the Ceugant. It cannot last.

Both my lords shall return

Therefore it is well past time I set pen to parchment, not only to mark the days in mourning and hope, but so the stories live. So you both will be able to catch up on the small details of your family's lives. Know what progresses here.

So. Tickhill's hall will be filled to bursting for the harvest-tide. Not only our own people, hanging mommets upon the eaves, but Alais and Otho are here with us. No doubt you, Gamelyn, would say all the better to keep an eye upon your brother in particular, and I can't disagree. But their son bides here, and it is nice that Alais should see him as she can; she misses him. And is breeding again, which worries me.

War is upon us, and the King has employed mercenaries, not only in Normandy, but here, in England. While some are said to be bound to the king by fierce oaths, there's no grounds to trust such men. They fear neither their God nor the Church, and heed no power other than hard cash and the promise of spoil. Only this past fortnight Gilbert advised me of several routs by mercenaries in the Peak Forest—his recourse being take them out by stealth and just as quietly get rid of the bodies.

Few of the lords fancy the King's decision; Huntingdon, de Ferrars and the Marshal in particular spoke against it, with the latter two preferring to install castellans bound instead of bought as they follow their liege to war with France.

Many are gone to war, husband, and we are vigilant. King John might have given oath to the Old Religion, but I'm not sure how long he will hold that oath. It is well he has been away from the Rites, for my own comfort, but it could mean that he heeds them less in the wake of other pressures, other powers.

And the Shire Wode's mystique lingers. Nottingham is now held by the third sheriff in as many years. The Hunt still rings those walls.

If only it could help us find Robyn.

We take care, and be assured I've no more compunction to send pirates—or grasping lords—to their hell than does Gilbert and our foresters. Mayhap I'll send a message north to the Moorlands, see about gathering a few 'privateers' of my own.

"Robbie? Have you seen your sister?"

"Nay, but I don't care." Her son sat ensconced upon a woollen rug in the solar adjoining Marion's bedchamber, gilded in morning light and surrounded by a litter of wooden horses and various figures. John had brought them to mark the season—his own work, of course, with that little hint of the magic he couldn't help but impart to anything he carved. "She went off riding, even though she promised to play with *me*. Marjory's too little, and Tom and Tibba're off with family down south. Unca John's gone back to his draughty old cave, and Auntie Aelwyn and Unca David's all busy, and all Ian does any more is practice riding his horse!"

"Well," Marion gave the tapestry beside the entry a twitch, "Ian has sommat to prove to his da."

"Ian's da thinks he's useless at riding. And he is, sort of."

"Hsst, boy! I'll not have you repeating such unkindness. Be compassionate to your cousin. We've all things we're born doing, and things we have to work at."

Rob gave this due consideration, shrugged it off beneath a new grievance. "Well, Ian's mam'll sometimes play with me. Eri used to play all the time, now she's just as bad as Ian at being off doing sommat. It en't fair, Mam!"

To be sure, Marion needed to speak with the shepherds, make sure someone could see Aderyn safely back. Surely she wasn't riding that far alone.

Then she remembered another lord's child, riding to Loxley every chance he could fetch. Gamelyn had been Aderyn's elder, but not by all that much.

And it had been only yesterday a messenger had come to ask help for the villages nigh to Mam Tor—and while Peveril and Castleton paid due to de Ferrars, the latter, as well as villages north and east, were under the protection of Tickhill. Most of them proper Heathens, as well. Her people, being threatened by a lot of Motherless Franks! It might be her great-granda's time all over again, with Willy Bastard's men ravaging the countryside just because they could.

And they weren't in the Wode, here, able to take them out from a well-chosen hiding place and scarper into the forest. Nay, this was a bloody great castle, hunched all bold and "come for me", and England was at war.

"—lately it's worse! I know she's all bent on sommat of late, an' keeping it from me, an' all the while haring after it, though I even found my extra horses just for her, since she never likes playing with soldiers, just the horses and the Hounds—"

True enough, a pack of tiny Hounds guarded the perimeter of wee Robbie's clash of figures. Special, these, fashioned from palest ash, though John had refused to overly detail them or tip the ears crimson, sure that embodying such things too carefully was unwise. Much had agreed; hearken to Nottingham, after all. But . . .

"Bent on sommat?" Marion gathered up all her wandering thoughts and penned them. "What would that be, pet?"

But Rob's attention swerved upon the solar's doorway. "Uncle!" he screeched, launching himself from the floor, Hounds as well as tiny soldiers scattering in his wake.

Much caught the child and swung him up on one shoulder—and that without so much as breaking stride or fumbling the ziggurat of buttered bread in one hand, Marion considered with an admiring smirk. Her man was clad for riding—Tickhill's burgundy muting the jingle of mail tunic and trous as he strode over, sword and scabbard swinging at his hip, gloves tucked at his belt.

"Aderyn's well enough, love," he assured. "I saw her heading out nigh t' sunrise with the grazers. I told them to keep an eye on her, see her safely back t—Hoy! Son! Who said this bread had your name on it?"

Robbie squirmed on Much's shoulder, making grabby hands. "You did! 'Cause you said you could smell bread so you were going to the kitchens, and did I want any, did you manage to fetch some this way."

With his lovely, infectious laugh, Much handed over a piece, crossing the solar to extend the remainder to Marion. "Just as you like it, love; fresh from the ovens five minutes ago, just the wee scrape of butter."

Rob already wore the latter from the thick layer spread over not only his piece, but Much's.

"At least we've butter a-plenty this year," she said, sliding a hand into the curve of Much's elbow. "Enough to satisfy two of my favourite menfolk. Are you off, then?"

"Soon enough, aye. We'll head across the Peak, and Gilly's to meet us nigh to Hathersage."

Marion nodded, mouth full of the fragrant, nutty bread. Bliss.

"We'll bear the messenger company back t' his place. And I asked young Ian to come along." Brows rising, he met her eyes. "Neither of us has told his da. We're leaving that t' you. 'Twill do the lad good, to quit the place for a couple of days, and should we see any action, he'll be well able without—"

Without his father lurking, Marion finished, silent, nodding. Otho and Alais weren't due to leave for another se'nnight.

"*That* 'un's sitting to sup with Huntingdon's man. I'm hoping he en't fetching any news you should already have."

"Nay, I spoke with the man upon his arrival yesterday. Both roads and weather have been forgiving, so his lord the Earl should arrive before market opens. He'll bring more news, not only about the North, but France."

"I wish I could go fight the bloody Franks!" Rob announced, waving a crust of his bread like a dagger.

No, you don't, Marion swore. Thank the Lady he was entirely too young for anything other than riding his pony and mastering the light recurve with which he practiced every day. He'd taken to it—'twere in the blood, of course—and moreover was spoiled for choice when it came to teachers. She smiled and snugged closer to Much's arm.

"It's not funny, Mam." Robbie misinterpreted her expression. "I want to be a knight. An archer knight, like the Saracens from Moorlands—mmph!"

Much had shoved another scrap of bread in his mouth. "I'll go with a lighter heart, love, do you tell me you've sent that message along t' Moorlands."

"I have indeed, and received hope we'll see a response come market day there, as well."

"Aye, well, then." Much swung Rob down with a fond smack to his backside. "You'll have plenty of support, even should I not return for market day. Himself the Earl's not about to travel 'crost country unarmed."

"Aye, well then," she echoed, twining both arms about his neck, and lifting her face to his. "Let me lighten that heart of yours even more before you leave, aye?"

A kiss, long and lingering, and when Rob tugged at her skirts she sighed, ignored him.

Until "Mam!" Another tug. "Aunt Alais is waiting at the corridor. She keeps pacing and looking around."

Ⓘ

"Your guard captain," Alais ventured, hesitant, "seems a goodly man."

"He is." Marion always spoke with consideration to her sister-in-law. They'd become friends, albeit not intimate ones even if Alais herself thought so. But nay, intimacy meant trust, and Marion couldn't. She held too many precious—too many dangerous—secrets.

"Has the man been with you long?"

"Aye, and with Gamelyn even longer." *Even back when Gamelyn's father held this place with his three sons and you, as Otho's wife the only lady. Much would have been nowt but a peasant boy to your like, of no notice save, mayhap, crossbow fodder.* "He served the Templars as Gamelyn's paxman the whole of their time in Outremer."

"Ah." Respect settled over hesitancy, if not wholly.

They'd retired to the lower hall, a bottle of wine shared between them and several projects to hand, enjoying a rare moment of quiet. Marjory slept in the upstairs solar under the watchful eye of Berta; Rob, toys long abandoned, had scarpered outside; even Alais' omnipresent maidservant had been set to sorting mending in the storeroom with several of her Tickhill cronies. Alais bent to repairing a tapestry. Indeed, the afternoon had proven a goodly excuse for Marion herself to catch up on neglected handiwork. A rush mat lengthened, bit by bit, over her lap, and she wove quickly and skilfully, hoping to replace several frayed nigh to bits.

"It's plain your guard captain is fond of you. And you, of him."

Since you saw us snogging—and aye, 'twere a foolish thing to be doing with guests about, even in me own solar—I think that's a proper tolerable description. Tempting, to just say it, but Marion just smiled, and kept working.

Alais shifted in her chair, put a hand to her gravid belly and stretched to one side with a sigh.

"Let me fetch you another cushion, aye?" Marion started to set her work aside, but Alais waved it away.

"I fear it won't help. I'll walk a few paces." She fetched action to words, heaving herself from the chair, her amble at first hesitant, then lengthening. "Ah. Better. You know how it is."

Marion nodded, though in truth she did *and* didn't. Coming to childbed meant pain and danger, nowt but. Still, Marion herself had been blessed to bear hers with comparative ease, even the wee, beautiful boy that hadn't lived past a se'nnight. With keen, wary eyes Marion considered Alais, who seemed overlarge for being due three months hence. Aye, not only that, but overly old for 't. Alais had already lost several between this one and Edyth, her youngest, and hadn't the conformation of a woman who'd ever bear children without difficulty. Too narrow and short in the cradle of her hip, despite a length of stride and reach—and that latter boded ill in Marion's experience as well, with an unborn bairn likely to be just as long of limb, easily entangled in a narrow space.

Alais was focused on other concerns, however. "Every castle has ears beyond our control, Marion. Even Tickhill. Especially Tickhill, I'll warrant, with all its . . . peculiarities and the resultant stories flying about. Mostly nonsense, to be sure. 'Tis true that any capable wortwife is looked at askance, but one in particular endures alongside that." Still pacing back and forth, one hand to the small of her back, Alais gave a meaningful and sidewise glance. "Even Otho has noticed the guard captain. He means to speak with Gamelyn, if"—a quick revision—"*when* he returns."

If. When. Marion found her fingers tangling in her weaving but said, light, "He'll be waiting a while, I fear. But even more, I fear your lord husband shall find *my* lord husband . . . unreceptive. And displeased by the interference."

In slow advance towards her sewing frame, Alais sighed and halted, squinting at a row of stitches. "I merely mention it for your own good." Her voice lowered. "There has been talk, in some households, how a castle of such vast importance as Tickhill needs a present and stable masculine hand."

Marion stiffened.

"I, of course, well comprehend the nonsense of such talk. You run this place with enviable efficiency—particularly when one considers your background." Alais peered over the frame at Marion, her smile gentle, wry—and thoroughly oblivious to what likely would have been an intentional dig from another of her class and privilege. "You and I well know who truly has charge over our demesnes."

Marion had to smile back. It was true enough, though Alais herself no longer openly displayed her sovereignty.

Well, then, she didn't have to, did she?

"I also comprehend how some aspects of marriage can be . . . unsatisfying. While some might think being wived to an absent lord proves more blessing than curse . . . well. Even Holy Church realises we have conjugal rights and needs. You and I are also lucky in that we're both very fond of our husbands. And truly your . . . frustration is understandable, what with Gamelyn absent so much, and inclined to . . . " She let it trail away, reseating herself and pretending to focus upon the tapestry.

"Inclined how?" Marion said, too sweetly. "Whatever do you mean?"

Alais slid her a look that plainly stated *you know damned well what I mean.*

"And 'tis a certainty that, unlike wives, husbands are allowed to indulge their inclinations." Marion shrugged, twisting at a recalcitrant reed. "I assure you, 'tis Gamelyn's absence as keeps him from my bed, much more than any other lovers he might fancy. And when he *is* here, he's loving and attentive as I could wish."

"Well, and there's no doubt in *my* mind who sired your children!" Alais's tone came as vehement as her jab with the thick tapestry needle.

Marion felt another, deeper ripple of disquiet. This remained the one spot never left undefended. Too much at stake, not only for Gamelyn and herself, but the children's future. "Nor in mine."

Alais didn't look up for a few moments, seeming lost in her work. Marion frowned as the woman shifted in her chair, but smoothed it away as Alais met Marion's gaze, a purposeful smile twitching her lip. "It's quite obvious to anyone with eyes that Gamelyn loves his children ever as much as his father loved him. And the only man I've ever known to bear a cuckold's horns with such serene acceptance is Joseph. I only mention any of this because . . . " She hesitated, angled forward—carefully—and covered Marion's hands with one of her own. "He has been gone overlong, and rumours fly like crows to battle. You need take care, Marion. That's all I mean to say."

Marion met her gaze for a long moment, then nodded.

"Here you are, my dear!" Otho's voice could fill a hall and did now, rolling up and reverberating the ceiling beams.

Several gwyllion perched there hissed; the remainder ignored him, watching Marion attentive as hounds.

Alais patted Marion's hand before letting go, with a smile rising to greet her husband. "Your timing is, as ever, perfect, Otho. I'm not sure this flax is quite the right colour, and as it's your favourite hanging, I thought . . . " Her hand gave a sudden jerk. The frame wobbled on its stand, would have fallen over had Marion not lurched forward and grabbed it.

Alais sank down, sudden, as if someone had kicked her shins. Marion leapt up, her own handiwork crumpling on the floor, and steadied her.

"Alais?" Otho strode over, claimed supportive duty with both arms. It gave Marion the chance to angle back and peer into Alais's face, pinched white save for a spot of livid colour high on each cheek.

In the next breath, Marion bent down and snatched her kirtles upward. Her thighs were stained damp; as Marion watched, another gush ran down to splat upon the flooring. Not clear. Crimson.

Alais wobbled again, and Otho grabbed her, said her name.

"It's all right, love. It'll be all right." Alais leaned hard against Otho; he grasped her hand and drew it to his chest as Marion looked up and met his gaze. She didn't have to tell him; he knew.

"I fear it's too early," Alais whispered, then jerked again.

Another contraction—not a good one, either. Marion watched it ripple beneath fabric. More blood, too.

"Take her—gentle, mind!" Marion ordered, lurching to her feet. "Your rooms'll do; they're warmed and clean. I'll have the hall man fetch Aelwyn!"

Without another word, Otho swept his wife into his arms, and carried her from the solar and down the hallway.

Ⓘ

Mam said you have the magic, stronger than most. But why don't you come back to us, then?

The child had returned. And the wyvern—recognising her, responding—once again played visual conduit between two worlds. Yet it did not wake, not fully, and the chain upon its neck vibrated, as if sensing something untowards broaching its spells.

She misses you. Da misses you. They want you to come back. Why don't you?

Robyn had already spent much of their scant communications asking after his people—and the time after rocking their memories close, mourning. *There's a spell as holds the Fae prisoned here. It holds me, too. But I want to find a way to break it.*

John said that Mam and Da tried to break it, several times. Da's been gone so long, to some faraway place to find. . . keys, he said. I want him to come home, I. . . Are there locks where you are? Uncle David's proper good at picking locks. He got one loose that Robbie'd fastened with the key inside, and—

Nay, girl. He didn't mean to be so brusque—he ached to ask after every name she uttered. And Gamelyn—had he left of his own accord, or under orders from those Templars he'd supposedly left for good? And how *dare* he go back to them, how *bloody* dare he up and leave their land! He was Summerlord, and with Winter banished, nowt to . . .

But she mightn't understand. And thisnow could, at any moment, prove enemy. He had to speak quick, plain. *Not a lock, pet. But like it, sure, and one even David wain't be picking. Is it autumn, then?*

Just past Lammas. Everyone's saying it's been uncommon warm all season, and. . . Something took Aderyn's attention for the briefest of moments; she looked aside, frowning. *Do you hear that?*

A shake of head. Robyn couldn't hear her side any more than she could his. *Look back to me,* he willed, suddenly aware of his pulse pounding out the moments: *one-and two-and three-and. . .* and kept saying her name against the Veil—as if 'twould help.

Finally, Aderyn did turn back to him. He took quick advantage. *Lass, don't turn away! I can't talk to you that way, y'know, and I need you to remember sommat for me. I need you to take a message for me, to your mam.*

The child didn't seem too sure of this; she kept glancing behind her, brows knit. *She doesn't know I come here. I'll be in a lot of trouble, did she know, and she mightn't let me come again.*

Robyn clenched his fists just before he signed something harsh, choked impatience back with the memory of his own scapes, most of which his mam had never known, and thank the Lady for that. *I think when you tell her why, she won't be so angry. Mayhap she'll come with you, aye?*

I don't think so. The child's face reflected more uncertainty. *She hates the Mere. I think I hear hoofbeats, lots of them. Can you hear?*

Nay, he couldn't hear a thing, and more, the Mere was misting up, the wyvern twitching, half waking, and sending silt upward in great draughts, and . . .

Hates. This, despite that the Mere was the Lady's, the one place remaining solely Hers. Questions gathered upon Robyn's tongue like the tiny bubbles of air peeling away from the wyvern's iron shackle.

He swallowed them, adamant. *If you tell your mam you saw me here, pet, she'll come. That I promise you. I really need you to tell her how we've been speaking. It's so very important. It might make the difference between me being lost here forever and coming home.*

The last bided more manipulation than any truth he could swear to. But it worked. Aderyn's eyes riveted to his—or what she saw of his through the water and silt, focused through a water-drake's eye.

She still didn't fancy it, that was plain, but his last words had indeed tipped the balance. *What do you want me to tell her?*

First, tell her what you've seen in the Mere.

What if she doesn't believe me? Sometimes people don't believe things. . .

She'll believe you. Just tell her what you've seen. Describe how you saw me, the sleeping wyvern, all of it.

The child bit her lip and nodded.

Right, then. If—

Sudden thunder reverberated through the Veil, felt in his chest rather than filling his ears. The child whirled, fell halfway into the water, and that, too, slapped his senses in an oddling, unsounded mix.

The wyvern twisted against the bottom. A cloud of silt covered Aderyn—or seemed to, because Robyn could still sense her presence there, full of fright. As the silt began dispersing into images, he knew why . . .

A sound of thunder filling the Wode. An armed cadre of soldiers, some mounted, some running. None of them none clad in a lord's colours—but all armed to the teeth and eager.

And the child, a darkling ghost between the mists, hunkering low in the grass until she realises: what they both see in the Mere is not nigh to the Mere. It's a Sight, a Sensing, riding the currents of possibility.

Invasion. The predators finding easy prey, upon the chase and stalk, and advancing upon a tall, white tower. Tickhill's gates are open to the weather, bridge down across the moat, and curtain wall hung with flags for market day . . .

I have to warn them! The child rose, half damp and all afraid.

Nay, lass! Shouted and signed both, Robyn hurled himself at the Veil, desperate. *Stay in the forest! Stay hidden until—!*

But it was too late. She'd already gone.

Midmorning had turned into afternoon, and now more lights were being kindled as the bedchamber darkened into dusk. Most of Tickhill lay quiet, oddly so—yet it was a false one, in the wake of periodic screams from the upper chambers of the keep.

Within that chamber, Berta was taking a turn in propping up

Alais, seated behind her. Aelwyn knelt between her legs, whilst Marion kept up the chanting singsong that every midwife possessed voice, administering judicious sips of tisane—a brew comprised of raspberry leaf and hyssop, laced with cohosh and pennyroyal. All of them whispered blessings between, both willing and witching that the bairn should turn beneath Aelwyn's gentle manipulations.

Aelwyn'd the smallest hands, after all.

More noise, now—a kerfuffle at the outer door to the chambers. It woke Alais, who'd slipped into the odd doze that often came between contractions. Her eyes sought Marion's, pleading.

"It's taking too long. It's too early."

"We know nowt until Aelwyn has the bairn turned. Here, take another sip, rest as you can."

More noise; it sounded like a man's voice? What man would dare to enter a lying in?

Alais twitched, but sipped and swallowed dutifully.

"See what's going on!" Marion snapped at Alais's maidservant— and to be sure, the girl had proven proper useless save for fetching the odd kettle of hot water and wringing her hands.

It took a further hiss and glare to send the girl bolting for the door. Marion followed her progress with a quick, harried glance, saw two other women there, barring the open door with their bodies.

"You can't come in here!"

"Then tell your lady I must speak with her!" David's voice rose plain into the rafters. "It's urgent!"

"He wouldn't barge in like this, lessen 'twere dire," Aelwyn muttered and Marion had to agree. "I can manage wit' Berta well enough the now. You'd best go see."

Still Marion hesitated, with a glance at Alais. Thankfully she'd nodded off again; she'd not know anyone had left.

The look on David's face, as Marion slid past the trio of fierce lying-in guardians, made her glad she'd answered. His plaint, however, didn't match his urgency—and was that young Ian at his shoulder, trying to peer past Marion to where his mother lay? What was Ian still doing here?

"Otho's raised the gates!" David growled.

Cheeky of him, mayhap, but . . . "Why are you coming t' me now, natterin' about the gates at sunset? We've his wife in"—*a really bad childbed*, she started to say, but a quick glance to Ian's face silenced it—"in some straits, so she needs me about now . . . and what are you *doing* here, Ian-lad? You're supposed to be on the road with Much!"

"I stayed because of Mama, Aunt Marion, and David has tried, he really has, to tell Papa, and so did I—"

"Milord's brother brushed me aside," David put in. "Even though I tried to tell him how the lass en't returned!"

"The lass—"

"Aderyn! She rode off on her pony this mornin', and the stable lads en't seen her since, and *still* milord the poncy bastard's ordered the gates closed!"

"Sweet Lady," Marion breathed.

A wavering cry rose from behind her. Ian flinched and craned his neck, trying to see. David looked away.

No time. No *time.*

"Send several of the lads out."

"And if Himself says no?"

"Otho has no authority here!"

"He seems to think he does, lass."

"Marion!" Aelwyn's voice, quiet but urgent.

"Then tell him I can abandon his wife just so I can come and slap his thick head from his shoulders, or he can demonstrate he is, after all, more concerned for Alais than pissing on our gates!"

David nodded. Ian looked a mix of pleased, troubled, and fascinated.

"Tie *him* to a damned pillar if you must." *And only fitting, seeing how he did the same to Gamelyn once.*

"I'll send several of our people out to find her." In the face of support, David took heart. "Ones who aren't so a-feared of th' Wode."

"I'll go." Ian said, stout. "I'll go, and take several of the soldiers who stayed behind."

"Ian," Marion started, "I can't ask you to leave now, and—"

Another cry interrupted her, turning into a wail. One of the women came running up, tugging at Marion's arm. "Aelwyn needs you, milady."

"I can't do anything for Mum," the boy insisted. "You can. And I can do this."

"Marion!"

Marion allowed herself to be dragged backward. "Help him, David. And Ian . . ."

"I'll find her," the lad vowed. "Just like you'll see to my mum."

- Entr'acte -

It hadn't happened, not yet.

Aderyn wasn't sure how she knew, but she did. If she could just make it home, get there fast enough, maybe she could stop it from happening.

She'd stopped at the crossroads to give Rutterkin a quick breather. The pony, conditioned to long jaunts at a good trot, wasn't so keen with the desperate pace they'd taken. Sweat matted his thick coat, his breathing came huge-quick, and he didn't seem all that interested in the spring grass, even.

Come on, boy, she willed, counting each heave of his sides and willing them smoother. *You can do it. You have to.*

As if he'd heard, Rutterkin twitched his ears. She patted him as he lifted his nose southward. It made her uneasy. And sure enough, only a few breaths later, a shout and an answering bark of laughter echoed up and over the trees.

Friend? Or foe? Please let it be a friend, one she could trust to take the message swifter than pony legs could manage. Save her home, save Rutterkin from running himself into founder!

Nay, Daughter, these are no friends to you. Time to go.

The Voice had been with her since she'd left the Mere; not in her ears, but in her head . . . in her bones. It sounded like her Uncle Robyn had looked: dark and full and . . . deep, somehow. Not all broad and solid like Much, or her da, but still. Powerful.

Mayhap it was Uncle Robyn, and he'd found a way to be with them, after all.

Aderyn drummed her heels against the pony's sides, but Rutterkin baulked.

A tiny half-growl half-hiss purled in her throat, and she kicked harder. The pony trotted on a few paces, but she couldn't get him to canter no matter that she kicked until the blood pounded in her temples. The trot slowed, became a walk. She tried screaming at him; of course, it escaped in a hiss and sob of breath. Tears burning her eyes and hiccupping her chest, Aderyn unwound her belt and used it on his broad buttocks.

Rutterkin merely set his jaw and haunches akin to stone, sulled up, and refused to move another step.

Run, child. Leave the pony! Come into the Wode!

The riders were closer, the sound of hoofbeats and voices drowning out whatever the Voice had to say.

A sudden wind, stark and nigh howling through the clearing, rippled her tunic and threw her hair upwards. Dirt spattered at her legs. Rutterkin whirled on his haunches. Aderyn grabbed mane, but found her hands closing on empty air as the pony slid out from beneath her and she hit the dirt.

It spangled stars before her eyes and hoisted the air from her lungs. Aderyn lay there, eyeing trees and sky and willing just . . . one . . . breath . . . Finally it came, a sudden raspy cough. It took several more before she could roll to her feet.

'Twere then she saw the haunches of her pony disappearing off the road and behind a gorse. She didn't need breath to curse, as silent but imaginative-fierce as ever Uncle David had when Uncle Much beat him at toss-bones.

The wind died, as if it had never been there. The ground trembled with the approach of the mounted men.

And the impulse, the compulsion: *Flee.*

The riders trotted round the far bend just as she made a fallen-down elm, and she spared a glance mid-scramble atop the log.

'Twas her undoing.

Soldiers, some mounted and some afoot. But more, her cousin Ian rode with them, tall in Tierce's saddle between two of the mounted men. Relief filled her and, ignoring any warning Voice, Aderyn slid down the log and started towards them.

The soldiers saw her, pulled up.

Ian's eyes met hers, and widened from surly to scared. "Aderyn, no!" It was shrill. "*Run!*"

One of the men turned, swinging a ham-sized fist. It caught Ian along the jaw, should have knocked him from the saddle. It didn't. Aderyn saw he was tied to it. Tierce bolted forward, but only managed an abortive leap before he, too, jerked back, haunches swinging. Two ropes were fastened to his bridle, held taut by the men riding on each side of Ian.

The leader peered at Ian, then Aderyn. One bushy eyebrow climbed upward and disappeared beneath his helmet. Then he shrugged and growled, "*Aller chercher!*"

"No!" Ian shouted. "*Run, Eri!*"

But Aderyn was so angry to see Ian slapped sideways again that she actually started for them instead of away.

Two horsemen broke ranks and started for her.

Aderyn turned and ran for the trees.

Not that it did any good. They came crashing after her.

Aderyn took refuge against the fallen elm and threw stones at them. Hit them, too; curses spewed into the air. One horse, its rider urging it to jump the elm, decided it had enough of stones from the sky and refused, spinning away; the rider nearly went headfirst over the elm's broken upper branches. More curses. The second rider lashed his horse forward, leapt the log that sheltered Aderyn, and spun to face her. Aderyn tried to dart sideways. The massive body whirled and bunched, blocking her. She tried again, and again, but to the same ends. Shod hoofs tore up the moist earth, the horse's breath heating her skin—the horse was that close—keeping her cornered against the fallen log.

The man let out an exasperated sound, and bent over in his saddle, snatching her by one arm. She bit him, hard. He dropped her with another, viler curse. Leaping the log, Aderyn headed back the way she'd come.

Instead she nearly ran into a wide, bay shoulder and a mailed leg hanging beyond. The horse danced in place, champing its bits, but Aderyn didn't so much as look up. Instead she dived beneath the horse's belly, hit rolling, and came up running.

Laughter echoed in the trees, mocking. Within a stride the bay was upon her. Broad fingers tangled hard in her hair, hauled her up in the air to dangle like a trout, then flung her face-down over the saddle pommel.

She wanted to scream—of course couldn't—and settled for kicking and squirming. Her captor merely laughed and tangled his fingers tighter, shoving her face against greasy leather.

"*Petit chat sauvage!*" one swore—likely the one she'd bitten. She knew enough Frankish to know it wasn't complimentary. Her captor merely gave another laugh, said something altogether unintelligible, and spurred his horse into a canter.

And while Aderyn had done her share of cantering—that and a full out gallop were her favourite gaits—she'd never done it slung over the pommel like a sack of grain. It knocked the breath from her, sent sparkles before her eyes. Only a matter of a few strides, but as they reached the remainder of the company, Aderyn struggled for breath. The reek of the leather filled her nose, and her lungs refused anything but hoarse, shallow gasps.

"Don't smother it, now. It might prove useful, just like the boy, aye?" The leader's voice—in Frankish again—but Aderyn's captor didn't answer in same, his talk full of syllables that rang almost musical. His laugh, however, was guttural, harsh against her senses as the man hauled her around to sit up.

By the hair, again. She hissed and started struggling. Ian caught her eyes and shook his head, albeit slight. The bruises on his face, the cut on his lip, his ripped tunic—all coerced obedience.

And she could breathe, again.

"So, boy," the leader drawled at Ian. "Who is this we've found, eh? May it happen you know some grubby peasant child, and one worth more of our time than to break its neck and toss it aside?"

Ian growled a gutter curse and angled forward. Tierce rolled air through his nostrils in warning, gathering on his haunches and spoiling for a fight.

One of the men holding the stallion's rope shanked his nose, hard. It merely generated more fury. Tierce bared his teeth, dancing in place, snaked his head and snapped—and he'd have grabbed and shaken the man if the other hadn't held his rope taut.

"Stop it," the leader said, flat. "Can't you see it's a warhorse? Control your mount, boy, or we'll cut his throat and the child's as well."

Controlling Tierce had never been Ian's strongest gift. Aderyn watched, willing the horse calm, unwilling to so much as move. But Ian lifted his chin, relaxed into the saddle and lengthened his leg. The horse calmed, somewhat, but the eye he slid his captors proved him ready for the attack, when it came.

"Good, boy," the leader approved. "No doubt in my mind you're exactly who that one guard babbled on about, but—"

The look on Ian's face pinched sudden and grey.

"—who is this child?"

Ian looked . . . sick, almost, and that frightened Aderyn even more.

Uncle Robyn, where are you?

But no Voice vibrated her bones this time. She sensed nothing but her pulse, pounding her ears all fearful-hot.

Meanwhile, her captor was picking at the hem of her tunic with sallow, nimble fingers, and rumbled something all smooth-quick.

The leader nodded. "My friend is correct, eh? Boy? Or do you not understand the Slav's talk?"

Ian turned his face away, grey smoothing into chill. Aderyn watched, her stomach doing flip-flops.

"Yaro says she is no peasant child, not with clothing so fine. So, lordling, tell me: who is this black-eyed little wildcat who bites my men, eh?"

Ian refused to answer. The leader kneed his mount closer and grabbed a fistful of sandy hair, yanked sideways. "*Who*, boy?"

The bruises on Ian's face went all the more livid, crimson against pale.

Aderyn's captor—Yaro—spoke again, and the last phrase sounded like her name.

The leader gave him an incredulous look, then smiled.

And the Voice returned.

Be strong, Daughter. Wait, and hold fast.

- XVII -

This much of the ordeal, over and done. Hours of pain and blood, only in the end to lose the babe—and just as likely the mother, too, before it was done.

Death and birthing, as her mam had always said, lay fiercely intertwined.

Marion and Aelwyn had stopped the bleeding, at least, dosing and packing Alais fore and aft with the most powerful tools in their combined kits. Berta massaged Alais's belly—carefully, and with more powerful unguents. Clinging valiantly to the same life her bairn had given up before he'd seen light and air, Alais was alive . . . but only just.

Father Tuck—well, Dolfin, and the only priest Marion let roam the upper chambers of Tickhill—prepared the too-small, stillborn babe to lay shrouded and anointed beside his mother. Dolfin had given unction to the mother too, not only for her soul's protection and comfort, but also in preparation for the worst. Alais did seem comforted, particularly after they assured her several times over of the poor mite's baptism. Marion had done that herself. Dolfin took Alais's hands and prayed with her, and Marion noticed he called upon the Dark Lady more than once.

All Hallows after all, had been long sanctified Hers, and Dolfin as well.

I pray you see this wee soul to the otherworlds, grant him rest and rebirth from his labours. Protect my sister as she wanders Annwyn's halls. Marion gave, silent, her own request, and as her eyes wandered towards the sunrise illuminating the chamber's high window, added, *O Horned Lord, I beg you, protect my child. See to your daughter, and see her safely home.*

Mayhap she is home.

Not the god but his mate, and the soft utterance sent a shiver through Marion. How apropos that the Lady would be here, close, in this room of birth and dying.

Is Aderyn safe, in our forest?

Where is safe, O Mother? What is safe? Mayhap the only safety known to humankind is within the otherworlds.

Another chill rippling down her spine, Marion rose. Realised her hands kept up a persistent writhe in her overkirtle, and it stained with birthing-blood.

She had to change. Eat sommat. Take her own riders, go to the Wode, help the riders find her daughter, now that her duty here had finally been discharged.

She was growing sick of the word: duty.

"Marion?" Aelwyn kenned her thoughts, came over and grasped her hands. "You've had no sleep, and not much to eat. I know you're worried, but you can't think of haring off after without so much as—"

"Where are you going?" A new voice intruded, ragged and rusty.

Not for the first time, Marion's emotions ran their strange gauntlet of pity and resentment over the man who'd finally been admitted to kneel by the bed. Otho'd one hand upon the tiny, shrouded form, the other stroking his wife's fingers. The latter, however, didn't stave off one fact: Otho's first question as they'd let him into the room had been, not about his wife, but whether his son had been given last rites.

Well, and such things were important to their like. Their god condemned innocent bairns to perdition for no reason other than a priest hadn't touched them.

Dolfin had assured Otho, and in the next breath reminded him, stern, that his wife had as well. That set the thoughtless git back on his pins. He'd sunk to his knees beside the bed and wept into his wife's palm. While Alais had comforted *him*, before falling into a fitful, drugged sleep.

"In case you've forgotten," Marion countered, heading for the door, "*my* child is missing."

"And you sent men a-horse last night, looking. You can't leave Alais like this!"

"I've done all I can for now. She'll have the best of care—Aelwyn can see to that as well as I, and—"

"Nay, *you* must stay with her!" He stood, began to follow. "You owe her this much, with what has happened, and you're supposed to be the best midwife in the shire, little good though it did my son!"

"*Alais's* son"—Marion snapped the words like a whip—"came too early, brother of my husband."

"And if you think we didn't want to save him," Aelwyn protested, "you're proper mistaken!"

"My lady." Dolfin stepped between them. "My lord. We're all exhausted unto death, and your tiny son's deathbed is no place to air grievances."

Again, pity and contempt twined, and Marion shook her head, turned away. "Aye, you're ri—"

"You will not leave her!" Otho shouldered his way past Dolfin, pale save for two crimson splotches upon his cheeks. "Send your common Captain to find his little bastard, but you will stay here as you ought! You'll tend to one who was lady of this castle when you were nothing but a wolfshead's whore!"

"My lord!" Dolfin gasped out

Aelwyn snarled a whispered curse.

Marion took in a slow breath, turned around, and stalked the four steps between she and Otho.

The punch hit square against Otho's jaw, staggering him nigh back against Dolfin.

Who backed discreetly out of the way, Marion noticed with no little gratification.

Eyes wide, Otho raised one hand to his jaw. The fingers trembled.

Surprised, my lord? Though you should have known all along that this *"wolfshead's whore" has teeth.*

"You are distraught, Otho, and not yourself," Marion hissed. "For that reason alone, we shall consider my blow adequate recompense, instead of the challenge you've so shamelessly made, and I'll be disremembering what you said.

"Dolfin, I think it necessary that you stay here, give comfort to the bereaved."

The priest nodded, blue eyes lit with satisfaction.

Marion returned the nod and turned to Aelwyn, took her hands. "You know I've every confidence in you. Nap as you can, but please attend Alais and give her the tisane. You know how much, and when."

Aelwyn's eyes also shone, approving. "Aye, Lady." The title purposeful, even as was the negligent tilt of Aelwyn's head towards Otho as she strode past Marion and to the door. A pause, with a waft of instructions to the women outside, having to do with preparing some food, and horses.

"And as to—"

The gatehouse bell drowned her out, its flat *clang-clang* scratching and trembling the stones. Shouts rose, urgent but unintelligible, carrying in through the window portals.

"Good God!" Dolfin breathed. "What now?"

Marion didn't bother to answer; she bolted from the bedchamber, unlacing her soiled overkirtle as she ran.

"Horses coming, milady, an armed cadre!"

The chief guardsman met Marion halfway, both of them dodging and weaving through barely controlled chaos. The bell kept up its anxious clanging. People had started pouring through the gates and into the bailey. Here and there shafts of sunlight broke through clouds, but the clouds were winning; likely rain by nightfall. They'd have to set up shelters if the outlying villages were being raided . . . but surely those people were from the outskirts of Maltby? That village was a good five miles, too far to have responded to the bell so soon.

The guardsman followed her gaze and nodded. "They were the ones as gave the warning, milady."

"How many?" Marion asked as David and his grown son, Lewis, came running up.

"Enough to chase the whole of Maltby into the countryside, the headman says. Son, go help at the gates. The folks're crowding too much. Be kindly, but there's time, tell 'em."

With a nod, Lewis sped away. Maltby's headman and his wife tried for Marion's attention as they passed.

She slowed. "Are you both all right? How many soldiers? From where, could you tell?"

"Nay, milady. They en't proper soldiers; all gauded up with gold and gems, wearing no colours."

"Mercenaries, then," David growled.

"A big lot of 'em, rounding us up mid-night, chasin' us like sheep!" The headman had a bruised jaw, held one arm close to his ribs.

"We had to leave everything behind," his wife put in, "and come this way, to warn ye and for shelter."

"You did right," Marion assured them. "Did everyone make it out?"

"Aye, milady, they did. T' bastids told us to run, t' tell—begging your pardon, milady—t' tell 'milady wolfshead her time's up'."

Fury rippled behind Marion's eyes; with a gentle touch to their hands, one then the other, she turned on one heel and started for the stair.

"How's milady Alais?" David asked, soft, as they climbed.

"Alive so far. The bairn was stillborn."

"Poor little mother," David sighed, and made a blessing in the air. "'Tis out of your hands the now."

"And this shoved right in 'em." She mounted the stair to the wall walk above the gatehouse. "I intended to ride out . . . " Her voice tried to choke; she steadied it. "Have we heard anything, David?"

"Nowt. Which could be a blessing," he added, encouraging. "Our bonny lass doesn't just look like Himself; she's the Wode's lore, aye?—and straight from the teat, like. T' lads'll find her."

Marion's smile came a bit forced and she knew it. Leaping the

last tread, she strode onto the wall walk, settling her hands to the
lime-washed stones. A banner hung just past—they'd started
readying for market—and it waved in the fitful breeze, welcoming
a different trail of people inward. Her people, being chivvied into
protective walls, and few of 'em given so much as a chance to
gather their belongings. It set a steady burn in her heart that they
shouldn't lose what little they did possess.

Milady wolfshead. The wolf-bitch of Tickhill. Aye, she'd claim
that and more.

No group a-horse as yet, and they'd see such a thing from two
miles distant. The surround to Tickhill lay wide and mostly flat.
David's assessment was accurate: they'd time to get the stragglers
in and close the gates. Then, the wait.

"We don't have enough men on hand," David muttered, "do it
come to cases. The sergeant in charge—Jocelin?—well, he's already
sent two of his fastest riders to warn the outlying villages. And
one westward, to Much."

Marion nodded. Standard procedures, those, detailed years ago
by Much and Gamelyn in case the unlikely indeed happened.
"What do these mercenaries mean to do? Just have a good time
disrupting the countryside? Use up our resources? For what?"

"And in th' doing give us the warning," David agreed. "Surely
they know there's nowt left but siege?"

"And a siege makes no sense. They have to know we're prepared."

"Not many are, though, what with the war. Mayhap they're
thinking of that. By the Horns, none of this makes sense!"

"Aye. It's all so . . . ill-timed. We've market three days hence,
and people coming."

"Not if they see armed troops. That'd be a blow to our purse,
like."

"But also ensure the siege would be reported. Not to mention
the Earl of Huntingdon, heading down from the North with an
entire retinue of armed soldiers!"

"Mayhap they don't know that. And sure's iron folds in forge
heat, I'll wager they don't know about the Moorlands' cadre."

"So they've no hope, whatever they want. All we have to do is
wait, and—"

"Do you have guards upon the postern?"

A new voice, somewhat subdued, and Marion turned to see
Otho taking the last stair onto the wall walk.

"Why aren't you with your wife?" It wanted to snap, still angry;
Marion forced it reasonable.

"They sent me out, said 'twas women's business." Otho
shrugged, looked out across the long, rolling swell of land to the
southeast. "And so it is, well enough. I'm of more use here."

"Like closin' the' gatehouse when our wee lass was away?"
David growled.

"Like holding out against a better-equipped siege than any

band of mercenaries might offer!" Otho retorted. "I know this castle's defences better than anyone. Including, milady, your husband."

"Now see here!" David started, subsiding as Marion raised a hand.

She didn't take her gaze from Otho, staring him down.

He met her gaze and matched it. "You know it's the truth. He's rarely here, is he?"

"He's here enough to sire my children," she said, low.

Otho looked away, but only briefly. "My apologies. It was uncalled for, and I'm . . ." He took a huge breath. "I'm better able to protect Alais here. She's in God's hands, and either you or I staying with her when we're under attack won't help anyone, least of all her. I know the tactics of siege. Moreover, I know this castle, inside and out, and you're being foolish if you can't see that much."

He was right. Despite David's bristling and Marion's own affront, still simmering. "I'm many things, but I'm no fool."

Otho peered at her for a moment, then nodded.

The people of Tickhill saw prospective invasion coming long before they could ascertain how many actually sought that invasion. The approaching group flew no banners, rode no formations. Their horses bore no wagons behind, only riders astride and stirrup men in plenty. Chainmail and weapons glinted, dull, in the sun.

In short, they gave no hint of being anything other than what they were: marauders.

"Warrant the gates!" Otho shouted down. "Warrant all approaches!" His orders returned in tens of different voices, confirmation echoing down and around the circumference of Tickhill's outer wall.

Any remaining clouds had fled to the horizon. One of the women had brought Marion a wide-brimmed hat to shield her from the late morning sun. Otho had, several times now, tried to convince Marion to retire into the gatehouse—or at least into one of the hoardings that hunched, several lengths of protective wood and arrow-loops atop the front bastions. Marion had merely climbed the gatehouse stair and stood sentry there.

David rolled his eyes at Otho—he knew better—and followed her. Grumbling, Otho too followed.

"Twenty-four of them," Marion muttered; she'd the longest sight. "Mercenaries, all right and . . ."

And.

The words stoppered off into a whimper, and she clutched at the merlon beside which she stood. It was either that or fall.

"Marion, what is . . . ?" David asked, and almost at the same time Otho swore.

"God's teeth!"

He, too, had seen what rode amidst the marauders.

Ian, his sandy head bare to the breeze, his horse being led—on a taut, careful crosstie—by two others. And besides that, astride the pommel and snugged in the meaty grip of a swart fellow that made five of her, rode Aderyn.

"It can't be," whispered Marion. "Nay, nay, *nay!*"

As they came closer, the children became visible to everyone atop the ramparts. Curses echoed now, up and down the stones. Closer still, and Aderyn's eyes sought her mother's, wide and fearful.

Marion whispered, invocation and curse both. Aye, and if she had her way, these Motherless sods wouldn't see any coming dawn.

The final approach seemed forever. Finally, the cadre of horse spread beneath them, with the front rider holding up a hand. The troupe came to a halt just beyond a telltale scar in the earth.

Once it had been the no-one's land of another siege. Seven years now past, King Richard's siege of Tickhill had gone into legend and hearkened not only its castellan's—Otho's—disgrace, but Gamelyn's reclamation of the home denied him.

Beginnings, aye. But also an end, in its way, of an outlaw band led by Robyn Hode.

The scarred ring of earth lay just outside the range of any crossbow.

Marion's fingers stung; she realised they'd scraped and left a carmine smear upon the crenelated, white- and ochre-washed stones. To her right side, David also muttered promises into threats.

You said she was safe! Marion flung outward.

More like they'd abandoned her. Again. But nay, no such luck.

What is safety, Mother-Maid? Where *is safety, when you bung yourself in stone, deny Our Lady and My forest?*

I have never denied you, or the Wode! You would punish our child for—

Punishment? Truly? You've even started thinking *like them. . .*

"Hallo!" the frontmost rider called as they came closer. Frankish, the lot of them, speaking a patois as foul and mocking as Marion had ever heard. "I would speak with your leader, O mighty Tickhill!"

Otho stepped forward. "What do you want, villein?"

They'd agreed this first exchange would be his. And about now, Marion wasn't sure her voice would work.

She had to admit, when Otho used his authority it passed altogether powerful. His voice rang the stones, layered with generations of overlords' contempt.

"We're no villeins, *nobleman"*—the mercenary leader's voice dripped its own scorn—"and I've no need to speak with *you*. I'm looking at the bitch behind you. Hardly what I was expecting, that a red-haired cunt thinking herself able to hold Tickhill alone should hide behind her betters."

"Watch your tongue, you filthy sod!" David hurled back, and along the wall, Tickhill's men echoed his rebuke. Otho, demonstrably silent, slid a chary gaze towards Marion.

She found herself grateful for the insults—and his lack of response. It loosed a chilly anger; it held her steady, legs and voice. Giving Otho a silent, penetrative look, she turned her back on him and put both hands to the wall, leaned forward.

"How charming. How *telling*, that a man's insults always involve a woman—and straightaway give grass to what problems he had with his mam."

Several of the mercenaries hissed. One even smirked. The leader's expression showed him less than amused. Shocked, even, that she'd sassed back.

So Marion kept it up. "Poor, poor lad. Mayhap 'tweren't mam, but your wet-nurse, then, as fetched you a sugar-tit 'stead of the real thing?"

This time, several of the mercenaries gave a sarcastic catcall familiar in every soldier's barracks. Tickhill's guardsmen echoed it, standing ready with their cross-and shortbows. The leader's face flamed.

Otho grabbed her arm. "Are you *mad*, to antagonise them?"

"Nay, look to th' bairns," David growled.

Ian's face was turning, from white-scared to disbelief, into gratification. Aderyn, mayhap, didn't understand the exchange so well, but she too had eased from terror into curiosity, watching the mercenaries have their fun at their leader's expense.

But a few vile curses settled pack-order, soon enough, and the furious leader rode a few paces closer. His horse's front hoofs stepped just past the old fire-boundary.

As one, Tickhill's bowmen leaned in.

"You'd best think well upon your situation, milady wolfshead!" the leader called. "I have hostages, as you can see! It's well known that the majority of your soldiers are wandering the Peak!"

"It's more well known that Tickhill has market in less than two days!" Marion called back. "Do you intend to greet our incomers at the gate, then?"

"We thought at first a better strategy might be to join them. You'd never have known—never will, from here on out, eh?—which of your guests holds an assassin's dagger."

"Have you forgotten what castle you confront?" Marion leaned over the wall. "Tickhill's own lord *is* an assassin!"

"*Was*, is how I've heard it! Dry bones bleaching in the desert. Which makes you a widow. King's property, eh? And him giving it to us, eh?" A gesture, vulgar. "To . . . hold, eh?"

"Good luck with that!" David growled back. "En't just Templars as guard this place. There's plenty living here as are more than *you* can take!"

"Moreso," Marion supplied, "than cowards who capture children!"

"Ah, but a coward's way oft proves fruitful—as much as these hostages shall, I think. Approaching your fair keep, we thought our first plan a good one. But what with babes like these wandering the woods . . . "

One of the men holding Tierce made a kissy face at Ian. He puffed up like a goose and Marion gritted her teeth, willed the lad to look back at them, not make trouble, not *now.*

Otho clenched his fists. "I'll kill them."

"Aye," David muttered, "I'll join you."

And Aderyn—*good lass!*—didn't take her eyes from her mam.

"So, milady wolfshead, our plans changed. Became more . . . direct. I'm sure you understand. And I'm sure you'll understand why you're to open the gates! For it's either that, or"—he raised a hand, and knives were drawn—"you'll see your heirs with their throats cut before you!"

Silence fell over the wall walk. Several of the guardsmen cursed, quiet, looking frantically to their own leaders. Marion didn't drop her eyes from the mercenary's, didn't waver, didn't falter . . . right now she couldn't so much as bend her neck. This mangy pack of dogs at her stoop would scent weakness like rotting meat.

"God's blood, but what choice do we have?" Otho growled, low. "Our children . . . and *you* sent Ian out to—!"

"Shut up!" Marion snarled back without dropping her eyes. "Let me think!"

One of the mercenaries rode to his leader's side and spoke. The leader broke eye contact with Marion, and she took the opportunity to consider every detail, every bit of terrain. Her gaze once again fastened upon the leader—his horse's hoofs, more like, just past that faint, demarcated ghost of damaged ground. A smile twitched her lip. "David. Hearken where they're standing. A wise precaution to take, for crossbows."

"Aye," he answered, curious-slow as perception dawned. "They are, aren't they? Just out of range of a good crossbow, no question."

She met his eyes. David tipped a nod, turned on one heel, and sped for the stairs.

"Well, milady wolfshead?" the leader bellowed. "Are you going to open the gates, or do we have to ensure it?"

"If I open my gates, what guarantee do you give that you won't hurt your captives?" Not *my bairns,* but *the captives.* It was the only way to not call down earth and sky and raze them where they stood.

If you can, the Lady spoke softly, as if She hadn't been altogether silent since Marion had walked away from the Mere after Robyn had been taken. *You have wandered altogether far from Me, daughter.*

No farther than you from us, Marion retorted. *But there is one who will not see His firstborn sacrificed.*

Are you so sure of that, Mother-Maid? came Her retort. *What are we, all, but sacrifices?*

And She was gone.

Marion didn't let it so much as quiver her limbs, and leaned even farther over the gap between the merlons.

Otho muttered an oath and grabbed at her sleeve—did he think she meant climb up and jump, for pity's sake? She twitched free, kept her eyes on the leader.

Who laughed, making several quick gestures. "I make no guarantees!" About eight of the mercenaries peeled away, one direction and the other. "Unless you promise results!"

"They're heading for the postern!" Otho hissed. "Get back, I have to—"

"I'm not going to fling meself from the bloody wall!" she shot back. "Go, I'm all right, do as you must!" *As will I, better without you nigh.*

Otho hesitated, peering at her, then shook his head and turned away, gathering several guards by eye. He tendered quick, muttered orders, and they, too, ran down the wall walk towards the back postern.

But he didn't leave. Likely didn't trust her. Fair enough; she didn't trust him, either.

No matter. Taking a huge breath, Marion let it swirl into thought.

Into words.

"I promise you results, all right!" she called back. "I can guarantee that any who have taken our own are cursed. Any attempts to breach these walls will be cursed. Followed in life by fire and storm, covered in death by earth and rain . . . *If*—a hiss—"death does find you and agrees to the bargain. For believe me, most have begged for it and been denied."

And bless His horns, but thunder rumbled in the distance, where a small gather of clouds had turned from white to grey.

Silence.

Otho muttered a slight prayer. Several of the mercenaries crossed themselves.

"Witch!" The leader snarled. "Open the gates, or the children die."

"Then I've no choice, have I?" Marion straightened, braced herself against the wall. "See to the gate, Otho."

The words rang into further stillness, broken only by ragged breaths coming up the stair tunnel, and soft, hurried footsteps as David sprinted back up into the light from below stairs.

More rumblings; this the Horned Lord, satisfied at what David held:

Several strung longbows, and a quiver-full of peacock-fletched arrows.

"My God, woman!" Otho hissed. "What if you hit the children?"

She didn't take offense; 'twere an honest fear, fluting his voice all trembly. "We were Robyn Hode's, aye? I think we wain't hit nowt but what we mean to."

He paled. "See here. I know—"

"Go on." She smiled, more supportive wortwife than castle lady. Nonthreatening. "See to the gates. We'll need them open, soon enough."

Otho hesitated, took a deep breath, then gave a curt nod. He turned on one heel and headed for the stair.

"I grow tired of this waiting, woman!" the mercenary leader shouted. "Open the gates!"

"I just gave the order!" Marion called back as, beneath cover of the gatehouse's nigh merlon, David slipped Marion her longbow, settling the quiver down between them.

The gate wheel began to groan, accompanied by the grate and rattle of the bridge lowering. *Slow*, she counselled, pulling a handful of arrows.

"Your choice, milady." David was doing the same and nearly sang it; all too plain he'd missed this sort of dalliance and danger.

Marion—though her heart also sang its own descant of fury—hadn't. Not in the least.

Not that it mattered, in thisnow.

"I want the sod who has Aderyn. You take the leader, then we'll both take on Ian's problem."

"His hands are bound."

"Aye. It'll have to be the ropes." Marion yanked a couple of hairs from beneath her hat. With both herself and David watching the coppery strands like hawks, she set them adrift on the breeze. A dip as they wafted outward from the castle, with a lift and curl as another tiny breeze took them out of sight. With a pluck at her bowstring—keeping weapon and hands low, Marion nocked it with a peacock-fletched arrow, fisting several more.

David ordered, "None save the two of us shoots until the bairns are out of range, aye?"

The other archers were busy ensuring their own weapons; answers came, quiet, in the affirmative.

"We loose on three, then." David took a breath, half-primed the massive longbow; Marion did the same. "One . . . two . . . three."

A jerk full upright between the merlons, a push into full nock, sight and loose . . .

The longbows did as they were made to do in skilled hands: cover distance with accuracy. David's arrow found the leader's heart; he gave a gurgled shout, thrown backwards from the saddle.

The passing of Marion's arrow gave a wiffle to Aderyn's hair as it sank into her captor's throat.

Another quick breath, another nock and push. Twin arrows sped towards Ian's captors before the first targets had so much as fallen from their horses. Both ropes gave a harsh *spang,* sailed sideways, and dropped.

Chaos ensued.

Arrows flying from Tickhill's walls; only two bows, but more than enough to mill the mercenaries like hens thrown a handful of corn. Rough shouts rising. Horses wheeling, panicked, as their riders tried to control them.

Aderyn's captor sagged sideways, dead weight pulling the horse in a tight circle. Aderyn writhed, trying to free herself of his hold. The horse stumbled and went down, both riders with it, and Marion's heart leapt into her throat.

But nay!—Aderyn scrambled and rolled clear. Leaping to her feet, she ran.

Nor was she the only one. Tierce realised his freedom in the same instant as Ian, and the stallion turned on one of his captors, rearing and striking. One rider fell, a slash of blood across his face. The other tried to untangle from the cut rope enough to unsheathe his sword—to no avail. David shot him from his horse. Yet two more threats met the same end from Marion's bow, one curling up and falling with a shout, the other flipping off his horse's haunches like a street jongleur.

The riderless horses whirled, fleeing Tierce's punishment; the stallion shook his head and looked for more. What a warhorse he would make! Marion thought as she dispatched another mercenary. Ian half-lay, bent, over Tierce's neck. Trying to regain control of the stallion, or injured, Marion couldn't tell. But Tierce wobbled and checked, dancing amidst carnage. As one of the mercenaries started to make good on the still target, crossbow primed, the stallion whirled on his massive haunches and leapt forward again, galloping mightily for the castle . . .

Nay, towards Aderyn.

It all happened in the space of a few breaths. Several more mercenaries, weapons drawn, spurred their horses forward—clearly intending the same. They hadn't a chance; David was picking them off as quickly as he could nock his arrows. The other archers awaited their chance—closer, within range—whilst Marian targeted, not more mercenary scum, but Ian's chestnut warhorse.

If Ian indeed lay injured, and the stallion out of control, she'd shoot it out from under him before it had the chance to trample her daughter.

Aderyn spun, let out a cry as the stallion bore down upon her. Marion pushed, nearly loosed . . .

Nearly.

At the last moment—or so it seemed—Ian sat up. Tierce

collected himself from a full-out gallop, gathered on his muscular haunches and spun around the little girl. Ian leaned so far towards Aderyn it looked as if he might fall. She reached up and grabbed the crook of his tied-off near arm. The momentum of the stallion's spin and leap forward did the rest. Aderyn swung over and landed astride the horse's croup, clung like a cocklebur against Ian's back as he angled forward and gave Tierce his head. The stallion exploded forward in a mighty gallop towards the castle.

"Open the gates!" Marion screamed. "Open them *now!*"

Several crossbow bolts flew after, ill-aimed. The mercenaries still dashed about, in chaos, over half their number felled by the deadly reach of the longbows.

The other half, nigh as one, decided on retreat.

"Don't let 'em go," Marion growled.

"We could use one alive," was David's terse reply.

Marion nodded, sighted her next shot just that much lower.

Tierce reached the bridge too soon—but no doubt this time that Ian guided him in a long, looping turn, waiting as the grind and rumble below the gatehouse increased and the chains clanked faster. The bridge struck ground with a heavy sound like thunder. Tierce came 'round and shot forward, hoofs seeking then ringing upon the thick wood. He clattered across the bridge, from rout and a hail of crossbow bolts, into stone walls and shelter.

And of the twenty-odd mercenaries who had ridden from the Peak to take a castle held by a mere woman?

Not one escaped to boast of it.

Ⓨ

With David detailing men to collect the few survivors, Marion sped down the gatehouse stair in a fashion over which her mam had oft sworn she'd break her neck. Yet again she proved that worry false, alighting upon ground level to a tableau of relief.

The children sat astride Tierce, who sweated and blew and obviously enjoyed every bit of attention from the small throng crowded about. He stood like a rock as Ian submitted to one of the guards cutting his bonds with a knife. Otho was there, too, speaking to his son with more animated pleasure than Marion had ever seen. He held the stallion's rein and occasionally gave a fond slap to the arched, sweated neck. Tierce endured it—despite being a fussy sort and normally demanding singular treatment— likely because Ian kept rubbing his crest, smiling down at his father. No question but he was the hero of the day, and Aderyn just as brave, to do what she had.

Marion's heart gave a lurch and jerk as a tousled, black head popped out from behind Ian. Aderyn sighted her mother in about the same breath—another fetch of Marion's heart, that—and the child slid off the stallion's rump. She disappeared into the congratulatory throng for a few breaths. A small blur erupted and ran smack into her mother's skirts.

Marion picked her up, whirling her about and not caring if they whacked a passerby in the crush.

"Mam! Eri! Hey, watch your feet, Eri! I told you you'd catch trouble, riding all over—"

"Robbie!" Marion snatched the little boy close as more jubilant people began rushing the gatehouse. "What are you doing away from the keep? Berta swore—"

"Berta went to the garderobe. Several times in fact; puking her guts and more, said she was that scared, and the last time she stayed there for the longest while, so . . . " Robbie shrugged, grinning. "I wasn't about to miss this for anything—Ian!" This as the lad came striding over and gave Marion a sudden embrace.

Marion forgot, for the moment, that she fully intended to smack the taste from her son's mouth. Ian's hug was that strong, and the shaky whisper he gave melted her heart further.

"Thank you. If you and Uncle hadn't agreed to let me come here, ride with Mistress Sarah—"

"More should I be thanking you!" Marion replied. "You helped save your wee cousin's life, did you know that? I'm so proud of you, how you rode Tierce!"

Aderyn was in plain agreement, tugging at Ian's tunic and talking as fast as her hands would allow.

Ian tousled her hair and gave a brilliant smile. "Well, I had to. They'd tied my hands, and he knows leg cues, only I'd never managed it so far, and"—a pleased flush crept over his cheeks—"Papa said he'd never seen anyone ride better."

"Your mam'll be even prouder, once she hears of what you did."

"How is she? Da"—Ian lowered his voice—"wouldn't say."

"She's holding her own, lad. She—"

"Riders! Riders on the ridge!"

"God's blood!" Otho's voice echoed in the gatehouse tunnel. He burst into the daylight, shoving Tierce's rein at one of the gatehouse guards and looking up to where the call had come from— the northwest bastion. "Not again. Is there more of them?"

"Call the men back!" Marion shouted, starting to pull Robbie, Aderyn and Ian towards the gatehouse stair.

"Nay," the latter said, "I can help!"

"Then you and Lewis"—David's boy had joined her orbit as well—"spread the word. Ian up the stair, and Lewis to the gate. Tell the men to fetch those survivors in, now!"

Obedient, Lewis ducked and dodged through the people milling the forecourt. Ian leapt the opposite gatehouse stair three at a time.

"Warrant the bridge!" Otho bellowed. First to the gate keepers, he then addressed the forecourt, where celebration was quickly turning anxious. "Clear the way, all of you! Back, and see to your—!"

"No alarm! My lady! Marion!" This from David, still watching from atop the gatehouse. Marion ran inward, the young ones still with her, and looked up to see him waving his arms. "No alarm! There's riders, to be sure, but also bannermen and wagons! 'Tis Huntingdon's banner—the Earl of Huntingdon approaches!"

The surrounding people began to mill again, with a back-and-forth of relieved chatter. Marion peered at Otho, who'd one foot upon the stair and ready to climb. Robbie and Aderyn each started to chatter—in their own way, of course. Otho allowed a swift smirk. Marion started to laugh.

And if it had a slightly hysterical tinge?—ah, well. It had been that sort of se'nnight.

- XVIII -

"Thank t' Lady's grace, but milady Alais sleeps well enough for t' now." Aelwyn kept her voice a bare murmur, mindful of Otho and Ian beside the bed in visitation. "No fever. Some bleeding, to be sure, and she passed the afterbirth."

"'Twere all there?" Marion eyed the tableau as well, her words just as soft.

"Aye. I feared it mightn't be, so I made a proper careful go ower it. Put a hex-breath 'pon it, too, and gave a bit to the fire. I'm boiling a bit down for the medicine. The rest I sent, wrapped all proper, to be buried 'neath a birch."

Marion nodded approval. "I knew you'd be best with her."

"Not the best, but good enough."

Leaning forward, Marion kissed her cheek. "More than just 'enough', my lass. But we en't out of the woodlands. She's proper weak, and if she takes fever we'll lose her for sure. I found Hilda—she and her people came for shelter, aye?—and she says she'll linger a while, spell us."

Aelwyn's relief showed, palpable, in the slump of shoulders and a gusty sigh. Hilda had been around when Anarchy had pillaged the land. Though she practiced her trade but little these days, the old midwife had forgotten more than most would ever know. "That'd be a blessing 'bout now. I'm reeling and so are you, love."

"Aye. We've got to get some sleep, what with market in a brace of days. Plus Huntingdon's been sighted. They'll be riding through the gates any time now."

"Faith! Surely you en't going to fête any guests before you've rested?"

"I have to greet them at least. But nay, I'll sleep soon enough, and Aderyn with me, I'm sure."

"I heard what was happening—hard not to—but all I could do was tie a knot and hold on, aye? The lad looks to have grown up in an afternoon"—she tilted her head Ian's way with a tiny smile—"but how's wee Aderyn fettling?"

"None the worst for it." A grateful sigh, then Marion frowned. "Though she has been keen upon telling me sommat. Not that I've had time to give her half an ear."

"And no surprise, that!" Aelwyn tendered a fierce hug; as always, she gave a bolster to tired limbs and spirit.

"My lady?" A soft voice, and a tap at the lintel. Hilda, ready to spell the exhausted.

Marion returned Aelwyn's hug, hard, and they clung to each other for a few breaths. "Fetch yourself some sleep now, aye?"

"Oh, and aye."

(ᛈ)

"A true Northern lass, who takes out her enemies and in the next breath welcomes family to her gates!" David, Earl of Huntingdon, tipped his goblet: his toast was purest respect. "And we are family, you know. Your boy . . ." This gesture towards where Rob skipped about the hearth—and baby Marjory's pallet—on a stick-horse. "My word, but he looks so much like to your husband—and *his* mother. More even than the lovely wee one as bears cousin Marjory's name. We must speak of fostering him, aye? Allies are never remiss in our world, and my dear wife would love . . . Alas, my dear! You're pie-eyed and falling into your wine—which is most excellent, by the by—but you must go to rest, surely. Did the bastards hang on that long?"

Marion's lassitude certainly engendered itself from lack of sleep, but the vibrant magnetism of her guest's presence sucked all the breath from the room—and she'd none to spare at present. Another force of nature, David of Huntingdon, but so wildly different from the one possessing her brother.

"Nay, my lord," Marion answered, shaking herself back to some awareness. "A long and sad childbed. My marriage-sister, lady Alais, Otho's wife."

"God help us, she's—?"

"Nay, my lord," Marion voiced it quick, unwilling for even the words to hang in the air and gain strength. "Alais does well enough, despite losing her bairn, and we hope that she'll do better."

"We shall all pray for her, then. And I pray you, my lady, to go and avail yourself of some sleep. I will do well with my nephew's company"—this as Rob made a circuit about them both, with his stick horse bobbing fiercely and his tongue busily clucking the triplets of galloping hoofs—"and that of your seneschal, and cousin Otho and his son when they depart their own dear lady's side. You and your people have already tendered to mine well past any obligation. Off with you, aye? Take some needed rest!"

"I'm grateful for your understanding, my lord." Marion bowed and went to do just that.

ᚦ

Sun rafted in, between the hangings and through the doorway to tickle at Marion's cheeks. With a grumble, she tried to move out from under it.

Couldn't. She was pinned to the bed as if with some weight.

For half a breath, she thought to panic. Instead she took quick stock. Recognising the weight and slight rasp of breaths, her nostrils tickled with additional familiarity: first the herbs she used to freshen the clothing presses, then the sweet oil she used to tame the wiry curls that seemed inevitable with most of her children, then a distinct, not-so-pleasant whiff from the bedding.

Marion opened her eyes. Sure enough, Aderyn was nose-to-nose with her, curled against her left side with one leg and one arm flung across her mother, hair still—somewhat—braided and her nightshirt rucked up around her waist. And Robbie—well, he snored blissfully within the coverlets on Marion's right, despite having twisted and reversed himself in the night, his head pillowed upon her hip and his feet against the headboard. His toes brushed her pillow, but it wasn't that which prompted Marion to sniff again and give a resigned sigh. He'd wet himself. What with all the excitement, Berta'd no doubt forgotten to drain the boy before bed. With a tiny quirk of lip, Marion started the process of creeping her way out from under the children. Without waking them.

Thankfully, neither budged.

Shrugging into a robe, Marion crept into the outer solar, making sure to close the bedchamber door behind, and strode over to the hangings and threw them back. She squinted against the sunlight and leaned upon the sill with a great sigh.

One could scarcely credit it was approaching Hallows. Below, the courtyard seemed washed in the golds and greens of summer, and bustled with not only the beginnings of another beautiful day, but also the packing up and leave-taking of those who'd taken sanctuary from yesterday's attack.

The westmost shadow of the keep lay short; it was well into mid-morning, and she'd overslept. Right now, basking in the reflected light, she wasn't sure she cared.

But, things to do. Important guests. Two more days 'til market.

And . . . Alais. She held her breath, whispered a small blessing—*let her still be alive, and doing better*—but surely someone would have come by now, had Alais died in the night.

Marion dressed, and went to make sure.

(þ)

"You look a sight better this morning, lass."

"I feel it, David, believe me."

And Marion did. Alais had sat up long enough to take some warmed gruel. David had not only fed their guests, but seen to a spot of late-morning hawking for the Earl and his closest retainers. Tickhill had birds, of course—as much necessity as appearance—but a man like David of Huntingdon travelled with his favourites, to be sure.

Otho had gone along. Ian, deciding he'd enough goings-on for a se'nnight, instead offered to sit with his mother. He'd fed her that warmed porridge and even coaxed a tiny smile by telling her his adventures from the day before. Nor did he forget a sombre and respectful reflection upon the soldiers who'd died in the ambush, trying to defend him from the mercenaries.

Aye, Ian would be all right.

So Marion could take some time and enjoy the breakfast David served: a thick slab of ham, bread still warm from the ovens, and porridge lashed with plenty of cream and honey. David hummed a bawdy old lay as he did it, and afterward sat across the board with a pint and a crust, still humming.

Energised from yesterday, as sure as Ian chattering to his mum. Marion grinned into her mug, recognising the symptoms.

She was a bit chuffed herself, to be sure.

"Down ower half our men, and we still routed the bastards, aye?"

Her grin widened. "With proper longbows. You've not lost your eye, David."

"Nor you, fair Maid; an archer worthy of the Hood's band and no question!" A tiny squinch of eyebrow—memory always there, if fading with time—and he lifted his pot in small toast. "To th' Wode, what taught us!"

"T' Wode," she echoed, and drank.

David gulped half the mug and wiped his moustache. "Ah!— that's fine ale on a finer morn. 'Tis a fact that Much wain't be half-pleased to've missed the ruckus."

"After he makes sure it never happens again, if I know my man." Marion spooned up several mouthfuls of porridge. "Hopefully he's cracked a few skulls t'ward Castleton to make up for it."

David snorted agreement. "How do you think they knew we were down arms?"

"'Twere no secret, the men riding out."

"But twenty mile south? Mayhap they were raiding to draw our soldiers out and afield? And them wobbling their gobs about coming into market, bold as brass and . . ." His shoulders twitched, awareness of a target sighted, and his eyes turned to opaque cerulean glass. "Aye, lass, you make sure of the gates, and I'll see to those two bastards in the underkeep. We'll have the truth out of 'em."

Too many found it altogether easy to mistake David's gentle manner—and his unabashed interest in the 'more womanly' pursuits of hearth, home, and herbalism—for weakness. Marion knew better. David had been one of the keenest wolves of the Shire Wode.

David leaned over the table, voice lowering. "Marion, I know I've said this before, but it bears repeatin'. I don't half care for how that Otho lords it about here."

"Well, he is a lord. He used to be lord of this castle."

"Seems to me he's not thinkin' in terms of 'used to be'. And with his wife abed, he's worse."

Marion nodded. "I know. But I can handle Otho if I must."

"And make him resent you the more for 't. His like're vipers. Sunning 'emselves all pleasant on the rocks, merely to bite you when you're not looking and slither away, all th' while waiting for the poison to take you."

"Serpents are of the Wise, in our ways."

"But not in his, aye?"

Marion took another bite, mulling it over.

"At least Himself the Earl fancies you." This said with no little satisfaction. "Treats you like kin, offering to foster young Rob, speaking to you like a sister, aye?"

She'd not had overmuch chance to contemplate the sincerity behind the Earl's offer. There wasn't much that passed David's notice.

"So cultivate Huntingdon like damn. You know Otho will— already is. Out hunting!—with his wife ill as she is!" A derisive snort. "Use their ways against 'em, lass."

"I thought we were."

"So we are. But there's several hard facts, aye? To our folk, you're our Lady in human form. To them, with their ways and laws, you're nowt 'but a woman' and too much woman, at that, with too much power for any man not up to you to bide quiet over. If that Otho's his way, he'll be finding some slithery, sneaking, behind-your-back way to take charge of this castle, leaving us with nowt but hell to pay, and our rightful lord finding himself having to take it back again . . . " A shrug. "No question Himself could, at that, if he . . . " David's mouth twisted, and he flicked a cautious glance towards Marion.

"He'll come home. I know he will."

"I believe you, lass. But no telling when he'll return at this rate. And you know the Christians, lass. They think no woman can—or should be—allowed to control too much."

"Alais said there were . . . rumours." Had it been only yester's morn? "That I should be careful."

"Milady Alais knows her own. I can only hope she lives out the se'nnight. She's an ally we never thought to have. And," he smiled, genuine, "I like her. She's a good sort, despite her upbringing."

"She is." Marion stirred her spoon widdershins, then back earthwise, considering how alike—yet unalike—was his echo of Alais' words . . . and again, just yester's even. "I hear you. I'll be careful."

David tipped a firm nod. "Aelwyn and me, we're watching th' man . . ." And the words trailed quiet, the dangerous gloss to his eyes skimming away, just like that. "If 'tisn't two of our favourite lasses! Did you finally decide to greet the morning, pet?"

Marion turned to see Aderyn, still rumpled from sleep, a drowsy Marjory hefted on one hip.

David rose from the board, brushed a kiss to Aderyn's forehead and relieved her of Marjory. "Haven't you had quite th' adventures these past coupla days! Enough to spawn a host of appetites! Sit, pet, and Uncle David'll feed you. As to you, wee miss, are you hungry?"

Marjory nodded, one finger in her mouth.

In record time—complete with a scowl to ensure Marion kept seated before her own repast—David had Marjory in his lap making vast inroads into porridge, and Aderyn beside him doing likewise. Minus her little sister's bairn-type mess, of course.

Marion watched the children eat, her stomach tight and her heart full. Her daughter was safe. *Safe.*

And soon enough she began to realise her daughter also had something on her mind. The mid-morning meal was Aderyn's favourite; Much had once said she could shovel in half her weight after a night's fast. Not much would put her off her feed. Nevertheless, she stared into space as much as she ate the porridge. And, upon noticing her mam's gaze, Aderyn's own chased away, a small and familiar quirk between her brows that had long signalled *too much to think over.*

Well, and no wonder, with all that had happened.

"Marion? Marion!"

She turned, rising as Ian burst into the hall.

"It's Mama! She wants you, and . . . Please, Aelwyn's there, but you . . . you have to come now!"

David cursed, then said, quiet, "I'll fetch Father Dolfin."

Alais had few words left, those soaked more in blood and pain than sense—and despite both Marion and Aelwyn doing their best. This time, of the ending there remained no doubt. Alais lasted long enough to see her children one last time and ask for her husband before she exhaled her last, and grew heavy in Marion's arms.

"She's free," Aelwyn whispered, choked with tears, her arms filled with Alais' two youngest. Marion echoed it, backing from the bed and wringing one bloodied hand in her kirtles. The other encircled Ian as he drew close.

Dolfin's prayers rose into the chamber, mingling with hearth smoke and incense.

He'd the easy part, administering to the dead. It was left to Marion to see to the living.

Ian seemed grateful of Marion's arm about him; he leaned hard against her, fat tears rolling unabashed down his face. Nigh tall as herself, he was, and it seemed barely a se'nnight ago he'd been a wee lad running in the woods—*like a bloody Godless Heathen"* his da had complained, with Alais delighting in her son's overfilled heart and quick mind. All the while, mayhap remembering another tow-haired lad like to him, she'd always stood firm between son and husband.

How easy, how quick, can open hearts be bruised and made hard, she'd said, more than the once.

"She was doing better," Ian protested. "I know she was. She sat up and ate all her porridge, listened to me and held my hand. Hers was strong, and well. Then she just . . . faltered, and blood everywhere . . . There's got to be something we can do. Mayhap . . . " He trailed away, slid a sidewise glance at first Dolfin, then Aelwyn and his younger brother and sister, then Marion. "If . . . "

"If what, pet?" Marion said, gentle—and wary.

Her wariness proved apropos as Ian leaned closer, murmured, "They . . . they say you can . . . I've heard the peasants—the people—say as much. That you've . . . powers."

"What people say isn't allus to be relied upon," Marion said, gentle. "Oft such things're more dangerous than any truth, aye?"

She saw understanding, then disappointment kindle the boy's green-grey eyes. Thankfully, more in league with than against her.

"Believe me, pet, both Aelwyn and I did all we could. There's no magic as can save a soul when it decides to leave."

Ian swallowed hard, hoved closer against her shoulder.

"No magic could save me brother, lost to us seven years ago, and sometimes there en't enough praying, belief, nor hope enough in thisworld to alter *tynged.* Fate," she clarified as a puzzled light leapt further in those resigned eyes. "Me mam's people called it so, in the Barrows of the west."

"Ireland? No, wait, your people were Welsh, aye?"

"So they're called now."

Ian kept watching his mother, as if hoping—praying—a breath would lift the still chest.

"You know childbirth's a dangerous undertaking, and your mam was . . . " *Too old for it,* she nigh said aloud, but nay. Ian already owned a sufficiency of uncertain feelings towards his da. No sense laying this one down, as well.

And it had been Alais's choice, this. Her choice, and her pleasure. Not that any would give her that. Nay, this would be down to sin, and woman's treachery, hearkening back to the first mother the new religion even bothered to acknowledge.

"Your mam wanted this babe," Aelwyn spoke up, reaching with one hand to push the sandy forelock from Ian's brow. "And she loved her menfolk just as hard and fine, so she'll be waiting in the otherworlds, aye? Holding to this bairn, and the others. And, in the end, you too."

"But she won't know me." Ian's voice broke on a sob. "I'll be all grown, and she won't have seen it!"

"Here, now." Aelwyn kissed his temple, hiked Nicolas up higher on her right hip and snugged Edyth close, giving Marion a sombre smile. "I reckon things'll be managed a sight better than that." She turned away, murmuring to both the children, taking them from the room.

It had been the exact right thing to say, whatever one's notions of an afterlife. Ian took a huge, rattling breath, but that breath was easier, calmer.

Dolfin folded up his stole and kissed it, peering over at Marion and Ian. One duty done, yet much remained.

Marion kissed Ian's temple. "Stay, if you like. You can help me and Dolfin do right by your mam. And when your father comes back, I'll be there, to tell him. Aye?"

Another sigh escaped the boy, this one relieved. Ian hugged Marion tighter for a moment, then extricated himself, padding over to stand beside Dolfin.

"What an utterly foul span of days Tickhill has endured. I'm so sorry, lady Marion, that we're intruding in your time of grief."

True to her promise to Ian, Marion had ensured she'd have word the moment anyone sighted the hunting party's approach. She'd met them there, gently tendered the sombre news.

She also made sure to send up a goblet of watered, well-doctored wine after Otho's precipitous departure—a mild sedative, nowt more, but enough to ease him in the afters. Already she'd done as much for Ian and sent him on to bed.

She and Huntingdon, however, sat beside the hearth in the main hall, working their way through an unspiked—and unwatered—bottle. The vintage was potent, a Frankish variety of which the Queen Mother, Eleanor herself, would approve.

"I'm glad you've come, my lord," Marion insisted, ruffling her hand through Aderyn's thick curls. The lass had come in and, despite their exalted company, had insisted upon curling up in the round, cushioned chair beside her mam, clinging tight with reddened eyes until she'd fallen asleep. It wasn't just her; all the children were upset.

Edyth and Nicolas had cried themselves to sleep, sharing the bed with Robbie, who'd tried so hard to comfort them that he'd worked himself into a like state. Marjory, too, had been so fitful that both Berta and Marion had been at wits' end as to how to appease her. In the end, Aelwyn took her off to bed. The baby adored her auntie—and Aelwyn missed her own bairns. Tom and Tibba were off for a season's stay with their grandmam in Lichfield.

"Well. If you choose, we'll make our visit brief. Or stay on through the market as originally planned, if you'd rather that. I know you're short more than your share of guardsmen at present, and things are difficult enough on your own—nay, please, hear me out, I mean no criticism! I've no doubts you're as capable of overseeing your demesne as my own lady love is with Fothering-hay. Nevertheless," Huntingdon leaned forward, refilling her goblet and his own, "it can be overmuch for a lone woman to manage an entire honour in her husband's absence, *and* deal with the pique of his relations."

Marion peered over the rim of her cup at Huntingdon, wondering how much the canny dog-fox had sussed out. Or been told, considering what David had said only that morning about the strategy of cultivating powerful relations. Otho hadn't subtlety counted amidst his virtues, to be sure.

It made Huntingdon's next question all the more telling. "So, my lady, we must speak of cousin Gamelyn. When was he due to return?"

"He said a year and a day. If . . . " She trailed away, unwilling to conjure any sort of ill within a house that had seen enough in the past few days.

"If," Huntingdon echoed, soft. "Aye, and that's the question, isn't it? I've sent many prayers for his safety. He's in God's hands."

Marion felt her hands tighten about the goblet. *Is he, then?*

A waft of heat across her breast, like a ripple upon the hearth fire. Or the breath of a stag in a misted forest. Or the doubts of a god. *I cannot feel him, so far away. He is in Her hands.*

That inspired little confidence, seeing as how she'd used Her other consort.

Aderyn gave a little whimper and huddled closer. Marion grimaced; she'd thought her daughter slept.

"Go to bed," Marion told her, soft. "You know better than to heed things as en't yours to hear."

A pause. Then, *Mam. I have to talk to you.*

Marion resorted to like speech. *Soon enough, I promise. Today en't been a good day, pet.*

Aderyn peered at her, then hunched down. Her lips quivered and her eyes slid back and forth beneath lowered lashes. Not an unfamiliar sight—and Marion had long ago decided Gamelyn's observation was best: their daughter seemed to hold some fierce arguments with herself.

If it's important, we'll talk, anon, Marion promised.

Aderyn shook her head, eyes still flickering.

Marion gave it up. "For now, my bed or Aelwyn's. Off you go, aye?"

Sliding a dark look first to her mother, then their visitor, Aderyn rose, curtsied and padded away.

"Does the child read lip shapes?" Huntingdon ventured. "I see she makes signs with her hands. Extraordinary."

"My lord, Aderyn isn't deaf. Only unable to speak." The slight reproof, fit for chastising an Earl, nevertheless cut sharp with a mother's protectiveness.

"My apologies, to you and the little lass. Assumptions aren't amongst the cardinal sins, but perhaps they should be. So easy . . . and so short-sighted. I'd not have spoken so had I thought the little one could hear."

"I thought her sleeping," Marion admitted, and lifted the bottle. A small sliver of carmine remained; she poured it into Huntingdon's goblet. "Shall I find another bottle, my lord?"

"Nay, lady, I'm well enough lubricated." A grin. "I think we're best away to follow your daughter's example. And . . . shall I prepare to leave come morn? I will do so, if you require."

"I wish," Marion said, and meant it, "that you would stay."

"Then I shall retire, and bid you good night my lady." Huntingdon stood and tossed back the remainder of his wine, then bowed. Turning, he made his somewhat-unsteady way for the stair and his berth within the lord's chambers.

When Marion entered her own solar, Aderyn was already deep in sleep.

- XIX -

M arion's Book of Hours
Waxing of Lammas, 1202
7 years, 7 months, 24 days
11 months, 24 days
<u>Our Lords Shall Return</u>

Alais, Noble Lady of Stainton, was laid to rest upon 19th July, 1202, with full ceremony in the chapel of St Nicholas, amidst the family that became hers. She died in childbirth at the age of 43. Administrator of her demesne, benefactress and patroness of All Hallows, wife to Otho, Lord of Stainton, and beloved mother to Ian, Nicolas, and Edyth...

She will be greatly missed.

So many here, to do her honour. The entire vill of Stainton, the monks of All Hallows, the Lady Maud of Hallamshire (her husband, thank the Horns, is in Normandy), not to mention the scions of Pontefract, Conisbrough, and Huntingdon.

(The latter has adopted Tickhill as a regular stop upon his travels north. I suspect it's not only his brother the King of Scotland he visits,

but several of the Northern barons who are be-coming more and more disaffected with the governance of our shires. Whilst I feign empty-headedness when the subject is even hinted at, I suspect Huntingdon in particular doesn't be-lieve my pretence. But it's safer. Whatever my sympathies, I well know who owns the lands upon which my family depends.)

Yesterday's morn, it was, and market opens today. Preparations that couldn't begin yester's eve, what with the funeral and its arrangements, began in earnest at the dawn. The flags are flown, the gates flung open, the courtyard bustles with comings and goings—notably Gilbert, who brought his own sort of cheer into our sad house-hold: a tun of mead from old Wulfstan down south, a tithe suitable for the season. It looks to be a reasonably warm and sunny day for this time of year, and, well...

Life must go on, mustn't it

Yet I've no heart for the brave faces and gaiety of a market day, little spirit left for the coming Solstice. Mayhap it's foolishness. I'm not alone here—I have, after all, my children and what remains of the Shire Wode wolves about me.

What remains. That's the finger in the sore.

I want them back, all of them. I wish it were possible to see Will and Arthur again. I want my brother back, and the doubts plague me, more and more: will I will ever see him again, in this life or any other? Every day I pray to whatever gods will listen for Gamelyn to come home, alive and well. I wish John found our new home more welcoming than the caverns beneath Mam Tor, and Much... on so many days I long to run away with Much and be no more than a common wortwife in some tiny, unknown vill.

I miss Alais more than I thought I would. Her quiet strength; her fierce opinions; her skills at managing everything from her estate *to her children to her man; her love for all of those. It's upon me to do the best as I can for her children, and for Otho… though I doubt that things will go well with him now she is gone. He's lost, and no wonder. Huntingdon has suggested Otho would be better back at his own place within the se'nnight. Yet I hate to suggest it so soon. It seems… indecent. Not to mention how Stainton is more capably run by Alais' castellan, and I've no doubts 'twill suffer 'neath Otho's management.*

Forgive me, sister. I hope I'm wrong. I hope he stands beneath this burden instead of folding. Go to the otherworlds knowing your children shall be well cared for. I cannot do the same for your husband, I fear. I have my own to look to; all my prayers and wishes must be for him and his safe return.

O, Gamelyn, please, please come home to us. They say you're dead, but I know you're not. I know.

And in thisworld, a woman can only do so much.

Marvellous, after the previous wretched fortnight, to race along the North Road at full speed. Marion leaned forward, mindful of the bow at her back but urging her gelding on. He obliged mightily. The chestnut mane slapped her cheeks as, about her, a full concert filled the air: hoofs pounding an explosive rhythm against the wet earth; Gilbert's welcome laughter as he tried to keep up with her and keep an eye upon his sighthounds; the rat-tat of the horn; the bugle of scenthounds in the far distance.

And while the Earl of Huntingdon preferred hawking, claiming this sort of hunt was more a younger man's game, he was proving no more averse to leading a mad gallop across the countryside than Marion herself. Her mount's nose bobbed at the near haunches of his black courser, and both his burgundy cape and his wheat-and-silver hair flew in the wind. Beside him, keeping pace easily, rode several of his trusted lieutenants, as well as de Lacy, a few acquaintances from York, the earl of Conisbrough and his lady, and Otho. The latter, of course, had been Huntingdon's companion more than once at Tickhill and, to Marion's surprise, he rode quite well. She'd assumed his scorn of Ian's slow-blossoming horsemanship no more than a mirror of his own inadequacies, rather than the reverse.

Huntingdon sat up in the saddle, raising a hand. They all slowed down to a trot, then a walk that took them into a wide meadow past a bend in the road. They halted. Gilbert whistled his dogs to heel; tongues lolling, they obeyed. Marion's lip tilted, exchanging the smile with Gilbert. They both knew once the dogs sighted something, good luck with that!

Several arrows' flight in the distance, a telltale banner waved from a copse of trees. The bell of hounds had gathered behind it, and the horn blared a repeated rhythm. Gilbert had coaxed forth a small group of beaters from Tickhill's surrounding villages. Not an easy sell during harvest, but the promise of meat for their larders, as well as Marion's oath spread far and wide: their lady would steer the hunt towards the cleared roads and meadows, away from any vulnerable crofts.

A willing oath. Marion didn't much care for this sort of Hunt in the first place—and that's what it was, all in capitals, more a noble's pissing contest than any true search of sustenance. She'd been on the other side, knew what happened to the crofts who happen to be in the way of such things: trampled crops; panicked beasts who went missing or refused to milk; children knocked down; a quarry mad with fear leaping into windows . . .

Yet going with Huntingdon this time meant Marion could claim a bit more of the hunt than normally came within the grant of Tickhill's Lady and Sherwood's Keeper. It meant replacements for feeding the mourners, as well as venison and pork for the larder, and her people gaining meat through lawful means.

The last was very important. Gilbert had brought ill news with good mead. Forest Law had, beneath the shire's Sheriffs and no doubt the blessing of both chief forester de Neville and King John's leave, become all the harsher.

A blow of Huntingdon's horn pulled Marion from her musings, its blasts signalling: *Understood!*

At the edge of the tree copse, the banner stilled, and the far horn went silent.

Marion's gelding dug at the ground with one hoof, impatient to keep going. She soothed him with a tug and scratch to his mane then attended to her own, coming loose from its braid despite sweet oil and a securely wrapped veil.

"No doubt they're worrying we'll spoil their efforts by arriving too soon." Gilbert drawled, sidling his horse beside Marion's. "I prefer a proper hunt and stalk, but 'tis nice to see your eyes shining, fair Maid."

"It's been a proper dismal fortnight," Marion admitted, reaching out to take his hand, brief and fond. "I'm glad you're here."

He grinned, raised her hand to his lips. "I'm always glad to return to the bosom of my family."

"Or to Maud's?" she teased softly. That courtship, begun with cold-eyed intention, had softened into a courtly romance to which their favourite trouvère would have tuned a fair ballad. De Furnival's absence had fanned it from smoulder into flames.

And Maud was blossoming beneath the attention. Gilbert treated her gently. Hopefully by now he'd shown her that pleasure could be had in rutting, that 'tweren't merely some battering ram intent on nowt more than breaching the gates.

Gilbert chuckled, acknowledging the dart yet tossing it back. "Aye, well, milady's fair bosom, whilst not as impressive as yours, is still well worth a return! And then to find her here, amidst my favourite and beloved?"

"Cheeky sod," Marion warned, though it was amidst chuckles. "Ah, Gilly, I've missed—"

"A glorious day for a ride, eh, my lady?" Otho's voice, nigh at her right stirrup.

"It is indeed, my lord." Marion assumed a quick and amiable smile, slid her gaze sideways. Otho was treating Gilbert to a frosty glare that surely had no cause. As she loosed Gilbert's hand and turned, Otho's broad face smoothed pleasant—just that much too late.

"You ride like the fabled Valkyries, my lady." The words came quick, covering, she was sure, the unreasonable pique Gilbert-ward. "I'm sure I've never witnessed a woman so fearless in the saddle."

His tone bore either a subtle barb or compliment. Marion decided to go with the latter, though the former remained more likely. "Aye, well, I have to keep up my end of Tickhill's equestrian reputation."

"No worries there, gracious hostess," Huntingdon also had turned in his saddle. His smile touched her and slipped, slight, as he turned his gaze to Otho. It lingered, the earl seeming lost in some sombre thought. In the next breath, however, sombre gave way to more cheer. "I wonder at my own foolishness at not asking you to accompany us before! You ride hard as any man!"

"Indeed," Otho was quick to second.

"My lords, you are too kind." Marion took the compliment with what spirit it was meant—though not without an inward roll of eyes to shame Gamelyn's own favoured expression.

And wished he was here, about now.

Beside Marion, Gilbert's eyes danced as he conceded the majority.

"How about as hard as any woman?" Matilda de Warenne had ridden closer. Her husband William had stayed with de Lacy and company. She, too, was a first-rate rider, retucking a flyaway veil end over her dark hair whilst keeping her prancing, overexcited palfrey to a walk. "I rarely see any man so hampered by an overabundance of fabric!"

The men chuckled, again demurring in the lady's favour.

"It's been too long since I've had a good chase!" Matilda continued. "My thanks, lady Marion, for the courtesy—particularly after hosting so many." Her smile curved with understanding; Matilda knew. Her husband's elder by twelve years, she'd brought a shrewd steadiness as well as d'Aubigny lands to the marriage. "I'd hoped the lady Maud would accompany us; she is no poor horsewoman and 'twould do her good. Or has that husband of hers decided he can make a long-distance curtail of even the smallest liberties?"

Well, Matilda could afford to be blunt. Not that Marion didn't agree with her.

"Her young son is ill," Gilbert offered, the quick defence plain to one who knew him.

Thankfully, Matilda didn't, but she did shoot the cheeky forester a speculative glance. Marion also eyed Gilbert, who shrugged, albeit slight, and let Marion continue, "I gave the wee one a dose, and Aelwyn's on hand, but lady Maud chose to stay with her bairn."

Matilda frowned, distracted. She'd no children, and it seemed the one chink in her determined armour.

"My lords!" Gilbert pointed towards the copse. "They're signalling again. Quarry coming this way!"

The alaunts milling at his feet needed no signal. As a pack they alerted, quivering-eager. No doubt they heard the crash and crackle of brush in the wake of their prey.

Huntingdon dismounted, as did the others, spreading in a line across the clearing. Otho, with de Lacy and his companions, took crossbows from their guardsmen, as did Huntingdon. Both de Warennes preferred short recurves. Marion stayed put with her own shortbow; she and her horse were both well used to shooting from the saddle. Gilbert's longbow hung 'crost his back, already strung; he held out a nonchalant hand for Marion's bow and, as she handed it over, stepped it.

Unlike his younger brother, Otho was no great shakes at dice. He seemed . . . well, affronted, somehow, by the ease with which Marion and Gilbert worked.

But then, he'd been proper odd since Alais' death. No fault to him for that.

"Wups, there they go!" Gilbert quipped as the hounds, silent and nigh as one, took off towards the copse. "Good dogs!"

And the woodland erupted into motion, tawny hides bursting from cover. The deer leapt and darted, trying to wheel and bolt back into cover. Some even made it. Most were foiled by the beaters close on their heels: carrying staffs and tunics tied to staffs, pitchforks waving, beating drums made of bowls and stout sticks and, in one case, a round wooden shield. One of the deer put up a fight. He'd retained one of his three-pronged antlers and, using it with intent, he stamped and charged at three of the beaters. They weren't fools, Marion was glad to see, diving for cover as the stag whirled and disappeared into the thicket, tail flung high.

Crossbows cracked, first Huntingdon's, then Otho's. Gilbert paused long enough to whistle a 'good dog' peal as his hounds downed a large hart, took aim at another. Marion brought up her own bow, sighted, and loosed.

Mayhap no honour lay in taking down one's quarry in such a fashion—to hunter, or hunted.

But they would eat well for some time.

ⓚ

Later, Marion wandered amongst the slain deer, touching a smooth hide here, a lolling head there. Twelve taken today, and a boar. Otho had taken charge of the guardsmen and Gilbert's under foresters, directing the breaking and parcelling for the trip back. She blessed them all, men included. A few of the latter gave proper responses, albeit covert.

Necessary, of course.

"'Tis womanly of you, to be distressed," Otho said, a bit gruff, as Marion passed him. "But we have to eat."

Again, barb or compliment? This time it truly seemed the latter.

"I'm not distressed." Marion looked him in the eye and thought, not for the first time, how thoroughly unalike he was to Gamelyn. "I'm thanking them for their gift."

"Gift?" He seemed startled.

"Their lives for ours. It matters, milord."

A frown. "Again, 'tis kindly of you, but they're mere beasts. Thank God, who led them to us."

She smiled, turning away. "Oh, I am."

His bewildered gaze followed her.

The other lords—and lady—had gathered to one side of the clearing for a quick tipple. Of course, earls and barons didn't casually perform a hunter's work.

Marion had given polite demurral to Matilda's invitation to join them. The woman had meant it kindly—and sincerely—but one of de Lacy's comrades from York hadn't bothered hiding his dismay.

Curdle my wine with that face, you would. Marion wished she'd a wee bit of purge-root to slip into *his* wine, to be truthful.

Better company to be had with Gilbert anyway. She strolled over to where he'd parked himself on a large rock. Orders long since given to the under foresters, he doled out choice titbits to his hounds.

Several of those sidled up, tails waving and ears flat in doggy greeting. Marion stroked their sleek heads, making as much of them as Gilbert, who was cooing, "Good lass, good lad. A lot of overspent *jongleurs*, you are!"

Indeed most of the hounds, tongues lolling, had sprawled theatrically sidelong, as if another step might finish them, then and there.

It didn't stop them from snapping up what Gilbert tossed their way, though. And even the ones who'd greeted Marion, once done, flung themselves down on the grass. Aye, well, they knew when the parcelling was done, they'd fetch a better share. She threw Gilbert a wink and grin; he touched his cap and gained his feet, jerking his chin to a space behind her.

Marion turned to see Huntingdon, who tipped his head to her, addressing Gilbert.

"Good hounds you have there, master forester. And a good bow arm, as well, though"—his blue eyes twinkled towards Marion—"nigh out-matched by your lady keeper."

"Thank you, my lord Earl," Gilbert returned, with a graceful flourish and bow. "Both are compliments of the highest order."

Marion shot Gilbert a look of *don't overplay it, lad* and shrugged at Huntingdon. "I taught me brother, after all. Though Robyn certainly surpassed me."

A lift of salt-brown eyebrows at the open reference, then a slight bow. "Touché, my lady! 'Tis easy to forget . . ." He trailed off, discomfited.

"Where I came from? I never can, my lord, though you in particular have shown a gracious and forgiving nature."

"Hah! You, my lady"—a stress upon that latter—"are a necessary and welcome reminder as to how intellect and competence are to be found everywhere." Extending a gloved hand, he continued, "Moreover, you're family. In my household, that matters. As to forgiveness and grace . . . well. Our Lord would have us demonstrate both, aye?"

"Aye, indeed. But not so many of His followers practice it, in my experience." Marion smiled, alighting her hand upon his. "You're a good man, my lord."

"I try to be, despite a world where few good acts go unpunished." A wry smile accompanied the statement, and a quick glance outward, over the field. "I do listen, my lady, and that is considered kindness to many. Sometimes I hear things I wish I hadn't. I imagine in your position, as healer and lady of your folk, you've experienced much the same."

He started walking further from the field; when Marion would have hesitated, he took her arm, stayed her. "Walk with me, my lady? Mayhap this will not be done with impunity, either. But I feel I must make mention of it." His tone changed, edging closer into the Scottish curl that never lay too far away.

Marion knew him well enough by now to recognise the unease it signalled. A frisson of alarm shivered down her spine; she sublimated it by knotting one hand into her skirts and lifting them from the damp and mud, better to match the earl's long strides.

Had she been shorter of limb, she would have been hardpressed. It didn't ease her anxiety. Huntingdon usually proved very keen upon such courtesies.

When he did slow, it was nigh to the woodland's edge and some distance from the others. And when he spoke again, it lay soft and familiar, nevertheless with that unguarded lilt. More warning.

"My lady cousin. Your husband's brother has spoken to me. Not in confidence, mind, but he is family also, aye?—and thought to seek advice upon a particular matter of . . . " Again, the uncharacteristic hesitancy. "Well, of you."

"Me, my lord?"

Huntingdon slid his gaze to take her in, and frowned. "Stainton is of the firm opinion that 'twould be to both of your best interests, should he take you to wife."

Marion halted, wondered for a breath if she'd misheard. "Otho . . . intends . . . "

"To marry you. Aye."

"But . . . " Marion's voice failed her; she tried several times before words came past her tongue, and those rather high-pitched, disbelieving. "But I'm already married."

"He believes . . . " Huntingdon turned towards her, obviously uncomfortable. "He believes you a widow. That his brother has long been—in his words, mind—'bones long bleached and buried in Saracen lands'."

She stepped back and shook her head, staring at him.

"I'm sorry, my dear, to speak so frankly on such an unhappy subject. You and Gamelyn got on very well together, I know. I would not easily give up on the hope of my own wife's return, did something happen to take her from me." He meant it: regret edged his eyes and laced every word. "With it being past the promised year-and-day, with most of that time not even the Templars able to find word of him . . . well. We have to consider the possibility. The realities of your situation."

The possibility. The situation.

Marion turned away, fists clenched and heart hammering. The trees towered over her, bare-branched and quiet, creaking with the slight breeze, steadfast and waiting and *there*.

And she went from bewilderment to rage, all in the space of counting thrice.

All this time, she'd watched her back and kept her eyes on the horizon, wary. All this time, she'd given her husband's brother a forgiveness said brother had been wary to bestow in return. Had let him freely wander her halls, suffered his overweening arrogant resentment and envy, deflected the expectations that had all but ruined his firstborn son. Overlooked his passive-yet-belligerent incompetence at running the manor his brother had bestowed upon him, and gritted her teeth over his bloody-minded insistence on keeping his wife pregnant though he knew 'twould kill her in the end . . .

And now, with that wife barely dead a fortnight and upon the assumption that his younger brother was likewise, Otho had decided to make a final play for what he had, all along, considered his.

All of it threatened to spill over, scream heedless and vengeful as a *baen sidhe*. Again, Marion choked it back. Control around one's 'betters' might be a hard-learned lesson any peasant woman had damn-well better heed, but all the while Marion realised another proof in it. She'd indeed come up in the world, hadn't she? Just like any mid-caste noblewoman, sweet-faced yet scheming upward all the while . . .

Instead she growled out a suitably-edited version. "*His* wife and newborn son are barely a fortnight entombed!" she shot back, low. "How *dare* he?"

Huntingdon sighed, looking off into the woodland. "I advised him to consider carefully. He said he has, and more, that he has not only the support of the Prior of St Mary's, but that of Hallamshire."

"The . . . Prior." And his brother Brian de Lisle, the ex-Sheriff of Nottingham looking for any way to extract vengeance from the Hood's sister. Marion refused to give it voice—no doubt to one such as Huntingdon, 'twould seem mere fancy. "And de Furnival? That one's about his own aims, nowt but indulging a covetous regard for Tickhill!"

"No question that Cousin Otho would be Hallamshire's willing envoi within." Huntingdon's eyes gleamed. "Gerard de Furnival has always been . . . ambitious. His wife is kin, as you know, and while lady Maud will heed me?" A shake of head. "Her husband's no longer a raw youth willing to the wisdom of his elders."

"More fool him!"

"Hm. Well. At least Conisbrough and Pontefract aren't so rapacious. Cousin Otho has also approached them."

Marion clenched her teeth.

"You needn't fear overmuch on that score. William is disinclined to see a good neighbour disrupted—and hardly comforted to see a vassal gain more than he already has. Roger is also less than willing; he remembers Otho's tenure here, including the foolishness of the siege. He realises that Otho has culled some favour from King John—the opposite side of that same siege—but also that you, at present, enjoy more." A shrug. "Thus, as Conisbrough and Pontefract are unwilling to lend support, Otho—as my cousin Marjory's son—has appealed to me. He says de Furnival is willing to carry a letter to the King."

Surely Marion's teeth couldn't clench any tighter.

"If you are—please forgive me, dear lady—but if you are indeed a widow, by law you are in gift of the King. Your dispensation, in such case, is the King's to decide."

"And my assets, naturally." It was flat.

The gleam deepened. Not amused, not at all, but appreciative. "Naturally."

"Which"—through her teeth—"obviously forbears my lord of

Stainton to the disagreeable possibility of wiving a woman who was not only once a peasant, but outlaw, and sister to the most notorious wolfshead in the land."

"Do not overlook," Huntingdon pointed out, approbation beginning to tinge his voice all wry, "that he is mindful of your . . . ah, 'scandalous past', and feels he would be a settling influence upon you. That he" —his voice took upon the stiff, nasally tenor, Otho at his more pompous— "well understands how such wayward and fiery humours accompany such physical colouring, and surely such a woman needs—nay, longs for—a stern hand to tame her.'"

"*What?*"

"He feels it is both his obligation and duty to step up in the circumstances—"

"He . . . actually *said* this?"

"—and that surely"—Huntingdon put one finger alongside his nose—"the price is worth paying, as he would not only regain the honour of Tickhill, once his, but a younger and obviously fertile wife."

Her bow. If only she'd her bow to hand. She'd ease Otho from his bloody damned 'duty' with one sure loose.

"Too many witnesses, lass." The Earl of Huntingdon finally betrayed a quiver of lip beneath that gingery, well-trimmed beard. "Better to use a wortwife's means, do you mean to do for him."

A laugh burst from Marion, short and sharp.

It was simply too ridiculous.

"Marion." It was the first time he'd addressed her so familiarly, and his tone no longer twisted wry, but earnest. "Mightn't it be an option to consider?"

"My lord—!"

"Please, hear me out." He raised his hands, placating. "If the King decides that your husband will never return from Outremer, then rest assured he will not leave one of his most valuable assets in the hands of a widow."

Into mine, he might, Marion thought, but kept her expression smooth, listening. *The King still believes in the otherworldly Kingship, believes it his, mayhap even over the Angevin's worldly legacy. He thinks of all others as Substitutes for him, Sacrifices to his power in thisworld, and we've used it well.*

Until now, it seemed.

"What of my son? The heir to Tickhill?" she challenged, though speaking it felt too akin to conjuring ill. "I'm not the only mother to safeguard her children's assets until they come of age. I have done and will, believe me."

"I do believe you. And it is one solution—though not the easiest. Gamelyn was given Peak and Welsh lands in fee simple; those are in your control, an inheritance for his son. Tickhill itself, however—"

"Belongs to the Crown."

"Make no mistake, dear lady, your situation here could prove chancy. And I cannot be here to defend you as my conscience would like." A smile, this time. "Though I well know you're capable of defending what's yours with no assistance from me! Good lord, the tales are starting to travel up- and down-country: the she-wolf of Tickhill, taking down a mob of mercenaries with a longbow! But trust to 't, the honour of Tickhill is plain incitement in this latest move."

Thoughts racing, Marion nodded, flicking a glance towards the clearing and their companions.

The villagers were helping Huntingdon's men load their take onto the sumpter horses. De Lacy was speaking—as usual, expansively and with great gestures—and seemed a worthy opponent for Matilda's forthright manner. The latter in particular seemed to spark husband de Warenne's easy-going amusement, Otho's mild dismay, and the horror of the men from York. Over near the horses, Gilbert was in conversation with his under foresters and several of the villagers; Marion saw a small flash from Gilbert's hand to the latter, welcome tender. Yet all the while, Gilbert kept glancing Marion's way, eyes sharp beneath the cover of his hat.

Unfortunately, Otho also watched her palaver with Huntingdon, when he thought she wasn't watching.

Huntingdon, of course, stood mindful as well. Scanning the clearing, his voice lowered further. "The northern barons are restless . . . Now, please, I well know you've loyal informants, and a canny brain to process that information beneath your respectable matron's veil. Let us not pretend otherwise, one to one. I tell you, it is only a matter of time before the northern barons cease wrangling amongst themselves and join forces, act. They are unhappy that their taxes go to finance a war that was, in truth, a waste of resources long before our present King sat on England's throne. Many Northerners have little investment left in Normandy and Anjou, including my brother. This is our home— here, upon this green island."

Marion nodded. "I hear you, my lord."

"Aye, and Alexander has already considered the possibilities of Northern alliances. This past trip he made it clear that he wishes me to do likewise." Pretending to view the gathering clouds, he furthered, "And to find those with . . . common cause. Which, despite a king's fickle favour, I believe you have."

"And since I do, and particularly since Tickhill controls partial access to the North—"

Huntingdon smiled approval.

"—and could well be an important factor in such a conflict?"

"Factor—or hostage. Despite any she-wolf upon the battlements." He eyed her, solemn. "Or mayhap because of that she-wolf. You remain, my lady, one who has the favour of our King, and your lord's son in residence. But he cannot hold for at least another ten years."

Marion put both hands to her belly. It seemed she could feel the lurch and drop of it against her damp palms. "Mayhap I'd be better off retreating back into the Shire Wode."

"I would recommend you first come to my home at Fotheringhay, should you choose a strategic retreat."

She let out a shaky laugh.

"Marion, I mean it. Your brother's legacy might haunt Sherwood, but ghosts and reputations are poor substitutes for solid walls about you. I can only hope my candour—foolish, mayhap, to speak so to the head of a household so fiercely loyal to the Crown—impresses my affection for you and the children. I will be glad to foster your son, for his protection and yours. And if any of you ever need sanctuary, you can—"

"My lord earl! My lady!" A soldier loped over to them, slowing as they turned. "Riders coming, from the north!"

Gilbert and his foresters were already stringing their bows. De Warenne and Otho were giving orders to the cohort, whilst lady de Warenne, shortbow in hand, gestured to several of the villagers to gather the horses. The remaining soldiers were armed, ready.

Of late, a mounted group upon the road could be nothing. Or anything.

A welcome sight rode round the far curve of the North Road, banners flying. Recognisable, and welcome, this grey banner of running horse, crescent, and cross.

"'Tis the Moorlands' folk!" Marion crowed.

The patch known as Moorlands lay northeast of Tickhill and south of the Humber, and had over the past several years become a refuge to a small enclave of folk who'd emigrated from the turmoil of war in the Holy Land. Some converted, many not, all had come to England beneath a diverse range of purposes and decided to stay for reasons just as varied.

They also acknowledged Tickhill, beneath yet another variety of motives, and occasionally sent reinforcements at Marion's request.

This group, however, seemed much larger than she'd expected. She hadn't long to assuage curiosity—moving at a good lick, they were. As they drew closer, not only Moorland's banner, but the burgundy-backed oak of Tickhill fluttered in the winds of passage. Marion's stomach gave a joyful lurch as she recognised the three riders heading the cavalcade; two bare-headed, one with a *keffiyeh*, and the remainder fanning out behind, dressed much the same.

One of Huntingdon's men let out a friendly whoop, and several answered it. The cheerful racket carried across the fields, echoing against the trees Marion ran over to the road. The riders slowed as their leaders pulled up before Marion.

"We are here!" Once Siham set herself to commanding something, she usually succeeded—and the Anglic tongue had been no exception. "As you can see, we also brought some laggards we found upon the road!"

Marion's gaze found and clung to Much's, a communication silent—and comprehensible—as her daughter's own:

I've missed you.

You look knackered, love.

I am. I'm glad you're here.

Gilbert, meanwhile, had loped over to Siham's mount, offering to hand her down as if she were garbed in samite as opposed to road-worn mail and leathers.

For this courtesy, Siham flipped a smack at his head. "Not before my men, foolish creature!" Then, smiling so broad it seemed her kohl-traced eyes would disappear, Siham swung a leg over and strode to Marion, both hands upon her breast.

"I bring the best fighters of my people, to aid and assist my lady of Tickhill."

Impossible opportunities. Chancy situations. Marion couldn't help a slide of eye, first to Huntingdon and then over to Otho and the other nobles, who seemed stunned.

- XX -

Marion showed her newest guests to the stables upon the bailey. Her gaze kept seeking Much; finding him there, she kept smiling. Kept talking to Siham. "You like it there, then."

"It is home," Siham said, simply. She'd pulled the wrap from her face, and kept flashing small and even teeth—the same smile that had never left her eyes. "But here shall be home for a while, yes? For I owe much to that dice game your good husband played with my lord of Pontefract."

Gamelyn had tried, over several years and without success, to buy Siham's service from Roger de Lacy. It had indeed taken a game of chance—along with de Lacy's belief, ultimately mistaken, in his own consummate gambling skills—to enable Gamelyn to acquire that service—and then give it back to her. She'd served Tickhill for some time regardless, but finally had travelled to the Moorlands: a place named—somewhat inaccurately—for its residents, and more appropriately towards the land upon which they wrangled a living.

"God requires we pay our debts," Siham continued, with a squeeze to Marion's arm. "Though this debt raises not the least hardship, believe me. We are all glad to help you in your need."

Her compatriots agreed. Siham turned and queried them in a smattering of tongues, nodding at her second-in-command. He gave orders in Arabic. Leading the docile, fine-limbed Eastern horses that Moorlands raised, the men headed for the stable doors, weaving a careful path amidst the visiting marketers and the stalls attracting them.

They knew where, and what to do.

Placing the welfare of her other guests in Aelwyn's capable hands, Marion took Siham and one of her companions, as well as Gilbert and Much, to the lord's stables beneath and beside the great mound.

Lit only by carefully-tended torches, the cavern surrounded them with scents of earth and manure, hay and corn. A stable lad seemed to materialise out of the darkness, eager to help; Much nodded towards their guests and led his stallion into a nearby box. The habit of Templar Rule lingered, and he always cared for his own mount. He quickly unbridled the stallion, who snatched at the waiting fodder.

Gilbert let the stable lad take his horse, but lingered. "Can I stand you a drink?" he asked Siham. "Non-fermented, of course."

She smiled at the courtesy, but her gaze slipped away to meet with her companion's, who'd so far waited tall and silent at her shoulder. That one's eyebrows tilted, one higher, one lower, with a glint of mischief in amber eyes. Another woman, Marion realised.

Realised further, at the look the two women exchanged, that Gilbert was doomed to disappointment.

"I have duties to see to, Gilbert, my friend." Sliding her arm free of Marion's, Siham gave a polite dip of head. "Another time, mayhap? And Captain?"

Much looked up.

"I and my riders will report to you, once we have seen to our horses."

"Aye, well, then."

Following the stable lad, Siham and her companion took their mounts deeper into the stable with a clip of shod hoofs on packed clay.

Gilbert watched after, shrugging. Turning, he grinned as Marion started inching closer to where Much tended his horse. "Shall I wait for you by the doors? See that you're . . . undisturbed. For a short while, anyway. Then mayhap you and I can have that drink, Marion. I've some forest business to discuss with you."

Marion nodded, and watched him saunter away as she approached the half wall of the horse box. She leaned upon it, chin upon hands, smiling at Much.

"T' lad from Castleton weren't exactly from Castleton," Much slid two of the packs from his horse's withers, settling them athwart his own shoulders. "He were in the pay of that lot of mercenaries."

"We've been . . . um . . . hosting several of them in the under-keep," Marion answered back, lightly. "David's set to fetch some useful information from them. Eventually. The rest of 'em lie buried in the fens."

A sly grin tried to take his face. "I heard sommat to the like, on the road back. We stopped being in such a hurry."

"You were in a hurry before?"

"Damned straight we were, until we heard Tickhill lay safe enough. Y' see, the lad who weren't from Castleton? He tried to sneak away once we arrived nigh to Hathersage, but Gunnora's grandson caught him. Tied him to the anvil, and we made a few threats with a warm poker. That loosened his tongue proper." A snort. "T'lad wouldn't've lasted a day in the desert. We en't so much as touched him, yet he was all ower singing who'd given him orders to lure us out, and the hows and whys. Well, the ones he knew, leastways." He slung the saddle over the stanchion. "I said he weren't from Castleton, aye? He were from Knaresborough."

Marion stiffened. "Again."

"Aye, he'd de Lisle's smell all ower him. Like that blacksmith lass." He slid a disapproving eye her way. "Should've never let that 'un go."

"What was I to do? Hold her for months on end?"

"Bury her in t' fens, like all the other scum who think t' threaten our lives here."

"So, did you let the lad-who-weren't-from-Castleton go?"

Much shrugged, uncomfortable, and began brushing the stallion. "Mm. Thought so."

"He weren't much older than our Ian. De Lisle's our target."

"Hard to draw sight when he's ower in Normandy."

"Mayhap, but t' lad were too scared we'd mar his pretty face to be lying."

Marion leaned against the stallion's rump; he grunted and kept eating. "And de Lisle's brother en't. In Normandy. He's Prior at St Mary's not half-a day's ride south."

And somehow willing that Otho marry me. . . why? So de Furnival can worm his influence into Tickhill through Otho, and oust us?

"Though I should think that hiring mercenaries would be beneath Prior Willem."

"Because he's a prior?"

Marion snorted. "Their lot would hire mercenaries for a lark, did it put more coin in their own pockets. Nay, because Prior Willem has allus followed his brother Pontefract's lead. De Lacy long ago cut off ties with de Lisle. He'd no patience for his brother's obsession with ex-wolfsheads."

"But the King showed some patience, when they were here last. The Prior and de Lisle both, in Hallamshire's company."

"The King wanted men for Normandy."

Much's expression settled grim. "Like Hallamshire's wanted Tickhill for ages. Maybe *he* put up the money for 'em. Mayhap de Lisle encouraged it, like, and convinced his baby brother to the deed. After all, the King's all ower hiring such scum. The like of such things trickles downstream, aye? Once it were known you'd ower half your soldiers gone—and I wain't be making that mistake again, believe me—I'll wager whoever 'twere couldn't resist a proper plum for the pickin'." Much shrugged away the questions with a choice expletive and a shake of head. Instead he reached out to run a finger down her cheek, tipping her chin up. "Or so he thought. Silly sod, he underestimated a wolf bitch protecting her pups."

A fierce kiss completed that tip of chin, one long and hard enough to fire her belly and weaken her knees. Marion gave back as good as she got.

Much broke the kiss, nuzzled into her neck. "Surely," he breathed, "what information I've brought milady is enough for a proper soldier's welcome."

"Proper? In a stable? With guests waiting?" Despite any tease, it had all started to sound proper perfect. Especially as he began working his way down her front.

"'Tis been the while, lass. I won't last long."

"*You* won't last." A snort. "And what about me, then?"

"Aye, there's that."

She nipped his ear, hard. "So I should think you'd best have sommat else to sweeten the pot."

"Some women en't never satisfied." A grin belying the woeful words, he pulled away—slight, just enough to reach and tug the second pack from the saddle cantle.

Marion took it with a small "Oof" and a "What do you have in here? Stones?"

"Aye, well, I brought a few on home, as we en't enough hereabouts."

Marion wrinkled her nose at him and peeked past the flap. Grinned. "Gunnora's elderberry wine!"

"She knew you were pining. And I wanted to ensure that proper welcome, aye?"

"Well, you have and then some."

He leaned closer, pressed her against the fodder bin. Hard, he was, from his broad chest to the thighs that pressed between hers—aye, and that, too, even without the mail trous. One hand ran down her back to cup one buttock, knead her closer; tilting her chin up, Marion nipped at his lower lip with a grin.

"Uncle Much!"

Blue-grey eyes met Marion's, chagrined and amused. "I should've known even Gilbert wouldn't hold that lad."

"Uncle Much!" rang once more through the stables, and Rob burst into the gloom, leaping up on the stanchion and into Much's chest. The bay stallion jerked up from his fodder and rolled air through his nostrils.

"Mind yourself, boy!" Much growled. "You know better than to be such a fool about the horses!"

"Aw, lad, I'm proper sorry." Rob held out a hand to the bay stud. After a stretchy-necked peer at the flying sort-of-boy-thing that might eat horses, the stallion decided it was just Rob, after all, and went back to munching.

"Here." Much tossed Rob up on the stallion's croup, handed him a wisp. "Do sommat of use more than screeching and leaping."

"I'm just so glad to see you, Uncle."

And so was Aderyn, who, mindful of the horses, had slowed her pace, but slammed against Much and clung just as hard, once she was there. Much swept her up and hugged her tight.

"Aye, and I've missed you both considerable. You and wee Marjorie and your Mam. Everyone, really."

Aunt Alais died, and her bairn.

"That I'd *not* heard." He peered over Aderyn's black head at Marion. "Faith, what happened?"

"Ian's really sad," Rob said, scrubbing at the horse's sweated back with two hands and the wisp. "He spends a lot of time up on the walls, just walking about. He en't ridden in days. He keeps saying said God's wrong, to take her away, and I said 'twere the Lady as took souls, and he looked at me all funny."

"It were a bad birthing. We did all we could, but 'twere no use." Marion's eyes stung. Aderyn wriggled down from Much's embrace and went to her mother, hugged close.

"Faith, but you've had a hellish week and no question, love." Much reached out and stroked her cheek. "Anything else I need to know?"

"Other than I missed you terrible? Anything else can wait for market's end." A tilt of head towards the children.

"'Cept what Aderyn said," Rob put in. "She said she'd seen Uncle Robyn in the forest!"

This was met with resounding silence. Marion looked at Much, who seemed just as bereft of any comment as she herself.

"She told Edyth," Rob said, eager. "'Course, Edyth doesn't understand all Aderyn's talk, but I do. I saw what she said. She went to the Mere, and talked to Unc—Hoy!"

The fresh horse turd made a satisfactory splat against the side of Rob's ginger-gilt head.

"Eri! I were just—!" Two more balls of manure hit him: one in the chest, the other in his open mouth just as he started to whinge, "Mam! I—uhnf!"

And before either adult could intervene, Rob was sliding down from the stallion's brown rump for his own weapons, and the fight was on. Balls of fresh and dried horse manure were flying. Aderyn backed in the aisle for better aim. Rob chased after, making up for in missile quantity what he lacked in accuracy.

"Enough!" Marion finally found her voice, but it wobbled and squeaked, useless. She couldn't believe what she'd heard.

The Mere? Saw. Uncle . . . Robyn?

Much ended up wading into the battle's midst, grabbing Rob around the waist and swinging him over one shoulder—with a whack to his rump for good measure when he kept wriggling and growling. Aderyn was about to let loose another manure ball. Much pointed a finger at her and she froze mid-motion. Dropped it.

Marion tried to speak, again. Again, her voice cinched itself tight.

"Be still, boy!" Much growled—and it was some satisfaction that it, too, came out all hoarse. "Aderyn, your Uncle's gone. There's all sorts of rumours flying"—his eyes slid to Marion's, giving notice that he likely knew what she and Gilbert had been up to—"but I were there, see? They took him from us."

I knew you wouldn't believe me—

"It's nowt to do wit' belief, pet. That Mere is treacherous, like, it shows you only what it wants y' to see, and your mam and da have spent ower much of themselves trying to fetch Robyn back—years of it, y'see? But he's gone, lass, gone for good, and all of it for nowt!"

Frustration overrode the hoarseness—and told more than he'd surely planned. Marion stiffened, peering at Much for a long moment.

His eyes touched hers and slid away.

Marion let a long breath out through her teeth, turning to Aderyn, who knelt in the straw beside her. "Was this what you tried to tell me before?"

Aderyn looked down. After a pause, she nodded.

"Mayhap it's time you told me all of it, then."

ᛦ

For Robyn Hode, tactical retreat had long formed itself into an essential habit.

In his Shire Wode, where swiftness in the ways of foray, strike, and withdrawal had long proved best in outwitting—and out-weaponing—heavily armed troupes.

In communion with his god, where the wandering and the isolation gave him a strength even his beloved ones couldn't, settled the forest's magic deep within—and repaired what damage endured from holding to the tail of an Infinite.

In the action before him, crafted, always, from the moment and the movement, driven by instincts and nature's pulse.

All of it survival, of a profound and visceral kind.

Only no pulse throbbed here, no eternity expressed in any living echo, no familiar Spiral, only thisnow spinning itself out so linear, so frayed, so . . . *unnatural.* He'd no moment, no move-ment, save to wander with his little guardians into deep, empty, timeworn caverns. Avoiding the ones who'd brought him here, avoiding the inevitable, mayhap, and all along avoiding a conflict he couldn't win, mending an abraded spirit against another inevitability.

It couldn't be inevitable. He wouldn't breathe the reality of it into even this stale air, spin power-filled breaths into *tynged's* pulse.

Wouldn't imagine Marion's child growing into a world grown so harsh-spare and selfish. So bereft of the magic as . . . as . . .

As here, in its own fashion.

Save for one cavern Veiled with spells, holding a wyvern spirit old beyond time, waking into visions and conjured up by a little girl's undeniable power.

So, now, habit became purpose. Moment, movement, and Robyn's own feet took him unerringly to a solitary cavern, where a solitary old man sat beside a solitary hearth.

The scene bided so natural, even if his own mentor was long dead and mere bones mouldering in his beloved earth. But nothing about thisnow or place lay normal. Robyn wondered what in bloody damn he thought he was doing. Debated, once again, retreat.

The elder looked up from the pot as he stirred, and the clouds across his eyes gave Robyn further pause. Magus was the memory-keeper—

memory. . . not just thisnow, but others, where heartbeats ramping up—

one-and, two-and, three-and—

—counting a time that doesn't-couldn't-didn't-wouldn't exist!... All of it bleak-black, rising about him, tasting of ruin and fear, war and subjugation and. . . and. . .

Robyn strangled it breathless. Considered that in the other paths of Magus's memories, there might lie something other than a world's ruination.

Robyn had to believe in sommat, and his god weren't here, about now.

So he halted at the lintel and offered the blessing and, when invited in, settled by the fire with his little beasties perched around him.

Magus didn't so much as move. As if he'd been expecting Robyn, settled all cross-legged at the fire with an ease Robyn hoped to have at half that age. Apparent age, 'tennyrate.

Not that he'd any expectations of growing so old, or seeing a pack of children growing about him, let alone grandchildren. 'Lessen they were Marion's and even then Gamelyn could handle 'em; he fancied the little beggars, after all.

The old man spoke first. "'Tis powerful you be, indeed, drawing fire magics in the Veil's damp." A shrug. "But still, staying there be reckless."

"Aye, well, I thought I were Hob."

The gwyllion curled about Robyn's neck gave a small growl and poked its head out from underneath black tangles. Magus blinked, startled. Well, 'twere true it lay there more akin to a Barrow torque than any living creature some days; even Robyn had grown used to its negligible weight.

Magus peered at the gwyllion. It peered back, gave a little string of scolding chitters, then flipped its tail and withdrew into Robyn's hair. The old *dryw* shook his head and gave a grumbling sigh. "What have you told the changeling Maiden?"

Robyn cocked his head, decided upon his own advance. "So she *is* a changeling. I thought she were ower young amidst the rest of you."

"She is not being the only, but the last, aye."

"The last as your kind took from the outerworlds."

"When we could still be riding and making the Rade. When the Veil was allowing us to draw it aside, here and there."

"What gives you the right to steal children?"

"What was giving Robyn Hood the rights to steal things?"

Robyn bristled, and several of the gwyllion hissed.

"What the master of beasts be feeling, the creatures be mirroring?" A snort. "Master, mayhap, but more fool. Still. When tiny souls be valued less than things, we are having every right. To be taking something left exposed on hillsides, left starving and slowly dying? Madness, it is being, to throw away a soul merely because it is being born different, or as a she! Sacrilege!" With an angry growl, Magus leaned forward, picked up a stick, and gave a judicious poke to the coals beneath his cookpot.

Robyn understood the anger. "Madness, aye. But mayhap there's sommat else. Mayhap those souls chose their *tynged*. Chose to have the livin' short and hard in amends for such wrongs as they might've done in other lives. What if in saving, you're interfering? Swerving their path into a dead end?"

"It is not being—"

"En't it? If they're here, they wain't die, wain't be reborn. They canna follow the Spiral or accompany their people ever on. Here, everything just . . . stops."

"Whereas *that*world be such as values only things and possessions, like magpies preening. Even you, Hob-Robyn! Thief and magpie—no wonder you would be pining for such a place!"

"It en't perfect. That's the point, old one. Nowt's perfect, but it's mine. My land. My *place*. I belong there."

"So certain"—the old man's eyes lit with a sudden, uncanny gleam—"you are being."

"Aye, I am."

Magus leaned forward, tending his hearth. "Mayhap Hob be realising his mistake in choosing thatworld. Doomed, it is being, its only change towards destruction."

"Then why do you want it brought in here, old one? If it's nowt but ru . . ."

ruin. . . wreckage. . . devastation. . . smoke hanging in thick, fiery skies. . . ashes gritting against his tongue while a roar and rumble deafens, an approach over a burnt horizon. . .

Water, a splash against his face that dampened the ash, tasting of salt with an echo—

water is our life—

—from . . . from *somewhere.*

The echo of it faded into the caverns, silty water—like the Veil—pooling into the corners of his eyes. Robyn sat up, slowly, for Magus crouched over him. He held a small cup in one hand. It still dripped.

"The changeling maid said as much. It is troubling her, that the Bowl visits you still."

"What . . . is it?"

"An augury." Magus rose and padded to where a wide-mouthed pot jar squatted against the wall. "A rift in thisnow."

"Like the . . . Veil." Robyn wiped at his face.

Magus shrugged and dipped into the jar, brought the cup up all wet. "The Veil is being drawn closed. The Bowl remains open—to Seeing, not passage. It used to be our telltale of otherworlds passage. Now?" Another shrug as he squatted beside Robyn and proffered the cup. "Now it is being more turmoil than guidance."

"So. It's"—Robyn drank from the cup as the elder man frowned, insistent—"not real."

The elder's snort confirmed what Robyn, unfortunately, suspected. "In some things, the Bowl is being all too real." He kept feeding the tiny fire—this time, with a grumble. "Destruction. Chaos. The Hob be bringing such things here, but in this much He is being right: such things must be part of life. Else life is *not.*"

"That's the most sensible thing I've heard anyone say in this place."

"I am being memory keeper, Hob-Robyn. Fool, I am not. Foolish, it is being, to spin unrest in smallish bounds."

"Only if you accept the bounds. Mayhap there's little hope of one soul—or a dozen, at that—changing what wain't change. Mayhap there's only the try at shaping a place for our own kind. What's worth saving and what's worth nowt but letting go! What needs cherishing! 'Twere why I stayed in my forest, let 'em call me outlaw—not to steal *things*, but to make a place for my own kind. I became Robyn Hode for *those* cast-off souls."

"Huh. And this is what you have been telling your changeling Maiden?" Magus plainly had his own method of advance, consistent.

"Mostly, I told her how she *en't* my Maiden."

Surely the old man had to run out of snorts sometime. "And so you keep up this game, claiming no Maiden? Disrespectful, it is being. Profane. Unnatural!"

"So I've heard. Ower and ower, and I thought t' people of Barrow lines, at least, wouldn't be so bloody stupid."

Magus drew up, offended.

Robyn didn't give him the chance to protest. "You say 'claiming', like some lass belongs to me simply 'cause I've a knob to poke her with—and if that en't a lie told by conquerors, what is? And then you say *natural,* as if there en't bucks who'll rut other bucks or, in fact, a list of creatures long as my arm who fancy their own or any? There's other ways to bring life and living than making bairns, and if my soul alighted into mortal lands fancying tackle out 'stead of in, 'tis *my* nature! And *you'd* best take care, old man! Fool I may be, when the moment comes, but at least I en't sounding all pious and tight-skirted, more a Christian monk than any Barrow mage!"

Magus stared at him, then carefully hawked and spat upon the fire. "Do not say that name here! It was being the Cold People, the stealers of holy places, the makers of sin, iron, and bells—they be bounding us here, thinking to cage what they couldn't control or take." He leaned forward, gave another stir at his pot. Said, low, "Wrong, I am, to say such things to the Hob. It is just being . . . unusual, for Horned God's creature to spurn a mate."

"I en't spurning nowt. I've no shortage of rutting when I need, to the Horned One's pleasure or my own. As I told all of you"— and bloody damn, but the memory of that place and the milky, stone bowl of Seeing chilled him to marrow—"twould be a lie, did I do so. So I promised my god, a thousand little deaths into the one, with blood and seed and salt, and furthered that oath by giving our Maiden the choice. *She* chooses who seeds the coming year, and I stand by her, make 'em prove their worth. It en't some bloody cockfight ower chattel."

Robyn expected more debate. To his surprise, Magus smiled, nodding. Taking up a cup, he ladled up a portion from the pot and offered it over. Robyn accepted. The stuff was colourless, with only the tiniest of scents to tell him what it was: a porridge of grain and milk and honey.

"From Crossroads places, where the Veil be thinned by offerings or rites. We can no longer be taking such gifts ourselves, of course, but ones like *those,*" Magus nodded to the gwyllion "and others of their kind be aiding us. Thankfully, the need for sustenance be seldom, as you no doubt be discovering."

"And there's none to be had in your forest. No life. No death."

Magus made a furtive sign against his breast. "It is not being a word we speak here."

"Death?" Deliberate, and a raised eyebrow as the sigil was repeated. "Aye, but seems to me that's your problem and then some."

Magus didn't pursue it further, merely scooped up pottage for himself. "The forest . . . be waiting. For the Horned One to be returning, breathe it green anew. For life. Death." Deliberate, but still with the gesture. "For you, Hob-Robyn. Instead, you be denying it, be telling our children we are dust."

"Shouldn't all of us be, in t' end?"

"What else were you telling the changeling?" Again, the advance. "You upset her. She is wandering our forest, seeing it not."

"Mayhap now she really does see it. She thought she'd been brought to the underworld. Annwyn's realm."

"And you are so certain it is not being that?"

"I've been there." Eyes level, words sharp between his teeth.

"So have I." Magus met Robyn's gaze, unbending. "This be surprising you. But once, I was being chieftain of the *Dryw* of the Attecotti. Do you doubt me?" he furthered as Robyn didn't so much as blink. "There were, then, being as many *dryw* throughout our land as there were being cattle upon the plains of the Brigantes. Death"—again, the sigil—"was being our friend, our teacher. Our way inward, to the wisdom of one of the most hallowed Rites of all."

"Yet one by one, you've lost those Rites. So much that you don't even admit to a death you can't touch, and spin forgetfulness with greater lies than any Christian priest could conjure—"

Surely the man had to run out of wardings; this one made fierce and vehement. "It is not being my place, to decide upon what my Priestess thinks best to tell Her children! It is not mine to be deciding where next we stand and fight. I am the story-singer, the memory-keeper—"

"I'd dare say, if everyone else has forgotten, you en't done your job ower well."

A curl of nostrils betrayed affront. "If memory is being of sorrow, Hob-Robyn, what is being the curse of one who brings it forth?"

A troubled frown twitching his brow, Robyn eyed him.

Magus merely took a sip of porridge.

Robyn looked down, did likewise. The porridge coated his tongue, flat and somehow . . . chill, though it steamed from the fire. *Crossroads, y' say, and rites and belief to open them. What if I've found a Crossroad? One made with the magic of the* Ceugant? *What would you do then, O keeper of Memory? Silence it, keep it buried underground, and all for your Ravening Mother Sow who keeps clutching to the chains of this dying fortification she's erected?*

Nay, not merely from her own doing, O Hob, but fashioned by necessity from the iron stones of a manifest gaol. What would you do, in her place? What would any of us do, to protect our own?

He'd heard the Lady seldom enough in his lifetime; here the power of Her overfilled him, driving rain to flood the fens. The gwyllion at his throat quivered, wings rustling. Robyn set his porridge down with trembling hands; it was that or drop it.

"You be misunderstanding, Hob-Robyn. Still. Even though our Priestess be making a choice of which even the Hob should be approving. A gamble, O Trickster, with the last magics remaining to her." Had the old man also heard the Lady, to be reinforcing her words so? "Priestess gave oath, long ago, to all of her people: to be protecting us against a world of pain and sorrow. What would you do, Hob-Robyn?"

"I'd protect them, aye. But deny them their rights to living?"

"She was not being the one who did that!" Magus retorted. "With the last of our magics she sheltered us, made for us a haven within this earth. But the magics have long been . . . faltering. Fading. The Dancing Spiral long weaves sideways, stumbles. And the forest . . . "

"Is dying," Robyn whispered, because he knew Magus would not finish it.

This time, Magus did not make the warding sign. "So, Priestess made another oath: to be bringing life to us. She used the Arrow you gave us—and it being wrapped and spelled in *your* promise, Hob-Robyn, your life-blood, your oath! She be making one last attempt, even if it meant to be forfeiting any more chances we might be having. Even if it be making more solid the power of the Veil that holds us. We have lost our way to any Crossroads, but we are gaining the best beloved of the Horned Lord's creatures. Hob-Robyn is being change, aye? Only . . . " He looked away, and Robyn saw his eyes glitter in the firelight.

"Only," Robyn said, soft, "you didn't count on *my* oath, nor on thisnow's incarnation of the *Ceugant*. She didn't . . . none of you kenned it, how my magic is balanced upon the knife-edge of that oath, not whole without my Knight and my Maiden."

"So," the old man sighed. "Our Mother's ultimate gamble be without fruit, and her power unable for the ultimate purpose: to be bringing life into the wasteland." He leaned forward and, with one sinewy, strong hand, gripped Robyn's arm. "Prove the gamble, O godling spirit, O god's son, O man. Be letting in the forest. Be bringing to us the full magics. Find a way and be breaking the chains. Be conjuring new crossroads. Be bringing the chaos and the living." Another shake, this to make his teeth nigh rattle. "It is being your spirit's path, Hob-Robyn."

Chaos. Another Voice, conjured by Memory's Keeper. *Woken by Chaos. It is what you do best, My Own.*

Robyn peered at Magus. The gwyllion at his throat purred, soft, its heartbeat a faint-slow arrhythmia to match his own.

Chains and spells to quell a spirit's flight—indeed a people's heart. New crossroads, where Veils would thin before Rite and Rade-right. Tricksters conjured from the eternal into form and function, dancing widdershins a Spiral of life into death into . . .

Life, from a wasteland.

"And, O Magus, what if it means an ending. Death?"

Again, no warding sign. Magus loosed Robyn's arm, but held his gaze. "Then the Dancing Spiral would be turning, at last."

- XXI -

"How do you know it was your uncle? You've never seen him, you don't know what he looks like."

He looks like me!

"And you've heard us say that many a time, pet."

This is why I didn't say. Because you wouldn't believe me, even though he said you would. He said if none else, you would, because I'm your daughter and you'd know. . . how I know. . . because you know things and. . .

Aderyn's hands had flown so fast it took all Marion had to understand—and that had been the convincing factor. The child believed what she had seen.

Much, however, had remained unconvinced.

"You think its all useless, don't you?"

"I think it's ower and done. It's been years! Your brother en't coming back, love, and mayhap 'tis time we faced—"

"Aderyn Saw him, in the Mere!"

"And what if she's nobbut dreamin' things from sun and shade? She Sees the spirits, aye, but what if that means nobbut Robyn's dead and gone, or good as?—and in that case all your wishing and hoping wain't bring him back. All of this, doin' nowt but haunting your waking days! It even sent milord back to that damned sodding desert, mayhap to die and for what? Dreams?"

Much hadn't received that proper soldier's welcome, after all. And Marion, lying awake and solitary, rose at first light, donned men's clothes and snuck down to saddle one of Gamelyn's desert-bred mares. Small and fast, they could go all day.

She'd let Aelwyn know, and David, giving them charge over the guests' entertainment for the day—and a good excuse for their lady's absence: an urgent matter she had to ride out personally to see to. It was the truth, to be sure.

If Much had kenned her departure, he'd not admitted it. Had, in fact, stayed in the soldiers' chambers just past the construction of the curtain wall that King John had agreed to finance only that spring.

Was it too much to hope Much hadn't slept, either? Or mayhap he slept altogether sound, since he seemed so willing to shrug off everything that mattered.

Fine. She didn't need him.

Anger surely kept her from noticing she was being followed—not, at least, until she started to lead Farasha out of her box and heard the second set of hoofbeats trailing behind, unshod on the hard clay.

At first, she figured it was the stable lad taking his charges to graze, or that Much had followed after all. Marion turned, ready to give him what-for.

Her tongue went limp as she beheld Aderyn, her pony trailing on a loose rein.

Not only that, but the child's garb proved she'd done this often: boy's clothes all layered for comfort and warmth; a set of hobbles, a rucksack, a full waterskin tied across Rutterkin's cantle, even a headcollar beneath the pony's bridle.

Marion shook her head. "Nay, lass. Not this time."

I have to!

"Aderyn . . ."

But the child didn't back down. *I need to come with you. I started all this. I saw him. I told him I would tell you, and I should at least bring you, too!*

Marion peered at her daughter for long moments. Narrow chin stuck out, thin shoulders thrown back, black eyes simmering—and sweet Lady, but she was the spit of Robyn! Determined to face whatever consequence, whatever course.

And just like Robyn, Aderyn scented weakness the moment it flickered into possibility. *I'm the one who Saw him, Mam. You've tried. Da's tried. What if I'm the only one who can See him?*

Again, words failed. Marion peered at her daughter for long moments, gave a sigh. "Aye, well, then. Rutterkin isn't up to the pace we'll be taking. Unsaddle him; I'll help you tack up Sadiyya."

Aderyn's face filled with delight. *I'm to ride a real horse?*

ᚲ

Dawn sent frosted fingers across a backdrop of gatehouse stone, and two riders waiting.

If Siham and Tafsut were surprised by Marion's travel

companion, they didn't show it. Unlike Siham, who'd been born in the camp-cities of Syria, Tafsut was of the Berber folk: tall, dark, and lean in the tunic and shalwar many of the Moorlands folk wore, but with bits of silver twisted into ear and nose, her black hair even wirier than Marion's own. Marion knew this, for the previous day over a shared meal, Tafsut had tugged at her cinnabar braid with a brilliant grin, and demonstrated that solidarity by pulling the wrap from her own head.

Now, Tafsut nodded at Marion's hair—with bits and bobs already beginning to worm their way loose from plait and headscarf—and smoothed at her own bare, short-cropped head.

Aye, 'twould be easier to manage, at that. "My man would skelp me."

Tafsut grinned wider. Siham suggested, wry, "Better, then, to have no man."

"This morn, I'm agreeing with you. Other morns, there's benefits."

Both laughed, and Tafsut flung her headcloth over her scalp, tying it as she knelt down to Aderyn. "You are small, but you must indeed be a woman, now, to ride with us. Can you ride fast?"

Aderyn nodded. Tafsut boosted her into the saddle, saw her settled with a pat, and mounted her own horse.

As one, they filed out the cavernous gatehouse of Tickhill.

Nigh to the river's edge they halted—within protection of the trees, but out of plain sight. Hallamshire's demesne, after all, even though this stretch of Loxley Chase belonged to Tickhill. None were likely to take such a well-armed group—even Aderyn had a bow tied to her saddle—but best to stay wary.

Siham nodded, taking the rein from Marion as she dismounted. Tafsut was bent down, saying something to Aderyn before she, too, took the girl's horse and turned away. All of it, tacit agreement to respect, and a calm consent to waiting outside the bounds of their friends' sacred places.

Marion, grateful for their understanding, took Aderyn's hand and slid deeper into the trees. The sparse sun dimmed further, gleaming grey-rose across the mists, those caught like hanks of unspun wool upon the bare branches. Morning always came later to the woodlands.

Aderyn's hand was cold in hers; Marion rubbed it against her woollen overkirtle, peered sideways. The look on the child's face betrayed more eagerness than apprehension, and it quirked a smile at Marion's lip.

Halfway in, she halted. Aderyn turned with a curious frown, which loosened in some comprehension as Marion began to divest herself of what bindings she could. Too chilly, this morn, to untie hose from braies, but she discarded her belt and unravelled her hastily-plaited curls. Aderyn, still eager, did the same.

Just beyond, the sacred trees arched overhead, gateway and ceiling, some evergreen and some bare, some with leaves clinging stubbornly in the mild weather, unwilling to give up just yet. Several flourished here, in this place they should not so easily grow. Barrow Mere spread out beyond, silent and sacred, nourishing the Lady's magic.

A shiver claimed Marion as she took her daughter's hand once more and led her inward. Aderyn had come here more than the once, it seemed, but how long had it been since Marion herself had walked this path?

Yet she forgot nothing, gave the Mere Her due. Circumnavigated the edges sunwise, giving each of the sacred trees tribute: from Alder swaying in the upper breeze like a young girl, to ancient Oak girdled with ivory skulls, to Willow rustling beside the deep-black water. All of them, really, and Marion noted how Aderyn followed her lead with a grave deliberation.

No berries had ever graced Holly's thick, dark green, but He waxed fat-sharp, protective. It seemed a sign: Robyn was alive. Waiting.

Damn Much anyway, what with his doubts and her so much as listening to them.

The banks of the deep pool lay sere, but the lap of water, back and forth, showed moss sprouting upon mud. Aderyn plumped down with the nigh-boneless ease of her age, and looked out across, propping her chin against one hand. Her eyes sought the stream's edge, burbling afresh with recent rains and spilling over rocks to roil the pool from beneath, whilst the Mere itself shimmered, green-black, from tree shadows and the depths in its midst.

Marion also knelt, albeit more measured, and breathed calm, asking the Mere for Her blessings. All the while unsure she would receive them—not now, not here—when she did lean forward and look, she saw nothing. Only grey eyes amidst a face still dense-freckled from a long, fair summer. Only the top of Aderyn's black head. Only reflections in a wide, still pool.

If only it would open, become the mirror her daughter had called it. Show her Gamelyn's fate, or let Robyn see they were here, trying to find him.

Reaching out, she drew a palmful of water and touched it to her lips. Cold, crystalline . . . it, too, revealed nothing.

You must come to Her with an open heart.

"*My heart is open—*"

Your heart is angry. Oft your Wintering brother finds heart in heat, be it anger or passion. But you? You are not he.

Marion looked up, but the Horned Lord was not there—only the power of memory. Still, she sought Him, told him, *And now our daughter has Seen my Winterlord—here, where the Fae took him with the Lady's consent! Does she See true? Or does she see but fragments of the memories left of him, in this place?*

The place lay still but rarely silent, what with the stirring of small ones in the trees, the flip-splash of a feeding fish, the breeze sighing through the Sacred Grove. It smelled like rain. They'd likely fetch some damp on the way home.

But the Voice came, faint and faraway, as if underwater. *Our first daughter is. . . unique.*

Marion looked up, gaze flitting side to side. But nothing seen, only heard, with the treetops swaying in a light breeze, and Aderyn's fingertips tap-tapping the Mere's surface as she watched the stream dance.

Her tynged is patterned upon what the Ceugant could—and should—accomplish. Result of your first hallowed working and manifestation. Hardly surprising that such a soul would choose to return, seeded into thisworld through the magic raised in the Sacred Marriage, born to it by Sacrifice. She is, by her nature, as tied to the Archer's fate as to you, her Maiden dam, and the Summering Knight who would stand as her father.

So she did See Robyn!

Did you doubt it? Or did the Champion, your lover, merely voice your own doubts?

Heat sprang behind her eyes, hands balling into fists. It lay unwelcome, the truth of her own anger—not only with Much, aye, but also herself. And what of Gamelyn?

Mayhap he has fulfilled his purpose. Cold as the breeze filling the trees, as the *splish* of water upon Aderyn's fingers. *Or, not.*

Aderyn's breath sucked in with a quick, hoarse gasp, and she scrambled up, wiping wet fingers against her leggings. Marion looked up to behold an antlered silhouette, rising from the mists and trees. She reached out, offering comfort. Yet Aderyn took her mother's hand almost reluctantly, and did not drop her gaze, even when the Horned Lord glided from the shadows.

He was . . . different.

No longer the tall, darkling man, He appeared more stag than any human form, His pelt a soft, grey-tipped black, His horns ivory streaked dark. His eyes, however, still gleamed both familiar and fearsome: fire-gold backed with pitch. Those eyes never left Aderyn, who stared back. Her hand lay chill within Marion's, but lax. It didn't so much as tremble.

She does not fear me, the Horned Lord said, curious—and respectful-soft in this place not altogether His.

Why would I? Aderyn wanted to know, and Marion fought the smirk that longed to claim her lip.

The antlered head cocked, first one way then another, regarding the child for a long while before his gaze turned upon Marion.

You will have to dredge deep to find Her, here.

Marion blinked. This was the Lady's place; this, above all else . . .

Places sleep when they are not tended. Gods fade when the sound of their names remain uncalled. . . or changed.

Aderyn tugged at Marion's tunic, and when Marion looked down, signed, *Is He saying it's our fault?*

"He's saying," Marion returned her gaze to the Horned Lord's, "that the fault is mine."

Is it not?

"I did not turn from Her first."

But you did. Turn away.

"I refused to follow and beg when She abandoned us, aye."

Still, you are adamant.

"She requires my belief. She has always had that."

Has She. The antlers arced, seeming to sweep the clearing.

"She decided nigh seven years ago that our people's needs were to be sacrificed to some other purpose."

Seven years. Apropos. Lammas approaches, with scythe and basket. Time again, for the winnowing and gathering. We must prepare for Winter's coming. The seventh year is one of both dread and awe.

Marion didn't allow the ice tickling her spine to fill her limbs. "And what shall you require, Lord?"

The gilt-edged eyes flickered, from Marion to Aderyn and, slowly, back. *I do not lament what I am becoming.*

"But?"

But. Laughter echoed across the Mere's surface, soft and tinged with rue. *You know me too well, Maiden-Mother. It is not as it was when Robyn Hode roamed the Shire Wode. What I was freed to be, again, when a callow boy offered a wager to set Allworlds a-tumble. Save in doing so, he proved himself no mere Foolish lad, but an elder force of Chaos, called into thisworld by his Maiden twin and his Rival. Thus a story old as We who plait the fateful threads re-emerged from the otherworlds, set a-whirl by an oath—by a will puissant enough to raise a power thought forever lost.* His voice faded, dampened by mist and swallowed by the Mere, then returned, wafting upon the mists. *By blood. By fire. By wild, wild magic. . .*

It, too, faded, gave way to the rustle of wings and air against the branches, the burble of the Mere's feeder stream, the heavy, enduring presence of the mists and the earth.

"Do you want him back?" Marion finally said against the quiet. Aderyn's hand twitched in hers. "Do you want the Ceugant? All of us?"

When the Horned Lord spoke, it once more vibrated with power, striking the mists and trees. *Aye, I want him back. I would have Her return to Our places, Allworlds and all peoples conjoined. I would have the three of you raise and hold Our power, to protect our Wode until the stars burn cold!*

Then, *Why do you think I led the child here?*

He'd waited, uncertain. Not only of thisnow's passing, but for the wyvern to stir, if only a little, and open one rainbow-shimmered eye.

It was not in Robyn's nature, to wait, but he knew the way of it. The lessonings had been hard-learned and rather vicious, but they had taken. Had been augmented further by this place, thisnow. And thisnow—for that's all there was, truly—the waiting simmered within him still-quiet, a place none could penetrate without his leave.

The gwyllion waited with him. The ones closest to him, as if lulled by the darkling flat-calm their human exuded, settled tranquil about him. His little familiar curled at his throat like a green-gold torc, unmoving save for soft breaths and a tiny, sluggish heartbeat that seemed to echo Robyn's own.

Conversely, the outlier gwyllion seemed even more twitchy, occasionally fluttering into the Mere and hovering about the wyvern's black shadow, or grooming themselves upon several ledges, or curling into restless sleep merely to wake, hungry, and fish the Mere.

All of it, floating past and through him. Did the child come back, Robyn meant to be here.

Open your eyes, he suddenly urged the sleeping wyvern. *Hear me and heed me, Old One. We are one in spirit, you and I.*

And the Old One answered him. Not in anything that could be called words, but in feelings darting, or ideas drifting. Sedate one moment—if there were moments, here—and another, wild and incoherent.

As if dreaming. As if the barrier holding them apart had started to thin.

Robyn lurched upright—and stumbled, he'd sat there longer than he thought, with legs all chill yet afire with hundreds of minute pinpricks. Fell, in a heap of clinging gwyllion, with flailing arms and tottery legs, and whacked his head against one of the stalagmites edging the cavern.

Robyn growled, trying with little success to clutch to the slippery surface, ordering his legs to behave themselves. Finally, they obeyed. He shoved away, blinking as something dark smeared his vision, and slung his hair from his face.

The gwyllion shrieked and fled upward. Even the one at his throat launched itself, wings tangling in his hair and claws digging into his nape. When it did wrench free, it dropped off his shoulder, wings extended, and soared upward, circling him with tiny cheeping cries.

Robyn blinked at all of them, and shook his head. That hurt like bloody damn, too.

He gave up on all of it—save the one thing. The important thing. Old One? he queried, moving towards the Veil.

The wyvern's black tail tip moved, back and forth. Silt rose, murky clouds upon the current, back and forth. The gwyllion continued to perform their aerial acrobatics.

Even a frown hurt. He must've bashed himself a good one. Robyn ignored all of it, reached the Veil and leaned against it, first one hand, then his forehead, then the other hand.

Found himself nigh inhaling silty water as his head passed through.

Robyn staggered back, biting back an instinctive gasp until his face was in air, not water. It sluiced down his face, trickling salt across his open mouth . . .

Salt? The Mere was fresh water.

He blinked away the water—a scum of dark clouded one eye— and found his hand marbled dark crimson. Curiously, he wiped at his mouth with his unmarked hand and, upon drawing it away, found it too splotched with a mix of water and blood. Wiped again as his temple gave a fierce throb. More crimson.

Of course. Head wounds could bleed like damn. Gingerly he probed; this one lay shallow, but let loose like something thrice its size. He started for his clothing, dodging the excited gwyllion— though actually, they were dodging him—and began rummaging for a bit of cloth to staunch the . . .

Blood. And fire. And wild, wild magic.

He stopped, turned slowly to eye the wyvern. It was eyeing him back through the drifting silt.

Had it spoken, or were the words mere memory?

"Through your spells you opened the way, through your blood the Veil let you pass."

"Well, if that's what it takes, then. . ."

This, indeed, was memory. The Priestess's words . . . her anger at him . . .

How had he forgotten?

"Is that all it takes?" he whispered. "Is that all I need?" Robyn made his way back through the frantic, soaring gwyllion—who despite their antics, did not touch him. Odd enough in itself, that— as if they dared not, and did that have to do with blood, too? His blood, for which the Priestess had been so careful to make amends when one of her own had unwisely spilt it.

Mayhap the whys of it lay here?

He held the wyvern's gaze, raised his bloodied hand to the Veil.

Passed through, farther than he'd gone before. To the elbow and up his bicep, skimming his hand back and forth. The wyvern's eyes gleamed, cold fire in the depths, and when Robyn put his face against the Veil . . .

The Veil let him in.

He pushed forward eagerly, submerging to his shoulders. The Mere hummed, and he tasted silt, felt the deeps filling his ears. An almost-panic came with the sensations—Swim! Escape! Air!—

and he reached outward with his arms, trying to push farther yet, find the surface, and now, if he could . . .

Instead he was pinned in place, not only by the Mere, but by a deep Voice.

Why do you think I brought the child?

It entered his consciousness and echoed about him, a muted waft against the fierce pressure in Robyn's ears. It opened his eyes, required he focus through the currents and the silt and the blood trail lingering, somehow.

He froze, hair wafting about his face and eyes sprung wide.

Saw clouds and muted spills of sunlight against winter-stark trees, all of it floating just beyond and above him. It shuttered for a half breath as the wyvern's gleaming eye slid shut then opened again, tilting unreal light into murky water. Clearer than ever, the Mere's banks wavered into focus, one side and the other.

Upon one stood The Horned Lord—more stag than man, an aspect of Him Robyn had never envisioned.

And upon the other, a black-haired child.

Aderyn.

Older, mayhap?—certainly leggier, and dressed warmer than the last time. Restless feet shifting sodden, dead leaves, she came closer, peering at the Great Stag with more interest than dread.

And approaching beside her, holding her hand . . .

The breath left Robyn's lungs in a gout of bubbles, all of them containing a name.

Marion!

ᛦ

Why do you think I led the child here?

The query brought both respite and dread; the first that it hadn't been the Lady who'd tricked Aderyn into coming here, the next that her eldest had been pulled into the close orbit of the Wild God.

A tug to her hand, sharp and quickly followed by several more, and Aderyn's fingers describing arcs into the air. *I see him! I see!*

She went to her knees on the bank, and Marion followed, crawling forward to peer into the water. Aderyn leaned out over the grassy bank. Clearly, she saw something.

Yet Marion saw only her own reflection, and beyond that, merely a shallow, sandy bottom disappearing into the depths.

She sat back on her heels, heart sinking. Beside her, Aderyn didn't seem to notice, gesturing *I brought her! I did!*

Across the Mere, the Horned Lord bent as if to drink . . .

Wheeled and started all in one, leaping into the shelter of the trees as, in the middle of the mere, something began to emerge.

Marion made an instinctive snatch at Aderyn's tunic even as she realised 'twere nowt more than bubbles and foam, as if some deep-laired monster had turned in its sleep.

Mayhap the monster, the black wyrm Gamelyn had called forth the night Robyn disappeared and Aderyn had been born.

And borne upon the oddling rash of bubbles came a sound, and with the sound a name.

Marion! it whispered.

Her brother's voice. Robyn's voice.

She wobbled. A last-moment prop of hand was all that saved her from a sideways sprawl. Her gaze fixed itself to where that burble of water had planed itself into a hundred tiny ripples. All the while, her heart pounded up into her throat, nigh choking her.

She came to find her skirts were being tugged, and Aderyn making her little inward hisses of frustration that said *Someone listen to me!*

With some effort, Marion paid attention.

Mam, did you hear him? Did you? Did you?

"I . . . I heard," Marion rasped, then repeated, wonderingly, barely above a whisper, "I heard him."

ᚲ

The wyvern pulled from the bottoms. It moved sluggish, wings fouling upon the chain about its neck. But it was moving. Rising. Sitting on its haunches, it gave a torpid shudder, not unlike an elderly dog shaking off a nap.

No longer did its gaze pierce Robyn. Instead its wedge-shaped head tilted upward, eyes luminescent against the silt—which conversely could not dim their gleam, or obscure the vision of Above, floating in the depths to taunt him.

So near. So far.

No more waiting. No time to waste.

Mayhap if he could reach the wyvern, it would take him upward and out.

He strained, wriggled and pushed until his ears hummed and his eyes skimmed red-black. But no matter how hard he tried, there was no going farther.

Calm down, Robyn told himself, and *What is she saying?*

For he could still see the child, leaning close, hands flying so fast he could scarce follow. Marion was nowhere in sight—had they left and Aderyn come back again? Had . . . ?

He felt dizzy, blinking and straining against the silt, chest aching. Lack of air.

How could he run out of time in a place that knew it not?

What do I do? Aderyn seemed frantic. *What do I do? Mam can't see you, but she heard you, and what—?*

She pulled back, out of view. Robyn pushed forward. A few more air bubbles escaped, but still, no farther.

His heels and head didn't agree with where they were.

The wyvern rose, shedding clouds of sediment.

Something tugged at Robyn, like tens of tiny hands upon his tunic.

And everything started to go black.

More bubbles, boiling, and steam heating the surface of the Mere.

This time Marion grabbed Aderyn and dragged her back. The child fought; Marion merely tucked her closer, pulling them both back from the water's edge.

Aderyn kept fighting, trying to go back.

"Stop it," Marion growled, holding tight. "Stop it, now! We'll see what . . . "

Her voice trailed off. Aderyn went limp in her grip.

The waters parted from a dark, serpentine gleam. It rose above them nigh silent, peering down with eyes a-glitter. Water rained down upon them, shedding from the beast as its wings extended, quivering.

Aderyn's chest heaved against Marion's arm. Marion dizzily realised she herself had ceased to breathe.

The wyvern started and exploded upward; the draught from those great wings buffeted Marion and Aderyn with wind and wet. A heavy audible clunk! and it jerked it back into the Mere with a fierce shudder and splash, writhing, its mouth opening to expose a row of teeth curved and keen-edged as Gamelyn's shamshir.

Surely a sight to haunt the worst and best of nightmares.

Yet no roar came from the open maw, merely a small, strangled purl. Those wings, large and tipped with claws, were fouled in sodden weed and a length of rusted chain; those and the irons about its neck had halted it from taking flight. Where it had faced off against Gamelyn's cold steel upon that long night seven years ago, angry and defiant, now it seemed . . . diminished. Plaintive, somehow.

Aderyn bolted forward. Marion only then realised her grip had loosened and, with a muffled curse, lurched after.

There was no need. The creature towered over the girl for a mere breath, heaved another low and heavy groan, and slowly lowered itself into the water, extending its neck and head as carefully, as close, to Aderyn as it could.

Chary of her? Or of the land?

Aderyn reached out.

"Take care," Marion cautioned, her approach even more so. Even the gentlest of beings, wounded, could snap.

But the iridescent eye closest to them lidded, and the creature gave a long, burbly sigh as Aderyn knelt beside it and stroked its nose.

Marion came closer and knelt beside them, pity twisting her belly as she noted the scars upon the wyvern's neck: some whitened with age, others new and raw.

Is this. . .? Aderyn paused, hesitant, *Is this Uncle Robyn?*

An impossible thought. But in Allworlds, where gods walked and possessed peasants, where those peasants could be taken into another time and place as geld to a goddess . . .

Mayhap it were more a horrible possibility.

Marion found herself leaning closer, murmuring the same sing-song she might to a wary horse. She rested a cautious hand upon the wyvern's nose. Long and bony, indeed akin to a horse's skull—a water-horse, what else?—it extended beneath her questing fingers smooth as well-tanned leathers, or the soft-sleek hide of a snake.

Aderyn was peering into the Mere. *I think it is. I can't see him.*

Marion reached out again, this time with heart and mind. Asked, though she hardly dared hope, *Robyn?*

No response. The wyvern lay rapt beneath their attentions.

We have to do something, Aderyn protested. *He's in pain.*

"He isn't now, at least," Marion soothed, caressing the wyvern's neck, avoiding the abraded flesh nigh to the iron collar.

No one should be shackled like this!

Marion tried the iron charms of her own learning—and some of Gamelyn's as well. She hadn't much hope of them—they'd not worked so far, after all. Still, gathering them on her tongue and breathing them down her arm, she curled the hex-breath about her fingers, and traced those fingers along the rusted, thick iron.

It creaked. Warmed. Shivered.

The wyvern, too, shivered. One eye irised open, slow, the rounded pupil narrowing to focus on her.

"Coom by," Marion whispered. "Let me help you."

For, beneath the shackles, the abraded flesh had begun to shift, and spark blue-white

Aderyn gasped.

A smile lit Marion's face as the magic did its work, sucking infection from the cut flesh, knitting it together. But her smile began to fade as the iron gave one last resistive shudder, and remained whole.

The wyvern also shuddered. Head cocking, both eyes opened to whirl and steady upon Marion.

Healer, it said. *Sister-healer.*

A thrill-chill sped up and down her spine. "Let me do more. Tell me how."

It lay there, watching them both. Its head rose, came level with Marion's own. Still watching.

"Are you, somehow . . . Robyn?" She almost couldn't bring herself to ask it.

We are wakened, one and all.

It wasn't really an answer. "Why can't I see him?" Her voice broke.

The beast made no answer, sliding further into the water, tail and wings lashing it backwards.

No, wait! Aderyn started forward. *Don't go!*

Again, the innate snatch and snag of her daughter's tunic hem, holding her as, all the while, Marion's eyes were fastened to the wyvern.

And the wyvern's upon her.

Free the Wild Girl, and the Wild God, the creature said. *Free me, and release the Hounds.*

Then it slipped back into the water, and disappeared.

- XXII -

"It's neither wise nor safe, a woman travelling alone."

Marion stiffened. Aderyn peeked around Farasha's hindquarters, dark eyes wide. Marion raised an eyebrow, considering, and turned.

Otho came walking down the stable aisle. A frown marred his brow, reflected in the torchlight. Until he halted before it, blocking it.

"She wasn't alone, milord." This from Tafsut, across the wooden stanchion where they had, all, tied their mounts. She gave a tiny "Oof!" as Siham nudged her, hard.

Siham's instincts were proven as Otho slid narrowed eyes at Tafsut, then rolled those eyes—ah, mayhap he and Gamelyn did have sommat in common—and otherwise refused to acknowledge her.

"As Tafsut said, I wasn't alone," Marion pointed out. "I thought you were going hawking with the earl?"

"Mayhap 'twas a good thing I didn't." Otho held out a hand to Aderyn and chirruped to her. He always did, and not even Alais had been able to stay him. As if Aderyn were simple. Or a dog.

Aderyn dipped a tiny curtsey. What was required and nothing more, and afterwards she retreated behind Farasha's rump.

Marion wished she could do the same. "Aderyn, love. We'll finish up here. Go on to the kitchens, find yourself a bite."

The child, all too happy to obey, scooted past Otho and ran for the door.

Watching her go, Marion turned back to the mare and busied herself with the girths. "You're in my light, Otho."

He moved away and, unfortunately, towards. "Let me help you with those."

"I'm perfectly capable of unsaddling my own horse."

"Your capabilities with a horse aren't in question, my lady." Otho's tone—quiet, reasonable—persuaded her to agree with his assistance. "Though you should let your stable lad earn his keep, to be—"

"I sent him on an errand." Instinct bade her snap, ready for battle, angry with capitulation. *Only yester's even, you spoke with Huntingdon. Yet here you are, giving in to this. . . usurper!*

And I know what battles are worth the fight. She let those instincts tilt her chin and square her shoulders, comportment secure. Rationalised, tart, *This en't one. Yet.*

"I see." Otho wound the billets and pulled the saddle, woollen pad still attached, from the horse's back, flinging it onto the side rail. "Well, it isn't as important as you gadding about."

"I was on business." Marion reached past him to the groom box and, taking up a brush, started to strop Farasha's sweated sides. "Not 'gadding about', as you say."

"No business is worth such risk. And what legitimate occupation would require a woman to dress in men's clothing?" His gaze flickered to her companions, negligently to be sure, then wandered to her leather-wrapped legs. Lingered there, surprised. As if he'd not expected to like what he saw.

Marion had the impulse to grab for a cloak, and hated the meaning of that impulse. When his gaze finally sought her own, she met it with a level, impassive stare.

He looked away, brief but telling. "Surely those damned mercenaries at our gate were adequate reminder of what danger lies rampant in the countryside." His voice turned reasonable, coaxing attentiveness, concurrence. "A woman and child have *no* business on the road alone at any time, but particularly now. Two female servants, however mannish, aren't enough."

Marion looked past him to her companions, found a scowl on Tafsut's face to mirror her own. Siham raised an eyebrow in Marion's direction and kept on with grooming her horse.

Otho extended an imperious hand over the stanchion. Tafsut paused midstroke, blinked at it.

"The brush, woman!"

Any small hint of refusal was covered as Siham bent down to snatch up another one, handing it over. As Otho took it and went to the other side of the horse, Tafsut's gaze sought and fastened, with smouldering intent, upon a precise area just between his shoulder blades.

Marion's lip quirked. Gamelyn wasn't the only desert-honed cutthroat to bide at Tickhill, after all.

"Please, my lady," Otho continued, working the mare's other side, "you must take care. I fear my brother's lenience has made you heedless. Perhaps it was to be expected, considering your"—a delicate pause—"previous status. I realise he allowed you many liberties, but—"

"*Allows* me." Easier—*wiser*—to just let him mouth his self-important harangue and go. Yet this protest refused silence.

Otho turned to her. "I beg your pardon?"

Let it go, the rational inner voice nagged. *Save your weapons for when you're prepared to use them.*

But this wasn't rational. "You said 'allowed'. Past tense."

Faith, but Otho was no great shakes at dice. But then, he'd never had to be, had he? A nobleman—*man* being the definitive there—and liable only to *his* betters. The expressions that ran across his face but proved it: confusion into bewilderment, then patient indulgence.

"Marion, if you would—"

"My lord." She drew up, eye to eye. "It is not fitting, such familiarity to your brother's wife."

A small snort came from Tafsut's direction. It might have been the horse. It might have been her clearing her throat, nothing more. Otho's glance didn't even flicker her direction—well schooled, he was, in ignoring lesser beings.

Or too busy biting back what he truly wanted to say. Not only manners, but some sort of sense prevailed—and with it, a cunning she'd not thought Otho possessed. Playing it nicely, he was, and courteous. No sense, after all, in overplaying one's odds, or prejudicing the woman beforehand.

Thankfully, Huntingdon had warned her. Otho had never been hard to read; Marion had just never bothered to do so. Alais's problem, not hers.

Only now, it *was* hers. And the man a clueless git who wouldn't recognise a rebuff if it kicked his stones. Mayhap he did need a kick to the stones because Sweet Lady but it was like dealing with Will Scathelock all over again! Even to his chaff-coloured, hard head!

And sure enough: a few beats of consideration, then an unyielding return to the original tack. "My lady, I apologise. But surely you realise we must be realistic about such things. I realise he's rarely here even when he bides in-country, but this?" A shake of head and sigh—unfeigned, to be sure, but also unregretful. "Even the Templars haven't heard from him. The Master Preceptor has given up any hope."

The words sent a quiver of apprehension up Marion's spine. How did Otho know that? He hadn't been here when Hubert had last come to Tickhill; had never, to her knowledge, even met the Master Preceptor . . . and that one prowling like a hunting cat the last time *he'd* bothered to accompany Hubert to visit Tickhill . . .

Where was Wymarec de Birkin now?

"To give up hope is their choice, my lord. It is not mine," Marion countered, tacking on, "I didn't realise you knew the Master Preceptor."

"I met him at Sheffield one day; he and his men were travelling through, enjoying milord of Hallamshire's hospitality upon a journey south." Otho shrugged it away. "It is of no matter; better we should—"

"Milady?" Mild and quiet as always, both infuriating and cherished—and flawlessly polite, in company of what he considered his 'betters'. "Begging your pardon, but you've an important visitor. They wish to speak with you, urgent-like."

Marion turned to Much, saw him exchanging a meaningful glance with Siham and Tafsut. Marion entertained a moment of irritation at being so managed; the absurd awkwardness of the situation left her more grateful than cross. "Thank you. I—"

"How dare you interrupt us?" Otho snapped.

"He is not interrupting any—"

"Beggin' your pardon, milord, but milady said I was to tell her did any—"

"You're still here." Otho strode over, blocking him with arms akimbo. "Interrupting us."

For one foolhardy and beautiful moment, Much stiffened. The difference between soldier and noble—the latter every bit as tall and broad but past his prime, blurred about the edges, unfit—was painfully obvious.

And of course, it only made Otho more angry. "You're. Still. Here. Leave us, man. *Now!*"

Much shot Marion an odd, trapped look.

Then he obeyed.

Obeyed.

A ridiculous situation, nowt but, yet humour seeped away as surely as Much's retreat into the dark corners of the stable.

Fury took its place. "You have no rights to dismiss anyone from my presence!"

Otho answered it, like for like. "The man is insolent!"

"So insolence is now defined by obeying my orders?"

"He interrupted our conversation."

"There was no conversation! Only you telling me your understanding of my place. In. *My*. Place. As if I were one of the children! You've no cause to—"

"I've every cause, considering the man in particular pays you more attention than is proper. More, you *let* him!"

"He swore an oath to my husband!"

"As did you, my lady. Your relationship with such a man is far less seemly than me calling you by your given name."

Foolish, indeed, to overplay his hand this early in the game.

Not that Marion cared. She stalked over and shoved her face into his. "Any 'relationship', as you put it, that I may possess with anyone under this roof is nowt I wouldn't be laying before my husband with a clear conscience!"

That set him back, but only for a moment. "And as your husband is not here to contain your behaviour, it is up to me—"

"Up to *you*? And when have you ever had the luxury of an opinion over the management of my husband's fief? Or *his wife*?"

"Your husband, my lady, is lost to the desert!"

"You. Have. No. Say." This accompanied by four jabs to his chest. "Either over my staff or my management of this castle. And if my husband is indeed lost to us, then it is his son who will be Boundys of Tickhill and I, as his mother, who will make any management decisions, and it will be in the same fashion I've made since we were given holding to this castle!"

"*His* . . . son . . . ?" Otho wanted to say more—he'd already said the like after all, hadn't he?—but choked the words back. Stepped back. Tried to regain control—over himself and the situation.

Which Marion knew she, too, had let get past her. Still, she stared him down, fingers snarling—clenching—in her tunic.

"My lady," he finally ventured, subdued. "I have been . . . inconsiderate. Pray accept my apologies, and consider my actions were done in concern for your wellbeing."

Shaking, she was, with humiliation, fury . . . in fact a passel of other emotions with no true description. Back in the Shire Wode, she would've punched him.

Or skewered him, she thought, and it put a tiny quirk to her lip. Robyn Hood's sister, after all, and it would put paid to the problem of him.

That smile, however slight, unfortunately seemed to give him leave to keep on. "Well. Now you're safely home, I shall beg your leave to go. The earl is still hawking, after all, and expects me."

She stared him down. Kept it up as he bowed, turned, and departed in the resultant silence.

With a low growl, Tafsut broke it. "But say the word, and I will end him."

Marion laughed, short and sharp. "Which him?"

Tafsut chuckled. She'd never ceased her grooming; it had evolved into stroking around the mare's liquid eyes.

Siham tsked. "Marion. What else could Much have done?"

"Mayhap not undermine my authority?"

Siham leaned on the stanchion. "It seems to me that undermining *his* authority"—she jerked her chin in the direction of Otho's retreat—"twould have made matters far worse."

"Worse than Otho thinking he has charge over this castle? And me? As long as I have authority, I can handle Otho."

"She is right, my lovely Arrow," Tafsut told Siham, giving small tugs to her mare's fluted nostrils. "If she must by necessity play a man's game, it surely requires a man's rules." Her hand dropped away; the mare nudged her, encouraging more.

"Yet is there nothing *but* a woman's rules, managing such a man as that?"

Tafsut muttered something about Otho's manhood and how she should be glad to remove it.

Siham grinned and shrugged, but her dark eyes held to Marion's, grave. "I pray you, my friend, do not forget: for any woman in this world, 'whore' is a worse epithet than even 'witch'."

She nigh ran into Much as she climbed the narrow, winding stair from the stables and into the keep. He'd been waiting, in the shadows of the first storey's landing.

And when Marion thought to shoulder past him, he didn't let her.

"Aderyn were right. You didn't even see me; you en't watching your back as you ought."

"*Aderyn* said—"

"Nay." Much's expression was hidden, the torch just past him backlight instead of illumination—though he clearly saw the sudden disquiet on her face. "Nay, she never said such a thing. But she were worried after you, so she came and found me." A shrug. "I were looking for you, anyway. John's arrived, not an hour past."

"John?"

"I told him you'd lit out early, so he settled in for t' wait. Faith, he's a queer stick of late, but this time he's in some fearful state. Insisted on waiting in your chambers. Not to be disturbed until he speaks wit' you, alone."

Marion frowned.

"I ken, 'tis ower odd." Another shrug, and a hand held out. "Mayhap 'tweren't the best idea I've ever had, to come out the shadows, like, and interrupt His Ponce."

And if that didn't set her anger back from simmer to boil. Marion pushed past him this time, started to climb again.

He followed. "Marion?"

She whirled on him, snapped, "Why bother coming at all, out the shadows or whats'mever, if you were all ready to do as Otho ordered?"

The torch now lit the narrow space in her favour; she could see Much's face, plain. Not that it did any good. Whatever emotion had released itself in voicing her name had smoothed away, and he peered upwards at her, calm and collected as ever she'd seen him, for several breaths before replying. "You seem to think I've a sight more power than I do."

"I think it's nowt to do with what power *you* possess!"

"I thought" —and did she truly hear a slight scratch of desperation in his voice?— "all things considered, 'twould be best not to throw pitch onto a blaze."

"More like pissing in t' fire. You were well enough staring him down, weren't you?"

His gaze lowered.

"Until it came to cases, and you bending your neck wit'out even a look to me to countermand or give leave!"

"Sweet Lady . . . *Marion*—"

"Don't be calling 'pon Her whilst you're doubting me!"

"Doubting—"

"All along, you've doubted me. And this the latest of doubts, letting bloody *Otho* order you around!"

"All along I've—?"

"All along." Said between her teeth. "Aderyn saw Robyn. At the Mere. She *Saw* him, and I *heard* him, and the beast rose in the Mere to speak with us!"

Emotion, this time; no disbelief but fear. "The black beast that milord stood against? The one as appeared the night our wee lass were born?"

"Aye, and the same! It all but put its head in Aderyn's lap, quiet as a hound. Begged us to set it free, though who knows how I'll manage that, if Gamelyn's truly gone from us."

"You said he en't." Fear lit a different, intense corner of Much's eyes. "You said you *know* he's not gone—"

"Why believe that, when you don't believe what else I say, or do?" Marion shot back. "I've the fight of me life to gain my brother back, and you're doing nowt to aid that fight! All 'milord' and 'by your leave' and tugging your forelock to the same man who'd like no more than to wed me, bed me, and get brats on me—and that to dun the inheritance from what he thinks're my 'bastards'!"

"*What?*"

Surely the shock on his face should sway her. All it did was make Marion angrier—not only at a man's world, but the men who seemed determined to ride it into founder. All of them: Otho as well as Hallamshire, de Birkin and de Lisle and his brother, the King . . . Even Much and Huntingdon and Gamelyn! Off tilting at ghosts and promises, chasing after distant fires like insatiable, oblivious moths drawn to a candle.

"Aye, pet. Think on that, next time you're ready to hop when milord Otho says 'hare'. Much more of it, and you well might be doing it for keeps!"

Marion turned away, leaving him in the narrow stair with his mouth half open, and tears stinging, hot, behind her eyes.

Ⓜ

"De Birkin. You *saw* him."

John nodded. Remnants of a good meal lay on the sideboard, barely touched. He'd clearly been pacing a furrow in her solar until Marion had arrived, intending to have a good, short cry before going to the Great Hall where her guests awaited the evening's meal.

Instead, John had nearly leapt upon her as she'd entered, in more a state than she'd seen him since Robyn had been taken.

And no wonder.

"How did he even *know* of the caverns?" Marion sat down with an ungainly *thump!* on the hearth bench, by habit alone twitching a nonexistent hem clear of the banked coals. She hadn't bothered to change. "Mam Tor, aye, but we kept the caverns secret to any but the covenant. To heed 'em as owt but a hole in the ground—"

To any as have power, they'd see the wards, did they go looking. And that one's the power, all right. John settled across from her, squatting on his haunches with a sudden, grim smile. *But not to break 'em, though he tried.*

"What could he possibly want?" she murmured, staring at the coals.

That's why I've come. After he was unable to enter, I went out after. I followed him to Peveril, where he met up with three other Templars, and a monk who came late to the fête, all sulled up on a cart with a driver and five soldiers to guard him.

Marion smirked. "Comin' through the Shire Wode all prepared, weren't he?"

There was also a man wearing Hallamshire's colours.

Of course. "Who was the monk?"

John shrugged. But Marion thought she knew. The Prior of St. Mary's. De Lisle's brother, Willem, who was working with Hallamshire and now, it seemed, with the Master Preceptor of all England.

All of that, to take down a peasant-turned-noblewoman, and her frantically holding to a magic that seemed, more and more, to slip through her fingers?

John was onto other game. *The Templar tried to violate our place, Maiden. The Horned Lord demands his head. All I need is your blessing, Maiden.* He reached up to unsheathe the small dagger hidden at his nape.

"I wain't give it. John, you can't leave, not now!"

Marion hadn't meant for it to come out and rise so: nervy, almost panicked. But John halted in his tracks and lowered his hand, peering at her.

She could only sit for long moments looking up at him, overwhelmed by all of it, uncertain where to even begin.

"Robyn" was all that escaped her chest.

His eyes went huge, and he knelt beside her.

She told him, all of it. From Robyn speaking to Aderyn and the wyvern's rising, to the mercenaries, then Huntingdon's warning about Otho and her suspicions about how all of it might tie in—including that meeting at Peveril, and her disagreement with Much . . .

Found herself crying, huge silent sobs that could express nary a sound, hands fallen open upon her skirts.

John had moved to sit beside her with his head against her shoulder—an even-more-silent empathy of misery—until Marion had cried herself into small, snuffs and spasms.

How apropos he smelled of earth and silt and river water—with salt tears as spice.

He leaned harder. *If I wait, I could lose the trail. They were heading south.*

"Likely to Normandy, like almost everyone else." She kissed the top of his head and wondered if it would be that easy. Give the word, let John take out the seeming mastermind of their ruin with a blade in the dark. Free all of them, including Gamelyn, from bloody-minded Wymarec de Birkin.

And now, Robyn. The wee lass saw him. Saw him. I don't know what to do. John pulled away slightly, gaze wavering into some distant place, pupils dilating into dark moons. Suddenly he gasped, reached out. Marion lurched up and took his hands.

Nothing for a half breath. John let his head fall back, let a soft whisper escape his lips. Calling it forth, and Marion Saw, then. The breath took hers, commingled, curled about them like smoke, trailed across the hearth and spat it into open flame, where beyond that . . .

Nothing. Nothing Seen. Nothing Sensed. *Tynged* moved out and away, multi-hued weave unravelling, undone, and strands floating—disappearing—as if the fire had burnt them to ash and smoke.

Not darkness. Not brilliance. Emptiness.

John opened his eyes, a numb stare that he turned to meet her own. Said, measured-soft, "Have you Seen the like? Before?"

Marion gave a slow shake of her head. The only thing she could compare it to was when she'd been in Worksop Abbey, a damaged mind with memory far strayed.

He tried to speak, shook his head, and pulled his hands from hers, gesturing. *I have. When Robyn lay dying in the caverns, and we thought you and Gamelyn dead. I saw it, over and over. As if there was some. . . fissure in the Wheel. Like tynged's fabric kept rending itself, uncertain. Or—* the words came slowly, simply, mused more than the once *—like all the futures were in flux, merging and changing with every breath, so nowt could be held, or Seen.*

"My gramma said . . . faith, but I was just a little girl but I can recall it now, plain as that." Marion gestured to the fire, still crackling. "'Twere my mam's mam, who said how what would come allus shifted, and could change upon a breath. We know that, to be sure, but she also said there were times the futures shifted so fast, a person couldn't so much as catch 'em. And that mayhap too many shifts could even make the Old Weavers falter, and *tynged* itself unsure." Marion wanted to reach out, take John's hands—yet she refrained. It was more for her own comfort.

Experience—first with John himself, then her child—had helped her ken long ago: in doing so, she would silence their voice.

Instead she leaned against him, a small smile tilting her lip as he shored back against her, needing the comfort as much as she.

When his next words came, they were slow, considering. *All this time, Aderyn has been the key. Not some faraway land, or an initiation in some cold Temple. It's. . . her.*

Marion started, gaze seeking his. "I . . . don't understand. Are you saying . . . ? Nay, John! I'm not sacrificing my child for any—"

"Nay." Spoken, as he all the while shook his head, eyes faraway and brows drawing tight. *I'm not meaning that. But 'tis what she is, wain't you see?*

Marion kept shaking her head, turning away. She wouldn't listen, not to this. Not when it clutched so, scraping her heart with icy fingers.

"Maiden," John growled, "look at me!" The fierce insistence pulled her to obey, to stare at the frantic gestures he made. *Mayhap you're too close to it. Mayhap I've pulled away enough that I can See it, even as your bairn Sees 'twixt and 'tween the worlds. What else does that mean but Aderyn's the crux, the deepest binding! She has to be. En't Aderyn, when all's parcelled, the result of the last working the* Ceugant *wove, truly together?* His eyes, finally, slid to hers. *Wasn't she?*

It made perfect, horrible sense. "I will not," she said between her teeth, "make such a choice."

Thinkin' like a mam, and so you should. But it en't a choice, not that way. If They wanted her, They would have already taken her. Blunt, but no more could Marion deny it than the truths John had already unearthed.

They didn't take me, either, when They could well have. His eyes once again clouded, distant, fair whirling with all the thoughts in his head.

She let him go . . . away, her own thoughts too troubled and crowded for any comfort. *The last working the* Ceugant *wove . . .* Had the past years been for nowt, then?—and this, the seventh, the final failure or success?

Gamelyn, come home. The year's winding away.

A tug at her skirts, not unlike her silent child's. Only this was John, his face settling mule-stubborn, and all-too-familiar.

Marion gave him her full attention, setting herself for battle.

Sure enough—*Mayhap we should return to the Mere. Aderyn can call the beast, and if I can ride it down and into—*

"Nay!" Marion stiffened, grabbing at his shoulder. "Nay, I wain't have you even thinking such a thing, John!"

If between us we could gentle it, then it's worth the try, aye? If I could, and bring Robyn back to us—

"Nay! What if you can't get back, either? We'll have lost you, too!"

He returned her frantic look with startling calm. *But mayhap I would be with him.*

"Or dead! With*out* him! If you don't remember how you nearly drowned, I do!" This time she did take his hands, the silencing purposeful, her own voice faltering. "We've lost . . . lost too many, John. I don't think I could bear it if I lost you, too."

Brown eyes blinked, started to fill.

"Promise me. Promise me you wain't. We'll find a way. We *have* a way, now, to speak with Robyn. Plan. With him."

Without our Summerlord. John shoved away and lurched up, throwing his hands up in the air, more eloquent than any scream. *All he felt he had to do before, I understood, but this latest journey? Leaving us like this. . . leaving you. And now he's gone, and it's likely we need him worse than ever!* He stopped abruptly, peered at Marion, suddenly culpable. *I'd curse him, and be justified. . . but I can't. I've tried, and I can't.*

"I imagine," Marion's voice caught, a wry choke, "that I've done for you."

The floorboards creaked beneath John as he resumed a back-and-forth pace

"Aye, we don't have our Summerlord. But John, we have *you.*"

John halted and turned, slow, to face her.

"You've loved Robyn the longest, even as he's loved you. You have, all along, stood up and held the Horned Lord's power. For him."

What if love isn't enough?

Marion drew in a halting, staggered breath.

Sometimes it isn't. Not all the wishing and wanting, not all the love to fill one's soul. What if we lose again?

"What if," Marion said, soft, "we never try?"

His lip quivered.

"You're the one who told me I had to believe. And it's true. Even on the foulest days, I have to believe. If not for myself, for all of you who look to me. For my children—and believe me, John, if I'd no hope or chance of seeing it, I'd take a dose to scour my womb barren, and never bring another child into thisworld. This frightening, tragic, *beautiful* world."

He turned away. Dust motes whirled as he walked over to where the streams of sun filtered in, and raised his face to it.

Signed, *Then best we take care of what's in our way. Those who have threatened you.* John turned back to her, the motes settling about his dark curls not unlike fireflies.

"For Otho, you'll have to fetch yourself into a queue. For de Birkin . . ."

Slight and unprepossessing, aye, but the sudden and predatory gloss to those brown eyes reminded: Little John remained one of the Shire Wode's most deadly wolves.

Padding slowly over, he knelt before her. Spoke, slow and clear. "Pass sentence, Maiden."

Once, it would have been the Hooded One to wield an axe, formed from copper and engraved with all the death songs. Then the Hood and the Horns had intertwined in an apropos dance of creation and destruction, the Horned Lord's avatar bearing bow and arrowflight, walking the blurring line of opposites, holding to neither and touching both. Now a Maiden bore both gilt Arrow and horn crown, and the weapon to pass a traitor's sentence?

An outlaw's dagger pulled from a hidden sheath.

John kissed the tiny dagger and held it out, hilt first.

Marion composed herself, cupping her hands before her face and breathing across her palms, stroking the breath over his crown. She touched the fingers of her left hand to the hilt, closed her eyes, and spoke soft the words she'd never thought to say, in a language older than the castle in which it was uttered.

Silence, with the fire still crackling, in tongues of blue-white cunning-magic.

Marion took a deep breath, let it out. Said, quiet yet firm, "Be back by the gibbous moon. No more than a fortnight."

John rose. *If I can't track him by then, the trail is too cold.* He grimaced. *If it isn't already.*

Something . . . *walking* over Robyn. Tens of tiny, clawed feet upon his back and haunches. Here and there, tugs upon his tunic, and it mostly clinging to him, sodden to the waist, and his hair spidering all wet over his face as, hands beneath his shoulders, he shoved upward.

The gwyllion went scattering. His little familiar, however, didn't spook so easily, hanging midair in front of his face, scolding him all the while.

The wyvern, rising. The child.

Marion.

Robyn lurched drunkenly upwards. His gwyllion familiar gave a startled *cheep*, belatedly grabbed a sodden hank of frizzled black hair, and hung on as Robyn rushed the Veil.

Yet the wyvern lay there, curled up and eyes shut, as if it had never moved. No vision, no displacement, no small Maid with her Mother peering into the pool, trying to find him. His mind had come adrift again, that and nowt more.

Save for his tunic, half-sodden. Save for . . .

Cheeks heating, heart starting to pound in something altogether close to panic, Robyn felt his temple. No blood, not so much as a seep, and no pain. But the gash was there, even if it had closed up, healing like a wound made a se'nnight previous.

The gwyllion cheeped softly, and curled about his nape. It hadn't been so calm when he'd bled.

Maybe the head-knock, and nowt more, had prompted all of it.

Then Robyn noticed the sediment drifting just past the Veil, descending thick. As if something had risen, muddling the thick bed.

He stepped closer, his heart a swift drumbeat against his breast, blood throbbing just beneath the skin, pounding. Blood.

Mayhap he should bash his head open again, or take the chert knife at his hip and . . .

His hand had drawn the knife, heart a drum against his breastbone, and the gwyllion starting to spiral about him, the one at his neck tense, ready to fly.

blood, and fire. . . and wild, wild magic

—says a voice, so faint-soft in memory
as marion holds out a hand and says—
he is bane, he is to be cast aside, waste upon rocks
—and her voices wavers into the void, to be replaced as
gamelyn comes forward, tracing foreign sigils into the air, speaking words that have no meaning, but all of power that
leaves arianrhod with the arrow in her hands—
your oath to us, hob-robyn, be not taking what is not yours to abandon. . .

A stagger, and a gout of air escaped his lungs, leaving Robyn dizzy-weak.

It is not so simple, is it, Hob-Robyn?
The wyvern?
Nay. The Lady.
Would you turn away from what lies here without a care? Turn aside from Me, even as your sister has done?

"My sister has . . ." Robyn shook his head, growled, "Mayhap she's hopeless as I am, 'bout now. If I canna be taking what en't mine to abandon, then what does that say about *you* taking what en't yours?"

His voice echoed in the caverns, but parsed itself, answering back:
The Horned Lord possesses my body as He sees fit, and the Lady my heart as She wills.

See? The Lady spoke, soft and chilling against the Veil. *You* are *mine, Horned Lord's creature. All of you, in the end, are mine.*

Robyn's voice grated and cracked when he finally answered. "So I'm to be left here to rot."

Our people need balance. All of our people, Hob-Robyn. Not only darkness but light, with the liminal rays and greys, dawn and dusk. They require their lord, as do I. All of them. Balance, not stagnation. Existence and agency, instead of lurking in the corners, forgotten. Invisible. What is left without the balance but collapse and destruction?

"Aye, the same as what will happen to the outerworlds, do our people pass from it, leave it and abandon it?" Robyn hadn't acknowledged the vision aloud, hadn't wanted to so much as make an echo in his voice.

She seemed to wait to answer, and for so long Robyn wondered if She had retreated. *All worlds fade, in time. Yet the Circle, the Spiral, never does: going away to come back around. Stars fade and die, to make new stars. Winter nips the eager buds, but they return. Children come, and the sire dies. As long as the wren can forage through the winter, the robin needs not worry it will see the spring again. They find a way within the Spiral's Dance. Life finds a way, even blasted to earth and dust.*

Earth and dust. The ground beneath Robyn's feet seemed to shift, his head ringing—nay, throbbing—with the sudden rhythm of his own heart's beating—

i will never cross the sea again

—gamelyn says, and
please come home to us
—marion cries, as
the world heaves and shudders, all dust and ash, all metal and fire. . .

And Robyn found himself on hands and knees, fighting hard to not totter onto his face.

Should you win free to the outerworlds, my Own, 'twill be no easier. Your leman would call it. . . hell upon earth.

"There's no such thing as hell. There's only what we bring with us."

And what would you bring with you, Hob-Robyn? What will you do, what will you promise? How will you make Us live again, in thisworld or others?

"If I'm there—" Robyn's tongue stuck, dry, against the roof of his mouth. Was Herself saying 'twere, after all, possible? "I can stand, if I'm there. I can bait 'em, mock 'em, lead one mother of a fight."

Even in a war you stand no chance of winning?

"Well, 'tis better than doing bloody nothing bunged up here!"

There, or here, Our ways are daily rived from Us. The Hermit broods, unwilling to loose the hem of your spirit garment. Your outlaws conjure your ghost behind every tree, and give Our people cause to whisper your name when stray gifts are left upon their doorsteps. Your Maiden turns from Me and takes up the horns Our Summerlord abandoned to her. Your leman wanders across the Sea and courts death disguised as My other face. All for you, Winterlord.

"What d'you expect?" he shot back. "I'd do no less! Have done! We were the *Ceugant*, have you forgotten? The trine and embodiment of Allworlds! *You* allowed us that, freed our most beloved souls to follow us and raise its power! Yet in the end you brought me *here*, where there's no otherworlds—*no Spiral*—to let us find each other again! Are you turning into the likes of Gamelyn's god, so eager upon punishment after all?"

You have forgotten what you yourself set in motion. What spells you wove into a woodland, a stone castle, a willow Arrow. A breath drying his curls, chill as a snow-heavy morn. Survival. For all of us, or none of us.

"All of us, aye. For surely you knew, O Lady Huntress, from the three of us and spiralling outward into our most beloved, that we were all made, ever on, to be with each other? To *love* each other?"

The Horned Mother, the Apostate Warrior—and you, the Trickster, agitator, Hob. *Who twists his oaths and weaves of them a puzzle fit to game a god. Would you, then, heedlessly shatter this one? Would you—all of you—ride the Return into destruction? Continue fumbling in passion's darkness and, in the end, find the only remnants of Our ways be carvings upon stolen temples, or an unbroached mother chained voiceless in stone? See your ancestors and what remains of your people vanish, never to be known again, even in tales and legend?*

"What good are legends?" The caverns rang with his cry.

Indeed, was her reply. *What good can such things do, in a world that knows them not?*

Then, silence. The caverns went still, and cold, and Her presence sucked away from Robyn's perceptions.

He hunched there for some time, heart pounding and thoughts whirling like a Beltane fire dance. When he finally rose to stand, cold and shaken, it was leaden-slow, and he quivered from the tips of his fingers to the marrow of his bones.

The gwyllion at his nape was strangely heavy, also still and cold. Robyn wondered, suddenly, if he'd knelt there while the world had passed him by . . .

As if to prove him wrong, the little beastie stirred and nipped his ear.

Robyn gave a sharp hiss and tugged its tail. "Leave off, you."

With a burble that sounded suspiciously like a giggle, the gwyllion uncurled itself and flittered over to the Veil. With that weird *pop!* it sailed in, diving at the group of fish that had gathered about the wyvern's neck.

Robyn frowned, and followed. What were those fish doing?

Not that he was about to see, because they all scattered as the gwyllion gave chase. Well, almost all of them; his familiar came bursting back through the Veil, a sizeable trout in its claws.

Sediment still floated about the wyvern. It hadn't been that long, after all. The fish—a small net's worth—nigh as one returned, hovering about the iron upon his neck, fascinated.

Nay, they were picking at him. Cleaning, feasting upon castings of hide, old skin sloughing away from the new-made skin. Robyn drew closer, frowning . . . aye. Beneath that lay a blue-white tinge that, even on this side of the Veil, he knew.

His sister's magic.

Your Maiden turns from me and takes up the horns Our Summerlord abandoned to her.

"Well done you, Mari," he muttered. "Why not?" Then, "Is she still there, Old One?"

One eye half-opened, lazily, to expose a vision hanging in the still-floating silt. The little lass, again, sitting on the grassy bank.

Aderyn had her arms wrapped about her knees, rocking in the sunlight, watching the trees. Waiting.

As if no time had passed, or as if a year had come and gone, and the child wandering in Lammas-tide again . . .

The breath hissed from between Robyn's teeth, questions flitting and darting swift as gwyllion, and possibilities clicking after those like tumblers in a lock.

The Spiral, shut from him. Only not, for he'd a connection to it after all, waiting in the spirit of a little girl, seated rapt upon a mere's edge.

You have forgotten what you yourself set in motion. What spells you wove into Tor and woodland, a stone castle and a willow Arrow.

A spelled arrow, bringing down an iron-manacled gate. The Wild Hunt, called in a rage of loss, trapped in the stones of Nottingham Castle. A royal forest known as the Shire Wode, where none dared pass without the leave of Robyn Hode.

A child brimming over with the magic, spirit kindled into life upon the *Ceugant's* first triune working.

Robyn had forgotten.

Survival. For all of us, or none of us.

His blood upon the Veil, weakest upon the waning of winter's tide . . . What might it do upon the waxing, and the time when the Veil of Allworlds lay thin?

What would you bring with you, Hob-Robyn? What will you do, what will you promise? How will you make Us live again, in thisworld or others?

Merely another taunt?

Or, mayhap, a challenge?

Robyn smiled.

Legends, Herself had said.

Once it had been rumoured there wasn't a trap Robyn Hode couldn't evade, no gaol he couldn't break.

Wellaway, then. Mayhap 'twere time to prove his right to just one more legend.

- XXIII -

The Moon
Temperance, reversed
The Wheel, reversed, upon
The Emperor…
A year and a day, you said.

A year and eleven days, now, with half of that year passing without so much as a word from you, and far too many convinced you're dead. I can only hope your days are being counted towards your return.

Our days, unfortunately, continue to be fraught.

Not only the cards with their strange marking and warnings. Not only the Horned Lord's riddles. Not only our people gathering about us, and the guardians of Tickhill alert to treachery from without. Not only your brother's machinations, with his wife barely interred within the chapel...

On the heels of losing Alais, we nearly lost Maud's son.

Only two mornings ago, it was, and for once I was glad de Furnival had made it back from Normandy to find his wife gone to a funeral at Tickhill. He followed her, no doubt intending to snatch up Maud and scarper—and no doubt I'd have closed the gates after him just as willingly—but the youngest boy, not more than several months old and sickly, turned worse. I'd already moved them from a lower room in the Great Hall to the upper storey closest to the hearth flue. I'm not so lost to sense as to invite any de Furnival into the family keep, but I do want Maud comfortable, with her bairn in a warm place.

We were lucky, and the Lady decided to withdraw her cloak. That last night, though, I feared we'd not save him, and poor Maud... Well. She accepted our comfort, at least. And upon the dawn, when the bairn drew easier breath and the fever broke, she was nigh delirious with joy.

A terrible thing to be grateful for, in truth, but 'tis also true that hard things either bring people closer, or rive them apart. Maud has been softening towards us for some time—and that Gilbert's doing, I know. I'm not sure exactly when spy became smitten, but there's no doubt of it, seeing them together here before His Lordship's truculent face poked in. I'm thinking it's for the best. I hope Maud enjoys our Gilly, but more that she takes care now whilst her husband is in residence. He's not the type to share anything he considers his.

Well. In truth, because of Alais's funeral, we've ended up with more company than we'd counted on over Lammas-tide. Thank the Horns a recent hunt saw us with meat in the larder. Add that to several rounds of harvest that've *already been put up, and more grain coming in, and our stores are, for a wonder, nigh over-filling. Everyone we can spare is out in the fields to see to it. Those who have been staying within the walls have been doing another type of gleaning in our gatehouse hall. Not hundred-court, this time; aye, we'd usually be holding it after Lammas between harvests of grain and fruit, but no chance of that within the next fortnight. Nay, with de Furnival returning from the thick of things in Normandy, and many still here showing respect for Alais, I've agreed to host a number of male-type councils in the Great Hall, and those held long into the night. Grumbling discussions over the war in France and the crippling amounts of tax such things demand; what to do with the real danger of the mercenaries the King has left here—all of them aware of what happened at Tickhill just over a moon's passage ago; the Queen's oddling ways (she sounds a proper witch, and I mean that in admiration and optimism...), but the new respect tendered the King after the way he rescued his mam from Mirebeau and captured the Duke of Brittainy in one fell blow. Yet there is still talk over how he thinks himself above any laws, even his own.*

Like that should surprise any of them. He's a bloody king, isn't he?—and I've yet to see a one of them who charts any decent course. Frankly, most rich men tend to dismiss what they've never lacked, treat those less fortunate no better than animals, and all the while whinge about heark-ening back to 'better times'. Ha! Like such things ever exist, save in snatches.

At any rate, something seems to have been decided. First the Baron de Lacy took his leave of us, then Conisbrough and his wife (the latter tendering a personal invitation to join her upon their next hunt). Only this morning, the earl of Huntingdon also departed, with several well-meaning caveats. None are, unfortunately, practicable at present save a few:

> *I have sent my own appeal to the King regarding Otho's intent. Much, Siham, and Tafsut are always on hand. And I keep the inner keep well secured, with the fighters of Moorlands joining—covertly—the soldiers of Tickhill.*

A light tap at the door. Marion turned, fanning at the still damp ink. "Yes?"

It opened, motes of dust dancing in the morning sun as Siham peeked around the thick wood. "I apologise for disturbing you. But the lady Maud says it's urgent."

Marion rose, frowning. "Please say it's not the babe . . . ?"

At Siham's prompt, Maud crept through the doorway, shaking her flawlessly draped head in soothing negative to Marion's alarm. "He's fine, my lady. Thanks to you and mistress Aelwyn." She peered around, mien strange—cautious?—before she lowered her head. "I have something I must discuss with you. In private."

Leaning back over her writing table to flip a cloth over her parchments, Marion eyed Siham over Maud's veil.

Siham shrugged, clearly just as mystified. "Shall I send for some wine?"

"I've some already here, thank you."

Siham slid another wary, penetrative glance Maud's way then, still frowning, retreated, with a careful close of the door behind.

Not all the way, though.

Hiding a tiny smirk, Marion gestured to the bench by the centre hearth. "Please, my lady, sit. I'll pour some wine."

"I fear . . . " Maud paused and just as quickly composed herself, folding her hands against her skirts. "Thank you, lady Marion. A drink would be most welcome."

As Marion poured, she made an attempt to ease her guest. "I understand your lord husband will be travelling soon back to Sheffield, then?"

"So he told us this morning, aye."

"I'm glad you decided to stay. For the bairn's sake."

"For the bairn's sake." A whisper, almost an echo, and as Marion ambled back over, she realised her decision to pour them each a healthy drink had been sound. Maud's hand shook as she accepted the goblet.

"Whatever is the matter, lass?" Too familiar, mayhap, even coming from a child's shared sickbed, but Maud didn't so much as rail at it.

She did, however, take a long quaff of the wine, then a longer breath. Fortifying herself for something. "The men are away, and there's no reason I shouldn't come to see you about my wee Gerry." It was defensive.

"He's fettling, though?" Marion sat across from her.

A rare smile blossomed across the pale face. "He is. Had a proper tantrum, all red-faced and all, and only a bit of cough!" She took another drink—and that putting the roses back in her cheeks, as well. "We owe his life to your care. My husband mightn't want to admit it, but I know."

Marion smiled.

A pause. "You told me, d'you remember? Told me that I'd a place here, and little to fear. I didn't believe you, then."

"When life comes hard, belief comes harder." Marion reached across, topped Maud's goblet. "If you don't mind me sayin', you seem a bit fearful the now. Is there owt I can do?"

Another healthy quaff. No doubt she was girding herself up for sommat. "Nay, my lady. I think 'tis time I did for you."

"There's no debt between us, save friendship."

"You seem to have many who'd claim that. I'm glad you have some of those watching out for you." Maud tilted her head towards the edged-open door, and Siham's shadow lurking just past. A frown marred her brow. "But . . . so many of them . . . Well, they are—"

"Rogues, Saracens and outcasts?" Marion finished, with a tiny grin. And likely not her imagination, that slight snort from beyond the door. "Just call it . . . a hearkening back to earlier days."

Maud bit at her own lip, looking down. "Aye, and . . . Well. Do you trust them?"

"With my life."

"You might be doing so in truth. Please be sure of them."

"We've seen too much, all of us together, to turn our backs or cloaks on each other."

"Just take care with any trust, however given." Maud's voice steadied; plainly she'd decided what she must do. "As you know, both my lord husband and lord Otho have left to escort my lord of Huntingdon to the border."

Aye, Marion knew. Either courtesy or cheek—and Marion thought the latter—to do so. Either proxy, or assumption, as if Otho still held the name of Boundys, and with it the post of border keeper given to every lord of Tickhill. Marion should have gone, with a cadre of guards and her son, to prove the point.

But, however unpalatable and infuriating, it would have been unwise in the extreme. Marion knew that, too.

"I was in the inner upstairs chamber last night, seeing Gerry comfortable. My husband and lord Otho were talking and drinking alone, by the hearth in the attached common chamber. They'd dismissed the attendants out into the hallways, were speaking of the topics that have been on everyone's mind of late. But then they turned to more . . . private matters." Maud raised her gaze to Marion's. "You, my lady."

Marion took in her own, resigned breath, let it out with a nod.

Her composure obviously confounded Maud. She leaned forward, cheeks heating against the hearth fire, and exclaimed, "They're both planning that Otho take you to wife!"

"Huntingdon said as much."

Maud sat up, her hazel eyes narrowing. "Yet he rides away and leaves you alone here?"

"He knows I'm not alone. And an earl has other matters than my safety to see to. particularly at harvest time. Particularly since any claims of widowhood will have to be proven before the King."

"But the King is in Normandy, and my lord husband intends, within a se'nnight, to return there. He promised Otho he would gain the King's ear regarding your situation."

"I've sent my own appeal to the King."

"Surely"—Maud's expression mixed awe and pity—"you don't think a peasant-turned-noblewoman has the ear of a king?"

This one does, albeit slight.

But that one, whispered the Horned Lord, *is far away. Even as your own are, wandering the otherworlds. Neither Summer, nor Winter, nor a Plantagenet King-Fool who would claim thisworld can help you now. You must grow your tines, little budhorn.*

A shiver traced up Marion's spine, and she lifted her chin, twitched her shawl closer.

Maud misinterpreted the gesture. "Mayhap my husband is right in this much. Being raised up past your place has turned your head—"

"That has nothing to—"

"Please, don't be angry. I don't mean to insult you, only to—"

"My kin were worth ten of the likes of Otho. There's no shame to where I came from. Or insult given."

"And I've no intentions of slighting you. Alais, God rest her soul"—a quick touch of fingers to forehead and breast, signing the cross—"loved and trusted you. You've come to my aid more than once, despite my husband's enmity. You saved my child, and I shan't forget it, ever. You manage this honour with a surprising grace. You've learned a new place very well, indeed. But not well enough, nor as you should. As you would, were you *born* entitled."

"Your like isn't the only kind who must ask their lord's permission to wed."

"Serfs must ask, aye. But as long as it doesn't complicate the work, or infringe on another lord's rights, they have much more liberty of choice in their marriage bed. More than I ever had, or shall."

Marion understood the bitterness. "I was no serf, but yeoman-bred. My father was a forester, a free man."

"And therefore neither fish nor fowl, with no proper place—or so my father used to say." A rueful smile. "He didn't approve of such things, I fear . . . nay, please. Let me finish."

The entreaty of that last in particular bade patience. The lass was right in this much—Marion had neglected, of late, the wisdom of keeping her tongue behind her teeth.

"Anything you've done or will do, Marion, comes too late. Gerard and Otho have no intention of waiting for the King's permission!"

"Surely Otho, even with your husband's support, can't—"

"Surely *you* can't believe that women are anything but pawns in a man's game!" Maud sucked in a breath, held it and shook her head. "You see, this is what I mean. You weren't raised to this. But through chance and luck, you're married to a powerful baron who is not only connected to the innermost circles of the Knights Templar, but holds possession to one of the most important bastions guarding the border of the midlands and the North. Unfortunately, most believe your lord husband dead by now—forgive me—which makes you a very wealthy widow with a perilously young son . . . and, by law, in gift of the King."

"Which, as I said, gives me protection beneath that law."

"Aye, if laws weren't only for those who can't buy their way out from under them."

Marion went still. Hadn't she been writing about this just before Maud had come in? And hadn't her brother said it, many a time, about laws only applying to those who could afford to heed them? Not to peasants. Not to Heathens. Not to *women.*

Granted, she'd been occupied of late with more important things than . . .

Damn Otho and Hallamshire! She hadn't time for this idiocy!

"Marion, you have to believe me! To listen!"

"I do." Wooden. "I am."

"Only last night, my husband detailed to Otho what should be done. You see, all they truly have to do is present the King with a *fait accompli.* There will be substantial fines, of course, and a proper royal snit, but in the end?" A wave of one slender hand, which dropped to fist in Maud's fine-woven kirtles as she rose, came about the hearth, and knelt down to take Marion's hands in her own.

"They told me to invite you to sup this evening in the Great Hall, and to keep you there until the ringing of Vespers. They mean to return at dusk, and ostensibly retire most of the escort to the outside encampment, where they will wait for a signal. They intend that only a few men should be within the walls at first, not enough to rouse suspicion. But enough to take the Great Hall from the inside. And you."

"By t' horns, but we should just up the pitch and raise the gates! They'll pay hell fetching 'emselves in—and we've the best archers in the country sitting here!"

Much's fury at said treachery had done its share in easing Marion's aggravation towards him. In fact, he'd termed both lords

"Bloody skiving bastards, good for nowt but arrow fodder!" and stomped from the tower. It was obvious he meant to kick any arses that weren't on proper alert.

Siham plainly agreed. She sat cross-legged by the hearth, waxing her bow strings with a singular focus.

Their council was small, in truth, missing Much as well as Tafsut and David, who'd followed him out. The former had followed Siham's orders and the latter Marion's own: to assist in any way possible, and round up the best of their fighters. Aelwyn was helping Gilbert; they both stood over the massive board by the east wall, sorting a pile of arrows. Gilbert had come straight back after escorting Maud to the Hall.

The children were exempt, naturally, and occupied by Berta in Marion's chambers. Save for Ian, who'd been requested to accompany Huntingdon's escort to the borders. Unaware of the undercurrents, or so it seemed, he'd agreed, eager to impress his father. At the time, Marion had thought Otho's demand no more than another shot over the 'heir to Tickhill' bow.

More like fetching *his* heir from any firing line.

Marion stared into the flames, arms crossed and fingers tugging at her sleeves. Choices had come to roost. What would be Ian's, were it put to him so harshly? Marion had her hopes, but they were merely that.

Either way, she didn't want the lad hurt. Didn't truly want anyone dead from sommat as this—save on off days, no question. Not to mention, if people were killed for stupidity and arrogance alone, there wouldn't be many of 'em left . . .

"What is your plan?" Siham asked, peering at Marion. "From the look to your face, you have one."

Marion smiled. "The beginnings of one, aye. I'm hoping you lot will sort it for me, make sure it's feasible."

◇

The cavern was deeper than Gamelyn remembered.

Of course, at the time he'd been nigh out of his mind with infection and thirst. Likely he'd wandered no farther than the marks.

All traces of habitation had been scoured—he'd expect no less from the Badāwī—and as Gamelyn held up the torch, he watched its light slip and curve over the cavern's walls.

The glyphs, too, went farther in than he remembered. They were incised quite deep into the rocks. Tracing his fingers over several, he shaped the sounds of them with his lips.

"Do you know what they say?" Tariq stood at his elbow, curious and patient, holding up another torch.

"Some of them. Some of them I don't."

Tariq made a small circuit, around the back of the cavern and back. "Were these made by my forefathers, do you think?"

"The forefathers of your forefathers. Before the Prophet Muhammad, before the pyramids, even. An old, magical language . . . " He trailed away, scrutinising the marks.

Tariq forked an evil eye, caressing the blue bead hanging on a thong at his throat. He uttered a small prayer.

"You're wise to be cautious, lad. But I'd wager since you've seen no harm in this cavern, it must consent to your presence. Places have as much power as people, aye? And these glyphs . . . they seem more of protection than any harm." Gamelyn pointed to one. "See this?"

"It looks like a rope tied at the bottom."

"It is *Shen*. It is protection. And this glyph, *Sesen*, is the lotus flower, rebirth. And this . . . "

There are waves where there are no waves, the Relic's voice agreed. It seemed to echo within the cavern. *It is Iao who unbinds you, Adonai who sets you free. I remember, do you?*

"Gam'alīn?" Tariq prompted.

"Some of it is Coptic," Gamelyn forced out. "Others are more ancient, still."

Ancient, indeed. A place where all shall know me, and none shall find me. Remember, O wanderer. Remember the Sesen, *rising red against the sunrise, when you raise your arms against a faraway sky, and speak the words of unbreaking. Your task is complete. You will be whole.*

"It is speaking to you, isn't it?" Tariq whispered.

"How do you know?"

"Your face gives it away. Since you were so ill, in this very place." The lad seemed uneasy, but determined. "You think this is the place where we must hide Him?"

"I think there is none better."

◇

A forever sky, here; one to raise one's arms upward in supplication and gratitude. An immeasurable width spun of indigo-and-crystalline to a fabric of nigh perfection, with a gibbous moon rising to mark the desert in brilliance nigh to daylight. Easier, though, to mark the sands and shadows than beneath a relentless, glaring sun.

Aye, Gamelyn would miss these nights, so different from ones bordered by green boughs, or even those upon the wide moors of the Peak, where moonshine was more likely to be misted than stark.

Riding the Badawī mare into the west, it was as if a great weight had been rolled off his shoulders; his step lighter, his heart greater, ready for anything. His dreams, whilst of blood and fire, ended not in destruction but a rebirth, red-gold, from the ashes.

"Rubedo," he whispered, tracing the cinnamon mane of the mare he rode, and the stitched zags of crimson woven into his abeya, fluttering in the night breezes.

Sesen. *The lotus unfolding. The peacock's tail covering sight to give Sight. Death and rebirth. The unity of opposites, the mythical patterns, the phoenix rising. The blood of a Divine King who gives his life so others might prosper.*

You made the pilgrimage, the sacrifice. You died to yourself and rose from fire and ash.

Shen. Transcendence. To be whole.

"*Beauséant,*" he murmured.

No outside Voice, this, but his own. The covenant's people had called him Scarlet, in the Rites. He hadn't understood, then.

"What are they like, the Ismaili?"

Tariq had held quiet the past couple of days, either lost in his own thoughts, or realising the same held his companion. It had made for a comfortable journey, both of them adequate to the task, fewer questions and more just getting things done.

Gamelyn hoped Remegius had long since arrived home, with stories to tell. That Marion was all right, and all his loved ones still safe . . .

I'm alive, he Sent into the depths. *I'm coming home to you. I'm coming home to all of you, and Robyn. . .*

"Gam'alīn?"

He shook himself back to the desert, and Tariq. "Well. I've told you somewhat. They are formidable. Hard, but fair."

"There are so many stories." The grey mare sidled, sudden, towards Gamelyn's chestnut, ears pricked and nostrils flared; sure enough, a patch of sand shone dark under the moon, its footing likely treacherous. Tariq murmured, "Well done, Dancer" and gave her withers a scratch, sliding a curious gaze at Gamelyn. "Surely such tales cannot all be accurate. But . . . formidable, aye. That is a word to use, if but one of the stories are true."

"Some of them are. And while the new da'i is not of the same mettle as Elder Sinan, he has his own, no question." Gamelyn paused, furthered, "I think he, too, heard the Relic speak."

Tariq muttered a prayer, leaning forwards to brush quick fingers across the blue bead tied into his grey's mane. "Why would a holy man fear such things?"

"Any man should have a healthy dollop of caution towards elder powers."

"And did he fear you, O sorcerer of the Ifranji?"

"More like he was wary of what I represented. It is a simple thing to be so terrifying: honouring another's faith and expecting the same in return."

"But . . . that is a thing of faith, of beauty. Why would anyone fear such an honourable intention?"

"Think of it, Tariq. It means there is no one truth. It means there are no bounds other than those that people try to capture each other within."

"But as there is no law in Paradise," Tariq argued, "should God's people not then fulfil His plan upon earth?"

"Yes. But which people?"

Tariq's eyes widened, gleaming in the pale light.

"And if an Ifranji can be considered brother to the Asāsīyūn, or a peasant can hold rich men at bay and stand up to a King, or a half-Syrian woman can bear a bow and stand as equal to any Ifranji soldier"—he'd told the lad a little of both Robyn and Siham—"then what does that mean but we *all* are people, worthy of our god's blessing?"

Tariq fell silent—more thoughtful than offended—and remained so as dawn crept over the horizon and into midmorning. There was a small cistern with a cliff and cavern nearby—a water source Tariq had used before and made mention of during the night crossing—so they had been heading that way all along. Unfortunately, it had also caved in, somewhat. Fortunately, they found another opening in the cliff face, still sound enough for two wanderers and their horses to shelter against the worst heat of the day.

They'd fed the horses—and themselves—with dates and flatbread, then padded the dirt with saddles and rugs, lying down for a rest, before Tariq spoke again.

"It sounds as if the Nizārī Ismaili give scant welcome to outsiders."

"They are protective of their own, with good cause. To be fair, the da'i gave me a chance to prove myself."

"A poor chance!" Tariq snorted. "I've heard like tales, where Ifranji throw people into water to prove witchcraft! If they drown, they're innocent, if they float, they're guilty—and a waste of good water amidst foolishness!"

Gamelyn chuckled. "Well. Aye. But the da'i could have thrown me from the ramparts just as easily."

"That also would have been a waste." Tariq went silent, seemed intent upon the sandy ceiling for long moments before asking, soft, "Were you close? You and the brother Asāsīyūn, who gave you the water skin that likely spared you?"

Where was this going now? "We were close, aye."

"Did he owe you a lover's oath as well?"

Gamelyn blinked, slid his eyes sideways.

Found Tariq peering back. Rolling onto his side, the lad propped his head in one hand and said, quite serious, "Because such things, like family and God, make bonds where others fail."

Gamelyn considered all the truths that could lie beneath the spoken Arabic, then decided upon one by a silent and more telling language. Tariq leaned in, eager and intimate, his eyes luminous as his name.

"Tariq. I have no wish to overstep the bounds of one who has been a guest in—"

"Do not guests deserve all the comforts a host can tender?" Tariq extended one broad-knuckled hand to touch Gamelyn's fingers. "You are lonely, far from your own people. You have lived with us, eaten with us, sat to our hearth as one of us. I would give you comfort." He withdrew the hand. "Only if you wish, of course. I do not mean to insult one who was an honoured guest to the Banu Saleym. I know your people are not so open about such things. But you were a brother to the Asāsīyūn, where brotherhood is no little bond. And"—once again, he raised that naked gaze—"your eyes tell me that it would not be . . . unwelcome."

Gamelyn realised the breath had snagged in his throat. He spoke past it, admitted, "Not unwelcome, nay. Surely you realise how lovely you are?"

Another of those gamin smiles. "I have been told, from time to time."

"Then please do not feel insulted, or rebuffed, if I tell you I cannot. Any other time I would be honoured and pleased to accept such a gift. But I've sworn to the prophet I would remain . . . unbroached, during my time here."

A year and a day, now past, an inner voice prompted; whose, Gamelyn wasn't sure. But he also wasn't sure he'd the liberty to adulterate what *al kimia* had forged of him, through privation and death and rebirth, within his soul.

For Robyn, this. Though Robyn would surely cry him a fool for turning aside such a lovely, willing gift.

Tariq's expression ran the gamut: first a slight affront, then regret, then grudging comprehension. "Eh," he finally said, "I understand. Oaths are not taken lightly. It would be wicked of me to expect you to lightly cast one aside. But . . . mayhap I am wicked. For I am disappointed."

"Then we are both wicked, Tariq." Gamelyn held his gaze for a long, silent moment.

A huff of breath, a shake of dark curls, and Tariq reached out to brush fingertips against Gamelyn's sleeve. His expression once more flickered with varied emotions. "Mayhap it is a sign, also. My father says it is long past time I put aside boyhood. That I am a man, and therefore must act as a man. He is wise, and just, and I . . . " He trailed away, clearly unwilling to continue—but just as clearly troubled.

Not for the first time on this journey, Gamelyn wondered how it was that he should be the elder, the guide. He didn't know enough. Wasn't sure enough of too many things, and even his own peculiar arrogance lay inadequate to this sort of advice.

Yet the lad kept . . . *peering* at him.

Advice, nay. Comfort? Mayhap. Gamelyn kept his tone light, albeit serious. "It is a difficult place to be, when a father's wisdom and advice is . . . insufficient. To one's confusion, or even one's nature."

A frown, as Tarik's eyes flicked aside.

"In my home, I had"—Nay, damn it!— "*have* a beloved. A brother to my soul. He opened my eyes to many things. One of the most important being that I should respect my mother. The mother of my children. All mothers, in truth."

"I . . . do not understand."

"Neither did I, at first. But I came, over time, to see his meaning. How can it be true that either of us is made less a man by whether he mounts me or I mount him?"

Tariq's eyes widened. Because of the frankness of speech, or the suggestion that a grown warrior allowed such things? It scarcely mattered, only this:

"Tariq, if we are contemptuous towards any man who 'takes the place of a woman' . . . though it is not, is it? We are men, and it is not some unvarying place, but a preference, a choice of pleasures. How can it be anything *but* of ourselves? And to scorn it as a woman's role . . . ? Well. That is truly no more than contempt of woman."

A frown darkened Tariq's brow. Yet again, it was born of thought, not denial.

"Is your grandmother not a woman, and one worthy of much honour and respect? Did not our own prophets have women around them—wives, mothers, companions—whom they loved and trusted, sometimes with their lives?"

"You make it sound so simple." Almost sulky, Tariq had turned to contemplate the cavern roof once again.

Robyn and Marion's mother had long ago accused him with nearly those exact words. "Such things are never simple, nay. I've just come to my own peace with it. As you will."

The lad sighed, throwing one arm upon the saddle and behind his head.

Gamelyn felt his stomach knot tighter. Not from any thwarted desires or possibilities—he was well used to dealing with those—but memory. "To be a man also means that we make hard choices. It is difficult, sometimes, to be a father's favoured son. So much to treasure. So much to live up to."

"I am no favoured son. I am but seventh amongst nine. My father well loves me, of that I have no doubt, but I . . . I have no . . ."

"Place?"

Tariq seemed surprised by the understanding.

"I was the youngest of my brothers. Though my father loved me, there was little place for me, either. In the end, I had to make my own."

Tariq thought this over for some time. Just as Gamelyn was beginning to doze, Tariq spoke again.

"My grandmother's sire—indeed all her people—have long followed the ways of 'Alî. Do you think the Asāsīyūn would take me?"

- XXIV -

Otho and Gerard de Furnival approached Tickhill, complete with a small mounted cadre, just as the sun began to settle across the fens.

Marion didn't see it, but from within the Great Hall she heard the gatehouse bell tolling the sighting. After that, a quick series of whistles passed along the wall walk. Nowt unusual to that—such signals were always in use.

Nay, 'twere what the whistles signified.

Aelwyn, standing at the door and ostensibly seeing to the service for the meal, met Marion's eyes. Marion nodded. Aelwyn stepped just outside the door, giving orders that the next course be brought—but also, Marion knew, sending a quick gesture to Much, pacing on the wall walk just above the Great Hall: *All well here.*

"I've arranged an especial treat for everyone here. With your leave, of course, Lady Maud."

"You are our host," Maud said, with the same detachment she'd shown throughout the meal—and hardly a tremor in her girlish voice. "To refuse any gift would be churlish."

Well done you, Marion thought as two maidservants, heads properly lowered, came in with two silver trays. "Our bees have been proper generous this year. We made enough for all your people—with your leave of course, my lady."

Both the trays were piled with sweetmeats. One was set before Maud; Aelwyn took the larger and lingered politely, as if awaiting the lady's decision.

Maud had to take in a calming breath, to be sure, but managed a level "By all means."

With a cheery bow and smile, Aelwyn moved towards the door. The other two maidservants stepped back, each going to take up a place on opposite walls. One of Maud's attendants started to reach for the large tray; Aelwyn danced aside and wagged an admonishing finger. "Ah-ah. There's plenty on the table for all of us here."

The bell rang again: the chapel tolling Vespers, this time.

Maud had extended one hand for the smaller tray; she hesitated, shooting Marion a tiny, worried frown. Marion smiled reassurance. "I had some earlier, whilst they were making them. Pray indulge."

"Well enough. We'll have prayers after the meal is finished." Maud took one and beckoned her ladies, encouraging them to as many as they liked. Marion sat back and didn't have to fake—much—her own pleasant expression.

All of it, accomplished slick as grass through a goose. Including the doorman, a quintet of de Furnival's men, privy to the plans made the previous evening, guarded the outer entry. The tincture mixed into the sweetmeats—with the larger of the trays much more potent—would see the guards easily dealt with and tied up in the undercroft, with Marion's own people wearing their tabards, faces hidden beneath those wonderfully-concealing helmets de Furnival insisted his soldiers wear whilst on duty. Maud had the four personal attendants—one of those Gerry's wet nurse, a peasant woman in the bedchamber—and these three looked to be little trouble, the way they were scoffing up the treats.

Marion had been adamant on that. Better for Maud and her ladies to be victims rather than possible conspirators.

It seemed to take forever, the approach—but that was just as well, giving the sweetmeats time to work their magic. Maud's slight nervousness had abated; she drank her wine slowly, savouring. One of her attendants moved over towards the small arrow-loop opening and looked out at the gatehouse. A matron well into middle age, her regard severe as a hawk and her loyalties, according to Maud, with lord instead of lady.

"Well, my lady, your lord husband will soon reach our gates. Mayhap I should retire to my own place, and let you greet him unhampered?" Just to see the look on the matron's face, Marion began to rise.

The matron turned. "But I'm sure milord wishes to speak with you, milady!"

"Would he? How odd," Marion replied. "He's never been all that keen upon my presence before."

The matron, who hadn't so far cracked anything resembling an expression, definitely was beginning to feel the effects of the sweetmeats. Her look of panic was unadulterated. And satisfying.

"Will you check on my son before you go?" Maud's words came unforced, just casual enough. "My lord will no doubt wish to leave come morning, and I would like to know whether my lady wortwife also regards Gerry safe for the journey."

Marion allowed herself to be convinced. The matron was smiling at this proof of planning; she gathered her two cohorts by eye, nodded them to either side of the inner door.

Marion did likewise to Aelwyn, who'd come to stand just outside the entry and the two maidservants waiting opposite. "See to it that my lady Maud's husband and companions are made welcome, if you please."

The three dipped curtseys—two of them less than graceful—as Marion followed Maud into the inner chamber. The matron lingered behind. Marion gave a tiny tug to Maud's kirtles; when Maud frowned her way, Marion slid her eyes to the outer chamber. The matron was heading towards the door, albeit unsteady. Nevertheless she, more than any lord, might notice the guards' substitution.

"Rowena!" Maud called, purposefully light. "Will you bring the tray in here, please? I'd like another of those wonderful treats for Gerry. He's awake."

Gerry had just finished nursing, clinging to the young peasant maid and treating the newcomers to a serious look. It held no hint of glassiness, and the baby put up a bit of a fuss as Marion took him from the wet nurse and dandled him, checking him over.

"I wouldn't give him anything so rich as of yet," Marion said as the matron came in with the few remaining sweetmeats. "But you're welcome to have some, pet." This to the nurse. Marion well understood the ravenous hunger of nursing a bairn—and it would take the poor lass out of suspicion's way, as well.

Marion took her time examining the bairn, who had decided the lady holding him had nice, bright-coloured—and very grab-bable—hair. Having had more than one child hoist themselves upright via said braids, Marion had long given up on being tender-headed, and let the lad occupy himself as he pleased. Not long, though—with a belly full of warm milk, he soon slept in her arms.

"He's well for any trip, though keep him warm and dry," Marion told his mam, who smiled and riffled slender fingers over the babe's flax pate.

The youngest—and greediest—of the ladies fell asleep first, nigh unnoticed on a chair in the corner. Soon the second followed her, wilting onto the bed.

The matron was a tougher customer; she marched over to shake the second lass off their lady's coverlets. Aelwyn followed and, making sure Maud was occupied with the baby, put a hand to the matron's shoulder and breathed the sleep spell against her ear. The matron collapsed like wet laundry.

The wet nurse snoozed in her chair as Marion lowered Gerry

into the basket at her feet. Maud daintily covered a yawn just as the bell tolled.

Visitors at the gates, this time.

Another set of whistles answered it, and Marion smiled, interpreting. The soldiers following de Furnival and Otho would, as chance came, be picked off one by one by Siham's dark-clad assassins. Dubious, that they'd all follow their lords into the Great Hall. More likely they'd their own sneak-thief orders.

Marion, with Aelwyn's assist and a bemused Maud watching, set a bottle of wine and several of their best silver goblets upon the table, along with some bread and cheese and another tiny, tempting dish of sweetmeats. Insurance.

A groan of iron hinges, as the massive downstairs doors were flung open. Male voices carried upward. Rather loud for a supposed invasion, mayhap?—but nay, sound did carry in the huge Hall. Whilst the ground floor chamber was nigh its full footprint—with only a few rooms closed off in the back, the upper storey made up only half, with only the open gallery running the full length out and back around. The doors closed, were bolted from the inside. Men mounted the stair—more than two, but less than six, from the sound.

It had been Much's main worry; that more would be inside the Hall than Marion and Aelwyn could deal with on their own, did things go awry. Which was why Siham and Tafsut were dressed as the two extra maidservants, and the guards just outside the chambers had been replaced with their own.

Marion and Maud stood waiting at the head of the board, with three maidservants standing attentive just behind.

Some small discussion was held with the guards just outside the door. Marion's heart skipped a beat, but the door swung open. De Furnival first, with Otho and—bugger and blast, but Marion had hoped Ian would have gone on to the stables, or lingered at the gatehouse, or something! He stood by his da, all hunched and surly, and when he would have met her eyes, looked away with a tiny wince.

Otho had a grip on his arm.

Three other men followed—not common soldiers, not quite—their clothing finer and their belts hung about with telltale Sheffield steel.

Marion wanted to order them out. Instead she smiled, albeit through clenched teeth, and ignored them. "Greetings, my lords."

They answered, pleasant enough. Ian looked around, frowned as he saw the two with Aelwyn and started to speak. Marion had a moment of panic, but Otho's fingers once more dug into his arm. There'd be bruises tomorrow, no doubt, and Otho seemed to decide bringing Ian had been an error, for he ushered him out and turned him over to the guards just outside the door.

Who would undoubtedly hustle him away, somehow. *First mistake,* Gamelyn would have said. *You only have two more.*

"Husband!" Maud went to him, holding her hands out, and de Furnival took them, with a bow.

"I see you did as I asked." The words weighted themselves. De Furnival addressed Marion, "I told her she should have some company and gaiety at times."

"And what better way to do so than with the woman who saved our child's life?" Maud's tone was a bit more straightforward than she'd intended; her husband threw her a frown.

He glanced around, gave a second look at their attendants. "These aren't . . . Where are your ladies, my dear?"

"They're in my chamber, readying the bed." Maud didn't have to feign a jaw-cracking yawn. "Struth, but I'm sleepy!"

"A good meal and all the worry over your bairn this past se'nnight 'twill do the like," Marion said quietly, her fingers brushing the board, her eyes never leaving the two lords.

Funny, how Otho couldn't meet her gaze. Or, mayhap not, considering.

"Then, my lady wife, by all means you should follow them," de Furnival said, releasing her hands. "We've something to discuss with the lady Marion, as it happens. Would you kindly excuse us?"

Maud glanced at Marion, who nodded and gave her a tiny curtsey. The younger woman repeated it, turning for the back chambers.

"And send Rowena, if you would, when you've finished," de Furnival called after. "Another woman," he explained to Marion as the door shut behind Maud. "So you don't feel overwhelmed by too many of the male sex."

Marion cocked an eyebrow, reaching for the wine. "You seem to forget, my lord, that I spent some time with a surfeit of the male sex in Sherwood. 'Tis difficult to overwhelm me."

"Surely," Otho offered, "it's to your credit that we do forget?"

"I'm sure some would say so," she countered, beginning to pour the wine into a cooled serving pitcher. Truly a dangerous game, this. Not for the first time she thanked the gods for not only Aelwyn's presence, but Siham and Tafsut, proper bulwark and sentinel. And sent another brief prayer after—tweren't betraying hearth law, to foul treachery and protect her own. But still, it rubbed close.

"There's no need for wine." De Furnival held up a staying hand.

Marion refused to be stayed. "Surely we need wine and some sustenance"—a gesture towards the well-supplied board—"to conduct business. After all, that's why you're here, aye?"

It knocked Otho for six, in truth. But de Furnival's regard turned, just like that: disconcerted to discerning.

"In which case, you don't need those big strong men with their shiny knives." Marion finished pouring the wine, set it aside and inspected the two goblets. "Surely two men are proper adequate against a handful of women, does it come to cases. Frankly?" She set down the goblets, took up her own, only half emptied from the hour previous, and took a sip. "I'd rather it didn't come to that. You don't know me very well, milord of Hallamshire, but I suspect you've heard overmuch. Surely milord Otho has told you that, despite my upbringing"—she tipped her cup to Otho and drawled it, purposeful, into the dialect of that upbringing—"I'm not daft. No doubt you've also heard I've an eye for a chance."

Otho looked as if someone had slacked every ounce of wind from his sails, and the respite of it coming a surprise. De Furnival was equally gobsmacked.

"Please. Sit, my lords. Let me serve you and then we can have our little, ah, *private* discussion. No better way to discuss possibilities, after all, than over a good meal and fine wine."

Otho, after a silent eye-to-eye agreement with de Furnival, dismissed the threesome lounging against the entry wall. The latter seemed plainly content to malinger outward as in, and filed through the door. Otho closed it, but didn't lock it.

Marion let the smallest of tilts claim her lip, and shared it with Aelwyn as the men seated themselves, one to each side of the board, and tucked in. Marion served the wine with her own hands, put the bread and cheese and salt cellar before them, gave a top up as they drained the goblets.

"Brandywine, milords, brewed by my Aelwyn, here, and from several bottles that were gifted from the Temple. The Commander told me they were from stocks favoured by the Queen Mother herself."

"Dry, just sharp enough," de Furnival commented. "Excellent!"

"And these sweetmeats, the honey comes of our own bees. Though we've not managed to outdo our southern villages in making mead."

"I told you." Otho seemed to reprove de Furnival. "Told you it was suitable."

"Ah." Marion put the pitcher onto the board. "Let's speak of suitability, then. What do you propose?"

The two men blinked at each other.

"We . . . aren't exactly prepared to make any . . . uh . . . *full* . . . proposal," Otho confessed, shielding his consternation behind two of the sweetmeats.

Marion hid her own smile. De Furnival was watching her closely.

"Frankly," de Furnival drawled, "we believed it was inevitable that we might have to . . . shall we say, overplay our hand this evening."

"Well, I'd be lying if I told you I hadn't caught wind of sommat. But 'tis better for both sides if we come to some agreement, aye?" Speaking it aloud gave Marion a chill. She leaned forward, topped up both their cups and continued, blunt, "Better for our purses, too, unless"—this time she did smile, purposefully sweet—"either of you have discovered some way to settle the King's outrage at eluding his assent?"

Again, she'd gobsmacked them.

Sadly, it wasn't actually physical.

"I must confess, you gave me no reason to believe you'd be sensible about this." Otho's confession came slow, as if his mouth were numb.

The drug was starting to work.

"Pray realise, milord; I was taken aback you'd even consider such a—"

A short cry from just outside the door, and a series of heavy, solid thumps.

The two lords tensed, turning to the entry. Marion hoped she was the only one who saw Siham's hand fall to where her knife must be, or heard Tafsut's Berber mutter.

"What is it?" Marion called.

A pause, then a muted voice answered "He's fallen down the stair!" Another series of thumps followed—surely a rush to the fallen one's aid, nowt more.

Or so Marion hoped her companions would believe. Faith!—but her folk were supposed to take care of any problems *quietly.*

Aelwyn had slapped a hand over her mouth, eyes betraying not only apprehension, but wry amusement. Marion had a like impulse, firmly stifled it. She didn't dare look at the other two.

Thankfully, neither of their supper guests seemed overly concerned—particularly Otho, who'd started to slump sideways on the bench. With a slight shake of head, he straightened.

De Furnival had thankfully turned back to Marion. "Well. Since you're being reasonable about the, ah, situation? Surely there is no need to risk angering the King. In fact, I must return to Normandy in a few days. I can speak on Otho's behalf—your behalf as well, now, and openly put the matter before our liege." His normally-keen gaze had begun to blur about the edges—but not much more.

Whilst her mouth had sucked itself dry, sweat tickling at the small of her back. Nerves. Marion took another sip from her own cup, glancing towards Otho. His eyes were trying to close.

He was so much stouter than de Furnival. Surely the latter had to succumb at any . . .

Marion grasped at another frayed straw of conversation. "I have some concerns of my own, milord, that need to be discussed before we can solidify any plans."

"Of course," de Furnival gave an expansive wave with one hand. "But surely that can be arranged in the meantime between you and Otho, so you . . . " He'd turned towards the latter, trailing away as Otho slumped forward upon the table and began to snore.

"My lord?" Marion leaned forward, all solicitude.

"God's legs, but he usually holds his drink better than this.

Shift yourself, man!" Leaning towards Otho, de Furnival shoved at him. "Wake u . . . !" His voice scaled a surprise as the shove fell just that much too short and toppled Otho sideways. De Furnival then turned an owlish gaze upon Marion, even as the goblet slipped from his hand. It rang upon the board, a piercing cry that spewed carmine across the board and de Furnival's hand. He stared at that hand, watched the wine drip and glint in the torches, its truth putting an equal light in his eyes.

Marion tensed. The most dangerous moment, this, and unpredictable.

"You *bitch.*" Lunging up from his bench like an angry bull, de Furnival went for her. She darted aside, Aelwyn a close shadow, both keeping the table between them and their pursuer.

Siham ripped the wimple from her head, sword in hand even as Tafsut shrugged from her overdress, daggers in both hands.

"You . . . " De Furnival staggered, flung his hands against the table to stay upright, speech slurring. "You . . . the wine was *drugged,* by God!"

"Nay, by the Maid of Sherwood," Aelwyn told him, sweetly, as he collapsed across the table. "But it comes to the same end, aye?"

The bodies had barely hit the floor before the door burst open. Much, along with two of Tickhill's guardsmen—no longer in Hallamshire colours or helmets—burst in, cheeks flushed and just looking for another scrap.

They seemed disappointed to not find one.

"Tie them up," Siham ordered the guardsmen.

One produced both a grin and a length of rope, jerking his head to his companion.

"Those men who came out, they were proper trouble," Much informed Marion. "But we settled them."

"And the noise?" Marion raised an eyebrow.

Siham snorted.

Much shrugged. "Aye, well. He fell down the stairs."

"With the assistance of the Commander's fist," one of the guardsmen pointed out, grinning.

"You owe Marion and Aelwyn an apology," Siham furthered, mock stern. "You promised to be quiet."

"Is it my fault the motherless git overbalanced?"

Marion let out the laugh she'd been holding overlong, and Much grinned and winked at her.

Siham, meanwhile, gave another snort and backtracked to the doorway. She had a quick discussion with the remaining guards, and leaned out farther for a moment before lurching back in, pulling a gagged Ian along by the scruff of his tunic collar.

"They held *this* one," Siham informed Marion, "and did not hurt him."

"Yet." Tafsut spoke offhanded, eyeing the torchlight as it glimmered upon her long, curved knife.

Ian merely gave her an exasperated look and started tugging at his gag.

"Maybe you, like your sire, would like a new *maman*." This from Siham, spoken with all the scorn Norman French could muster.

Plainly this was news to Ian. "I'd like a *what?*" He seemed only then to take in the tableau before him: his father and de Furnival, sprawled senseless, with the two guardsmen binding them hand and foot. "Da . . . ? Lord Gerard . . . What is going *on?*"

Marion took pity on him. "They're fine. Just sleeping it off. For now, we've a lot to do and a spare amount of time to accomplish it. I'll explain on the way."

"An explanation would be helpful," he agreed, somewhat sardonic. "On the way where?"

"Out," Siham answered, warning. "We'll be tying you too, *petit*, until we're sure of you."

"Sure of . . . " Clearly at a loss, Ian didn't struggle, his gaze clinging to Marion's.

A whistle rose, echoing almost painfully from the interior cavern of the Hall. *All clear*, it said; when answered in kind from outside the Hall, Marion felt the rest of her muscles, finally, relax.

Even though they weren't clear yet.

Meanwhile, a grinning Tafsut—aye, and she'd been waiting for just this moment—strode over to Otho's unconscious form, bent down, and hefted him over her broad shoulders.

"Lord Gerard wanted to send me to Hallamshire with several of his men," Ian told Marion. "But my father refused, saying 'twas time I helped instead of hindered him. I'd truly no choice than to follow them back, with my father giving me nowt but surly words and once a blow when I questioned. If I'd known what they intended . . . "

Riding beside Ian, Marion reached out and touched light fingers to the bruise upon his cheek.

"Surely you can't believe I'd be a part of such a . . . !" Clearly trying to find a suitable descriptive—and failing—his gaze slid, outraged, to Tafsut and Siham.

"You were with them, boy," Siham pointed out. "He is your father. You owe him a son's loyalty. It only follows that we had to be cautious." The two women, along with three other of Moorlands guardsmen, closely tailed the procession.

And procession it was. Resembling a spearhead, it was headed by Much on his favourite palfrey, with a small group of Tickhill's best trailing after, some walking, some riding, all armed. Most carried torches to light the night, with the two in the middle leading horses burdened with two odd packs: Otho and de Furnival, slung senseless across the saddles, coarse sacks over their heads.

The lady Maud and her women would be sent home the next day, under suitable escort. Hallamshire's guardsmen and the three mercenaries had already been dragged unceremoniously to the edge of the fens, with David detailing how lucky they were to still be walking, as the last who'd thought to take Tickhill were rotting in said fens.

Ian's eyes gleamed even without the light of the torches. "He is my father, but my mother taught me better things."

"That is well." Tafsut nodded. "Your mother was, truly, a woman."

"I thought we were going on to Hallamshire after." Ian continued. "For a visit. Instead we were joined by more men and rode for Tickhill. My father refused any answer about what was going on. De Furnival flat out lied to me. Said we were going to bolster up Tickhill's forces."

"Hold up," Much said, low, from the front. The wide night sky of fens and fields had given way to scrub, a thick, green-black tangle of woodland scratching at the stars and bordering either side of the road. Sound echoed off the thick growth and travelled easily, here.

Prime outlaw territory, were not the Hood's presence still here, growing like the trees. Not that Marion would lose much sleep if their captors were set upon by outlaws, but . . .

Nay. Proper perfect, this solution.

The rear guard stayed on alert, whilst Much and his lot got to work.

◇

"You can come back with us, you know." Marion told Ian. "You don't have to stay. Much has detailed men to stay, make sure they don't end up as wolf bait."

The lad had settled onto a fallen oak, peering at the coppiced elm a mere stone's toss away. His father and Hallamshire had been trussed to it—indeed, like wolf bait. Heads lolling, knees up against their chests, they still slept, deep in the influence of the doctored wine and sweetmeats. Even the noise from a nearby stream—the frogs, silent when humans had first tromped through their domain and now commencing their shrill and reedy courtship—hadn't wakened them.

"I'd rather go back with you," Ian finally said. "But . . . my mother would have wanted me to stay. She loved him. I owe her that much."

What the boy didn't say?—nevertheless said volumes. Marion

looked over Ian's downturned head at Much, who shrugged. *Did you expect owt less?*

Nay, she hadn't. But . . .

"Ian." She knelt. "Mayhap you should come with us. You'll be . . . out of range. I'll have to disseise him of Stainton. With what he's done, I've no choice."

"I know."

"I hate to do it to your home."

"Tickhill's that. Particularly with Mam gone . . . Stainton's no home."

Marion sighed. "If you were older—"

"Well, I'm not. And I've no more head for running an estate than *he* does."

Much snorted and put both hands to the lad's slumped shoulders, squeezed. "You're nobbut twelve, lad. Your balls en't even dropped. Give it a few years."

Ian smiled as if Much had handed him the sun. "You think so?"

"We all know so. Aye, pet?" Much slid a glance to Marion.

"You're your mam's boy as much as your da's," she answered. "Mayhap more. Never forget that. I just wish you weren't plonked amidst all this. I'm sorry."

"Why are you sorry? It isn't your fault, but theirs." Ian sighed. "Either way, 'tis likely I'll be at Tickhill's gates before you know it. No choice left but to place myself upon the mercy of my relations."

"No mercy." Marion kissed his forehead. "Just love."

A groan from the elm. De Furnival, likely coming 'round.

"As Herself said, lad, the guardsmen are lurking," Much furthered. "Case you have any trouble. We wain't leave you here alone in the dark."

"I'm not afraid of the woodland."

"And so the Wode shan't touch you," Marion said, soft. "You have its blessing and the trees shall know you, allow you passage."

Another groan, this time from Otho.

Marion dug in her pocket and pulled out a small folded parchment, striding over to the elm. With one of the daggers they'd piled beside the two men—noblemen's blades, all of them, made of the finest steel Sheffield could produce—she pinned the parchment to the elm, right between their bound-together hands. Otho twitched—aye, coming to. Time to leave. With a satisfied huff towards the parchment, she turned away.

Ian watched, eyes hard with his own sort of satisfaction. She'd read it to him on the way here.

Nowt official—that would come—but still the most essential of messages, with contempt roiling not only in its tone, but its patent lack of signature:

> *Anyone who sends mercenaries to my gates*
> *had better come ready for battle. Anyone who*

> *brings mercenaries within my gates? They are*
> *declaring war.*
>   *So be warned. The curse of the Shire Wode*
> *is upon you. Should you wake from this night*
> *to rise against my home again, you will be*
> *more than sorry.*

"Blessings be unto you, lad," she told Ian.

The boy nodded and, from his seat upon the fallen oak, watched them disappear into the trees like so much mist.

- XXV -

Waning of Mabon, 1202 CE
Dhu al-Quida, 598 AH

Rain had fallen upon the valley oasis. It rose sparse mists unto the dawn, dancing in the wake of their horses' passage, and dispersing as two riders crested the hills, looking out over Acre—and past.

Gamelyn watched Tariq. He'd told the lad what to expect. Still, he well remembered his own first sight of the sea.

Forever, that skim of silver and blue and mirrored light; it seemed to go on past the end of the world. Even when one knew the great African expanse lay beyond, and this sea was but a smaller echo of the great ocean that crashed Africa's western shores, and provided both battering force and cradle to a small, homely cluster of green-washed islands farther north.

Nigh indescribable, both the sight and Tariq's reaction. He leaned against Dancer's neck, elbows quivering. His mouth hung open, working—he'd pulled the wheat-coloured scarf from his face to sniff the brine-laced air—and his eyes were sprung wide-white.

Gamelyn smiled, gave Lioness a nudge with his calves, picking their way down into the valley.

It took a while for Tariq to follow, at the last trotting up on a wider stretch of path. By then he'd found his voice. "Truly, Gam'alīn, you must forgive me, but I did not believe you."

"It is an unbelievable sight. One of many, never to be forgotten."

Tariq cocked his head, peering sideways at Gamelyn. "You are . . . sad. I thought you were joyful, grateful to be returning to your family."

"I am. But . . . Won't you be sad if you petition the Ismaili? Won't you miss your family?"

The dark eyes met his fully, then. Tariq nodded understanding, and turned back to the sea.

They rode in silence for some time.

"So *much* . . ." Tariq let his mare pick her way, staring out across the water. "And none of it fit to slake one's thirst."

"I'm afraid so. But in that brine lives an entire world's worth of creatures, perfectly adapted to their lives. As we could be to ours, did we choose."

"Sometimes there is no choice."

Gamelyn nodded. "So we have to grasp what choices come our way."

Not turn them aside. In ignorance, or fear. Not that either are so different from one another, aye? The Lady's voice filled him, so strong he gasped.

"Gam'alīn?" The tone—and the expression accompanying it—had become familiar. Tariq understood that his Ifranji friend spoke with spirits; it didn't mean he had to be comfortable with it.

"The leg." Gamelyn gave it a rub; healing well enough, but in truth an uneasy partner still.

Tariq frowned. "I will see you down to Acre."

"You will not. 'Twill be dangerous for you, coming back alone."

"Less for me than an old Ifranji soldier limping his way through Acre!"

"Hold on there, I'm not *that* much your elder!" Gamelyn aimed a half-hearted swat at Tariq's pate.

A duck of head with that heartstopping smile—this time, full of mischief. "Anyway, I want to touch the sea. It will be a story to tell my grandmother!"

Tariq got his wade in the sea.

The two mares weren't so impressed. Lioness in particular snorted and puffed up and backed nigh halfway up the beach as the waves rolled in, convinced that the strangely shifting "ground" had one mission: to eat unwary horses.

So Gamelyn took them up from the surf line and let them have a good roll in the velvet sand, whilst Tariq splashed and yipped and danced in the surf like . . .

Well, like Robyn would have.

So beautiful, so *quiet,* this cove. Within site of the harbour, just far enough past Acre's eastern land gate to be a haven of sorts.

Upon the narrow, southward jut of peninsula rose the Templar stronghold, all brilliant white in the sun and visible for miles. Nevertheless, it was dwarfed by the expanse of sky and sea.

Gamelyn had already reported to the Commander there, a staid, weary man who'd nevertheless been quietly thankful that one of their own had been returned to them—and successful, in the end, upon a holy mission. The Commander had offered Gamelyn the kiss of peace, a berth in the dormitory with his Brethren, and two reassurances.

The first, that the Badawī youth who'd saved the life of a Templar certainly deserved sufficient and safe escort back to his desert. The second concerned the Templar galley floating gracefully in the U-shaped harbour. It waited for cargo and a fair wind to take it westward towards Cyprus, then Spain, then Normandy and England.

Home, Gamelyn vowed and grinned as Lioness got up with a grunt, shuddered sand all over him, then collapsed for another roll.

Tariq finally came tramping up the beach, several lengths of limp seaweed hanging from in a large shell he'd found. He laughed at how Dancer stood over Lioness where she had nestled, sternal recumbent, into the sand. She'd curved her neck around Gamelyn, who stroked her forelock, having accepted the offer of a couch made of sand and her white-splotched shoulder.

"She already misses you, Gam'alīn."

"I shall miss her. And you, Tariq."

"You know I shall miss you." Tariq crouched, scooped the seaweed from the shell and offered it to the mares. "But you will see your family, eh?—and that's what matters."

Dancer smacked her lips, bobbing her head up and down at the strange texture of the "grass". Lioness, never one to let a meal go to waste, had inhaled her portion and was looking for more.

"And your family?" Gamelyn asked. "Will you go to the Asāsīyun after all, or return to them?"

"I will go and give the Nizārī your message, as I promised."

They had discussed it on the road . . .

"Tell Masud Abbas ibn Malik al Abd-El-Kader that Gui abd'Hariq aljinni alshier al-ghaba returned the Prophet to his homeland, and in doing so, found his own truth. He now journeys home to fulfil it."

"Will you stay there?"

"I'm not sure." The lad's eyes had darkened. "I miss my grandmother. My sisters and brothers. My . . . people. I'm not sure I want to give them up just because I feel . . . different sometimes."

"I understand," said Gamelyn, and closed his eyes.

Tariq nestled down beside him like a pup, and Gamelyn slept for a while, lulled by the sound of waves against rock, the warmth of sun and foam against the sand, and the smells of horse and brack.

Dreamed of rain, and green-wet boughs, and caverns rising from the mists, their depths drip-drip-dripping into nigh-forgotten pools.

⊕

"So. You be returning to us."

Robyn said nothing, merely held her gaze from the cavern's entrance. The Priestess returned the favour, neither of them giving way, with only the drip-drip of silt water against stone, and into cloudy pools. The silence lingered, even those gathered held still and silent at their work or watching.

Behind her, one of the Crones leaned forward. She didn't seem to speak, but the Priestess tilted her head as if listening.

Finally, the Priestess lifted one hand, gestured. Robyn entered the Grotto.

The remainder of her gathering was not so sanguine. Fewer this time, they turned to each other, their quiet murmurs echoing into the depths. Some milled about like hens after corn, others glared at Robyn as he padded in, towards their leader.

Glares became startled exclamations as his clutch of gwyllion sailed in after.

The wildcat paused—it had been drinking from a small bowl—ears flattening briefly before returning to the bowl.

Otherwise, an ordinary day, aye?—if the previous one had even ended. Exchanging chatter and unspent moments, or giving due to powers that could no longer hear what voices were raised, or shaping statuary doomed to moulder away, unseen. A circle, to be sure; but one closed, unaltered, and . . .

Wait. There was a difference. Magus was conspicuous in his absence. Grey Eyes, too, was missing. And of the two ubiquitous Crones, only the white-garbed one lounged beside her Priestess.

The one who'd held him against the Bowl. A shiver claimed Robyn as he glanced towards it, hunched solitary in the shadows.

Those peopling the Grotto seemed the same: no more, no less. And the guards—including, emphatically, Skull Face—glowered at Robyn, were behind the low dais in full force.

Robyn ignored all of it, coming to stand before the Priestess and settling to his knees, haunches upon heels. The gwyllion alighted about him, muttering and jostling for place. His familiar uncurled itself from about his throat and perched upon his left shoulder, a tiny sentinel.

"Why return, Hob-Robyn?" White Grandmother growled. "Why now, when you have been avoiding us? Mayhap we are not being pleased to . . . "

Her voice trailed off as the Priestess sat up from her own reclining posture, leaning on one arm to peer closer. "You are being changed. Somehow."

"Like a man, he is being," sniffed White Grandmother. "Wanting something, always."

Robyn shot a glance at her—unable to help it—and the Crone smiled victory. First at him, then the surrounding folk, who answered amongst themselves with whispers.

So he tucked his chin, forelock falling over one cheek. "Arianrhod." Low, persuasive. "You must hear me."

More whispers as he spoke the name, more akin to a small clutch of owls hissing at each other across a forest glen than any human voice. Curious. Confused.

The same mirrored itself in the Priestess's face, and the Crone's; nigh as one they sat up as the latter demanded:

"Why do you be speaking that name, boy?"

"Because I know it and I am not a boy." A purl of thunder accompanied the words, and echoed beneath a ceiling that had never known such.

The Crone's eyes widened, slight. Again, the smile tipped her lip.

Again, the gathering of owls hissed, wary.

The Priestess leaned back upon her couch, ran small, strong fingers through the fur of the wildcat as it returned to curl against her hip. "And why must we be hearing you?"

"Because I am the Horned Lord's chosen. To dismiss me is to dismiss life—and death."

Her eyes narrowed, gleaming, and the Crone made a sign against the furs. Around them, the people drew closer, hisses growing into murmurs: confusion turning, displaying a threatened edge.

Conversely, the wildcat slitted its eyes and began to purr.

"Yet you be denying both," the Priestess countered, "in this very place."

"*I* en't the one in denial. What I refused weren't yours to take."

"You be seeking to turn the Wheel widdershins."

"Aye. Constantly."

Skull Face muttered a curse and lowered his staff, clear threat. His companions, likewise.

The gwyllion around Robyn's throat returned it with a growl, wings quivering, rising. The other spirits crouched upon their own perches, defensive. Ready.

The guardians wavered, gave ground. Save for Skull Face, who paled, and stood firm. Two of the others seemed to shake themselves, and stepped forward again.

More murmurs, these shocked. The wildcat spat at the guardians even as the Crone turned on them, slicing an angry sign into the air.

Grudgingly, the trio stood down.

The Priestess spared them a thin glance, her mouth taut. She rose, slowly, from her couch, her eyes boring into Robyn's own. "So. You be seeking my place, be displacing Her will."

"Is that what you really think?"

"I be thinking Hob-Robyn has become a creature of sire's blood, after all!" the Crone sneered. "You will not be finding it easy to—"

"Enough of this." Robyn didn't move a muscle, though the gwyllion nevertheless quivered, ready. "I want nowt from you save the respect of one entreaty."

"Entreaty? We have been telling you, more than the once. There is being no escape fro—"

"Return the Arrow to me."

Coming to an abrupt halt on the edge of the dais, the Priestess stared down at him. "The . . . Arrow."

The owls muttered. The gwyllion hissed, with Robyn's familiar a soft echo, all the while craning its neck back and forth.

Still, Robyn didn't move, merely peered up at her. "I could've nicked it, you know. I en't called the 'Thief of Sherwood' for nowt, after all, and easy enough to find." He gestured in the direction he knew it lay, hidden. "Nigh t' rest of your mouldering carvings, like 'tis nowt more'n a trinket of some ancient, futile war. I could've had my little beasties fetch it. They trail me like tiny hounds, could pop in bold as brass, snatch it up and be away before anyone could so much as draw breath.

"But nay. I'd do me little friends no service, did I ask their help, since *your guardians*"—he purled the word all mocking, this time gesturing towards Skull Face and his like—"find little hardship in making threats towards 'em. Surely, and some refused, but the same one as spilt my blood raised his staff! Against spirits as were old here when our people first crawled out of the swamps! And the very ones as bloody well help you survive this barren tomb."

The White Grandmother seemed angry indeed—but not at Robyn. And the Priestess kept watching him. Staring, she was, uncertain now instead of proud. Wary, as if he'd sprouted two heads.

Robyn merely kept peering up at her, rump upon heels and hands resting—light but ready—across his thighs. "There's more to 't than that, aye? To nick sommat implies the one doing the taking has no proper rights to it." He held her gaze, watched her pupils contract all tight, counted the sluggish, if strengthening, pulse at her throat. "You and I? We know better."

"You be making the offering, not I. You be swearing oath upon that Arrow."

"Aye, I offered up the Arrow to you—"

"'Twere your magic you be offering up to us!" Magus' voice rang into the Grotto, accompanied by the *tap-tap* of his staff and the scuff and shuss of his bare feet upon the stones. The small gathering made way.

This time, Robyn was cognizant of the mix of emotion upon their faces: resentment *and* respect.

If memory is being of sorrow, Hob-Robyn, what is being the curse of one who brings it forth?

Magus came to stand beside him, peering at him as if kenning his thoughts . . . but his next words proved there were no "as if" to it. "You thought you would be turning my head . . . and so you were, in your way, making memories turn and burn. So here I am coming, Trickster—and never are we forgetting you are just that, O Hob. I mean to be reminding you of your own words, so the bargain you mean to be making rises fair, and true." One blue-spiralled arm rose, and the fingers gave a small twist into the air.

A whisper floated into the caverns, a ghostly imprint of Robyn's voice.

M' magic is yours, as much as me own. I have called you to ask this much: keep it safe. . . until I return for't. . .

"And I have returned for 't," Robyn voiced as the echo faded. "My making. My magic."

Silence. Even the everpresent *drip-drip* seemed to slow, mute itself.

"Trickery!" Priestess shot into the stillness, albeit a quavering loose from an unsteady string. "We be holding it safe, and you would be bringing the end of all our hopes!"

"You have done, no question it lies safe. But also useless, aye, where it lies? And 'tis one of m' natures, chaos . . . but ending? What lies in an ending but more beginnings?"

"Not here. Never here again."

"Why not? You're one as threw the bones t'wards your own shrewd wager: bring the Horned Lord here, in the body of His own, trick the trickster into making life within your dormant caves." Robyn laughed, both rue and sweet. "Sweet Lady, Lady, did you never think there's more'n one way to do just that?"

Her pupils expanded, this time. "You are bein—!"

"Mad as a buck in autumn. Aye, well, mayhap I am. But that Arrow brought me here. My blood and my magic opened the gates enough so your folk—not the gwyllion, not any of the other spirits, but *you*—could cross over just long enough t' snatch me in. You watched—because you could watch, at least—and waited for the proper time and place: Solstice, when the light comes back and the Winter King sleeps." He rose, kept holding her gaze, eyes meeting eyes. "So, Lady. What if the Arrow's flight can pierce the Veil again? What if the Crossroads can be opened—and mayhap held open in the same time as holds this place?"

The cavern went silent as any tomb. The Priestess drew back, as if expecting a blow.

The wildcat watched Robyn and the gwyllion through half-shut eyes, once again beginning to purr.

Thanks for that, Robyn thought, and fought the impulse to smirk, however slight. "Aye, and what if—at the proper time and place—the lord of the Hunt calls upon the power of his Maid and Knight from the other side? What if the Arrow is let fly into the night—and not just any night, but the one when the Veil between the worlds is thinnest?"

"Samhain," said she, into the quiet.

The Crone wasn't so restrained. "Fool, Hob! The Rade of Samhain be long away and lost to us! If we cannot be so much as touching the tides, surely we cannot be knowing them, finding them, riding them!"

"You did once."

"For once and final, that wager was being, and we lost," acknowledged the Priestess. "The portals were drifting away, allowing only sparse glimpses here and there. Soon there were being none. We are blinded here. As you said."

"And what if we *could* touch the tides?"

"What is meaning by 'we', tall one?" the Crone asked, all too sweetly.

"He knows what I mean." Robyn pointed to Magus, eyeing the Priestess. "I'd wager you know. How *many* secrets have you kept, pet, even from your own people?"

"The child." A tiny, bare breath. "Made in the magic of Allworlds, that one. Once, when you were sleeping, we heard her song through the Veil. I captured it in my hands. I can hear its power still."

"She's reached out again, past the Veil. I've spoken to her."

And he could see, in the sudden gleam of her eyes, this she *hadn't* known.

The owls, watching, began to murmur.

"Impossible!"

"Aye, it is being so!"

"None can be *speaking* across the Veil!"

Without a word, the Priestess motioned them back to silence. She never once took her eyes from Robyn.

"My sister's child is t' gateway." Robyn gained his feet, swift grace, and began pacing. "But then, how can she be otherwise? 'Made in the magic of Allworlds', as you said. Forged out of the Great Rite, by *Ceugant* brought forth, into flesh. Out of blood and sacrifice, by fire and wilding magic." Deliberately he turned his back upon the guardians, faced them—Crone, Priestess, and Magus. "She can tell me when the Veil grows thin. She can tell me when Samhain looms."

He had her. The cold sepia of her cheeks had gone sallow, yet her eyes had softened with something he'd never seen: the raw pain of hope and, trickling about the edges, fear.

"If this is coming, then you must be making the Bargain," Magus crossed to the dais and urged her, soft. "There must be a bargain upon which to make the Rade."

"This will be no mere Rade, old man." Robyn's voice came just as soft, though it could cut steel. "This will be the Hunt."

And it lay upon the rocks, smouldering like the iron to which none of them would dare draw close.

Save the gwyllion upon Robyn's shoulder, who began to croon. The Priestess blinked, and a tiny smile tried her lip.

"To be leaving here, Rade or Wilding Hunter's Ride," Magus

finally insisted, "means there must a bargain be. As we did for Hob-Robyn. As we always have done, from beginning times. Sacrifice must be given, always, to be working the deepest magics. You be knowing this. Hear them, Hunter's Own and master of beasts?"

Indeed, the gwyllion had been joined by the others, circling a-wing and upon the rock ledges, soft tones echoing, beginning to grow.

"It cannot be working. None of us can be leaving here!" The Crone shook her head, backing away.

"With the Arrow," Robyn insisted, "I can. My blood. My bargain." And silent, he added, *I'll take the future back. Thwart the darkening skies, deny the pestilence of smoke and poison. Ensure my Wode stands, and endures.*

The Priestess stood toe to toe with him, watching, unblinking. Waiting . . . and what for?

"If you be passing outward," Magus hovered between them, so close Robyn could smell the oil in his hair, the mint-and-soil tang of woad. "If you be joining your Horned Master, be leading the Rade and Ride the Hunt? Will you also be breaking the iron curse, unshackle the ancient spirits and loose their chains, set your people to once again roam their lands freely?"

"Free my Arrow, and me. I'll show you."

The small gathering had begun, once again, to mutter amidst themselves.

"And if you cannot?" The Priestess still watched, with an expression Robyn wasn't sure he fathomed. "This battle is not being one you can win, Hob-Robyn. Do you think we have not been trying before? The future shifts, unplaits and weaves itself, but this remains: if we are being what remains of our kind, then you, indeed, are the last of us. Choose most carefully."

"Lose or win in t' try, or do nowt? Stay *safe*?" He curled it scathing.

And now he was damned sure he didn't care for the way she eyed him. It seemed almost . . . pitying. "You will find the outer-worlds . . . changed."

Wellaway, that much was clear, with Aderyn being a lanky child 'stead of a sizeable bump beneath Marion's kirtles.

"And not only *tynged's* flight around you, O Hob-Robyn, but *tynged* itself. You have lived outside it; when you return to it, likely you will find it . . . unforgiving."

"Life en't altogether forgiving. I understand that, and likely better than you, Lady."

"Do you?"

"We be having no place in that world," the Crone countered. "Have you forgotten the Seeing, Hob-Robyn? It is death!"

Hisses and signs traced against the unspeakable. Though the shudder went deep, a crawl of chill over his flesh, Robyn breathed it in. Smiled, grim and grace. "Aye. It is."

A tilt of lip, then head, and the grandmother turned aside, going back to settle upon her furs. "Then your place is being here, waiting for your return."

"If this works, I'll see you next in the otherworlds, and the Wheel shall return."

The expectancy in the caverns had grown, palpable, voices rising with hope and fear.

The Priestess raised one hand.

And from the shadows, they came: the indigo-garbed Grandmother and Grey Eyes. The latter, eyes downcast, cradled the Arrow upon a nest of wrappings; the former held a great, ancient bow.

"Only the Hob would think to change Allworlds," Indigo Grandmother said, holding out the bow. "Merry met, Hooded One."

Robyn frowned, took it, eyed it up and down and up again. Said, ruefully, "This en't likely to last the pull."

She shrugged. "Hob-Robyn you be. Horned Lord's creature, woodland spirit, Archer of *Ceugant*. All you be needing is one."

Well, all right, then. As long as the bloody thing didn't break in that one. Robyn nodded to himself, started to reach for the Arrow.

But White Grandmother had risen and, swift as a mouse, put a hand to his chest, staying him.

"There must first be the bargain," she said, soft. "Be making the bargain, O trickster Hob, O Gwyn son of mist, in whom the spirit of Annwn lives lest the world be destroyed."

The words threaded a chill up Robyn's spine. The gwyllion hummed, as if in answer, and the sound reverberated against his hand, stirring the wood of the ancient bow.

"He will not be spared, nay," Indigo Grandmother finished the ancient phrase. "Even so, be making the bargain, O Arianrhod."

"The robin, or the wren," the Priestess said. "Winterlord, it is your *tynged*, your *dihenydd*, your fate past all other bargains. The sacrifice must be made. And while you have set Creiddylad free from a father-god's control in otherworld's time, in Allworlds still must Winter and Summer together do battle, and seek Her favour every *Calan Mai*. So the Wheel must be turning, and so you must be returning the Horned Lord's promise to us. Let in the forest, pull aside the Veil, free the Old One who must guard our gates!"

"But?" Robyn queried softly, with a stroke to the ancient bow, and as the Priestess arched one brow, continued, wry, "There's allus a 'but' to every bargain."

"Aye." Magus, this time. "If you be losing in otherworld, bound you will be to return to thisworld. For this much is being true: should the magic be fading, no other place can be sustaining the Hob."

No light warning, this. But 'twere no light wager. Robyn held out his hand for the Arrow. "There's one place at least, and some things worth dying for. *Anadl tynged*."

"Then the bargain," said the Priestess, settling back into the furs not unlike the cat beside her, "is being made."

⟨ᚱ⟩

Make the bargain. . .

He walks through a grey, stunted woodland, dry-eyed though he wishes to weep, shackled though he wants to run, pinioned and hooded though he longs to fly.

The hood has never kept you prisoned, the Voice says. So soft, nigh inaudible . . . weakened, somehow. Yet Robyn hears the god, at last, at least. *It is your strength. It is your centre. Your focus. Your purpose.*

And my shroud.

Aye, in the end. But not yet. Roll the bones, Hooded One, Horned One. Make the bargain and dance the Spiral's return. Open the gate and let Ride the Hunter's Moon!

But . . . I cannot do it alone. No one can do this alone.

You will not have to. Your Maiden waits for your call. Let voiceless be the truest voice indeed. Tell her. Your Summerlord has wandered the wilderness, died and made the initiation, found his own power. He returns across the sea, coming back to Us. Call him. Call them!

The drip-drip and hiss of blood upon hot rocks. The fire, leaping and licking upward into the rippling green-grey light of the cavern. The wyvern's eyes, opening against the silt, guardian and . . .

Gateway.

Robyn inhaled the sacred Fire, opening his eyes against the blooded, blue-fire smoke. Held it, there, prisoned within his lungs until a cough knocked against his chest, then released it as, from the other side of the Veil, the Old One met his gaze.

"Call them, *Ysgawen,*" he purred. "Take my words to other-worlds, let the voiceless be Our voice."

Another breath, deep in and released out.

"Tell them there is no time here; they must call me forth, even as I call them now to the bargain. Tell them I shall wait."

A last breath to make it three, a triad, a brined point upon a triskele arrowhead. Allworlds. *Ceugant.*

"Tell them *Samhain.*"

⟨ᚱ⟩

Tell them.

Old dreams. Old nightmares, thought long forgotten. Ones to sink the damned into deeps and hold them there, lungs nigh bursting, ears filling, blackness humming, until breath betrays and water rushes in, and . . .

A hand grabs and hauls him backwards—always, somehow, it won't let him just *die*—and blood-filled water spews over his habit, where the cross has gone black, bleeding crimson into white. Yet the voice is not the same. Not Much, holding him close, insisting all choked and fierce that he must live, he has to live . . .

"Da?"

Nay, this voice is one he's never heard, not with his ears. Nevertheless, he recognises it. *Knows* it.

"Da, it's time to come home now." Aderyn bends over him, quite serious. "We need you. Mam needs you. Uncle Robyn needs you . . ."

Gamelyn woke with a strangled shout, twisted and hanging. Tangled in rope, trapped, confined in a land where there was no sun, only wet and cold and impassable tunnels leading to a dying Wode . . .

"Y' all right, Brother?"

Another voice, but this one full of reality—sanity—as well as a bit of pain. The Templar galley, Gamelyn realised. He was in the Templar galley, swinging in an upper hammock for a bit of sleep, and he'd accidentally kicked his lower neighbour.

"Sorry. Nightmare," he murmured.

His lower bunkmate murmured back a reassurance—he knew, all soldiers knew—and rolled up to help Gamelyn untangle himself from the hammock.

"Better?" the man asked, through a friendly, gap-toothed smile.

"Aye. Thank you, Brother."

As his neighbour rolled back into his own lower berth, Gamelyn stretched out in the hammock, relaxing into its drift and sway. About him, men shifted and muttered and snored in various stages of sleep. It made fitting accompaniment to the creak and flex of the galley's wooden hull, her broad beam settling into the waves. Soothing, all of it, for now: the sea reasonably calm and the current running with them.

Gamelyn took in a long, deep breath, the nightmare beginning to fade.

Save the one thing, tickling odd behind his eyes.

Aderyn had spoken to him in the dream. More, he'd recognised it. Somehow. How such a thing could be possible kept drifting from him, as if on dreams . . .

Her voice, carried upon Fae dreams, Gamelyn realised, slow. With *Robyn's* voice lingering beneath, fiery and fierce as mulled honey wine, to scorch an echo faint and undying within Gamelyn's skull.

Undying.

Tell them they must call me forth. Tell them I shall wait. Tell them. . .

"Samhain," Gamelyn whispered into the dark.

- XXVI -

M arion's Book of Hours
Waning of Mabon, 1202
7 years, 9 months, 25 days
1 year, 1 month, 25 days
<u>*Our Lords shall return*</u>

After the storm, some peace. All we can do now is wait, and watch.

No doubt by now my message has arrived to the King. I intended to send Gilbert; instead 'twere Hubert and a handful of Templars as ended up accompanying Gilbert—and my missive—to Normandy.

Hubert stopped at Tickhill a bare day after the business with Otho and Company. En route south, Hubert naturally wondered why Tickhill's defences were at maximum. Of course, I filled him in on what had happened. In turn he told me that he was going to London on business, from there taking ship to Normandy to meet with Master de Birkin (already there and, I suspect assisting King John in his wrangling with the French king) and more Templars.

So, Gilbert and two of Siham's best fighters travelled south and on to Normandy with Hubert—who insisted—and quite rightly so—that a Templar Commander's statement would give substantial weight against what suit Hallamshire has, no doubt, laid before King John.

For aye, Gerard de Furnival—humiliated and in no little dudgeon, according to his lady wife—left for Normandy not four days after we deposited him in the Shire Wode.

I drafted the notices of deseissment of the vill and manor of Stainton, and Otho slunk in de Furnival's wake back to the keep at Sheffield. He won't allow Ian to return to Tickhill—another development we hope the King will remedy. Ian is safe, but unhappy, I fear, and little improved in circumstance despite his father being allowed to take up a place as seneschal. All of this, of course, is from Maud's pen. She too is safe, thank the Lady, and her husband suspecting nothing of her own involvement.

Yet my own security still lies in some doubt. I go nowhere outside Tickhill's walls without a bevy of guardsmen, and Much, free to companion me without Otho lurking in our family quarters, rarely leaves me. He's worried, I know, whilst we wait for word from Normandy. While it's unlikely the King will ignore a missive backed with a Templar's word, it's quite possible that Hubert's master could foul the works.

John sent word. He found Prior Willem—and no doubt sent him to his hell. Unfortunately, Wymarec de Birkin was already gone to Normandy.

I try to ignore it. Try to pretend that, at present, I cannot truly be Maiden to the Shire Wode, but must instead be hemmed in, a pretender to nobility, a woman whose success—and freedom—are tempered by stone walls.

Aderyn, too, frets at what she considers imprisonment. She can't truly understand the danger—and I'm glad—but curtailing her wanderings means I'm not in her good books. Thankfully, Tafsut has rather adopted her—a better and more ruthless guardian than I could ever prove. Together they often "sneak away" for a ride across the countryside, though it is always accompanied by a covert tail of Moorlands folk as would do credit to a small army. Aderyn rides Farasha always, now, and is nearly as smug as her brother Robbie, who has graduated to riding Rutterkin on his own, beneath Sarah's experienced eye.

The Mere is off limits, for now. Aderyn agreed, once I promised her that we will be there, at the proper time. That we will help her Uncle Robyn come home.

So we prepare for the coming of Samhain, and together, John and I plan what we must do. We cannot fail this time, even should Gamelyn not arrive...

He has to. We will not fail.

We're running out of time, Gamelyn. I know you're alive. I can only pray you're on your way home.

*Dark moon 'twixt Mabon and Hallows, 1202 CE
Barfleur, Cherbourg, Normandie*

It seemed that alighting upon the land of his father's people had always prefaced great transformation.

First, in banishment from Blyth Castle, bereft by the wake of Loxley's destruction and his father's death, Gamelyn had been here by his eldest brother as scutage. Kneeling upon the chill earth of a Templar's tent, Gamelyn had sworn his sword to Hubert de Guisborough, smothering grief beneath an assassin's cloak: Guy de Gisbourne, hammered in Outremer's forge.

Then, the return. In the wake of King Richard's ultimately futile attempt for Jerusalem, both Hubert and Guy had waited on the docks of Barfleur. Then, too, they had stayed at the *Croix*, awaiting the storms so they could travel home, to Hirst.

No idea, then, what had been waiting. Another massive—and just as painful—transformation. But this one had been from Guy and back into Gamelyn as the dead had, seemingly, come back to life: first Marion, then a pagan wolfshead known as Robyn Hode.

And now?

Now, more waiting. Both wind and current had set themselves against the great Templar galley; *Magdalena* was one of several that lay restrained in Barfleur's harbour, listing to starboard with wind and rain. Barfleur itself literally teemed with humanity: soldiers, sellers, smiths and seamstresses. King John was in residence at Chateau Gaillard, a half day's gallop inland, and Normandy was at war.

Gamelyn was sick of war. Sick of everything, his only focus arriving home as quickly as possible.

Standing aft, Gamelyn peered out at the thick curtain of wet and grey, water dripping from his cowl, and wondered if the dinghy would be able for one more trip ashore. The sea had quickly turned from threatening swells to foamy whitecaps, while *Magdalena* tossed beneath him like a horse with a burr under its saddle. And how apropos was that?

The difference between this and the sparkling, azure warmth of Acre could hardly be reckoned. Still, it was exhilarating. He grinned, kept a hold of both his cowl and the galley's railing, and drank the rain like wine.

The only sobering thought was the weather. No question, but this crossing bided changeable, treacherous. Wind and weather had laughed at even Willy Bastard's might, and kept him bogged in place for nearly two months, delaying what would be a permanent conquest of Saxon England.

Gamelyn's hand slipped on the wet railing, tightened with a squeak. He had to get home by month's end. Somehow. *Putain de merde*, but one could *see* England from here, did the day dawn clear! Not much more than swimming distance, it was, to the shore beneath the stark white cliffs—those, of course, invisible in the murk—and doable, surely! If one discounted waves that could curl higher than a ship's mast, or water chill enough to freeze the knob off a stone gargoyle . . .

"Brother?"

Gamelyn turned to meet the captain's half smile. Rain and a close-pulled cowl nigh hid the latter—and definitely hid a sergeant's black habit underneath, the same Gamelyn himself had once worn.

Still grinning, the captain nodded to Gamelyn's perch. "I fancy this sort of weather more than I should, meself. Of course, 'tis usually in port and not the middle of the ocean. Fickle, I am."

"I would say smart."

"Smart would be staying on dry land. Or so me brother would claim." A tilt of the wet cowl. "'Tis time, Brother. The last dinghy's here. We'd best take it now, what with the weather turning worse. Only a skeleton crew's to stay aboard, and we lucky ones are away to have a decent meal and dry off at the *Croix*. Coming?"

With a last, longing glance past the waves, towards the cliffs he could not see, Gamelyn ducked his head against the rain, and followed.

⑤

The *Croix Cramoisi* was, as its name suggested, an inn that catered mostly to Templars, but it also boasted its share of Hospitallers, and was capably run by two Templar Brethren who were oath-bound to Château de Gisors. Mayhap not as noisy as the inn just down the lane, but cosy, for it boasted two hearths, plenty of wholesome, hot food and, tonight, a pair of minnesingers accompanied by drum and lute, with light songs to charm away the heavy rain runnelling down the roof tiles.

The short trip for *Magdalena* to shore had indeed been the last possible, and nigh *im*possible. If not for the captain's skill at the rudder and the four remaining passengers manning the oars, they'd still be out there, carried away and foundered, likely. But their sopping garments garnered them a place by the fire and an offer of dry robes, with hot mulled wine, coarse bread, and enough pottage to nigh overflow the substantial wooden bowl a potboy placed before Gamelyn.

In companionable silence, they fell to.

The minnesingers were well able to fill the small hall, from one song to another, with stops in between for comments to and for their audience. One table in particular was quick with the back-and-forth; they seemed a bit . . . well, rowdy. Particularly considering that most Templars and Hospitallers had learnt restraint as a habit, one rarely shed in any public place . . .

Ah. These weren't Templars, though they must be accompanied by them to so much as make it past the front doors. Well dressed, two seemed well-paid guardsmen, and the other mayhap some merchant, groomed to a fault, with wavy dark hair falling just so past the collar of his tunic. As he rose from the table to drop a coin into the minnesingers' hat, that tunic was revealed as the same, rather expensive shade of green that had so pleased—and been so pleasing upon—Robyn.

And aye, several Templars accompanied him, seated at his table with drinks in hand—and all bemused by his ebullience. They'd been companions a while, 'twould seem. Six, counting both Templars and guardsmen . . . nay, a seventh relaxed in the corner shadows, fingers tapping out the minnesingers' rhythm upon the head of a cane.

Familiar, somehow; mayhap something in the movement. Gamelyn's attention swerved as the green-garbed man laughed and swooped a courtly bow towards the drummer.

The pot nearly slid out of Gamelyn's hand. He knew the music of that laugh.

"Brother?" The captain reached towards him, frowning. "You look as though you've seen a ghost."

"I think I have," he murmured, and lurched to his feet.

The green-clad man turned—quick as that, with an awareness no mere merchant needed to possess—and no questions remained. Save the one.

"*Gilly?*" Gamelyn blurted out.

Gilbert stared, and blinked, and stared again. "It's impossible . . . it can't be . . . fuck me stupid, but it *is* you!"

Then all was confusion. Gamelyn wasn't sure who approached whom, but they met in the middle somehow, the drummer snatching his drum out of the way—barely—and them colliding into a hard embrace surely to knock the breath from a man, all the while babbling half questions and even more broken answers.

"How are you here—*alive*—and—"

"I just came in this morning, I can't—"

"We're here to take the Templar ship back to—"

"*Magdalena?*"

"Aye, that one, and we beat the rain from Chateau Gaillard, stuck here for the wait."

"Me, too, since—"

"*Gamelyn?*" The voice came from Gilbert's table. Ragged-hoarse. Disbelieving. And . . . and *frail*, somehow, when it had once filled a room.

Gilbert shoved back, releasing Gamelyn, with a self-conscious smile curving his lip and a tilt of head indicating that shadowy corner . . . to where a silver-haired Templar sat bolt upright from the shadows, his peacock-headed staff clattering to the hard-packed floor.

Somehow, the room had gone silent—or mayhap it was just their corner, their sudden-small world where nothing existed but the meeting of eyes across a room. No romantic love, this, but love nevertheless, and fealty and . . .

All the while Gamelyn's eyes never left Hubert. And for his own part, Hubert didn't speak. Didn't rise, or so much as move.

Gamelyn stumbled over, lurched to a stop. Then he sank to his knees, crumpling forwards, his head falling into Hubert's lap.

⑤

"You're back. You've come back to us."

Hubert kept saying it, with a gentle reach and touch of fingers to Gamelyn's sleeve, as if touch alone could convince him of the words. "You're back. She will be so glad."

Scalding heat kept rising behind Gamelyn's eyes, making Hubert—indeed, the entire room—swim and blur. Yet he couldn't speak—words were inadequate to the task, so he reached out and grasped Hubert's hand. At first firm, Gamelyn slackened his fingers, sudden-gentle, as the grip within his own proved . . . precarious, somehow.

But it tightened; thinner, mayhap, but no less hard, and Hubert clasped their hands together into a knot. "I have prayed for this moment. Over and over, and yet to have it come here? We will send word to her. She needs to know. We have birds here, so we must send word"—a frown towards the rain-lashed windows—"when wings can fly, that is."

"Another round, O potkeeper!" Gilbert sang out from Gamelyn's other side. "'Tisn't often a man returns from the dead!"

The entire inn had fallen under the sway of reunion, the brethren one by one drifting over to pay their respects. Hubert was well known and loved even here, and the story of the Templar who'd taken the Saint's relic back home had, until now, been told as a cautionary one. Even the minnesingers had changed their tunes, bringing out a lot of cheerful lays surely more suited to a sunny meadow concert than an inn battened down against pouring rain and driving wind.

The latched shutters creaked and banged nigh in time, at that.

"Apropos, I would say, my lord Commander." Gamelyn finally could force words over his thickened vocal cords. "Since my very first meeting with you was not far from here, and in much the same conditions: on my knees, wet to skin from foul weather and a rough passage."

"On that day 'twas naught *but* mud, as I recall, from here to Argentan," Hubert mused. "Dear God, but it was a foul se'nnight, only"—he leaned forward, kissed Gamelyn's forehead—"only fairer than most, for aye, there *we* met, my *Confanonier.*"

And the heat spilled, runnelling down over Gamelyn's cheeks.

"Aye, me too," Hubert agreed. "I never thought to see you again in this life, my son. And this life, no matter our hopes for the next, is the one we best know and love."

"Thisnow," Gamelyn agreed, soft, "is all we have."

Gilbert's frame twitched, amidst passing out more drinks, and his gaze slid to take in Gamelyn, one brow describing a perplexed arc.

The inn began to settle down, all congratulations and well-wishes expressed, the excited buzz calming to normal speech, backed by music and the howl of the wind and rain just past the warmth of the dual hearths, and the solidity of well-wrought cob-and-wood walls.

For long moments, it was enough to sit, silent and heart-full, between two men Gamelyn had thought he might never see again: one who'd been a father, and one who'd been more a brother than any blood relation had proven.

"Did you find what you sought, my *Confanonier?* What you needed?" Hubert's whisper was meant only for Gamelyn's ears, but Gilbert heard as well, fixed a sidelong gaze upon Gamelyn.

A reminder: the question had import to him, as well.

Gamelyn met Gilbert's eyes and nodded, albeit slight, as he spoke to Hubert. "The Relic is returned. It lies, quiet and fulfilled, in the desert, where none shall find it but all shall know it."

Hubert's lip curved. "And?" Leaning closer, it seemed his gaze sought to bore through Gamelyn's own eyeballs and into the back of his skull. Or, more likely, his soul.

Gamelyn met it, matched it. Said, "Death knows my name. She showed me the lunar light and the dawning, and dragged me into darkness. When I woke, 'twas naked in Her arms. She clad me in the *rubedo* of Her kingdom, gave me the words of returning, and granted me leave *to* return."

Hubert raised Gamelyn's hand to his forehead, then kissed it, returning it to the tabletop with a small, asyncopated tap. Released him, and reached for his drink.

Gamelyn did likewise, the heat sprouting once more against his eyes. Leaning back into the shadows, he settled his spine against the wall where Hubert had first sat, nigh hidden.

Beside him, Gilbert's fingers also made a tiny dance upon the tabletop. Not overt, more likely part of Gilly's preference to move even when he sat still, unless stillness meant survival.

Gamelyn frowned, realising it had naught to do with that. Gilbert was speaking to him with the old signing-talk.

—wish there was some way to send a message a-wing. This bloody weather has to let up sometime, aye? Hubert is right, Marion will be elated to see you. The children. Much, and John. . . bloody damn, all of us, so glad!

Much. Marion. John. The children. David and Aelwyn . . . his true family, all waiting. And then . . . Gamelyn took a drink, but didn't straighten up. He was tired, he realised, tired to bone. Nevertheless he focused on what Gilbert was saying: little things, mostly, a necessarily-scant recap of how everyone was at Tickhill, with the promise of a fuller reveal before they arrived back home.

Then, *We have to get home. We both—but particularly you—have to return to the Wode, and before the moon of Samhain.*

Gamelyn nodded. *I know.*

Then he closed his eyes, and let himself fall into a light doze, propped against the wall between trusted—and beloved—ones.

At first, with all things considered and spoken—not only with Gilbert, but Hubert—Gamelyn thought it necessary to ride to Alençon and petition an audience with the King. Indeed, it looked as if he might even have time to undertake the se'nnight's worth of hard riding back and forth on muddy roads; the wind stayed persistently and aggressively uncooperative.

Hubert negated it by sending two of his Templars instead,

carrying missives marked with his own seal as well as Gamelyn's. One was meant for the King's eyes, while the other was addressed to the Master Procurator of England who, along with his Normandy counterpart, were attending the King. Both said, to effect: *The prodigal is alive and returned, and will, by my own order, accompany me back to England and our holy preceptory, to attend our business in all matters.*

Unsaid was the understanding: *And he cannot risk missing ship back to England.* Hubert knew something was in the wind, that it involved the feast of All Saints—Samhain—and, as he always seemed to, understood.

Meanwhile, Gamelyn spent too many nights drinking with Gilbert, catching up on a year's worth of triumphs and slights that would have—if Gamelyn hadn't already known it—convinced him that his wife was a pearl beyond any price, his brother in need of a damned good thrashing, and . . .

And John, holding the horns. Whilst wee clever Aderyn?

Had spoken. To Robyn.

Gamelyn wept altogether too easily these days, and didn't care a damn.

Instead he passed out the moment he rolled onto his mattress—such normalcy in a cot across from his Master's, knife beneath his pillow, sword hung at his head and observances twice daily, whilst away from the preceptory—and slept more soundly than he had in well over a year and a day.

Dreamed soft, rain-filled dreams, where voices lifted in soft and eerie song, and bonfires hissed as tree-rain spattered them. Where rune-marked cards fluttered in the wet wind, and turned to leaves, shed against a waxing moon. Where Marion walked a moonlit meadow, damp skirts tucked up, arms bare, bathed in silver and copper. Where John lifted the horns to the cloud-tossed night and placed them, reverently, on the leaf-littered ground.

Both of them, looking. Both of them, whispering unto morning: *It's time to come home, Gamelyn.*

Yet *Magdalena* remained tethered to Barfleur's harbour, and Gamelyn paced the docks like a caged lion, hair and cloak whipping in the wind, beneath a moon hung hidden behind thick clouds.

He felt its movements regardless, from dark and into waxing.

They were running out of time.

⑆

Time.

Occasionally it would reveal itself through a shaft of sunlight, strafing the Mere all too quickly and into darkness.

Mostly it just stuttered, sighed, and lagged in place, spinning itself into nowt.

Sometimes Robyn paced the caverns; sometimes he sat and breathed the stillness; more often he ran circles, hopped up and down like a madman, danced about the fires and conjured *tomorrow* into the cool caverns. All the while, his gwyllion swirled and spun and settled about him.

All the while, the wyvern watched; awake, now, but strangely quiescent in the shadowed bottoms.

Waiting, as Robyn was.

It weren't his truest nature, patience, but Robyn had learned its lessons through unforgiving means. And now?

He could wait forever. He had time. 'Twere his loved ones as didn't.

When it came, 'twere more sudden than he'd thought possible— or mayhap it weren't, because, well—but nevertheless the moment lingered. The wyvern rolled upon its watery couch, and projected a vision of a black-haired child standing upon the banks of Barrow Mere.

Mam says we'll be here. At Samhain, we'll be here to guide you home.

⑤

Finally, after a se'nnight of foul weather fit to tear sails to ribbons, the clouds scattered and fled, taking the storms with them. Gamelyn woke to peace, and observances held against a dawn that bathed the sopping harbour in gold and roses.

The stillness seemed deafening, in fact, after so many days of creaking—and sometimes, leaking—walls, banging doors and shutters, and rain pummelling the roof.

But the chance had come, and *Magdalena's* captain sent word: they should prepare to take it, in case the wind turned.

So Gamelyn—not without an occasional, impatient glance towards the harbour—ensconced himself in Hubert's chambers, and prepared. It was a rather-sodden task. The damp had encroached everywhere: lingering upon the walls; settling mildew in bags and gear; smoothing a dank chill into every bit of extra clothing. Body heat and stints at the hearth were all that kept worn clothing from doing the same. Even their blades had miniscule patches of rust. Once he'd packed away the clothing, Gamelyn, with an impatient glance out towards the harbour, made himself sit down to oil not only his, but Hubert's steel.

Mayhap the wind on board ship would help dry everything. Assuming they weren't delayed again.

They couldn't be delayed again.

A light step scuffed at the entry. Without turning, Gamelyn said, "We'd best see that everyone's blades are well-oiled as soon as possible. Ours were trying to rust, and . . ."

No further steps inward, and he trailed away as the silence

expanded just that much more—brooding, somehow, an inimical presence. Lurking. Gamelyn stiffened, instincts clicking in place—shivs to hand, two well-oiled daggers on the bed, accessible—and turned.

Of course. Who else would it be?—yet the reality of the sudden appearance settled upon Gamelyn: improbable.

Yet, mayhap, inevitable. Particularly in thisnow.

"I reckoned," said Wymarec de Birkin, "I'd time to catch you before you left. The weather, and all."

That weather seemed to have made little inroads upon the Master Preceptor—indeed, the spotless repair of his garb suggested he'd stopped to change. Of course. Neither did Gamelyn's threatening posture seem to touch him. Indeed, Wymarec leaned against the doorway, crossed one foot over the other and arms likewise, eyed his Templar fore to aft and plainly found him wanting.

Are you, still, his Templar? The Voice—hitherto lost, gone, silenced—blasted into his consciousness with all the force of tossed and pitch-soaked mangonel fire. Gamelyn's knees wanted to totter beneath the force of it; he didn't allow them.

Instead he wiped the oil from his hands with a rag and sheathed Hubert's sword. *You picked a fine time to appear. Lord.*

Just a reminder to whom you do—and do not—belong. A deep chuckle resounded behind his eyes: the Horned Lord was Amused.

Wymarec, however, was not. He gestured to the packed gear. "So you think to leave without tendering me a report, Templar?"

"I followed the chain of command, my lord Preceptor. I gave my Commander my report, which he tendered to you via missive."

"Hubert"—a drawl, insouciance personified—"has been known to exaggerate your abilities. From time to time."

"Whereas you, my lord Preceptor, have always been keen as a good blade upon my limitations. Mayhap they remind you of your own."

Several blinks, confusion settling into a flare of anger, then into stone. Wymarec had never had a winning face when it came to throwing the dice. Of course, he'd never had to, had he?

"Obedience, Templar." A chide. "Of course, that has never been *your* strong suit, has it?"

"To your gain, I should think. It has accessed places you never would have trod, otherwise."

"The Heathen cult, you mean." Wymarec shrugged and clucked his tongue. "Yes, you did marry the witch-woman and play her lethal game of rutting, birthing, and dying for her pagan gods. You gained access to their secrets for not only the Temple, but the Crown. Though the latter, at present, is more bent upon wailing *mine! mine!* over his damned Frankish patrimony than renewing fealty to the land that truly owns him." The pale eyes lit with a spark that seemed more damned than divine. "Because of that misfocus, his land shall claim him all the quicker."

Venomous, soft, it twitched a chill at Gamelyn's nape. Treason and no less, to claim a King's death. But while Wymarec hadn't the Sight that Hubert possessed, there was no doubting this much: King John's *tynged* had been Seen and sealed.

And their own?

"But of course, you," Wymarec's gaze sharpened once more upon Gamelyn, "have also spent more than a few waking hours trading favour with earthly kings, all to ensure your own earthly power."

Gamelyn shrugged; he saw no need to deny it.

One of Wymarec's eyebrows arced upward. His next words proved he'd decided to go for the throat. "You never did bring me the druid, alas. But upon consideration, that could hardly be tallied as your fault, would it?"

Instead, Gamelyn smiled. Said, very soft, "Hardly."

Another blink, a flat stare, and silence. As if Gamelyn were merely a base element of some alchemical conjuring, weighed and measured and ready to render—mayhap commingled with others—within the hot centre of a firepan.

"Hubert," Wymarec said slowly, "was right. You left something other than the Relic in the desert. And found a few others. But then," a shrug, "Hubert usually is right, at the end of it.

"So, Templar. You will ride with me to Alençon."

Of all the things Gamelyn had thought would happen, this was not among them. "Nay, my lord Preceptor. I will not."

As if Wymarec had waited—nay, hoped—for just that reaction, his lip ticced sideways. "Obedience, Templar. You will do as I say. And I say you will gather your belongings and come with me. East, not west, or indeed, wherever I shall beckon, including the steppes of the barbarian hordes, should I command. You went to the desert a child, have returned a man who speaks with the Unknown and Unknowable, who has faced death and instead found his power. I—*we*—have need of you. Here."

No more insouciance. No more the lean against the lintel, or the crossed boots and arms. Wymarec had straightened, fists clenching, a light behind that flat, reptilian gaze that Gamelyn well recognised—though he'd rarely seen it shunted in his own direction. Avarice . . . nay, covetousness. *Lust.* Not for any bodily delights, but for what secrets the heart and mind alone could hold.

It is why he wanted Robyn. The Horned Lord's Voice reverberated soft, this time, shivering beneath Gamelyn's skin and sinking in, bone and sinew. *It is why, when we bring Robyn back, this one must never know. He would pin our Winterlord like some insect, and eviscerate him with hardly a qualm. All for what Robyn possesses, and what this supposed "Master" knows he never will.*

And now—thunderous-quiet, a warning—*he knows you* have *it.*

It?

Don't be more the Fool than you were destined. You know. You have fallen beneath its embrace, risen cloaked into its Power. You have walked the halls of Annwn, spoken with the Seven Demons, burnt in the cold fires of the ifrit *and* djinn. *In Death's arms, you have glimpsed Eternity and broken beneath its weight. You are. . . whole.*

Nearly, Gamelyn reminded.

The Horned Lord let out a soft breath across Gamelyn's nape and fell strangely, pensively silent.

"I am needed elsewhere at this time," Gamelyn straightened, meeting and matching Wymarec's gaze.

You will not keep me from my people. You will not keep me from her. From him.

Wymarec took a step forward. "You forget, Templar, who and what you are. You forget who holds your leash."

"I think it is you who forgets, O Adept of the Inner Circle, who and what I am."

Another step. "You are Confanonier and Knight to Temple Hirst, and therefore under my orders."

"I have been those things, but in thisnow?" Gamelyn used the old term light—and deadly—as an arrow laid at nock. "I am also an equal, Adept of the Inner Circle, and even the Grandmaster of the Temple cannot take rip that cloak from me. Once sworn, always sworn, unto death—that is our Rule, for our protection as well as any puissance, and it exists, as you well know, within the Inner Temple solely, and so that one man's blind intolerance cannot touch or think to corrupt the whole."

The Master Preceptor was turning a distinct and angry shade of carmine. "Neither shall we allow a hair-triggered crossbow to corrupt our purpose!"

"God is in everything; god is in nothing. Corruption depends upon judgement; we judge not, lest we be judged."

"Do not quote me gnosticisms I taught you when you were a base and soiled youth!"

"Then have faith in what you taught!"

Odd, how this moment—thisnow—was the first time Gamelyn truly felt himself a Templar, soul as well as body. Intriguing, how this jealous-warped soul thought such a thing could be taken. Worth remembering, that there had been a time when both of them had been little but mirrors of the same fruitless search for perfection.

Instead, all along and for too long blinded, Gamelyn had found nothing but untold beauty in its lack.

Only now could he realise it. Nigh too late.

Nay, he reasoned with himself. *I am going home. It will not let it be too late.*

It is never too late, be it this world or the next. The Lady, this time, and the scent of roses alighting upon the small, dank, dark room. *Send the little man upon his way.* Then, in soft tandem with Her Lord: *It's time to come home, Gamelyn.*

"The land must have a King. The King must be the land." Gamelyn turned away, started to roll up an overtunic—Hubert's, it was. "I, O Adept, am going back to *my* land."

There was every possibility that the man would jump him— there was that much sudden and murderous fury in him, a silent blast licking bloody flames into the sodden room. Silence held, counting out the beats: one, two, three. Anything was possible, in this moment.

Including the sudden vision: when they did finally take up arms against each other, Gamelyn would kill him.

But not this day. Instead, Wymarec turned upon one heel, and was gone.

- XXVII -

The Honour of Tickhill, Yorkshire Bounds
Waxing of Samhain (gibbous), 1202 CE

To the lady Marion of Tickhill, greetings:

*The King has, in His wisdom and mercy,
given verdict upon the matter of Tickhill.*

Likely there'd been more silver marks involved than wisdom
or mercy.

*As you are now a widow, in gift of the
King, and as the King desires that such an
honour as Tickhill not be left solely in the
hands of a woman who has come late and by
marriage to her status, the King has decided
that the best solution for all is the one that I
myself and my lord de Furnival attempted to
present you: marriage to the remaining lord
who once held Tickhill so competently against
His enemies, and in a time suitable to maintain
the security of our holdings.*

*You have proven yourself stubbornly loyal
to my brother's memory, and I've no doubts*

*that you will respond to this missive in as wil-
ful a fashion as ever. Still, you are a clever woman, and surely realise that it is in your best
interests to accede to the King's commands. I
give you adequate time to prepare, and shall
make the journey to Tickhill a se'nnight after
All Saints, when we shall kneel together in the
Chapel of St. Nicholas before God and in the
King's ordered service.*

*Otho Boundys de Blyth, now by grace of
the King mesne lord of Tickhill*

The amount of venom lying, even beneath words penned by a scribe's careful hand, was mayhap understandable.

Well, then, Marion had some of her own. She tossed the missive aside and pondered the other that had arrived the previous morn. In Maud's own hand, it had been carried by the only messenger besides Gilbert that Maud trusted:

M-
Word came via wings: the King has relented.
Prepare yourself.

Already in lockdown, Tickhill had as of yesterday begun preparing for siege.

Marion glanced over to where, upon her bed and a fine woollen cloth, the oddling parchments lay in a circular spread. At the top was the Hanged Man: Sacrifice. At the bottom was the Wandering Fool. In the middle was the High Priestess, and the Tower beneath her.

It couldn't have been any more apropos had she searched the bloody things and placed them purposefully in that order.

Sweet Lady, what had gone wrong? Gilbert and Hubert had surely arrived to plead her case. Their ship had set sail two days later than de Furnival's—and just in time, as storms had closed the ports for nearly a fortnight after. She had received word via wings, and Seen as much, too.

Just as she'd Seen, with the help of the parchments, that the storms had abated in Normandy. But that was all, as if *tynged's* curtain had been drawn against her, the futures in such flux and motion that none could surface, clear.

Yet she didn't need Sight to ken that Otho had received word from Normandy, and in the same fashion Marion herself expected. Of the pair of birds Gilbert had taken, surely one would have arrived by now? Their home roost lay at the All Hallows dovecot, and Father Dolfin knew to watch for them.

"All Hallows," Marion murmured, letting the larger missive spring back into its roll. Tempting, really, to feed it to the fire. Instead, she turned to her companions, who'd brought the missive and stood by, pensive and silent, as she read it. "Otho says he will come after All Saints, to take possession of the castle—and me."

It is time to rid ourselves of him, John signed.

"I en't after killing a lord." Much might have been a tall bulwark behind John's slighter form, but less menacing for all that. Until he continued, one hand going to his sword, "But in this case, I think we'd be best to end this 'un."

Marion shook her head. "I can't order Ian's father simply killed out of hand."

Ian hasn't returned. Do you owe him loyalty?

"Likely he can't, with what's going on. He's a child, John."

I were younger than Ian when Da sold me service to Gamelyn's sire. Your brother had whip scars on his back when he were Ian's age. If the lad's still a child, it's because he's been kept one a-purpose.

Marion hadn't an argument to any of it.

Much, however, did. "He's a nobleman's lad, Johnny. Their likes makes us over, aye and no argument there, but they've also ways of making their own lads into men, and none of 'em any more pleasant."

John huffed. *Mayhap a stray arrow will find Otho, does he come to take our gates.*

"The se'nnight after All Saints, he said," Marion interrupted the back-and-forth. "All Hallows comes first. And by then we will have found something much more important than a minor lordling pissing his claim to our gates."

John nodded. Aelwyn and David had already been sent, with Siham and a mix of well-armed guardsmen. They carried not only coals from the Sacred Fire, but a message to all their people: in every village, kindle the bale-fires from her bowl, and that Barrow Mere would be sacrosanct to the Maiden to one purpose. The Wild Hunt would ride upon the full moon of Samhain.

"And if Gamelyn en't here?" Much's voice quivered, tentative but determined to say it, nonetheless.

He has to come. He will.

"Have you Seen it?" Marion asked John.

You know I haven't. No more than you.

Much crossed his arms, his face shutting into several layers of stone. But he was right, and Marion knew it.

Said, gently, "All Hallows is three days hence, John. It's the only window we have."

But which All Hallows? We could wait until Gamelyn comes. In Their hands, Robyn wain't know how long it's been, months or another years, aye? We'll be sure of success, that way.

"Nowt's sure with any of 't, Johnny," Much muttered. He understood John's true worry.

As did Marion. "You've the *rights*, John. By my leave and His—who else has been able to hold the Horns outside the Rites since Robyn was taken away? Between you and me, John, we've kept Him with us and for our people, even with Summer and Winter wandering from us! I've faith in you, even if you've little in yourself."

John looked down. *I just. . . I don't want to wait, any more than you do. But. . . I don't think I can bear it if we fail. Again.*

Marion understood that all too well. "But can we afford to wait? Now that the King seems determined to pass Tickhill around like a willing courtesan?"

Mayhap that's changed, too. Mayhap Gilbert and Hubert have succeeded and we just don't know. Not that it matters. If we have to, we go back to our Wode. Where we belong.

"Mam!" Rob's reedy voice rose up into the rafters, stirring the gwyllion into a flap and flutter. "Mam, where are you?"

Marion took in a huge, quavery breath, let it out. Called "Where am I normally, this time of day?" and shot a wry, rather-forced grin towards Much and John. The latter gave an eyeroll and the former a head shake as not only one, but two sets of heavy-loud feet pounded across the midkeep atrium.

"No wonder downstairs is deserted . . . everyone's here!" Rob announced as he burst in—at a heedless pace.

The reason why became immediately apparent as Aderyn came chasing after. Her hands gestured a blue streak: apologies to her mam for the interruption, to her brother recriminations as close to cursing as a child would dare go in the presence of adults, mostly meaning *I told you Mam wasn't to be bothered about now!*

Much grabbed Rob and swung him over one shoulder, holding out a hand to Aderyn. "The pair of you, no better than you should be—come on, then, your mam's got business to attend to."

But I didn't do it! Aderyn plainly thought this unfair.

"And mam needs to know there's soldiers approaching!" Rob protested.

Much nearly dropped him. "What, lad?"

And as if on cue, the bells rang.

"See? I told you, Eri!" Rob sniped at his sister from over Much's shoulder. "I'm faster than any soldier, and she needed to know right aw—"

"Whist your bloody gob, boy!" Much snapped and, tossing him onto Marion's bed, whirled and raced out the door.

Surely the man hasn't come already? John frowned at Marion. *Not that it matters, we're ready for him and*—a peer at the children—*and I've an arrow with his name on it* he finished so only she could see. Then, with a nod to her, he followed Much.

"Mam, didn't I do the right—? Mrmph!" This as Aderyn dove for the bed and stuffed a cushion over her brother's face.

Marion rescued the parchments, snatching her veil from its wall hook. "Where is Berta, lass?"

She went with Marjory to see the hens. Rob was supposed—another shove against the pillow as her brother, growling, tried to free himself—*to be asleep.*

"Rob." Stern, Marion's voice, and cold as ever Guy the assassin could summon.

And Robbie listened, sitting up all big-eyed and worried as his sister let him up.

"You will, both of you, go to the nursery. I'll send Berta to you, and you'll *stay there* until we know what's happening. Aye?"

"Aye, mam." Subdued, so she knew he'd obey. Even when Aderyn grabbed his wrists and hauled him off the bed, he didn't so much as squirm, but let his sister drag him out the door.

Winding her veil over her curls, Marion followed.

Ⓢ

Surely Otho would come better prepared than this.

Marion had mounted the gatehouse side stair in hasty two-at-a-time leaps, but her pace slowed as her line of sight cleared the wall. Almost thoughtfully, she came to stand beside Much.

He, too, peered across the wall and outward, watching the approaching riders with a frown ticcing his brow. Siham stood an arm's reach to his left, bow in hand; she nodded to Marion. John was to Much's right with a pair of longbows—one Marion's own—and a quartet of strings hung around his neck. He, too, had a frown, albeit slight.

"I see maybe seven, eight," Marion said, leaning her elbows on the wall, squinting as sunlight broke through a patch of cloud.

"And the glint of steel." Siham pointed. "The forerunner mentioned arms, but he ran here too soon, didn't stay long enough to check. Fright makes for fools."

"No banner." Much crossed his arms and frowned harder.

Behind them the bailey resembled a beehive at sunset, driven by the echo of the alarm bell's rhythm: *immediate danger, take shelter now!* The closest fields had emptied quick as that, the last of the people filing in whilst their farthest compatriots took shelter in the northmost carr. Everyone settled in, giving way as Much's guardsmen darted here and there, protective, alert, all business. Efficient in the circumstance. Of course, of late they'd too many chances to practise.

Much shook his head, muttered something beneath his breath as the last of their people filed inward. Called, "Close up!"

It repeated around the wall, everyone taking their places—including Siham, who strode to where wall and gatehouse met, plucking at her bowstring. The bell gave one more half-hearted *clang* and stilled, vibrating into the air. The huge gate mechanism made up for it, lifting the bridge with a metallic, heavy clatter and groan as the gates swung inward.

Wordlessly humming to himself, John began stringing his and Marion's bows.

The riders came closer, first at a brisk canter that ate up the distance, then settling down to a trot. They had to know the castle was armed and ready. Would have heard, if nowt else, the preparations echoing across the long, low fields from there to here.

The sun wasn't helping. The remaining clouds had scattered, leaving harsh light blazing down to send the riders into shadow. Marion stood on tiptoe, peering outwards. She usually had the longest eye—save for one of their younger archers, aptly named Peregrine.

But this time it was Much who reacted, leaning over the stones with an oath. "Sweet Lady's pa . . . !" It trailed away into a gasp.

Marion turned to him, started to speak, couldn't. Much's face was that white, eyes nigh bugging from his skull, mouth working.

Then he whirled and ran for the stair. "Stand down!" he hollered. "Stand *down*! Open the gates!"

Open the . . . ? "Much, what are you—?"

He fled downward so fast he was nigh tripping. Not that it mattered; he leapt the last few and raced into the gatehouse shadows.

Marion exchanged puzzled glances with John and turned back to the riders, raising a hand to shield her eyes from the sun, peering . . .

Staggered back a few steps. Said, "Oh."

John dropped her bow, and she couldn't so much as chide him for it. He, too, had seen.

Beneath them the stone rumbled, the gates lowering on their well-oiled tracks as Marion and John both bolted for the stair.

(s)

Marion was the first to emerge from the cavernous entry and walk between the flung-open gates. But Much was on her heels.

Not protective, this time. Eager.

Eight riders in total stopped at the moat, the lead horse giving a prance and paw at the edge of the bridge. Covered with road dirt, all of them—plainly they hadn't stopped since they'd landed— yet five white habits gleamed, nevertheless, beneath the sun. Even those were no patch on the lead rider's bared head, all but set ablaze in the fierce autumn sun.

"My mission was a success, you might say," Gilbert was grinning from the leader's left stirrup, and to his right Hubert dipped his head, weary but satisfied.

Marion took one step—one only—upon the bridge. It creaked. She sucked in a deep breath and, lacing her fingers together across her abdomen, let it out.

Said, stern, "You're late, milord."

"I know," Gamelyn replied, then smiled. *Smiled.* "But I always manage to return in good time, aye?"

"You *said* a year and a day."

"There were . . . difficulties upon the road. Surely my lady can understand the trials of such."

"Your lady, milord," Much tried for severe and failed, miserably, "has had little but trials of her own, of late."

The boyish grin disappeared, as Gamelyn and Much peered at each other for long moments. "I know." The answer was soft. Then Gamelyn turned to Marion again, the smile reappearing, less bold but nevertheless full of charm. "Will you please, milady of Tickhill, allow your husband and his guests within?"

"Your guests are surely welcome," Marion retorted with an incline of her head. Hubert and Gilbert returned it, the latter with his own cheeky grin. "But as for you, lord husband?" She managed a shrug, somehow, and her shoulders didn't so much as shake. "*You* had best make your apologies phenomenally good."

Gamelyn swung down from the horse. Somehow John was there, taking the reins and peering at Gamelyn as if he were the sun, not some mere reflection limned in white and copper. A glance shared and stayed—a bare breath that seemed to linger— before the green eyes slid to Marion, held. Gamelyn made slow advance onto the bridge, one step then another, until he stood before her.

"I'm sorry," he said, and "It's been a year of hell, hasn't it?"

Marion wasn't sure how it happened, or exactly when, but they were suddenly wrapped around each other, with Much and John and Gilbert and Siham pressed close, and whistles and cries of appreciation from the castle walls, and the bridge creaking beneath them as everyone gathered round, all questions and answers, embraces and tears.

"DA!!!"

As if some magician had parted the waters, the gathering swirled and dipped, giving way as first Rob, then Aderyn came racing across the bridge, nigh sending their sire arse over tit into the moat as they leapt upon him, crying and burrowing in.

"I promise, I'm really here," he kept saying into Aderyn's hair, against Rob's ear. Then he peered up at Marion, eyes a-glimmer, to repeat, "I'm here. I'm home."

⑨

"What will you do?"

Gamelyn peered at Hubert across not only a goblet of wine, but two sleeping children. Only two, because Marjory would have nothing to do with the sun-bleached stranger who had descended into her world. Even now, despite being half-asleep in Marion's arms, Marjory eyed her sire with grave suspicion.

The best chairs had been brought and cushioned: one for Gamelyn and another for Hubert, plus a settee shared by two stiff legs.

"Sleep." Not the most satisfactory of answers, to be sure, but the truth. It had been a damnably long, hard ride from Sandwich. "As should you, Hubert."

"I mean after All Saints."

Marion tensed, and Marjory burbled sleepy complaint. Gamelyn met the grey eyes—beloved, the memory of them never far, and couldn't stop a gentle smile. *Nay, not even Hubert knows. Because he would have to tell, if asked.*

Hubert tsked. "I would have to be in my dotage indeed, if I didn't realise something important was to happen. You and Gilbert, both in such a hurry to return, for one of your peoples' most important festivals to honour the dead." He shifted in the chair with a slight grimace. "I merely ask your plans afterward."

Marion was still eyeing Gamelyn. No doubt she wondered that as well. There'd been little time to share any close thoughts since their return.

First, baths by the fire, with a bevy of hot kettles brought by a seemingly never-ending round of people, all eager, it seemed, to do their newly-come lord and his guests this service. Supper afterward, for it had taken until supper to get all that water heated and poured. And now, just him with his most trusted and loved: Marion and the children, Much, Gilbert, and Hubert. John had, oddly enough, disappeared after supper—though no one else seemed to think it odd—and David and Aelwyn also were absent. Not yet returned from business regarding Samhain, or so Marion had whispered in his ear when he'd inquired after them, concerned.

Odd, though, that Hubert should ask this now. Here. They'd had the voyage if not the ride—the latter had been too urgent for talk. But Hubert had said little even during the voyage, eyeing Gamelyn with what might be termed wariness, if it weren't Hubert.

Yet he'd the same look, now. "I know you spoke with Master Wymarec."

Again, Marion frowned and tensed, just a little. Gilbert lounged on a fur by the hearth, the nonchalance of frame belied by his gaze, sharp and missing nothing. Much spent his own curiosity in refilling Hubert's goblet. From a different pitcher, Gamelyn noted; mayhap that was why Hubert seemed so . . . relaxed.

"Then you must know what was said."

A shrug. "He did not share it with me. I garnered it was not pleasant." A smirk, sudden and wolfish. "For him." Hubert took another drink and set it aside, addressing Marion. "You will note that the ring upon his finger can never be removed, unto death. Nor can the initiations of head and mind. Aye, Maiden, you understand; amongst your own people you too have such."

Gamelyn frowned. Aye, he trusted implicitly every single one present—well, mayhap it was best the children had all fallen asleep—but this? Unprecedented. Hubert seemed . . . anxious, somehow, to lay it out before them. So that they would know.

"The habit itself, though? When tattered and ill-suited, one's garb must be mended. Or replaced with another. Garments, cloaks, outer skins, no more and no less—and sometimes need be laid aside, in service of the Great Work. And now, having been winnowed from base elements into something more powerful, it would seem this lad"—the blue eyes sought Gamelyn's, held—"that I have loved so dearly and seen grow to manhood? It would seem he has more important roles to play within that Work than remaining a mere Knight. As above, so below."

Gilbert repeated it, soft.

Marion bent over, nestling the sleeping Marjory into her basket, then rose and padded over to Hubert. She knelt beside him, took his hands in her own.

"Mayhap, milord," she told him, soft, "it is no 'mere' Knight you have mentored. Mayhap the Summering Knight *is* his greatest role. And one that *you* have made possible."

Hubert smiled. Marion kissed his hands and rose, taking the pitcher from Much, offering it with a smile.

Smiling back at her, Hubert drank deep.

Settled back into the cushions, and fixed his gaze upon Game-lyn: steely, now, and severe. "So. Will you at least come to visit an old man, after All Saints?"

"Some oaths are impossible to set aside. One of those?" Gamelyn held up his goblet. "Is you, my Brother."

Ⓢ

They put their sleeping children down in Marion's bed, with her watching as Gamelyn tucked them in. He even got to hold Marjory, albeit dead asleep.

And after, when they walked hand in hand across to the lord's chambers—his chambers—and Marion clung to him in the hallway, it seemed more a *so glad you're here* as opposed to a *take me to your bed right now and treat me with gentle roughness.*

When she merely kissed his cheek and pulled away, bidding him good night, he started to reach out, frowning, curious. Worried.

They had always enjoyed each other. Had this left, as well, in his absence?

Marion took his hand, brought it to her cheek and kissed his palm. She said nothing, but her expression—patient, waiting—ensured that he made the connection.

Once she'd been a novice nun—though it hadn't been her, truly, with her memory and so much of her strength taken after Loxley's destruction. Still, she remembered. All of it. And despite the circumstances, despite being a prisoner of the woman who'd tried to destroy them, a small part of Marion remained grateful for the austerity and restraint that had allowed her shelter, and healing.

She understood that her Summerlord must hold abstemious, self and power, for this most important of Rites. They would need that power, to ride forth on the night of the ancestors and retrieve Winter's King.

Feeling an absolute fool, Gamelyn kissed her hair and wished her goodnight. Marion, more than most, understood the power that underlay self-denial.

John, on the other hand, was much a harder sell.

- XXVIII -

Sigils, traced in the wind . . .
there is wind when there is no wind
Coals, lit then tossed into the Mere, to steam and bubble—
there are waves where there are no waves
—and light the fires, primed with agaric, crackling against the sunset.

Six bale-fires ringed the Mere out past the trees, tended by their people; the seventh one burning bright here, between them, laid in the small meadow surrounded by the sacred grove beside the Mere.

Seven fires, one for each year of sacrifice, and about that last, the covenant of the Shire Wode waiting as their Maiden—
wodewose wylding lady, moon-crowned mother
—wields with bare arms a staff topped with agaric, aflame, and their Knight—
not dryw, nor hooded, but horned and robed as magician, fool, king
—throws his arms to the sky, wields a gilt-trimmed dagger and and speaks words to curl across the Mere like smoke—
the sound of seven snake heads, they rose from the sea
it is iao who unbinds you
it is adonai who sets you free
And the horn blows, winded by a child—
black-haired godling daughter, born of blood, and fire, and wylding magic
—to call the hooded one home.

Ia! Ia! By the shield of Solomon and the Horns of the God; with the chalice of the Lady and in the name of the Magician in the wilderness. In Allworlds the Ceugant *bides, and by chains of iron and fire I shall bind you all the tighter, do you not. . .*
Mi argyllwdd rhyddhau. *Release. My. Lord!*

The words purled across the Mere. The horn echoed, carried, and behind them another three figures—David, Aelwyn, and Gilbert—swayed. Hummed the note, urging it forward, keeping it in thisworld as John tapped the drumbeat to carry it to the next.

Gamelyn put one hand to Aderyn's curls, the other sliding to squeeze Marion's shoulder.

"Now we wait," Marion said, soft.

Gamelyn peered out over the Mere.

Whispered, "It's time to come home, Hob-Robyn."

He'd been sharing a meal with Magus when he felt it.

They both felt it, the magics shivering the rocks like thunder. Or the sun's light burning holes through earth and stone.

Robyn leapt to his feet, snatched the nearest torch, and ran for the Veil.

The gwyllion clung to Robyn's shoulder with wings belling, crooning with excitement. Its eyes fairly lit the way, fire-coals in the dark to rival the torch spitting and flaring in the wind of their passage. The blood runes seemed to catch the light, black ash then white-hot.

Robyn stared at them for several breaths. The gwyllion appeared in the dark, eyes glowing, shrieking and stooping about him. His familiar swatted his ear—hard. Robyn closed his eyes against the burning runes and shook himself back into action, nearly overshooting the next corridor leading down. He corrected his course with a slide and stumble and a grip of bare toes to set him to rights.

Whenever he blinked, he could see the runes, ghosts of fire, hanging against the crimson of his eyelids.

As they dived down the last tunnel leading to the Veil, the gwyllion's croon transformed into a thin, high-pitched quaver, one more felt than heard. In the skull, reverberating against bone, driving the quickening of heart and breath and outward.

All of it, quavering, urging *There's not much time. Not here, not thisnow.*

Hurry.

Crepuscular grey beckoned from ahead, filling the cavern. Robyn leapt for the rockslide, clambered over and leapt down . . .

Skidded to a halt, feet skating on damp stone. The torch dropped from his hands, rolling and hissing, guttering. Robyn threw his hand up before his face, eyes squinting, watering, at the raw light, *new* light . . .

Changed.

The cavern's pale, adamantine witchlight had given way to golden sunlight flaring downward, brilliant reflections, mirrors and shards chasing shadows farther into the deeps. Fish scattered, bolting for cover in a dazzling and uncertain world, a mist of murk roiled upon a spiralling current, and . . .

And the wyvern was awake, writhing against the bottoms, burrowing deeper with wings unfolding to cover its eyes.

Robyn blurted out a creaky negation, staggering forward. It had always been through the Old One's sight that he could See.

In the few rapid heartbeats of advance, legs wobbling, the sunlight began to wane.

Robyn lurched against the barrier, slapping his palm against it, a choked "Nay!" escaping.

Yet the magic—it was magic, he could feel it even through the thick surface of the Veil—didn't wane with it. It expanded. Filling the Mere, unforgiving sunlight transforming into the softer haze of firelight. Not as vivid, this light, but no less intense. No less penetrative.

The wyvern stilled, pinions slowly—ever-so-slowly—vaning closed, revealing eyes whirling wide, reflecting fire magic. The gwyllion crooned—not just one but a fairing's worth of them, clinging to the stones with eyes aglow.

And, sketched in the mirror 'twixt worlds, Robyn could see great, golden bonfires upon a faraway shore. Smoke hanging in the Sacred Trees, a gauze sifting starlight to trace the barest edge of a dark moon, sparks soaring upward. The Mere's rising sediment echoed it, framed it hanks and haze, revealing a faint silhouette: the girl-child held a long dagger in her hands like a sword, and behind her stood two shadows, and more behind them.

It's time to come home, Hob-Robyn.

With a growl, Robyn rammed his shoulder into the Veil.

Which, of course, didn't budge.

The wyvern kept writhing. Upon its neck, the irons seemed to shimmer, light to dark in the roiling silt.

"It is being afraid." Sliding soft from behind him, the voice, as the Priestess walked up to the Veil. She'd one hand raised to shield her own eyes. "In pain."

"So we all are being, thisnow." Magus' admittance came equally muted.

Robyn spared a glance, saw none else had followed. None else had likely dared.

As if the motion had been a signal, the gwyllion launched itself from his shoulders. Claws scored Robyn's throat; he staggered back a step and clapped a hand there, felt wet warmth seeping through his fingers. Several other gwyllion let out a cry and dropped from their perches, joining their fellow midflight. They spiralled the cavern once then, as one, dove for the Veil, bursting through, inward.

"What are they . . . ?" Magus trailed away as the small creatures skimmed a quick circle upon a quicker-moving current.

Robyn shook his head, bewildered. "I—what in sodding . . . ?"

This as the gwyllion dove at the wyvern's head, resembling crows attacking a hawk. The wyvern burrowed deeper and, when that didn't work, reared back with wingtips unfurling in a cloud of silt.

The gwyllion kept diving at its head. Several latched onto the fetter about its neck, their odd, voiceless keen quivering—and penetrating past—the surface of the Veil. The not-sound seemed to further madden the wyvern. The water clouded heavy and dark. The iron at its neck left bloody furrows as it struggled.

The bow. He needed the bow! Robyn scrambled over to the ledge that held it, and the Arrow. Snatching up both, he turned to the Veil, fingers scrabbling for the flax string tucked at his belt. A twist had the string free; another spun it straight. Inexorably, quickly—carefully—he stepped and strung the bow. It complained at the pressure, but held, and Robyn breathed more strength into it: *Just one more, just one.*

More gwyllion were joining the attack upon the wyvern, a rainbow-hued flight diving downward—downward? The wyvern sloughed its great head, trying to shake them off. It struck the Veil. The great wall of water shook, bulged.

Magus tottered back a few steps. Priestess sucked in a sharp breath.

Robyn flashed them a sudden, ruthless smile and tossed the forelock from his eyes. Raised the ancient bow. "Well," he murmured, and reached for the Arrow. "All right, then."

It nestled in his palm, familiar, secure.

Thisworld tilted upon its axis, flooded . . .

Into thisnow.

Heart speeding, lungs heaving, a-sweat and panting, to race the life suddenly speeding through him, no more thisnow, but *then* and *this* and *next,* into the rage and pain of years fled past

Into voices—

As the Great Mother wandered the river valleys and deserts, weeping and seeking her mate, so we have wandered and returned, light dawning, to awaken the fire, to cast silver into gold. Return my lord, my brother—return unto me!

Into visions—

A black-haired child raising a blade into the night, reflecting flame into the Mere, heart-song claiming what silence cannot speak: *I am a breaker threatening doom; I am a tide that drags to death; I am an infant, who but I peeps from the unhewn dolmen arch?*

Into visitation—

Spirits wand'ring, never finding, gathering at the gate so eager:
Is it possible?

And into a vertigo of fire magic: kindled by a sorcerer Knight,
woven by a witch Maid, channelled through manifestation and
fed by sacrifice . . .

Upon the Arrow, Hob's bargain, Hob's blood in this place, at this
time

*Spilt in ancient halls, to seal the bargain, to feed the fires and make
the magic. Return the god to us, Robyn Hode, return to us the Wode!*

Answered in thatnow, with love and pain and sacrifice—

*You took him! Took him from us! Give him back, or we will seal
the doorway forever!*

And thisnow . . .

Dissolves.

and hob-robyn staggers back, black eyes golden, blood-magic
shaping the gate, feeding upon fury and fire enough to char a
world . . .

my lord annwn, would you burn your own hall to save theirs—?

magus wails

Burning is cleansing, more times than not. This—

thunders dark winterlord

*—is no longer my hall, but an existence let slide, from fallow into
rot!*

but priestess stands tall, faces him, reasons *where could we go?
what could we do?*

as fast as rage kindles, it ebbs, and *i know—*

purrs the god—

*i know. . . the gaol has closed in, more and more, and what is left
as the trap closes, more and more?*

not even hope—

magus says, and lowers his head as the god places his hands
there—

promise? threat?

ah, but neither, as the god's breath whiffles grey locks, and a
kiss lingers, as the hot-gold gaze turns upon the one who does not
bow, who holds a gaze of hot-gold with one remote, moon-cool as

She stays Him

i called you here, o hob, o archer, o darkling lord—

goddess says—

*to be bringing in salt and seed, be bringing in the forest, for a when
that this, here, is all that is left unspoiled*

in that when—

god agrees—

i shall be returning, so i have sworn

and goddess holds out her hands, palm up—

*first, it must be made to live again! be returning to your forest, lord
of chaos, and be remembering your oath!*

god puts arrow in his hair and lays bow at her feet to cover
her palms with his own . . . bends, retrieving the bow, a stain of
crimson smearing her open palms, marking oaths left behind—
return the god to us, return to us the Wode!
as to veil he turns, nocks arrow to string, whispers—
arise, old one. . .
Pulls the bow, sings it, again, grasps iron-spells with fire and
blood and magic—
dihunoch, ysgawen—
Lets fly.
Arrow pierces Veil, sinks home into iron with a flare of
blue-white. Iron screes, lights all a-crackle. Boils, seethes . . .
Shatters.
Old One rears up, wings flaring outward, straining its chains—
or trying to, as Iron bursts, leaving no more than a cloud of smut
and stain.
He cavorts, whirls, spirals through the water with gwyllion-kin
beside him, through light and shadow and . . .
Stops.
Peers up, haunches quivering, ready for flight.
Turns his eyes upon priestess, upon magus, then upon archer,
who alone returns Old One's piercing gaze, broken bow in hand,
as gwyllion burst back through Veil in wild, aerial displays . . .
Rade is being nigh!
priestess says—
go whilst still you can!
and hob-robyn answers—
nay, the Rade is now!—
as gwyllion and ghosts pour around him, pulling him through
the Veil.

✆

Black, it ascends: an ancient spirit spreading wings of translucent
smoke, a shade beautiful and fearsome and unspeakable, to rise
wet-gleaming from Barrow Mere.
And it is not alone.
Wraiths pull sodden from the shallows, tread grown heavy as
thisworld drags. Ghosts long captive flit through trees. Creatures
with tattered, rag-bag wings take laboured flight, whilst wingless
others swim, leaving oily, sooty trails behind them. Fae skim and
soar across the waters, a wake of luminescence. Wind sucks in a
breath and exhales fierce upon the hallowed copse; trees creak and
moan with the sudden wind, living echoes of ghostly passage . . .
And human flight, from gatherers ill-prepared to behold such
visions—and whilst Maiden's command holds some, others escape,
in silence and in screams.
Stay! Watch! Wake!

Old One opens ebon wings into the wind, lashes tail, uplifts. Upon its back a figure straightens, clad in darkness, cowled, horns shimmering—alive—against fire-lit darkness. Around Him empty wraith-eyes fill, sentience stirring, intent fashioning, steps lightening; sensing life, drawn to breath and heart's beating.

Panic stirs, only Knight's will and Maiden's holding circle firm, magic steady.

For there is beauty, amidst the ruins.

Wake! Be Free!

Not merely twinned evocation, this, but incantation from Old One . . . nay, Old One's Horned and Hallowed Rider.

Free!

Like to human voice but somehow . . . not. Purling upon water and trees as huge, ebon wings beat into the wind, glittering copper and gold; as little beasties shed their shadows, wing rainbow trails about bonfires; as wraiths turn from life-envy to Horned Lord's promise: *Wode between worlds is free, drawn aside, unveiled. Ride with me. Rade with me. We shall Hunt Our enemies upon this Wylding night, by storm and fire, and I shall lead you to your fate—weave your tynged, one and all, at last!*

Voices freed, again, yet full with wonder as well as fear; amazement, even joy. Beasties fly spirals about their lord, and fireflies dance upon the Mere. Gatherers advance, swaying to unheard rhythms, enthralled.

Maiden steps forward, cinnabar hair blowing about her bare arms, and holds up gold-and-silvery dagger: reminder . . . promise—

Warning—

—as Knight takes dagger and spins it, holds it, speaks a word only he knows.

Everything goes still. Everything goes silent.

Old One turns, swivels neck and head to stare into Knight's eyes. When Knight stands firm, Horned One's eyes catch sudden fire beneath hood and horn, fierce and furious-wild, scorching all they would touch.

Always, you defy me.

Aye. Smile glints against gold. *It is my . . . tynged, is it not?*

First-caught flame to blazing, and Horned One gestures. Gold-gilt dagger is jerked to fly from Knight's hands; Horned One snatches it mid-air, raises it to strike.

Recoils before blow is thrown, shudders, looks down.

Sees Child standing, bare toes in Mere, one hand upon His cloak, one holding His hunting horn.

Old One nudges Child; she strokes His nose and meets Horned Lord's eyes. Shakes her head.

Smile flashes within hood, dims flame-hot gaze. Instead of a blow, the knife wings through the air, end over end, to land between Knight's booted toes.

Then Old One dips, offering winged shoulder, and Horned One leans down, one pale, sinewy arm extending, darkness into fire-light, markings scrawled like indigo snakes; they hiss and writhe, spiral up and down as He says:
Little wren, Hunt with me?
Child mirrors smile, starts forward—
"Nay."
One word, spoken to break silence and spell: this not only Maiden, but Mother.
And another steps forward: the Maker-Holder, with gilt-touched eyes and outstretched hands: *I will go, until the child is ready.*
Horned Lord hesitates, golden eyes darkening, smile softening . . . less god. More . . . human?
Takes horn from Child. Pulls Maker a-pillion.
Says:
"I have been where the soldiers of Prydain were slain, from the East to the North; I am alive, they in their graves!"
Cries and gasps from the gathered; as it floats and echoes into the trees, He continues:
"I have been where the soldiers of Prydain were slain, from the East to the South. I am alive, they in death!"
Leans again, reaching, and instead of Child grasps Horn.
His shadow-mount noses Child. Turns, crouches. Leaps into the air, and soars away, with Hunt fast beside and horn sounding, its bell lingering long after Wylding Hunt disappears into Wode.

Awed silence remained within the Circle, long after the Hunt took flight and vanished like mist into the trees.
Awe was all that held Marion upright. Yet it wasn't awe, but exhaustion, that surely took Gamelyn to his knees. Nay, neither; 'twere misery, as sent shudders through his frame and tilted his voice wooden. "He's . . . gone. He's taken John with him, this time, and we . . . we've . . . *failed.* Again."
"Nay." Marion went to him, and Aderyn as well, clutching to her mam's skirts. Resting a hand upon his head, Marion curled it across his cheek and down to lift his gaze to meet her own. "You silly sod, we haven't failed. Robyn's not gone—"
"*Then where is he?*" The bark of a surly dog, underlain with a threatened whine.
Marion understood. Spoke soft, reasonable. "That I don't know. Here, love." She reached over and tugged the thick cloak snug beneath Gamelyn's chin. "Faith, but you're cold and no wonder."
The magic had taken its toll on both of them. She felt as if the blood iced her veins, whilst he shivered, pale as frost, hands trembling akin to an elder forced to the plough several days straight.

It was Aderyn, this time, who tugged at her sire's tunic. *Listen to them, Dada.*

With a shaky smile, he touched her cheek, and listened. Marion, too.

"The Hunt, did y' see?"

"And His hounds—"

"I saw them! White, they were, with ears afire!"

"Aye," David's voice, to Marion's right, was satisfied. "Can you not feel it? He's back in thisworld."

"Then why did I feel so . . . empty?" Gamelyn murmured.

Aelwyn came forward to kneel beside him, skirts pooling about her like grass. "Because you're daft. You've forgotten how much a Rite can take from you. This one, even more."

As Aelwyn stood, Aderyn took her place, hugging close.

*I saw him. The wyvern carried him—*the child pointed east—*that way. The* gwyllion *followed.*

Marion looked around; no question, but the gwyllion had vanished from the clearing.

"But . . . why couldn't we see Robyn, you and I, if he was there?"

"He was there." Marion's insistence warbled, hoarse; only then did she realise her breath still came hard, blowing like a horse that had night been run to founder. "Aderyn's right. The beast carried him."

He was the Horned Lord, upon the Hunt. Aderyn insisted, furthering with a shy smile, *He wanted me to go with him.*

Marion was glad she'd nipped that one in the bud.

"But . . . John."

"Our wee Johnny's carried the god this far," Gilbert told Gamelyn, soft.

"'Tis likely he's the only one as would survive such a thing." Aelwyn nodded, putting an arm about Marion. Marion leaned in gratefully and held out a hand to Gamelyn. He took it.

"Robyn won't let him be hurt," David added. "Gamelyn, leave off, will you?—we've done it! Brought our Robyn back!"

"Now we've only to find him." Gilbert smirked.

"Later, mayhap," Much warned, putting a steadying hand to Gamelyn's shoulder. "For now, you'd best look to the gathering."

And aye, their covenant needed them. The god had broken the Circle. Those on the peripheries—the ones who'd stayed and not fled, anyways—were milling like tethered goats, ready to panic.

Gamelyn leaned his head into Marion's palm, held Aderyn closer. As if it were a sign, Marion gathered David and Aelwyn and Gilbert by eye. They melted off towards the surrounding people and Marion stepped forward, re-establishing control.

"Good people, we thank you. The Horned Lord rides, so stay close by the fires. It is done."

"Maiden, will he blight us?" One voice rose, prompted others.

"The horse had eyes of fire! His cloak had wings!"

"He held a spear!"

"He's angry, surely!"

"Angry, mayhap—but not at you." Marion tried to step forward, gave a slight stumble. Much appeared beside her, snaking a supportive arm about her waist, allowing her to raise her hands, palms out and beseeching. "Never shall His anger be for you, who helped free Him from the Fae lands."

They believed her. Most of them kept drawing nearer, coming back to shadow the bale-fires . . . only not too near, eyeing the Mere as it swirled, restive.

Behind her, Gamelyn stood. And when he wobbled, their child held firm—as if she could shore him, did he take a tumble. Marion smiled as he let Aderyn think she could.

"All who stood here this night are blessed! All who aided the Hunt will see their people thrive!" Fierce, nigh breathless, Gamelyn's voice nevertheless travelled.

"So must it be!" David sang out into the night, and the gathering echoed it around the bale-fires, rising into song.

- XXIX -

Time was . . .
     Time shall be . . .
Time . . .
Is.
He escapes from darkness and grey stones into sodden leaf litter and gentle rain, the tart aftermath of lightning rising his nape, and thunder rumbling amidst the bare trees.

Alone. Confused.

Hunted.

The latter is all too familiar, somehow.

The air hangs . . . *clings.* Not with the sweet lift of springtime, but autumn's soft nip. Slicking heavy-wet and cool into heaving lungs, it lingers smoke and ash within his nostrils and upon his tongue. At the last, a shudder traces his spine and pops clammy sweat over his skin.

From crofter's huts to castle wards, the Horned One rides with an unearthly host: dark and small and painted blue, they run in the black horse's wake, follow the Rade and make it their own. Into night and stars racing, following the moon as light starts to tint the east, then stopping, turning. Facing the sun as it starts to rise, the heat, the golden light, and realise they are. . .

Freed.

Freed. As is he, somehow.

One hand props him; the other raises, slow, to brush at his chest, clutches at woolsey fabric of a well-worn, unremarkable brown. He studies those hands. Somehow too pale—they've not recently seen the sun—yet broad and capable, with work-sprung knuckles and long, clever fingers. A tangle of unruly ebon falls over his eyes; he shakes it back. Realises he's a hood upon his head, which sinks against his shoulders in the lax willingness of well-used leather.

The forest is more familiar than his own thin, shivering frame. Yet it, too, seems over-strange.

Souls shall be winnowed this night, and spirits gathered. Many lie in darkness, shivering against what they do not know, their hearts as dark-clad as the one who Hunts them, and He gleans their nightmares to give them more. Many light fires against the night; He marks the valiant ones, who greet the ghosts and pray safe passage for their souls; who honour the ancestors with fire and song; who set the night alight with bonfires, and guard the lintels with rowan and oak galls, so the Hunt shan't take them, not just yet. They are wakening. You are.

He is . . . wakening? Has he been sleeping, somehow?

A rustle from behind, and instinct bids him swing about. No more than remaining dry leaves clawing at their limbs, surely, but 'twere loud—*so loud.* In accompaniment, what must be the fluttering and trilling of birds, mayhap a squirrel's bark of alarm. The trees creak, harsh with branches clacking, grey fingers a-clasp then spreading to scrape at sullen clouds beyond. So grey, here, always grey and overcast . . . nay, wait! The clouds part, letting in shards of light to set him blinking, dark lashes attempting to filter brightness into something bearable.

A stumble; he manages to find footing only to stumble again. Clumsiness, a foreign progress; he kens this even as he recognises this place. For he has known it, even if not in thisnow.

Thisnow, the forest groans about him, loud enough to make him cover his ears with a grimace as it continues, *Are you sure?*

Sure? Only of this hyperaware, oddling pain. Sure? Of nowt including his own heart's beating.

Rising into the trees, lifting the black horse's mane, billowing its rider's cloak like ebon wings, fluttering the red ears of the snow-white hounds as they bell, and give chase.

Warning.

Mere thought becomes a power-filled breath, aching, seeping inward. Every slip-thud of his heart—sluggish before, but thisnow racing thick behind his ears and rapid against his ribs—nevertheless bides singular. Significant. Every faltering step, every stuttered breath a tiny tick of beads upon some abacus, an indentation upon wax, a step along a clandestine trail. Every lurch and lean: marker and gauge.

Mayhap a deeper magic has slipped the noose further still, cast him somewhere unknown . . . some *time* unknown? Instinct, again, bids him snatch at any semblance of that magic—he knows it exists, knows it will answer, knows it, unlike himself, possesses a name—

Tynged
—and tries to clothe himself with it, ground in thisnow.
Only thisnow . . . isn't. Yet is, utterly.
Tynged weaves answer, a smothering cloak with its hem just as swiftly unravelling into maddening, separate skeins. Too many; they tug, trip, slide around and draw him along in a frothy-thick current. And when he tries control or capture, 'tis as river water through his fingers, innumerable whirlpools of faint recall—somehow his, somehow not—marking the weight of him, taking him.
Measuring.
Memory.
Blood-price taken, and teind paid.
A serpent chained, bound to the Mere, never to be free again. Never. *Never . . .*

Break my chains, Lord.
Release him!
You be of no power here, son of iron and bells!

Knees totter, reel him forward on shaking hands. Clutching at the damp loam, seeking merely to find more perception, more . . . *awareness . . .*

Am I not? Is she not? Are. . . we. . . not?
You will release my Winterlord!
Yours? He is not being yours, Maiden-sister; as you be choosing Summer over Winter, as Winter be home to us.
I am Mother, not Maiden, not thisnow, and he is mine! *My brother, my son, my soul and heart and body!*
Blood. And fire. And wylding magic. . .
The promise, O pwca. Be remembering the promise, for thisworld be drifting further in; time will measure but here and there, hard to see even for such as you, within thatworld of measure and reckoning.

Thatworld. Thisworld. Measure.
Tiny parts of thisnow spinning away, out from a web into a never-ending skein of reckoning and *thens.*
The Old One roars into sunrise, and the Host answers it, ghosting away into the trees, as the horn calls one last time and the Rade. . .
Is done.
A tiny, mewling sound. With some sense or Sight, he comes to realise his body is curled akin to a hedgehog threatened by dogs, with hands at nape, eyes squeezed shut. His heart thuds—*one-and two-and three-and*—familiar, aye, but not beneath this awareness, this inexorable crimson-black thunder behind his eyes . . .
Nay. A Voice pulls the weight of breathing from his lungs. *Too deep.*
Deep? How? Who? Where? Who am *I?*
You are Me. Warmth enfolds him, spreads upon his breast like fresh blood. *Fy Annwn ei wrogaeth.*

The words scratch at the tally consuming his mind, and he clings to them, repeats them, *Aye, you. I am, and I've done my homage to Annwn.*

You have. My own has now twice been as dead and returned, to me and to his rightful place, through the Ceugant's *promise. Three shall fulfil its power, but not yet, not yet. . . Rhyddhau, release it, let it go, O pwca.*

Pwca. Names are power. This one embraces him, a cowl of protection shouldering the extreme twist and surge of consciousness. It allows him to push upward to hands and knees, to feel the earth as earth and his breath as breath.

No more, no less.

Is. Was. Shall be.

Aye, O pwca, *you are My avatar, My own. Trickster, Hob. My breath in the night, you have returned from Annwn's hall to once again ride, a demon to My enemies.*

A flinch and totter beneath the heft of the Voice; overmuch, a beckon to the weavers who would spin out *tynged,* nigh unbearable: Existence, Debt, and Memory . . .

You are being the last of us!

Ia! Ia! By the shield of Solomon and the Horns of the God; with the chalice of the Lady and in the name of the Magician in the wilderness. In Allworlds the Ceugant *bides, and by chains of iron and fire I shall bind you all the tighter, do you not. . .*

Mi argyllwdd rhyddhau. *Release my lord!* . . .

Into an everlasting tally:

Was.

Is.

Shall be.

One-and, two-and, three-and. . .

It breaks him, would take him, but Voice becomes Presence, impassioned and *here,* curving along his spine. *Be easy, My Own. Hold fast, and We shall bring you safe to home.*

Breath sears his nape, and bone-hard fingers tangle in wet-frosted curls, drawing his head back, bringing him upward to his knees upon the soft loam and it is warm, so *warm.*

O Pwca, O darkling lord of my wylding Wode. I have missed Us sore.

Missed you. . . God, I have missed. . .

The voice is another, somehow familiar, with a glimpse of russet light and laughter—it is now? Is it to come? Or merely a memory meaning to buckle him? He resists with hands splaying outward and upward to scrape against then clutch, hard, at velveted bone . . . nay, antlers. His own, his lord's? But he has no lord, is no one's lord save when the possession comes . . . possession? Aye and no matter, both and neither. He falls into the moment—no counting, no reckoning, only heat and breath and *claiming.*

Make the magic, lord, and claim him home.

Another snap of *one-and, two-and, three-and* but memory's bite dwindles beneath a faraway purl of thunder, a lingering shaft of brilliant sun through treetops and, more, the hot growl at his nape. *It is* mine *to weave the last spell. Ours to ride this Hunt.*

In mindless instinct back arches, hands take fierce hold of antler, submit to/with flesh and bone, between earth and sky hung, speared and shivered upon a phantasm of breath and blessings.

In the name of darkness and light and all shadows between, you have returned to Us!

Us. There is more . . . ?

Nay, too much—*too much*—as, teeth gritting like sand in a mortar, fingers digging into the moist loam, he surrenders within the presence of Wode and god, piercing and surrounding, grounds lostling spirit into thisnow.

Falling to earth, he lies there, panting.

And so We remain.

With a gusty sigh and rub of cheek against the sudden brilliance of sun-drenched grass—still damp, like a fur flung to dry upon a fireside bower—he realises he is naked, wet to skin, and nigh boneless.

A tiny smirk tips his lip.

Aye, usually you are the one to tame me. Thisnight you needed taming. Together we grounded Our power, breathed it back into thisnow, claimed it.

The smirk broadens. Claimed, all right. The Horned Lord has never fancied *that* before.

Somehow, faint-far, he knows this too.

You are me, I am you. How shall I not?

"You'll have Her mad at both of us, more like."

Mayhap I'll give Her cause to love me the more. As she does your Knight, who finds his truest pleasures rutting buck and doe.

The laugh comes easily, but sobers to slide beneath puzzlement. "My . . . Knight?"

Patience, O pwca. We remain. Thisnow will find you, anon. Warm arms snug him close, and the Voice fades upon a warm, greensap breeze as he sinks inward.

Pwca. Aye, I am. Pwca.

And lets it go, curling close, taking a deep gulp of damp breeze, forest green, and thisnow.

✝

"Aye, and the Hunt was abroad last night, no question." Father Dolfin seemed pleased, if unsurprised, to see them. "Rattled the stones and guttered all the candles, blowing leaf litter all the way across the altar. Not only that; I seem to have acquired a new tenant." He waved a hand towards the Lady Chapel, where a sinuous, dark shadow slept at Her feet.

Gamelyn blinked, and Marion gasped, "The Old One!"

The wyvern raised its head to peer at them, eyes gleaming in the dark before it settled down again, head beneath one wing, and faded into the shadows. The remainder of All Hallows lay just as quiet; it seemed the monks had stirred for Matins and retreated to their cells to pray.

"So last night *was* your doing," Dolfin said—rather mildly, considering. "I thought it might be."

"It was a . . . wild night." Gamelyn's venture was cautious.

"Hm." Dolfin crossed his arms. "Did you tell the beast he could come here?"

"I'm not sure"—Marion's retort came more tart than cautious—"that it's wise to 'tell' an ancient spirit anything."

Dolfin raised an eyebrow, started to answer. Instead he frowned suddenly, eyeing them up for long moments before coming to some conclusion. "Both of you, wait here."

Marion and Gamelyn watched him go, somewhat at a loss. With a tiny shake of head, Marion paced an unsteady path towards the Lady Chapel.

"Marion?" Gamelyn followed her, realising his own step was none too steady.

"We're on the right path, at least. Robyn said there was one of the Old Ones lying in the earth here, sleeping. I guess the water spirit came where his own kind were . . . " She trailed off as Gamelyn came to stand beside her, but it wasn't his doing. She was staring at the Dark Madonna.

Who sat aside the wyvern's back . . . yet it wasn't Her. Or was it? She looked nothing like to the goddess Gamelyn had witnessed before in these walls. Dark, aye, her skin gleaming bronze beneath the torches, her pale eyes gleaming amidst—but instead of being clad in thin-spun samites, She was garbed in woad and moss, fine-tanned leathers and silk-soft furs. Her ebon hair was long, but instead of being combed smooth as a raven's wing, was oiled and twisted with leaves and wooden beads.

"The Wodewose," Marion breathed with no little reverence, and the sound of it raised the hairs upon Gamelyn's nape and arms.

As if the naming had sparked motion, She stood. With a mere—and disparaging, no question—glance towards Gamelyn, She paced slowly over to Marion. She barely reached Marion's chin, but it didn't matter; of Her power in this moment, thisnow, there was no question.

Suddenly She smiled. Raising her left hand, She laid it flat just above Marion's left breast, over her heart.

Marion gasped, staggered. Gamelyn started forward; the Wodewose woman slid him a glance that said, clear: *Stay where you are.* Then, standing on tiptoe, She pulled Marion with Her other hand, to whisper in her ear.

Marion bent, listened. Her shoulders shook. Going to her knees, Marion took Her hand and kissed it. In return, She kissed Marion's head and traced a sign upon her crown.

"Here we are!" Gamelyn whipped around as Dolfin's voice boomed into the chapel. "I've brought . . . " It petered out.

Gamelyn whirled back around to see only shadows, and Marion kneeling amidst them. Taking a deep breath, he turned back to where Dolfin stood, bearing pitcher and tray. A young monk followed,wide-eyed towards the Lady Chapel, bearing another tray.

Mayhap they'd seen? Mayhap not, and neither did it matter.

"I didn't mean to interrupt your prayers," Dolfin murmured as Gamelyn walked over to take the pitcher from him. "But you're both pie-eyed and staggering. Wherever you're going, 'tis likely you'll fall off your horses if you don't eat."

Gamelyn's stomach gave a lingering growl.

"I'm proper famished," Marion's voice came from behind him, tiny and quavering.

Dolfin gave a satisfied grunt, gestured them over to the side table, and started parcelling out eats.

✝

"What did She say to you?"

Marion slid her gaze towards Gamelyn. The look seemed gauging, almost stern; indeed she peered at him steadily for so long that he wondered if he'd overstepped, somehow. Was prying where he'd no business.

"She said several things," Marion said, finally, with a pensive look, playing with her horse's mane. "She said that the Hob had fulfilled his bargain, and so She had returned him to us, for a time."

"For a time." He wasn't sure he liked the sound of that.

"'Tis all we have, aye? Thisnow, and our time in it."

Which made it all the more urgent to Gamelyn. They had to find Robyn. And John.

"We need to head southeast." Marion left off the mare's mane and gathered her reins. "Towards Loxley."

✝

Thisnow. When. How.

Time . . . is.

He wakes, alone, with only a small depression in the moss to suggest he lay last night with another being. His god has left him to catch his bearings, and he does. It takes longer than it should, somehow, but he knows this path, this stretch of wood.

Changed, aye, as things do.

Loxley Chase, the Voice whispers within him, while distant memory fills in the remaining blank places. His feet follow a well-worn path along the river's westerly edge, heading north from the Hathersage road, towards the charcoal burners' kilns. The smoky remnants of the latter still hang in the moist air; not that they'd be burning now, with heavy rain passing through and still hanging, clouds of damp promise, along the horizon of nigh-bare treetops.

Though the smoke seems thicker than it should.

No matter; he has to find them.

Whoever they are.

Tell me who, he pleads of the Voice. *Tell me why.*

Yet not so much as a shiver of thought or feeling rises to response. Only his own heartbeat, threatening to magnify to fill his ears—*one-and, two-and, three-and. . .*

Nay, he tells it, *not now,* and thankfully it subsides.

Mayhap in grounding him, his god has spun protection; like willowherb and bulrush fluff to cushion new-laid eggs in a basket. Mayhap he cannot know, yet, who or why.

The question is in his name: *Pwca.* The answer? Keep moving.

The wind picks up; with it carries the scent of added rain. And smoke. The farther in Pwca treads, the more the latter wafts about him, tingles alarm like a bad memory. Tells him: nigh to Loxley, what else to expect? The last time he'd been there, it had been . . .

Long ago, Horned Lord murmurs.

Pwca halts mid-stride, another memory surfacing: green summers and long winters, with the work hard but affection leavening it. Two children—two?—running wild as hares, let free by their parents' love.

Long gone. The otherworlds move different skeins of tynged's loom.

Otherworlds. More memory. Through a veil of fog and ice, someone had called, come for him—does he seek them, then? Why? How?

You will know soon.

"*When?*" he snarls.

Smoke thickens about him, carrying upon it the singe of well-fed flame.

Loxley, the Horned Lord whispers, and bloody *damn* but names indeed have power, with 'when' and 'soon' meaning overmuch in thisnow, reeling him beneath memory upon a half heartbeat. Where time was. Where *he* is . . .

Just past *fourteen going on for forty,* as his mam allus says, a lad who barely escapes being slaughtered with his village, panicked by smells and shouts, pursued by the sensate crush and surge of hate. Blood and brutality all about, and a weight in his chest he doesn't/does understand:

The death agonies of those he loves.

Father dragged off his horse and hacked to bits, the god's antlers broken, stripped of adornment.

Mother bound and forced to her knees, beheaded upon the sacred stones.

The fear-dread-*knowledge* that another beloved one is its cause, however unwitting.

He will betray you—

—and so he himself has brought down this ruin upon them.

Agony courses through him, in the half-blinding power of a winter storm.

In the next breath he lurches forward, twisting grief and rage into instinct—*as always, pwca*—no thought, merely action.

The forest bends before him in odd deference of headlong pursuit. Hot breath scorches his lungs, horn weights and chills his brow, and belly-deep a wolf snarls menace. The smoke leads with acrid scent, throwing gilt flickers amongst the dawn, then a rush of sound to dwarf even the sound of his own gasps and heartbeat ticking off *one-and, two-and, three-and* . . .

Voices rise, command and response. A heavy-bladed axe bites with that familiar-particular *ring-thunk*, accompanied by the slap and slash of dragging brush, the hiss and crackle of flames fed by dry needle and leaf.

And beneath it all, the god's fury: *Treachery. Violation.* It sets slick-black thunder rumbling against his ribs with *one-and, two-and, three-and. . .*

The deer path, known as intimately as the string calluses upon the long, hard fingers of his left hand, winds then curves then winds again. On the last bend Pwca's feet ken what to do before his mind so much as registers: they slow him effortlessly into a nigh-silent creep, to take refuge against a huge survivor of the original devastation. An oak.

This, too, has import though he kens it not; instead he moulds against rough bark, and crouches behind autumn-sapped bracken, peering across what had once been Loxley. Where, faulty memory supplies, the forest herself had claimed ruin from desecration.

No more.

Black with soot, men swarm through thick smoke and tread the overgrown crofts and tofts akin to ants disturbed from their mound. Most have kerchiefs over their faces. What trees withstood Desecration—the word hangs, entitled, in his mind—either lie in smouldering ruin, or shudder and quake beneath the ring and snap of hand-axes. One elm in particular, on the far edge, is nigh uprooted, cut to heart and festooned with rope; four oxen lurch in harness, trying to fell it.

Every axe-blow seeks to topple, not only Forest but Pwca. Every creak, every moan and call—for the trees are crying out, begging . . . *screaming.* Can these blind, stupid murderers not *hear?*

He sinks, overwhelmed, hands clapping to his ears—fool, to think he can stop it, any of it!—before he lurches forward on hands and knees, retching.

Nay. You are more than this. The Voice fills him, sets back wayward and panicked thisnow upon a firm axis. *This place is sacred with Our blood. It belongs to no man, no plough save Mine Own!*

Fury seizes nausea, shakes it and breaks its spine. Rage glimmering behind dark eyes, Pwca rises.

Silent. Considering. Predatory.

Three fires all told, two smouldering and a smaller one flaming hot. A wide swath of forest already cleared, a jagged scar ripping past what had once been Loxley. Raked and hacked, the brush lies heaped and tangled. A second team of oxen drags felled logs over to a pile already well started, a thickset man droving with shouts and the occasional flick of whip. A well-dressed lord on a sturdy rouncey barks commands to the first quad hitch toppling the elm. Axes ring through the cleared ruin, prompt the snap and cry of wood being rent. Four men are busy at the chopping. Several hounds mill about the rouncey's hoofs, whilst a slight man passes back and forth, feeding and tending the fires.

A snarl kindles in Pwca's chest, and banks into a low growl. Never has he seen such as this. No sense to rip the forest asunder, raze it flat and clear, then burn half of it as waste!

They take. They have no right. They do not belong here, in our forest, in the realm of the Hood's covenant!

Another name-claim, familiar. A vicious smile tilts Pwca's lip, and he tugs his hood over his curls. Nods as his god purls *This will be* our *justice. Our right.*

"Milord!" A shout breaks the Voice's spell; that and the crush of footsteps drawing closer.

Hand falling to the copper knife in his boot, Pwca ducks into concealment. His gaze fixes upon what the approaching man bears athwart his back: a recurve bow and a flat cache of arrows.

His smile broadens.

"Milord! This one?"

"A beauty, to be sure!" The man a-horse ambles closer, speech betraying guesses for truth: a noble, of lesser rank perhaps, but nevertheless in charge. "We'll take this as well." He gestures towards the oak. "They pay plenty at the coast for one large enough to keel a ship."

"Nay, 'milord'." The whisper escapes, muted beneath axes and smoke, beneath the cry of the elm as it splinters and cracks and refuses to fall.

Yet the bowman treads closer, head cocked as if he'd heard. Pwca watches the bow, its lovely, deadly curve limned by the grey, unfiltered light of ash and torn-up earth. Waits.

No Voice, this time. His god is sunk within, breathing his breath, rising his heartbeat, possessing him utterly. Pwca rises, graceful and soundless, senses bruised and tingling tight-sharp. "Coom by, man." A whisper.

Frowning, the bowman whistles up the brace of dogs. Obedient, they leave off their gambol at the rouncey's side and trot over.

A silent breath, this time, let out in just-as-silent entreaty and a twitch of fingers. An arrow-flight away, a stand of bramble shakes in answer. Then another rustle, several ells past that. Then farther.

Bait, and one no prey animal can resist. The dogs leap to the chase.

The man starts a curse, doesn't finish it. Instead his words gurgle and choke as Pwca leaps from cover, drags him out of sight, and employs the knife.

The bow is unfamiliar, somehow—undersized, Pwca kens, and the arrows fashioned for a shorter reach and draw. But he caresses it like a lover, steps it with startling ease, and finds himself knotting his hair and caching a trio of arrows there, fisting two others as he tests the bow.

It won't shoot far before the aim wavers; it can't pierce chain-mail—somewhere, somehow, he remembers another that could—but 'twill do, at that.

"Alfred?" Another man, coming close.

Pwca ducks into hiding.

A third follows, swinging his axe to rest upon one massive shoulder. "Did he send 'em away, after sommat?"

The other chuckles. "Aye, or they scented a coney. Bloody dogs."

"Well, we en't needing 'em." One claps the other on the back, both turning away. "If his lordship would just bestir 'imself and bloody well go hunting, leave us to our work . . . "

The timbre of their words gives pause. These are peasants; working men akin to his own da. What choice do they have but to follow orders, do their lord's bidding? Misgivings pull the Horned Lord from his soul like a splinter from infected flesh. Pwca winces, shudders, leans hard against the oak.

Its touch brings awareness, strength and protection, and hesitation shivers away beneath the Voice. *They are complicit in the barrening of our sacred forest, and for what?*

The last words sear and simmer, derisive.

Our charge is yours, to give by rite and right. The Hood's justice, do you yet remember?

Memory burns, sinks the Voice within, conjures the *one-and two-and three-and* hammering behind his ears—

"—call 't Hood's justice. *Mine to bear and I'll give 't, I will—*"

Time . . . shall be.

Pwca twists, rolling along the tree trunk to its other side, and whispers the hex-breath along the arrow's shaft. Licks the cock-fletching, feels the sting of a thin slice, tastes blood and sees the stain of it, dark, on the vane.

Raises the bow, eyes riveted down the shaft.

Breathes—"*Bodolaeth*"—and looses.

The two villeins fall, one with a shout and one without a sound. Another turns, eyes wide-wheeling; before he can sound any alarm he, too, falls to a silent, deadly arrow.

Time . . . was.

"*Coffadwriaeth.*" And the breath takes the nobleman off his bay with an arrow to the throat; sends the two-hitch drover ducking for cover.

Alas, they've scraped away anything within reach that might provide just that.

Pwca smiles and abandons his hiding place, walks into the clearing. Looses another arrow.

Watches the man scream and tumble.

The two-hitch bawls and takes flight.

And a dark, huddled shape flits around the four oxen hitched to the elm, ducking behind. His voice is plain, though but a murmur, invoking calm to his beasts.

Bow half at nock, Pwca follows.

Smiles grimly as chase becomes game, with the oxen and their bespoiled tree trunks the safety 'round which predator and prey dart, back and forth and . . .

Pwca backs, waits.

Finally growls "Coom by, man," again with the Voice beneath his own, and pushes the bow.

Slow, cowering, the drover obeys, clinging to his cart-traces as if his legs won't hold him. His hands are gentle upon the oxen— caring, albeit trembling. As he comes into full view he gives a tiny moan and drops to his knees, hands clasped above his head.

Prays "Milord! Milord Robyn, please—"

Robyn?

The bow, quivering-ready, wavers and wobbles from full nock.

"—'tweren't my doing, 'tweren't my wish! I'd nivver give cause to anger ye . . . t' anger the Horned One. But me wife, me kids, me parents unable to fend for theyself. *Please*, lord Robyn, spare me!"

Robyn.

The bow looses with the sound of a hundred angry bees.

The drover shrieks and staggers, sure he's dead. Instead he finds himself alive, pinned to the front of his cart by the arrow through his loose overtunic. The oxen shift, blowing, threatening panic as the hooded figure stalks close.

But Pwca murmurs to them, gentling them though he himself is anything but, heart timed like a rapid hammer in his breast.

Time . . . *is.*

"I follows the Old ways, I does," the drover babbles, voice climbing with sudden hope. "I warned em, see, I warned 'em of the Hooded One's justice. Please, milord Robyn, spare me for me woman's sake, and me bairns."

Robyn.

Time is.

Was.

Will be.

One-two, two-two, three-two. . .

"*Go!*" A snarl. "Tell them what happened here. Tell them! Warn them all!"

The man rips his tunic from the arrow shaft and flees.

Silence.

Only the untended fire, small warmth against a cold, smoky day. Only the bay grazing, riderless and rein dragging. Only the remaining oxen, calmed and stolid in their traces.

Time . . . *is.*

And only the remainder; he whispers it: "*Dyled.*"

Several are tried and tossed aside before he finds an axe that bites flesh readily as wood. Two heads, four, with the fifth the nobleman who thought to claim the oak, and all the while Time rings in his ears to the cadence of his own heart's beating . . .

One-and two-and three. . .

Bodolaeth. Coffadwriaeth. Dyled.

Existence. Memory. Debt.

The rhythm is all, and it sinks further within, threads faint amidst *tynged's* darkling strands which, all at once, beg and deny holding.

So he holds nothing, merely sways and lets it wash through him, fill him, judder and shiver and take the breath from his lungs.

Time was.

Is . . .

And senses fade back into some semblance of sanity beneath the Voice, pulling separate to fill the clearing.

Who are you, My Own?

. . . Shall be.

"Hob-Robyn." Taking in the breath-voice, he let it swirl in his lungs, heated and spent, releasing it to exhaust outward like mist . . . nay, not like mist. For as he watched it, it drifted and commingled with the smoke, between the piles of smouldering, raked-up brush. "I am Robyn."

Robyn the Hooded One, King of the Shire Wode, avatar of the Horned Lord, brined point of the Ceugant's *fierce arrow.*

"Where are they?" Robyn murmured, but knew. A different path. Mayhap, a different time . . .

Nay. Please, not that.

Unsurety brought the rhythm, the awareness, the *one-and two-and three-and.*

Be ye still, the Horned Lord purred in the old tongue. *There is yet* dyled—*the debt*—*to pay.*

And the rhythm muted, slow, into blessed silence.

Eyes closed, he stood there for long moments. Then Robyn Hode bent and took up the severed heads, carried them dripping to the well, and hung them upon the ravaged stones.

- Entr'acte -

John came back to the glade and found it empty.

Hardly surprising, once he considered it. The madness had been contagious, last night. Robyn had seemed more Horned One than any mortal, unsure of what or who he was, and . . .

One could only hope he'd woken sober, and in his right mind. Did Robyn mean to make himself scarce, John wouldn't find him. Still, it made him uneasy, to think of Robyn lost and unsure.

Lord? he sent into the green, asking. Nowt but the rustling of dead leaves and the creak of branches in the breeze at first. Then he heard it: the blast of a stag, and a cheeky chirrup from a robin.

Aye, but the Wode would take care of her lord.

John shrugged the brace of rabbits he'd downed from his shoulder and, crouching down, began to skin them.

By the time he'd started a fire and propped the rabbits over it, the breeze brought more clouds, and a hint of smoke. John peered upward. Mayhap leftovers from the bonfires last night.

He smiled, remembering. It had been a ride unlike anything he'd ever had. And he'd lived to tell the tale.

Of course you would. You and I have become. . . acquainted. Aye my Janicot?

His covenant name sounded warm and fierce. Once, the Horned Lord had been a cold, fearful presence. Now?

Aye. They were . . . acquainted.

The fire flared, sparks flying as a pocket of sap opened and caught. John reached, thinking to tend it, but halted midgesture.

Shoving the dark hair back from his forehead, he bent closer, a frown twitching at his brow.

Reached out again—cautious this time—and wiggled his fingers over the fire as if warming them.

Sat back, frown tilting deeper and fingers unconsciously framing a hex-ward into the air. It hung there, a shimmering ghost that refused to fade away.

The Fae had ridden last night, freed to Rade with the Wild Hunt. And whilst he might hold the Horned Lord's spirit and ride His mount a-pillion, he'd made no such accord with Them.

Their magic lingered deep, and this coursed altogether strong and otherworldly, soaking into the earth like spilt blood, creeping over his skin like chill. Yet . . . 'twere familiar, this, to sparkle 'gainst the ward so. *Familiar.*

Again the fire flared, sudden and high, blowing bits of ember and char against John's cheeks. One stung his lower lip; he flicked a negligent hand at it, falling back on his buttocks to stare beyond, into the trees, where one of their shadows . . . walked.

Nay, no trees walking. Mayhap a Wodewose creature trod forward—that tall, that cunning, but slow despite its length of stride. The shadow thrown, behind and to the left, bore antlers, and rose against the late morning, tall and straight as a yew.

"I know you," the figure said, soft. *Beloved.* "M' little John."

"I . . . know . . . you." It creaked, rusty from disuse. "*Robyn.*"

- XXX -

"I'm sorry." Robyn traced a thumb across John's singed bottom lip where a blister had started—and from which, earlier, John had winced whilst Robyn kissed him dizzy . . . but only for the moment. Their coupling had been frantic, awkward, pain as much as pleasure, familiar and not. "I en't sure I ken what's come of me yet, but . . ."

But this. Aye, this. He nestled closer to John's body, closed his eyes as kisses were laid, like sacraments, to each of his ribs.

Spoke the words he'd feared. "How long?" And bloody damn if they still didn't stutter unwilling. To ease the rusty choke of them, Robyn trailed his fingers across the lovelocks at John's left temple, his cheek, his eyelids. There were more ghosts in those eyes as well, but not so many lines, really, as to imply . . .

John ducked his face into Robyn's hand and curled closer—they well might turn each other inside out, they were clinging so. With another kiss, this to Robyn's neck, John signed, *It seemed forever.*

"Aye, it did. But"—he forced his throat to obedience—"how long?"

A shrug, as if to deny the sorrow dulling brown eyes. *Seven years.*

Seven. Years. Robyn's head sank against the furs they'd tangled and propped against, a weight too heavy, suddenly, to bear. "But 'twere a month, mayhap, or a fortnight more. At times"—his eyes met John's and held—"aye. Forever. And nowt, all at once."

They let you go. 'Tis all that matters.

"They did . . . and They didn't. I had to promise—"

You made a promise to Them? Fear traced a quiver along John's body.

Robyn scooped him all the closer. "I had to . . . nay. I needed to. I think." He frowned. "Me memory's still patchy, 'm afraid. Like everything's sideways sommat, then straighter than ever. Like time was . . . "

Time was.

One-two, two-two, three-tw. . .

Only a matter of several breaths, but when Robyn shuddered free he found John atop him, slender fingers tangled in his hair, nose to nose with brown eyes boring, *seeking.*

"Can y-you hear me?" Hesitant-soft as always, John's voice, yet the magic that trickled into Robyn's heart and gently tugged him free was strong and pure.

That, more than anything else, told of time's passage.

"Gamelyn isn't the only one who's learnt sommat," Robyn murmured, and John's cheeks flushed.

Well, then, the only one as didn't realise how powerful a *dryw* John was, was John.

"Gerroff, love, I'm fine. I am." Robyn insisted as John hesitated. "It's just . . . I think me head and me feet aren't quite acquainted with each other yet. Not really here . . . nay, that en't right. More like I'm even more . . . here . . . " He trailed off with a puzzled shrug.

Aye, well, John scooted over. *You are here, with us. We made Them let you go, and that's all that matters. Whatever comes, we'll cross it, together. From here until the end.*

"Aye. We will." Robyn buried his face in John's tangle of hair, breathed deep. "But first . . . tell me again, love. Tell me again they're all right, that we'll find them soon. Tell me . . . everything."

Aye. But we'll eat first.

Odd, how Robyn didn't realise how hungry he was, or the trembling in his limbs that wasn't just the afters of hard pleasure. Until now.

A smile curved John's lip, and he rolled to his feet and bent over the fire, where two rabbits were roasted nigh to perfection.

Ⓟ

"At least we know we're on the right path." Gamelyn couldn't help the satisfaction in his voice. Even as he raged at what had begun this, he knew what—who—had finished it.

Marion didn't answer. Dismounted, skirts tucked over one arm, she wandered through hanks of damp, dead smoke. Her booted feet crunched the scorched grass, picking the way through what had been waste fires; she leapt felled trees, pausing, here and there, at the headless bodies.

Aye, those skulls upon Loxley's crumbling well were a proper giveaway.

Marion ran a seeming-idle hand along the empty trace roped to a huge elm. Unsteady, her gait; her lips grey and tight-drawn. Fighting not to heave her guts.

Gamelyn understood this, too. The ruin was sickening enough; that it lay *here* . . .

A soft rain had come, chasing over the far hills, with sunlight breaking, here and there, through mists and smoke. As Marion moved away from the elm, a stray shaft found and haloed her hair like fire. She bent her head beneath its warmth, whispered a prayer that runnelled, silk and more fire, along Gamelyn's nerves. As if in answer, the elm creaked and swayed.

Made apology to the Lady of the Shire Wode: too girdled to recover, yet too rooted to fall and free its spirit.

Marion turned away with tears glimmering on her cheeks, shaking her head.

"We'll send someone," Gamelyn assured as she approached, took up her mare's rein and stepped up, arranging her skirts as she alighted in the saddle. "Spare it misery, honour it in our home."

"Aye, 'tis for the best," Marion sighed. "We're near to them."

Gathering up the reins, Gamelyn nodded, eagerness once again fingering his heart. "Let's go."

"To the caverns," Marion said. "They'll be there." But she stood unmoving, still peering out across Loxley's second ruin.

"Marion?"

"Who gave them leave?" Marion's gaze slid sideways, clashed with his.

Her frown not only pinked, but drew blood. "Marion, you *know* I would never countenance this! Even if I'd been here long enough to—"

"I didn't mean that." Her cheeks coloured, betraying the pale gilt of downturned lashes. "But since Loxley Chase is under custody of Tickhill . . . "

"Otho." It was a growl. "To trade on speculation is not beyond my brother."

Marion thought of the letter, of the King's permission, and gritted her teeth. "But how could Otho have sanctioned this so quickly?"

"That's"—a growl as Gamelyn put spur to his horse—"what I'd like to know."

ᛈ

Still out of time, they were, Robyn knew. Just as he knew they had to get to the caverns, find their place, hold their ground. Wait for all the threads of *tynged* and time to splice back into weave.

Instead of walking or running, they stole a bridle from an

over-large stable, and a horse from a small herd of them grazing upon Sheffield's park. Hallamshire's horses, John had said with no little satisfaction, as they headed to the Peak ridge at a round gallop.

Mam Tor rose above them, bathed in sun, her hem carpeted in dusky heather past its prime bloom. Robyn had never thought to see her again.

And the caverns took them in.

Then, and only then, did thisnow seem to shift into place with an almost audible *click*. Then, and only then, did Robyn sense them coming. More ghosts biding behind his eyes, but these living-warm, and O, so desired.

John stayed behind, smiling shy understanding as Robyn denied any wait, climbing the small bluff just above the cave and taking the path east.

How apropos that he first saw them, two riders dwarfed by Mam Tor's shadow as the sun set below her. It had, after all, been here that they'd first wielded their magic together: the *Ceugant* in all their power.

His heart in his mouth, pacing *one-and two-and three-and*. Likely sommat from a jongleur's tale that he should start running—not only to quiet it, but because he was done with waiting. And more, that the horses should leap into a gallop as Gamelyn saw him, then Marion too, all three of them racing to see who reached the ridge first.

The horses won, of course, but Gamelyn kept coming, thundering down the hill nigh atop Robyn. Just before, Gamelyn set the palfrey to as pretty a stop as could be accomplished, downhill as it was, and leapt off in a body tackle of Robyn. Which of course, set them rolling farther downhill, more grunts and laughs than any attempts at embracing until they landed at the bottom with Gamelyn atop and Robyn nigh squashed, and Gamelyn taking his face in both hands and kissing him so he couldn't *breathe*.

Nor did it matter.

But it was mayhap a good thing that Marion came up, for they had to take a breath. Robyn leapt up to grab her in a huge, hard hug, swinging her round and round until he wasn't sure whether that made him dizzy, or Marion's grip, so tight it hurt . . . but hurt damned fine.

"You're back. You're here. You're back!" she kept crying.

"Oh, God," Gamelyn kept muttering, over and over. "I was afraid it would all be for naught, that you weren't . . . weren't *here*, somehow, and we'd failed again. All of it, just to fail and—"

"Shut t' bloody fuck up, Gamelyn," Robyn growled, reaching out to yank him into a hard and gob-stopping kiss.

He usually wasn't one for riding pillion; he liked to be in communion with the horse, not mere passenger. But this time Robyn rode behind his lover, arms wrapped tight, spooned up all drowsy and compliant as if he were some damsel from a jongleur's tale, and mayhap one just rescued from a very hungry dragon.

He was bloody exhausted, and bloody surprised that he didn't just topple off the horse.

Well, Gamelyn would catch him. Or John, with whom Robyn kept sharing an absolutely daft smile. Or Marion, who rode on the opposite side, close enough they could reach out and travel hand in hand.

Robyn longed to stay at Mam Tor forever. He longed to ride like hell to Tickhill and see all his most beloved. He longed to ride through the Peak forever. He longed, most of all, to disappear into his forest—his green, verdant, *alive* forest—and never emerge.

Forever.

Or at least long enough to fetch his strength back. The air was . . . heavy, somehow, within his lungs. The sky seemed over wide. Gamelyn's familiar smell lingered in Robyn's nostrils just that much too heady-close. The woollen tunic beneath his hands was just that much too abrasive, as was the crunch of grass beneath their horse's hoofs, the bark of a startled woodcock, or the *chirrrump* of the frogs in the fens, just that much too loud.

And the gwyllion, somehow and still wrapped tight-close about his neck, seemed as heavy as a handful of gold.

Weak as a blind and suckling kitten, he were, and no question. No good thisnow towards another fierce longing: to rut Gamelyn until he screamed.

So, for now? Just being here, leaning against his lover's back and letting it all wash through him? That was enough.

The stars had begun to peep through, the frogs singing in the fens and the grass crisp beneath the horses' hoofs as they approached Tickhill. The castle glowed in the gloaming, flickering gold and black and crimson, tens of torches and bonfires leaping up against the coming darkness, to lead them all back home.

Gilbert was the first to approach Robyn as they came in the gates—though 'approach' seemed an unimpressive description for his shriek of joy as he ran over, pounced, and nigh dragged Robyn from Gamelyn's horse, hugging him until both their bones creaked.

Gamelyn knew; he'd heard.

Gilbert the first, but not the last—John and David, Aelwyn and Siham—as they clung together, huddled close: the remnants of what had once been Robyn Hood's band of outlaws.

The castle's inhabitants cheered and slapped the castle stones in approval. Some of them knew what was happening—most didn't—and it didn't matter.

It put a choke in Gamelyn's throat and a sting behind his eyes. A hand stole into his; Marion still a-horse next to him, her own eyes glimmering as she watched. With one last squeeze, she dismounted and walked, slowly, to the small, close group. Was let in.

Gamelyn, still bemused, dismounted. Much came beside him—after directing several lads to take the horses—and linked an arm through his.

"I once told Marion," he said, a bit hoarse, "that 'tweren't worth it. You nigh killing yourself in t' desert, her spending every waking thought upon it, gnawing on memories like a hound at a dry bone. I figured him dead or lost forever, and none of it worth another life to try an' defeat t' past."

Gamelyn snugged close to him. "And now?"

"Now." Much shrugged. "I wouldn't trade this moment for nowt. How 'bout you, milord?"

A smile tipped Gamelyn's lip. "Maybe one moment. Alone, in my chambers. Tonight, I hope."

"Well. You allus did fancy a bit of rough trade." A grin, Much stepping forward as first Marion then Robyn turned, gesturing to them both.

Come here! You belong here with us!

Still smiling, Gamelyn followed Much and joined the gathering.

A feast awaited them in the tower—not one fit for any king, but a proper board filled with homely things: bread still warm from the ovens, pottage, mutton, sweet herbs and wine, as well as a rack of venison provided beneath the lord's grace, and that of his lady's foresters. Also, a goodly tray of sweetmeats—minus, of course any sleep enhancers.

The latter was unnecessary. Once they'd eaten their fill, Gamelyn kept yawning his head off. Marion, too. And Robyn . . . well, he kept listing sideways at his place between Gamelyn and John—and he didn't even seem to notice the children hanging on his every word. They'd be hanging on to his arms, if they'd their druthers, but they'd been warned.

They'd have time to acquaint themselves with their newfound uncle. There was all the time in the world, now.

Torches everywhere in the tower's main hall, and the main hearth fed like the bonfires had been at Hallows. Instruments brought out, with impromptu tunes and even a little dancing. Gilbert was trying—and failing—to make a pleasant sound from a small, beautifully-carved wooden flute. John finally nabbed it back and began a jaunty little air. Someone handed Gilbert a tambour as consolation, which he at least could swing in time to the drum. Marion managed to coax her brother into a small turn about the hearth, and Gamelyn took one, too, though gave up after he found himself more dragging Robyn than dancing with him.

Supper lasted long into the night, but the guest of honour went to sleep, propped up in the lord's chair and snoring.

ᛈ

Robyn woke to the rays of morning and a scent he'd nigh forgotten, all musk and spice and sweet gathered and pounded. His limbs were tangled in blissfully soft linens, with one arm and leg thrown across his own personal forge fire.

Opening his eyes, Robyn found Gamelyn peering at him. Couldn't, for long moments, speak past the ginormous lump that filled his throat.

Then Gamelyn said, green eyes soft as Robyn had ever seen them, "You're here. It's real."

So it followed that Robyn should make it more real, and lurch atop Gamelyn, and kiss him until they were both giddy and air-starved and—aye! finally!—trembling-hard as good corner posts.

He wanted to go slow, to make this one count, but found himself lurching atop Gamelyn like a boy overready for his first go.

Gamelyn grabbed his wrists and shoved him onto his back. For a moment, Robyn was afraid he was going to come up with some sort of monk-type excuse—*sorry, love, it's a fast day and we're not allowed to eat meat or roger the peasantry, not on this day.*

Instead Gamelyn bent over, slid one hand down to grab Robyn's knob—just enough rough, and just enough care—and kissed him again. Again, just rough enough, but a bit less care. Eager. Greedy.

Skin so warm, like velveted flame, and tiny, gasps into each other's mouths, and . . .

A harsh, just-gone-flat sound clanged its way into the silence: the gatehouse bell.

A rap on the door came a mere breath later. Both of them frozen mid-tangle, whilst the bloody, god-forsaken, mothering traitor of bell kept ringing, and the fist upon the door made its way from rapping into a heavy pounding.

"Gamelyn!" Marion shouted from the other side. Both frantic and apologetic—and aye, she should be that, but . . . "Gamelyn, he's here! Otho's riding towards the castle!"

Gamelyn twisted off Robyn and shot upright, flinging away the coverlets, stalking to the door and wrenching it open.

Marion was braiding her hair, her robes askew—plainly she'd also had a good morning interrupted. Her eyes met her brother's, stricken. "I'm sorry, pet, so sorry, but he has to come this time, there's no way 'round it."

Much came behind her, just as dishevelled and confirming Robyn's own theory. "Milord?"

"Warrant the gates," Gamelyn ordered. "I'll want a tally as soon as I arrive."

"Aye, milord." And Much scurried away.

"If I could have done this alone, I would have," Marion started, paused as Gamelyn reached out to touch her cheek.

"I know. But you're right, this time you do need me."

She looked him over as if for the first time, grinning. "I'd suggest dressing." Blowing a kiss to Robyn, she whirled on one heel and out of view, her bare feet tapping across the hall to her chambers with a breathless call for the maidservant.

"Bloody Otho has one more to answer for," Gamelyn growled, with a slam of the door.

And, well, but Robyn was fair lost at this point. "Otho? Your brother Otho?"

"The same." To Robyn's dismay, Gamelyn didn't come back to the bed, but stalked over to the clothes press.

"Sod that. Your bloody brother can bloody well rest his heels in the gatehouse or sommat. Wait milord's pleasure—and I mean that, because I mean to bend you over and send you his way all satisfied and smelling of—"

"It's not that simple." Gamelyn snatched a clean pair of braies from a wicker basket next to the press and shook them out. Stepping into them, he seemed a bit off in the left, and that was when Robyn glimpsed several long scars, and muscles still wasted, before Gamelyn yanked up the braies and began tying them. All the while, that lovely, freckled knob tried an impatient butt at the linen, just as indignant by virtue of interruption as Robyn himself. "Marion's right. I have to be there."

Robyn counted ten—no, five—then growled "*Why?*"

Gamelyn told him. All the while he kept dressing: pulling on dark hose and securing them; snatching up the tunic he'd flung over the footboard merely to grimace and toss it aside; heaving the lid of the press to shake out another overtunic—and that sumptuous, all fine weave and embroidery, no question 'twere fit for a lord.

In fact, Gamelyn looked no less than that as he finished telling Robyn about Otho's plot, all the while strapping on his sword belts, shrugging into a thick, burgundy cloak and velveted cowl, and layering a gold chain of office over that. A quick comb of wet fingers through his lovely copper hair and beard completed it.

Robyn had already started to pull on his own garb. He wanted to see that gormless sodding git of a brother fetch what was coming to him; aye, that he did.

Morning dawned stubbornly grey and heavy and *cold*, as if in denial of the slats of sun and clear sky peeking over the horizon. Fitful breezes carried, every now and again, a waft of drizzle. It merely emphasized the approach of winter, slow and inexorable as the armed retinue approaching the curved entry arch of Blyth's gatehouse.

But nay, 'twere Tickhill now, names changing as surely as nobles' garments, and if the approaching soldiers weren't a proper progress: rich cloaks, mail oiled and gleaming, banners a-fly. Tickhill's banner, with Hallamshire's behind . . . and, aye, several Templars bringing up the rear, a piebald contrast to the colourful foreground. 'Twere as if the castle's dye vats had upended in the night, to spill out the massive main bailey and across the approach, undiluted by sodden grass or misted air.

Robyn reached for the longbow that John had kept for him, well-oiled and used just enough to keep it supple—and decided he'd step it after all. He didn't like the look of that cadre. Armed to the teeth, they were, and neither one of Gamelyn's brothers had proven anything like to reasonable.

Lurking the wall walk beside him, avoiding the fitful gusts of wind behind a merlon hung with several sodden banners, John plainly agreed. He'd already stepped his own bow.

Well, they did occupy a prime place to take out a few of the bastards: atop the gatehouse with a clear shot to where the gates had been lowered. All his own, beside him again, longbows to hand and ready for anything: John on his left, Gilbert to his right hand . . . even David, who'd never looked back upon leaving an outlaw's life behind, had plainly kept in practise.

Robyn spared a mournful thought for Will and Arthur, wondering where they were and hoping they were content. It flitted away as Marion walked onto the bridge, Much, Siham, and Siham's lover at her heels . . . and faith, but did his sister have to walk out there so bold-like? Robyn quickly finished stepping his bow, snatched up a palmful of arrows—two in his hair, two to hand—and heard the creak of Gilbert's bow as he sighted down a clothyard shaft, feeling the wind.

But Sweet Lady, Marion held her veiled head as proud as any noble with their fancy harness and cloaks and flags. Put them to proper shame, she did, dressed in a velvet cloak that nigh matched the cinnabar braid peeking from beneath a mantle of rabbit's fur; and beneath that a full gown the colour of spring leaves, shimmering at neck and sleeves with cerulean embroidery.

Gamelyn, wearing his own garb and status with heady, insouciant ease, waited beneath them in the shadows of the gatehouse. No patch to him did he yearn to make a proper entrance, considering. But then, Robyn amended with a smirk, his poncy ginger paramour had never shrugged off a chance for drama.

And while Gamelyn's appearance was surely a thing worth

watching—and maybe stripping down later for a bit of fun—it more rubbed raw against several facts.

These people were his: kith and kind, and none of Robyn's.

Robyn chuckled against the rue. Gilbert slid a glance his way, emotive as any caress. Robyn reached out and tugged at one of the locks that always wanted to avoid what careful coif Gilbert demanded. "Bloody damn, but the best place to deal with *this* lot were in our forest, aye? Set 'em down to a simple meal, shake 'em down, and turn 'em loose in nowt but their skin."

A tiny smile touching his mouth, John leaned his head against Robyn's shoulder, the smile chasing away. *Better that, than be just one more of the wolfsheads milord of Tickhill claimed and tamed!*

The virulence of the signing surprised Robyn. His lips began to move, albeit unsure what to answer, or how.

Instead, all the air left him. Ears pounding, heart quickening, eyes clouding . . . all of it no mere response but attack. His heart leapt in his chest—*one-and, two-and, three-and*—and the rhythm took him, flung him from thisnow and into . . .

The stones of the wall walk will shift and roil beneath him, fade from bright washed-white and ochre and green to an ancient, crumbling, weather-beaten grey. Past him, the crowded bailey will shimmer, desert itself, buildings will melt and moulder to rubble, brambles will twist and tangle across well-groomed sward whilst the chill, wet wind groans . . . not through a proud bastion, but scattered stones, eroding an octagonal keep until only a few, crumbling walls and the mound remain . . .

None of it matters. None of it stays. None of it will do. . . any. . . good . . .

Helplessness takes him, a great wave to pull his legs from under him, towing him into the deeps before . . .

No more. No. . . More. . .

Before he forces his mind black, and blank.

The wave broke, threw him back into thisnow. Robyn found himself flung a-sweat upon the wet wall of the walk, hands skating, white-tight, over slick stone. His companions had gathered close, David and Gilbert bent over him, John tugging fierce at Robyn's tunic and stuttering "I'm s-sorry, I didn't m-mean—"

"It weren't you, love." It creaked from between Robyn's lips like an off-true wheel, a voice somehow his . . . and somehow not. Robyn gave it up, instead concentrated on unknotting his limbs. Mostly succeeded, with a totter and flail. One hand gained purchase on a bit of stone painted proud white and red and ochre—not crumbling, not grey—and he clutched tight, pulled himself upright. "You didn't do it. I . . . just don't think I'm all . . . *here,* yet."

Gilbert and John steadied Robyn, held to him until his limbs bided steady enough. A gust of wet smacked his cheeks; Robyn closed his eyes, held his face to it, grateful.

David's sudden hiss of warning cleared Robyn's head. He fastened bleary eyes upon the cadre stopping just that much too close to the lowered gate. Twenty of them, in Hallamshire's colours—or what had been that lord's colours when Robyn had known them—all stopping just out of reach of crossbows, and clearly not thinking that Sherwood's finest might be waiting with a brace of longbows.

Horses shifting and stamping, a quick back-and-forth between the three frontmost riders; the sounds were carried by the stiff breeze and up the walls—sometimes fitful, here and there. Then a man who could only be milord Otho nudged his horse forward. Another man followed, bearing the banner of Tickhill. And if that weren't insult enough, Otho had obviously prospered, dressed all fine and riding a finer palfrey, but he was greyed at the edges, gone to fat like any nobleman who'd had his way fair paved for him.

Gamelyn would take him down in two strokes and use him to wipe horseshit from the bridge.

Just behind milord and to his left rode a sullen, tow-haired lad of about thirteen—Robyn wondered, suddenly, if 'twere milord's son. However downcast, the boy had Gamelyn's eyes and chin. On milord's other side, a broad-shouldered guard captain reined to a halt.

The wind gave one last, fitful cough, then died.

Robyn smiled. All the better for a clear shot.

While milord Otho clearly expected Marion and her own small cadre to just let him mount the bridge and saunter through the gate, she had other ideas, though they made Robyn reach for his bow and nock an arrow. Marion stepped in front of the horse, and Much put a hand to the bridle.

"What can I do for you, my lord?" Her voice echoed against the wall, clear and reasonable.

"Let loose of my lord's horse, you!" This from the soldier just behind milord Otho.

David paced down the walk, looking for a better vantage. John's lip curled. Gilbert tsked, and pushed into his bow.

"Gamelyn said we were to wait," Robyn counselled, though he gave an eager sort-of push at his own.

"Oh, aye."

So where was Gamelyn? There was making an entrance, and there was taking too much for granted.

"Things have changed, milord," Marion was saying. "I'm afraid you'll find no welcome here."

Milord Otho rolled his eyes in a fashion that made it plain who his younger brother was.

And where *was* his younger brother?

The guard captain, meanwhile, had been eyeing the walls. He

clearly saw the men at readiness, and it was just as clearly something he didn't care for. He nudged his horse closer to Otho, muttered something. As one, they set their gazes upon Marion. The young lad had also started up a protest at his father, leaning forward in the saddle. Milord spun and growled at him to shut his face.

Much was keeping one eye on them and one back towards the gate. Siham and her lover were looking less than sanguine.

Where. The bloody fuck. Was Gamelyn?

Pulling up his hood, Robyn moved into position between the merlons, bending his longbow and taking aim. He could see for miles—and they could see him, plain, should they look up. It was his intention that they should. So he hollered down:

"If any of you so much as breathe wrong at milady of Tickhill? I'll propel you backwards off those fine palfreys with an arrow through your wishbone. Before you can spit, mind."

They looked up, then—milord Otho as well as all his men. Robyn grinned, knowing it was a fearsome sight:

His archers had followed his lead without words, each at a gap atop the gatehouse wall, each wielding a longbow and sighting every man in the front line.

Marion glanced up—hastily, to be sure, she wasn't about to take her gaze from Otho and his captains. Neither did she back a single step. But humour trickled into her voice. "I'd advise you, milord, to stand down immediately. Pray listen to what I have to say."

"There is nothing to say!" Otho's veneer of calm showed damage; nevertheless, he began to slowly back his horse down the bridge, attention flitting to all points. "Nothing you *can* say, woman."

"You really shouldn't call her that, in that tone of voice," Siham's lover drawled.

Robyn smirked.

Otho was not amused. "My lady, you are ordered, as a widow in gift of the King, to admit me, and—"

"Well, brother, that's your first mistake." The voice carried outward, reverberating, from the tunnel. "I usually only allow one, mayhap two, more. I pray that will be unnecessary."

"Bloody damn!" Robyn growled. "But if milord the sodding poncy git of Tickhill hasn't finally decided to make his entrance!"

A smattering of chuckles rippled across Robyn's nearest and dearest as Gamelyn strode across the bridge and into view below. Strangely minus his cloak, his mantle and chain of office still seemed intact, if mayhap askew.

Milord Otho was so gobsmacked that he nigh tottered off his horse.

Marion turned to him, and Robyn saw her mouth *You're late. Again.* There was a story to be had from that, to be sure, and she looked none too happy at his shrug.

"G . . . G . . . *Gamelyn*?" Otho blurted, leaning against his mount's neck. "You . . . You're . . . alive?"

"Again." Gamelyn responded with a tilt of head. "I have, over the years, proven somewhat hard to kill. I'm sorry to disappoint you."

A surfeit of emotions played across Otho's broad face—and they were honest, all of them: doubt, anger, regret—and relief. The last one surprised Robyn.

Otho dismounted and strode towards Gamelyn. All the bows creaked, ready; he halted after several steps and held out a hand. It shook. "I'm truly glad to see you, brother. I never wished you dead, never—though I did believe you were, else—"

"Else you'd never have listened to Hallamshire, and tried to use me to take back Tickhill?" Marion growled.

"It was a reasonable option!—and one that you refused past all sense, to what . . . " Otho trailed away, undoubtedly realising that he wasn't in the best of positions to argue his case.

"Aye, let's talk reason, shall we?" Gamelyn crossed his arms.

And powerful arms those were, too. Robyn kept his arrow close, but gave a slight lean against the merlon, watching quite happily.

John snorted at him, brown eyes dancing.

"But of course," Otho agreed—a bit hastily. "I have only ever wanted to be reasonable, brother. I shall immediately send word to the King, as his writ has been—"

"Made unlawful, aye. In the eyes of not only King but Holy Church, as *my wife*"—stated firm—"is not a widow. The only word you need direct to the King is an apology for wasting his time, as I've already sent my own missive to our liege, written during my wait in Normandy. The Templars delivered it to him, as I'd a ship to catch. I've no doubts they'll fetch his receipt to me in good time."

A good reminder, that he had the Templars on his side . . . wait. Gamelyn was still involved with the Templars?

"As it stands, it's well I did make haste, as you clearly came ready to lay siege to my walls." Gamelyn gestured upward to those walls. "You seem to forget that I have powerful allies, high and low."

This time Otho peered upward at Robyn in particular, frowning. Thought about recognising him for a spare breath, then shook his head and decided it was quite impossible.

Instead, he protested, "There's no need to be unpleasant, brother! I thought you were dead. Tell me you'd not do the same in my place."

"Try to steal your wife and family and home? I think not, brother. I've only ever reached for what was rightfully within my grasp." Gamelyn's voice was soft, level. Deadly. "I was taught from a young age that to do otherwise meant risking more than I had to give."

The young lad was looking even more surly, though it hardly seemed possible. And worse, the cadre of guardsmen was getting anxious. Robyn hissed for everyone to keep a close eye on them.

"Gamelyn, you don't—"

"Nay, Otho, I think it's you who doesn't understand. You owe me satisfaction. You have tried to take what matters to me. Even my children."

"What?"

"You know what I mean."

Otho plainly did, for he shot a quick, angry look at Marion, but remained silent.

"Do you hear me, all of you?" Gamelyn paced towards the end of the bridge, speaking now to Hallamshire's men. "This man has wronged me. I demand satisfaction. He will give it to me"—he whirled back on Otho—"through fealty, or battle."

Aye, and *that* set a cat 'mongst the pigeons. Best to do so, as well, because if that twenty-odd decided after all to charge, there could be casualties. Gamelyn needed to piss out his territory, and do it right sharp.

It only helped that the difference between the brothers—one hard and lean from months of desert survival, the other soft and unfit and unlikely to have picked up a sword with intent in months—was painfully obvious.

Nevertheless, Robyn hoped Otho would choose combat. He rather suspected Gamelyn did, too.

The Hallamshire captain tilted his head and made one step of retreat. Only one, but its message, too, was obvious. The guardsmen settled.

The lad, however, did not. "Uncle!"

Marion went over to the lad, spoke to him in a soft voice.

"There's no . . . I don't . . . I . . . " Otho was stammering like his priest had caught him *en flagrante* with four whores of various gender.

Gamelyn strode closer. "Make. Your. Decision."

To Robyn's unsurprise—and disappointment—Otho went onto his knees, fumbling at his sword belt. It seemed to take him entirely too long to unsheathe the thing, but once he did he held it out, flat upon shaking hands. "I am a widower, with children to think of—"

"Should've thought of his children before he dragged our young Ian 'crost county and made him witness this," David growled.

"—so I have no choice but to ask for mercy, and give due fealty."

Starting to take the sword, Gamelyn hesitated, gesturing at Marion. She was still over with the lad—Ian—and she frowned. As Gamelyn repeated the gesture, she ambled over, albeit cautious.

Gamelyn stepped back and said, soft and smooth as silk—if silk could poison, that was—"You will give it to my lady, and through her, to me."

Otho flushed nigh scarlet, but tightened his jaw and handed the sword to Marion. She took it, then handed it to Gamelyn.

Who then stabbed the blade point-down into the earth between Otho's knees. To do him credit, the man didn't flinch, but he did angle back as Gamelyn leaned closer, murmured something for Otho's ears alone.

A tight nod: understanding. Only then did Gamelyn back away and tilt his voice to reach everyone. "It is agreed, then, before witnesses. There's only one more thing to settle before you leave my fields."

Otho was frowning as he rose—slowly, clearly thinking *What now?* Robyn wasn't sure, himself.

"You have my foster son in your entourage. His fosterage was an agreement between our households and approved by King John. I would suggest he be allowed to stay here, along with his younger brother and sister, as well."

And that brightened up the lad Ian, had him hiding a sudden smile against one shoulder.

"Do you not trust me, brother?" Otho looked honestly affronted. "I gave you my sword in all honour!"

"I merely make the offer, brother, since you are a widower. Children need a woman's guidance. It's about giving my nephews and niece a proper place in our family's home. It's not about *you*."

John snorted again—this one soft, so it didn't carry.

"More like about not trusting Hallamshire," Gilbert muttered. "If Otho had your inclinations, O fearless leader, he'd be on his knees for that man every chance he got."

"Hey!" Robyn protested, "I fetch my share! Not that I don't mind a stint on me knees from time to time, back or forth."

Gilbert started laughing and hugged Robyn to him. "Sweet Lady, old son, but have I missed you!"

It took very little time, actually, to finish things up. Though Marion's nerves were taking far longer to settle than she'd like, to be sure. Not that she hadn't managed just fine on her own, but no question that things had come to a fair head this time around.

Arm in arm with her brother and Gamelyn, all their people clutched close, Marion let them lead her back across the bailey to the keep. Her thoughts just kept whirling, wouldn't stop. Odd, now that she was able to shift some worries onto other shoulders, how she suddenly seemed to actually feel the danger, heart racing and breath coming short as if she'd run herself to exhaustion.

Maybe she had, in a very real sense.

But things *were* settled, at least for now. Otho had the choice:

stewardship at one of Gamelyn's northern holdings, or stay with Hallamshire. Marion hoped he'd go north, out of any influence from de Furnival, and at a small holding he couldn't damage too much. But no matter that, Ian would be coming within the week, bringing Nicolas and Edyth to stay.

"I made the mistake of leaning against the wheel cog for the gate mechanism." Gamelyn was saying—and aye, but he did look somewhat abashed. "My cloak got caught."

Another round of laughter. Marion shook her head and brandished a fist at him. He caught it, kissed it.

"One of these days, my lord, you'll not arrive in time."

"Nay, Maid of my heart and Mother of our children. I'll always arrive in time. It's what a Knight does, aye?"

"You still haven't said what you told the daft sod!" Gilbert was waggling his own finger Gamelyn-ward.

"I told him, did he once again treat my wife as no more than a commodity, it would be the last time. That I'd hunt him down and cut his lying throat."

As conversation stoppers went, it was a class one. But the silence wasn't disapproval, nay. More like respect.

"I'm famished," Robyn said. "Any chance of a meal in this sodding great castle?"

- XXXI -

"An earl is coming *here* t' stay? Next you'll be telling me Count John has sat at your fire and toasted bread over it wit' the wee ones!"

Gamelyn didn't answer Robyn, lost in thought as he read the parchment Marion had handed him—not just once, but several times in quick succession. He handed it back, eyeing her. "Can we be ready?"

She nodded. "Of course."

The young messenger awaiting her smiled in relief. Mayhap he'd been set to sixes by not only the Lady of Tickhill in residence, but the lord. He'd come in just as they'd sat to board, muddy from the road—and ravenous, from the eager way he watched Marion cross to the sideboard and fill a heaping platter of victuals for him, as well as a goodly pot of their best ale.

Even hunger couldn't stay his surreptitious glances towards the man who'd spoken, however.

The rumours had already begun—and looked likely to continue, from the lad's stunned expression.

Marion smiled, gestured him towards the door and thought, *Shut it, Robyn, 'til I see him away.*

Robyn took a drink of ale.

His namesake, of course, hadn't so much as sensed the undercurrents. "He's King John, not Count John," Robbie informed his uncle around a copious mouthful of bread. "Hey, that's a fancy necklet, is it really yours? Or did you steal it off some churchman?" Peering at the gold torc about Robyn's neck, Robbie scooted closer.

This, naturally, put a distinct light of panic into Robyn's eyes, as well as a sly curve to Gamelyn's lip. Marion knew her own mouth was twitching as she escorted the messenger, platter in hand, to the door of the solar. David waited there and, with a meaningful twist of eyebrows, guided the young man back towards the stair. He'd see to the messenger's remaining comforts, including a berth, did he need one.

"Don't you know the difference, Uncle? I mean—!" Robbie yipped as Aderyn flipped a smack at the back of his head. He turned to her with an offended huff, rubbing at his ginger-gold mop.

Which stuck out at all angles despite comb and water. Marion sighed.

From his place beside Gamelyn, Much was smirking at her, eyes dancing as he dressed his fish with vinegar. Beside him, Siham and Tafsut were exchanging giggles mixed with a smattering of Arabic and English commentary.

"Well," Gamelyn ventured, reaching for another piece of bread, "I'm afraid Robbie's right—"

The boy preened and stuck out his tongue at Aderyn.

"—even if his mouth is unhinged. What's the first rule around people you don't know, boy?"

"Awww . . ."

"Answer your da." With a flick of skirts, Marion settled back onto her bench.

"Best take care, you two," Robyn muttered. "You're behaving proper parents."

"Fancy that," Gamelyn aped right back.

Oblivious, Robbie ventured, "But Uncle Otho says we en't got a da—OW! Eri, that hurt! It's true, even Auntie Aelwyn once said—" He gulped it back as Aderyn, black eyes glinting, merely threatened a third smack.

"Your Uncle Otho was being an arsehole," Robyn told the boy, shifting sideways—and away. "Y' do know that, right?"

"And I did say," Aelwyn put in from her end of the table, "that no man can claim to've sired a Beltane-got bairn. It don't mean you en't any da."

"Aye, carrot-head," Tom interrupted, "And you've to mind your da, 'cause—Hoy!" This as Tibba delivered a rebuke like to Aderyn's.

Meanwhile, little Robbie flushed until his freckles nigh vanished, lips pressed tight.

Aelwyn threw an apologetic glance Marion's way. Marion hid a smirk behind her hand and persisted, "Robbie. Answer your da."

Heard, as strong as if Robyn had said it, *Bloody damn, sister, but you sound like our mam!*

And bloody damn, but my son sounds altogether like you, brother.

"When outsiders are about, keep your tongue behind your teeth and your mouth shut." To this recitation Robbie added a pout as seasoning, then returned to dragging his bread through the swirl of honey Marion had given him.

Mayhap ruthless, seating Robyn and his precocious nephew together with a shared platter, but then Robbie had begged for the chance. The messy allocation of honey couldn't be helped.

Nay, if Marion were truly ruthless, she'd have settled her brother next to wee, warbling Marjory, who'd pulled herself upright against the board to reach for more bread, singing all the while, her honey-smeared cheeks giving "messy" an entirely new meaning.

Robyn flicked a jaundiced eye over Robbie's leavings, then merely reached over and nicked honey from Gamelyn's platter. "At this board, I'd take proper care on calling anyone out on being ginger-haired, lad," he advised, waving his bread at young Tom while fetching a sideways smirk to his sister and his lover.

Tom flushed and paid sudden attention to drinking his ale. At the far end Gilbert let out a hearty laugh, Aelwyn joining in. Siham grinned besides a likewise grinning Tafsut. John smirked, nudging Robyn. Marion chuckled, as much retort as that my, but it was proper entertaining to watch Gamelyn turn all goo and porridge in the wake of Robyn's theft and smirk. More even than the shenanigans that signified family mealtime at Tickhill . . . and for the first in far too long, *everyone* had gathered to break their fast about the huge board.

David returned soon enough, as well, and Marion rose from the table. Her hearth, after all, and a matter of pride to see to her people. Aelwyn started to help; Marion shook her head with a smile and refilled her brother's plate. She couldn't help a stroke of his black curls and a quick alight of palm against his shoulder. Needing the touch, the reminder: he sat here, with them.

Gamelyn's green eyes lingered upon her, satisfied and perceptive.

"That lad's proper respectful for a king's messenger. Gave all the auld signs!" David marvelled, reseating himself beside Aelwyn with a quick peck to her cheek. "He's more messages to take on up North, so he regrets he cannot enjoy your invitation to an overnight stay, and tenders his utmost respects to Tickhill's lord and lady. His horse was spent, so I offered one of our swiftest rounceys. I 'spect"—David reached for the cream jar—"the lad's not likely to miss a tournament. He'll bring the horse back within the se'nnight."

"A *tournament?*" Tibba squealed, and it set off all the children into excited jabber.

"Can I down the flag for the mêlée?"

"Can I be squire?"

"Can we—"

"If none of you shut it, how can we make any decision?" Aelwyn interrupted.

Voices lowered, but the amount of whispering didn't abate. Gestures, too. Little wankers, they were keen to use Aderyn's speech when it was convenient. Marion hid a smirk behind her hand.

"A fortnight's notice." Gamelyn had retrieved the parchment, musing. Its wax signatory dragged, heavy, over the board. "And Huntingdon's already on his way. A couple of days, mayhap, before any arrivals?"

"Likely," Much agreed.

"It doesn't give us much time to be ready. A tournament!" Gamelyn rolled then tossed the missive in David's direction; the latter deftly snatched it midair and opened it, mouth tilted thoughtful as he read.

"Aye, well, we do have the only licensed ground in the North. I suspect they're looking for more recruits for Normandy." Marion regained her seat in time to rescue the honey pot from Marjory's predations; to circumvent a resultant toddler storm, she offered another trail of sweet across bread. "And, dear friend, you've forgotten the way things work. A fortnight is luxury compared to what King John would give us to prepare."

"King John would . . . give you?" Robyn nearly coughed ale up his nose.

"Aye," Much drawled, "Though the King, he'd likely travel sixty miles in a day. A-horse, no hard chore, but how he manages it with a train of wagons and whatnot?" A shrug and wry grin at Marion.

"They follow, ever dutiful," Gilbert pronounced. "I'm glad to be a forester."

"Last time we'd barely a day to prepare for the Royal Progress." Much reached for the ale pitcher. "That lit a proper fire t' soldier's hall, right enough."

"And my kitchens—wup! No chance, lass." Aelwyn rescued her ale cup from Marjory.

Robyn resembled a crofter lad witnessing a dart-prick tournament for the first time: eyes back and fore, back and fore. "You mean the man's come before, then?" Just as clearly, her brother was appalled. "Stayed here beneath your roof? Ate and drank at your hearth?"

Gilbert also seemed dismayed, more with a *My word, haven't you told him?* glint in his eyes. John's expression showed his own distaste for the subject; he wouldn't have elaborated upon this in particular. But it remained how there bided too many things to fill in for Robyn, with some shrugged away or skirted around for later by necessity.

Or preference, Marion had to admit.

Aderyn, on the other hand, gestured eagerly, and Tibba chimed in, "It was so exciting, Uncle! All those horses, all the wagons, and all the people, coming *here* to pay court!"

Hardly exciting, seeing to all those hangers-on, but Marion had no wish to dash the light shining in her girls' faces.

"The King travels as he pleases, and where." Gamelyn's speech drew tight even as his eyes stayed soft. In recall of how long Robyn had been gone, and regret, and clearly dreading an inevitable confrontation. "And whilst Marion has certainly had to accommodate those visits more than I—"

"He stayed here whilst you were away t' desert, then? With Marion unprotected?"

"She weren't unprotected." Much's reply tinged itself with affront.

And it would be all too easy to maintain that affront; instead Marion smiled at her brother and leaned forward, elbows on the table. "I'm pretty fair with a longbow, aye?"

"They still tell the story hereabouts," Robbie put in, anxious to dispel the tension, "of how Mam held off a whole army at our gates with nobbut her longbow!"

"Is that so?" Robyn eyed his namesake with a twist of brow. "Wellaway, I en't surprised at that. Your mam allus were a proper shot." He added an apologetic glance, not only to Marion but Much. All the while, he avoided Gamelyn's gaze.

All the while, Gamelyn tried to catch it. "Tickhill is a royal castle, Robyn, held in our family by grant and consent of the King. We don't exactly have the liberty of refusal."

"It's only ever . . . I never thought to see the day come where you'd offer hearth rights t' same bum-boil as nearly saw both of you strung up in Nottingham and burnt!"

This caught the children's attention.

"Hanged, Da?" Robbie burst out. "You and Mam were almost hanged?"

Aderyn's face echoed the outrage her fingers expressed.

"Aunt Marion," Tibba put in, "was it when—"

"I'll tell you later," Marion overrode all of it. "I promise, aye?"

But she heard Gamelyn's low, snapped-out words. "He isn't coming now, he's in Normandy, and we don't have to worry about this for some time, do we?"

"But it en't just him, is it? Now you've some earl coming—"

"If you find it that hard to understand, then mayhap you should make yourself scarce for it! Go hunting with Gilbert and John!"

Once, Robyn would have risen to the challenge willingly, all bluster and blow as the argument rose, was hashed over then done with. Instead his eyes flickered to the torchlit sconces—nay, the walls—but all clouded-strange, as if they were . . . turning inward, Marion could think of no other way to describe it. Lips vibrating with an unheard whisper, his fingers twitched against the board, rhythmic and tiny.

"Mayhap," he murmured, "I will."

John glared daggers at Gamelyn. The latter's expression seemed torn; iron resolve sparking to culpability's flint.

"Take me, Uncle?" Robbie tried to scoot closer and somehow couldn't; closer examination revealed Aderyn's hand clutching his tunic. He wriggled, glowered, then furthered, "I en't gone hunting yet. 'Tis time I learned!"

"Not yet, my lad," Marion interposed. "Give it a while yet. You're nobbut five."

"Aw, Mam, I'll be six soon eno—"

Robyn, with a muttered apology, rose from the board and retreated from the solar. John followed, quick as that.

Gamelyn's body angled forward, clearly desiring likewise. Instead, face smoothing, he took out his ire upon an unfortunate cut of meat.

"Nowt to worry," Aelwyn was telling the youngsters. "If the Horned One speaks, Robyn must listen, aye?" Which set Tom and Robbie into another of their back-and-forths, only this time over did *they* hear the Horned Lord, could they leave the table so abruptly and not fetch trouble for it.

The rest of the meal's discussion concerned the upcoming visitors. All the while, Marion's thoughts followed Robyn, and she knew Gamelyn's tracked the same.

ᛒ

John caught Robyn just as he cleared the ditch bridge edging the motte, grasping his sleeve to halt him. Likely John had paused just long enough for another glare Gamelyn-ward. Silence, of course, being typical for John, with it all over the *types* of silence, loud as any shouting.

Nowt you can do, love, go back now, leave me be, Robyn gestured.

John didn't obey right away, peering at him so direct as to flense Robyn's already-raw senses. Realising the latter soon enough, John flushed like a young lad caught skiving. Leaning his head against Robyn's shoulder, after several breaths he straightened and turned away.

Heading for the stables, *not* the motte.

Ears pounding, Robyn watched him go. Tempting, to follow after, but even a beloved one's company seemed overmuch when . . . when this . . . whatever-it-was happened.

You will find the outerworlds. . . changed.

Memory, this, with the Priestess's voice curling about him as if she were there, beside him. Though 'tweren't Rite or Rade, and if not impossible, unlikely.

You have lived outside it; when you return to it, likely you will find it. . . unforgiving.

The gwyllion lying at his throat twitched, ever so slight, then let out a long sigh and slept on.

Robyn strode out across the sward. Thankfully the wide bailey lay peaceful-quiet, the gates just flung open—and his relief at that surely seemed overwrought.

It was rather early for visitors, though far from deserted. Tickhill's residents had begun their own tasks, and thankfully, he was invisible amidst them. An elder man picked scattered dung into a cart, and several women knelt in the kitchen gardens, their bairns playing in the rich earth. The cloth dyers along the nor'east wall were setting up the day's operations, the mix of salts and stale drifting on the breeze. A lad greeted Robyn cheerfully as he sauntered past, leading a trio of sumpters with picket ropes hanging from arms and belt.

Plenty to graze in the bailey, at that; patches of green flourished upon the edges of thoroughfare and outbuildings. The reassuring sight didn't match the sudden, slow-heavy cloud of sorrow enveloping Robyn, slowing his steps until he realised: not his own. This emanated from a squat, cross-shaped building west of the keep.

Aye, he remembered this chapel, oozing more purgatory than any paradise. Its bell began to ring, tolling the Hours.

The little gwyllion might have indeed been copper and gilt about his throat, gone cold and still. Conversely, the sound scraped against his own already-raw senses, vibrating in his chest, strangling breath, setting his heart leaping and stuttering as if some gauntleted hand squeezed it.

Being careful of the iron and the bells, sweet Hob!

Drawing a blessing-breath by sheer will alone—and it felt as if his lungs were filled with mortar—Robyn loosed it, watched it drift across the bailey. The grass and earth beneath his toes supported him, whilst the sky pressed down and over the chapel with a tiny roll of what could have been thunder. Responding. Reminding him that a power remained, one greater than any building could hope for.

His own sudden weakness drained itself away. Nevertheless, Robyn put as much distance between himself and the chapel as he could.

Instead he skirted the riding area, taking in more welcome odours: hay, grain, chaff, manure. In the sandy ride, a young man— nay, a young lass, dressed in leathers and loose tunic—put what was obviously one of milord's warhorses through his paces. The grey reminded him of Gamelyn's first warhorse—old Diamant— and gleamed with good health. Willing to his rider, he moved nimble as any dancer, his muscular back and haunches well up to the requested tasks.

Would the guards at the bloody gatehouse even know him, consent to let him out? Robyn considered turning about and making a try at the postern gate; more his style, at that. But this time there mightn't be a punt at hand to take him across a stinking shithole of a moat, and he wasn't rescuing a queen from gaol and to his forest.

Bloody damn, but he'd best get used to going in the main gate, at that.

He didn't try for silence as he sauntered past the wall guards and into the gatehouse tunnel, though the habit of such lay too strong. The guards alerted, of course, but upon recognising him gave a polite tip of their helmets. More, the stouter of the two standing at the entry gave the sign—*Bendith y mamau*—whilst the other smiled and offered, "A lovely morn for a wander, lord Robyn. It'll rain tonight, I reckon, but nowt serious."

Lord Robyn from one of his own, in his forest, didn't sound as odd as a mailed soldier saying same, no matter his pleasant, familiar manner of speech.

"Nowt serious since Hallows," the other offered, also recognising him with a tip of his helmeted head—and those had changed as well while Robyn had been gone, though he wasn't sure exactly how. "'Twere a chancy thing, that storm."

The other nodded and forked an evil eye towards the south, all the while eyeing Robyn with a mix of awe and wonder.

A quirk trying his lip, Robyn exited the flung-open gates, the bridge giving a soft creak that echoed into the moat. And while part of him hoped Gamelyn would come after, most of his heart just wanted to go, put these stone walls behind him, and vanish into his forest.

A conundrum, when he'd spent so much time and effort just to *get back.*

So 'twere in truth an odd and hesitant uncertainty that bade him go no farther, lean on the lower bridge and watch the sun cozen the bare tips of the eastern grove, licking sideways across the fens to light them ruddy as Gamelyn's hair.

A lovely morn, indeed. Merciful, this, almost timeless . . . or at least a time that didn't gather in his throat and rate his heartbeat. The Wheel had no end or beginning; tallied nothing akin to a conqueror-people's foolish, linear notice. The Wheel shrugged such things off and went its own fancy: going to come back 'round again, go and come back 'round, a never-ending spiral.

His tunic tugged sideways, and he started, one hand dropping to his knife. He forced it to relax as he saw who stood beside him, one hand upraised for another tug. Faith, but the wee lass had crept up on him silent as a hunting ferret.

And bloody hell. Tess was gone, too.

Robyn gave Aderyn a wary eye. The lass stood unafraid beside him, her dark-dark gaze serious. Of course, she and Tibba made the eldest of the Tickhill brood, not like the others—and being around *those* akin to walking a jongleur's tightrope, with the wee bairns the worst! Like little Marjory. Sweet as stolen honey, aye, but bairns were so *small,* their necks fragile as wilting flowers; no question but he'd drop one if ever he held it. And the toddling ones moved so damned *fast,* grabbing with hands that surely wouldn't let go once they had you, and just like the swaddling bairns, they always went for his *hair.*

Robyn slid a quick peek at the guards. They might be worried after Aderyn, following after an ex-outlaw, after all. But nay, his own imagination was working too hard. Their expressions held no judgement, only observation. After all, she'd an inclination for sneaking, this one. More, her sneaking out had been Robyn's deliverance—and he knew it, even if they didn't.

Mayhap it was why she didn't seem a child to him—one to be avoided if at all possible.

Da isn't angry with you, she signed. *You know that, aye?*

Robyn had to smile, squatted down to answer in kind. *Lass, you're not to worry ower that. Your da and I've spent more'n a few days brassed off wit' each other. We did it long before you were born, and no doubt we'll not leave for the otherworlds wit'out a punch or two.*

The gwyllion burbled at his throat. He stroked it, feeling its heartbeat quicken against his fingers. Aderyn's eyes followed the motion and, with gentle, podgy fingers, she reached out to touch the gwyllion's sleek sides. Moreover, it let her, purring not unlike a cat, soft pleasure undulating.

Robyn frowned. "You see it. You don't see a torc."

A what? We've gwyllion *all within the castle, and I see them all. . .* Her fingers stuttering, Aderyn mimicked his frown. Realising, mayhap, that this one existed more concealed than most. *It came with you, from there, didn't it?*

Robyn nodded.

One last pat, then the lass turned her attention out over the moat. *You're going to go back to the forest, aren't you?*

Robyn blinked.

If not today, then another. You have to go, aye, because He needs you as much as Da and Mam. The Horned Lord, I mean. Da only holds him for the Rites, like, but now you've returned. . .

How old are you again? The words murmured behind his teeth, but he was glad he'd not loosed them, voice or sign. Instead he wanted to slap himself. Now who sounded like someone's mam?

Instead, he gave the answer she deserved. *The Horned Lord is. . . here.* Robyn gestured out over the landscape, then scooped it to his chest. *Whether I'm in the forest or in this castle.*

Her eyes slid sideways towards him, puzzled. *Always? But he wasn't. . . before.*

And I wasn't. . . here before. If you follow me.

The frown twisted a bit; she didn't, quite, though game for the try.

Do you remember what you Saw? Robyn furthered. *In the Mere? A lot of things couldn't fetch themselves, in or out, where I was. Caught, just like me, in. . . thisnow.*

But you were. . . caught. . . seven years ago. Not thisnow. That's what Mam said. You were taken the night I was born.

Seven years, whilst he'd bided . . . how long? Even now, he wasn't sure. And proper difficult, to explain, but he'd best give it a go. *You know the Wheel?*

She nodded.

Well, everything is upon it. But 'tis like the Wheel turns. . . slower, out upon its rims. Right? And closer in, at the hub, goes around just that much faster. Allworlds bide, all of 'em on the Wheel, but on different places. Different. . . rhythms. You know rhythm, aye?

A quick nod. Shrewd, this one, gauging what he said most carefully; she was her parents' bairn, to be sure.

Well, the Barrow folk are on the outer edges of the Wheel, like. They're our kin from long ago, only it en't that long to them, because they're living a different, well, rhythm. They're trapped there. More, they lost the Horned Lord when they were trapped.

Aderyn's eyes widened.

Aye, they were stuck there without him. Without the lord of the dance, there's no seed, no sap. No life. No death. And he added, silent—for this bided no fit weight for even a clever child: *It's why I had to help them, and make a bargain I'm not truly sure I understand.*

He rose, giving her black hair a tousle. More silence, as she peered up at him, and the sun sank across the sky.

Cantering hoofbeats resounded against the bailey walls.

Aderyn merely turned to greet them, whilst Robyn leapt like a hare with the urge—both nurture and nature—to duck or flee. Denying both, he laid a protective hand to the child's shoulder. The hoofbeats scattered to a halt, sliding on the mossy cobbles beyond the gatehouse. Several murmurs echoed outward from the tunnel—conversation—then a slower *clop-cla-clop-cla* resumed. A horse emerged from the shadows, and the outer guards' sudden attention told even more of the rider's identity than the coppery, bared head.

"Aderyn?" That head tilted. "What are you doing out here? Your mum's looking for you."

The child nodded, smiling. Sliding another darkling glance at Robyn, somehow both chary and cheerful, the smile held as she lit back the way she'd come.

Gamelyn watched her go. The good humour hinting at the corners of his mouth vanished as he turned to Robyn. A nudge of calf cued the horse forward—the same nimble grey Robyn had seen earlier. Obviously His Lordship had co-opted His horse from His rider for what he'd imagined a lengthy jaunt. More, His Lordship appeared more come into his own than Robyn had ever seen. Whilst Robyn, uncertainty less a thing in thisnow to dare and laugh at than a reality that somehow cut to bone, stood at the gate to a castle he'd never thought to openly enter.

Save, perhaps, by the leave of His poncy ginger Lordship of Tickhill, who stared down his nose at the peasant mucking up his front stoop.

The horse pawed the ground.

"Clearly," said the peasant, "you promised him a proper run."

A blink. A roll of eyes. "Step up, then," said the lord at his poncyest. "Heaven forfend I should disappoint the horse."

Neither Gamelyn nor Robyn should return before afternoon. Not if Robyn had any say about it, leastways. And all to the better, that; a bit of a shout, mayhap a few punches flung and a couple of bridges burnt to ground, then the making up . . . aye. That'd set them both to rights.

More importantly, 'twould fetch them out from underfoot whilst Marion put her demesne in some semblance of order.

She knew, of course, she'd several burning bridges of her own to cross in that direction. Eventually. But for now, all Marion cared about was that her brother was home. Robyn was home, and with them, and with his freedom had come others:

The Lady of All Hallows had changed Her aspect. The Wodewose Maiden inhabited the ancient and hallowed earth below the church stones, companied by two of the Old Ones: the Wyrms of Earth and Water. Forged chains had been loosened enough that the Fae could once again broach the sacred places. There was nothing that they couldn't stand against, together.

So, for now, Marion set to. Shutters and curtains pulled back to let in the fresh air and sunlight. Tapestries hauled down to be taken outside and whacked free of dust. Orders given to the kitchens. Messengers sent to the neighbouring fees and fiefs, with a list of necessary supplies and foodstuffs for the upcoming tournament. A lengthy conversation with Gilbert and his under foresters regarding the explicit permissions for the hunt to supply the rest of their needs, as well a discussion with David as to the expectations of the event itself.

Once that was all accomplished, Marion took a quick walk of the bailey grounds to clear her head--also ensuring the livestock were either out to graze or headed that way. The exception, of course, being that one mule who always slipped her traces and wandered the bailey as she pleased. Old Watch-Ears, the children called her, for indeed the old mare had once brayed warning of an intruder having a mid-night go at the sally port.

The children, of course, had been set to their tasks for the day. And a beloved, staunch figure trailed her: Much, one hand resting upon his sword hilt. He was humming. Happy.

She felt it, too. The sense of wellbeing trickled through the entirety of Tickhill: another danger routed, the Hunt putting the fear of old gods into the surrounding lands and blessing those as believed, the lord returned.

Both of them. Marion had written it only that morning in her Book of Hours:

Waxing of Mabon, 1202
My lords have returned!!

- XXXII -

The grey stallion had a good run.

As did Robyn.

And aye, but a rough bout of sex made one satisfying way of settling a disagreement.

Heart still racing against his breastbone and up behind his ears, Robyn merely bided thankful it came from proper exertion this time, not some damned, overweening Tally.

"You have never played fair," Gamelyn complained against the tree roots. His fingers were still covered with green and mud, tracks laid in the moss, soft as any pillow.

"Aye, milord, I know exactly how to bend that stiff neck of yours," Robyn whispered into hair of copper silk, and almost added, *I were thinking of breaking it, ower this.*

But nay, not yet. There'd been enough shouting ringing the bare branches as 'twere . . . and *ower this.*

"Their like, in our places? Our rites?"

"We'd precedent."

"Fuck me, but I'll give you 'precedent'."

"'Twas Gunnora who reminded us, how once the rites had been open to—"

"And they used it to slaughter most of us!"

"We had to find a way to safeguard everything! It meant there were prices to pay!"

"Aye, but some en't worth the cost!"

"You don't know that! You don't know any of what we've had to do, or why!"

Gamelyn's voice had wavered and cracked, then, betraying a chink in the armour Robyn had despaired of breaching save with longbow and a well-aimed arrow. Or rutting . . . aye, but it did the trick best; one of the few things as *hadn't* changed.

Thank the Lady.

Beneath him, however, that freckled neck and spine were showing the beginnings of more protest. Robyn ran a hand across taut ribs, smoothing down and over one buttock and thigh. Felt Gamelyn's muscles shiver lax once more.

"You don't understand."

Nay, I don't. But neither do you, I'm thinking.

As if he'd heard, Gamelyn shoved upward. Robyn rolled onto his back, a root catching him in the arse end, grinding a yip from him as Gamelyn pinned him there, repeated, "You don't understand, Robyn. I need you to understand."

"Hard to understand owt with a tree root up me bum—"

Gamelyn's mouth ticced in what might have been amusement, or more likely exasperation. He lurched sideways, half-sitting up against the tree, Robyn dragged in his wake. Not that it was a bad place to be, curled and nestled against chest and hip. Just a shift and scoot downwards, kissing that trail of gilt fur, and then see if milord wain't falter . . .

Gamelyn stopped it with a nigh bone-breaking snug of arms.

And aye, the leg was weak from those scratches—a lion, he'd said—and ribs still showed from desert privation, but . . . bloody hell, 'fighting trim' didn't quite begin to describe it. Robyn's lip curled, appreciative, and he managed to suck in enough breath to coo, "Ooo, milord, but en't y' so broad and strong—"

"Shut it, you tosser, I'm being serious."

"I take any mouth job proper serious, in case you've forgotten."

Gamelyn's brows drew together, stern, whilst the rest of his anatomy responded to the words with a tiny quiver and, in one particular case, a definite rise.

Robyn's smirk broadened.

"There are a few things, you know, that aren't solved with a good rut."

"Precious few, by my lights."

"Well a few of your lights dim when it comes to this."

"Mayhap. But yours"—Robyn gave a purposeful squirm and nipped at Gamelyn's belly—"blaze all t' more."

A hand snarled in his hair, tightened and yanked so that Robyn was forced to meet Gamelyn's eyes.

"Robyn. I *need* you to understand."

"Do you, then? What exactly am I supposed to understand?" *How t' nobles are playing at mummers' masques in the same places they defiled? Or. . .* Robyn started with a glare fit to slay even Templars, but it wavered at the strange, raw uncertainty in Gamelyn's eyes, and dropped.

Nay, not now, he couldn't parse this any further or 'twould come to blows, no question. And when all Robyn wanted to do was hold to Gamelyn like a drowning man. "I mean, how can I understand owt when you're chatty as a sulled-up mule and allus have been, keeping so close none can—"

"As if it's easy to even begin to fill you in on . . . Christ, Robyn, it's been *years.*"

"And you think I don't ken that, if nowt else?" A snap and growl, and this time Gamelyn let him pull away.

Another difference; for the first since Robyn could recall, a heavy-dour, infuriating, sulled-up silence didn't follow.

"*Years,* Robyn. Waiting, working, selling myself to anyone who would buy upon the smallest of hopes, more often than not losing that hope. Both Marion and I biding our time and all the while breaking our hearts. Planning, scheming, working it for all its worth so we could find a way to fetch you back to us. And all the while making a home, a safe place—"

"And has this bloody 'Eden' of yours been worth it? Has opening up *our rites* to the same Motherless sod as tried to kill us been worth it? Or putting Marion in such a—"

"To hell with the King! He's an occasional pustule on our behinds, aye, but we've problems closer than him! Just look about you, Robyn, and see what we've *won.* Marion hasn't been 'put' anywhere she doesn't belong, or agree to be. She wields the power of any goddess, not only in the rites but our home! She's lady of a great estate, running it with a grace that others envy and covet . . . Marion's *content,* Robyn. Bloody ecstatic, in fact, now that you're here and we're all together. Our children—the god's children—are healthy and strong. Our people are satisfied, well fed, all—"

"All in servitude to a lord. *You,* milord."

"For God's sake, Robyn, we all have to make deals with devils to just survive! We're *all* bound to something. Even you, *Robyn Hode. Bound* to the Shire Wode, and to the Horned Lord!"

Bound all the tighter, now, Robyn thought, shuttering his gaze and stilling his tongue. Felt the rhythm of his heartbeat—*again*—ramp up behind his eyes, and a shudder curled up his spine as he gritted his teeth, swayed, *drifted . . .*

To come back to thisnow with a harsh gasp as strong arms gathered him, shook him hard. Contrariwise, Gamelyn's murmur rippled soft, entreaties surely more akin with a too-serious, naïve nobleman's son, and not any ex-Templar assassin that memory would attempt to suggest. "—you all right? What is it? None of it matters. All that matters is you're back, here with us . . . here with *me.*"

Where was he? *When?* Robyn splayed his hands—one on freckled skin, one upon moss and roots—and leaned fierce against all of it.

you're here, we're here
—the woodland told her lord

And Robyn's world tilted back into its proper path. "Aye, I'm here. *I am.*"

Another shake, this small and not so teeth-chattering, but it set Robyn further into his right mind.

"Ask me, then." Again, more the eager boy who'd literally stumbled upon Loxley and into ways he'd never dreamed existed. "We'll make up for lost time this very moment. Ask me anything. *Anything,* and I'll answer."

As Robyn peered into that juniper-green gaze, he finally grasped what Marion had meant when she'd reclaimed her own memories after Loxley and found her brother still alive.

"How'd you get so much older than me?"

The answer bided the same but never easy: choices, hard gambles, bitter decisions. Points and places of reckoning he'd not witnessed and never would.

Years.

And the ... the *awareness* of it, a harsh tally of thisnow, reminder to fulfil Reckoning and waiting, in the wings: *one-and two-and three-and...*

Gamelyn just kept peering at him, as if he'd all the time thisworld could spin.

Well, there were none as could say Himself the Templar hadn't any patience, or endurance.

Robyn's throat finally loosened, though his voice grated faulty. "Too much time. Too much yet too little, and we've spent it trying to hold on even as it disappears past our view. And that only because we en't the sense to know it's never gone, its only ever comin' up behind us again."

"The Wheel goes and comes 'round, goes and comes 'round." Lips forming the syllables as if tasting them, Gamelyn's brows twitched and furrowed together. "Every incarnation of the Lady I've ever known has told me that. Including your mother."

"Our Lady knows that t' more we try to pull *tynged,* plait it into sommat as we can manage, cobble up things to separate ourselves from ourselves ... the more we're buggered." Robyn cupped a hand over his face, let a soft breath heat his palm to dull compromised senses.

Touched it to his lover's forehead, smoothing worry—or trying to. "Gamelyn. Every time rivalry or riddle's lain between you and me—twined us or separated us apart—the other's suffered, aye? From the very beginning of it, and I'm not willing to that again. Questions, you say, and pet, trust to 't you en't the only one avoiding his share. I've no grounds faultin' you if you've made hard deals with harder devils. I'd some choices meself, bargaining my way back to thisworld."

"No more secrets, then. No more riddles." So strange, this, coming from Gamelyn. Yet he seemed more relieved than wary.

All right, then.

"The only riddles I see," Robyn answered, "are the ones we've to answer, together. Aye?"

Gamelyn smiled, not the boy's smile but a man's, broad and, in that moment, unencumbered.

Robyn leaned forward, kissing the corners of that smile. "I think Marion en't the only one who's found some measure of content."

The smile quivered. Gamelyn peered at him, unsure.

"Stop thinking like a bloody nobleman, all weighing and measuring," Robyn growled.

"I *am* a bloody nobleman."

"Well, I en't, and what sort of mean and grasping sod would begrudge the happiness of sommun he loves? Even if 'twere without me." Another kiss, this to Gamelyn's forehead.

"I begrudge it, some days."

"Well, you've allus been difficult."

"Difficult," Gamelyn told the tree tops. "He says *I'm* difficult."

It seemed, for a half-breath, that the trees had decided to answer. A sound lifted and tore itself upon the upmost branches, then settled downward into a low vibration, not unlike a hunting horn. Gamelyn stiffened. Robyn started to ask *What the bloody damn?* only to choke it back, unsaid, as a rhythmic *clang-clang!* accompanied the horn: three counts pealed, three counts waiting, then another three . . .

With a foul curse, Gamelyn lurched upright, snatching at his braies and leggings. And when Robyn thought to protest, cut it off with a terse "Visitors. We have to return."

"But Milord the Arsey Earl en't expected for—"

Gamelyn laughed, a sudden peal to outdo the horn and send Robyn's limbs all wobbly. "God, but I've missed you." Clothes in one hand, he extended an arm to pull Robyn upright. "Just that. The advantages of privilege. If Huntingdon has sent messengers to other vassals, and those messages arrived before ours did? It could be the first of a wave of guests. Even a few Templars might be riding on ahead, to witness the mêlée and do business."

"Templars." Of course.

"Several of the lords call us the King's tame moneylenders."

"Us."

"Only a few know what the true connections are—and only because they, too, are tied into the knot."

"Knot." And bloody damn, but Robyn loathed it when he parroted things like some bairn. Even wandering Fae lands hadn't accustomed Robyn to this much come-by-and-catch-me. "You mean these, um, 'few' are—"

"With us. Aye."

Robyn bit back what he wanted to say and swallowed it whole.

Wondered if Gamelyn, with all his talk of prices and precedents—whatever the bloody damn that last was—could manage to comprehend how "with us" had long meant "against them".

Aye, a price, to be sure.

"Believe me, I'd rather be here." Gamelyn finished tying his braies, peering at Robyn. "With you. But we've left Marion's platter full enough as 'tis—"

"You do know me sister, aye?" Robyn shrugged away disquiet with a purposeful snort, bending to fetch his own clothing. "She's likely glad we're out the way."

Another laugh, this one shorter—but aye, so sweet-familiar it curled Robyn's toes. "True enough. But she will have my ears if she's left to play milady of Tickhill on her own and I'm within shouting distance. And rightly so. You"—the green eyes met Robyn's own, suddenly chary—"can stay here. If you'd rather."

Robyn thought he would, rather.

Mayhap better to *stay* dead, known only to the ones as mattered. Be a ghost haunting the Wode, linger in castle walls only long enough to mayhap startle a few visitors and, of course, bed his lover. Be the shadow, the fate none could feel, the mystery wrapped up in riddles . . .

Be a legend? A soft whisper tickled his nape. The gwyllion twitched.

Oddly enough, Gamelyn hadn't heard Her voice. He did frown at the torc, as if he'd seen the movement, then shrugged it away with a tic of lip; he'd obviously followed Robyn's thoughts. "Tempting, aye? You could stay ours and ours alone, haunt the green Wode as you choose. Though rumours have already begun to proliferate."

"Let 'em, then."

The twitch of lip broadened, but turned into a grimace as Gamelyn twitched his hips—mere aide to shifting his hose, of course.

It also gave Robyn cause towards giving his own yank to those hose. Off.

Gamelyn realised it. The grin returned and turned rather diabolical. "Later, pet. Surely you don't mean I should keep important guests waiting?"

"Fancy that should matter to either of us!" It was Robyn's turn to laugh. "Or are you saying you want to flaunt me, like a prize horse?"

"Oh, you're a bit more than that, pet."

"Watch it, now, you're startin' to sound like a shire crofter."

"Or a notorious ex-outlaw. Who's unbelievably starting to sound like he doesn't fancy being flaunted." Grin tilting, it flashed wide. "Eh, Robyn Hode?"

Well, then, and 'twould sure enough be a proper "sod-off". Fancy the look on Himself the Master Preceptor Templar's face—or his

Royal Arse-Pain-ness—when such a notorious wolfshead showed up alive!

"See here." Gamelyn sobered, uncertainty echoing in the draw of brow and pinch of nostril. "I have to go. You don't. Likely it's no more than some minor and local vassal. There's time."

"Not here, there en't," Robyn muttered, in the next breath sorry for 't, and hoping Gamelyn hadn't heard.

But he had. Silence skulked in, long and lean as a hungry wolf.

The bells broke it, pealing the same flat rhythm, the same message. Gamelyn reached out, trailed one hand across Robyn's cheek and back, a brief tangle-tug in Robyn's curls.

With a gusty sigh Robyn finished tying his own clothing about him.

"Looks like rain," he said as he mounted up behind Gamelyn, who eyed the darkening northern sky as if it had offended him, then turned the grey's nose for Tickhill.

ᛒ

As Robyn had predicted, rain swept in just as he and Gamelyn galloped through Tickhill's gates.

But Gamelyn's predictions proved faulty. Their visitors, whilst not royalty, were almost as important.

Robyn found it easy to slide off the grey stallion's rump and disappear into the gathered locals as Gamelyn dismounted, striding over to clasp arms with the nobleman.

The nobleman seemed elated to see him, with a kiss to both cheeks and an enthusiastic hug. The big falcon on the nobleman's arm, however, weren't best pleased to have his perch shaken. Robyn smirked understanding, dodging behind the smithy just off the bailey stable before Gamelyn had a chance to notice he was missing.

The Earl of Huntingdon usually made a stop at Tickhill, and not just for the sake of some nobleman's games. It seemed Gamelyn's mother had been a close cousin and, being a man who held family as fierce-close, David of Huntingdon had become not only a powerful ally, but a friend to rely upon.

Or so Marion filled in for Robyn later—much later, after settling all her guests in for the night. She'd brought a late-night repast to her quarters after nigh running headlong into her brother, who'd been sneaking up the hidden stair from the stables below and into the tower's uppermost storey.

Aye, but it might have been a night from their childhood, with rain pattering the roof and beading moisture on the sills, cobbled up together by the hearth and fending for themselves whilst Mam and Da were away.

Save, of course, for the fact they'd never broken bread or swapped fireside stories in any bloody great castle. Nor would any of their kith or kin dared call an earl by his given name.

"How'd you know I were hungry?" Robyn mumbled around a mouthful of cheese curds.

"You're allus hungry." She tipped more mead into his pot. "Anyway, you'll need your strength when Gamelyn comes to bed. Devising strategies makes him boisterous. Or so John seems to think. I think John rather fancies it." She grinned. "Me, too."

Well, and Robyn had already spent an afternoon of quiet bliss down in the stables with John, and left him curled up in the hay ricks, too snug and warm to wake. Proper tempting, to just stay there. In fact, he'd meant to just steal up and steal Gamelyn down to them—but no such luck. The lord's chamber had been empty, the hearth banked low, and when Robyn had padded across to peer out the tall, narrow window, he saw where Gamelyn had gone. Fires illuminated the Great Hall across the bailey as if 'twere day.

"If Gamelyn does come to bed," Marion mused. "No question, but milord David was full of tidings—and ones the King won't be hearing, I'll warrant. The Northern lords' brew is taking its time, but 'tis distilling into sommat proper powerful."

Mayhap he'd leave a note on Gamelyn's pillow, then. Robyn grinned, took another drink. No doubt the like would appeal to his poncy ginger paramour.

"But then, according to some folks, we do nowt in the North *but* brew trouble." Marion continued, thoughtful, carving a joint from the side of goose. A fancy fat one, too—it filled half the platter.

Robyn peered at his sister where she knelt on the huge rug. She seemed to be devising a few strategies of her own—despite having shed her fine bliaut and silk veil for thick woollen robe and slippers. Her hair, glinting even more cinnabar than the fire crackling in the hearth beside them, tumbled over one shoulder, no longer contained by veil and an impressive weave of plaits. A few faded strands were starting a gather at her forehead, and while hearth-tending and childbearing had steeled her spine while softening breast, belly, and hip, in truth she bided more a lovely Mother Goddess and no less Queen than the one who'd borne a proper brood of Franks. Including this latest, who'd seemingly claimed the throne and would no doubt drive them all spare.

Marion sipped her pot and contemplated the air, frowning—albeit more pensive than cross. Content, aye, but also fierce upon sommat. She'd always thought about things overmuch. Just like Gamelyn. And Robyn himself either racing ahead or falling behind.

Like now. "Do you need me t' understand, too?"

A blink and start, then Marion turned to him. "What, pet?"

"Eh, sommat Gamelyn said."

Marion met his eyes, questioning. He'd no answers, only more questions. More *riddles*, after promising his lover they'd have none.

"The rites," he said, deliberately.

And watched as she dropped her gaze to the hearth, and tension runnelled up and down that straight spine.

For aye, but where Gamelyn couldn't truly understand this one? Marion could. Did.

But Marion didn't speak for some time, leaning forward to fiddle with the hearth. And didn't even seem to notice when a lock of hair fell from its hasty knot and nigh into the flames.

Robyn leaned forward, tucked it gently back. "You'll be catching fire, pet."

A short laugh. "It wain't be the first time."

Again, silence.

Robyn watched her for some time, then decided to broach it. "You know, when I was lying in the Hunter's caves after Loxley, mostly trying to die and somehow not managing it, Cernun told me stories. So many stories, and me so fevered I couldn't now tell you the half of 'em. Such a loss, that."

"*Bendith*, Cernun," Marion whispered to the fire, and still didn't meet her brother's eyes. "May your soul walk a gentler path t' next."

Robyn nodded and flicked a fingerful of mead at the fire, his own offering. "I remember a fair amount, though. So many of the stories were about when he was a boy, and then a young man, bearing the weight of the horn crown." He took a drink, eyeing the fire, and Marion. "One in particular comes to mind now. Cernun told me about how the countryside were ravaged whilst two spoilt nobles both vied for the same crown. As usual, their sort weren't giving a damn as to what happened with common folk; they just wanted their patch, and t' hell with those as got in the way."

Finally, Marion's gaze slid his way. Her brows twitched—confused, mayhap, but also curious.

"Cernun told me how most people living then, they believed their god were sleeping, or had abandoned them. And, as people do, they started looking for sommat else. Hearkening back to better times, even if those times weren't so much better. Memories can be sweet or cruel, but they're also liars. All we truly know is thisnow, and even if we rarely can hold that, we've to make it count."

"Robyn, I'm not sure I under—"

"I'm thinking you've been amidst t' conqueror-people overlong, love." And realised the same could be said of his own time in Fae lands, with those words—*conqueror-people*—branded into his own speech. "Since when do stories have to make sense at the beginning? Or hold your hand and lead you through all careful when you're capable of sorting it on your own? En't it the point of a truly fine tale, to wend you through some answers as sprout hard questions? Mayhap to break you, so's you can sort the pieces and figure what they mean?"

She sat back, arms about her knees, that one vagrant curl

framing an expression full of *All right then, O Arsy One, I'll wait for it.*

"Well, people can be fickle, aye? Just as it's our nature to wander, mayhap it's just as bred in us to be angry when our gods don't live up to what light we cast upon them."

Marion's frown deepened, sketching more uncertainty.

"Cernun told me how those people, then, they started returning to the Heath, to the old gods. Searching for what they'd lost—and who can't understand that? Some of 'em were even noble-born, searching for the ways of their ancestors. Some of those even meant it, for whilst the Barrow runs strong in our ways, there's also old All-Father and the runes. Or even the ancient Mother who lay with her dead brother-husband and conceived the sun. Aye, so many of the first ways, runnelling together like streams to a sea—and Cernun thought: who am I to turn them aside? Or so he said, at the time." His eyes sought hers. "Our mam and da never told me; mayhap they told you? Gunnora remembers, according to Gamelyn."

"Mam and Da said nowt of such things. They allus tried to protect us. No blame to them." Marion tucked her arms and legs tighter, closer. As if in defence. "But aye, Gunnora told both me and Gamelyn that tale. 'Twere what aided our own decision, knowing how Cernun opened the covenant, as had been done long ago."

"Aye, to all as would swear oath: to harm none, and keep it close. The masks were worn, no longer just ceremony and the play, but concealment. Aye, that last, because trust can be a slippery path. People tend t' sway to the easiest wind, not allus the soundest or best. Mam and Da never breathed a word of any of it, particularly what happened next. Cernun did."

"Gunnora told me sommat about it," Marion agreed, cautious. "She was just a wee lass. The stories came from her people. The Sun went into shadow, and King Stephen were captured. Some thought it a sign. But like too many once-born folk do, most of 'em looked into the mirror to decide what the sign meant."

"Aye. And the Church used it, desperate to gather their wandered flocks back into fold."

"The worst?" Marion murmured. "Anarchy kept on for years past any dance of sun and moon, whilst Christ and all His saints slept on. And why should we 'spect any different? As long as the gods have their due, they sleep, sated on our blood."

The statement held as much rue as acceptance—and the former didn't proper seat itself with the sister he'd known. Robyn's turn to frown, this time, but he continued. "Well, 'tis sure that several priests—one of 'em a bishop with more money than his god—decided they needed a bit of that due. 'Tweren't hard, or Cernun claimed, to find a few souls willing to exchange the lands they'd lost for information about the covenant. Sounds familiar, aye?"

Marion said nothing, staring into the fire.

A log fell sideways with a shower of sparks. Robyn took up the poker and wheedled it back into place. Said, soft, *"Þa wealas flugon Þa Anglan swa fyr."*

This time Marion flinched.

"They've hunted us, always. They've turned on us, always. If their priests demand it, they'll see us all dead or banished. They have the power."

"Which is why we're gathering it to *us!*"

Robyn fell silent, watching her.

Marion swallowed, hard, and turned to him, grey eyes muted-forceful, like storms building across a choppy sea. "You don't understand how it was."

"So Gamelyn said."

"It was the price we had to pay, Robyn. Surely he told you that, as well."

"Aye, he did, and I've heard it too much of late," Robyn said. "Prices to pay. Teinds. Even in Fae lands . . . "

As he trailed off, Marion put her chin upon her knees, eyeing him, obviously sensing what lay beneath. And whereas he might, with Gamelyn, play the game of reunited lovers frantic to let only fair things surface?

Family were different. You became sommat other, for good *and* ill, with those as had fed you, wiped your nose, and nappied your bum.

Marion continued, keeping her eyes steady upon him. "'Twere a price both Gamelyn and I agreed upon. Once we realised his magic were tied not just into the old ways but the new, and how both were fighting each other instead of commingling? His way inward had to be different. He realised it, went back to the Templars. He had to, to find his way." A wary tremor started once again to thin her words. "I didn't think it a wrong choice. Cernun treated with them. You yourself agreed to treat with Hubert, and—"

"Hubert en't the bloody Master of England, aye? Though he could be. I thought he might be, then." Robyn took up his cup from the hearth, drank. The warmed mead slid down his gullet, leaving a pleasant trail of fire. "So. Gamelyn makes his own dare with the Templar's god, and finds his magic in the stones and the sand. Aye, well, we knew they allus spoke to him."

"You remember, don't you?" Her voice quavered, a plea.

I need you to understand.

Memories can be sweet or cruel, but they're also liars.

"Surely you remember, Robyn, how even after that first Beltane—our first, magical Beltane that gave us our Aderyn—can you recall how it was with Gamelyn? Even when we'd raise the magic, it weren't the same as on that Beltane. As if a door had shut itself within him. And then . . . we lost you." Marion's hands kept twisting in her robes, white-knuckled. "Things were bad, that winter. We were all trying to cling to sommat. I'd a new bairn—Aderyn—and a householding to manage, and Much. John retreated to the caverns, kept the Horned Lord in thisworld by sheer will. But Gamelyn . . . his grip kept failing him. He had John. He had Aderyn, and me, and Much. But it weren't enough. Not beneath the blame he laid across his own back. He felt responsible for being unable to open that door, raise his power when he most needed it. When *you* most needed it."

"Mari—"

"Every time he'd learn a new way from the Templars—and believe me, that bloody-minded de Birkin only fed him bits and scraps, like a dog he wanted kept hungry! Every time he'd return with it, and we'd use it. Scrape it all together, try to conjure you back. Five times in as many years we went to the Mere and raised the power . . . but 'twere never enough. The Horned Lord was with us, but the Lady betrayed us, every time. She let Them take you, then all but vanished from the Mere!" She dropped her chin, and Robyn saw fat tears spill down her cheeks, glistening against the firelight. "Well, She's had her jape and we've found that we, too, can dance for it. Our truest magic, the soul we opened the doors to and gave welcome the one time we were allowed to truly work together? Aderyn was your way back to us. Our best working, together—and the foreign magic Gamelyn managed to conjure—was what loosed the chains to the Old Ones, and the wylding spirits."

Rue and sweet all sifted together in the words. Robyn did the only thing he could: reached out and pulled her close against him.

"Funny, en't it," he murmured, "how the past has a habit of repeating itself. Mostly because we learn nowt from it . . . but mayhap also 'tis the consequence of riding the Wheel, of bein' us, able to only attempt grasping this place. Thisnow."

Marion curled against him. "I knew 'twere flying in the face of what had happened, over and over. I knew you might think your freedom won at too great a cost—"

Love, he thought, *you en't the half of it.*

"—but we're no longer some stroppy lad's club wandering the woodlands. We had to protect what was ours! Our people, our home, our bairns! And it's *working.* We've our own covenant, our own people. We've the Inner Circle of the Temple hallowing our ways, as well as a select few of those in power—believers, all. We've a landed King who willingly claims kinship with a Frankish witch. King John might be the latest in a bad lot, but he follows the old ways and looks to the Templars—"

"For his own ends, no doubt—"

"As do we. The King of England, Robyn. He defies Church rule as he can, knows it to be what the Templars call 'The Great Lie'. He willingly made the blood pact with the land."

"No doubt that one knows," Robyn drawled against her hair, "there's plenty of peasants to stand in for him, come t' Sacrifice."

Not funny—not at all, considering—yet Marion hiccoughed a sudden laugh against his chest. "So Gamelyn keeps reminding him. That sommun else is paying the price, when Himself has his royal arse kicked before the fires."

"And no doubt thinking he's above it. Too important to pay what's due." Robyn's gaze escaped towards the hearth, watching the flames leap and curl over the wood, hungry and alive.

It was what had been missing in the Barrows. No hunger. No *fire.*

Time stretched upon it, slowing, grew thin beneath the weight of that bloody-damned inexorable . . . *Tally* pounding *one-and two-and three-and* trying to purloin his perceptions. The walls closing in, his spirit sifting itself away, mayhap up the roof vents like so much smoke, thisnow snaring him further and farther behind.

Nay, he couldn't give in. Couldn't lose. Couldn't turn away. Their last chance, it were . . .

"Robyn?" A hand covered his own. Marion's, warm and strong, whereas his own shook, ice-chill. "Robyn, what is it? Tell me."

He opened his mouth, but the Tally but grew louder, a surf pounding sand, drowning any chance at voice—funny, that, as if he even knew what to say.

Warm hands cupped his cheeks, giving his head a firm shake. Aye, might it shake his mind loose just enough, to rattle and break the counting for good?

"Robyn!"

He reached up and grabbed his Lady's wrists, met the grey eyes, let both be a line hauling him to safety from a drowning pool. "I'm here." It was a mere breath—also a promise. "I'm here."

"You are now." Grey eyes glimmering, she bent forward and kissed his forehead. "Is it the castle? The stones?"

Mayhap. He wasn't sure, and that disturbed him worse. "She said—the Priestess of the Fae," he explained as his sister frowned. "She said I'd find the outerworlds . . . changed. I didn't ken. Not then."

Marion held silent, peering at him for long breaths, her hands twisting to hold his. Trying to understand.

I need you to understand.

He wasn't sure he did with this, either. "Since I returned, things are . . . nay, I don't mean larger, though they are, somehow. Nor faster, though sometimes they are. Too close, mayhap. Sharp. Like shaving with a blade you've honed over-keen, one as'll cut you proper if you en't steady-handed. And my hands are shaking, all the while."

Her intake of breath was hoarse, soft.

"'Twere so . . . You could barely feel yourself breathe, in that place. Only occasionally did you notice your heart beating, because then you'd have sommat to count the moments, but even then, you'd forget to count. Like having a bit of mushroom and letting things just slip away. Only you never stop . . . slipping . . . "

Her hands gripped his tight, gave another fierce shake, and aye, but he'd nigh done it again. Slipped.

The Tally thudded soft behind his ears and in his throat, threatening. He gritted his teeth, said, "Time is . . . thicker here. Like water, and me pushing my way through. Sometimes," he added—had to, she looked so anxious. "Not always."

"You don't have to stay, Robyn."

Mayhap he did. *The stones*, his sister had said. *Be breaking the power of iron and stone*, the Priestess had said. *Be piercing the Veil, setting spirits free. Be bringing us Home.*

"You can go back to the Wode. And you certainly don't have to be here for any tournament."

He couldn't help the grin. "Mayhap I should set meself up on the road, shake down a few passersby like old times."

"You can . . . disappear. Visit us as you like. Be nowt more than a rumour," Marion continued, her hands firm against his.

Robyn slid his gaze to meet hers. "So I told Gamelyn."

"And so you should. The Horned Lord has returned, in all his power, to uphold the blessings of our Wode."

"Like at Loxley?" His eyes caught hers and set alight.

Loxley. The Horned Lord echoed, a whisper faint against the stones, and they both heard it.

"Now, and then." The hearth sparked and spat, dim against the sudden return of flames in her eyes. "Oh, aye."

"Even if Gamelyn wants me here?"

"Gamelyn thinks too much like a noble sometimes!"

"Well, and en't he? En't you, now?"

"I'm sommat between, neither fish nor fowl. And *you* en't some spoil of war!"

"Sure of that, are you?"

"*Robyn!*"

He turned over her hands, kissed the palms one by one. "So, pet. What do you need me to do?"

"No more than you be here as you can. And try to understand what's come while you were away."

"I'm not sure I do, altogether. But I trust you. Only a few people in thisnow I trust with me life t' way I do you. So. What d'you *want* me to do?"

Marion closed her eyes for several breaths; she'd known what he was asking, even if she wanted to avoid the necessity of an answer. "I want you here, with us. I want both of you here, never to leave again."

"But?"

"I don't know, Robyn. I don't know what's wisest, but I do know the best way for you to avoid being entangled in all this—"

"I'm already knotted fair tight, Mari."

"But you don't have to be! Stay 'dead', Robyn Hode. Be a ghost in the green Wode, and creep our corridors o' nights. Live in the forest when you're tired of stones and soft beds."

"I en't' that daft, pet. Who'd tire of proper soft coverlets and feather ticks when they can have 'em?"

"I'm being serious, Robyn!"

"So'm I. And it sounds as if *you're* feeling proper trapped in what's come while I were aw—"

"I'm not." Deadly serious, she was. "My life isn't perfect—nowt ever is—but it's mine. I'd not willingly leave it. But I'm not you, and . . . and . . . " A shake of cinnabar curls. "I'm fearing for you, Robyn. What *our* life will mean for you. And Gamelyn . . . he'd set the world afire to keep you with him—but he'll end up using you in the bargain. In this game we're playing, he'll have to. To protect all of us."

- XXXIII -

Head Forester de Neville arrived two days later, in the company of several lords' sons eager for the tournament, and asked to speak with the Keeper of Sherwood and the Peak Forests.

Considering the clearance at Loxley, Marion had a few words for him as well.

"It was good of you to take the time to speak with me, milady. Considering your workload must have quadrupled."

Marion inclined her head. They were meeting in the Great Hall, nigh a mirror of their first discussion over a year previous, even down to the scribe settled at his table and Marion's own carefully faultless appearance. This time, however, her chief forester stood with her. Gilbert had several agisters' rolls and woodwards' tallies in a pouch slung over one well-brushed shoulder, and three of their foresters at his shoulder.

"There is only one recent incident we must discuss, but it is an urgent one." De Neville had turned his eyes from the writing desk to the board stacked with rolled and flattened parchments. His appearance back on English shores had, it was rumoured, been prompted by the King: to hold several courts and—no doubt—squeeze more cash from the convoluted permissions of Forest Law.

"I beg your pardon," de Neville continued, fingers riffling and searching the pile, unrolling and twisting and tossing aside. The scribe, polite and patient but in the end despairing over what his lord was doing to what organisation he did have, reached towards a certain pile and handed a parchment over. "Ah, yes, thank you, James. Read it out, if you please."

The clerk did so—in rather droning Latin. With a bare twitch of lip, de Neville flicked a keen gaze at Marion. Definitely assessment—but destined for disappointment, he was; she knew Latin as well as any scribe, and returned his sort-of smile with a gracious tilt of head.

She wasn't quite prepared for what the scribe read, however.

"'A tall, black figure, with eyes that glowed like fire. He shot arrows that never missed, milord. He wore a carapace of horns, but they kept appearing and disappearing, like. First a man, then a beast . . .'"

With no little effort, she kept her expression pleasant, smooth. She daren't peer back at Gilbert. Mayhap de Neville hadn't meant to catch her out with the Latin, after all; he was still watching her akin to a recently-unjessed tiercel.

"'I tried to hide, I did, but He found me—'"

"Move on to the end, please." Bland, the interruption.

The clerk blinked, squinted at the parchment, running an ink-stained finger down it, lips moving as he tried to catch himself up. "Ah, here we are. 'He spared me, told me t' spread the word. Then he beheaded them, one and all, and hung their skulls on old Loxley well. I ran, then, fast as I could . . . Aye, I did as He commanded, my lord. Spread the word that He'd returned. All through the valley and over the heaths, down into Sherwood, His place . . . not that he ever left, see, but now wild Robyn's taking His due, He is. Past time and—'"

"That's enough, James."

The scribe shrugged, put down the parchment then reweighted his own, picked up his quill, and waited.

Gilbert shifted, foot to foot.

De Neville also waited, eyeing Marion.

She let him, extending a hand to request the deposition. Another surprise for de Neville; he covered it by giving her the parchment. Marion scanned it, making a frantic gather of her own thoughts.

"With my lady's and my lord's permission?" Gilbert stepped forward. "I but recently informed my lady Keeper of a slightly differing version of the tale."

Marion wanted to kiss him; instead she joined in. "Aye, and 'twere even more fanciful than this." She waved the parchment.

"Mayhap no mere fancy, since there are rumours spreading the shire like wildfire. Some incidents are spoken of in just that tone: Due. Justice. Yet it is not. Justice. Like the matter of the Prior of St Mary's in Nottingham, found staked out and slain in his own churchyard—"

Marion tucked her chin and allowed nothing to show on her face.

"—and Nottingham is in lockdown. The Sheriff has retired to his tower and won't come out. The villages from there to the Upper

Peak are talking of black horses galloping o' nights, with flame-eared dogs." De Neville seemed to realise his tone had changed; with a shake of head and a clench of fists, he regained his carapace of iron. "It would seem this notorious, ah, figure that the villein spoke of—named, in fact?—has indeed resurfaced. Even amongst your own people here, at Tickhill proper, do the tales carry." He folded his arms. "Your brother, lady Marion. Robyn Hood."

"Tales of my brother continued long after his death. No doubt they will continue on. People always need something to hope for, do they not?" Marion replaced the parchment on the board, letting a hint of aggrievement colour her next words. "Yet it seems there is more to this tale than fancy and rumours."

Gilbert shifted again behind her.

"Is there, my lady?" De Neville rested both fists on the board and leaned towards Marion. She might call it eagerness—if his face were less akin to a stone cairn.

"I worry more over the unacceptable events that prefaced these tales, my lord. Specifically, the injury to lands within Tickhill's rightful fee. As to the results?" She shrugged. "If, indeed, one of my husband's . . . agents—"

De Neville glanced at Gilbert, who'd come to stand beside her, chin held high and gaze level upon de Neville.

"—took recompense for spoilage? Well, he merely acted with Tickhill's rights in mind. This abuse is a serious matter in truth. As you know, my lord husband has recently returned from pilgrimage to the Holy Land, merely to find his trust disabused on several fronts. He intends to personally write our King about such outrages."

"Indeed," de Neville concurred, "all such things are a matter for the King. I can say nothing to the other . . . eh, outrages your husband has suffered, and I'm sure he will find satisfaction for those. But the exemptions of assart for Loxley Chase were deeded by the King himself. In result, it is myself, as Head Forester of England, that must see our liege's wishes are fulfilled."

Beside her, Gilbert let out a long hiss of breath between his teeth.

Marion's thoughts were already buzzing overmuch; at that last, they slid into a deathly stall, focusing on the only possible quarry. "You gave leave to assart Loxley."

"Under gift of the King. Loxley, as well as several other places along the river." De Neville tilted his head, gave the swift twitch that passed for a smile. "It gave good timber—or will, once I find a cadre of workers who aren't scared stiff of a few skulls hung upon a well."

"Surely the King wouldn't—"

"Come now, my lady, you know the King as well as I. Better, mayhap." No jab but insult, this, should Marion choose to take it.

She didn't. Instead she lifted her chin and gave him back stare for stare.

"Our liege is aggressive in his protection of his royal forests—and rightly so. But we are at war with France. Our King is bent upon enlarging his maritime presence. That requires old growths of large timber, which the forests along the river south of Sheffield have. Some choices must be made and held to. I understand you have some fondness for Loxley in particular"—altogether reasonable, his tone; she could almost hear the *Kindly don't waste my time with any irrational feminine predilections, if you please*—"but don't you think it far past time for the land to be opened up for meaningful development? Fire drives soil fertility. The growth there has been considerable, and new seedlings grow apace. With this assart and its permissions, it will be possible to allow your peasants back onto the land—and that will only profit your lord husband, my lady."

"Then, my lord Forester, I shall assume you have the writs available for inspection. My lord husband shall desire to see them, I assure you."

"But of course. James? The assarts?" No attempt at search, this time. As the clerk bent over the trunk laid at one end of the board, de Neville continued, "All part of the business planned for this evening's council, but since it has come up already?" He paused to take the roll of parchment from the clerk and hand it to Marion. "Kindly give this to your lord husband. Both of us will know the lay of the land, so to speak, before proper negotiations."

"It might have been better to send word before acting, my lord." Marion palmed the roll and didn't open it.

"Our liege's rights take precedence, and he impressed upon me a need for haste. Rest assured, lady Marion, I've the greatest respect for my lord of Tickhill. I'm extremely glad he has returned safely." A lift of eyebrow—a suggestion of discomfort, mayhap. "You see, my lord of Hallamshire has been, shall we say, tapping upon my door? More than once."

"Hoping to reacquire the Loxley valley."

"My lady is well informed, indeed."

"I find it necessary amidst my duties, my lord."

The brow squinched back into place. "Well. As Keeper of Sherwood and the Peak, it is another of your duties to contain lawlessness. It's quite possible that your lord husband's . . . agent"—and my, but if the tone beneath that didn't scrape threat all along Marion's spine—"indeed merely carried out what he saw as his duty. Though the boundaries of such . . . eccentric behaviour? It might be difficult to condone. Particularly since it has added to our difficulties."

"How is that, my lord?"

"Again, as I'm sure you realise, 'twill take some skill to convince superstitious villeins to live in a place they consider ill-fortuned."

She kept her eyes upon him, allowed, "I'll look into it, my lord."

"I hope so." A shrug. "Such things, after all, are bad for business."

↑

"Hugh de Neville?" Robyn repeated. "Who's he, then?"

"The master forester." Marion smiled up at Gamelyn, accepting the offered pot of warmed wine he held out to her.

"And well on his way to becoming one of the most powerful men in the kingdom." Gamelyn sauntered over to where Robyn sat cross-legged on the lord's bed, the parchment held down by one foot and one hand. "Should I read it to you? You'll go squint-eyed trying to decipher it overlong."

Robyn treated him to a scowl and held up his empty pot. "Well, and t' squiggles should fetch easier wit' more wine."

"You've had three already," Marion put in with a hint of concern—and not without some justification, considering.

But the black eyes held a plea, albeit tiny, towards Gamelyn. As Gamelyn acquiesced, silent, Marion muttered a sigh from her place against the east wall.

Of course, she'd not witnessed what came most nights. How Gamelyn came to bed reeking of costly liquor and even costlier accords. How he often found Robyn riding the night mare, and woke him, rutted him until they both fell into thankfully-dreamless sleep.

If the wine helped, then so be it. Bad enough that Robyn had been by circumstance reduced to skulking the stone tower unseen, waiting the lord's pleasure in the lord's bed.

"I can read, y'know," Robyn challenged, eyeing them both over his cup. Thankfully, Marion didn't see how his bow-hardened fingers, so keen upon bowstring or dagger, clutched the pot slightly a-tremble. Gamelyn did, though. "Amidst all the useless jabber, this means you've no longer control ower Loxley, aye?"

"So," Gamelyn's voice tilted into a growl, "it would seem."

"Whereas," soft, Robyn's whisper, a breath that nevertheless echoed against the stones and flickered the hearth flames, "I do."

Gamelyn turned, slowly, to peer at him. Marion, on the other side of the hearth, had stiffened.

"I might've been a bit . . . well, mad, I fear. Mayhap I still am, for I en't regretting what happened there."

"Nor I," Marion stated into the quiet. "Well . . . all right, mayhap I am regretting what trouble'll be fetched from it." Suddenly, she grinned. "And aye, but isn't the man proper worried about how all those superstitious peasants mightn't return?" She tipped the goblet to both of them, leaning upon the long, cushion-padded couch like some decadent resident of ancient Rome.

"Well," Robyn purred, matching her wry humour, "and if they do, they'd best be mindful of the proper rites."

Gamelyn laughed and went over to the board just past the

window, settling the pewter pitcher bedside the leftovers of their meal. A tapestry hung behind, crowded with trees and knotted vines; he ran a hand up and down the nap of it, eyes wandering to its avatar just past the narrow window.

Robyn followed, twining arms about Gamelyn's waist to curl up behind him and nestle his chin onto one shoulder. Beyond them, a copse of trees—nigh a league beyond the pasturelands—swayed in the wind. Upon those pastures, just outside the bailey walls, a virtual encampment of people had begun to park themselves, readying for the tournament with their wagons and wares, turning the grounds from sodden fawn and emerald to muddy sepia.

Even that led, a strange and trampled path, back to the woodland. The Wode.

"It beckons, aye?" Gamelyn whispered. "It craves closer acquaintance. It always has. And if I feel it, what do you feel?"

Robyn didn't answer, just nuzzled Gamelyn's ear and pushed away.

Gamelyn started to follow, was diverted by a slight figure who, pack over one shoulder, strode towards the gate. Hardly noticeable, save that he turned, as if beckoned, and peered up at the tall, octagonal tower. Nodded, as if in acknowledgement, and turned away, kept walking.

"Where's John going?" Gamelyn's query interrupted a half-teasing, half-serious back-and-forth between brother and sister. Robyn had sauntered over to pour himself another pot of warmed wine.

"Back t' our Wode," Robyn answered, giving Marion a victorious smirk as Gamelyn leaned behind her and merely handed Robyn the pitcher.

"But I thought he'd . . . " With an exasperated glare at Gamelyn, Marion padded over to the window. Her steps turned mincing. "Damn, but t' floor's *cold*."

"Then wear shoes, pet."

"Why should I be the only one who en't allowed to indulge in sommat as en't good for 'em? Mayhap I should do what our eldest used to."

"And what were that?"

"Stand on my feet." Gamelyn curled an arm about Marion's waist, pulling her close and watching John melt into the crowd about the gatehouse. *Robyn's staying, then.*

The thought both unnerved, and delighted.

"Only Robyn's are bigger."

"Well," Robyn smirked, "of course—Hoy!" This with a yip as Gamelyn aimed a swat at his pate, swerved it into a snag of curls to drag him close, too.

Realised, in this moment, he'd all he'd ever wanted: Robyn, Marion, a broad keep and their Wode about it, with all it meant.

But part of *all it meant* had disappeared into the shadows of the gatehouse. *John*, he mourned, with a breath into Robyn's hair, and a tighter snug at Marion's waist. "I'd hoped he'd stay."

"I thought you'd go with him," Marion said to Robyn, grave and quiet.

"I thought to stay," Robyn muttered, "until you brought that parchment. Thought to throw it in their teeth, let 'em know you'd one more reason, one more brined point to your quiver, pawn to your King and Queen."

"Pawn?" Marion was indignant.

"A Bishop, at the least," Gamelyn conceded, soft, unsure where any of it was going. "Since you're perverse enough to go 'most any direction."

Marion shoved at him. "Are you trying to be funny?"

"He's trying to play your game," Robyn answered, oddly quiet. "En't he? And I thought it might be the best thing to do, aye? I'll get used to everything, wain't I? Eventually."

Marion laid her head against his shoulder. "You don't have to, I told you, you don't."

"I want to be with you. All of us, together, that's what we all want, en't it?"

Yes, Gamelyn thought—or at least part of him, with the other protesting, *and no, not if* . . .

"Then, *that* came." Robyn pointed to the parchment. "You couldn't save Loxley. Even a lord can't save Loxley." He turned back to face the woodland, gilt sparking beneath his half-closed eyelids. "But I can. *I* can hold Loxley, and tens of vills like it, if none'll so much as go nigh without t' Horned Lord's permission. Just as I held t' Shire Wode, and the Peak. I held it stronger and safer than even a lord. Wearing t' Hood. And Horns."

Marion had opened her mouth to speak, shut it with a small *pop*. Whilst Gamelyn couldn't speak, only stare at Robyn.

"You told everyone I were dead, aye? Even your . . . masters, t' Temple."

Gamelyn took a breath, held it, let it out. Said, a bit curt, "It suited my purposes."

Robyn looked out, silent, for some time. He took a deep breath and turned around, settling his back against the wall, peering at his sister and his lover for some moments.

It didn't alleviate Gamelyn's unease, not at all.

"Well," Robyn finally said, "mayhap it could still suit. Only this time, 'twere for *all* our purposes. Aye?"

- POSTLUDE -

Sun drenched the courtyard, radiating swatches of both heat and cool from the wall walk. It felt marvellous, beating down onto Gamelyn's shoulders and bared head. He'd changed from brushed woollens and thick-napped cloak to light, colourful linens. No cloak.

Tempting, to go find a sunny spot and just doze. He hadn't fetched much sleep last night. Robyn, too, had been yawning as he and Gilbert waved and left Tickhill's gatehouse behind.

They'd disappeared into the trees some time ago, yet Gamelyn kept watching after.

Aye, and mooning would do him no good. He was being foolish. Robyn would be back after the tournament, when Tickhill had settled down into normal.

There was another party on the approach, as well. Flying the banners of . . . Gamelyn squinted, then gave it up, looking past the approaching party, into the copse where he'd last seen . . .

"What are you doing here?"

And damned if Marion didn't possess the ability to creep up like a stalking bitch fox, most days. Gamelyn whirled about, pretending a clutch to his heart.

She'd dressed for the warm weather as well: a light sleeveless overdress of pale blue over fawn linen, and a lightweight veil. Snugging an arm in his, she repeated, "What are you doing here?"

"Seeing Robyn off?"

"That doesn't answer my question. I thought you'd be going with him."

"Um . . . I thought we'd discussed this yester's even. I'm staying here with you, seeing to the responsibilities to you, to Tickhill—"

"And I appreciate that, but as you might recollect, both Tickhill and I managed quite well without you, thank you very much—"

"Here, now—"

"—And neither I nor Tickhill shall fall apart if you're gone a se'nnight." Marion frowned. "Only that, mind. You've a tournament to preside ower, after all, and 'twould be best were you here, aye? There's still rumours I'm pretending you're alive."

He'd tried several times to speak, but Marion hadn't let him so much as utter a word. Of course, by the end of it, he was starting to grin, his eyes wandering to that copse where Robyn had disappeared.

Marion kissed his cheek. "Now, go on. Much is waiting for you."

"Much? He can't—"

"He wain't. But you're keeping him waiting, and I've things for him to do." Marion smiled, and kissed him again.

Gamelyn peered at her. "I love you, you know."

"I know. Off with you. Only a se'nnight, mind."

Not only Much waited in the cool of the gatehouse, holding the reins to a grey Arab-bred mare, but beside him was Siham and Tafsut, already in the saddle and waiting.

"I need to stay and help milady," Much said. "But I fancy these two'll see you proper to where you're going, and take the mare on."

Gamelyn peered at the two.

"We'll be back for the tournament," Tafsut explained. "But we need to go to Moorlands for a few things in the meantime."

"Dare I hope there'll be an archery contest?" Siham asked with a grin. "Dare I hope you've disallowed a certain archer's attendance?"

Gamelyn chuckled, taking the rein from Much and stepping up. "I'm afraid I can't promise anything where Robyn Hode is concerned."

"Where today?" Gilbert asked, taking a swig from his drinking horn then passing it to Robyn.

Wulfstan's good mead. His Gilly-lad knew how to travel in style. Robyn drank deep and passed it to John, who did likewise.

"South," Robin finally said. "We'll head south. I've heard Nottingham's Sheriff is a right sod. Mayhap we'll give him a few more nightmares, aye?"

Gilbert retrieved the horn, toasted it into the air. "That I'd pay good marks to see!"

And I, came the Voice. Robyn turned to see the Horned Lord, upright with tines branching dark against an oak dappled in sun and shade. *It is good to see you wandering Our Wode again, Hob-Robyn.*

"It is, isn't it?" John said, soft.

"Aye," Gilbert agreed.

Aye, indeed, came a soft whisper through Robyn's hair. *In thisnow, for thisnow.*

The Lady, and he couldn't help a tiny shiver.

From the road just behind, cantering hoofs echoed inwards. A loud snort from the oak; the Horned Lord morphed into an ebon deer, who took flight into the trees.

"Hallo the Wode!" It echoed through the woodland. A light tenor, unprepossessing, mayhap—did not one know the man whose voice it was.

They all stared at each other for a moment, Robyn frankly baffled.

Gilbert had to answer. "Here, milord!"

More voices, this time, back and forth for a snatch of moments. The horses' hoofs sounded again, this time retreating.

Robyn ambled a few steps forwards, then halted as a broad-shouldered figure came striding through the autumn trees. Resembling the young lad who'd first wandered towards Loxley, Gamelyn was garbed in twice-worn tunic and leather trous, with a well-patched cloak half-covering the rucksack at his back, and boots worn shiny.

"What are you doing here, milord?" Gilbert crowed. "And dressed like a knave of a forester, at that! I thought you were to be fetching your castle ready for a fancy tournament!"

A shrug of those broad shoulders. "Well, Marion wanted me out of her way. Just as you always say, Robyn."

Robyn still couldn't say anything. He blinked at Gamelyn rather owlishly, wishing his tongue wasn't glued to the roof of his mouth.

Even John's silence was . . . well, more silent than usual.

"Hm." Gamelyn seemed nonplussed by their lack of reaction. "I thought that I might be able to convince Robyn and John more easily to allow my presence in their bed o'nights . . . I guess it's a good thing I knew Gilbert mightn't be so inclined." He shrugged the pack from his shoulder; threaded along the length of one strap were three drinking horns. "How about if I come bearing bribes? More of Wulfstan's mead."

Joy burst in Robyn's heart, brilliant as the sun spraying through the tree branches, shoving startlement aside. He pounced on Gamelyn, hugged him, bussed him fierce, and only then pushed him back. Said, his voice trying to crack, "What do you think, lads? Do we let this nobleman join our merry band?"

John linked an arm through Gamelyn's and nodded, grinning ear to ear. Gilbert took the mead—of course—and gave Gamelyn a graceful, quite courtly bow.

"With such gifts, milord, your presence is always welcome. And aye, I'll forgo what nightly delights you might offer and claim one of these as mine own."

Arm in arm, they started through the woodland.

"You have me for a se'nnight," Gamelyn said. "I do have to be back and show my face for the tournament. Those are my orders, and it's more than my head's worth to have my wife all cross."

"Aye, well enough." Gilbert grinned. "That should be enough time to rob a few deserving churchmen, at the very least."

They made a mile or so in companionable silence; John and Gilbert ahead marking point, then Gamelyn and Robyn.

Until Robyn snugged closer and nipped at Gamelyn's ear.

"So, milord," he said, low. "About this tournament."

"Yes? And don't call me that."

"Will you, *milord,* by chance be holding an archery contest?"

"If I was, I wouldn't invite you."

"Well, that's the point, en't it?" Robyn grinned. "Since when has Robyn Hode ever waited for an invitation?"

"Robyn Hode just might find himself tied hand and foot in the middle of the Wode, should he think to try such a stunt."

"Oooo," Robyn purred against Gamelyn's ear. "Promise?"

"Hoy!" Gilbert had turned around, arms akimbo. "Are you two coming, or what?"

Robyn grinned at Gamelyn, who rolled his eyes then ran to catch up with John and Gilbert.

⊕

AND SO DID ROBYN HODE,
WITH HIS MERRY MEN,
DISAPPEAR INTO THE GREEN WODE

- END BOOK FIVE -

- Author's Note -

I have spent much of my life wandering the greenwood with Robin Hood.

And I have spent over forty of those years telling stories about what would become Robyn Hode.

Some of those stories were acted out. Most were written down. Some weren't 'my' Robin. Most were. All of them, over the years, helped me grow as a storyteller and writer.

So how to contemplate "The End"?

Finishing a series arc is beyond description. There remains only feelings that one attempts—feebly—to describe.

Giddiness. Relief. Gratitude.

And also:

Mourning. Grief. Emptiness.

It has, after all, taken me a long time to shepherd Robyn and his merry band into the outside world. I think I can forgive myself for feeling as conflicted as a certain russet-haired Templar. Still, it's time. Time to move camp, to find new hunting grounds, to hunker down and take shelter during the storm . . .

To tell more and different stories by the fire.

One cautionary tale, however, I would like to share with you now, if you'll permit.

Our Mother Earth will find ways to control us, if we cannot control ourselves. Upheaval is a symptom of a society's illness. And so much of what is going on in thisnow is what happens when we ignore our histories, and decline to question the status quo of established narratives.

Robin Hood, whoever they might have been (or never been), has *never* been about accepting the status quo. And while the greenwood is a sanctuary, wolves also lie in wait over hard winters. In this newest, chaotic fluctuation of *tynged's* strands, hunkered down in our own sanctuaries, we're surrounded daily by sobering reminders: that history can lie, *will* lie to suit a corrupt narrative; that yes, there are people who will relinquish their souls and follow some 'great white father' anywhere; that an elitist system based on consumption, genocide, and racism can't help but totter beneath its own weight.

Yet still, even a flawed history has much to teach us. And there are more things to learn from those many histories that still remain obscured, many purposefully made invisible. A literal rainbow of people are hunkered down in *their* sanctuaries—their Wode!—with stories too long ignored . . . to humanity's shame and peril.

The good thing is, that means there are so many stories left to be told! All we have to do is listen. I'm looking forward to hearing them. And, of course, telling a few myself.

Robyn said it: All we have is *thisnow*.

Let's make the most of it.

I have spent much of my life wandering the greenwood with Robin Hood. And I have spent over forty of those years telling stories about what would become Robyn Hode.

And I can't imagine I'll stop just because I've finished a series arc. But that's a story for another time . . .

Thank you for coming with me on this journey. I am humbled and thankful to have shared it with you.

J Tullos Hennig
Summer of 2020

Find this and the rest of the series (paper, ebook, & audio)
at your favourite retailer & Forest Path Books
https://forestpathbooks.com

~~~

Stay informed on Forest Path Books' releases and news!
Join the newsletter group at:
https://forestpathbooks.com/into-the-forest/

~~~

Interested readers can catch up on the
latest news and releases by joining
J Tullos Hennig's Reader Group at:

https://subscribe.jtulloshennig.net

and/or by visiting
https://jtulloshennig.net
You can even nab yourself a free story or two!

J TULLOS HENNIG

has always possessed inveterate fascination in the myths and histories of other worlds and times. Despite having maintained a few professions in *this* world—equestrian, dancer, teacher, artist—she has never successfully managed to not be a storyteller. Ever.

Given a heritage of forest-dwelling peoples—Choctaw, Chickasaw, and Scots-Irish—the decision to make a home base in NW Washington State with the Amazing Spouse was a no-brainer. They live alongside an equine 'pasture potato' on a retirement pension, a wolfhound who alternates between leaping over the sofa and snoozing on it, and a press gang of invisible 'friends' Who Will Not Be Silenced.

Active in conventions and genre literature in the 70s/80s/90s, Jeanine returned to the authorial fold with the publication of an award-winning series of historical fantasy novels She is a member of the Author's Guild, the Historical Novel Society, and SFWA. In 2018 she was presented with the Speculative Literature Foundation's juried Older Writers Grant.

Her historical series *The Books of the Wode* presents a truly innovative re-imagining of the Robin Hood legends, giving emphasis and reality to both pagan and queer perspectives.

https://www.jtulloshennig.net

www.ingramcontent.com/pod-product-compliance
Lightning Source LLC
Chambersburg PA
CBHW030658190726
48286CB00001B/88